WORLD ONE

WORLD

ONE

TIMOTHY COOPER

THE AMERICUS PRESS

Washington, D.C.

1990

Copyright © 1990 by Timothy Cooper
All rights reserved under International and Pan-American Copyright Conventions.
Published in the United States of America by
The Americus Press, Inc., Washington, D.C.

Library of Congress Cataloging in Publication Data
Cooper, Timothy, 1953–
World One.
I. Title
87-73424
ISBN 0-9619914-0-2

Printed in the United States of America
First Edition
Composed by Maryland Composition Company, Inc., Baltimore, Maryland
Printed and bound by R. R. Donnelley & Sons Company, Harrisonburg, Virginia
The text of this book was set in Electra Cursive and Baskerville.

This is a work of pure fiction. Any resemblance to persons living or dead is wholly coincidental and runs contrary to the intent of the author who conceived the work as entirely imaginative.

For Jo,
who makes all things possible

WORLD ONE

1

The human-dogs have just come by. We have been warned and given an ultimatum. We must surrender this place, our marble home, by the beginning of tomorrow's long night. We must be on our way and out the door before the new moon climbs the hazy dead sky and frowns down on these silent waterways here in the capital city. I will not tolerate this. I will not let the human-dogs get the best of me. Elizabeth and I will fight them, for we, like Thomas Jefferson, have sworn upon the altar of God eternal hostility against every form of tyranny over the mind of man.

That is why we live under Thomas Jefferson's bronze feet. We live in a manmade cave below his proud statue here on the edge of the ever running water, the perpetual river. We've staked our claim and now bandits have declared their intentions to have it, because they too like Mr. Jefferson's famous frame and high domed sanctuary. By right of possession, this place is ours. By right of all that is right, we should be left alone.

Today is the four hundredth day since America died on the eve of the many explosions. It is enough to say that the old America has passed on, been laid to rest under these high seas which cover the wounds of war. America died and other nations across the globe went down and under during this period of too many explosions of nuclear bombs.

Elizabeth and I have survived and become strong and have made a life for ourselves here on these waters which give us sustenance in the form of fish. We dine on fish and we fish for fish and we get through it despite the paddling human-dogs who try to attack, sometimes. But I possess a rifle of very high intensity and I own bullets. The human-dogs respect me. That is, they respected me until today, until many banded together to rob us of our home.

I'm setting out our predicament to help me face the facts. The facts are these: We have no real place to go. By tomorrow night we will be overwhelmed by forces greater than we. But most important of all to me is the fact that if we go, if we run for safety in search of a new home, I believe that my dream of Americus will die.

What I dream of is to set America right again. I dream that the high waters will recede and that the days will go bright again and that the never ending haze will lift from the sky and that a new age will come—a second chance.

Elizabeth claims love for other ideals. She's got it in mind to bear children, despite the circumstances and the hazardous surroundings. She won't admit to herself that she is sterile, caused no doubt, I have no doubt at all, by the great war of the titan nations. Elizabeth is a hunk of woman. She's weathered the mightiest of storms. There were more storms than days in the month following our catastrophe. The waters rose and the sky went dark and winter set in and too many people died.

That was then. This is now. Now the human-dogs want our house and we must decide which way to go or what to do. Even now we are faced with grave choices.

Is there any way to hold our ground? Is there a way to defeat the tyranny which threatens us and is soon to be upon us? I'll mull these questions over, deliberate on them, turn them to one

WORLD ONE

side and then another, think them through and come up with an answer or two. As the champion for Americus, for a better world out there, it is my self-appointed responsibility to overcome these difficulties and find other means to put aside these alarming threats of tyranny.

We'll take a ride outside. We'll cruise above the grizzly waters and meditate and see some sights. Right now Elizabeth is inside packing. On another day she would stand fast; she would arm herself with jagged stones and let them fly at the bands of human-dogs approaching. But today the odds for victory are less than none. Only a demented idealist would stand to be cut down.

The air's so cool and breathy. The skyline's a purple shade of black. My canoe's slipping across a barrage of waves. I paddle lightly as I should. In this decimated city of high water, rooftops are like islands, floating strangely above the steady stream of an anxious river. And on these rooftops, people live. Human-dogs plus others. The difficulty comes in trying to separate the human-dogs from the rest. In the four hundred days since the end of all beloved things, tyranny has had the upper hand.

I slow to miss a careening tree, felled and rotted long ago, now making its way to a broader sea outside the limits of this capital city which right now is the capital of nothing. I try to spot the dim blue moon which grotesquely hangs sometimes in a foggy cyan sky. I keep my eyes sharp and scanning east to west, contemplating that at any moment I might sight the silhouettes of marauding types looking for some violent action.

There is a kind of claustrophobic serenity out here. For just so far and not one yard farther, it seems safe. In that one tangible area it seems peaceful and at ease. But I know that beyond that temporarily pleasant line of sight, danger runs its rounds. I know that human-dogs are killing people, murdering them for food and drink and high places on which to rest and scan the sea world from. I know it as surely as I know that that form which just passed me by was a human body floating out to sea. It may have been destroyed by current forms of warfare. I can't be sure. I can't really know. That could be me, and probably will be.

Inside and warm, basking in delicious afterglow, we are. All's not lost, not when Elizabeth's so smooth and spicy and breathing lightly by my side. She's thinking here, right now, even as I think, that this is the time when she's finally become pregnant. But even if it were true, what then? What kind of place is this to bring a child up in? Our little child would have to hide behind my rifle, learn how to kill with heavy stones. From an early age, he would have to learn of human-dogs and how they prey upon all others who play by rules, who have regard for others living in this pool. One day a child might come. One day the world might be reborn. All these dreams are possible, even my one dream of Americus. But until those days arrive, I'll watch my way and paddle lightly in the dark.

Standing watch outside, in the grand old open, under a wretched sky. Thomas Jefferson stands straight, eyes fixed as usual, steady and ready ahead. Once again I walk this hall. Its pillars seem to shine, its dome swirls, its floor lies hard and cold. And in its midst is this awesome statue of a man, dead and gone to history. Who remembers him? Who cares that he once lived? I care. I love that man up there. I have sworn eternal hostility against every form of tyranny over the mind of man. Jefferson and I. C.J. Jones and Mr. Thomas Jefferson. We are comrades in history. He had his hard times and I have mine. America was his fine dream and Americus is mine. How can I ever abandon him, leave him here for the human-dogs? If only I had a barge, a broad platform on which I could lower his noble form and slip him out to sea. If only I were well equipped to deal with the human-dogs and make these thoughts unnecessary. I have little time to fantasize. I am failing in my dreaming. Americus will not rise out of this dirty lake, this sad, sick place. Violence is not so easily ended. War between human beings goes on and on, despite the rupture of all civilization. I close my eyes and then open them. All is as before. But in one dream, on one refreshing night, I'll open them and see a world of passivity, yes, a world released from harm. And it will have come to be because Americus led it there, took advantage of its second chance.

I hear a howl out there. A high wind is kicking up some

WORLD ONE

waves on the running water. I smell the stench of seaweed which is always here, no matter what. I am sitting on my marble step, Mr. Jefferson solemnly behind me, and am wondering what our fate will be and when it will take hold.

Elizabeth and I have just had a flaming argument. I'm really not surprised. The tension here is more than we can take. I'd rather stay and take the dogmen on. Jefferson inspired me. Eternal hostility and the rest. Elizabeth says that our time here is through. Haven't I gotten that, yet? I'm feeling strong this hour. My rifle's ready for repeated action. I'll stand on my steps and take the daylights out of them. I'll even take a stone or two, die if I must, I will. Elizabeth laughs at this. Then where will you be, you and your handsome dream of Americus? Good question. I'll be dead and so will Americus. Damn the human-dogs. Damn this filthy basin of human animosity.

I'm sober now. I stood by our doorway for a while and looked out on the night. I must live if Americus is to someday come to life. I must try again in some other place. I must recruit patriots where I find them. I must be patient and choose my confrontations well. This is not one of them. I and my cause would be better served by bowing to these overwhelming circumstances, and leaving this island of nobility. Elizabeth is right.

We are bedding down for the night. Elizabeth is near the surface of her sleep. I am all eyes and ears, though there is nothing to see or hear. I feel panic in my heart. This night, I am thousands of days and weeks away from where I want to be. But at the end of this time, I see a thought made real. I see all the human-dogs meek and tamed. They make music. None of them howl.

Sure, some may think I'm dreaming. I dream Americus will sound the horn, write the anthem, charge into the light and lead the way to life without violence and all that that entails. Elizabeth has been caught by sleep. She's swimming in a liquid dream of warm water and perfume. She's in a forest populated by children. It's time I followed her. It's time I put the world outside in its proper perspective. I won't let it interfere with my thoughts about tomorrow. On and on I go, into the color of my tomorrows.

Up early, frying fish. To eat, we fish. I spear fish for a living. They glide by and I harpoon them. I stick a blade between their ribs. I pluck them out of the dark and murky waters and store them in a canvas bag until Elizabeth takes charge. Probably we stink of fish. There's fishy smoke about. Sometimes we dream as we eat of fields of melting butter. If I were granted one chef's wish, it would be unlimited access to pounds of butter, bright yellow butter with which to moisten our fish and spruce up its monotonous flavor.

Elizabeth has requested a last boat ride. We're packed and prepared. I see no harm. One last tour. One last meditation on the remaining sights of this capital city.

Floating by the great man Lincoln in the inky day. We see people up on the hands of the statue. Someone waves. We wave back. We float on.

Turning south toward George Washington's monument, buried part way up by the rise of the water. No life is apparent up at the top where windows look out on the desolate waterways, on the drowned, dead city. On we glide, over where a green mall used to be. On we row toward the Capitol dome, past vast buildings of a past civilization, past places which represent thought come to nothing—the graveyard of failed thinking. Elizabeth's crying quietly in the stern. The dark city, the flooded ways, the many buried bodies below these dark waters. Nothing came of something. Americus must rise from nothing.

Not nothing. From Thomas Jefferson's high ideals. A human body passes by, face down and decayed. Find peace in the sea . . .

WORLD ONE

We've turned back. Soon human-dogs will be out and we don't want to tempt them, incite them by our presence to commit violence. This morning a bit of a breeze is up and I like it. We both like it and have commented on it to each other. More broken trees slide by. Garbage litters the surface like fleas on sick animals. Nothing came of something. Americus must rise from nothing. Not nothing. From Thomas Jefferson's high ideals.

I'm out here having a word with Mr. Jefferson. No one's around so it doesn't seem weird. He's up there on his pedestal and I'm down here on the marble floor looking up at him, at the high dome above him, at his great words which ring the lower edge of the dome. "I have sworn upon the altar of God eternal hostility against every form of tyranny over the mind of man." That's my slogan for Americus. I'll put it on the flag. It'll be at the top of the constitution. It's what my new nation will stand against, against all forms of tyranny—against all war, all violence, all of it.

Something bothers me. I'm trying to put my finger on it. What I'm trying to get to is this: when am I going to begin? When am I going to start with my notions of Americus? If not now, when? If not now, will I ever? Thomas Jefferson is looking down at me. He is watching me think. He is definitely influencing my thinking. I am in my right mind but I hear him speaking. He speaks to me. Me, C. J. Jones. History is present. And the future is here as well. We've all come together. In this moment.

He's right. Now's the time to act. Now's the time to raise up a flag and hold our ideals high. It's worth my life. It's certainly worth a try. And I'll have Mr. Jefferson behind me. He'll see me through. I'll confront those human-dogs. I'll lay down my laws of reason. I'll quote Thomas Jefferson to them. And I'll back that up with some imagination. I have to be clever. I have to be shrewd. I can't simply give up my life for no reason. And I'll send Elizabeth away. I'll send her along. I'll be okay. But I must start right away. Now is the time for Americus to rise. Already its sun is beginning to gleam in my eyes. I am the first forefather of Americus, the nation which brought peace to the world.

Elizabeth won't let go. She won't leave me alone. She won't ship off without me, and I won't go. So here we are. One forefather and one foremother standing tall under the graceful stare of Mr. Jefferson. No sign of the human-dogs yet. It's still too early for them. They sleep late so they can carouse on the dirty waters till dawn. But we'll be ready for them. Somehow we'll be ready and waiting, driven, of course, by our love for Americus.

Still no sign of them and the day is moving on. My rifle's at my side. Elizabeth's on my left, her dark eyes locked on the steamy horizon. We'll take them on today or any other day. I'll drive a bullet through any one of their violent brains. But hopefully I won't have to. I'd really rather not. I'd give anything to talk my way of out this. I need to muster up a speech. I need to get it right the first time out. What's that? Shapes on the waters? False alarm. Nothing's wrong. Elizabeth and I are here standing next to our great friend, Mr. Thomas Jefferson. If he were here, he'd find a way to put a stop to the coming violence. If he would only speak to me. If he would only put words in my mouth, bright, beautiful words—words of a historic nature.

I caught Elizabeth nodding off to sleep. I kissed her on the cheek and that made her wild and awake. Now she's circling our monument, watching out in all directions. She deserves more than this. She deserves some peace.

This is what I'll say to her. We'll take this stand today for a better world tomorrow. Then we'll go on holiday. We'll set out on a pleasure cruise before the winter hones in and creates discomfort. It'll be a breezy cruise toward the western seas. There are mountains in the west, many mountains which couldn't possibly have been flooded up. We'll go in search of real trees. And if our luck holds out, we'll put our hands in soil, black, rich loamy soil up there on those mountain tops. We may never come back to this place again. We might give up old Thomas Jefferson for the daily sight of trees and soil and what not. Oh, I like this plan, this second gorgeous honeymoon. And up there in the mountains Elizabeth just might, and I underscore just might, conceive. This is nice. Just being here thinking about those mountains in the west.

WORLD ONE

Elizabeth went berserk. I told her of the honeymoon and she lit into me with her finest passion. Out here in the open. If I'm going to die today, my exit will have been worth noting. I love this woman. She's as fine as any mountain top. And the two together . . . that combination would make me cry and ask out loud, "Why's life been so good to me?"

A stray human-dog just passed us by. He's not one of the pack. He's a loner, I can tell. I held my fire and he didn't raise a hand to threaten us. That was good thinking. He would have been one wet, dead dog if he had even for a moment tried.

The human-dogs have come. Our horizon is absolutely littered with them. Boats and rafts bob here and there in front of us. They're fifty yards away from us. They're stalled out there on the flat surface of the sea. What are they waiting for? What are they doing? No doubt they see my rifle which gives them pause and allows for some reflection on their definite mortality.

Human-dog #1 is speaking. And Elizabeth and I are listening.

"Put that toy away, old man. Stick it in the river. We are here as your companions. We've brought fish to share and bottles of fresh water. Stick it away, old man. Eat our bloody fish. Drink our water down. You have something that we want. Give it up. We have something that you will like: a means by which we can spare your lives. Truce, old man. Drink and eat, old man. Evening comes and the waters go calm. Trust in brothers. We share your constant misery."

Human-dog #1 is resting. He is weary from so much creative thinking. "Truce, old man." Whatever could he be thinking? Whatever could he be dreaming? This human-dog is not living up to his reputation. Elizabeth runs her brilliant eyes across the way. There must be fifty doggies out there in the twilight. I hear her say to them, "I'll feed you with my stones."

Then I hear Thomas Jefferson speaking. I hear a voice right next to me. It's his voice. Elizabeth nudges me. Talk back to them, she's ordering. But I'm listening to Thomas Jefferson and will stand no interruption.

I am to challenge them. Test these human-doggies and try to end their tyranny. That yapping statue has got a lot of nerve.

I'm out here with Elizabeth exposed to fifty human-dogs and he's up there hard and cold and made of nearly indestructable bronze and he wants me to test these dogs with reason?

"Disarm and advance. We want no warfare. We want reason and safe peace. We want a pleasant order. We want what's ours, our home."

Human-dog #1 again.

"I want your sanctuary for America! We remember how it was. Shining lights. Good nights. We want to recreate it. Start again. Is that so unforgivable, old man?"

Elizabeth again.

"You want our blood. You want us drowning right this very second. I'll give you shining lights and good nights."

Now Elizabeth fires off a stone. It floats and falls behind Human-dog #1. He says nothing. He simply lifts his canvas bag of stones and releases it into the dim and trashy waters. Then he shouts at all his doggy men, "You, too."

Mr. Jefferson is bringing out the best in him, this Human-dog #1. The human-dogs unload their bags of stone. Each and every one. Stones follow stones, into the dim and trashy waters. And after that, the spiky weapons, the boards of shining nails and thorny branches. They float on the sea, all of those carefully crafted weapons of tyranny. Now he puts it to me.

"We've done it, old man. Look for yourself. Open your eyes. Woman, can't you see? Shining lights and good nights. We'd like to get it right. Now, ditch the toy. Stick it in the river."

I do no such thing. Instead, I take us out into the river, out to confront the doggies face to face. I hold my violent weapon close. And Elizabeth and I go to meet our fate out in the dirty twilight.

Here we are now in the open, Human-dog #1 and me. Elizabeth holds my rifle and trains it in a gentle sweeping motion from one human-dog to another. It is only fair; they outnumber us. Human-dog #1 greets us with a blissful smile. It lights up this dingy twilight. What bright clean teeth for a man who lives by violence. He could use a day or two to shave. He could use a tailor of superior abilities to frame his burly body. Still, this dog has a solid presence and his eyes shine out like green moons.

WORLD ONE

"Why don't you stick it in the river? I would trust you more, old man."

"Why don't you leave us be and find some other monument to claim?" I quickly say.

"Let's eat, my friend, and remember civilization."

And we are eating his bloody fish and washing the small bones down with fresh water and the mood on these waters is changing. Human-dog #1 is a sentimental one. He remembers green acres in this city. He recalls parks and forests that lie wasted underwater now. We all remember these places that once were. But that was long ago, before four hundred and one days ago. He seems to want to get to know us. He seems less violent up close. In another time, I would probably have liked him. I might have been his neighbor. But now, out here in the open under a dirty dark sky, I trust him little and like him less because he is a threat to me, to me and Elizabeth and our dream of Americus.

Some human-dog is breaking out some liquor. The bottle passes from hand to hand. It reaches us and Human-dog #1. We all drink some and the mood is even better. The night seems merry now. The sky is lighter than before. Human-dogs are singing. They are howling at the moon. But all the while, Elizabeth has her finger on the trigger and the barrel is pointed at Human-dog #1.

The bottle goes around again and then another floats by. A smoky moon is up and we all seem satisfied. I feel a bond now. I sense a kinship with this man, this burly man across from me. And under the moon, in this boat and at this particularly difficult time, I am certain I can communicate with him. One human-dog tells a funny story of how he survived the floods by floating for days and days in a plastic bucket. Another recalls living in an apple tree for weeks while the waters rose above the ground. And these tales are of some interest to me. We are sharing life struggles in the middle of a catastrophe. But I am not here for this. I am here to live. I am here to make some peace and avoid deadly confrontation. I am here because Thomas Jefferson is back there, back standing in the center of his monument. I am here to change the world by beginning it all over again. And Americus is my means to this, to this noble, endless peace. And if it is to ever be, the human-dogs before me must have a change of heart, must make Americus rise and lead the way to a spirit of global peace never before realized.

But how? How am I to do this? How am I to win their hearts, make them live in peace? These human-dogs, they seem to thrive on anarchy. They love this lawless land. They'd love to war forever, war in all parts of the heavens. But are these evil men? Are these human-dogs more evil than any of the others who've come before?

I look at where I'm sitting. I'm sitting in an evil soup, concocted in part by all of mankind's history. There's no doubt, no doubt at all, that these doggies have contributed their fair portion to its insidious composition, but to be fair the blame must stop there. We've all contributed to it. We've all added some morsels to the soup. How could it be otherwise? We should have ended war while we had the chance. We should have killed it off. Put it and us out of our common misery.

Basically, I think this. War is tyranny. And tonight, tyranny must end. The human-dogs and I will end it by working out ideas. Ideas for peace. A plan for peace, a plan to end the evil.

I will take advantage of the mood here. It is presently a mellow mood made rosy by bottles of liquor. I will move these human-dogs by theatricality. I will move them with some literary tale which makes my point, describes my message well.

So let me change into my costume. Let me dictate a literary tale. Let me entertain the human-dogs before me and teach them all about a world of peace and how we all might get there.

"Human-dog #1," I say. "Let me add some light to this long, long night. Let me tell a tale which might enlighten you and give you a modicum of hope for the lives of your children."

"That'd be fine, old man. Give us a treat tonight."

"I will.

"This is the story of the end of war and of an age called Whitsuntide. This is the story of the Lord of War and how he came to die. This is the story of the birth of peace as seen through Satan's eyes. Now quiet. Now listen. He speaks."

WORLD ONE

There was a place I once lived which was high above the earth in the days when man was ignorant of the means for the greatest destruction which his mind could make. Now at this time my father put a dream into the sacred harbors of my sleep. He planted this dream in me and I took the bait and I ate the bait and it makes me sick to think of it. God, wise God, beloved father, universal being, creator and giver of life, of sickness, of plagues, of sun and stars and waters and rivers and filthy streams, sent angels into my dreams, into the quiet fields of my subconscious and tormented me while I rested above the world. Angels, sickly angels with swords of fire and tongues of flame and crystal eyes honed in on my private avenues of thinking and told me of a certain prophecy. And fool who I was took it as truth. Gospel and truth it was to me, who for many ages believed in the logic of dreams and found solace in their various messages.

Angels said to me on that bitter night when I was caught unaware of the plots of God, "You, son of God named Satan, will unearth the first secret of your father's universe. When two hands split mass and create force and light and storms of hot clouds, take this secret, and deliver it to man so that he might pass God's test. God has said that before man comes to his destiny out beyond the stars he must first pass this test of wisdom over war."

Angels, bloody angels, departed then, left me to dwell upon this message in the heart of my sleep. And I did. And when I awoke I knew what must be done. So I did it. I went down to earth and found a bit of mass. This mass was the smallest of the smallest things on all the earth. And when I had found it, I went up to my rosy resting place above the round, round world of man and grasped it between my fingertips and squeezed it until it snapped in two as the message of the Lord had said it would. And then all things happened. With the breaking of the bit of mass the world about me was shattered with light. Hot light it was. Hotter even then the strength of one hundred suns before my eyes, my happy eyes. And with the light and heat and force there rose up before my feet the highest cloud of the hottest flame that I had ever known. I breathed in the acid air. My lungs feasted on it and sucked it down, deep down the acid air was sucked until it became a part of me. In my blood it found a home and till this day I can taste it when I wish. So be it. It is a means by which I remember what power I possessed and what glory I had for a time when this secret was all mine.

Ever higher did this cloud of my creation rise on that day when I put God's message to the test. And then I understood what I had done. I had been given the greatest secret of the universe: the secret of splitting mass in two to create the power of God's divinity.

But if I had been satisfied and kept this secret to myself and disobeyed the will of God I would have had all power for all time. Endless power had been my dream, and God knew this to be so. But he was shrewd. He knew my ways. He knew that I would obey his command because I was not one for leaving well enough alone. I would see that man possessed this knowledge of great destruction and I would see that he would use it in the fields of war, and I would see that he would not come to his destiny out beyond the stars, for I would always have my company down on earth and would never wish to live alone.

So on this day when I discovered this secret of the universe, I went up to God. I called to God after many steps across the universe and I said to him, "My father, father of us all, I have done as you have wished. I have seen the secret of the power of splitting mass in two and by your word I shall deliver it down to man and we shall put him to the test. But what rewards shall there be for me when I have accomplished this? It is only fitting that I shall gain by this monumental effort to serve the gladness of your will. What shall it be, my father? Have you another kingdom over which I might have dominion?"

Now God the Father hid his face from me. Never had I seen his face, not then, not ever. So be it. I would never see his face until I died and entered into Heaven which I had not the least desire to do. But I had heard his voice. I heard it then. I will tell you what he said.

"If you do this thing and do it well, my son, then you shall have a reward which matches the talents of your labors. Give this knowledge to man and together we shall watch his progress. But remember man is young. Do not let this

WORLD ONE

knowledge spread too quickly, or you shall have no company down on earth, for man is still plagued with war and wisdom is still the miracle of dreams."

I was eager to assist. What a lovely battlefield there would be if man took hold of this first secret of the universe. What lovely clouds I would see, if man used this force sparingly. What a lovely thing it would be to see man make merry with atomic weaponry.

And so I went my way with the glory of my father's voice ringing lightly in my ears. I went down to earth to pass on the thing which I had come to know in dreams. But all the while I never thought that God had meant for me to serve his will in another way.

I was and am a fool.

I drifted into the dreams of the greatest of the great men of scientific minds who lived in the land which I had marked for the execution of my purpose. Slowly these great minds discovered the secret which had been passed down to me from God. Slowly they saw the wisdom of my implanted calculations and then more quickly set about to accomplish the task. And there was a need for this. To the east of the land where I had come, a continent was decimated by the surges of a long lasting war. And to the west of where I had come, a new trap of death was opening. To east and west the wars of man were reducing him to the rank of predator, and I could only see that by introducing him to the first great secret of the universe he would sink down further in yet another way. So be it, I said. So help him, I said. But God is working his purpose out and I have no reason to interfere. I am a son of divinity and have only been born to serve his will in the ways that I can. Truly, I was fit for this. Or so I thought before I knew.

Rapacious minds consumed my spicy bits of information and soon a bomb was built. A triumph of my instruction, it is fair to say. Never was there born a nobler saint of education. Never was there born one who instructed with such subtlety. I was the champion of a new divinity. I was he who changed the destiny of man and guided him to the riches of universality.

So be it. It was done. By plan and compromise it was done

and I should have been given my seat of royalty. I was not. I sit at the feet of my father and tell you my story which I will describe as a pathetic calamity.

Now when the bomb was tested I was exalted by the pupils of my class. The heat and force and light of this thing which made night day in the desert so impressed all those who had engineered it into life that they feared all that they had done. And why not? Such a cloud you have never seen. Such heat you have never known. I had delivered the finest of fears into the hearts of these men whose minds were as brilliant as the light of this manmade sun. It was then that I had a glimpse of what it was that God wished be done. So fearful was this thing which consumed all air and made night turn white that man trembled at the burden of his discovery. This then was God's purpose. With the knowledge of divinity it had been his fantasy that man would lay down all weapons of war and come to terms for peace. God vainly believed that by his generosity he would shake all men out of the wilderness of war. Such a fool was he as I am now. Scientists see light where governments see death. So, quickly I turned this situation to my clumsy advantage. I would see that the government of this land that I had marked would be the first to use the magic of this power. And so it did. The threat for peace became the signature of death and I recognized the enormity of my supremacy.

I went down to the place where the weapon had struck on the day of its delivery, and even I was horrified by the decimated symmetry of the city which had lost its luck to my revolutionary source of divinity. So complete was the annihilation that I shuddered to think what the evolution of this secret would bring. So quiet was the land that my footsteps still echo in the traces of my memory, and I have no sentimental feelings for history.

The sky was stained and the land was empty of all signs of civility. A child whimpered here and there and the waters steamed around the edges of the silent city which was a tomb

WORLD ONE

where the commiserating winds were free to roam and soothe the scalded tissues of the dead.

Imagine what it was to see the fruition of my father's undying generosity. Imagine how easy it was for me to go so naively onto the stage of my father's trickery.

Quickly and foolishly I went to meet my father high up in the heavens to tell him of all that I had seen. I would not disguise my feelings with regard to his devious plan which I had been a party to. I called out to God and my voice was filled with self-righteousness. (I suspect he knew all of what I had to say even before I came to rest at his shiny, lighted gates.) "Father," I said, "your gamble to bring about the end of war has failed. With the passing of the knowledge of splitting mass in two, man has become the monster of the ages. Had you witnessed what I have seen you would be as sick as me. As your agent I have delivered to man the single greatest weapon of total misery. Even I must have respect for this thing which makes rubble turn to ash. What is your purpose, my father? What are your calculations?"

Father said to me most pleasantly in a voice which betrayed nothing of his insincerity, "What purpose could I have? What calculations could I make? I have no power over man. I only wish to see him well. I have told you of my plans. Man's destiny is the purpose of my calculations. But man must take the step."

I was content then to believe the superficial testimony that my father handed down to me. True it was that he had no power over man. And true it was he wished to see him well. But still I could not understand the nature of the compromise which had been set in motion upon his universal stage. And when in time I came to know what he meant by "Man must take the step," it was too late. My time was done. So now I think of it and tell you how I came to sit in pain in this place of death.

I was glad that man had failed God's first test. Peace for man did not seem natural to me. But when I went down to earth after this most pleasant conversation with my father, I was aghast to learn that the end of the wars to the east and west had come. My father was not such a bloody fool. He had seen light, where I saw death. I was embarrassed by his victory. I would see that it would not happen again. I would challenge man's destiny.

My father had no right to make a mockery of me.

I would make man pay dearly for his peace. I would make him eat his atomic weaponry. I would watch him feast. War would one day come again among the nations of the earth, but from this time forth it would be a war of nuclear majesty.

I was not content then to leave well enough alone. The trickery of God had left its mark on me. I would see to it that many nations of the earth possessed these glorious instruments of death. And why not? All is fair in life and war. All is fair in battle between father and son. All is fair when secrets are revealed by the one who creates all dreams and sons and wars. So be it, I said. So help me. My father shall have a little more respect for me.

In time I made my way around the world dropping secrets here and there, dropping spicy bits of information to even out the balance. Some men were slow to learn, others picked it up more quickly, and still others caught on almost instantaneously. Men's minds were not an even lot. So help them. The quickest learn how best to survive. The slowest meekly hang their heads and worry. Such are the ways of man.

Time had come along with me as did the progress of mankind, and despite some simple, bitter skirmishes the world at large was in an age of peace for years. I believed my father thought his fantasy had at last come true. No nations down on earth would dare to confront each other with weapons of this kind. A logical impression for him to have, considering what man knew. But I knew more. I knew man to be a fool. I waited high above the earth for the day of his annihilation. Man was not a beast who could restrain his temperamental actions.

WORLD ONE

And through this time of fragile peace, I would report to God, my father, and let him know the day-to-day events of man on earth. I kept him well-informed. "Father," I would say, "your wisdom sits well with man. Have you not seen the product of your skill? Aside from simple, bitter skirmishes, man now lives in peace. You have made man fear the power of your creation. Only a fool would tempt its force. And man is no fool. He was created in your image."

But I was to learn later on in life, that it was I who was the fool. I was on the stage of his almighty compromise. But then I did not know what part it was that I would play.

Daily now in the seven nations of the earth which had so gratefully received the infusions of my sacred knowledge, the stockpiles of atomic weapons grew like weeds between the grasses. Watering weeds instead of grasses was what it was to me. Such a luxurious funeral there would in time be. And how I looked forward to the day when I would be victorious over God's claim to man's destiny. How I looked forward to the day when all the rubble of all the world would be disintegrated down to ash—and could be used to soothe the scalded tissues of my feet.

But God had other thoughts than those which I was thinking. God was not blinded by the encouragement of my observations. One day he called me from on high and requested that I come to visit him. And so I did. I took flight and met his light at the lighted gates. "Satan," said he, "both you and I are wise. We see that man is not. Look down upon the stage of nations and you will see that this age of peace is only temporary. Though man fears this revolutionary source of power, he will use it in his time of greatest fear. Too many nations have this power. How this has happened you might care to tell. But what is can never go unchanged. You have a problem far beyond your understanding."

I bluntly said to God, "But what problem could there be? I have lived to serve your will. Could it be that you have made miscalculations? Could it be your plan for man is but a fantasy?"

Then I was struck by his kind reply. "All things are possible. All things at once can be true or false. But think on this, my son. If men should come to war and use against each other the gifts of my creation, then surely all the world shall die. You shall be left forever without your company. You shall have no minds of men to tease. You will be my lonely son, and I so wish you to be happy. My suggestion to you is this. Take care to protect a portion of the people of the world. Take care to hide them from the ashes of the coming holocaust. Perhaps it will not happen, but then again we both know the tempers of my children. Do this and you shall have a time of happiness in old age. What say you to this, my son?"

Then I should have known what it was he wanted. Then I should have known the true purpose of his suggestion. But I was young and easily influenced by one of greater intelligence. I said instead, "By your suggestion you admit the possibility of defeat. I am shocked by your honesty. But, as you say, what is can never go unchanged. Perhaps you are a little more impressed with me? I have accomplished something in this time of man's tranquility."

And my father said to me, "Yes, I am a little bit impressed with you. You have the power to administer all of man's defeat. But do take care to keep some company. Man has been such a pleasant friend for you."

I thanked my father then for his kindly offering. I turned away and went back down to my place above the earth. I weighed what he had said and concluded he was one of decent generosity. By his plan I would have all that I would wish: to see the world drown in the lights of atomic weaponry; to be among my people for eternity. I accepted his suggestion. I would protect a portion of the people of the world. I would keep them out of the range of war. But where? What place on earth would be safe? I would have to think on this some more.

I rested then on the winds above the world and fell into a graceful state of dreams. And in these dreams I saw a ship. And in this ship I saw a portion of the people of the world whom I had taken care to save. And then all at once I saw this ship floating out across the fields of God's eternity.

I had my answer then. I knew it even while I dreamed. I

WORLD ONE

saw the place where I would go with the last of mankind for eternity. What beauty could be found in dreams, I thought when I awoke. What mysteries I will come to know.

How lucky then I thought I was to have a father who chose to keep me well.

I went down to earth to pick and choose the members of the human race who would be spared the coming evening of incineration. I went from east to west, from north to south and picked them up and put them down in a lovely land of flowing green. It was an island of breathless majesty. It was an island fit for kings and queens. I loved it while I lived on it. It is a pleasant memory. So be it. It is now a swamp of ash.

Now on this island there ruled a queen who was wiser than all the other men of governments who led their nations down to death. So wise was she that she took my message as the word of God. I slipped into her dreams and warned her of the end of all and asked her sweetly to undertake the building of a ship which would house the people of her land in worlds that she would come to know out beyond the stars. She did not hesitate. She was a woman of considerable ambition. She had sensed the fate of man was near. She was a woman whom I would choose to bring to bed. I would be father to her children. I would take special care to see her well.

She is my most beautiful memory. I sing to her at night.

She set about to build a ship which would take the people into the safety of my net. She did not know that she would be the one to bring about my death. How could she? Even I did not know. I would never have believed it even if I knew. She was a wise unwitting servant of God's will. Glory to her now that I am dead.

On the morning after I had gone into her dreams and directed the patterns of her thoughts, I became a blinded beggarman and walked the streets of her royal city and listened to the talk of my kinsmen. She, the wisest of them all, had made a declaration that man must meet his destiny out beyond the stars. Therefore, she commanded that a great ship be built, a ship of vast dimensions which would house all people of her land until a new age of man had come. I listened with affection to the recitation of this, her first decree, and marveled at the way she so gracefully turned an authoritative phrase. Truly I had hit the mark when I had chosen her above the others. Surely I would be rewarded by the one above my head. Or so I thought. I remind myself of my stupidities.

I have said this queen was wise. I will tell you she was wiser still. After her enunciation of her policy of destiny, she ordered the kingdom of the island closed. "No other people will take this flight of God. We are the chosen people. We live to serve His will." A stroke of genius I would say. She seemed to understand so well. In the streets I praised her name. A queen so ruthless was worthy of my name. She would keep her people safe. She would deliver them high into my hands. She was the leader of my sacred race.

Now I went up to God and informed him of my progress. I told him of the things which I would do. "When the ship is built," I said, "I will bring man's world to war. Other than the people of this chosen kingdom who will by then have set sail, the children of your glorious creation will die with rubble in their mouths. It will be a most horrific sight. But then again look what we have to look forward to. A new generation of mankind will be born out beyond the stars. It will at last go in search of a greater destiny. Perhaps this is what you've planned. Tell me, father of us all, is this not a portion of your plan?"

God said this to me. I remember it so well. "You are generous when it comes to battle plans. Yet you yearn for company in your older age. Do take care that the last of men do not destroy themselves. Eternity is eternity. And loneliness is a bitter price to pay for your undying generosity. I put to you a proposition. It may intrigue your heart. It may entice the subtle nature of your mind. Will you listen to what I have to say?"

Gladly would I listen to this one who stood beyond the lighted gates. And gladly would I air my views on the subject

WORLD ONE

of his proposition. Thus far all of my father's suggestions had kindly served the purpose of my will. In all his thoughts he showed great respect for me. I had become enchanted by his choice of words. I had come even to long to see the beauty of his face. So help me. I had changed. From the time that I learned the art of splitting mass, I was never the same.

God said to me, "Here is my proposition. Man has failed to pass my test. I reveal to him through you the first great secret of the universe and he turns it into a statue of idolatry. He knows the fear of it and still he persists in coming to the evening of incineration. I had hoped he would find the way to peace. I had hoped he would discover the second great secret of my universe. But I see no hope of this. Not while he lives on earth. So take the last of man away, my son. Keep him safe out beyond the stars. Preserve him for your company, and treat him as you must. But as he will have a new beginning, why not put him to the final test? Why not play for the highest stakes of all?"

And I said to God, "What stakes be these, father of us all?"

"Eternal life and eternal death," said he.

The substance of my father's proposition was this. He asked me to give the last of mankind one last chance to learn to live in peace. One last chance out beyond the stars. Either mankind learned to live as one in peace or be condemned to live at war for all eternity. I was amused by the nature of this proposition. Why not indeed? I asked. I was intrigued. What a field I would have in which to play. What a time I would have with my art of interference. But then my father said more. "Winner take all will be your or man's reward." Winner take all ... Winner take all ... At first I would not think of it. I was not one to place myself in jeopardy. But then again when I weighed the balance of his equation, I knew I had all of history sitting on my side. I said this to him. "Father, you are a master of intriguing propositions. But how can you believe man will ever find the way to peace? Look to his past. Look to the present. Time and time again he falls down foolishly. What can you expect of him? What miracle of thought will bring him to this time? Surely I will win. What then would be the nature of my reward?"

God the Father said to me, "If the last of man defeats himself by his art of war, then you shall have all power over him. I shall turn my back on man and be glad to hear of him suffering eternally under your net of misery. But if by some miracle of chance, mankind finds the path to peace, my son, then you must surrender your eternal life to me. You must relinquish all your powers which have guided you thus far into the time of eternity. Winner take all, is my proposition. Either man is at last free of you or you shall rule his everlasting destiny by whatever means is suited to your liking."

I went away from God that day thinking only of my victory. I went away from God that day and walked into the beauty of his deadly fantasy.

I floated high above the earth and met with my conscience for a while as the winds blew hither and thither. What my father had proposed might mean everlasting power for me over the minds of men. If the last of mankind could not resist the tasty temptation for war, then I would reign supreme. There would be no God to interfere with me. I would have all that I had dreamed. The competition would at last be eliminated. Oh, what a glorious time would be in store for me. I could not resist this challenge. To rid myself of God's charity to man had been my dream since birth. And now before me lay the way. I would pledge myself to God. I would accept his deal now that the death of man on earth was a certain reality, thanks to the ignorance of man and the generosity of God and my gentle art of interference. But I would ask my father for one important concession. I would ask him to allow me to destroy the atomic weaponry that the people of this kingdom possessed. I would not wish to see the last of my people consumed in the lights of this holy fire.

"Eternity is eternity," I said to my father. "I do not wish my people to die suddenly out beyond the stars. Allow me to take away this force, so they might live throughout the time of my eternity." And God granted me this wish. He understood the wisdom of his son who cared for the lives of men.

WORLD ONE

As I have said, my father was one of generosity when it came to the blood of his kind.

And so the deal was sealed. Man would be put to the final test. And I, in time, would have my dominion over him, for the miracle of chance that he would find the way to peace was as small as the smallest of the smallest things on earth.

I proceeded down to the land where the people of my kingdom lived. And there I found the greatest of the great men of scientific minds constructing the ship which would take them out into the fields of eternity. How high and glorious did this ship rise out of the pastures of green. And its wings were like the wings of the angels of God. And it was made of steel and glass, and the steel was reflected in the glass, and the light of the sun lit the glass, and the ship rose up like a little ladder toward heaven. Like a father, I was proud of the work of my children. These men had more dexterity than I. How I wished then that I could be one of them. But my genius was of another kind. We all had our gifts from God. We all possessed a portion of his omnipotence.

I wandered to and fro in these days on earth before the time of the end of all. I witnessed the people of this kingdom of green gather great stores of food and water for the journey which was to come. I watched in spiteful ecstasy as all the members of the human race whom I had chosen for this expedition joined hands with the people of this kingdom to make ready for the time of my everlasting destiny. Here lay the seeds for everlasting war. Men of nations next to men of other nations would bring about catastrophe. Some day far away, I would see these same people lust for power and turn against each other and inflict the damage which would lead me to my victory.

On that day I would call out to God, my father. "Father," I would say. "Remember the oath that you have made? Mankind has come to war. It has not found the way to peace. The likes of man cannot live side by side and float in harmony. Now it is you who must relinquish your powers over man. No longer may you interfere, even obliquely, with his fate. The time has finally come when I am free to choose the destiny for these, my precious people."

But that day was not now. There was work to be done. As the ship of steel and glass rose higher still and stood like a tree blooming in the dawn, I went on my errands. I went in search of this kingdom's stockpiles of atomic weaponry. I would destroy them deep underground so that these children would have no temptation to bring them on the journey, and use them foolishly when they came to the day of disharmony.

My senses were keen. I found them quickly. And with the power of my sources of divinity, I wrapped them in circles of fire. And there were a thousand fires on that day and by the end of the day I had accomplished my wish.

Weary of setting fires in this kingdom of green, I took my leave and went up to my residence to find a moment's rest. I lay down and fell right away to sleep. And then I let myself dream. I dreamed of the sight of ten thousand lights of atomic weaponry shattering the surface of the earth. In this dream there was more light than I had ever seen. This light was like the light of God at the gates of heaven. It was as though God himself had come down to earth and destroyed all those who had worshipped weapons of idolatry. Perhaps . . . but the dream went on and darkness came until I dreamed I saw the features of my father's face. That was when I first felt the excruciating pain of this, my eternal misery.

I should have been more adept at reading dreams. I should have known what was to come. I should have known what my father had in store for me. But I was too intoxicated by my dream of victory. In his way my father gave me fair warning. He was telling me in dreams what my fate would be. But I did not hear the message in the winds. I could not conceive that man would ever come to peace. I underestimated man. I underestimated my father's art of interference. I should have known. I should have known. The meaning of the ending of that dream is now so clear to me. It said I would see my father's face. I would come to know him. I would come to sit at his feet and tell this story of how it was I came to die at the hand of man and by the will of my father and by my own devastating stupidity. So be it. It is done. I am no longer a merchant of the dead. I am the scribe of immortality.

2

I awoke too late to see the glory of man's last creation completed. I awoke too late to see my Queen lead her people and the other members of the human race into the ship which would take them out beyond the stars. But I awoke in time to see the ship take flight. From high above the earth I saw it break away from the green island surrounded by seas. I saw the ship move past me and above me and higher still it went until it vanished altogether from my sight. It parted the blue skies and its fires stained and made crimson the white clouds below it. And when it was gone on, when it had traversed the high dome of the sky, I raised my hand and commanded that the world of mankind come to war. But I will tell you that it was not by my hand alone that the end was made real. I had great power over man down there on the surface of the earth, but so, too, man had power and man likewise commanded that the world come to war. And it did. I was witness to its ultimate destruction. And I loved the beauty of the fireworks which glowed in a multitude of colors and deformed all which lay below. The scent of the earth was changing as I sat above it, and I watched its foundations rock and sway, and I heard the winds moan, they moaned so pathetically, so bitterly, so relentlessly. My eyes feasted on the turmoil of light, but my stomach was twisted and I tasted blood on my lips and my hands sweated profusely as I listened to the sirens of the dead weeping in the winds and screaming for revenge.

I closed my eyes and allowed the pictures of the lights of the world to linger in the depths of my imagination, and those lights which I had seen on earth were the very same that I had dreamt. I had pictured them perfectly. I knew why. I had been the first to see the horror of the power of the first great secret of the universe. I had been among the first to see its early primitive performance under the aegis of man at the time of the last great war. I was satisfied that I was one of singular vision who could look into the future and see destiny in dreams.

Soon the fires died down and the stench of the earth was bearable and I went down to it out of a sense of duty to my father who had made all this possible. I walked the earth. I am the sole witness to the days after the winds had cleared the debris and I saw the valleys of the dead. I saw the seas of mortality. I saw the men who had died with rubble in their mouths, and it was not pretty. It was not like the vision of light that I had seen. It was far different. There was no beauty in the world where I walked. I became sick with grief and had pity for the dead. I had changed most violently, for even I could see what insanity this had been. No longer would I look. But I wept with the winds which circled the world and I regretted that I had come this far to see my kingdom of hell on earth. If I had known what misery I would bring by passing this secret to the nations of men, I would have done otherwise. I really would.

But I found out too late. I stood by and watched and did nothing. How was I to know that the end of all would make me so sick? How was I to know I would be changed when I went down to earth and saw what lay under the beauty of

WORLD ONE

those ten thousand lights, the glory of which I had witnessed in dreams? Enough. This was done. It cannot be changed.

I left the fires and wounds and destruction of the earth and made my way into the channels of the long dark seas of eternity. I was meant to follow the last of man. I was meant to take his temperature for war. I was meant to rule over him without interference should he lose his way to peace and find more war and fail in his pursuit of his God-given destiny. I waded through the dark and the seas and flew past the glory of stars and the warm lights of moons, and I trembled in the cold, and bathed in the heat, and rested in the places which were mild and quiet and calm. And soon I lost all memory of what had happened to the world of mankind. Soon the sights which I had seen glowed dimmer than the farthest stars, and I was not haunted by the images of the dead, soon I did not mourn for the loss of the green islands and the great seas and the little voices of children. I restored myself and thought only of what it would be to reign supreme.

What fate would I choose for man when he failed? What tasks would I conceive for him? What pain would I inflict on him? I might blame him for what he had done to the earth. I might deform all features of his face. I might make him breathe the air which I had breathed on earth when I went down to see it out of curiosity. I might put into his imagination the images which I had seen. I might make him feel the pain of all those who had died. I might allow each man over time to witness the day on which his brothers were left behind.

I would consider all and any punishments; I would consider all means for pain. But in the end no pain could be greater than for these people to see what had happened on the day they went safely into the frontiers of eternity. If they could see this day, if they had known what had happened, they would cease all war, they would find the way to understanding and to live in peace. They would find it and stand by it and not stray. If I had been God, I would have made them see this day. His threat of incineration was not enough. They should have been made to see the day of ten thousand lights and the night of extinction.

On through the dark I sailed and there were no sounds in the dark, so I made sounds for I began to be lonely as I went on in search of the last of mankind. I recalled the heavy noise of seas crashing by the shores; I recalled the way the winds sang in the moment of dawn; I recalled the way the old world awoke to the sounds of living activities. I recalled all sounds which I had heard in my time on earth, and with each sound I became more lonely, for the dark channels of God's seas stretched out before me and still I had no sight of the ship which carried my people into the silence of eternity.

But when at last I had travelled the distance of the light of a star, I saw the glory of man's last creation. I saw the ship of steel and glass. I saw the windows of light made bright by the dark—and for one moment from afar I thought I heard the voices of the people singing in praise of the Lord, my father.

They would pay for that noise to God. They did not yet understand that I was their king. No matter. In time they would soon fall down and my father would keep his promise and all would be well in the land of my making.

I went forward into the wake of the ship and there I disguised myself once more as the faithful blinded beggarman so that I might blend with the people on board. I made myself a citizen of the kingdom in a brilliant instant and magically slipped through the glassy windows of the drifting tomb of civilization. If I had had a mirror and could have made myself see, I would have been astonished at my sudden transformation. I would have seen the face of an old man who had been blinded by snows in his time on the mountain. My clothes would have been the clothes of a man who had been torn apart by the wind. And my back would have appeared as though it had been broken a dozen times or more. But I had no mirror, and I could not see.

Within the ship I felt the dark. My senses were beyond all other men's. I could hear for many miles and I could taste

WORLD ONE

the air and feel the light of stars and the night of the endless seas in which we all travelled toward a time in eternity.

How happy I was to have caught up with the last of mankind in this ship which was at one time only a glitter in my fertile dreams. But I must share the credit. Without the handiwork of man it could not have been made. It is man who shares in part the glory of his destiny. You see, he was correct to go on. He was correct to journey out beyond the stars. If he had delayed, he would have died. All men would have died. And I would not have had even this short time with them in these dark fields of silence. Enough. My story goes on.

I, the blinded beggarman, walked through the cities of the ship while all men rested and slept and dreamed. As this decrepit old man I was free to come and go. If I was seen, I was paid no attention. These men had better things to do than to care for an aging old man. Or so they thought. But I was a particular old man and they would all come to know me and respect me, for blinded men have the power to look into the future and speak with many tongues and see into dreams. This is what I did.

On the night of the day I entered into the ship, I walked into the dreams of the last of mankind. I had expected to find new dreams and new ideals flourishing within the multitude of these minds. I found no such thing. I found the same dreams, the same dreams of fear and hate and treachery. I was not surprised, really. I should have known. The nature of the beast had not changed. My chosen members of the human race all envisioned a world beyond where their kind would have supreme power over all who lived among them. The ambitions in these dreams were the very same as they had been on earth: to climb the towers of great power, to rule and be master of the human race, to preserve their own kinds of legacies. Here I had given these miserable people the chance to escape the threshold of hell and still they persisted in acting so foolishly in the privacy of dreams. My father must have known that this would happen. How could he have wagered so much on so little hope? Perhaps he felt that it was his duty to provide for man one last chance before he handed him down to me. I did not know then what he had in mind. I wish I had, so help me, I wish I had.

The people in the south of the ship dreamed of the deaths of those who lived to the north. And the people of the north dreamed of the deaths of those to the south, and so on and so on. All were bitter from old grievances which had not been settled before the time when the ship set sail. How easy my task would be, I thought at the time, to spark the flame which would bring about the war which would gain me my prize. But surely even I must have a challenge. Surely I must have fun before the greatest triumph of my destiny became a reality.

Firstly, I practiced the art of language so that I could speak to all races of men. Divinity has its privileges and the art of language is one. How my father would have been impressed with me to hear me speak so effortlessly all words in the vocabularies of men. How I wish then that I had treated him to a display of my talents. Such is the curse of a son never to have his father near when he performs at his best.

I would consider further how I would split the nations of men on the ship. I would consider the tactic which I would employ. I had found on earth how relatively simple it was to exploit the differences that divided mankind. They all had a nose for the scent of war. One way or another I would lure mankind into battle. And my task was made easy by the proximity of the forces. At this time my thought was that my father was slipping. Perhaps he had grown tired of the burden of man. Perhaps it was his true wish to begin again with a new form of man. Perhaps I was to be his executioner for the last of mankind. I could hear him say to me on the day of my victory, "You have fulfilled my great wish. It is you who shall now worry over the souls of these men who could not find wisdom. For myself, I must start over again. I must create a better man, a better, wiser people, and see from the beginning that they learn their lessons well."

Whatever his thoughts, I knew mine. I was never known for my indecision. I would go to God and ask a favor of him. You see I was generous. I would live up to the spirit of the arrangement that I had made with my father, the Lord. I

WORLD ONE

would allow man to have his final chance to come to peace. It is only fitting for divinity to show grace in the dawn of victory. I would make sure that man would have his chance before I interfered with his destiny. And why not? I was the son of the father who had made all things. The individual man lived for such a short time. I had immortality. I had all those years behind me and all of those ahead. I could grant mercy when I knew that I would eventually win.

So I left the ship in the night while my people slept and confronted their fears and ambitions in their dreams. I changed myself and shed off the skin of the blinded beggarman. I gave myself sight and journeyed out into the wilderness of the heavens and flew toward the gates of light. I expected my father to receive me respectfully. After all, I had accomplished much since the last time I had spoken to him. I reviewed all that I had done. I had chosen my people. I had selected an able leader for my sacred race. I had spared other members of the human race and found the means by which they would all survive the onslaught of atomic weaponry. Now these people drifted safely through the nights of eternity. It had all gone according to my wishes and plans. What father would not respect this success? I knew I would be greeted respectfully and be granted the favor which would heighten the glory of my victory. I relished the thought of my conversation with God. I relished the sight of the lighted gates which I would soon see. I relished the time which I would spend with the people of my world once they had suffered their last tragic defeat.

Finally at the lighted gates I called out to him. "Father," I cried, "though you will not allow me to set sight upon you, I have come to list all my accomplishments. Or is it possible you know what I have done? All I have done, I have done for you."

Of course, I knew that he knew. My father had eyes. He could see. I knew he could even hear my thoughts. He knew why I came. He would wait for my next question. So I spoke.

"I have come to ask a favor of you. Thus far, I have followed the letter of your commandments. I hope to do more. But you have made my job too easy. I hear what the last of mankind are thinking. They have no trust in each other. And why should they? They all think the same, the same as they thought on earth. The nature of the beast does not change. Yet, as you, I am generous. I do not wish for easy victories. I wish for man to have his final chance. Grant me this favor, oh, father. Tell me how man might learn to live for eternity in peace. If you tell me the answer I will share it with man. Tell me the wisdom and I will hand it down. Let man fight me with wisdom. Otherwise, the thrill of my triumph is none."

God moved himself to speak. I had touched his holy nerve. I could tell even he thought highly of a son who thought well of fair competition. The lighted gates shone bright and his voice was rich and respectful. He said this. "I will tell you, my son, of the second great secret of my universe. With this knowledge in the minds of men, I must warn you, it is possible for you to suffer defeat. But then again, man already knows of this knowledge. It is his choice not to pursue it and take it up and live it. Thus, it is likely that you will remain safe, even if you impart it to man."

And I said quite sincerely, "But at least the contest will be equal. My talents will be tested. I am a fairer son than you might think. I ask only that you allow me to take this second great secret to man and announce it to him, so that he might not fall down so easily. Without it I have merely to speak and wars will come and I will gain my dominion over him, and he will be lost to you forever. Surely a father must have the chance to influence his children and steer them away from damnation."

He said to me, "A sense of nobility has come to you in older age. Of this you can be proud. I have a little more respect for you, my son. At this time, you are a credit to my kind."

I bowed down then with my thoughts rushing. I was coming to the moment of which I dreamed. To have his respect was to have peace in my soul. By a single gesture of generosity to man (for which I would lose nothing) I would

WORLD ONE

gain a delight which I could take with me into my time in eternity. I had wished for this and now I was beginning to have it. I shook as I spoke. How nice it was to hear him speak to me dearly. "I live to serve your will, my father. You have been most generous with me. You have given me the chance to win clear title to the human race. For this chance, I would do anything. I am your most gentle creature of divinity. I love you for your word and for your faith in me. It is a pity that mankind does not know you as I do. Surely if they heard you speak, they would understand the beauty of your ways. I am sorry you have suffered such great disappointment. Perhaps in another time you will be more pleased."

Hearing now what I said to him then, I sound like a bloody fool. In my defense, I can only say that I was caught off guard. I was slipping into my deepest fantasies. I walked before his lighted gates blind, as blind as a blinded beggarman. It had not occurred to me that I was a puppet in all he had planned. It had not occurred to me that I had then consented to my death. No, I thought only of my perpetual fantasy which I believed was at last coming to a time of reality. So be it. I was no match for God.

He said to me quite honestly, "Listen then to the second great secret of my universe. It will not surprise you. It is as simple as it is clear. In the beginning, I handed down the law, and this law was meant to be a guide for the lives of man. But I speak now of a greater law. I speak of a law which governs the lives of the nations of men. Mankind is one, and so it must live under one law if peace is ever to come. Call it a universal law, call it the law of mankind, call it the wisdom of the ages. It is one and the same. My son, if the men of nations choose one law under which all lives are ruled, they will have their great destiny, and they will have their peace, for law is peace when accepted by all."

I thought then: Truly my father is such a simpleton. One law for all mankind is the naivest of dreams. What incentive would man have to live in this way? What would induce the nations of men to lay down their banners of pride and lift up this flag of true nobility and wisdom? I should have laughed then at his idyllic fantasy and told him to drift on alone with his dreams; but I thirsted for his respect, and I tasted the nature of what my life would be when I claimed my long-sought victory. I would entertain his naiveté. Gladly, I would do this for him as a token of my respect for him and because of his respect for me.

So I said to my father, "Then I have your permission to take this second great secret of the universe and hand it down to man? I am not sure it will provide a better chance for him. But if this is the best that you have to offer, then so be it. I will tell him that by this law he may have peace and come to his destiny and live in eternity. I will tell him in ways of my own what you have told me today. And let us hope that mankind will not be as blind to this wisdom as truly I am. Perhaps it is just that I have a better feel for the nature of man. For I do not believe, father, that he will see the wisdom in this law."

Father said nothing as was his usual way in departing. I stood for a moment before the gates as the light of his presence grew fainter and fainter the farther he stepped away. I felt pity for my father just then. He had such belief in his people. And I knew that they would again only disappoint him. But what was I to do? I had my own ambitions and my own destiny to follow. My father was growing old. Perhaps he had had his day. Perhaps he was resigned to defeat. Perhaps he was passing on his power to me, his fair and generous son, Satan.

So I went down into the floating ship armed with the second great secret of the universe. Once more I transformed myself into a blinded beggarman. Once more I walked about and went unnoticed. Who was I to them but a lucky survivor of the human race? I planned my entrance well. They would see and listen to me soon. Their lives would depend upon my words. This chance they would have. Great wisdom would come from the blinded beggarman. But still they would not know my true identity. They would not know until the end. On that day of defeat they would regret that they had not

WORLD ONE

listened better to me. They would regret it for eternity. A chance for wisdom and peace and they pass it up for war. How I could understand the pathetic nature of my father's plight. How I could see the coming of my victory. But one last chance, one last chance for man. He would have his chance for victory, and I, mine.

All the nations of men were awake when I came home. They had risen from their dreams, their nasty hateful dreams pretending to be so sweet and innocent when they strolled among each other. Such hypocrisy made me sick. I would like better to see them dead. But I controlled the measure of my disgust. I waited through the day. I wandered aimlessly from city to city while I prepared my speech. I would pay lip service to them all, and probably then they to me. I had no hope that they would hear the wisdom in my words. Father above me, I thought, why have men failed so miserably? They wade like oxen in the sea. A new beginning they have, but the end is so clearly near. One day my father would make better men for me. One day my objectives would be much more difficult to attain. I pray this day is not too near. I wish to enjoy the fruits of my dominion before I enter into a new race for the souls of men of wisdom.

The nighttime came and all men slept and returned to the haven of their familiar dreams. But I did not sleep. I am one who has no real need of sleep and dreams. My dreams are realities. And my rest comes with accomplishments. Divinity has its privileges as you shall see.

When the ship was as silent as the sea beyond the lighted windows, I moved into place the fulcrum for my scheme. I screamed. It was not a simple woman's scream. It was a scream of pure energy. Blinded beggarman was screaming into the night and all the people woke. You see, blinded beggarman had had a bad dream. Or so he told the people. In this dream he saw the coming destiny of the last of mankind, and with it he saw catastrophe, and with the catastrophe he saw floating death, a lifeless ship. Blinded beggarman saw the end of man in this dream and he spoke of it in all languages so that he would not be misunderstood by any of the men of many nations. Blinded beggarman said more. Toward the end of his dream he had seen visions of waters. They were blue, beautiful waters to begin with, but the blue turned black and the beauty disappeared and a stench rose up from them that he could smell even within his dream.

I screamed of death and treachery. I sang the tune of universal misfortune. And to enhance my credibility for prophecies, I told them all more. I told them that there was a source of light in this dream, and in this light there was a voice and the voice said to me: "There is a second great secret of the universe, blinded beggarman, that men choose not to see. With this second great secret, the last of man can have peace and eternity and destiny. Without it, they surely will die as you have seen in your dream. Tell the people that by law they may have peace. Tell the people that unless man learns to live in peace by law among the nations of men, he will see the day when your dream is no longer a haunting prophecy. Go tell the people, old man. I give you the power to tell them with many voices. I give you the power to tell them that this law comes from me."

Now all men of all nations listened to me. Before them stood this decrepit old man, yet they listened. Why would they listen unless I had performed my task perfectly? I had struck them with my prophecy. And for one moment I feared that I had done it too well. Might they accept what I had said? Might they come to see this wisdom over their selfish deadly dreams? I grew sweaty in anticipation of what they would say. I might have gone too far with fair play. With a universal law for peace among men, I would be dead. I was not ready to sit at my father's feet. I was prepared for everlasting life. I have heard men of great genius can do too well among ordinary men. It is possible for ordinary men to accept without question the ideas of these far-reaching minds. I feared this. I feared that I had done too well carrying the message of God.

This was not so. Man was as stupid as I had believed. Here I had provided him with the greatest incentive. I had said that either he learn to live in peace by law or suffer the end of all. What better incentive could there be? He paid no attention. Man believes in his immortality. It was a pity he had not seen the death of the earth. It was a pity I could not

WORLD ONE

draw him pictures of what I had seen. It was a pity he took flight too soon—he would have seen the end of immortality.

The first question these people asked was, Who was I? I told them. I was a servant of the Queen. I had praised her name in the streets of her city on earth. I had pledged my allegiance to her, for she cared for the safety of her people. She saw what no other men saw. She saw destiny when others saw death and destruction. I told these people that by my loss of sight, I had learned to see into the future. I had learned to hear voices in light. I had learned to receive the messages of the Lord. I was but a puppet in his play. So help me, I did not know how I was chosen for this task. But I ran errands for the God who created man's destiny.

These people were intrigued by the silvery truth of my prophecy. Perhaps, I thought then, the competition would be more fair. I had delivered to man what God had said. "Law is peace when accepted by all." I had imparted to man the great wisdom of the ages, and now it was up to him to either take it up and destroy me, or put it down and come unto my ministry.

The Queen came forth then to question me. After all, she was the leader of my sacred race. I welcomed her when I sensed her presence and knelt down on my knees. I could feel her hot little eyes upon me. Even a blinded beggarman has a feel for royalty. I was flattered by her intense interest. She said, "By your inference, my loyal blinded beggarman, it can be said that you are a messenger of God. God moves in curious ways. Let this be said. But also this. I, too, have heard the voice of God. It was His voice which has led us all into this time. It is He who has carved the way for mankind to find its destiny. Therefore, why should the people believe that you have truly heard the voice of God? What makes your nightmares prophecies? Why should we believe you are the chosen one? Why should we believe in these words of universal law? I see no spirits of war. I see no treachery and division. Our water is not poison. It would serve no one's purpose to make it turn black. I am the keeper of the peace. I am the law while I live. I will not submit the people's destiny to some ideal of universal law. I rule over peaceful men of many worlds. I see nothing to be gained by your ideals. I do not know you, blinded beggarman. And whomever I do not know, I do not trust. Before the people, I thank you for your loyalty. But we have peace enough without stirring up the waters. It is your right to reply. Speak, and we shall listen."

A ruthless queen was she. She loved the substance of her power. And why not? She ruled supreme, for now. Why should she step down from her gilded throne and submit her fate and the people's destiny to some unknown order of rule? She would not take the chance. It was true, thus far, she had kept the peace. But then, she did not know the deadly dreams of the many men of many nations who would love to seize control and satisfy their urge for power.

I spoke again, knowing she had won. I could count on her to lead my people down. She was the champion of my cause. I silently blessed this queen. I would mumble no more heresies. "Dear Queen," I said, "forgive me for my dreams. I am old and have been blinded. I am overcome by many dreams. I thought it well to speak of these. I meant to do no people harm. I will shut up. I shall scream no more. I shall remind myself to dream only of peace and conjure up images of this world's noble destiny. I believe that you are the law and guardian of the peace. One queen of peace is better than many men of law. I must admit, I may have heard the devil say the words that came to me in dreams. I am weak for devil's play. Rather would I cut out my tongue than speak such blasphemy again. I am your contrite and most loyal servant. Your power is the power for peace. All men of nations respect your glorious will. There will be peace in your time of rule."

The Queen seemed satisfied with what I said. I posed no threat to her. But what a fool was she. I had said the words of God. I had handed man his wisdom. I had given him the means to find his destiny. By those words he could have had salvation. But bloody fools are bloody fools. No leaders of men would ever give up such self-important power. Witness this queen. She would have none of it. Better she thought to

WORLD ONE

rule by might than by equality. I was fair and generous. But man was not. No matter to me. I had done what I had said that I would do. I had given man his chance to accept the words of wisdom. Now I would act. I would bring man into war. Let the worst be done, I thought. There is no time to waste. Better for all to end it quickly. The Queen interrupted all my thoughts.

"You are curious, blinded beggarman. In dreams you have the strength of ten thousand men. You have courage and conviction. But when I challenge you, you quickly turn afraid. What makes you act this way?"

I must be careful now, I thought. She is not acting so stupidly. I must measure out my words. I must bury my claim to prophecies. I stiffened my spine and spoke. "As you, my Queen, fear war and battle, so do I. We are the last of mankind and we must take care to preserve our destiny. As an old man I have seen many wars. For many years I have sought the answer to peace among men. This is why I dream so. I seek answers awake and when sleeping. I hear voices in the day and at night. I seek the way to peace and pray that I find it before the day that I die. I am not unlike you. I do not wish to hear of the repeat of the horrors of history. Old men would like nothing better than to die in peace and leave behind a better world. These are the thoughts which make me dream of answers that are unworthy of your attention. Once more, I ask forgiveness. Once more, I repeat, I am loyal to your rule. You have all power over these people. Nothing can change this reality. Think no more of what I have said. No God would ever speak to me. Gods choose to speak through kings and queens. You have said as much. I am silent."

I could not sense then what she was thinking. She might have been pleased with me. She might have wished to see me dead. As I was quiet, so was she. And no people interrupted the serenity of that passing moment in the night. I heard her turn and walk away as I lowered my head to the floor of the ship and listened to the light sounds of her steps. I heard ten thousand quiet footsteps as the people departed from the hall where I had screamed. I heard the murmurs of many languages blending together in discordant ways. I knew then that I would win. The Queen would empty my words from her thoughts. What worth are the thoughts of a blinded beggarman? And so, too, I knew that the people of the many nations would think nothing of it. They had other ideas to consider. But at least I knew that I had acted honestly. I had delivered to man his last chance for peace. And it had been rejected. And now there would be war and I was free to pattern its course to my liking. What war would I bring? I was thinking. All sounds of footsteps disappeared. I was alone. I was free. I would have my dream of eternity. I would have my everlasting dominion over these powerless people who saw sense in war but not wisdom. Oh, father, I thought. You deserve so much better than these . . .

I rested for an instant down there on the floor. Perhaps I was even a little weary of this easy game. Why was it, I wondered, mankind could not see that to have a destiny it must first learn to live as one? Why was it, I wondered. Why was it?

This question was of no consequence to me. It was simply a matter of curiosity. All questions of humanity intrigued me— this no more than others. Truly, I did not linger on it long. I set out to bring about war. And war it would be when my work was done. In this service, I was a specialist. Ask any casualty of man's history. He will tell you I am an expert tactician. He will tell you I am the lord of conspiracies. You shall see.

I had gone so far as to warn the people and the Queen of what would happen to the reservoirs of water. I was not believed. Blinded beggarmen have no credibility, and I was no exception. But this was soon to change. True predictions have a habit of enhancing credibility. But by then it would probably be too late. I would have snatched up the rewards of my victory and mankind would be left with regret. And blinded beggarman would have changed back into his true form. The people would recognize the one who is called Satan. I looked forward to this day, the day of the beginning

WORLD ONE

of my dominion. "Father above my head," I whispered, "can you sense the winds of change? Have you heard the rumors of my coming principality? Are you prepared to relinquish all mortals to me? I love to serve your generous will. So be it. I will."

When the sweet of night came again to the people on board the ship which floated fruitlessly toward some ignoble destiny, I was electric with energy. I felt ten thousand feet tall. I felt the power of eternity massage my fingertips. I impressed myself. I was soon to be a father of many children. I was soon to deliver mankind into the bliss of war. This is how I went about my duties.

I lifted up my nose and smelled the scent of still waters. I let this be my guiding light. I walked down through the avenues of the ship, past silent cities and sleeping people and a dreaming Queen, past warehouses stocked with food. I, the blinded beggarman, proceeded to my destination, the people's watering hole. I, in my divinity, had no need of it. No son of God has need of water. But people are of another breed. They have need of water in their veins. They prefer water without poison. I made the choice for them. Poison, it would be.

I spit into the reservoirs of water. I pictured the deep round pools turning black. Black they would be as this night in eternity. Poison they would drink for breakfast, if they were as blind as me. The fresh blue water began to stink. I put my hand into each pool and stirred the toxic waste. I felt my fingers burn. Attribute what I did to my art of interference, not to my fair play. But still I had an impulse for generosity. I left untainted three pools of water in the reservoir. After all, there must be something left to be battled for. Mankind must have its fight for me to obtain the glory of my victory and the happy home of my reward.

Understand this well. I would not have interfered had mankind accepted what God had said through me. It had not been my idea to toy with humanity so brazenly. I would have taken much more time. I would have created little skirmishes. I would not have dared to bring about the end of all, like I had done on earth. It was my father who played for the highest stakes of all. By his suggestion, we undertook to play this deadly game. I merely seized an interesting opportunity to be father to these children. And this deal was not without great risk to me. I had placed myself in jeopardy. If man had chosen to live as one under the light of universal law, I would have then consented to my death. I never again would have practiced my art of interference.

In those moments when the blue waters turned black, I was supremely confident. I knew what men would do when all the blood of life was poisoned, except enough for one nation of men. It takes little imagination to understand what fantasies would come true. I would simply sit somewhere and listen to it happen. I would then go and report the reality to the one who cared so much for me. "Father," I would say, "today mankind has bloodied its destiny with war. The last of mankind has been given its chance to learn to live as one, and yet, it has turned its face to me. Children seek their father. I am the one of war. It must be sad for you to hear me say that I claim dominion over them. From here and evermore, they shall be under my expert tutelage. And I shall thank you in advance for no further interference."

I walked proudly away from the stinking pools of water. When the morning came, mankind would know the power of my prophecy. I would be respected as no blinded beggarman had ever been before. But as I walked away, I felt a subtle weight of tragedy. In the dawn of my omnipotence, my heart felt some sympathy for the children of the Lord. They had heads for knowledge and hearts for beauty and souls for magnanimity. But they lacked the vision for wisdom, and so it was that their time was coming to an end, and I felt sorry for them.

I had struggled with God for the souls of men for so long that it made this, my last act, seem so trivial. After all of the ages that had gone by, it had all come to this. Drops of poison in pools of blue water. This was not the way I had envisioned that it would be. But then I had not dared to think that God, my father, would have grown weary with man and put him to the final test. I thought then that it must be that he had another plan. A new species of man was in the making. Yes,

WORLD ONE

I thought, this must be. It did not matter to me. I would win all for which I had worked. I thought back on all my horrors of history. I pictured all of the dead that I had caused to be slain on all of the battlefields that there had ever been. And now the ending to my quest had come to this. Drops of poison in pools of blue water. Nothing ever turns out the way you dream. Not in life. Perhaps in eternity. Perhaps.

I walked on through my journey in darkness and tried to stifle my sad sense of pain. But I was a sentimental fool. I felt tears in my old blinded eyes. And then tears were running down my cheeks and neck, and then I wiped them clean and dry. Perhaps it was I who had grown weary and old and sentimental. I knew then that I was in need of rest.

I found a soundless corner of the ship and lay down. I remembered how I used to rest above the earth and sleep on fine clouds. I remembered how it was to rest and wake and then, fresh, go down to the earth and spend my time among the people of the world. I knew then why I was so sad. I missed them. I missed all of the people of the earth. I missed that home. In that moment before I slept on the ship on the eve of my victory, I regretted what I had done to my friends.

3

When I awoke I remembered nothing of my sorry fit. I awoke to unholy screams which sounded throughout the ship. So the people had discovered their stinking pools of water. What a shame I had not been there to witness it. But the screams gave me a happy satisfaction. My prophecy had become a nightmare in reality. I would be praised. Now I wandered down to them as innocent a thing as you have ever seen.

With a raspy voice and sweaty palms, I called out to the people who stood terrified around the pools, "Last night I had a dream that this would happen and by the stink I know it has. Poor people, I told you of this plague. I should be put to death for not having warned you better. How did this happen? Tell me, I cannot see. Tell me, who is the perpetrator of this insane action?"

The Queen answered me. I had not detected her presence. When I heard her voice, I started. She had a strange power

WORLD ONE

over me. I cannot describe it well. It was as if she knew me. It was as if she knew this blinded beggarman who swore his loyalty to her. I turned my old, bent frame and bowed down to her, my Queen. She had her eyes on me, I knew. My sweaty palms were dry.

"My friend, the blinded beggarman, you are a man of prophetic talents. Just last night you told us of a dream. And now your dream is true. You see clearly in the dark. I am impressed with you. Perhaps I even fear you. By some unknown act of treachery all but three pools of water are of no use to us. This alone differs from what you prophesied. But then again it might give man his reason to go to war, man against man, nation against nation. What say you to this, my friend?"

There was something in her voice I did not like. There was something in the way she said my name. When I choose a leader, I choose her well. She suspected all and everything. I had better act accordingly. This was a dangerous queen. I lowered my ragged head.

"I only know what I picture deep in sleep. Thus, I am horrified to sleep. Do not let me sleep, my Queen, or I shall dream more, see more, scream more. I am cursed."

But then ten thousand people cheered. They cheered for me, the blinded beggarman, who could see destiny. And voices everywhere besieged me. Like the drumming of the rain, I heard each drop. And they were saying, "Tell us what to do, tell us what will happen. We have no powers of your kind. We cannot see our destinies. We have no gifts of prophecy."

I was flattered and amazed. The spirits of my children clung to me. Instinctively, they knew that I would be father to their race. They sensed in me my magic divinity. I would tell them who had done this thing to their blood of life. And each man would find my conclusions interesting. But I would wait to tell them for a little while. First, I wished to hear the tones of panic in their throats. My sympathy for them was spent.

But the Queen raised her voice above the crying people. She was more interested in me than them. She was the queen for me. Gladly, would I have gone with her to bed. Her children would bear the features of my face. They would all be as ruthless as she and I. What lovely company we would all be. But at this moment she thought differently from me. She said, "Still you have not answered my question, blinded beggarman. I ask it once again. Could it be that men might go to war over these last pools of water? Could it be that this might be the way to the fulfillment of your prophecy? If so, we must all act to prevent it, for a war among these people would be the last war for all mankind. It would be the very end to the human race. This will not happen. I dreamed a prophecy of destiny, not death. Our minds conflict in sleep, my friend. Give me your best answer."

I answered her. "Once a prophecy has been told it has the strength of life, and it will happen. Nothing can be done. The future comes inexorably."

She said, "But remember this, my friend. We have had two prophecies. One by you and one by me. How shall we reconcile them? Both cannot come true. One prophecy for death and one for destiny. It will be interesting to see which comes to reality. I pray to God for a miracle this day."

Before I knew what I had said, I said it too. Down on my knees I said it. Before the Queen and the people I said it, "I pray to God for a miracle this day."

I felt the creeping smile of the Queen. I felt her hot little eyes upon me. She knew with whom she conversed. She knew I was no mere blinded beggarman.

She went away. The stinking pools of water sickened me, as did my words to God. But I had said them quietly. My father might have heard me mumble, no more. My ruthless Queen had played a ruthless trick on me. I would see she came to regret it. I saved my sympathies for me. I would need them far away in some other time in eternity.

Now the men of nations came to me and called to me and begged with me to tell them of the future and of what would happen. I told them nothing then. I said I was a man of some delicacy. I promised to return to each city in the night and tell each people what I had come to know with my gifts of prophecy. To each I promised to tell my discoveries.

So the people departed as had the Queen and once again I was all alone. The air was putrid and the water worse and

WORLD ONE

I was pleased with what I had done. I stood up and walked about the reservoirs until I found the three clean pools of water. And with my hands, I drank some clear fresh water down so that there might be just a little less for the thirsty tongues of man.

How greedy I could be. I had no need of water, but I drank. Precious little there was, but I drank. But do not think of me too harshly. I was no worse than man. In fact, I simply resembled him. But then again, I had immortality. And with immortality goes responsibility. This was where the last of man was falling down. He feared his great responsibility. The human race would have immortality only with responsibility. I say enough. I uncupped my hands and lay down on the floor and pretended to have more prophecies.

I knew my Queen would try to put me to the test. I knew why she went away. She went away to conceive a plan to dispose of me. I could hear her thinking even from these miles away. She would love to see me dead. She would love to rid my father of his son. She had no hope of this. She had no hope for anything but death. She would look lovely still as stone.

But quickly I must act. I trusted her intelligence. She might even come to see that I had delivered the true words of God. I set about to precipitate the war of man. I felt the strength for victory. I went on my way.

And to each city of each of the nations of men, I went. "In my prophecies this night," I said, "I have seen the culprits of the crime. They are your neighbors to the north." And to the neighbors in the north, I said, "They are your neighbors to the south." And on and on I went accusing neighbors here and there. And when I had completed my errands for the evening, the fuse was set. Each neighbor pledged to see their neighbors dead. You see, I played upon their insecurities and the nature of their tempers. I knew that men often acted before they asked the proper questions. I knew I could rely on this, for the horrors of history provided for such good examples. Brother nations would go against each other. And the cities on the ship would be reduced to steaming pools of blood. And I would make the survivors drink from them, for after battle one is often thirsty. Their new father would look out for them. He was anxious to do his duty well. I would be so proud to be the father of many, many children. You have heard me testify. You have heard me speak the truth.

I had set my stage and was content to bide my time until the hour of war. Soon I would go to God to report on mankind's progress. I would break his heart with my news. The heavens would rain his tears. I felt even now for the coming of his tragedy. It is a pathetic sight to see one's father weep in misery.

Now while the minds of men were burning in their cities, I thought it would be pleasant to take a little walk. I peeled away the skin of the blinded beggarman and took flight into the long dark seas of the heavens. Never had I been so happy. I flew like a golden jet of light within the dark and pondered all the futures that there would be when man and I came to settlement. I came to wonder where our home would be. We would find some lovely place where all the land was green. And I would have my children build great palaces for me. All places would bear the imprint of my name. And all men would worship me as I had had to worship the one who created me. Even as I flew I heard my children singing. They were singing in honor of me. Though they would suffer devastating pain and eternal war, they would be grateful when I came to them and praised them for their daily deeds. And the women would scream for me. They would cry to have me in their beds. All women would have a taste of my sensuality. And more children would be born on this new land of green, and they, too, would come to love their father who had created them and given them his name. And they would all respect me in such a tender way. It might make me have some pity on a few of them. I might relieve some kind boy of pain. I might make fresh water for a pretty girl to drink. I might let some old man die who had had too many years of constant misery. I would maintain my generosity. I might even share my power among a chosen few. Inevitably, there would be those who excelled in battle beyond my expectations.

WORLD ONE

For them there would be rewards. They might rule a portion of the people. They might even be allowed to father children. But I must be wary of tendencies toward generosity. The new blood of man must be pure. And through eternity it must become yet purer. I must protect my sacred heritage. Yet the human race must multiply. I see a sea of a trillion children. They call my name. They sing to me. They love me all the same. I am one with them and they with me. I have freed them in eternity. I have given them immortality. I have made them sons of God. I sit upon my throne of ecstacy.

I flew and flew into this dream. It made me breathe so easily. I heard symphonies in the silent deep. I heard my tune of destiny. But then I wished for sleep. My travels had been long though sweet. I knew the time had come to return to my place of residence. I turned in flight and made my way back toward the lighted ship of humanity.

At a distance it was but points of light. It was no green land with many shores. It had no great palaces built for me. And the people did not quite worship me. They knew little of my strength, and still less of my generosity. But soon they would have me in their midst and I would be the light above them and they would know my name and repeat it for eternity or until I wished it to be changed. Though Satan was a luxurious name, I might do better. But I would not take the name of God. Never would I wish to hear his name again. I would have ruined him. I would forget him. I would not even remember what his name had been. And my people would not speak it. I would forbid it. Amen.

I drifted now gazing at the sight of my fine ship of humanity. To think this ship had been born in my dreams made it all the more magic to me. Soon I might hear the battle cries. Soon I might smell the scent of blood. Soon I might be making my way to God to tell him of the news. My heart was warm with contentment. My mind was cool with ecstacy. So many ages I had waited to sense the true divinity of God. It had been worth the wait. It had been worth—everything. My work, my life, my dreams were now coming to this conclusion, this stage of my advancement. If I had had to wait another million years, I would have done it.

Now I came close to the ship, this tiny ship which had

been God's last hope for man. I did not hear the battle cries. I sensed no smell of blood. I did not understand. I changed myself into a blinded beggarman and walked through the walls of glass. I went to see the children of my race and incite them on to victory.

But the Queen had taken advantage of my absence. She was strides ahead of me. She stood before the people and administered prophetic words. She was trying to out maneuver me. She knew I would be upset. After all, I had come to make man go to war. I was in no mood for pacifism. I was in no mood to hear her change her mind. It had occurred to her that the blinded beggarman might be right, that by law and law alone mankind might find the path to peace and to its destiny out beyond the stars. What made her change her mind I do not know. I should have stayed on board the ship and listened to her thoughts more carefully. I should have polluted her clear and hopeful thinking. I did nothing of the kind. I strayed away into the warm waters of my dreams instead of keeping watch over the players on my stage. I knew when I returned I had made a great mistake. My Queen had had the time to understand what the wisdom was to be in eternity.

Now before the people she spoke of the glory of the light of universal law. For with this law mankind is free to live in peace without the fear of war. Mankind is free to live as one. Mankind is free of me. With this law mankind is free to settle differences more artfully. As great as was my art of interference it was no match for the art of universal law. In fact, with this law I would be put to death. The Queen was now the messenger of God. She had taken up his cause. She had taken the first step on the path toward man's destiny. I would be helpless if she succeeded in converting all the minds of men. Now I knew what it was God had wanted from me. Now I knew why he had had a little more respect for me. God had set me up to deliver to man his law. I was the puppet of his play. I stood squarely on his stage of compromise. I was the pawn of his charade. The Queen and I would do battle for man's destiny.

I heard the chilly whisper of her words: "People of mankind, our time has come to learn to live as one. The time has come to end the ages of war. The time has come to claim victory over humiliating violence. The time has come to take up the wisdom of our universe.

"I believe the blinded beggarman is a prophet of God. He came to us to tell us of His decree. God wills that we should find our way into eternity. But we shall find it only if we go in peace. And to have peace we must create one great law for all mankind, one world of man for all eternity.

"Therefore, it is my duty to step down from my position of authority. I have led you to this place, but I shall lead no more. No one person should hold all the power. No one person should administer the law.

"Together we must create one great law for peace. Let this be man's miracle of the ages. Let this be man's miracle before God. It shall be a miracle of peace. And with peace will come mankind's immortality."

She seemed to say this so easily. And the people stood stunned. Here she had accepted the words of the blinded beggarman when before she had flicked them off like beads of salty sweat. Indeed, she stepped down from her throne in what I presumed to be my halls of victory. She went among the people as though she had never been a queen. Here the last of man was left alive without a leader. Here the last of man had been on the verge of war. And now they stood dumfounded without a voice among them. My Queen was not as ruthless as I had imagined. She had heard the truth in my damning prophecy. Now it would be up to the people to decide between peace or war.

What way they would follow I did not know. Would they take up this responsibility as God had dreamed, or would they bury it beneath pools of blood? I feared a confrontation with the Queen. She had put me in a box. And I knew she waited to hear what I had to say. I could not speak against all that I had said. I had been the first to speak in favor of it. I could not destroy my credibility. I could not damage the blinded beggarman's golden reputation. I had to destroy this woman who had been queen. Mankind could not learn to live as one. Mankind must wage its final war and grant me my long-sought triumph. Never would I have believed that God's words might be accepted by such mortal fools as these. I must have my palaces and I must have my children and I must have my destiny and immortality. I had no wish to sit with God and relinquish the beauty of my powers. I had come too far for this. I had paid my dues to be the father of my children. I would live to see them praise my name. I would live to see the demise of God, my father. I would live to see the former queen tried for treason and be sentenced to death. She had no right to challenge the nature of my destiny, and the destiny which I had claimed for the future of my children. Who was this woman to try to do this to me? Had my father known whom I would choose? Had he privately instructed her? Had she pledged to go along with me until this time when my art was to be tested? Perhaps God had planned for this to be my final test. I saw my father's hands everywhere. I suspected he listened to my thoughts. I cursed him for his treachery. I prayed to be witness to his death. I prayed that I would have the strength to defeat him and his children. I prayed mankind would not accept the former queen's decree. Why should they? They had other means to settle grievances that were more colorful and interesting. I must attack. I must bring my world to order. I must bring my children under my command. Time was running short for me and I would have no second chance. "Winner take all . . . ," I heard my father say once more. It would not be so easy for me. I would be challenged to the end. So be it then, I thought. A puppet, I am not.

    I grinned after a moment of reflection. I knew what I would do. Fury often inspired me to action. Rage opened the way to better thinking. I would break this former leader of my race. I would damage her integrity. And before the people would know what they had done, she would be a distant memory.

How then did I turn the people against their queen? How did I bring her to her time of trial? I accused this wise and gentle one of trying to bring the people to a state of war. I

WORLD ONE

declared, "We sit with Satan. She wears red velvet robes. I sense the colors by my fingertips. She speaks of everlasting peace, yet deceives us into war. Is it not she who leaves us leaderless in our time of greatest need? I ask you, fellow citizens, do her actions not smack of treachery? Are we to believe she wishes us well when we are on the eve of war? Satan would be glad to see us flounder in the deep. He would triumph by our misery. Remember, my good people, Satan wishes us to war. So, too, our former queen would have us take this step. Mankind can ill-afford a final war. This war may be our last. I will prove we sit with no mere mortal. I will prove she has the power of devious divinity. I will prove we have Satan in our midst. Watch the blinded beggarman!"

I heard these mortal men pricking up their ears. I listened to the congestion of their doubts. And I even heard the astonished thoughts of my beloved Queen: He has planned it well, for a blinded beggarman. He pretends he is for the destiny of man. He suggests that I seek to bring it to an end. I have touched his nerve. I have sorted out the truth. By law and law alone, mankind shall have its peace.

My thoughts were these: But you are too late, my Queen. I have powers to poison minds as well as water. I shall teach you never to cross the sacred will of divinity. You shall make the blinded beggarman see light. And with my sight you shall be condemned to death.

I blindly made my way through the throngs of humanity. I felt the fear on the faces of the people. Soon I stood before her. I did not kneel.

I said, "If we could be rid of you, we would see the end of war and death and annihilation. But first allow me to show the people all the powers that you possess."

I took her soft white hands. She did not resist. She could not resist. She did not know what I would do. If she had known, she would have ripped out my blinded eyes. She would have allowed my poisonous blood to flow upon the floor. She would have rinsed her hands in it. But she did not know. And I did.

I put her hands up to my eyes, my swollen, crusty eyes. I felt their warmth and tenderness, surely her hands were a miracle of God. I pretended to feel a surge of energy. I pretended to feel the heat of many suns. I fell down upon my knees. I crawled along the floor. I hid my face in shame. I cursed the sins of Satan and swore against his name. But then I looked up. And when I looked, all the people saw that I could see.

"The blinded beggarman can see!" they screamed. "She has the power of divinity. She was no mortal queen!" I now had the pleasure to look upon the icy face of my beloved Queen. I had tricked her, it was clear. She now wore the robes of unholy immortality. I crawled away from her. My first sight of the new world was too much for me. I could not bear the sight of Satan's face, even disguised as a queen's. "She has powers that we have never known. She is Satan come to destroy the last body of mankind. Hear me, people of the world, we have come face to face with the one who has made all true horrors in history!"

Now the Queen was thinking: Satan sheds the skin of the blinded beggarman. How happy he must be. Such trouble it must have been for him to walk so blindly in the dark. And now he crawls away like some disillusioned fool. But I am glad that he will see the fight.

Now I was thinking: She stands accused. What is her plan? What will her next dangerous move be? I cannot hear her thinking. Everywhere people are shouting and calling and making noise in many languages. I would shut their mouths if it would not reveal me. I have only to hear what she will do and I will counter it.

Now the members of the human race were thinking: We have no Queen and we have Satan. We have so little water and our neighbors stand accused. Better it would be to take advantage of this moment of confusion and turn against our brothers . . .

It was a glorious sound to hear the panic of the people. They pressed against each other as if on the verge of a cataclysmic explosion. How beautiful to sense the coming of my hour. How beautiful to know I had completely destroyed my sweet Queen's credibility.

By my accusations, I had made her sister to me. How satisfying it would have been to have her so close to me. If only she had been born with immortality we would have

WORLD ONE

enjoyed together the triumph that was coming; surely it was coming now, now that she was me, now that men were eager to defeat their destinies, now that they had no leader to comfort them and calmly guide them.

In vain I tried to listen to her thinking. What grand move would she attempt to make upon my stage? She had turned away from me and was walking far away. And the people let her pass, for they all had their eyes upon their neighbors.

This Queen knew me, but what would she expect of me? And how would she seek to check my play? She knew I would want to see her dead, this much I knew. Likewise, too, she would love to see me take my final breath. I cried out to her, "Satan, do not leave so soon!"

And with the repetition of my name, bedlam broke out. If I had been so disposed I might even have pitied these poor pathetic creatures of the human race. They were wise to understand that they had been betrayed by Satan. Though fortunately for me they believed that he was she. Only the true Queen knew from where the blinded beggarman had come. Only the true Queen knew that I meant to destroy the human race. But still, she was so ignorant of my deal with God. If she had known the consequences of her actions, she might have acted sooner. But she had not the privilege of communications with my father.

And neighbor went against neighbor. What better time for there to be a battle? And battle leads to war, nicely and naturally. Who could blame them, really? They had no leader, no trusted power above them. They had no means to settle grievances, they had no universal court of law. If I had not intruded, the Queen would have come to victory over me. Men would have come to understand the brilliance of the law. And God would have been so pleased that mankind had discovered his second great secret of the universe.

I alone was pleased. I alone had the upper hand. I alone was on the verge of victory. Bedlam to battle to war! A little longer and mankind would be mine. And mankind would have no hope for peace for the rest of all eternity. I would finally be content with my complete dominion over it. I would be content to lead it on and on into a perpetual state of war and bloody disharmony.

But still I was not satisfied. Over there, there stood a living spokeswoman for my father's cause. She watched me from afar. Perhaps she liked the color of my eyes. I had made them red for her to match her royal robes.

But I could not in all good conscience let her live. Too much trouble she had made for me by stepping down from her sacred throne. How I wished she had not been such a wise and ruthless queen. How I wished she had remained quiet and seated until my war for man was done. I would miss her in my bed. I would miss the children that we could make. I would miss the pleasure of her tender touch. But she would turn mankind against me, if she could. She had nearly put my plans in jeopardy. She had nearly done what my father had wished. But I was not prepared for this. Now or ever. Never would I be prepared for this. I was too young to die. She was not. I would demand her death. And then bedlam leads to battle leads to war!

I, the seeing beggarman, stepped out into the fields of victory and raised up my hands for quiet and peace. I said to one, I said to all, "Let us not forget our true enemy. Let us punish the one who has brought us strife. Let us do some sentencing for all her crimes against humanity. We will find peace if we rid ourselves of this fraudulent queen. I have heard in my dreams a message of God. He says to man, 'Slay Satan and peace will come.' It is only just that we follow this course. Let us at least see if peace will come when she is dead. Satan will die when all men agree to punish him. I propose we put this Queen on trial. I propose that if she be found guilty of crimes against humanity that she be cast out into the long dark seas where she will be lost forever."

The people were silent as I spoke. I commanded all men's attention. This was proper training for our time to be. Soon they would all bow down to me and utter words of praise. But this was enough for now. They heard me speak and weighed my words and seemed anxious to please the man of prophecies.

WORLD ONE

The people were thinking: We shall follow his lead and try the Queen and then meet our neighbors in battle. We shall live for as long as we can on the last of the pools of water.

The Queen was thinking: All goes according to his plan. He shall see me dead, and then rule. He is listening to me now, even as I am thinking. I have no plans for my defense. I have been outwitted by Satan.

And I was thinking of the eternal wars to come and of the nobility of my civilization and of the faces of my people as they toiled on and on from war to war. I was thinking of the entertainment that they would provide for me as my time over them extended on and on into the twilight of eternity.

I said to all, "It is right and fair that we try this one. After all, we are a generous people. History must see that we acted decently on the day we sentenced Satan to death out here in the fields of God. And think how God will reward us for our actions. Think what miracles we shall receive from Him at the hour when He looks down and sees that His unholy son is gone from the hearts of men. What rewards there will be is impossible to know. But the rewards will be plenty and we will find the means to live on and fulfill our destiny. What say you, Satan? Are you prepared for your last trial? Never before in history has mankind had this opportunity. And we shall make the best of it. I encourage you to do the same. You have so little time in which to defend yourself. I pray that you will do it well."

And now the people cheered for me, their prophetic servant of humanity. They loved me as a brother. I had saved them from their vicious Queen who meant to lead them into war. Little did they know that the bedlam was just beginning. Little did they know that I had other plans for them. Little did they know that God was about to abandon them.

4

And so it was I saw the people put the Queen on trial for crimes against humanity. These were a fair and equitable people when it came to prosecuting divinity. I was pleased to see that they would have been so fair to me had I been the one to bear the brunt of Satan's name. I sincerely wished my father could have seen these people. They seemed to act so reasonably as they went about their business of setting up the court to try her former majesty. My father would have seen mankind acting so responsibly to preserve the dignity of justice. But he would have been saddened to see the victim of its animosity. This Queen had not been born to be executed for my crimes. She believed in the wisdom of the Holy Father. She believed in the destiny of man. She believed that peace would come in the time when all men learned to live as one. But I was too much for her. I was too much for anyone. I was second only unto God. And he was far away and would not interfere. He had wiped his hands of man and now only

WORLD ONE

waited for the hour when I would come to him and tell him of my final victory over man. "Your children have failed to pass the test. They have met with final defeat. And now I am entitled to my children. Give them up and let me relieve you of this burden."

But at least the Queen would have one reward. She might die a dreadful death, but she would be granted entrance into Heaven. She would not be among my chosen children. She would not live for eternity in my new green place of hell. Better it would be for her to die now than to survive. She was a true child of God and she would fare much better in his presence. And she would tell him of how I tricked mankind out of its destiny. This would be important to me. Truly my father would have great respect for me when he heard of all the things which I had done to win the contest. And I had even played by the rules. I had played it by the letter of our agreement. I had given man his final chance for peace and he had turned it down. Yes, I deceived man thereafter with my accusations against the Queen, but I had made no promises to refrain from interference. My father would have expected this from me. He would have been astonished if I had done otherwise. I had fulfilled the terms of our agreement, and now only waited for the verdict of the court and the death of the Queen and the coming bedlam and battle and final war of man. How easy it all seemed. How pleasant it had been. I had simply had more patience than the Master of Eternity. And my reward would be to take his place and choose a different destiny for man which only I could appreciate.

I was anxious to get started. There was so much I had left to do. First on my agenda was to find a place where my children and I would live. I would search all regions of the universe to find the most picturesque of homes. I would settle for nothing but the best—the deepest green grasses, the tallest trees, the gentlest, most fertile valleys, the most graceful, rolling mountains. And the rivers would be as clean as the lighted gates of Heaven, and the seas would be free of salt and stocked with meaty fish. And there might be seven suns which circled in the sky, and night would never set in and darken the smoke of warring nations of men. It would be a most beautiful place for hell. It would be a land which would give me comfort in my golden, old age. It would be the land of all my dreams, the land which I was meant to know. It would be everything that the son of God should have. And my children would never wish to leave. They would be happy in their natural state of war. They would thrive and grow in battle and become the great warriors of the universe. And I would be their God and king. I would lead them into every fray. I would map out their strategies. I would restore the divine instruments of atomic weaponry. And I would invent other great weapons of incineration. But man would be made to use them more discriminately. I had no wish for man's complete annihilation. I had already been witness to that tragedy on earth. No, man would use his powers more intelligently, so that wars might go on and on inexorably.

You can see how I have pictured all this so perfectly. A lush green land, ten thousand battlefields, ingenious weapons of destruction. I saw the beauty of the future well. This was a part of the secret of my power. I had a never ending supply of imagination. In all fairness I must say, this was a gift from God. It was he who had envisioned the nature of the universe and created it masterfully. It was he who had dreamed of man and made him so cleverly. But as I had found, even God was flawed. He was too impatient for man to come to his destiny. He was too impatient to wait for man to come naturally into his age of peace. Perhaps if he had waited, mankind would have learned to live by universal law. But he did not. He chose to make a deal with me. "Winner take all . . ."

So here I was in the ship of glass and here I was with the last of mankind and here I was on the eve of my victory as men took steps to seal their fates. I was elected by the people to be my beloved Queen's prosecutor. I kindly accepted this duty. I thought to myself, what better person could there be to prosecute Satan than me? I knew his art so well. I knew all of his crimes against humanity. I was well suited for the task, this much I knew. But I was surprised when the Queen announced that she would act in her own defense. Every mortal knew the folly of this move. As wise as was this Queen, she had made a regrettable mistake. Her thinking was no match for mine. I had already proven this. Perhaps she

WORLD ONE

prayed that God would see her through. Perhaps she dreamed that I would show some mercy on her. Perhaps she wished to be solely responsible for her own death. She was a most perplexing queen. I would miss her when she was gone. I would miss her when she was dead. I would miss her by my side in the green wastes of my kingdom at war.

And now finally, the people chose among themselves the judges and the jury. Each of the nations of men was represented so that, it was said, all would share in the responsibility of condemning Satan to death. How poetic it all seemed. All men had joined together to try me and sentence me. I was almost touched by their fairness and sincerity. If I had been the one to stand accused, I would have felt much better. I would have almost believed that a sense of universal justice had come over the nations of humanity. They came together when all of their interests were at hand. Before this time, I would not have believed that this could have been possible. But now that I saw it taking place, I was proud of them. For the first time in history, they acted as brothers in an endeavor that was a noble cause to them. "Slay Satan and peace will come." They echoed my words, the words of the seeing beggarman who had been elected to prosecute the Queen. At that moment I was living on the stage of a new age in man's history. I shall never forget it. But always, always I will regret it.

"I have proven that we, the people, have been misled," I said. "I have proven she has powers beyond those of mortal men. I have proven she has taken all good men to the brink of war. But we are not fools. We have been led by Satan into death for too long. Now it is time to end Satan's rule over the hearts and minds of men. Now it is time to deliver Satan to a rightful death. And I ask this court of law to see that this is done. So help me, this may be our only chance to see that divine justice *is* done."

Thereafter, I called for the death of the Queen. With her death, I said, mankind would at last be free, free to go on to its destiny out beyond the stars of the heavens. And I thought then that the judges and the jury of the people would believe all of my accusations. Why should they not? She had abandoned them. She had led them out here so they would all die a miserable death. The people believed that Satan was before them. And so he was. But he was not she. I was he. She was the key to my victory. She was the beloved puppet of my play and I was amused to see her dangling before me.

Now the time came for her testimony. Now came the time that I had been waiting for. Speak, my Queen, I thought. Turn the people against me if you can. It is your last chance. There will be no other. I will be here to see that you die and never speak again of the light of universal law.

Now the Queen rose, and the judges and the jury waited for her immortal words. These words would be remembered for all eternity. I remember her every twist of thought. I remember each and every sentence. I remember the way in which she turned my children against me and brought me to this time at my father's feet. Listen and you shall hear the words which ended my time in eternity.

"It is my pleasure to speak to this court. There is nothing which I would rather do. There is no place in the heavens where I would rather be. For at this moment as I speak we put in practice what the Lord has decreed to be the second great secret of the universe.

"I have been put on trial for alleged crimes against humanity. It has been said that I have powers beyond those of mortal men. I do not think so. I have but the power of the word. It may not be enough, for the true Satan speaks with many tongues and in many languages and has a prophetic intellect. Nevertheless, I shall speak one last time of peace, and I pray that you will hear the wisdom of my logic.

"I say that I have brought peace to mankind. I say that I can prove that there will be peace now and forevermore. I say that by this trial mankind has found the way to wisdom and the way to live as one. I say that we shall have our destiny and victory. I say that Satan will be condemned to death before this day is through. Think of the future as I speak and you may come to understand all that I have to say.

"Have I not brought peace to mankind even now? Can

any members of the judges and jury see a battlefield? Can any members smell the scent of blood? Have we not found a means to settle certain grievances peacefully? Have we not established a court of law among the nations of men? Do we not, in fact, practice the theory of universal law? Are we not now acting and living as one? Look to the future, my people. Look out into the glory of our destiny. By the creation of this court of law to try me as Satan, to try me for all crimes against humanity, we now live in wisdom. We have done what it was that I wished. We have acted for the good of all men by coming together for judgement peaceably.

"I am not Satan. I have brought you no wars; I have shown you the way to great peace. Surely Satan does not speak of peace and law. Satan speaks of war. His tools are poison and twisted reputations. His tools are deceits among brothers. His tools are the weapons of war. And he glories in lawless incivilities. I propose law not war. I propose peace not death. I propose that Satan will die if we as men live under the light of universal law.

"I believe this choice will lead us to our destiny, and a great destiny it will be when we become like sons of God in the outer reaches of eternity."

I was shocked by her eloquent treachery. She had indeed brought peace to mankind in this court of law. With my consent she had done all that she had wished. I had never counted on this defense. It was so obvious; it was so perfectly clear. I had made a bloody mess of things, for as I looked about the court I saw that the people were about to believe in all that she had said. Truly, I had set it up for her. By my generosity I had given her the means for escape. After all of my planning, after all of my pain, I was now on the threshold of total defeat. I imagined that I could hear my father singing. I heard him sing from a long way away. He was singing to me, to his most unholy son, Satan. He was singing an alluring song ever so enchantingly. And the words to the song were compelling. They seemed to reach out for me. And I began to feel the world of my eternity closing in. Yes, the words called to me. Yes, they asked me to relinquish my powers. Yes, they called to me to come sit at the feet of he who sang to me so demoniacally.

I trained my sight on the Queen. This filthy beauty glowed and radiated before me. She knew that she had struck the golden chord. The judges and the jury had been appeased. They saw no devious divinity in her. All my claims had been reduced to annoying memories. These people loved this queen. I no longer held any power over them. I was the one who had been outwitted by the wisdom of this queen. I had no hope. I had no credibility. These people saw the light of the law of which she spoke. And all of it, all of it was my doing.

I would not let her live. She had destroyed all which I had made. I could not forgive her for this. I would not allow her to witness my death. I would take her with me. She and I would go and follow the song of my father and together we would be received by him. Together we would live for eternity. This would be all that I would have left. It was so little, but it would be enough. She would see not one single day of destiny. She had no right to take away my victory. She had no right to give mankind its age of peace.

I, the seeing beggarman, peeled off my skin of mortality and revealed the true splendor of my hideous form. I transformed my hand into a claw, a claw with bony, poisonous tips which I would use to tear out the heart of this queen who had done so much damage to me and my destiny. And as I changed back into my proper self, the people were transfixed by my presence. They had never truly seen me. They had never seen the features of my face, a once beautiful face which had been distorted by the will of God. And I howled at them, and my howl was like the screams of all men who had died by my will throughout my reign in history.

I went for the Queen. I took a step to meet her where she stood so proudly and serenely. And I lifted up my claw, and she gazed at me. And I lifted it higher still, and she still gazed deep into my bloody red eyes. And as I prepared myself to bring it down into her, bring it down to rip out her heart and take her with me into death, the people seized me.

WORLD ONE

And it took hundreds to tame me. It took thousands to restrain me. It had taken all of humankind to make me sit upon the floor so passively. I remember sitting there and I remember looking up and I remember the face of the Queen as she looked down on me and smiled her ruthless smile. She had expected this of me. She had expected that I would wish to take her with me, but even more, she had expected her fellow men to join hands to restrain my final play. And they did this for her. They did this to me. Together they were even stronger than I. I was a helpless fool upon the floor. I was a child in their presence. I was a child without my toys. And it was then that I wished for my father. I wished my father would take me away to some safe place far away where I could grow and live sweetly. I suffered down there on the floor. If I had not been a true son of God, I would have wept in that first hour of my defeat. Never had I been so lonely. Never had I been without the respect of my company of mankind. I had nothing then. I had failed so completely that I wished for death—a long eternal death where I would feel nothing and know nothing and be nothing. I wished for this death with the same will that I had wished for my dominion over mankind.

And then I heard voices above me, from high above my valley of thought, I heard the people calling me by name. It was good to hear my real name. I loved this name, this name, Satan. And I was proud that the people now knew it. I was no mere blinded, seeing beggarman. I was Satan, the unholy son of God and I wanted all men to remember me as I was. Put me to death but remember my name! They would miss me when I was gone. They would miss what I could do for them. They would miss my parades on the battlefields. They would miss my talents of interference. They would miss everything about who I was and what I did and what I could do. So let them miss me. Let them worship me in my absence. Perhaps they would change on some other day in a glorious future of which I had never dreamed. Let them go on and meet their petty destiny. Let them go on and meet their fate. What was it to me? My time had come to its end and I would be happy to be put out of my misery. And they perhaps would be happy for me. Damn them, damn them, damn them for all eternity.

But the voices of the people were calling to me and I heard them now, down there on the floor, and I heard what they said, and they accused me and tried me for great crimes against humanity. I let them have their victory and I admitted to it all. I revealed a million crimes and spoke proudly of my name and I told them that I was the one who had caused them so much pain and had led them triumphantly into all the wars of history and that I was glad of it. I admitted all. I admitted that it was I who had poisoned the reservoirs of water on board the ship to win my final victory over God. And I told them of my generosity and of how I had given man the first and second great secrets of the universe. And with great joy in my voice I told them all of what I had seen on earth on the day of war when all men died. And I chastised them for not having been there to relish the sight of the dead. And I went on and on with my stories of my crimes against humanity and told them everything, everything that I could possibly remember about my time on earth, about my deal with God, about the beauty of my plans for the future. I painted pictures for them of how it would be to live with me forever and forever, so help them, they would have enjoyed immortality with me.

Mankind needed no prosecutor in this trial. I confessed gladly to everything. And why not? It was important for me to have them all know who I was and what I had done. And toward the end of my testimony I turned to the Queen. I hated and loved her. She was the first person to ever surprise me. She had changed the world. She had accepted the wisdom of the ages and she had made men see the light of the law which would bring peace and harmony into eternity. Perhaps, I thought, she was a daughter of God. Perhaps she had been sent to earth to defeat me. But, no, when I looked at her she was not divinity. She was only wise. She was only mortal, but she had a vision of destiny which made her even more powerful than me.

And then I thought back to the time when God had handed down to me the first great secret of the universe. I understood now that at that time I had stepped onto his stage of compromise. He had been willing to sacrifice one world for another, one people for another, one age for yet another.

WORLD ONE

God had known that only in this way would mankind change and become his children of peace.

I wished that I could say that it had been God who defeated me. I could not. Man had changed. And God had helped him change, and together they found the path to peace. Together they had confounded me and defeated me. So be it. I was glad for them. Now I could die in peace and go on to a place of rest where I would not have the burden to make men play. It was not God who had become weary of man; it was I. I had lived too long and done too much. Perhaps it was the sight of the earth after the evening of incineration which had made me weak and tired and deeply weary of my role. Even I was saddened by such utter devastation and as I have told you I missed the green earth and my friends on it. I had never dreamed of the destruction which I in the end did to the people of that world. I was sorry that it had happened. I regret that it was I who made it come to reality. Truly I was not glad that it had happened. Truly I would be glad to relieve my conscience of it. It was time for me to die. I would go willingly. I thanked my father for bringing me to it.

And when I had no more confessions to make, the jury of mankind deliberated in my halls of misery. Their verdict would be simple, this much I knew. Guilty I was, and guilty I would be, and I would be condemned to death by the universal judges of mankind. Indeed, mankind had achieved much in its time. Here at this moment the horrors of history were likely to stop. Perhaps the Queen would even have her miracle this day. Whatever would come, would come, I thought. Let man have his triumph over me. All the triumphs had been mine for too long. Let man go it alone, let him live without my company, let him live in the boredom of peace. He would not like it for long. I believed that man loved his battles and wars. I believed he cherished them, for they gave him a reason to live and to die. They enriched his life and made it worth living. Man remembered his times of war more often than his times of peace. He, like me, enjoyed the thrills of victory. Even now the faces of the people were flushed with delight as they awaited the sentence that was soon to be handed down.

This court was a battlefield, only I was the sole enemy. What exhilaration they all must have felt knowing that they had finally defeated the greatest of all enemies. And they did it sublimely. They did it unintentionally. They did it in spite of themselves and their natures. Trust man to stumble upon wisdom without his knowing he has done it. So be it. It was done.

The members of the jury had no trouble making up their minds. My confessions were good for their consciences. They could be relieved of all responsibilities for the messes they had made in their time. But I would not let them off so easily. I would always want them to remember their contributions to the wars of history. Without their undying aid, I could have done nothing. I would not allow them to blame me entirely. I would make them remember that they were partners of mine, partners in all of the horrors of history.

They handed the verdict to the judges and the judges took counsel among each other and their decision took even less time. It seemed that they agreed. I was to be put to death. I was to be punished for all of my crimes against humanity. I was given no second chance. I was given no reprieve. I was given the sentence of death, and I took it gladly. Better to be dead then alive without my kingdom and company. Better to be dead and sit at the feet of my father than to mix anymore with peaceful men. I was never one for tranquility in life. Perhaps I would like it in death. I would soon see. I would soon see.

And now the judges handed the sentence to the Queen who had committed history's greatest crime against me. She read it magnificently. "Be it known to you, Satan, that the universal court of mankind judges you guilty of great crimes against humanity and therefore decrees that you be sentenced to death. Furthermore, this court directs all people to live as one under the light of law, and be at peace now and forevermore."

And then I said to her, "You have done much in your

WORLD ONE

time, my majesty. I pray that you will be rewarded for this. I pray that you will be content with your boredom in peace and your coming destiny. I will accept my death, I cannot do otherwise. I have no place among men without war. Perhaps I finally will have won my father's total respect for me. Perhaps in the end it is I who will have the final victory. I am sorry that you will never know. I would hope that you would wish me well.

"But before you are finally free of me, hear me. Hear some final wisdom of divinity. I am generous to the end. I have always been generous with my friends.

"It is true that by my art of interference, I have caused man much pain. I have also given him joy, for you, too, have loved your victories. But I was only one power in the glory of the universe. You were the other. Without you, I would have died many ages ago. It was you who gave me life and courage and my fine abilities. Without you, I would have wandered alone and accomplished little in my time. But with you, I was able to do great things. I was able to create monumental works of war that I hope you shall always remember. I did these things in unison with you. You were willing friends and I simply assisted you in your lofty pursuits. It was you who wallowed in a world without wisdom and it was you who made the great misery in life come true. Long ago you could have ended my days. I would have been out of your lives and you would have had your peace and tranquility. Now that you have the wisdom of the ages, now that you have all consented to live under the light of universal law, I am nothing. I am as good as dead. It is almost as if I had never been born. But remember, my friends, should you someday walk out of this light, then I will return. God will make me live and I will come to you and we shall live together again and create new works of war. Remember, my friends, that you are responsible for your own fate. God will not help you. You have the wisdom. It is enough. So go on, reach out, find your destiny whatever it may be, and be thankful that you live, for your time can come to an end when you choose to live with me."

I had said enough. I was finished with man. I wished to get out of his sight and go to my death. But before I would have them take me away, I had a word with God. "Father," I whispered, "give me safe passage to you, for I consent to die. Your children know wisdom and they live it. I am witness to the third great secret of the universe—that all mankind is one and has a destiny of peace somewhere out beyond the stars.

"For you, my father, I give up my powers. I look forward to mortal death. I look forward to seeing the light on your face and gaining entrance into Heaven."

And so it was then that the last body of mankind took me away from my halls of misery. Once they had been my halls of victory . . . Once they had been my stage of fantasies . . . Now they were the court of the law of humanity. Now they were the instruments of eternity.

I did not look back. I was carried down through the ship of steel and glass. I passed the cities of the men of nations who had once lived to see each other die. Farewell to the separate cities of man, I thought. Your lights will be the lights of all men. I will look out for these lights from my place in Heaven. I would be glad to see them pass by.

And down through the ship of steel and glass I went with the people guiding me by my hands. And the darkness of the passageways was cool and then grew cold, and I began to be afraid. I did not want to die. I did not want to come to know the features of my father's face. I wanted life! I wanted victories! I wanted the joys of sight and sound. I wanted to go with man to discover new green worlds where the land was fresh and clean. I wanted to go with man to see what his destiny might be. I wanted to take back my immortality. I wanted to snatch back my powers. But it was too late. Too late for this. Mankind had won. I was beaten and defeated. I screamed as they put me out helplessly into the long black seas of eternity.

And as I drifted I felt the touch of his hand and then I knew nothing. I do not remember my journey from then on. But it was in this time that I died and was reborn. In this time I

WORLD ONE

shed my wings and was transformed. In this time I was brought through the gates of Heaven which had never been open to me before. And when I came alive again, I stood before the light of God, my father. And my new eyes were transfixed by the white light which was everywhere and everything that could be seen. I stood as one changed before the father of us all who was within me and outside of me. Such a feeling you have never known. Such a feeling you will never know until the time comes for you to enter through the gates of Heaven and stand before the Great Creator. I cannot describe this world of light. I cannot describe the power behind all life and all death. But it is the one thing that all men must experience, for they have not lived until they do. And now I was living—the miracle of death had brought me life, everlasting life in an everlasting world of living light.

I heard my father's voice. It was the same. I remembered now. I had heard it before, long ago. In some other time I had heard it. I knew it from somewhere far away when I was another form. And then I remembered who it was that I had been when I heard him say, "Satan, my son, you have come."

I did not like that name Satan. It suggested vague unpleasantries. It suggested difficult memories from another time, a time when I lived for death. "Satan, my son, you have come." Again and again he said this refrain. And again and again the memories came, and I remembered a people and a ship and fields of stars and avenues of darkness and something floating free, something floating until a warm hand reached out and touched it. I remembered nothing more. I remembered no journey, I remembered no pain, only the easing away of my strength at some time, at one time. I had no strength before God.

But as he spoke all was remembered. I knew who I had been and why I had come. And I could see the past and the future. I could see all shades of light. I saw no dark. There were no shadows in these fields of eternity. There was only the music of life which was his voice, which was the rhythm of the changing tunnels of light. And I knew this music. I had heard it before, but now it was with me everywhere. Now it seemed to beat from the center of my heart, now it made me feel beautiful, like a child asleep.

My father said to me, "You have honored your word and therefore you are well and fit to sit before me. It was time that you came. It was time for your victory." I did feel victorious. I did feel the glory of triumph. Why? I remembered what I had been and what I had done and yet I felt like this. I felt the glory of triumph. It was the way in which my father said, "Satan, my son, you have come." He had respect for me! And he had allowed me to enter into Heaven and see his sacred avenues of light. I was witness to my father's face. I had finally been accepted by him. And I would live for him. I would give my soul to him for having forgiven me, for having not punished me, for saving me from the stillness of death, from the emptiness of nothingness, from the place where I had been. I no longer wanted to remember ... I only wanted to have him as my company. I had no need of anything more. I was content. I was happy. I was filled once more with the delight of divinity. I had it all.

But the music of my father's voice continued; it continued its tune of harmony. I listened. I wanted to listen forever. I wanted to live by the music of this choir, this choir which made music with light. My father said to me, "It was you, my son, who gave mankind its destiny. It was you, my son, who brought glory to my stage of compromise. By your consent you have changed history, a history that will now come to mankind. And I shall call this time the Age of Whitsuntide, for mankind has received the law and accepted it. You have done this for man. You have created a miracle in history. And in time, you will live among men. You will go back to your friends. And you will be received with joy and thanksgiving. They will all say that it was you who passed down the law and cleansed the people and taught them to live as one. They will all say that it was you who brought about the Age of Whitsuntide, this new age in man's history. You have my respect for this. I am a father who loves his son."

Now I was in ecstacy. All along this was what I had truly wanted. Truly I had wanted to be accepted by God, my father. Why had I done what I had done? To bring peace to man was a greater joy, a greater power than to bring war. If only

WORLD ONE

I had known. If only I had known I would have done it much sooner. I would have made my deal with God before . . .

But the music of my father's voice continued and I listened and though the melody was still beautiful, the words of the song had changed . . . I must earn my way back to man. I must become the scribe of history. I must tell the story of the Age of Whitsuntide so that mankind will never forget how wisdom came and how Satan was defeated by peace and law and unity.

My father said, "Tell this tale ten thousand times to anyone who will listen. Tell this tale to the generations that will come, so that the way to peace will be remembered for all time. This is your punishment, my son. You shall speak of peace and of law and of the Age of Whitsuntide when all men learned to live as one. And when this tale has been told ten thousand times then you shall be born among men and live with them and know the joy of what it is to be a man in a world of peace."

But I did not want to remember what I had done. I loved the light around me. I loved the beauty of the heavens. I loved the voice of my father. I wished to forget, not remember. I did not want to inflict myself with pain. I wished to be forgiven. I cried out to God, "But I have brought peace to man. Please forgive me now. Let me live without my memories. Let me go on and worship you and love your light. Or let me go to man now and live with him and love the peace of his life. Do not make me sit at your feet and tell my tale ten thousand times. Make me forget, oh, father! I have died and been reborn. I have fulfilled your dearest fantasy. I have brought mankind to its Age of Whitsuntide. Do not make me live in misery again. I have learned enough. There is no need to punish me. I now see the light and I wish to live with it. I wish to live among the sons of God. Let me join the glory of humanity! Erase my memories! Fill me with peace, oh, God!"

But my father would not do this. I would not reap my rewards so soon. I was to be suspended in a world of internal misery. I was to repeat my mistakes ten thousand times and tell my tales of the horrors of history. And so I sit at the feet of my father within his world of light and feel the pain of what I did to man and what he and God did to me. And I regret it all. I hate each thought, each word, each phrase of memory. I regret everything that was; I regret that I must tell the story which is told only to give pain to me, for far away mankind lives without me.

Sometimes my father will speak to me and lift me up out of my misery. He will tell me of what happened to the last of mankind after I was let loose into the long black seas of eternity. And I love to listen to this story. It makes my heart glad for them, my friends, my friends of humanity.

"My light went to mankind," he begins. "And with my light I brought showers of rain. And with the showers of rain I sent my voice. Man heard me speak through the rains. 'As a sign of your wisdom and your accomplishment, my rains will follow you until the days when you have come to your great destiny. And your food shall multiply and there will be plenty to drink and you shall have nourishment always. Witness that wisdom brings miracles to man. Witness that wisdom makes man sons of God. And know that mankind will have immortality for as long as it chooses to live under the light of law. So go forward, my sons. Go on to meet your great fate. You shall find it out beyond the stars, and it will be the one thing of which you have never dreamed.' And so it was, my son, mankind went on to meet its fate. And all wars and battles ceased between the men of nations. And mankind lives now in the heart of its destiny under the great hand of its new-found wisdom and life and peace are plenty."

All of this was long ago. I have now repeated my tale ten thousand times. You are the last to listen. I shall never have to repeat it again. I am done. Gladly, I am finished. I am proud of all that I have said. And now I no longer feel the pain. I have no pain. I am happy. I have paid for my crimes against humanity and my father has forgiven me. I am his son, one holy son of God.

Very soon my father will deliver me out of this world of light and into the mysterious world of the destiny of mankind. I will be reborn and live until the day that I die a mortal death. Then my spirit shall go on and be with my father

WORLD ONE

forevermore. But now I am relieved of my burden. I have had a long rest, and I am ready to join humanity, out there in its place of harmony. Now I will miss my seat at my father's feet. I will somehow miss these long labors, miss the telling of this tale. But you will remember it. And you will remember it without the pain of having to tell it.

Remember who I was and what I am and pray for what I shall soon be. Pray for humanity, pray that it will forever live under the light of universal law. And pray for all of the people in man's history. Pray for those who died in battle and in war. They were too young to know wisdom. And I was too young to know my true destiny. But pray that the horrors of history will never be repeated, that man will never lose the wisdom that he has learned. I could not bear it. I have paid for it too dearly. I have felt the pain for too long. It is enough. I never wish to know it again.

And remember how good my father has been to me. He is the fairest of all. He has forgiven us for all of our crimes and we have him to thank for our destiny. And always remember that wisdom leads to miracles, that wisdom is the key to immortality, that wisdom is the key to the great secrets of the universe. This much I know, this much I shall never forget.

Now I hear the music of my father's voice. It is time. He calls to me. I am ready for the journey to this place far away. And my father promises me that it shall be green and that there shall be showers of rain and plenty of peace. It is there that I shall be content. It is there that I shall dream the dreams of a mortal man. It is even there that I might find my queen. It is she that I am thinking of now. It was her spirit that kept me alive while I recited this tale and felt such misery. Perhaps when I come to her she will know me. Perhaps when I come to her she will forgive me. Perhaps she will love me as I love her. So often I pictured us together. I pictured the faces of our children and the fields of green where we lived under the light of a fresh sun.

It was the Queen who gave me hope. It was the Queen who made me wish for life even as I told this tale of death. If she is there, I shall love her. If she is there I shall take care of her in all ways. She will be one with me and I with her and our children will join us in the beauty of life. I wish for all of this, even though it will be for such a short time. Only humanity itself will have immortality. One man lives for such a short time. It is too little, yet so much. It is so much when there is peace among men. It is everything when there is peace among men and there is time for living, not dying.

I think of all humanity out there somewhere, out there where I will soon go, and I love them as much as I will love my queen and our children. They have come far in their time. And they achieved the greatest of all victories, the victory over me, me who was war and misery. But perhaps they have forgotten the horrors of history. I do not believe that it would be better this way. I believe that they must never forget. Better it is for them to remember their stupidities, even at the risk of pain. Even at the risk of everlasting embarrassment. I have paid for my crimes, thus it is my privilege to forget. But man has not. He found wisdom and defeated me. He was entitled then to his destiny. But he is not entitled to forget. Never should he ever forget the way it was when men of nations went to war. Never should he forget the way it was to live with me, for together we made war and found peace. This is the way the world was made, this was the way I died and was reborn. So be it. It is done. My father calls me to my destiny.

5

So much for Satan. So much for man's destiny...
   The human-dogs are still here with us in the dimming night. A stinky wind is blowing from the east. The waters rock rather pleasantly and I am feeling refreshed. Human-dog #1 has his eye on me. And Elizabeth has our rifle trained in his direction. The forty-nine other dogs sit silently in their boats, awaiting a noise from Human-dog #1.
   I lose his eye and turn my sights back to the statue of Thomas Jefferson. Across the waters it seems to float within an all black sky. His high domed sanctuary frames his magnificent form. Here in the night, here with the human-dogs who mean to take it from us, it looks like a flower in the wilderness. I turn back to Human-dog #1 and say, "Elizabeth and I have sworn eternal hostility against every form of tyranny over the mind of man."
   The forty-nine other dogs laugh at us. I don't suppose I blame them. Elizabeth and I sit facing might and we have only one rifle for our protection. Plus a bag of stones. But it is clear

now that we have something else. Human-dog #1 seems less resentful of us. He seems less inclined to despise our presence. Early on, before my tale, he would have drowned us merrily. Now he takes another drink and his green eyes glow again like moons.

Noises strike us from afar. Back behind the human-dogs other animals are heard. The fifty human-dogs turn to see the intruders on the lake. A band of twenty more bring up the rear, armed with spikes and stones and lavish knives. Elizabeth and I. Fifty human-dogs plus twenty. I must say, this is a most foul combination. But Human-dog #1 will have us live, so long as Elizabeth points my rifle at his heart. He drinks a bit more liquor; he sucks in the stinky air. It is early and clearly he is eager for more frothy entertainment.

"You are a sticky fellow. What is your name?"

"C. J. Jones."

"Then C. J. Jones, have you more to tell? What spicy tales are left in you? The long night settles in. And I like to dream with you. You see, I, too, want to build a better world. I want to sow the seeds of peace. I have no interest in mutilating my enemies. Not you nor she nor anyone. The world around us is all but dead. But still you have some hope. I like a heart like that. I like you, C. J. Jones."

Elizabeth whispers to me. "Let's disarm the rest."

There is merit to this suggestion. But while Elizabeth's hand is near the trigger, basically I feel safe. Safe from immediate death. For who knows how long.

Behind Human-dog #1 we hear sharp whispers which turn quickly to raging howls. And then arms are beating about and as suddenly as the sounds first came there is silence as the body of a human-dog drops lifelessly into the high water before us with a butcher's knife lodged exactly in the center of his bleeding chest. But Human-dog #1 doesn't turn round. He seems so assured of his position—at least among his dogmen. Elizabeth is not distracted by the commotion beyond. Her eyes are trained on #1. I, however, am queasy. I think of the dogman going down, bleeding down into the black waters. And although

WORLD ONE

I did not see his eyes, I see them now, underwater, wide and panicked with life-ending pain.

The eyes travel down and the dog body follows and soon it touches down and meets all the other bodies which died because of the many explosions of atom bombs four hundred and one days ago.

Recovering now, I speak to Human-dog #1.

"You have had one story tonight. Take it with you and leave. This is our place. We own it by right. By all that is right, it is ours. Our monument, our statue, our home and place of inspiration. Farther out, you have the Capitol dome in which to live. You even have the high end of Lincoln's Memorial. Leave us alone and there will be peace. You and I will both live. We can build a new state of peace, a nation of law and a world of tranquility. What better way to spend a life can there possibly be? Name it, and I will be your companion in it."

And with a great lung full of boggy air, #1 speaks, his arms rising in the shape of half moons on either side of his bulbous head.

"Fry up more fish and pass more bottles around to our guests. Everyone eat more and drink more. We have a new prophet in our bloody midst!"

And then the human-dogs howl. The wide throng of them sing songs marked by discords and Human-dog #1 basks in this cacophonous barbarity. I look aside at Elizabeth but she holds her gaze on #1 and reaffirms her aim in the process.

And yet another cry breaks through the night. To my left, two human-dogs are at it for some revelant reason until the thinner one, the one with no hair on his head is strangled to death by the other and pushed overboard into the black soup of the polluted basin.

#1 takes no mind of it at all. Instead, this act seems to inspire him. "Runners, go back. Run to our Capitol home and return with our wives. I want them to hear C. J. Jones. He will tell us another tale. But this time it will be—a tragedy. I am in the mood for a tragedy. Can you dream it, old man?"

The runners in the back of the line turn and row off. All the rest is left as before. The musical howls and the moist, stinky air and Elizabeth and me and my mentor, Human-dog #1.

"Here is the tragedy, you and I. We fight rather than dream

of the future. We must kill to hold our own, to survive. All about you is tragedy. Why would you want more?"

Human-dog #1: "Then give us tragedy and hope. Mix them together like a stew. Me and my people will eat it. We will wait for the women and children to return. Make it a story for women and children, too."

Out on the blackish waters beyond the human-dog line I can see flames. There is a line of flames above boats, many boats carrying women and children toward us. Human-dogs are humming. Human-dog #1 is resting. Elizabeth shifts in her seat and I turn round to have another look at Thomas Jefferson. He's a comfort in the night. And as usual, he's a source of inspiration.

Now the women and children are around us. Human-dog #1 is awake and greeting his wife and children. What a sight this picture is. This man with his wife and children. Elizabeth and I are introduced. Elizabeth refrains from shaking any hands. She hasn't forgotten her business. She's here to save my life. God, I love this woman. Other human-dogs greet their wives and children and soon before me, there seems to be a field of faces, not of warriors, but of desperate people searching for a source of inspiration.

What am I going to do? A children's story of tragedy and hope. Mr. Jefferson lead me true. For we have sworn eternal hostility against every form of tyranny over the mind of man.

A cry for peace, a call for inspiration, a children's story in the night . . . What am I going to do?

This. *"A young girl speaks; she speaks from a place far to the north, four hundred and one days ago, on a day called Wednesday . . ."*

Y ou must know that he was born on Hiroshima Day, that he was an American, that he died without a country and of his own free will. You must also know that his life was a

WORLD ONE

failure. He never achieved the one thing that was the most important to him. He never lived to see the world live in peace. But I am still happy for him. I envy him. I wish that I had the courage to die right now of my own free will. I do not. You see it is Wednesday. It is the dawn of Wednesday and from everything I hear on the radio it is probably going to be the last Wednesday of my life. But I will not be the one to take it away. There are others who will take care of that . . .

    I am in a little cabin on the Bay of Fundy, Nova Scotia. I am speaking to you, whoever you are, if you are, on this nifty recording device I've set up by my chair directly in front of the fireplace. I've been up all night listening to the broadcasts from the BBC in London, local news from Halifax, and blues music coming in vaguely from the direction of Boston. B.B. King has been fading in and out all night, clashing with what occasionally sounds like Beethoven's sonatas. The reception is dreadful and faded altogether now. Halifax is my closest and most constant voice of reality—if you can call it reality. That's why I'm talking into this nifty machine. It makes me seem real to myself—I know what I am saying is being recorded. It's kind of a reaffirmation of reality for me. All around me I sense insanity. The longer I speak, the saner I feel. So let the insanity be. It doesn't bother me. Not so long as I can talk into this nifty machine and sit by the fire and talk to you, whoever you are, and think about my dad who isn't with me anymore. It's my favorite time to think of him. When the dawn gets still like this in this moment before it breaks into day, I like to think I can feel him around this old cabin which he had built for me. Really, I guess he didn't build it exactly for me—my mom and he built it. That was before I was born. I always got the feeling I was conceived right here in this cabin. Probably I started my life right here one night, or one dawn just like this. I don't know for sure. That isn't something one ever asks one's mother or father, is it? I mean you don't exactly ask them questions like that. But I like to think it's true. I like to think of them here making me. Today is my birthday. I shouldn't think there'll be anyone to celebrate it with. I shouldn't think I'll even be able to celebrate it by myself. I shouldn't even think it will matter that I, or my father, or my mother, or you had ever been born.

I'm getting morose before I begin. I'm not usually this way. I was always a cheerful, bright little girl, but now I guess I'm getting cynical and morose at the age of fifteen. It's pretty pathetic, really you must admit it's pathetic for a girl like me to be caught up in a bundle of cynical thoughts before she's had a chance to get going in life and experience the good with the bad and shape her mind accordingly . . .

You should know my name. My name is Sonia Pearson. I am living just outside of a quaint, little village in Nova Scotia called Sandy Cove. It is not for the fishing that I came here. I hate the smell of perch and I detest eating it and so I am prepared to starve if I must. I would rather die nobly than eat fish. I was raised with a taste for the finer things in life and perch is not one of them. I'm complaining again. I'll stop the machine if I catch myself complaining. There is nothing more obnoxious than a fifteen-year-old complaining. My dad never complained. In all of those years he never complained. I always thought that he was some kind of god. He never said a word against those who persecuted him. He was a Christian, I guess. He wasn't a martyr or anything like that. He just had a broader outlook that made him see things others didn't. That's why I looked up to him.

I'm looking out the window now. St. Mary's Bay is beginning to brighten. The fog is its usual dreamy self. It comes and goes but usually it stays for most of the morning, until the sun fries it to death. Not being a native, I like the fog. If I had to stay here for the rest of my life it might be pretty depressing, though. Whoever heard of growing up in the fog? My mother said that it's good for the complexion. That would be one benefit. There are others, I suppose, but I can't think of any right now. I'll try to remember some more before I'm through—there was one other . . .

So what am I doing talking my heart out to you? Who are you anyway? I'm the romantic type and so I imagine that you have found this neat little recording machine at some distant time in the future. You obviously understand English or you wouldn't waste your time listening to me. You are probably not my age, although I would like to think that

WORLD ONE

there was someone my age interested in having known me. All of my friends are down in America with their families. They probably won't be living much longer. No one will probably be living much longer. I might have a few days left even after today if I stay inside and keep the windows and doors locked and as airtight as possible. And then again, I hear that I might last for weeks or even months. Maybe I'll just get so sick I won't even know what time is anymore and I'll just drift away one night while I'm asleep.

Do you know, I never had a boyfriend. Isn't that ridiculous? I'm fifteen and I haven't even had a date. Sure I've known boys and everything, but I've never had a date where we go out to the movies or stay at home and listen to music. I've only been in love once and that never really got anywhere. He was two years ahead of me and I was still an ugly little thing who insisted on braiding her hair. Everyone knows that boys don't much like girls with braided hair. They like free-flowing hair. It makes them look more tantalizing, more sophisticated and alluring. I didn't know any better then. I braided my hair and lost him to another girl. The truth is, I never really had him. I just wished I had him and plotted all sorts of ways to get him and never did. I blame it on my braids. You should take my advice, whoever you are listening to me. If you want the best-looking boy, let your hair down. It's the only thing that makes you look devastating. Of course I always thought I had charm, but that doesn't amount to much in the jungle of romance.

You probably don't want to listen to much more about me. I didn't start talking to you to talk about me. But in composition class my teacher always said that it's best to set the stage a bit. Who, what, when, where, why. By now I think I've covered the who and the where and the when ... or have I? When is now, this Wednesday. The reports on the radio from the BBC drone on about how the world is about to go to war over some things I don't pretend to understand. It doesn't matter anyway that I don't understand. I never had time to major in politics or history, or for that matter, I never had time to major in anything, except I did pass first-year Algebra with flying colors. Numbers are neat. All you need to know is the right equation, and pop! out comes the answer.

That's why I liked mathematics so much. Everything was so neat and orderly. Want an answer? Get your favorite equation and fit in some nice numbers and out the answer comes. It's really easy if you put your mind to it. I wish my dad could have seen how easy it is for me. If he had majored in math, he would still be here today. He would have known all the answers and no one could have disputed him. As it was, just about everyone in the world disputed him. He kind of stuck out like a sore thumb but not many people listened to him. I can't tell you whether or not he was right, but he certainly had his own opinions and that's a lot better than not having any at all. My mother had lots of opinions, too. But I never knew her. She died when I was born. I only have some pictures of her which I've always kept hidden under my scarves in my drawer. If I look at them I get sad. If I don't look at them I get sad. I've never been able to resolve this crisis in my life and I guess now I never will. I've been walking around all my life feeling guilty about the way that she died. I was born and she died. I tell myself that it wasn't my fault. My dad never blamed me, either. It's just the way it happened. It had something to do with complications and I don't have the words to describe them. But the result was that she died when I was born and now I feel guilty and sad and am torn between looking at her pictures and not.

    I always look at my dad's pictures, though. I knew something about my dad, and I don't blame myself for his death. I've already mentioned that he died of his own free will. A couple of days before he died, he mentioned that the Romans always killed themselves when they were defeated in a battle. They refused to surrender to their enemies. Probably they were too proud to live with defeat and this, I think, was my dad's problem. He was defeated by a world full of enemies and so he committed suicide so he wouldn't have to live with them. It's not that he didn't care for me. He saw to it that I was taken care of. I have lots of money and this place to live and his friend Mrs. Mac looks after me. He said it wasn't safe for me to live any longer in America. He said the same about Europe. He thought Nova Scotia might be the safest place, due to the westerly winds as he called them. I don't know what's safe and what isn't. Probably in the end it won't make

WORLD ONE

any difference. But I like to think that my dad took care of me as much as he could considering the way the world was then and the way it is now.

I forgot to mention that he killed himself because he wanted to be free. I know this sounds crazy but he once explained it to me. He said that no one in the world was free. Once he said his country had been free, but not any more. He said the threat of war which hung over the earth made every man, woman and child a slave to it. If there was one thing my dad wanted in his life, it was to be free. He not only wanted to be free but he wanted the world to be free and safe from death by war. But he couldn't manage to persuade the world that there was only one way to have peace. I'll tell you about all that later. I need to fix myself another cup of coffee. I never knew talking into a recording machine could be so draining. Before I switch off for a minute or two, if you've never heard of coffee, let me tell you it's one of the world's great delicacies. Girls my age usually don't drink it, but I began drinking it when I was ten. I suppose it's made up for my lack of boyfriends.

Switching off now to fix myself my favorite cup of coffee. Wednesday at dawn in Nova Scotia. Sonia talking about her dad.

Switching on now after making my favorite cup of coffee. You might like to know how I do it. I put in two lumps of sugar, one teaspoon of cinnamon, three tablespoons of Folger's Instant Coffee and a splash of cream that I pick up fresh each morning from the grocery down the road where Mrs. Mac works. Mrs. Mac refuses to believe all of the reports on the radio and continues to operate her store, oblivious to what everyone has to say. I kind of like that about her. She's old enough to believe that things will never change. That is, man will go on no matter what. Anyway, Sandy Cove is so far away from the rest of the world she probably wouldn't know whether the world outside changed or not. It could completely disappear and she would never know the difference. Isn't that wild? Whole continents could turn to sand and she wouldn't even believe the reports on the radio. She has what they call tunnel vision. She sees only what she wants to see. And all she wants to see is that the supplies and groceries she orders from Yarmouth come in on time.

She was married to the town preacher once. Pneumonia got him in the end. He passed away on the Wednesday before Christmas, just before high tide came in. Mrs. Mac never tires of telling me how he loved to watch the tides, the Hand of the Almighty taking care to see that the world was put in order. It may sound queer to you or me, but he was old and had been around for a long time and had a lot of time to think about such things as the ways of nature. I can't say he was right or wrong. It's true the highest tides in the world come in every night, depending on the cycle of the moon. Sometimes, actually, they come in in the morning, but mostly they come in at night. If the Almighty does have His Hand in it, He doesn't seem picky about when it does what it does.

I see nature and wonder about how it all works, but I don't see any particular mystery about it. It all seems so natural, like the way I just live. I just live. I was born and I just go on living till I die. Some people are afraid of death. But not me and Mrs. Mac. Death doesn't frighten us. We see eye to eye on that. We've talked about it plenty. But we have different reasons for it. She's not afraid of death because she believes in a life beyond this life. She says she's going to live in a big mansion along with her husband and the rest of her family just as soon as she doesn't wake up one morning. It all seems so natural to think about it that way. You just go on living somewhere else. She says it's going to be a better life in this big mansion. Her family will be there to meet her. She calls it moving on. She says spirits never die. Only people die. And spirits aren't exactly people. Spirits, she says, are our single force of energy. It gets complicated explaining it after that, but I think you can get the gist of my point. She'll just be moving on when she dies and she's not any bit afraid of it. I'm a little different. I feel like I've been kind of numbed to fear. I guess there's a reason for this but I haven't quite worked it out. Maybe it has something to do with the death of my mom and then my dad. But that's not it exactly. You

WORLD ONE

see, I've always lived with death hanging over me. By death, I mean instant death. That's why I don't feel any different today than I felt yesterday. Or the day before yesterday, or the month before last month. I've been walking around with death all my life, which sounds kind of strange but that's the way it's been. One day after another, I've been walking around with death smiling over my shoulder. I'm not the only one though. All the kids my age felt this way. It was just the way we lived. My dad said that it was because of the time we were living in. He said it hadn't always been quite this way. Sure, he'd say, there had been plenty of terrible wars and hundreds of thousands and practically millions of people had been killed at the time; but he said my time was different. He didn't blame me for feeling this way, either. He didn't think it at all weird when I said I had kind of gotten used to the idea of death. I appreciated the fact that he didn't call me morbid or something like that. Most parents probably would have said something like that, but not him. He understood those things. That's, I guess, one of the reasons he worked so hard trying to prevent what is probably coming. And what's probably coming is probably coming in the way the tides this evening will. They can't be stopped. Take me, for instance. If all I wanted to do in the world was to stop those tides coming into St. Mary's Bay, I still couldn't do it. It just isn't possible for one person to stop the tides—sure if a whole army of people set out to do something, they could think up some scheme to dam the bay and block the tides, but not just one person alone. You'd have to be God or something. The same goes for stopping the event that might be coming tonight. I mean, one person just can't cut it. And don't think I don't know what I'm talking about. My dad tried to do it. He had a little help, and everything, but it wasn't nearly enough. He needed a whole world of people to help him, and they didn't. Don't ask me why. My father explained it to me once, but I was probably too young to understand it fully and missed some of the more subtle aspects. He tried and it didn't work and it killed him. He couldn't live under the threat of constant death; he wasn't numbed to it all like I and my friends were. It made him go crazy. That's why he killed himself. He went crazy. He knew what was going to happen and why. If he were alive right now he'd be over in his favorite chair and nodding his head while listening to the BBC on the radio and he'd be telling me over and over again, "I told them this would happen; they knew that this was going to happen . . . It is happening and there is nothing that can be done." Well, I tell you. He knew that this was going to happen and now it is happening and there is nothing any one of us can do about it. Crazy, isn't it? There was a time when there was still time to do something about it and now there's no more time and people still can't do anything about it. Anyway, this is all to say that I'm not afraid of it because I've lived with it all my life and grew up expecting it, and here I am ready for it. It's a good thing because otherwise I'd be crying and carrying on and making a fool of myself just like everyone else is doing now that they realize it's just too damn too late. I'd hoped for better, but I'm glad I grew up to be a realist. Realists can more easily accept death and whatever happens after that.

Here I've been going on and on and I haven't touched my cup of coffee that I interrupted this recording for. Listen to me while I sip it. Maybe you'll see what I mean about how nice it is to have a good cup of coffee when you've been up all night thinking about what you're going to do to celebrate the last day of your life.

I'm *so* melodramatic. I'm sure I've got lots of days left to live out here near the Bay of Fundy. Anyway, I couldn't bear the thought of dying right along with all the others. I don't intent to be among the first of the pack. I'd rather wait it out with Mrs. Mac. Right up to the end she'd be telling me she wasn't going to die and I'd be telling her that if we were going to die I wasn't afraid of it because I'd been expecting it all along. I can see us now sitting together in her grocery and talking about how nice it will be to see the fall coming, and then, bap! she or I drops like a fly drunk on smoke. If she goes first, I'll just fold her hands on her lap and close her eyes if they're not already closed, smooth back her hair and say a little prayer over her before I go back to my cabin and wait it out. But if I go first, I've already given her instructions on what to do. I'm a realist and I like to plan ahead. She's been instructed to cart me over to a bluff which

WORLD ONE

looks out over St. Mary's Bay. I've already picked out the spot where she's supposed to bury me. It's waiting for me now. I've spent the last several weeks digging into the ground and preparing my place of rest. My white cross is made; I fashioned it out of two nice pieces of driftwood and painted it an all-purpose white. I nailed the two sections together so they won't be blown apart by the winds. I would have liked it better if I'd been able to have a place next to my mother and father but they're buried too far away from here and Mrs. Mac wouldn't have the strength to get me there, let alone bury me and cover me over with dirt. On second thought maybe I'll just go out to this place and lie down in my grave and wait it out there. There's probably no sense in getting too sick in my cabin and ruining my chance to have a decent burial. You know what I mean? I'd rather be prepared. It's always good to do things right, especially when you're talking about the last thing you ever do. That way at least I'll be looking up into the sky when I die and the last thing I'll see will be either a cloudy, rainy sky or a bright, beautiful blue one. I've fantasized that I might even see a flock of geese flying overhead just before everything goes blank. Can you imagine what that would be like? A whole flock of flying geese looking down at me as I die.

You must think I'm really out of it by talking like this. I don't care. It's my funeral. I can do with it what I like. I don't have to cry or anything if I don't want to. I can go gracefully if I want. There's no law that says you can't die the way you want to. My dad would think a lot of what I'm saying. He'd call it free will. Maybe that's the inscription I'll put by my grave: "She died of her own free will as did her dad." He would like that. He would be proud of the thought behind it.

Whoever you are listening to me now, you must be pretty lucky to be alive. I guess you're lucky. It seems like it's better to live than to die, if you can help it. But still, it must be difficult for you, knowing of all the things that have happened to the world since I died. I don't know what it is like for you being alive in such a different world. Is it anything like this one? I mean, do you see the moon rise over the bay around midnight? Do people still go fishing out past the cove? Do you have plenty to eat and drink? Does spring come anymore? These might sound like stupid questions but it's hard to imagine what everything will be like after today. Will you even know what Wednesday is? I'll tell you in case you don't. Wednesday is the fourth day of the week. There used to be seven days of the week and on Saturday and Sunday you were free to do anything you want. If you are still interested in listening to me, I'll tell you what some of these days were like. You might care to know because it'll help you understand what it was like to be living in the most beautiful spot in the world—before I had to go to my grave.

That pause on the tape recorder is for dramatic effect only. It's supposed to like, hang you up in the air for a moment or two while you go on and on and ponder what I'm going to say next. I learned that kind of technique in school in composition class. I can hear my teacher now: "Give the reader some air—let it hang—let them want to know more." By now you should be begging to know more if I've done it right. If I haven't done it right, well, it's just poor training. I don't have any excuse but that I didn't do very well when it came to writing out my thoughts. That's why, as I've said, this nifty little machine is a life-saver when it comes to self-expression. I like the sounds of words as they jump right out of my mouth. Words on a page are too much trouble to interpret. Anyway, for all I know, you who are listening to me right now can't even read or write. Consider yourselves lucky. That kind of thing got my dad into a lot of trouble when he was out there trying to save the world. His words followed him until his dying day. They just climbed right over him and put him in his grave and covered him over. Maybe that's why I never did too well in composition class. I was afraid of what those words might do to me if I learned how to use them too well.

But I shouldn't be afraid now. It's too late to be afraid, as I've mentioned earlier on in this person-to-person conversation. So are you ready to hear about the good old days?

WORLD ONE

The good old days mean the days when everything was just jolly and wonderful, when I could go out of this little cabin and climb one of those rugged peaks that look out over the Bay of Fundy. If you've been around these parts for a time now, you've probably been to the one that juts out from the end of the winding road up from the village. Chances are you've passed by Dead Man's Curve about halfway up to the place I'm talking about. That particular curve was responsible for at least one death that I know of—a lobster truck came shooting out of the darkness late one evening and rammed right into a van full of children from the old summer camp that's up from the perch that has such a devastatingly gorgeous view. The kids were okay. Only a couple of broken limbs and cut lips. There's nothing unusual about that when it comes to kids. They do that kind of thing all the time and it only makes them feel grown up when they've recovered and mounted their casts on their bedroom shelves. The driver of the lobster truck didn't make out too well, though. He swerved to avoid the van and plummeted down into a ravine and struck a big rural power line—one of many that traverse the countryside around here and cut right through the forest and ruin the natural beauty of the land. So this lobster truck driver dies and the kids from the camp are still alive and who knows where they are now—that being a couple of years ago—but at least they got to live a while longer like me and do things that they wouldn't have had the chance to do had they died along with the man who crashed down into the ravine.

So this perch with the gorgeous view is at the end of the road that passes by Dead Man's Curve and a ways up from there—say about a mile and a half—maybe more or less—depending on whether you're coming or going. Haven't you ever noticed that when you're coming back from a place you've just gone to the distance seems to be so much less than it was when you were going there in the first place? My dad called it an illusion of time, "the tricky distance of time" he'd call it. There's something to that, too. I might be only fifteen, but I feel that I've lived a long time. Since I've been going forward to a place where I've never been before—that is, I'm not returning to a place that I've been—it seems that my life has been much longer than what's represented by my age. Do you understand that? Take this tape recording of mine. If you can stand it, you just listen to it over again after you've heard what I've had to say the first time, and I just bet you that it will seem like it takes a shorter amount of time to listen to it and hear me drone on and on about how short it seems and all that. I'm an idiot. Right? Here I am about to die, maybe, and I'm talking about the tricky distance of time. If my friends heard this I would definitely be classified as a clod. A clod is an idiot—a clutz—a spaz—someone who you wouldn't go around associating with because you wouldn't have any other friends after that. Now that I think about it, when my dad died he didn't have any friends—but he was different. I know he wasn't an idiot. You just have to turn on the radio and pick up the crazy voices in London or Boston to know that he wasn't a clod or worse. He was right. He knew it all damn too well that the world would get itself into a tub of trouble with all these bombs that are about to go off. You can't call a man like that a clod—no you can't. He just had a way about him that made other people afraid. They didn't want to hear him lecturing them about how the world was going to blow itself up with big bombs. Sure, some of them listened to him and agreed with him, but they were hardly enough. My dad wanted everyone to know and get stirred up and shout down the governments and make them stop all the nonsense that they were indulging in. My dad called all these governments and the men running them "out-of-date." Get that? My dad was calling all the governments of the world "out-of-date." No wonder they got so upset with him. He was a threat to their concerns. There they were—sitting pretty in their little seats of power and making all these big bombs and pushing all the other governments around, all because each of these little governments thought that what they were doing was exactly right and just and good for their own people. Well even my dad said that he believed all these little governments *believed* that they were doing the right thing by their people, who they were responsible for. But the thing was, all the other little governments believed exactly the same thing and so none of them could come to any kind of agreement about what was right except by knocking and

WORLD ONE

shoving and kicking (so to speak) the others around. What a mess that has turned out to be. They just went on knocking and shoving and kicking each other around even after they got rid of my dad—and here it is. Wednesday. The day that it's all supposed to end because the big nations have finally decided to get around to knocking and shoving and kicking each other around because they believe they are right about some thing or another that is still ridiculously difficult for me to understand.

 I'll go on and on about all that quick enough, but first I was telling you about this place that you've probably already been to—the perch that looks out over the gorgeous view of the sea. Have you ever had to jump from rock to rock when the sizzling sea is coming in? You practically have to be an acrobat to do it without getting drenched. I usually bat around .500 on the average. That's when faded blue jeans come in real handy. They dry pretty quick no matter how wet they get—and up there you can even take them off without anyone seeing you and let them dry on a big rock that has been smoothed by constant slapping of the waves. Those are nice times up there. I can take off my clothes and run wild. I'm not a lewd person or anything. It's not as if I'd take off my clothes anywhere else but there—and only when they've been drenched by the sea. But it does give me an opportunity to feel like someone from an ancient, primitive world—a world in which they didn't have neat-looking blue jeans that felt good in all kinds of weather and conditions. It's at times like those that it's hard to believe there is any kind of time. I call it my Know Time. I know what it was like to be the first woman on earth. Maybe I'm not quite a woman yet but when I can go out on that perch and look all over the sea and taste the salt in my mouth and feel the sun tingle my skin, I have to tell you it must be pretty darn close to what it feels like to be a woman. That's one of the reasons why I'm not afraid to die. I've had plenty of time to live. I've walked across rocks without my clothes on. I've had barnacles cut my feet and not felt any pain because the air was so nice and fresh and the cold water soothed them and healed them almost overnight. That's something I hope you've had a chance to do if you've had the time. I don't know what you've been doing—you've probably been looking hard for food and been trying hard to keep from being sick, but if in between all those times you have a chance—go up the road past Dead Man's Curve and go on about another mile and a half and sit up on the perch and get splashed by the water when you're jumping between the rocks and take off your clothes and let them dry in the sun while you feel how it is to live like the first person on earth.

Dawn is doing its thing over the cove. My cup of Folger's coffee is depleted and I am sorry that it's gone. The second cup never tastes as good as the first. That's what my dad always used to say about smoking cigarettes. The first of the day was always his best and it practically got to be a ritual with him to go out onto the porch as the sun was coming up and light up one of those English brands of cigarettes that have the gold ring around the end. I didn't mind the smell of it like most people did. I thought it was kind of sexy—you know? I mean I got to watch the smoke curling up in the air (our cat liked to watch it with me) and then it would lift itself up like it was going to heaven or somewhere far away where everything was calm and gentle and relaxing. Do you think all things go to heaven? Or do you think some go to hell and others go to heaven? I've never really decided about it one way or another. I don't expect to either before I die. If there is a heaven then all the better for me and my dad. I'll go there and see him soon. That would be nice. He's probably trying to organize people up there like he tried to do on earth. I just hope he's having better luck then he had down here.

You want to know what I think would be heaven? I'll tell you since you can't answer me and say no. To me, heaven would be a place not too much different than this place where I'm talking to you from. There would be plenty of sea around it. There would also be a sun that rises in the morning but only sets for nighttime for a few hours a day. I don't much like the nighttime. That's why I've stayed up all night tonight.

WORLD ONE

I couldn't bear to dream away my life when things all around me were so uncertain. I figure that in the daytime things are much more certain. They have a tangibleness about them. Tangibleness is a good word for it. Is it a word? You tell me. I don't have a dictionary in front of me to look it up.

So heaven for me would be this place where the sun is up most of the time and nighttime is only a minor annoyance and there is plenty of sea all the way around. And I would have my dad next to me whenever I wanted. I don't suppose people would have to die anymore there. They would already be dead. And there wouldn't be a language problem or anything—I mean there would be one language which everyone would speak. Can you imagine that? What language are you people speaking now? I certainly hope it's English. My conversation wouldn't make much sense if for instance you were all speaking Arabic or Chinese or some strange African tongue. But since I don't know for sure, I'll just go right on assuming that you're speaking English. Do you believe in heaven? Probably after what has happened you don't believe too well, if you do at all. I wouldn't blame you. It's hard to believe in something like that when everything has turned out so rotten. It has turned out rotten hasn't it? From what they say in Boston and London it's going to be quite a grisly day all over the world. You might say this earth of ours is going to be the real hell. There's no reason to go anywhere other than this earth to find hell when the world is going to go up in smoke.

My dad wasn't going to stick around to see this. He had better sense than that. He was a man of much sense and he took care of himself so he wouldn't have to be disappointed in the way things worked out. I don't blame him, either. Why should I? It wasn't his fault that everyone went so crazy with their bombs. He was a man of peace. You may laugh—go ahead and laugh. But not everyone was so crazy as to think that they could go right on building bomb after bomb with no other way to get peace in a world full of big and little governments squeezed together like a bunch of ballbearings. That's the way it was, you know. The earth had shrunk and shrunk and finally there wasn't enough room and there were no other places to discover and people went right on fighting over this little bit of land and that little bit and that big bit and on and on and finally, like today, they decided that they all wanted to end it because they all couldn't have what they wanted. And no one could control the governments. That's the kicker. No one could control what they did and so they went about their own business of calling the shots and bang! They called one too many shots and it's all going to be over according to the men on the radio by the end of today, Wednesday. What a way to celebrate being alive. They didn't give me too much of a chance. Of course, they didn't give you any chance, and that's a lot worse in my opinion. Do you have governments now? I hope not. They turn out to be a pack of trouble when you get right down to it. "Too many governments spoil the world" is a phrase that I've coined from the phrase "Too many cooks spoil the broth." Let me explain that to you since you probably don't get around to cooking too much nowadays. If you have five or six gourmet cooks trying to make an Italian specialty—one wants to add more basil than salt and the other wants to add more vinegar than tomato sauce and so in the end they all start fighting among each other over the perfect recipe and what do you have in the end? Nothing. You don't have that special Italian dish that everyone dreamed of. You have a mishmash of different cooks' concepts of what the perfect dish should have been—and so you have nothing. That's the way the world is today. Too many governments, all thinking that they have the perfect recipe for how people should live and where they should live and each one of them trying to add a little here and there to their own particular idea of how it will turn out best—the broth being the world in this case. What a mess. So they can't settle on who is right, who has the best recipe, and they destroy what began with the best of intentions of how to make the best kind of world.

My dad could have explained it much better to you than I can. He was better, as I've said, at telling it like it is, but he isn't here anymore to do that and so I have to use my own words to clarify things for you and hope that you will understand what I'm talking about.

Have you ever sailed a boat? Outside my window I see the spearhead masts of any number of sailboats moored on

WORLD ONE

the shore of the cove. The dawn makes them seem so romantic. I'd like to climb up one of those masts and set sail for the middle of the sea and watch what's going to happen this evening. Can you imagine being in the middle of the ocean when everything goes puff! I bet it would seem like there are a dozen dawns going on right at the same time. I bet it would seem like the whole earth was being made over again. Anyway, I would like to stand up on that mast and see it all happen. It would have made a great story for my grandchildren when it was late at night on a stormy evening and they were scared of the darkness and thunder and lightning. I would have told them about the time I went out into the middle of the ocean and watched the world split at the seams. That would have shut them up. A little storm would seem like nothing to them compared with what I had to tell. That's one thing about these times. It puts everything in perspective. It's hard to get mad at anything or anybody over misplaced shoes or overcooked dinners or dwindling bank accounts when all the world is about to get sick to its stomach. In fact, it's hard to get mad about anything at all. I just get this dreamy feeling of being happy and grateful to be alive and nothing else matters but the seconds that are going by right this second and the light outside my window which frames the masts of the boats so nicely and properly.

Do you ever think about your own deaths? You couldn't be very afraid of the whole issue—what with you being the survivors of such a horrible incident. You probably are just enjoying being alive and doing all the normal human things that I like to do. If you ask me, it's not such a wise thing to think too hard about death when everything around you is teeming with life and sunlight and moonlight. Do you believe that we never die? That we have souls that go on after us and travel at the speed of light? I pretty much believe in that kind of thing. I can't say that I originated that idea, though I wish I could say that I had. My dad was a proponent of that kind of thinking. He'd go on and on at all hours of the day about whether or not his soul and the soul of his girl (me) would meet up one day while passing through the universe. Think about that idea for a minute. Two streaks of light travelling out in the happy unknown, meeting up with each other at some distant point. Would we shake hands? Would we hug each other? Would we recognize each other? Would my light be of a different color than his? These are all issues that we as people have to think about, because it's part of our faith in the living. I mean when you live you have to think about dying from time to time. And when you die it makes sense that you have to think about living from time to time. After all everything goes round and round and life comes about from death (you're not living when you're not born) and death comes from life. To put it all in perspective, you have to live to die and have to die to live. To me it's a pretty cozy arrangement masterminded by some one or some thing of a very superior intelligence who is pretty much in charge of it all.

    I think now that my dad was safe taking his own life and all. He believed in what I just said. And if you believe in a thing and have reasonable grounds for thinking that way, chances are that it's got to be most of the way true. I guess, though, I'm still avoiding the issue of why he decided to end his time on earth. This part might interest you. My dad wasn't a saint or a prophet or anything quite so extraordinary. I'm pretty sure of that. But he was a man who believed in the power of peace. That was a term he used over and over again. "The power of peace is the power that will rule the world." It's not as though he went around to everyone he knew and said stuff like that. He was more politic than that. Also I don't think he wanted people to think that he was too naive or even crazy. Lots of people have thought that peace was what the world needed and had to have to survive the wars that pop up through history. What made my dad a little different was that he believed that peace could only come through some kind of world law that could keep all the people safe from each other and able to live together as a kind of world family. He studied the history of war and the history of peace and in the end he discovered for himself that when men of whatever nation lived together under a common law they

WORLD ONE

could live in a relative state of peace. Hearing myself say this it doesn't sound too earthshaking or anything. I mean it's pretty straight forward when you get right down to it. The trouble is, or was, that none of the powers in power in the governments of the world would dare to go to the people and ask for their permission to create a big body of law that would oversee all of the actions of each nation as they related to the rest of the world. My dad's idea was that if the people of the world had the chance to understand the reasons for war and the reasons for peace, they would rally round and call on their governments to join other governments in forming a world law that would be for the protection of every nation on earth.

I can hear him now complaining about the outmoded, as he called them, methods for settling differences between nations. You see, just like right now, when things look very bad and bleak, there are men going round and round the world trying to settle the problems which are causing all of the confusion and difficulty today, and for plenty of days before this. That's called diplomacy. Representatives of each nation that have a problem get together with other representatives of other governments and try to settle whatever problem exists by negotiations. That means that the problem won't be settled until the nations make an agreement, or some kind of treaty. Well, my dad said that this kind of thing might have worked okay a hundred years ago or so, but not now. He said that the world had grown too small and too interconnected, and that in any case, even if a treaty were signed it didn't necessarily bind the nations to what they had agreed on. All of this is a little over my head, but I'm trying to explain it the best I can because I want you to know something about my dad before I die. He never wrote a book or anything about what he did, and besides after today there probably wouldn't be too many copies left around for you to read. Can you still read? Do you still like poetry? What are your favorite books? I used to like the movies, too. I miss going to the movies and watching a new world open up before my eyes. Some of them were good. I liked the Walt Disney films the best. They always had lots of good and bad people in them and in the end the good always won out over the bad. There were plenty of witches and sorcerers and wicked old people who had to do battle with young handsome princes who believed in the good and just things in life. Like life itself. These princes in these Walt Disney films would go to the ends of the earth to slay an evil dragon or defeat a wicked queen. When I was younger I always pictured the man that I would marry would be that kind of man. But thinking about it, I think that my dad was that kind of man, though he didn't make out so well in what he was after. It was just too much for him. No one man can do battle with the world and end up too well. But it was his dream that he would attract a lot of other people like himself who believed in the same thing, and that then they would attract even more people who came to believe in the same thing, and that eventually even after he was dead something would be done about the state of the world and the fact that it wasn't working very well the way it had been set up. What was happening, and what is happening now, is that all these governments that I keep talking about can do anything at any time they feel like it. So the world is in a constant state of agitation, and when things boil over wars break out and people like myself get killed and buildings and museums are destroyed and people go hungry and die a little later on when all the smoke has settled. What makes this situation worse (and I'm sure I don't have to tell you about this seeing as how you've been living for a long time with what will happen on this day) is that governments got so good at making bombs and forgot about getting good at coming up with some neat idea about how to make the earth a safe place for people like me to live. I don't blame the people like myself much. Well, maybe I do. My dad couldn't make the governments see what he was talking about, or if they did see, they weren't about to jeopardize their positions with their people by proposing some wild idea of a world where every nation was a kind of a state under one government which created laws to protect the people everywhere. He called it universal law. He said that there had to be a universal law which applied to all men of all nations on earth for there to be a just peace. That's the kind of man he was. He looked around him and saw that things weren't working, and that there wouldn't be anything left of the world when the day

WORLD ONE

came when the big governments started to fight over any one of a number of important details that affected their lives. But I'm seeing the day. Here I am in a little cabin in Sandy Cove, Nova Scotia, hearing on the radio about how the world is about to be as sick as it's ever been and there isn't one thing I can do about it, or for that matter, any of us can do about it, except to stick it out to the end and die with some dignity.

6

I'm going to take a minute or so pause so that I can step outside and get some fresh air. Switching off now. I'll be back with some news of the day. We can compare days. I hope yours is as beautiful as this morning promises to be.

Coming back on now after some fresh air outside in the dawn. My dawn is scarlet red framed by a bending bow of clouds to the east. The tide is low and the mud is thick in the basin of the bay. Already the sand flies are actively spinning around in what looks like a constant state of confusion. They never seem to know where it is they are going or why. They just circle round and round, as if they were in some kind of mysterious orbit. They must have a logic to them—I mean they must know what it is that they are doing—but it's impossible for an outsider to recognize it. I hope that they eventually get where they're going. They must be hungry half

WORLD ONE

the time. Maybe they feed on the air and it doesn't matter at all that they spin around like cats chasing tails. I was feeding on the air, too. It makes for a good breakfast. It's like the best fruit you've ever tasted or the freshest water you've ever drunk. You've probably been breathing dirty air for a long time. You probably don't know what fresh is like at all. Let me clue you in to the benefits.

First, it makes my head feel like it's lifting off my shoulders. I've been cooped up in this little cabin all night while listening to the rattle of the voices on the radio. But the moment I take a step outside I feel like I'm walking above the world. I could be a cloud—one of those bending bows of a cloud to the east. Do you know that I actually get thirsty for fresh air? I get thirstier for it than I ever do for water. I guess I was raised this way or something. I can just stand on the front porch for hours drinking it down. And then it's like I feel these currents in my blood. I feel it rushing around in every part of my body and this is when I feel like I'm floating above the world. I feel lighter. I feel happier. Take a deep breath now and tell me if you can feel the same sensation. Ready, breathe. What was it like? Of course, you'd have to be outside for it to count. If necessary switch me off and step outside and take a breath for me. I'd appreciate it. It's really been one of my most favorite things to do. I won't speak for a minute or two while you go ahead and do it. That will make it easier on you. You won't have to fool with any of these buttons again that make this nifty machine work.

Now I guess you know what I mean. You're probably a lot happier and will be able to listen to me for a long time now. I'll make a deal with you. Every now and then I'll give you a fresh air break. That way you can go outside and breathe in and out for a while until you feel good. Then we can pick right up with what I'm telling you.

You probably want to know more about what it's like to live up here in the country where everything is so gorgeous and alive. I don't mind telling you everything I can think of, but there will be lots that I leave out. I can't possibly tell you everything about it. No one person could do that. Like you.

You couldn't tell me everything about what it's like to live the way you're living now. So don't expect me to do better. I can only give you little bits and pieces of information. But if you close your eyes you might get the picture. Close them and think hard for a while. I'll try to lift you away and back into my world. Are you ready? Take a breath and go.

The forests are the ancient part of the earth. They seem to have been around since the world began. There are fields of trees that shoot up into the sky as if they were on their way to heaven. Their branches are like the wings of wild birds and they shelter the cool dark forest floor. Every leaf, every pine needle is different from the one next to it, and the one after that and the one after that. And these leaves and needles protect the trees and make them breathe like you and me. There are so many shades of green that it would be impossible to count them all. Once when I was much younger and wasn't too logical or anything, I tried to count the different shades of green on the trees on the bluff of the hill up the road. I got to the number 340 before it began to dawn on me that I might not finish before suppertime. I told myself I'd start again in the morning but somehow I always put it off after that and never took it up again. So don't worry about all the shades of green that there are. Just take my word. There are more than you can count.

The trunks of the trees are like the backs or hides of African animals. They're so tough that you can cut your finger on them or scrap your arm raw. Nature looks out after its own kind. Nature protects those who protect us. Honestly, I feel so safe when I'm walking in the forest. Don't you? Sometimes I might get a little scared at night, but that's not very important. I still feel basically safe. It's just that the wind sometimes stirs things up and makes unusual noises and things like that and I'm unaccustomed to it and so I think that someone's out to get me. But they never do. It's nothing. Every time I get scared it's nothing. And every time I get scared I just have to make myself remember that it always turns out to be nothing in the end so why should I be scared in the first place? Logic is a great protector when it comes to being in the forest at night.

Have you ever noticed how the sounds of the day are

WORLD ONE

different than the sounds at night? First of all, in the night there seem to be a lot more different little sounds than there are in the day. In the day I just hear the loud ones with a few occasional small ones thrown in if I really pay attention and listen. But at night you can hear everything in the forest. I hear the snapping of twigs and the rustling of branches and the noisy movements of squirrels and raccoons and restless birds. I have a favorite owl that I listen to every night. He must be a very grand and very wise old owl by now. I've heard this owl ever since I was a child and he still carries on in exactly the same way from exactly the same place as he did long ago. I suppose you have favorite animals, too. Have you ever seen a rabbit in the woods? I have. I've seen practically a thousand of them up here. They seem like the nicest, most human of the whole bunch. I've never been able to exactly catch one and make friends with it, but if I could I know we would get along just fine. They have sharp black eyes and finely tuned ears and can run like the dickens whenever they hear something they're not familiar with. And they jump like they're on springs. They practically bounce along the forest floor.

I've forgotten to go on about the forest in the night. I like sleeping on its pine needle carpet. It's more comfortable for me than any bed I've ever slept in. First of all it's always warm from the day. Bits of sunshine warm it up to just the right temperature for sleep and somehow it stays warm throughout most of the night. It's also so cozy and soft. I can put my head down and be wide awake and pretty soon I just seem to fall down into this gigantic pillow and then the sounds of the forest fade and then I start having this swimming feeling and then I'm eased down into a comfortable place where all I do is dream about whatever occurs to me. That's what I mean about the forest floor being the best bed in the world. Why people invented beds, I don't know. All around them they had all the beds in the world. But leave it to people to make improvements on things that don't need improving on. Even in the winter I don't mind sleeping out in the woods. Usually there's snow and the snow warms you up and makes you feel like you've got a blanket wrapped around you. To tell you the truth, I don't sleep out in the woods much in the winter, but I could if I wanted to. Do you sleep out in the woods in the winter? Do you have to? If you do, you'd probably agree with me that there's no place like the woods to find a bed—summer or winter. But it's probably not something everyone can appreciate. Only people like you or me.

I appreciate nature because my dad appreciated nature, and I learned from him first hand what it meant to live with her. If there's any advantage I think I have over city girls, it's that I know something about it. I may not have a couple of good-looking boyfriends to walk me home from school—any reasonably devastating blonde could have them—but I have all of nature to look out after me and keep me company. Some people might not understand that. But, fortunately, I don't have to explain anything to anyone. I just have to respect nature and it respects me. We get along. I don't irritate it and it doesn't irritate me. It's a handy relationship and I don't have to put on pink dresses to impress it. Nature is colorblind and etiquette blind when it comes to its regard for people. The general law about nature is that we all fit together. Don't you find that to be true? Think about it. We couldn't live very well without it doing all the things it does for us. Take my trees, for instance. I wouldn't have this ducky place to live without them. They gave me the frames for my windows and the floors on which I rest my feet. And even though we had to cut down some trees to have a place that is just about the nicest place on earth for me to live, I still feel a part of my natural surroundings. And where the trees have been cut down, others have grown back, and by the time I would have had children and a big family, those new trees would be as high as the ones that my dad cut down.

I mean it would be a crime and everything if we just cut down the trees and let the ground rot and get washed away by the rains. That would be unforgiveable. Nature would take its toll on us at one time or another. You can bet on that. But my dad had a respect for nature. He put back into the land

WORLD ONE

what he took. And now nature will respect him for what he did. There won't be any need for vengence. There won't be any need for hard feelings. That spot in the woods is being reborn even as I am talking to you now. Maybe just tonight it's grown back about an eighth of an inch. Think of it. It's growing in one way or another all the time, when I'm awake and when I'm sleeping. It grows as I grow. Nothing's going to happen to that spot in the woods where my dad cut down those trees so that I could have a roof over my head.

Are you growing new trees, too? I can't tell you what to do, but if you want my best advice about nature you'll try to do that as often as you possibly can. You won't regret it. You have to think about your children and their children. They have to have trees. They have to have shade in the forests. They have to have a soft spot in the woods to sleep in summer or winter. You have to think ahead and know the laws of nature before you can go tampering around with things that are a lot bigger and more powerful than you. My dad was always thinking that way. He said that you could take little examples like that and then relate them to the larger issues in life and know what was right to do. He said that this was what man should have done with the big secret that the governments discovered to make bombs. He said that it was fine to have discovered this secret—or it couldn't be helped anyway. But it wasn't so fine to use it to go against the natural grain of nature. But the governments were (and I guess haven't changed much except to get worse) bullheaded, and instead of using this knowledge for the good of everyone, they turned it against everyone just as soon as they discovered it. They just wanted to make sure that they had the biggest bombs so that they could be safe from all the other governments that had big bombs and on and on it went until today. I can't imagine how big the bombs are today. You will probably have a better idea about this than I. Were they really as big as my dad told me? Did they eat up the cities and poison the air like the men on the radio said they would? Have they destroyed all of the good things in life? Did they change the tides? Did they ruin the forests and shield out the light of the sun? I'm asking too many questions, I guess. But you can't blame me for being curious. All my life I've heard about these bombs and now it doesn't look like I'll ever live to see what it was they were supposed to do. So you can't blame me for being curious. It's a natural thing for me to be, considering the circumstances and everything.

I wish that there was a way we could exchange information more evenly. I'll try to tell you everything I can about the world that I've known. That's only fair to you, after all. You should know something of your history. You should at least hear the voice of one of your ancestors. But I wish we could think of a way for you to tell me what it's like to be in the time when you're listening to the record of my life. I wish my dad were here. He could tell you so much better about his general philosophy of how he hoped the governments of the world could live in peace. Maybe he could help you with your problems. No one ever said he didn't try to work out the big problems in life. At least I never heard anyone say such a thing. I guess there isn't a much bigger problem than how to get peace in a world full of governments that are constantly stabbing each other in the back. You could say that governments are the curse of the people. That may sound like pretty hot stuff, but there's a grain of truth in it. They never got very good at solving problems and much of the time they created more problems than they solved, so what's the good of that? I can't find too much good in it but maybe you can. I'd like to hear you try. I really would.

Are you happy now? Maybe if you're lucky you've gotten rid of all the governments. The men on the radio say that there won't be practically any governments left after today. And the ones that are left, they say, will die off pretty soon and there will be only a few people left alive. I admit sometimes it's kind of scary when they talk about mutilated people being born later on. You're not mutilated or anything, are you? I don't mean to offend you, if you are. You can't help being what you are. And it wasn't your fault if that's what's happened to you. It was our fault, the governments' fault, everyone's fault. But still, people weren't born to be mutilated. They were born in a certain way, like trees. Not everyone I've ever met has been beautiful. But that's not to say that they aren't beautiful in some other way. And sometimes those people who don't have a face like Cary Grant are the nicest of the

WORLD ONE

bunch. I've heard stories about the most stunning-looking women in the world who weren't nice at all inside. Even if you're mutilated by what has happened to the earth, you probably are still gorgeous inside. Nature has a way of protecting her kind in one way or another. What may have happened to you on the outside may have made you some kind of divine person inside. That's why whether you're mutilated or not, I'm talking to you like a friend. I don't have many friends up here, except Mrs. Mac, and she's a lot older than me and doesn't always listen to what I have to say. But you're nice, I know. Anyone who would listen to me would have to be nice even if he or she were mutilated on the outside.

Would you like to join me for breakfast? I've been planning out what I'm going to have all night. Breakfast is my favorite meal of the day and I won't miss it even to talk to you. But I'll keep right on talking while I fix it and enjoy it. You can't deprive a girl of her last breakfast, now can you? It's not every day you eat a last breakfast. I won't want to die on an empty stomach. You can understand that, can't you? You can understand it very well, I know. If you hear some rattling in the background that'll be me fixing more morning coffee and boiling my water for Quaker Oats—the cereal that sticks to your ribs and keeps you going all day long. I usually eat it with brown sugar and sprinkle raisins over the top to add just the right amount of texture to it to keep it interesting. I'll screw the lid on very tight when I'm finished with the canister. I'd like you to try it after I'm gone. All you do is boil the water until it's piping hot and then pour it carefully over the white flakes and stir it up a bit until it's real thick and appetizing. Then add the brown sugar and raisins. The raisins might have spoiled by the time you get to them. I won't be able to help that. But you can live without them. I didn't used to stir in the raisins and I liked the oatmeal just fine. I'm just saying that it adds the right amount of something to it and gives it the depth that makes it more than just an ordinary kind of cereal. You get what I mean? Quaker Oats and me go back a long time so I've had time to experiment with how to make it the best. I've tried strawberries and blueberries and it's true that they add flavor, but for me it's the wrong kind of flavor. I prefer something more discreet. It's got to blend in just right and raisins are the ticket when all is said and done.

You can also have some of my Folger's coffee if you like. Make yourselves at home. My dad always said that this little cabin was built to last forever so you won't find me possessive about it. I'm glad to be able to share it. My dad would be glad, too. He always wanted to make things last for a long time and I guess I've inherited that kind of instinct. So make yourselves at home and boil some water in my red kettle on the stove. If the electricity isn't working anymore, then build a fire in the fireplace. There's a rod that you can hang the kettle on and there're some safety matches in the bottom drawer of the far right cabinet next to the refrigerator. I know the milk in the refrigerator won't keep for more than ten days. So you won't be having any milk with it, but there are plenty of people who like to have it black. There is some white sugar in the canister next to the tea, so feel free to use that too.

Can you hear the water boiling in the background? Nova Scotian water is the purest water I've ever tasted, so it's perfect for the best cup of coffee in the world. Pretty soon you'll hear a high pitch noise that sounds like a cop with a broken whistle. That's caused by the steam rushing through a small hole at the top of the kettle that is there to release the steam. It might explode otherwise. I guess bombs are made on that kind of principle. Somehow the men who make bombs learned how to create a lot of pressure inside of a small object and because there isn't any small hole to allow the pressure to be released, it just explodes, shattering the casing around it. But when you hear the high whining in the background, you'll know that that's not going to happen. Kettles are for boiling water for hot coffee and Quaker Oats, not for making bombs.

I have to get down the porridge bowl and wash out my coffee cup. I keep the raisins inside the refrigerator to make them last for a long time. There is nothing worse than a

WORLD ONE

spoiled lump of raisins. A white hairy mold climbs all over them if they're left out for, say, a week or two in humid weather. That's how I can tell I shouldn't eat them. Mold is poisonous and shouldn't be eaten by anyone. You watch out for the white hairy mold—it will make you sick and you probably don't have too many doctors around to help you get over it. I'm not telling you how to live your lives or anything. I'm just suggesting that there are things that you have to look out for to keep alive. You probably don't have much time to read books about keeping healthy. But if you do, there is a tiny community library up the road across from Mrs. Mac's store and I know for a fact that there are books about medicine and keeping fit that you could find. You won't have to check them out with the librarian, I bet. And best of all you won't have to pay any fines if they're overdue. I must have been charged about ten dollars in books fines over the last couple of years. I just like having the books beside my bed and I can't bear to part with them after I've finished reading them. To me it's kind of like returning a whole world when I have to take them back. Some of my favorite people in the world have been people I've been fortunate to read about in books. They always seem to do the right things no matter how hard the circumstances of their lives happen to be. Isn't that nice? Against all kinds of odds they almost always come out on top and make everything right and make everyone happy and glad to be alive and living. My dad should have been a character in a book. He would have done much better in that kind of environment.

I wouldn't want to be in a book. I like being on the outside looking into the inside. And besides, I'm not an important person or anything so glorious as that. Maybe if I had lived a lot longer and travelled around and experienced the African deserts and been invited to Buckingham Palace to have lunch with the Queen and been a movie star, I could have been in a book. But still, I'm happy. I haven't missed that much. There's more to life than being in a book. That much I know.

As you can tell the kettle is boiling. It's a pity that you can't have some coffee with me. It's even worse that you can't share my breakfast. We would have so much to talk about and I'd try to be the perfect hostess. I have napkins covered with wild birds and two sets of candlesticks my dad left me. Have you ever eaten breakfast by candlelight? I know it's an upsidedown thing to do, but it's very romantic when the dawn is as pretty as it is today. If I had enough candles I'd even eat my lunch by candlelight. I wouldn't tell this kind of thing to Mrs. Mac. She's so formal about the way things should be properly done. But since no one's around to complain and make me do things their way, I eat breakfast by candlelight and dinner, too.

I'm sprinkling the raisins on my delicious oatmeal now. Now the brown sugar. Now I'm stirring it all up into a hot steaming soup. I'm going to pause a second and eat . . . It gets better every day, this breakfast. You won't want to miss it. Follow my instructions to the letter and you will be happily fed when you're through.

The candlelight makes all these neat shadows on the table top and brings out the color in the strawberry patterns on the tablecloth. This tablecloth used to belong to my mom. My dad wanted to make sure that I had it. Any mom who likes strawberry patterns on her tablecloth must have been a pretty special person. She would be glad to know how much I've enjoyed looking at it in the candlelight for all this time. There are things like this that I'd like to say to her. I can't help it, but I keep storing up things to tell her. It's hard to remember everything I've always wanted to say, but if I ever get to see her out there when I get to become light and travel into the universe, I'll do my best to remember everything I've ever thought of. Do you remember your mothers and fathers? Do you have things that you'd like to remember to say to them if you ever meet up with them? Maybe you ought to write them down in a notebook or something so that you won't forget. I did that for a while, but I lost it on the beach one day when I was swimming. It must have been covered up by some sand and then washed out into the bay at high tide. It made me pretty upset for a few days. All my thoughts to my mom were somewhere at the bottom of the sea, and I'd worked on them for so long. You can bet I'm not going to take this tape out with me if I ever go swimming again. I won't want that to happen to what I have to say to you about my dad and me. No one is ever going to accuse me of making

WORLD ONE

the same mistake twice. Only a fool doesn't learn from his mistakes. I don't know how often I heard my dad say things like that, but he was applying it to the governments, as usual. He never let up on those governments until they did him in by not listening to him.

My Quaker Oats are getting cold from me talking too much while I'm trying to eat. I'm going to be silent for a while while I finish up and enjoy the last of the last delicious bites.

One, two, three—I'm here again and happy as a clam. It doesn't take me long to eat, now does it? In honor of this conversation I'll keep the candles burning for a while longer. I might even let them burn all day in honor of my birthday. Why shouldn't I?

Don't you ever want to do something that's outrageously luxurious? Like burn candles all day long. Like go swimming in the rain at sunset. Like eat a whole bowl full of ripe cherries. I wish you could tell me about what strikes you as the ultimate in luxury. It's probably different for you than it is for me. Luxury to you might mean, oh, just eating at all. Maybe it's just drinking a glass of good water. I'm sure I take some things for granted all the time. Like I can go over to the water tap and turn it on and out comes the freshest most delicious water I've ever tasted. But you might not be able to do that at all. You might have to purify it, or boil it to get rid of contaminated particles that cause sickness and disease. That is what is so interesting about talking to you. It makes me speculate on what it's going to be like after today for the few people who will probably survive. Mathematically speaking, my dad always used to say that some people would survive. They might go hide in mountains for a long time until the air was good to breathe again. Then they might come out and start to rebuild what was left of the world so that they could go on living again. That's why I'm probably not an idiot talking into this nifty machine. I mean I would have to be an idiot going on and on about my dad and me if there wasn't any chance of anyone surviving the bombs. But some people might happen along to this little cabin in the north and turn on this machine just the way I left it, so I'll take my chances. I have to do something. I want someone to know that I was alive and kicking, no matter how few. There is something in a person that just cries out for someone else to know that he or she was born and lived on the earth. That's why, I think, painters paint pictures and composers compose music. They want someone at some time in the future to listen to or see what they've said with images or sounds. They're really just saying in the best way that they can, "I was here! I lived. Listen to me. Look at me." I don't think it's such a vain thing to do. You don't have to be great or anything for you to have this need, either. Mrs. Mac wants to be remembered by her grandchildren. That's very important to her. I've heard her say time and time again, "At least my grandchildren will remember me." Plus she has her store to hand down to her daughter. That was her creation. She spent all these years fixing up that store and running it and painting the outside every couple of years and polishing the brass doorknob, just so she could leave it to her daughter the best way she knows how. I have to admire that. It's not the most important thing in the world—I don't know, maybe it's just as important as anything else. She's not the empress of China. I know that for sure. But she's lived in her own mind like the empress of her own estate. Sure the empress of China had a bigger estate, but really when you get right down to it, it's still just an estate—the very same as Mrs. Mac's. And even the emperor of China is going to die. The empress will have to live alone like Mrs. Mac one of these days and the feeling won't be much different for her as it has been for Mrs. Mac. Do you understand what I mean? I'm talking about two people who are living in the same way but slightly different. I guess you could call me a reverse snob. Here I am comparing the empress of China to lonely Mrs. Mac and calling them practically equal. That's pretty snoby of me. I might as well say that I'm as good as Moses or something. But what I am saying is that people are people, no matter who you are. I've learned that from my dad. That's why he tried so hard to make the governments understand that they were neither

WORLD ONE

much better nor much worse than all of the other governments that they were at war with, or were going to be at war with. He started out by thinking that all men are equal in one way or another; that no person was always completely right no matter how hard he or she tried and that to live peacefully could only be possible if there was some kind of overall law for the people of the earth to live under, so that everyone's rights would have the best chance of being protected by impartial judges. That always made a lot of sense to me, but then, what did I know about the whole thing? My dad would always use the example of the Articles of Confederation to make his point. He would compare the world to America when it was getting started a long time ago. Then there were many states but each state could pretty much do what it wanted to do. And when push came to shove over a big issue that concerned all of the seperate states, the only means of settling the issue was to go to war. My dad said that this was the way with the world. There were and are all different nations around the world that can do exactly what they want to do. There is no law that holds every nation responsible for its actions and so there are constant wars between various ones. It's enough to make you feel ashamed for being so human. But when the Articles of Confederation were replaced by the United States Constitution, America lived under one law—it had a constitution that bound all of the states together. And ever since then you haven't heard of Alabama fighting Maine, now have you? You haven't heard of Florida fighting California, have you? That just doesn't happen because there is a federal law and if there are any differences between one state and another, they have to go to court to settle whatever it is that they're arguing about.

Now my dad always was thinking that if there was an overall law that the nations of the world invented to settle their differences peacefully, there wouldn't have to be any more bloody wars. Each nation could go to this big court and ask that the issue be settled one way or another. Then and only then would force be applied to the nation that wouldn't go along with the court's judgement. And then all the bombs that all the nations have wouldn't make any difference. They would have security, and all they would have to do is go along with what the court said, win or lose.

You probably know all about this anyway because you've seen what war is all about in the worst kind of way. That's one thing that you have over us now. You can learn by our mistakes without having to repeat them over and over again. We should have known a whole lot better ourselves. In case you didn't know, we already had two world wars and still they haven't been able to stop the one that's coming. People are so stupid sometimes. They have all the answers right in front of them and still they can't see them. The Almighty should have made people with bigger eyes. It would have helped a lot of us. My dad would have lived a lot longer too, if everyone had been born with bigger eyes.

Have I told you I have blue eyes that Mrs. Mac says are the color of the evening sky? She always told me that they would be my chief asset when I came of age. My time will come, she always said. My time will come. She always told me that boys especially like blue eyes—and eyes like mine, she said, would knock them for a loop. I hope she's right. I've been counting on some beautiful boy to tell me that I've got beautiful eyes. You can understand my concern. It's natural for a girl to want the best boy in the world.

I guess what I'll miss the most is getting married. Every girl who was ever born has dreamed at one time or another of finding the perfect boy and going to the altar with her dad. I could tell you all my dreams about how I'd meet this perfect guy, but my dreams probably aren't much different from yours. He would have to be everything, though. Not that he has to be a fancy athlete, or anything. Some girls like athletic types. I've got nothing against them, mind you. Why should I? There's nothing wrong with boys running around the track and catching the winning touchdown at the homecoming game. It has a sort of dramatic, sensational appeal. But for me, I want something a whole lot different. I don't even expect the boy of my life to have all the good looks, either. I

WORLD ONE

wouldn't object, but don't think I'd just go after some old beauty. I'd want him to be as smart as he could be. From what my dad always said, a man needs to have the wits of an Einstein and the heart of a saint. I would think that would have to be a pretty rare combo. Sure, I could find one smart fellow who knew how many miles it was to Venus and back. And sure, I could marry a clergyman who wanted to give all his money to the poor. I could find either one of those people and be happy halfway. But my dad told me that men of the kind he was talking about did exist if only you were patient enough to wait for them.

I'd wait forever for a boy like that. Who wouldn't? It's never a good idea to settle for second best. Any girl will tell you that. I'd like him to have some money, so that we could live any way we like, but then it's still not the very most important thing to me. How could it be? With a guy who has a brain like Einstein and a heart like a saint, I could always be happy even if we were living in the slums of a city—or the ruins of a town after a war. What makes life worth living for me is just to live and think over the meaning of things very seriously. I might like him to know how many colors there were in a rainbow. I might like him to know how many words there were in the Bible. I might like him to know how many notes there were in Beethoven's Ninth Symphony. Do you know how many notes there are in the Ninth Symphony? That would be half of what I would want in him. In the other half, I would want him to take care of a dog with a broken paw and a horse with a torn ear and a fish who couldn't get back to the sea on account of the low tides. He doesn't have to believe in God or anything, though. Although I suppose everyone pretty much believes in one kind of God or another. It's only natural and I don't see it as a sign of weakness. All you have to do is look around and you can see so many things that were made somehow by something that is more grand than you or me. Most people on earth believe in some kind of religion or another. People call it different things and say prayers in different ways—but still you have to admit it seems pretty darn likely that no matter what you call the God you believe in—he's probably the same one, just going by various names. Like languages—the word for bread is not the same in English as it is in French or Latin or Hebrew or Russian. I don't know how to pronounce the name for bread in all those other languages, but I can guarantee you it's not the same. But bread is bread and you can't get around that. What do you call the God you believe in? Do you still believe that there is a God? I wouldn't blame you if you didn't. It wouldn't make much sense for God to let the earth get in such bad shape. You wouldn't think that a being who made the world would let it just fall apart. So I don't blame you for not believing in an Almighty who made such beautiful things only to let them die. It just wouldn't make any sense at all. None whatsoever.

What kind of dreams do you have? Do you know what nightmares are? Do you know what daydreams are? I have lots of daydreams. I can't remember when I had my last nightmare. I was probably still a child and dreaming about being swallowed up by the sea. The sea always looked so big when I was young and my dad always warned me about rip tides which grab you by the legs and take you down under without any warning. That's why I dreamed those nightmares. Otherwise I wouldn't have. I would have been too busy daydreaming. I'll tell you my daydreams if you tell me yours. I've got practically a hundred favorite ones that I can pull out and think about any time I might be feeling low. What are daydreams for but to make you feel good when you're feeling bad?

Just before it got light today, when the radio was going on and on about the news coming from Europe and Boston, I was dreaming about how nice it would be to go riding along the trails over the backs of the hills around here. Do you ride horses now rather than ride around in automobiles? People used to ride horses all the time before the automobile was invented. My dad called the horse the only civilized means of transportation. He would have rather ridden a horse a hundred miles in the rain than ride an automobile one mile in the sunniest of weather.

Anyway I was dreaming about riding on the old trails at dawn and hearing the thunder made by the horse's feet and feeling the slap slapping of the pine branches as they were swept apart by me and my favorite horse. Any horse I've ever known has been braver than me. They follow their noses. They practically seem to smell the trail no matter how covered up it is. Or maybe they just have excellent memories and can remember the trail from the time before. I couldn't say. I've never been privy to a horse's private thoughts and meditations. But either they smell their way through the thickest of the forest's paths, or they have the best memory for details of any living things I've ever known.

Now I like riding along the trails pretty well—the trees are all around you and the air is filled with lots of oxygen and it's thrilling to climb towards the top of the hill on an animal running for daylight. But the very best for me is to run the horses on the beach at dawn. And high tide is better than low tide. If you've ever tried to run along the beach at low tide it's impossible, right? The horse's hooves get caught up in the mud and he naturally slows down and he gets tired out more easily and then again he might stumble and break a leg on some sharp stones. Anything can happen. You have to watch out for him very carefully. The most horrible thing in the world is to see a horse with a broken leg. You have to shoot them, because the leg won't heal properly in most cases and it's very painful, very painful. So the trick with riding a horse on the beach at dawn is to make sure there's going to be a high tide so he won't be tempted to run down into places where it's dangerous. And if you do this, you will have the time of your life. Have you ever seen a sleeping horse? I've seen 'em tired and breathless but I've never ever seen a sleeping horse. So it's okay to ride them early in the morning because they never seem to need much sleep. Don't take my word absolutely on this. But at least I've never come across a horse too sleepy to run on a beach at dawn when the tide is high and the sun is making its way up over the silvery line of the sea.

7

The clock over my bed reads six till seven. I don't think I'll turn on the radio anymore. What will happen will happen. I'm not about to ruin my day anymore by listening to all the men on all the stations countdown to the final minute of my life. What would be the use in that? That would be like counting the seconds while you were drowning instead of thinking over your life or whatever you're supposed to be doing in the time before you die. Have you ever heard of that theory? There is a theory that when you are dying all of your life passes in front of your eyes just before you sink down into the darkness, which is supposed to be the beginning of death. It's in that time, so the theory goes, that you take an accounting of your life, both the good and the bad. I suppose I wouldn't need as much time as some people older than me. I don't have a long history of good and bad. I wouldn't want to be in some people's shoes, though. Can you imagine having been really bad and having to face all of the

WORLD ONE

things that you had done just before you died? That could be a truly horrible sight. And on top of dying it might really do you in, for keeps. I wonder if the men who are going to cause the world to get blown up will see themselves doing that just before they die? That's probably about the worst thing a person could do in a lifetime—blow up the world. I wonder how they're going to feel when they see themselves doing that? I would think that they might come to regret it at that moment. I would think that they would wish for a second chance and maybe ask to be forgiven by the person they pray to and think is above them. I guess you could call those moments before you die and see everything you're supposed to see some kind of punishment and some kind of reward, depending on which way you went in your life.

I've tried to be particularly good for the most part, but I have some things I'm ashamed of. Nothing like blowing up the whole world and killing people, mind you. I wouldn't have the nerve for that. I'm mostly thinking of the time I hit that raccoon on my bicycle and broke its neck. It was practically the worst thing I have ever done and I don't like remembering it even now, but I suppose I have to face up to it this evening, so I might as well. I didn't mean it. He just scampered out onto the road when it was misty and very grey all over the place and the next thing I heard was a quick thudding sound and a little yelp, and then my bicycle swerved and I was knocked silly by the side of the road. I wasn't out too long. But when I saw what a bloody thing I had done, I was sick! I was sick for two days! You have no idea what it means to kill something that you didn't mean to. It's positively the most gruesome experience a girl could have, and I don't ever wish to repeat it. No, I won't ever. I'll be dead before then.

My dad must have seen a lot when he was dying. He's already experienced this theory, if it's true. I'd kind of like it if he could give me some kind of advance warning about what's going to happen to me. My mom, too. It's not every girl that's going to have to die alone. It's not every girl who's going to die without even a friend. But don't think I'm getting cold feet and am going to flake out on you. I've got more guts than that. I am my father's daughter, you know. And he had more guts than anyone. He went all the way around the world trying to make the men in governments make this universal law come true. And then when that couldn't be done, and when he knew that the world would soon blow up, like they say it is going to today, he knew what he wanted out of life. He knew he wanted to live or die by his own free will. So don't think I'm going to be scared when things get tough today. I'll take it which ever way it comes and meanwhile I'll just enjoy the day talking to you. I might like to go see Mrs. Mac, though. I don't know. You never know about old people. Sometimes they just like to be left alone. Everyone has a right to die in peace and in their own way and maybe that's the way she'll want it today. I expect she's been listening to the radio all through the night and is smart on what's going on. And she hasn't come to see me, so I expect she has her mind set about the way she's going to live out her last hours in Sandy Cove.

And if she believes in that theory I was talking about, I expect she's readying herself like me, so that she won't have any unexpected surprises jump up in front of her face when she's going down into the darkness or wherever you go when it's all coming to an end. Have you ever known any of your friends to die? Did it look like they saw something before they stopped breathing? I hate to seem so morbid and ask strange questions like this, but I have this yearning to know all that I can so that I'll be as prepared as I can be when the time comes.

I didn't have to set my alarm this morning. That's one good thing about staying up all night. I've found it hard to wake up to the buzzing of an alarm. I've always wished I had one of those alarm clock radios that wake you up to the sound of pleasant music. Do you use alarm clocks? When I sleep outside, I don't have any use for alarms or music. I wake up by the first light of the sun. I first feel kind of warm in my dreams and then begin to feel a bit thirsty and then I seem to swim to the top of my dreams and presto, I'm awake! And then I look up out of my sleepy eyes and there are the gorgeous tops of the trees and the sunlight shining through like golden spikes and then my hand feels the wet dew on the forest floor and then I hear the buzzing of insects and bees—there are always the heavenly sounds of birds. I guess

WORLD ONE

you could say that they were my music. But certainly I don't have to lay and listen to some jackhammer noise that makes me have last minute crazy distorted dreams. Do you think people sleep after they're dead? It wouldn't make much sense to me if they did. Frankly it doesn't make much sense to me to have to die when there are so many beautiful things in the world that you can go on appreciating as long as you live. If I could just get all those men in the governments to come up here and sleep with me in the woods and wake up with me the way I just described, they wouldn't dare think of making such a mess of things for everyone like me. And what about all the animals? It's not as if they have any choice in this matter, now is it? And what about you? You didn't have much of a say in this decision the men on the radio were talking about all night long. It's what my dad was talking about all the time. There's no justice. Men are slaves to these powers that have gotten out of hand. Men are fools for not thinking things out better.

You might think I'm pretty unforgiving. I apologize for sounding that way. A girl should keep her thoughts to herself most of the time. But then I don't have anyone around to tell me what to do so you can understand why I might get so uppity. My father should have sent me to boarding school. They give out what they call discipline and I suppose I need lots of that. Besides I might have met a boy by now and would have had someone to hold me tonight when things didn't start to go so well.

One of the most fun things I ever did in my life was to team up with some girls at the camp across the bay and raid the boys' camp on the opposite shore. You might think that this was no real accomplishment, but I'm here to tell you that it was. Everything had to be planned down to the last detail. We had to know the movements of the tides so that we could cross the bay around its rim without having to walk along the highway that now and then has traffic at night. We had to wait for the cover of fog so that some fishing boat wouldn't spot us and come close to the shore and investigate. We had to slip past the counselors and drive ourselves to stay awake until three o'clock in the morning. But I am here to tell you that it was worth it. You haven't lived until you've raided the boys' camp across the bay and done it successfully without getting caught. It's a very romantic thing to do. I'm telling you this so you'll know that I have courage. Courage is my best asset right now. You might not understand, not having the kind of background that I have. But right now I'm living through probably the most difficult day of my life and I will tell you it takes some kind of courage to not get upset and go off and do something I would regret.

The summer after some girls and I raided the boys' camp, it closed down and now it's been turned into a trailer camp. There are people living over there and sometimes at night you can see the fires burning along the shoreline. And I hear music every now and then—mostly it's music I've never heard before, but I like it fine. When the tide is down, the music is fainter than it is when it's up. The water carries sounds pretty well at night when it's full up. It's kind of magic that way. If I ever had to build a fort or a safe place to live, I'd build it in front of plenty of water. That way it would be possible to hear anyone that might be coming—whether they were coming to do you harm or good. You might keep this in mind if there are unfriendly characters stalking around here after I'm gone. It isn't good to be surprised when times are as rough as I imagine they'll have to be.

Anyway, I've never laughed so hard as the time we raided the boys' camp and got away with murder. And it wasn't as if they hadn't done it to the girls' camp first. Boys are mean that way. They are always causing trouble when you least expect them to. So I was friends with some of the girls at the camp and when I heard about all of this, I recommended that we do the same thing. It was kind of like we decided to go to war with them after what they had done. Later on I heard that the boys did it first because some of the girls refused to dance with them on the previous Saturday night. They felt they were justified to get back at the girls for making such fun of them. Maybe they were, I don't know. But I didn't hear about that part of the story until later. And even

WORLD ONE

if I had heard it, it might not have mattered—the things they did would have made any girl ashamed of knowing any boys at all.

So on this night when the fog had come in from the bay like a warm muffler over everything, and when the tide was down as low as it ever gets, I made my way to the rendezvous spot down by the canoes and there I met up with the most courageous girls in the camp. They all wore black—black shoes, black pants, black shirts and black scarves. And there we painted our faces with mud. I had seen that trick done in an old war movie when the British were invading a town in Germany. It worked very well considering we should have used a brick of coal.

It was muddy going almost all the time. And the headlights of the cars that were roaring down the highway on the opposite shoreline seemed like demons the way their headlights steamed through the fog. I wasn't too scared but there were other girls with me who were. But mostly we just went right on our way until we came to the dock at the bottom of the boys' camp. It was quiet there. Very quiet and still and it was like you could almost hear a hundred boys breathing. The little cabins were dark and we only heard the stirring of horses in the stables and the occasional drone of a car engine in the far off distance. So we went to it. We crept up the rickety dock and took off our shoes so we wouldn't make any noise as we walked along the gravel paths—and then we came to the spot where we wanted to be. We all stood in a ring around the flagpole and looked up at the empty mast. You could just taste victory. It's a thrilling feeling to be so close to victory. If you've ever been at war with anyone, you'll know what I'm talking about. Now one of the girls slipped out a pink brassiere. And we couldn't stop laughing. We were there in the foggy darkness laughing ourselves silly at the sight of this pink brassiere which was about to go up the boys' camp flagpole. We all thought that this was the most original thing we could do to get back at the boys who had been such a nuisance and had caused so much trouble. So we tied the brassiere to the flagpole and hoisted it up—and up and up it went until it reached the top. There wasn't much of a breeze so we couldn't see it flapping around the way flags do on battleships—but it was enough just to have it sitting there, waiting for the boys to see in the morning. They would be so embarrassed, I knew that. Boys make out to know more about sex than they do, and it might take them a second or two to figure out what it was—but they would, and boy would they ever go pink in the face and probably sheepishly walk away and wish they hadn't done what they did.

Well, we got out of there real quick after that. There wasn't much more to stand around for, except to gloat inside about what a good job we had done having made it all the way without getting caught. So we left and got safely back without a hitch. I said goodbye to my friends at their dock and went home sleepy and happy.

As I said, that's not the worse thing in the world a girl could do, but I imagine I'll see that episode flash before my eyes when I'm going down into the darkness. But my whole point about all this and why it's so interesting to me now is that there is a lesson in it, as my dad would say. And it applies to what he was always talking about. Here the boys went off and attacked the girls' camp because some girls wouldn't dance with them. And then the girls went off and attacked the boys because of what they had done to their camp and then when it was all over, the boys and the girls (including me) got into all sorts of trouble. I wasn't allowed to associate with the girls after that because the counselors said that I was a bad influence. What I'm saying is that everybody sees events differently. Like in the world. One country can see something differently from another. And because they do see it differently they react differently and then the trouble begins. They might absolutely believe that they are right in, let's say, attacking another country for what they have done to them. But then the country which has been attacked might have done something against the country because of something the other country might have done to them. You see what I mean? Everyone sees events differently, and that leads to misunderstandings and in the case of nations and peoples that can lead to war which gets everyone in trouble, like me and the girls and the boys. So what I'm saying is is that there should be some kind of way like my dad has always said of peacefully working out the problem. Like the boys should

WORLD ONE

have gone to the counselors and complained. And then the counselors should have brought it up with the girls' counselors and the issue of whether the girls should have danced with the boys should have been settled. And if the counselors agreed that the girls should have danced with the boys (after all, that's what dances are all about, and the girls did invite the boys) then the girls should have been made to dance or suffer some kind of punishment, like no canoeing for a week, or no archery for a month or something like that.

You might think this is a pretty small example of what my dad was always talking about—but it's the small examples that sometimes show up the bigger issues in their true light.

I wouldn't dream of doing anything like that again because I learned that there are always different ways of seeing everything and when you're in the middle of the problem, it's best not to make judgements that can cause big problems for everyone who's involved.

But still, it was one of the funniest things I've ever done, and I'm glad I got a chance to do it before today.

Are you listening to me at night? Or is it dawn or day or what? There are times when I like the nighttime the best and then other times when I like the daytime the best. Have you ever felt this way? Both have advantages and both make me feel differently. In the day I always want to do things. I want to go out and live and run up and down the streets and see people and go visit the sea. But at night I like to think. Then everyone else has gone to bed and isn't making any kind of sound and won't be around to bother you until dawn. So it's then that I like to make my cups of coffee and in the summertime sit out on the porch and watch the changing night sky. Have you ever thought of what it would be like to see the night sky from the surface of the moon? How would it look from the farthest star? I bet my life it would seem like an entirely different sky and you wouldn't recognize any of the lights above you. For instance, you might be seeing the back side of a familiar star that you might recognize if you were still down on earth. But from the back side the light would give off a different glow and it wouldn't seem like it was the same one at all.

But I guess you don't think much about travelling to other places in the universe. You probably have too much to think about already. That's why I'm glad I was born when I was born. I've had plenty of time to stay up late and think on the stars and the planets and just the darkness surrounding everything. There must be plenty of places to go out there. And I don't mind telling you that if I had the chance I'd just take off and go out there and find myself a new place to live. It would be better than sticking around here and waiting for tonight. I can't tell you how much I wish I could just put on some wings and go flying up into the world above me. I don't have a good enough imagination to tell you what I might find. It would sound silly even if I tried to tell you. But I imagine I'd find a nice place to settle down in eventually. There are just so many stars up there—and probably just as many planets and one or two of those planets must be as nice as Earth—maybe even nicer considering there won't be any men on the radio telling everyone that the planet's about to blow up in the evening. But if I could get up there I'd build a little cabin like this. I'd take some books with me so I would know how. And of course, I'd have to take some good food along to keep up my strength until I found the right way to go about getting food on a constant basis. I might need some water too just in case it took me a few days to find a reservoir—or a mountain stream. Also I'd have to take some matches—the wooden kind of matches so I could start my campfires and cook my Quaker Oats. But I wouldn't need very much to start out with. I've learned a lot about being by myself in the last few years and I think I could do pretty well on my own up there. Of course, I might get lonely and wish for company now and then, but at least I wouldn't have to worry about the world getting blown up on my birthday. That would be a great relief, I'm telling you. It's not every girl who has to worry about such things on the day she wants to celebrate the fact that she was born in the first place.

Don't think I'm feeling sorry for myself. I just think it would be nice to go to some place today where I wouldn't

WORLD ONE

have to worry—some place far away where there aren't any people around to get me upset and start me thinking about unhappy things.

Have you ever wondered whether we were at the center of the universe, or maybe at the end of it—or the beginning? Just where are we when it comes to a status in the over all picture of things? I wouldn't think that we would be very high up on the totem pole. What kind of people would go blowing up their place of residence when it gives them so much good stuff all the time? It's a question worth thinking about. You might take some time to think about it yourselves. I would think that we would be somewhere near the bottom. Like a child, we can't reach up very high yet—so we must be somewhere at the beginning. That's about as high as my dad would have rated us, too. He believed that there was so much more to look forward to. He kind of thought people were only beginning to realize their potential—that they had a long way to go, but in time, if they didn't blow themselves up and found a way to live together in peace, they could go up that totem pole and come to places and planets that they could only dream of now. He was pretty romantic, I guess. And I guess I take after him, but it seems kind of obvious to me when I get down to thinking about it. Here we have only been really alive for a few thousand years and the universe is billions of years old and will probably last quite a lot longer than that. And you would think that we have only begun to look into things and find out what it is like to live at the beginning of the universe, to say nothing of what it would be like to live at the end of it. That's something for you to think about when you get through listening to all that I have to say. I hope you can come up with some interesting thoughts about it too. It's important for people to think about what they've missed. You can learn a lot that way. I bet a lot of historians are going to be upset today. Everyone is going to destroy all of their history books that they spent so much time putting together. And now they're going to have to start all over again—it's going to be so much trouble that they might just forget the whole thing and do something else with their lives, if they survive. And if it's enough to make the historians mad, think how mad all the mothers are going to be. Every mother who ever had a baby is going to be sick. Here they devoted all of their lives to bringing up a child so that he or she could have a good life, and then all these governments just lash out at everyone. I'll tell you straight, I've been in favor of mothers running the world for a long time, and I just wish that they had gone out and done it. It would have made it a lot easier on the people like me.

Do you still have babies? I bet you wish you could take them away from here. I bet you wish you could take them up in the sky on a pair of wings and find some other place to live where everything is okay again. You might understand more of what I mean when you think of what you could have, and what you do have. That's one of the purposes of dreaming. You have the time to think ahead to what could be and not always about what is. My dad spent his entire life thinking about what could be—maybe he could have spent a little more time thinking about what is—but just a little. It's important to think ahead. And you can't only think ahead to one year or two. You have to think ahead to ten years and twenty and even a hundred years. That way you can make things turn out more the way you want them to. It won't be perfect—but at least it would help to think a little more ahead so things like what's going to happen won't happen.

So these are some of the things I turn my mind to when I stay up late and watch the stars and the darkness. It's kind of uplifting, if you know what I mean. I've always liked to do it—and since my dad's been gone, I've had the time to do it. Don't let things get you down. Just look up into the sky and dream for a while and you'll feel much better than you did before. It's kind of natural to do that—after all, we were meant to go to other places in the universe. We were meant to find out much more than we already know. You can just tell that by the feeling you get when you take the time to look up and dream about tomorrow.

What kind of world would make the bombs that the men on the radio are always talking about? I have my own ideas about getting rid of them so they won't be around to bother us

WORLD ONE

anymore. My dad thought it would be a good idea to destroy them all—toss them out into space or something. But really he always said that they weren't the real problem—the real problem was political—how war happened and how peace happened. I know he's probably right about what he always said, but I like to think about these things more romantically. That is, I'd like to see these bombs buried underground with the men who made them—or better yet bury them underground with the men who commanded that they be made in the first place. That seems like a simple solution to me. I can't imagine anyone else going ahead and building these bombs when they know that the people who made them before them had to get in the ground with them and sleep with them forever. People might get kind of discouraged about having anything to do with them if they knew that that was going to happen to them. Can you blame them? Think what it would be like to sleep with those nasty things. First of all, there might not be too much room for you to sleep with them because they are so big—they'd take up all the space, even underground, and you wouldn't have any place to lie down or stretch out. As I said, I'm pretty romantic when it comes to ideas like this.

Still, it might work. I wouldn't want them to be shot out into space. I wouldn't want to clutter up all the new places in the universe with things like these bombs. That's like throwing all the garbage into the sea or into the streets. No one should want to clutter their future home to be. Besides, if there were other people out in the universe somewhere, think what they would think. *They would have a fit!* And if ever they met up with us out there, I don't think they would be any too friendly considering what we had done to them in the past. They probably would send us back to where we had come from and never let us see all of the things that are waiting for us out there. I don't want to sound fresh or anything, but I don't think my dad was correct on this point. You have to think ahead when it comes to important issues like this and you sure can't take any unnecessary chances. It could get you in the end and then where would you be? You'd be far away from home with all these people who didn't like you at all.

You have to consider all possibilities with important issues like this. That's for sure.

There are other things you could do, too. You could cement them all up in the places where they're sitting right now. If you got all the cement mixers in the world you could do it in a couple of hours. And when the cement hardened you wouldn't have any more problems. They'd be stuck down there in the ground. And if anyone pushed a button to set them off, they might move an inch or two, but not any more. They'd be like sticks stuck in a bog. They'd probably steam up and then groan and then whistle and then go pop and drop dead. All the cement mixers in the world could do it in a couple of hours, as I said. That's one way to get rid of the bombs. You might have some suggestions of your own. If you were around I'd be more than happy to listen to them. I wish we could have talked about this before today. It might have made a difference. Then we could have gotten on the telephone to enlist everyone else's support, and then they could have gotten on their telephones and phoned everyone that they knew and pretty soon we'd have just about everybody in the world on our side about what to do with all the bombs, and then we could go right on and do it before it was too late. I wish I'd have given all this some more thought before today. I'm like everyone else. I'm always thinking too late. I have this funny pictures in my mind of all these cement mixers—American mixers, Hebrew mixers, German mixers, English mixers, Italian, Chinese and Russian cement mixers, roaming all over the world and stopping now and then to pour some more cement into the places where all the bombs are kept. It would be quite a sight. I would be proud to see that happen, I'll tell you that right now.

Don't think I'm stupid in saying all this. I know it's not that easy. My dad would have been the first to tell me that and I would have known that he was right. But it's not as if I can go around the world now and convince all these men with the bombs that they have to get together and make all these laws so that they can have some peace for a change. First of all they wouldn't listen to me and next of all they would probably call me some kind of nut and put me in an insane asylum and lock me up for years. And I wouldn't want

WORLD ONE

that. Especially since there's hardly any time left and there is so much that I would like to say and do. Anyway, I figure that some people who are older than me should have done all this in the first place and gotten us out of this situation. After all, I didn't make these bombs and I've never gone to war with anyone, except maybe with the boys' camp over what they did to the girls.

I keep telling you my dad tried to do this, but I guess he really didn't have much of a chance. One or two men aren't anywhere near enough to change things in this world. You need an entire army of people—more than an army, you need millions of people to get up their nerve to tell the governments off and make them settle down to live in peace. Everyone wants peace. At least that's what everyone says, but they sure didn't seem to say it loud enough and figure out the right way to go about getting it. Just listen to the radio if you don't believe me. I don't hear anyone talking the way my dad used to talk. He could have been wrong or something, but I haven't heard any better ideas, and the whole thing always made some kind of sense to me.

Do you ever get thirsty from talking? I'm pretty anxious to pour myself a tall cold glass of water and drink it down. Sometimes I squeeze some lemon in it and that makes it taste even better. There's something about lemon and water that mixes just right. You will excuse me while I go and get a drink? I won't be long.

I just had a thought on the way to the cupboard. We could drown the bombs. We could fill up the holes to the brim with water and lemon. The lemon would probably get them all rusty and eventually eat away at the metal and pretty soon after that they wouldn't be of much use to anyone anymore. That's a thought because water is cheaper than cement and lemon can be found at any supermarket and you wouldn't need all those big trucks to do it. You see, if you just think about things you can usually come up with lots of ideas about how to get things done. I know about this from experience because once I had some goldfish that I was very fond of. And one day I had to clean their tank to scrub off all the algae so they wouldn't get poisoned. So, I caught my goldfish one by one and put them in a glass of water by the sink. Well, when I had finished cleaning out the tank, I looked over at the goldfish in this glass and they were dead. At first I didn't understand it at all. They had been dancing around in it when I first put them in there, and then the next time I looked, they were dead. But what I didn't know was that I had put them in one of my spare glasses of lemon and water that I had forgotten to put back in the refrigerator. So I can tell you from experience that lemon and water can do things to things that can be very unpleasant.

Bombs and lemon and water won't mix. You can take my word on that.

I believe in possibilities. I believe that a person can do pretty much anything they really want to do. That's nothing new, I guess. People have been saying that for a long time and lots of other people have proved them right about it. But that's not why I'm bringing up the whole issue now. I'm in a situation where I can't do anything I really want to do. I guess I've proven those smart people wrong. Like I can't make this war go away. I *want* to make the war go away, but I can't. Therefore, it's just not true anymore that you can do anything you want to do. It's just not true.

I'm not crying in my milk over it. It's not as if I'm the only one who's in this particular predicament. But there is a whole lot more I wish that I had experienced when I get right down to thinking about it. You're probably having the same problem as me. Only you might realize how many things there were for you to do if you had lived at the same time as me. That's the kicker. You don't even really know how the world was and of all the possibilities that were just waiting for you if you wanted them. You might have some idea about them by the time I'm through talking to you, but still you can't possibly know them all. I'll tell you some of the things that I'll be missing. Maybe if I think about them and talk about them out loud it'll almost be as if I had lived them.

WORLD ONE

That's about the best I can do under the circumstances. Don't you agree?

One thing I'd like to do anytime now is to be a bride. In fact, to be a bride would be my first priority if things got better around the world all of a sudden. I'd go to one of the finest hotels in all the world and sit engagingly at the far back right table in the dining room and wait for the man of my desires to show himself and ask me to dance after a light supper of salad and white wine. And he would dance with me until midnight, or until the moon rose up over the balcony. Then he would escort me out onto the veranda and ask for my hand in marriage. You think I'm sappy, don't you? Probably I am. But when it comes to one's true love you have to be a little bit sappy for the whole thing to come off right. I mean, it's not as if you're going out to pick out a new car or even pick out a kitten from a litter. You have to let yourself go while you're being seduced by the man you're going to marry. Next of course would be the honeymoon in Paris. I won't go into detail about that. If you don't know what a honeymoon is, you've missed out on a lot. So I'm told. It's been said that French coffee is wonderful and that there are many places on the boulevards where you can sit out in the open and drink it to your heart's content. I would like to do that very much. I would marry a man who would like to do that too. You see, I am very picky when it comes to husbands and honeymoons. You only get one go-round, so my philosophy is that it had better be good and done just right. Anyway, that's the story I always wanted to tell my daughter when she was thinking about getting married. I'd tell her not to settle for second best; not in husbands or in honeymoons. Of course she might like to go to the Congo or somewhere extremely exotic and I wouldn't say I could see anything wrong with that either as long as she thought that that was the best choice around. I don't even know if the Congo exists anymore. I have a map of the world and it says there is a place called the Congo but the map is old and I think it's different now. But names won't matter too much after today. The whole world will probably be some kind of jungle—maybe the whole world will be called the Congo. Maybe only elephants will survive. I'd feel pretty stupid if I knew I was talking to elephants like this. I've never heard of an elephant understanding anything human. Have you?

So what comes next? We could have some children, or we might wait a while and go travelling. We could get in a car and go travelling to anywhere we wanted to go. And when we came to the sea we could get on a big boat and take it to wherever it was going. We might wake up one morning and land in the Orient and little Chinamen might pick up our baggage and take us on a tour of the country. I hear that there are more people in China than in any other country in the world. It's obvious to me that they like people over there, so it might be a good place to visit. After that we could get on a train and travel clear across Asia. There is a train called the Trans-Siberian Railroad that runs along the entire length of Russia. Russia, I think, is the largest country in the world with more wheat fields than Canada and America combined. Since I like the look of wheat, I'd like to see them. It must be a pretty sight and I would probably always treasure it, even when I got old and couldn't remember things too well.

Then maybe we'd go down to Europe again and see all the countries that are worth seeing. I imagine that would be every one of them. Every country has something good in it. Even if, let's say, you don't like the food or the weather, you might find something that you couldn't find anywhere else in that particular one. That's why travelling is so interesting to me. You see things firsthand. You aren't influenced by anyone else's opinion. You are free to like and dislike anything at all and come away from it knowing a whole lot more than you did when you went into it.

Then I wouldn't mind coming back home after, oh, six months to a year, and starting to build a big beautiful home. I'd like it to be on the sea, of course. And it would have to have hundreds of acres surrounding it and a view out the kitchen window of the sunset. It might take a long time to build this house by the sea, so we might have to live in this little cabin for a while until everything was put up just perfectly. I don't think my husband would mind. Anyway, you can't have all your dreams come true at once. What would you have left to live for if you had everything you always wanted in a second? Any man could understand this, I think.

WORLD ONE

If he didn't, I could always explain it to him and then there wouldn't be any problem. So the house by the sea would be next on my list of things I really want to do. Then after the house was built and I furnished the rooms the way I've been studying for almost my entire life, we could move in and have a child or two. I've read that having a child is plenty of work, and that may be, but from all accounts it's a worthwhile effort. I mean it wouldn't be much fun living in a big house by the sea without a child or two. And then you have to think about the world. The world can't go on without a child or two from people like me and my husband. Anyway, it's all part of nature's plan and it's worked best that way ever since people were around.

I can't think much beyond that. You can only see just so far ahead into the future and it's probably better not to make too many plans. Sometimes it's fun to change them and do something that you never expected to do. But still, I'd like to do what I've just described. It sounds like a good way for my husband and I to get started in the world before we learn more about how to help it solve some of its problems. You have to try to help the world with its problems if you can, otherwise living doesn't make so much sense, now does it?

I wish I could have helped it more than I did. I really do. My dad would have been very proud of me and that's an important thing to me. Ask any girl who has a dad. She'll tell you the very same thing. It's one of mother nature's instincts. And it's a good one.

I guess you could say my dad had good instincts, too. The trouble is, good instincts don't always get the best rewards. After all that he believed in and worked for, nothing came true. And what made matters worse, he was rejected by the very country he wanted to serve. They say that it is a very noble thing to try and serve one's country. But in his case, no one thought that what he was doing was noble at all. That was the last thing anyone ever said about what he believed. He was called a traitor, a Communist, a heathen, an idiot—a dreamer and insane. There were only a few people who stood up for him and told the world that this day would come—plenty of people wouldn't believe him. They said that no one would be crazy enough to set off all the bombs. I hope they've been listening to the radio today. I hope they've changed their minds. I hope they've grown up a bit and thought about what my dad always said. It's just too bad my dad isn't alive to see this day. Not that that would make him happy, but at least he would have had the satisfaction of knowing that he was right about the bombs. And I believe he was right about his universal law—and the stupidity of governments and the madness of unreasonable men. You would have liked my dad if you had known him. You would have appreciated his concern for people like you. But you might have felt bad for him after what his country did to him.

That's why he took me to this beautiful spot by the bay. He didn't want me to live in a country that had treated him so badly after all that he had tried to do. He wanted me to grow up in a peaceful place where the newspapers wouldn't know our name and where he would be safe from what he called harassment. But he was sick with pain and he couldn't bear to see the world come to an end. He just couldn't take it and I don't blame him. I don't blame him one single bit. If I were older I might do the same thing. Really I might. I'd just put a gun to my head and pull the trigger and go to be with my dad so we could talk about old times and he could tell me stories about my mom. I'm not even a little bit afraid of death. Anyway, it's better to die on your own than to let the world have the last laugh. Like, I don't want to be any part of a people that are going to do such dreadful things to the earth. I don't want to be any part at all. You understand that, don't you? You didn't have any choice. But I do. We all do. We all had a choice to fix things up before they got this bad, and no one did. No one took the one single step to make things all right for the rest of us. It makes me sick to think about it. Really it does. You are probably pretty sick yourselves. But I want you to know that my dad tried everything he knew how to make the world better for you and me. What more can you ask of him? What more can you ask of anyone? What else is there to do when you get down to thinking about

WORLD ONE

it? It is *the* noblest of causes even when practically everyone treats you like a dog for trying to do it. People have a lot of nerve. A lot of damn nerve. I'm ashamed to be a member of the human race. I really am. And I'm ashamed of the country where I was born. It was up to them to look ahead and determine the right thing to do. They had the most influence around the world. They could have fixed things up. They could have seen to it that the world went on. What right did they have to do this to us? I'll never understand that. Never in a million years. Well I hope that the Almighty punishes each and everyone of us for letting a thing like this happen. I don't think there's anything that He can do about it. It wasn't His idea to blow everything up. He only creates things; He doesn't go in for destroying them. That's what I think. You can think what you like. People get just what they deserve. Nothing less and nothing more. That's the neat thing about being a person. You have the choice to do whatever is right, if you really want to. I must sound like I was born in a church. Well, I wasn't. No more than you. But you can't help talking about the Almighty when it comes to issues like the death of everyone. It naturally leads one to thinking about who made everything in the first place. It's just logical to think that way. You might not understand logic anymore. Even now it seems to have gone out of fashion. And now it's too late to be logical anymore. What's the use. I might as well go mad. I might as well just go right out of my little mind and pretend I'm in another world where everything is all right and where there isn't anything to be afraid of. It's better than listening to the radio and hearing all the men in London and Boston going on and on about the end of the world. It's just not fair to people like you and me. We didn't do anything. We just happened to be born at a bad time. We just happened to get stuck in a world gone mad. I wish I had been born in the 18th Century. At least I would have had a better chance of living a more normal life—and I would have had a dad and he would have been here with me and we could have done a whole lot better—a whole lot better. I'd give anything to have been born a long time ago. I would have been happy to miss this entire problem. And if you had been born then, you could have been my friends and I could have talked to you face to face instead of through this recording machine. And you could have met my dad and you could have lived in this town with us and we could have been happy to be alive in a world without bombs and this kind of total death. That's a nice dream to have on a day like today. It makes me feel much better just to think about it. I wish I had thought of it before. I wouldn't have gone on about such nasty things and you probably would have liked me better for it. I apologize. It won't happen again. I'll just pretend I'm living in a dream when I'm feeling blue. You'll understand, won't you? I haven't got much time.

Have I told you I have red toenails? I polished them up last night while I was busy listening to Beethoven in between all the men on the radio. In this early morning light they are quite beautiful. Red is supposed to be the color of courage. I have red fingernails, too. People used to tell me that my hands were made for playing the piano. They were probably right. If I had ever learned to play the piano fast enough, my fingers would have looked like they were on fire, what with my red fingernail polish. That would have been the right effect to have. Red fire on black and white keys. It would have made a tremendous picture. The magazines would have been very impressed. It could have done a lot for my career. It's the little things that count. And that would have been one of them. Someday I'll compose a tune called "Fire on the Keys." It will have the sound of crackling driftwood on fire on the beach. It will be very explosive when I get to the end. And I will have a last crescendo that will lift my audience right out of their seats. You can count on something like that to make me famous. You see, I know what the sound of driftwood on fire on the beach sounds like. And all that I would have to do is to imitate it on the keys. It will be an experience you aren't likely to forget. Sometimes these ideas just come to me. I might be lying awake in bed at night and then suddenly I'll have a thought and that thought will lead to another thought and it's kind of like a chain reaction. And finally, when I'm through thinking, I've got the whole idea in my head and I'm ready to do something about it.

WORLD ONE

You know, with all the people in the world, you would have thought that someone lying in bed at night would have had a good idea about saving the world after all this time. You would have thought someone could have worked it out just right and made the rest of the people see what it could mean. You would have thought it—I mean if I can so easily think up such a small thing like I just said, you would have thought someone much older than me could have figured the whole thing out without much trouble at all. Maybe someone did. But it doesn't much matter anymore. That idea is now about as useful as that tune that's been running around in my head ever since that night when I couldn't get to sleep.

I'm wondering if Sandy Cove has changed since this time. I guess that depends on when you have gotten around to listening to what I have to say. Maybe it's a hundred years from now. Maybe it's just next week. But if you like, I'll tell you something about the people of the village. We don't have any movie stars or super cool jazz musicians or other glamorous personalities, but I like these people just the same. People are people when you get right down to it, and the simplest of people can be the nicest people you ever knew, and the neatest of people can be not very nice at all. Do you know what I mean? I'm sure you do. You're just not the talkative kind. You have all sorts of deep thoughts and are given to brooding silences but you don't talk much, do you? Anyway, even if you did want to talk I haven't given you much of a chance. I'll let up on you later on, but right now I want you to know about the people I know and what they've meant to me since I've been here without my dad. For instance, I don't think I'd rather die with any other people than these. Have you ever felt that way about anyone? You just know that if you have to die, it would be better to die with these people than with anybody else.

I've mentioned Mrs. Mac, haven't I? She's a peach. She's lived in this town ever since she's been alive and you couldn't take her away from it if the world was on fire. She'd just sit on that wooden chair of hers by the window of her store without so much as moving a finger or two. I call her a woman who knows her own mind. For the record, Mrs. Mac wears red quilt skirts that go all the way down to her ankles. She was born in another generation and back then they hadn't heard of anything shorter. I believe she still hasn't heard of anything shorter. Every time I give her a chance to talk she goes on and on about her dancing days and her most special beaus and what clean living she's done. She married a clergyman, as I mentioned. You wouldn't think by looking at her that she was ever married. It just doesn't seem likely. But she's got a picture of the two of them on their wedding day, so I guess I'll have to believe it. Does it sound like I'm putting her down? I'm not. I wouldn't think of it. I'm just trying to tell you the way I see her and that's all. Mrs. Mac is my best friend. And she was my dad's best friend, too.

Once when I was sick she took care of me. She made me what she called her healing soup and checked on me every two hours. She had to close down the store so she could come over here and see how I was doing. Not everyone would do that. I can always count on her to be there when I need her, though I try not to pester her too often. I wouldn't want to wear out my welcome. My dad taught me about that. A girl can only ask for so much. After that you get to be a nuisance and people don't want to help you anymore. Mrs. Mac also knit me a sweater for my last birthday. I'm hoping that the gloves she's been working on in her chair by the window are for me too. I don't know, but I suspect they are. She once asked me to try on a pair of gloves in her store, saying something about how she had a friend who wanted them and that she wasn't sure about the size. I haven't let on that I suspect those gloves she's been knitting are for me, but I hope so. The winters up here can get pretty chilly, with all the bay fog and the rain. I plan to stop by her store today and see if she has remembered my birthday. Then I'll know for sure. I guess I have my hopes up and I'm hoping not to be disappointed.

That's enough about Mrs. Mac for now. I'll get her to say something to you when I go to see her. She might be shy, but she'll at least say hello. She's not one for engaging in too

WORLD ONE

many one-sided conversations, but for you I'm sure she'll make an exception. She's generous that way. You'll find out.

I won't say much about my teacher from last year. She called me a snob one day and I haven't forgiven her. She might have been right but she shouldn't have said that in front of the entire class. It took me days to get over the embarrassment. And then she gave me a low grade in mathematics when I worked extra hard to get a B. What killed me was that I got a 2 for effort instead of the 3 that I deserved. So I'm not going to say anything more about her. I just hope I don't have her next year. She's enough to make anyone just quit school. And I'm not the only one who feels this way. You talk to any of the girls, they've had similar problems, only in different subjects.

But the librarian is nice. She lets me take out more books at a time then I'm supposed to. And then she recommends books that I've never even heard of. You can't get any nicer than that, can you? If she's still around when you get around to listening to me, go up the road to the library and ask for her. She won't let you down. And you can tell her that I sent you. That way you'll be treated better than you think. The library is on the top floor of the rickety white house two doors down and on the right side. There's a sign above the door that says, "Books are Man's Best Friends." Well, if books are man's best friends, I'd call the librarian the best friend of the best friends. She was born to be a librarian. I think the library should give her a medal or something.

Then there's the preacher at the church. He became the full-time minister after Mrs. Mac's husband died. Reverend Russell is his name and he scares me half the time I listen to him up there in the pulpit. Mrs. Mac doesn't get scared but I do. He's practically the only one in the world who scares me. You'd understand why if you had ever listened to his sermons. If this was Sunday instead of Wednesday I'd go to church and I'd take this nifty machine with me so that you could hear what I mean. Mrs. Mac says he likes to put the fear of God in youngsters. Mrs. Mac doesn't usually call me a youngster, but when I say these things to her about the Reverend Russell, the word just naturally comes to her. But I guess I shouldn't be too hard on him. I mean here it is

Wednesday and he's always been talking about how the world is going to end if people don't live better and it looks like he was probably right all along and I should have listened to him better and not been so scared of him. It wasn't so much what he said, it was how he said it. You'd understand if you heard him. But one time a friend of Mrs. Mac's baptized a baby girl up at the church. I was there because I was a guest of Mrs. Mac's. I could hardly believe I was listening to the same minister when I heard him speak about the baby so nicely. I was impressed with him then and I even made up my mind to have him say nice things about my baby when the time came. He was just a different person when it came to different kinds of services. I guess it's a person's privilege to change.

Doctor Elson lives down the highway from here and I haven't seen him very often except for the time when I broke my finger in the woods. Mrs. Mac isn't much on fixing broken fingers, so she called him in and he put a metal splint on it and taped it with white tape and gave me a pill for the pain. I felt much better then and sent him a thank you note. The next year he sent me a Christmas card and we've been friends ever since. It's funny how an accident can make you a friend. If I ever had a real emergency Doctor Elson's is the first place I'd go. And he'd remember me. After all, I wouldn't think he'd send a Christmas card to just anyone. He said I was one of his best patients and would be glad to make me feel better any time I needed it and would always be there to take care of me, along with Mrs. Mac.

I don't have any pictures of the people I'm talking about, otherwise I'd leave them out for you to see. But you'll just have to take my word that these are nice people who will take care of me at any time. All I have to do is ask them and they'll be there. Just like that. In a second.

Have you ever stopped to imagine the way the world was when it was being born? That may not have occurred to you, having been around only for the bad part when everything

WORLD ONE

got so upset and ruined. I wouldn't blame you in the least if that were the case. But I've often thought about it. You just can't help it when you're living in such a gorgeous place as this. You naturally have to think back to a long time ago when the world was coming into form. I understand that there was a lot of ice covering this part of the earth for quite some time. Naturally it would have been too cold to live here then. And naturally there weren't any people around to begin to muck things up, but I bet it was actually quite beautiful. The first trees would have been starting to grow after the ice melted away and formed the ocean and the bays. Then the sun would have made the grasses grow and warmed the fish in the sea—or made them come alive, and live practically the way they do now. I wonder when the first flowers began to spring up out of the ground and show their colors? That would have been around the same time the trees began to get taller and form branches with leaves, and ferns and moss and stuff.

Sometimes I think I would have preferred living back then. I know I wouldn't be living in this little cabin by the bay with electricity and a refrigerator and instant coffee. But I don't think that would have mattered to me. It just would have been nice to know that no one was going to blow up the world any second and ruin everything that was coming to life. I wouldn't have had any fears at all. And my dad could have stayed alive and been with me. He wouldn't have had to bother trying to save the world. He wouldn't have had to waste so much time on something that didn't work out in the end anyway. That would have been nice for him and for me. I guess we might have had to live in caves. There are a number of caves under the rocks by the sea and I bet it would have been pretty easy to find the best spot in the entire area for us to have a home. I might have missed the library and the music and Mrs. Mac and Doctor Elson, but no one else. If my dad were alive I wouldn't need anyone else. You can understand that, can't you? A dad is a very important person in a girl's life and I imagine she could get along just fine without anyone else but him.

There probably wouldn't be any horses yet, so we'd have to do a lot of walking here and there to get what we needed to live on. We'd probably have to wear tree branches or something to keep us warm in the winter. In the summer probably seaweed would do. Except for the rain, it's very warm up here. We could build a raft from fallen trees and go out into the middle of the bay and go swimming and sunbathing whenever we wanted to. Have you ever built a raft? There are all sorts of ways to do it right and I won't go into it now, but wherever there's wood, you can build a raft and use it for some of the finer experiences in life. A boat's nice, but a raft's just right.

There certainly wouldn't be any roads, except maybe animal paths. It might be hard to walk through the woods depending on how overgrown they were. But think of all the berries we would find. Think of how fresh, I mean really fresh, the air would be. It makes my mouth water just to think about it. It really does.

We'd have the only campfire on the beach, too. It's the prettiest sight in the world to see a single campfire on the beach at night. The red is so red and the black around it is so black that it makes for a picture you'll never forget. I suppose the sea would have salt in it, even back then. The salt makes the driftwood burn fast and makes the fire hotter and for all I know makes the red redder. I bet the sound of the waves would be as loud as a symphony orchestra right in the middle of my living room. We could count the number of stars above our heads. I wonder if the stars have changed since then. I wouldn't be surprised. Just about everything has changed since then, I imagine. Maybe the stars would have been brighter way back then. Maybe they would have been dimmer. Are we going towards the stars or away from them? Questions like that drive me crazy just thinking about them. Would we even know what stars were? We couldn't go trot off to the local library to find out. No one would have had the time to write the books.

My dad could have spent all of his time living instead of trying to help other people by finding a way to keep them all out of war. Back then there wouldn't have been any wars at all. The word for war wouldn't have even been invented. Think of that. There would have been no word for war. And peace would have been the natural state of things. Everything

WORLD ONE

would have been living and growing by mother nature's laws. And it seems to me that if mother nature works so well by living with laws, then man can too. My dad would have liked me to say things like that. He would have called that remark, "Very illuminating." Anyway, he would have had a much better life if he had lived with me way back when. Our work for the day could have been sitting around the campfire and thinking about the best way to make the world right from the beginning. We could have dreamed up all these fair laws for everyone to live by and then asked them to accept them or vote on them or something like that. I'm telling you, it would have been a far better thing for my dad and me to have been alive way back when. We could have started off everything just right and then a person like me wouldn't find herself in the position she's in now. And all because we followed mother nature's example of living together under some kind of laws. I bet by now you think I'm crazy. Don't think it for a minute. I may be young but I know that there's no better place to learn how to live than in nature herself. After all, we all come from nature. And we all have a choice to follow her guide. It's just natural that we learn to respect her and what she has to say about who we are.

I expect your world is a lot different from the beginning of the world or the world I'm living in. Does it ever get lonely with so few people left alive? Do you have your dads around to keep you company? Is the world all frozen over like it was in the beginning? I certainly hope not considering if it was, you can't be listening to me talk about me and my dad. But if it's not all frozen over then I hope you have some peace and have forgotten all about wars. They've never done anyone much good and they've caused lots of pain. But don't think about it now, or anymore. You must enjoy life while you can. And you must do everything you want to do. It's not fair to live without living. Like go and watch the sun set tonight. Or watch it rise in the morning. Do lots of things like that, so you store up some good memories. And take care of your friends and your brothers and sisters. Everyone needs to be taken care of. It's all part of mother nature's laws and she knows best. And don't forget to try sleeping in the woods sometime, winter or summer. There's no finer home than the woods—it was really everybody's first home before they got so smart and built all the bombs.

Today I'd like to be a bird or a swan or a goose or some flying thing that could rise above the earth and see everything. That's not too much for a girl to ask on her birthday, is it? If someone would just touch me with some kind of enchanting spell I would be happy to be a bird that could fly above everything and see the world all over. How long would you think it would take a bird to fly around the world? Could I do it in twenty-four hours? The length of time that it's my birthday? I'd hate to be caught over Mongolia and the Gobi Desert when the spell was lifted. It would be a long way down without my wings and I wouldn't have any way to get back to my little cabin by the bay. But still, I'd like to see as much of the world as I could, if I could.

Just suppose an angel or a fairy came down to me right now and gave me my wish. And just suppose I actually could turn into a bird for my birthday. Wouldn't that be the living end? Wouldn't that be something to tell my children? Wouldn't they be so proud of me that I actually had the courage to wish to be a bird which was willing to fly around the world?

It's not such a strange wish, you know. To my mind, it would be better to be above the world when all this happened then right down on it. First I would fly around to all of the places that I know so well around here. I've never seen the village from the air, for instance. I've never seen the bay from high up in the sky. I've never seen the woods and the low tides and all of the thousand things I know, from up in the air. It would be like seeing the whole world new again. Everything would look so perfect from up there. The woods would look so absolutely green and the sea would be its regular perfect mixture of blue and grey and the long highway along the coast would seem like nothing more than a mountain trail. And up there I would be able to spin around and around to my heart's content. I could go diving for fish or occasionally rest in the thickets of the highest trees on the

WORLD ONE

land or perch myself on the steeple of the church tower and watch all of my friends live their lives. And no one would recognize me. I would be just a simple perfect part of nature. I would just fit in to the natural state of things and would be as happy as I am now.

I am happy now. I have lived for a long time, so it's okay to die tonight, isn't it? I could have died when I was much younger. I could have died at birth and not even known my dad or this little cabin or Mrs. Mac or anyone. That would have been more unfair, don't you think? But I just want to do something today that is so special, something I've never done before. I'll have to try and think what it could be. I have to do the right thing. I have to. You have to take advantage of all the time you have and do the best thing with it, or else you can die with too many regrets about what you wish that you'd done in your time alive on this earth. That's why being a bird that could travel all over the world would be the right thing for me today. I would get a chance to see everything, see all the people throughout the entire world—in one day I could do this if I got my wish.

Is that the last thing I'd really want to do? I must think about this carefully, now. I can't make any mistakes. Is that the most important thing for me? To see the world? To see all the people everywhere? That is something, but is it enough? Maybe I would like to be married. Maybe I would like to have a child. Maybe I would like to have a birthday party. Maybe I would like to go and sit and talk with Mrs. Mac. You tell me. What should I do? It's morning now and the dawn is finally past and I want to do the best thing in the world today. Today is my birthday and I want everything to be right. You won't tell me, will you? That's okay, I understand. But remember that you're my friends. You are there listening to me and I am here talking to you and we're friends, aren't we? It's good to have a friend on your birthday. It's good to have a friend anytime. But especially today. Especially today I'd like to have a friend to be with me. That's not too much to ask. That's not too much to wish for. Is it?

Listen to me. Pretty soon we'll take a walk and I'll keep on talking to you so you can celebrate my birthday along with me. I'll take you to every place I know. I'll show you everything there is to show. And when you go there again you'll remember me. That should be nice for you. You must get lonely, too. You must like to have friends. You must like to live like I like to live.

I don't need to be a bird and fly all over the world. My world is right here. Right here in this cabin where I have strawberry patterns on the tablecloth and instant coffee whenever I want, and I can boil water for it and I can have lemon and water at just about any time and I can listen to the radio and hear my favorite music and I can go up to the store and chat with Mrs. Mac. I can do all these things. I don't need to be a bird and fly all over the world. I want people to know me. I want people to listen to me. I may not be very old but I've lived a long time and I have something to say. I take after my dad. I want people to know about him. It isn't his fault that things are going to be so bad. He didn't do it. He tried to stop it and make everything better. He cared about the world. And I care about it too. I want someone to take care of me today. That's what I want. I don't need to be a bird. I don't need to see everything go up in smoke from the air. It wouldn't be pleasant. It wouldn't be the best way to spend my time. I want to live and be happy and do good things while I can. That's not a crazy thing to do. I don't have to think all day about this evening. Why should I? There's more to life than thinking about death. There is so much to live for. You must know, otherwise you wouldn't be alive and listening to me now. You know what I'm talking about? You must know. You must understand. You must want to live very badly to be alive and see all the things that you see. Is it really as bad as they say it is going to be? Have you seen people dead everywhere? Are there really so few people alive? Have you been mutilated by the germs? Do you have children? What makes you happy? What do you eat? Are there still any wars? Are there still any trees? Do you sleep in the woods and sail on the bay? Has the bay turned back to ice? Are there still stars in the sky? Did you like my Oatmeal for breakfast? Do men still talk on the radio? Do they still play music in Boston?

Don't think I'm crazy for asking all these questions. I just hope everything is all right with you. You are my friends and

WORLD ONE

friends take care of each other and I want you to be happy and think well of me and my dad. It's time we took a walk. It's time we lived and were happy on my birthday. Maybe later we'll have a party and invite my friends from the village. Maybe we'll go for a drive in a car. I know how to drive. I'm only fifteen today but I know how to drive. Mrs. Mac taught me. She taught me so that in case there was ever an emergency I would be able to go wherever I wanted to go. We could go see my doctor. We could drive and drive along the coast. I could tell you what I see—I could describe everything. If it makes you happy, I would do all of this for you.

I'll be switching off now so I can fix myself a last cup of coffee before we go out for our walk. I've been up all night and I'm getting sleepy. And I don't want to waste the tape. It's important that I talk to you. It's important that you know who I am. It's important we stay together today—it's Wednesday and fifteen years ago today, I was born.

8

An infant wails in its mother's arms not four feet away from me. A dog-mother attempts to comfort him, this terrified little child who wails suddenly and for no apparent reason under the black face of the sky. Human-dog #1 stares across at me. Clearly, he is following the train of my story. Clearly, he is listening, and listening hard, to what I, to what Sonia, has to say.

The child will not stop its screaming. He is screaming about bombs falling and rising waters and long, long nights. Nightmares. But the nightmare still lives! It is before us. It is at every turn in our wretched lives. At my feet lives a nightmare. Above my head, there is one, too. It is a wonder that we are all not screaming, wailing, shrieking out loud on this night.

Human-dog #1 addresses the dog-mother.

"Give me the child."

And she does.

Now the terrified child is lying in #1's arms and he is whispering to it. It is impossible to hear what he says, but the wails

WORLD ONE

are beginning to lessen, die down, peter out. The boy is whimpering on the water. His tears are brushed by flame light, his young eyes devour the large presence of Human-dog #1. #1's wife strokes the child's forehead. She places a kiss on the top of his head. This is pretty to see. Dog-child is spreading a smile for all to see. He could be my son, he is looking so fine in the night.

I cast a look at Elizabeth. She raises her rifle a bit so as to avoid puncturing the child should she have to fire. Her face holds forth a light. No doubt it's a maternal light. She's reacting to this child in #1's arms. She is wishing that this boy were hers. She is wanting a son while holding this rifle of mine which is pointed in a singular direction.

But I don't want a son born to this. I don't want a child raised in this bloody soup of debris and human savagery. But this boy is smiling now so delightedly. Human-dog #1 has got him to laugh. He is ready to return to his dog-mother.

Dog-mother takes him back. No wonder #1 is #1. He has a flair when it comes to children. He has a flair when it comes to taking lives. How could those two talents be rolled into one? It's amazing to me that they are. It really is.

Elizabeth touches my thigh with her free left hand. I like that touch. It is an experienced touch I hope I will always know. I place my hand on her back and massage it ever so gently. I know that she aches, but this is all I can do. There's so little we can do out here exposed as we are. There is so little any of us can do, period.

I notice that Human-dog #1 is having a word with his wife. He tussles the hair on his children's heads. Human-dog-father #1, I think. Will he dare to bloody us in front of his children? Probably, he will think, that it will be a good experience for them. After all, this is a life experience!

"C. J. Jones, carry on. The boy's nightmare has passed. He is feeling good again. And so are we. Continue . . . please."

"I will be delighted to."

Debris floats by carried forth by a current of some unknown origin. Mashed paper rotted, bottles and branches circulating around and around looking for rest, looking for land. And for a moment I choose to remember green, the light green of trees, the sound of their young leaves making music like the surge of soft trumpets. A world of green, I am thinking, would be my idea of a good place to rest.

But to continue: "Sonia is taking a walk, on Wednesday . . ."

It's me again. Did you miss me? I missed you. I'm walking down the beach and the sun is high and the waves are nibbling at my feet and the sand is warm and I am happy again. I can take care of myself. I don't need any help from anyone but you. You are the best friends I've ever had and ever will, I guess. Can you hear the breeze? It's coming in from the north. The Arctic must be warm this time of year because the day breezes make me feel so comfortable and gay. I think I could probably glide on them if I really wanted to. I could just spread my arms and gradually I'd go up and up until I was practically in heaven. I'd take you with me, of course. I could tell you what I see. You could see it with me. And you wouldn't have to be afraid that you'd fall. You wouldn't fall. I'd take care of you and the winds would take care of me and we'd all be safe up there while the breezes made us feel happy.

Can you hear the sand crunching underneath my feet? It's the most natural sound in the world. You can probably recognize it, because I bet you know it from your own personal experience. We have that in common, I'm sure. If you wanted to, you could follow me on my walk. You could follow exactly in my footsteps and see everything I see today. If it's a whole lot different, all the better. You could see the world through two different pairs of eyes. Not everyone in life has a chance to do that. It might be a first. In your time, this tape could be a classic—one of its kind. The person who had this tape would be far and above the others—it would be like owning the only Rembrandt in the world, or having the only car to drive around in and show off to your neighbors. You see

WORLD ONE

what I mean? You will have an exact record of what life was like on this day a long time ago. Maybe it wouldn't matter to you a bit. But I'd like to think it would because it's all I have to give you.

I just picked up a shell. It's a puny little shell, not much bigger than my thumbnail. But the stripes on its back are stunning. They look like rolling sands that you'd find in the African desert. I've never been to the African desert, but the pictures I've seen in the encyclopedia look just about the same way. Isn't it funny how nature can copy itself in entirely different creations? Here, I'll put this shell on a rock opposite the hull of the ship that was wrecked long before I ever came here. There's a red rock just beyond it and I'll lay the shell on top so you can see it, and remember back to what I said about its stripes. I hope you'll agree with me about it being like the rolling sands—if you haven't seen a picture of the African desert, you can find it in my encyclopedia under "Africa." There's a color picture which will show you just what I mean. The encyclopedia is in my bedroom beside my bed. Make sure you look under the letter "A" in the first volume. You shouldn't have any trouble after that.

I used to be afraid to go near this shipwreck. It always seemed to me that someone's ghost would crawl out from underneath the hull and grab me by the leg and take me down under where I would have to live and be subject to some kind of underwater slavery. And I always imagined at night when there was a terrific storm out in the sea that I could hear all the people who had died in that shipwreck calling to the people on shore to help them. That must sound pretty silly. But I was a lot younger then and people had told me that story so I couldn't help thinking it was true until I grew up and knew better.

I'm down the beach where the boats are now. Do you hear them rocking and the water slapping at the bottom of their hulls? That's always been a comforting sound to me. I could sleep by that sound. Everything seems safe when I hear it. I should record some of it and play it by my bed when I can't get to sleep. It's like counting sheep—the constant thudding of the breaking waves against the hulls. I bet it would make for wonderful dreams to hear that all night. Do you like it? It's the most natural sound in the world to like. Of course you do.

I know you can't feel the sunlight—you certainly can't hear it. I can't even hear it, but take my word for it, the sun makes me feel alive and as if I were growing, like plants grow. I used to try to catch as much sunlight as I could when I was young. I had heard that it made you grow up faster, like plants—if you sat in the sun for the day, by nightfall you'd be a full quarter of an inch taller. Mostly I got a sunburn and nothing more. But when the summer was almost gone, I would measure myself and sure enough sometimes I would have grown an entire inch, sometimes a bit more. So it does seem as though the sun has some effect on how much you grow, only it doesn't work as fast as I was told it would.

Do you worship the sun? The Egyptians used to. They had sun gods and built temples to them. But they lived several thousand years ago, and they hadn't heard about God and the Bible and the disciples. But still, for not knowing about those things, they were looking in the right place. At least they were looking up instead of down. That was a start, you have to say that. And if you do worship the sun, don't worry. You'll get around to the other things in time. It just takes awhile for people to develop their religions and become sophisticated in them.

Can you hear me breathing in the air? I'll take another breath and put the microphone closer to my mouth—there—you must have heard that one. Here I am on the beach on my birthday breathing in the freshest air in the world. How many birthday girls can say that? I don't smoke or anything, so my lungs just kind of expect this kind of thing. But you might not be so lucky, even if you don't smoke. If the air is as bad as they say it's going to be, then at least you'll have some idea of what it was like to breathe it in when it was good and fresh and as pure as anything can be.

I'm going back to those boats for a minute. I want to capture that sound of the waves slapping at the hulls. So if you hear that sound for a minute or two, you'll know that's the sound I'm going to try to go to sleep by, if I can remember where to find it on the tape.

WORLD ONE

Can you tell what time it is by the height of the sun? I've never been able to, not even after I put in some time trying. I have to rely on my alarm clock in the cabin and the tolling of the church bell on the hour to know exactly what time it is when I'm outside. It just tolled nine times, so of course it's just nine o'clock. I've never had a wristwatch, not that I ever wanted one. You just don't have to think of time much up here, and that's a good thing. First of all, I wouldn't want to waste the day worrying just how many hours I had left in it before I had to go to sleep. Have you ever wished you never had to go to sleep? I have—plenty of times. If I could, I'd stay up forever. I wouldn't sleep a wink. I'd enjoy every hour I could be awake to the fullest. The only thing you can get out of sleep is dreams and I already have plenty of those in the daytime, so it wouldn't hurt me at all to be able to stay up all of the twenty-four hours in the day. Unfortunately, I wasn't made that way. Are you made that way? I would envy you if you told me that you were. Just think, you could live so much longer that way—you might live twice as long. It would be as if I would have lived to thirty years old if I hadn't wasted all that time asleep. I've tried to stay awake for days on end. I lasted for two days once. I never even closed my eyes to rest, but then after the 50th hour I was sitting peacefully on my porch—no I was sitting on the steps of the porch—and I just thought I'd blink some of my sleepiness off, and the next thing I knew I was waking up with a light rain sprinkling down on me. And the bell on the steeple was tolling nine times and I knew I had been asleep because I had been awake to hear the seven. I had to laugh at myself. What kind of girl falls asleep on her porch steps and wakes up in the rain? Well, you can count on me not going to sleep today. No matter how tired I get, I won't close my eyes, I won't give in to my fatigue. I wouldn't miss this day for all the dreams in the world. I'm going to be awake for the end of the world.

You're right if you think I'm walking through town—I say town, but really it's only a village—my village of Sandy Cove. I've just come up from St. Mary's Bay—that's where we found the sunken remains of the old ship. There is a white house on a very tall hill over to my left. I used to go there on the sunniest and clearest days of the year. From there you can see anything and everything. It's a place where you can imagine that you see the very edge of the world and then some. If I were an astronomer, I would build my observatory up there. From there I could see the farthest stars and the beginnings of the heavens. I would be able to see our friends coming from outer space. Go there sometime and tell me what you see. You might be very happily surprised. Really, you might be. To the right is my library which overlooks a grassy glen where the trees in the summertime are always blooming one kind of thing or another. I don't have my mother around to teach me the names of the trees, but I've heard they have horse chestnuts and apple trees and plenty of lilac bushes. When it snows sometimes in the winter, I go sledding down that slope to the glen. It's a very smooth ride, like going down curved glass. But sleding is for children and it's not something a young lady like me goes in for anymore. But I had my time, I had my time.

Do you know that in all of Sandy Cove there aren't many more than a few dozen people living here at one time? Less in the winter. A lot of folks can't take it when it gets cold. But the truth is it doesn't get very cold. It's more like very cool. It's not South America or anything so balmy as that, but then again it's not Antarctica either. It's something in between. A very likeable something in between. Of course, if you've been here for a time, you'll know exactly what I mean, unless the ice has come back and frozen everything over. In which case, I would suggest you travel down to the south and sit under some palm trees and listen to what I have to say.

When I was telling you about Reverend Russell and his church, I was talking about the Church of England. That's just one church here in Sandy Cove. There are three churches in all. Most towns in Canada have at least three churches in them, so you can have your pick as to which one is the best for you. But not all the churches have a cemetary like the one around the Church of England. That's where I've dug my grave. I will take you there so you can see what a good job I've done. I like picket fences, particularly white picket fences. That's one of the reasons I chose to dig my grave in the cemetary of the Church of England. It's the only one

WORLD ONE

which has a newly painted white picket fence. I've always been one for neatness. And the white picket fence is the neatest fence I know.

I bet you don't hear many sounds while I'm talking. That's because there aren't many sounds in this town. We have dogs—every town has dogs, and dogs do bark—but usually in the nighttime when everyone else is trying to get to sleep. I probably hear more dogs barking than anyone else because I stay up as late as I can so I can live as long as I can.

There aren't any movie houses here or any drive-in places to eat or any important museums or airports or railroads—nothing at all that can really remind you that you're living in the real world. It's funny that way. We are in the real world but it just doesn't look like it. Not a bit. There's only a bus that comes in every morning to pick up people to take them to the big town up the coast. That's Digby and I don't go there very often except with Mrs. Mac and she only goes twice a month for special things she needs for her store. We won't go in and see Mrs. Mac right now. I'll save her for later. She's less humorous in the morning than she is in the afternoon, and I want you to hear her at her best. She's a peach when she's in the mood. You just have to catch her at the right time. You'll see. You'll like her. She's the nicest woman alive, especially considering her age.

Do you wonder what the men do here in town? You'd think they'd be fishing all the time and smell like perch and raw lobsters. They smell nothing of the kind. Maybe their dad's smelled like fish, but not them. They smell like the earth. They go farming all the time—they know all about the soil and how to till it and make it grow foods. Reverend Russell says that these men are the backbone of our society and that they must be looked up to and admired because they are closest to the Almighty Himself. What do you think of that? The way I understand it, all I would have to do to be closest to the Almighty Himself is to pick up a shovel and start digging at the land. I might do that someday just to see what happens. I'll let you know if anything comes of it. From what I've heard about Reverend Russell, he knows just about everything there is to know about the Almighty, so you have to take him at his word. He's studied the whole matter through and through. So if you ever want to be the closest of your friends to the Almighty, pick up a shovel and start turning the soil and planting vegetables and things. You might be in for more then you bargained for and it's good to get whatever advantage you can in these matters. You never know when it's going to be all over for you and you can't afford to take any chances on not being the first one into heaven.

    That's enough about the town. Let's go to the places where I like to live. After all, towns are for the old people and the land is for the young. Switching off now while I take to the road and walk up past Dead Man's Curve. Why don't you take a coffee break? I'll be back and wide-awake. I wouldn't miss this day for anything. Not anything at all.

Have you ever been to the gravel pits? It's not the most glamorous place in the world. It's a place where they grind up rocks into little bits and pieces so they can use the gravel to lay down on muddy roads and make them passable. I'll take you there because it has a nice high view of the water and because it's one of the places I used to ride to on my horse that died last year. He didn't just up and die. He had to be put away. He broke his leg and they had to destroy him like you would a skunk or a troublesome fox. I was mad with grief for weeks after they had to do that. It was my fault. We had been there before and nothing had ever happened and I just didn't think anything ever could happen to him there. It was one of those cases where you think everything is going to be all right and then it turns out differently. I've never forgiven myself for what I did to him. Everyone said it wasn't my fault, but I was responsible for him and it wasn't as if he could tell me that he was afraid of those gravel pits. I know he liked the view from there, but he did always get nervous around the rim of the pit and I should have known that some day he might have an accident.

    I'll take you there. I'll show you where it happened. I'll take you there on one of the trails that we used to ride—in the evenings we used to ride this one particular trail. Nimrod

WORLD ONE

and I were so happy together for a while. And I always felt braver with him. He protected me from the hatchet-man. I could go anywhere with him and not be afraid. No hatchet-man would ever dare to come out of the woods and grab me while I was riding the strongest and fastest horse in the world. Have you ever heard of the hatchet-man? He's been around these parts for years. Maybe a hundred years. And he murders men and women and children. It doesn't matter to him. He will kill anyone that he finds alone and unprotected. I've only heard parts of his story. No one knows his whole story. But it's been passed down through the years and I'll tell you what I know so that you can be on the lookout for him and not get yourselves murdered—if he happens to still be around when you are alive.

They say he was born in a hidden cave on the mountain—not far from here. They say he was part animal and part human. It was because of this that he didn't think quite right. You see, he thought by murdering people now and then he was really protecting them. He was protecting them from each other. He didn't trust people. He knew they lied and stole and hurt each other and did wrong things all the time. So he wanted to keep people from all of the bad things that other people would do to them. It might seem crazy to you that someone would try to protect people by murdering other people, but I'm just telling you what I've heard. So because the hatchet-man was part animal and part human he would live in the woods and wait for unsuspecting and unprotected people to stray out alone, and when he found them he would sharpen his hatchet that he had made out of stone and then climb a tree, the highest tree that he could find, and then jump down on the one poor person who was all alone. And when he had done this he would chop up the body and scatter the pieces throughout the woods and it would be like the person had never been born. It was like there was no trace of the body—as if it had turned to dust or something. One minute the body was alive and well, and the next it had completely disappeared. I know this is a horrible thing to have to tell you. It doesn't make much sense, either—this person trying to protect people by murdering other people just in case they might sometime hurt someone else, but this is what I've heard about the hatchet-man and I have to believe that this was what he thought.

Last night I was thinking about him again. I never used to be afraid that he might come and get me until last night. It must have been the men on the radio talking or something that made me think of him. Because the men on the radio were talking about how all the governments had made all these bombs to protect all these people so that other people wouldn't hurt them sometime. But what was so strange and what reminded me of the hatchet-man was that all these governments were about to do the same thing that the hatchet-man has done. They're going to murder all these other people to protect their people, who in the end won't be protected at all, but murdered, just as if the hatchet-man had done it himself.

So I thought to myself, here we've had all these hatchet-men looking out for us all this time—and while I was afraid of the one in the woods around here, I should have been afraid of the hundreds of hatchet-men that were looking out for all of us around the world. So you can see why I'm not going to be afraid the hatchet-man is going to try to get me today. It wouldn't matter if he did. If he doesn't get me today, then the other hatchet-men are going to get me tonight— and one way or another, I'll be dead. So I'm not afraid and I'm happy to walk through the woods along the trail that Nimrod and I used to ride in the evenings. I'll switch off until we get to the gravel pits. If I don't come back on, you'll know that it was the hatchet-man who got me first. I'll be scattered all over the woods if that happens. I won't even have a proper burial. Maybe if he has mercy on me, he'll put me in my grave that I dug up for this occasion. If not, then at least I will be at home in the woods where I like to be. But it's not like the same thing wouldn't happen to me if, let's say, one of those big bombs fell on me. At least I would get to see the hatchet-man if it happened here. At least I'd get to see who murdered me. That's a lot better than getting murdered by someone far away who doesn't even have the courage to be his own hatchet-man.

Don't worry about me. I'll be all right. I don't really think I'm going to be murdered so early in the morning. I've always heard the hatchet-man likes to come out at night. He spends

WORLD ONE

all day sharpening his hatchet so it will be ready for the night. But just to make sure, I'll keep my eyes on the tops of the trees. I don't want to have anyone dropping down on me out of the blue. And as I said, I wouldn't miss this day for anything. Not even the hatchet-man could do that to me. He wouldn't dare.

I have not been murdered and I am not dead. I made it to the gravel pits without so much as a scratch on me. I told you I could do it. And I was right—the hatchet-man only comes at night. I won't have anything to worry about for the rest of the day. I will live to have a happy birthday. And you will come to my party and together we will celebrate and be friends. Can you hear the gravel crunching under my feet? I am standing on the exact spot where Nimrod slid and broke his leg. It's almost as if I can hear him screaming because he's been hurt. When he fell, I slid off of him one way and he slid down another way and that was the last time we were ever together. That was the last time he could feel my legs around him and feel my hand on his neck, patting him. I wonder if horses, like people, live on in some other way? I wonder, if that's true, whether he remembers me. I remember everything about him. He was white and his eyes were black and he had long tufts of fur on each of his ankles and he had a tail that swished back and forth, back and forth when he got excited by this view of the sea. Usually we were here at sunset and he would watch it go down with me—he would be as still as stone as we watched it go down and I could hear him breathe and he could hear me. We were happiest then. Just me and him standing together on the edge of the gravel pits looking out over our world. Someday I hope to catch up with him and I hope that Nimrod and I can stand on some other hill and watch some other sunset and be happy together without even having to be worried that the hatchet-man is going to try to get us.

Have you ever been to a deserted town—like a ghost town in the wild West, or a coal mining town in West Virginia that has been abandoned because the hills have been stripped of everything they ever had? I'm asking you this because the place I'm walking past now on my way down to the Bay of Fundy is kind of like that. It's kind of like a miniature ghost town the way the buildings are just sitting so still this morning—nothing much is moving—there's a banging which you can probably hear off in the distance, like a faint tapping caused by a spirit of yesterday. I'm walking through the old boys' camp that was abandoned last year when the owner died of cancer. I hear that that's a lousy way to die. You get pretty sick for a long time and the doctors do all sorts of nasty things to you to help you live a little bit longer, but in the end you die just the same and it was as if you never had a chance to begin with.

I never met the owner of the camp but I've heard that he built it just so he could live up here in the summertime. I guess that sounds crazy to build a boys' camp just so you can live up here for a few months, but grownups do strange things sometimes. Anyway, he's missed a beautiful summer so far this year. The rains have been light and the sun has been around for most of the days and it's not even August yet. If he hadn't had cancer this whole place would be alive right now and there would have been plenty of boys to ask me out to a dance, if I wanted to go. I might have accepted if a nice enough one had asked me in the proper way. But boys like that seem a long way away on a day like today. There's nothing up here much but memories that don't exist for me, but must for others. What I'm trying to say is that everything you experience exists when you experience it and then again when you remember it. So this boys' camp might be dead like its owner but it still actually exists just the way it once was for the people who once were here and once enjoyed its life.

I'm standing in front of the big house with the wide front porch—the main lodge—the lodge where all the dances were held. The girls always wore green and the boys always wore white when they got together on Friday evenings. Inside the main lodge they used to play records and the boys used to strum their tennis rackets as if they were playing electric guitars. They were very impressive, I remember. I liked the one who played lead, only he had his eyes on another woman

WORLD ONE

much older than me. Don't think I care. I have self-confidence. One of these days I'll find myself the one who is right for me. And I will know it immediately and there won't be any questions in my mind about him. He will be the one who comes over to me in the finest dining room in the world—somewhere in Paris—and he will dine me and then we will dance and I will put my hand on his right shoulder and then everything will be in its proper place. Then I will be his forever and you won't catch me frowning ever again. I won't have any worries. I will be free and he will take care of me like no one has ever done before.

You see what memories can do to you? Here I am standing in this camp where no one is anymore. The dozen little cabins are empty and haven't been cleaned for a year. The swimming pool is cracked in the bottom and couldn't be filled with water from the bay even if someone wanted to do it. And the stables are empty—the horses long gone—and the weeds have taken over and are choking everything. I imagine this is what will happen to our town after today. Pretty soon the weeds will take over and all the houses will be empty and no one will have cleaned them for years and there won't be any life around—not in the streets—not in the glens—not down by St. Mary's Bay. Nothing will be moving—it will be as dead as the man who got cancer and died. Maybe some of us will live for a short time like the man who was treated by the doctors, but all along we'll know we will die—if not tomorrow, then the next or the next or the next day. All in all it's better to remember what was than to look ahead at what's going to be. That's my point about bringing up all these memories. At least the memories are real. At least things were once much better when everyone was alive and living in the summertime in Sandy Cove.

I would feel bad for the man who died of cancer if it wasn't for the fact that he doesn't know what's going to happen today. He got off easy, I guess. He died before the others—he died more naturally. At least he died having made some other people happy. I wish I had been able to make some other people happy before today. It would have made my life have more meaning. I would have accomplished something worthwhile. Maybe you'll be happy listening to what I have to say. That would be worth something to me, to know that you are happier after listening to me tell you what it was like to be alive in a world that is beautiful and real. You won't otherwise be very happy, will you? I mean all the towns that you go to aren't alive anymore, right? You don't see normal people in the streets—coming and going—painting fences and sweeping their porches. You don't see people sitting in their windows in the evening knitting scarves for the winter or watching their cats lick themselves clean. You don't see the white smoke from the fires pouring up out of the chimneys. And you don't smell the smoke—that rich smell that drifts down past every open window and makes you think of fall. You won't know any of these things. You won't know how happy we could all be when things were the way they were supposed to be.

    I don't hear the boys making noises in their cabins. I don't see the flag up the pole. I don't hear anyone splashing in the pool and groaning because of the cold water. And I don't hear the music from the dances—I see boards nailed across the windows. I couldn't even get in to the main lodge and play pool. I haven't played pool for two years. I'd be pretty rusty I guess ... I wonder if the man who had cancer was buried up here? If he was, he probably had a thousand boys at his funeral. Probably every boy he ever knew would have come. He made so many people happy and they would have come to pay their respects to him, that much I know. I guess when I die there won't be too many people to pay their respects to me. I haven't had the time to make a lot of people happy. Maybe you will visit my grave anyway. You could bring lots of people with you. Would you put flowers on my grave? Would you kneel beside it and say something nice about who I was and what I wanted to be? I would appreciate that if you could find the time to do it. It would mean a lot to me. Probably I would know if you did it. I can't be sure, but probably I would know and you can't imagine how much that kind of thing would mean to me. And it wouldn't take all the time in the world. When you finish listening to me, you could go right out and do it. You know where I'll be. I'm not trying to put you to too much trouble. I know you've got lots to do and are probably hungry and tired—and it's not

WORLD ONE

the most fun thing to do, sitting by graves and talking to the dead—but I've tried so hard to make you happy today by telling you about all the nice things there are in life. I guess I'd just like to know that someone appreciated me, even if it's just a little. A little could be a lot, considering the circumstances.

Anyway, I guess the sight of this camp all empty and everything makes me sorry that the man died of cancer when he had everything in the world to live for. But since I'm remembering him and his camp, it's almost as if nothing were dead.

Sonia switching off while she goes down the cliff to the Bay of Fundy.

Have you ever thought about how much life there is in the sea? There's probably more different kinds of life in the sea than any other place on earth. The sea has everything. It's got porpoises and whales, it's got barnacles and shrimp, thousands and thousands of red walking lobsters with claws that pinch, perch by the millions, minnows and worms, crabs and eels—you get what I mean. The population of fish under the sea beats the population of life on earth any day, I'm sure. I would hope that at least they will survive. Did you know that people originally came from the sea? There's plenty of hope in that. Let's say everyone in the world does die. Maybe in more years than I can count, a new kind of man will walk up out of the sea and begin his life on earth all over again. That would be better than nothing, wouldn't it? Have you come from the bottom of the sea? Were your great, great, great grandparents some kind of fish which had fins for tails and gills for lungs? Did they have webs for hands? Did they survive on smaller fish? I don't mean to get too personal. I'm told that there is no greater nuisance in the world than a girl who asks too many questions, but still, I'm curious. If everyone does die in the world tonight and the fish survive, maybe in a few thousand million years everything will be all right again. People like you and me will start to live again and do all the things I've been telling you about. That would be nice, if nothing else works out. At least you could try again.

Why I've brought this new idea up is because I'm out here on the beach like I promised I would be, and I'm the only one here. There isn't a fishing boat in sight. The wharf that juts out into the bay is deserted, too. That's unusual for low tide. Mornings like this in the summer, I usually see men scrubbing down boats or hauling fish into trucks to take to the market in Digby. Not today. There's no one out there on the pier. And when I think about it, I didn't see too many people stirring in town, either. Did you ever have the feeling that you were alone when you weren't supposed to be? Well, that's the way I feel today. On any other Wednesday I'd be sure to see just about everyone I've ever known up here. I'd see the crab trawler and its captain. Two hoots of the horn would mean, "How are you?" and I'd throw both hands as high as I could into the air and they'd know I was all right. I wish you could hear those hoots. It's practically the most friendly sound I know. Also, I've never had a bad day when I've heard those sounds. There's something very special about them. Mrs. Mac says they must be a good omen for me, and I believe she's right. Maybe if I sit here a little while longer that crab trawler and its captain will find its way to me and give me the hoots for my birthday. I imagine a present like that would be the best one I could have on a day like today. Sonia is in need of a good omen. I guess that goes for you, too. We could all use a good omen today. Think of all the thousands and thousands of years it could save us if everything worked out.

This beach is my favorite beach for sleeping out all night. You must think I'm some kind of nut, liking to sleep outside in every place under the sun. It's not so strange really. I like communing with nature. It respects me and I respect it. We get along and that's that. I've been good to it and it's been good to me. Over on that pier is where I can catch about a hundred perch every two hours. I just throw in my line, wait for a nibble and up comes the perch. There's no waiting for hours and hours for nothing. It's not like fishing for trout in a stream or anything so tiresome as that. I used to think I just had a knack for it, but my illusions were soon damaged

WORLD ONE

by one of the fishermen who said that the currents were just right around the pier and that's why the perch congregated there and looked for food. Anyone can do it, I found out. You could too. That's a tip for you. If you are hungry and in need of nourishment, go to the end of the pier and make a fishing line with even a nail hook. Find a good fat worm and let it sink into the water. Count to ten and if I'm not mistaken, which I'm not, you'll have something for lunch or supper right away.

Now I can only foresee one problem with what I just said. Say for instance that you really have come up out of the sea after a thousand million years. And say you are people again. You would have to be careful not to snatch up too many fish, just in case you make the same mistakes our people made. I mean, if you decide to blow up the world at some future date, you would have to make sure that there are still enough fish in the sea to make it possible for people to come out of the sea again in another thousand million years. I wouldn't think you'd go out and make the same mistake our people did, but just in case, don't fish for too many fish. They're more like people than you and I think.

This is the beach where Nimrod and I used to ride. I've told you about him. And today I miss him again. If I really believed in ghosts I swear I would have to say I feel him. If I close my eyes and block out the sounds of the waves, it's almost as if I hear him—cloppity-clop, coming down the beach at a full gait. Horses are enchanted, you know. They are one of the most ancient animals in the world and they know many things that people don't know. They know fear before we do, for instance. Nimrod could sense danger long before I would ever see anything. Maybe he could smell the danger. I don't know. But when he got on to something, his ears would shoot back and then he would rear his head and his eyes would look all stormy and he would swish his tail like he was trying to battle a bee. Then I of course would know that something was up and that we should get the hell out of wherever we were. I did that every time, except for that one time up there on the gravel pits. I thought he was being spooked by the wind, and I never knew of any danger in the wind. But it was the sharp slant of the pit itself that Nimrod sensed danger in. He knew that we shouldn't be there. And he told me that we shouldn't be there. But I didn't pay any attention and before I knew what was happening, it was too late. You see how stupid people can be? Here I had a horse which I loved telling me to beware, and I went right on without paying any attention to what he had to say. I guess Nimrod was kind of like my dad. My dad sensed all the danger that was around, but no one paid any attention to him either, and then he went off like Nimrod and wound up dead.

If it were up to me, I'd rather be a descendant of the horse. And if people come back alive after today, then I hope that they all come from the horse family. Horses are smart and they are always on the lookout for dangerous things.

I'm looking down at the sun in the water now on the pier. I can understand why people thought it was a good idea to worship the sun. The sun makes everything shine, even the darkness of the water. It's shining up at me and I can see my face in it. It's not much of a face, though some girls are equipped with a lot less. Give me a few more years and I would have been the number one knockout. I would have had all of the fishermen in the neighborhood whistling at me from the sides of their lobster boats. If someone ever thought to have a beauty contest in town, I bet I'd win the crown. Queen for a day, a week, a month. I like the reflection of my face in the water because I can imagine it anyway I want it to be. Down there I can have lavender lips and arched eyebrows and a curvaceous profile which would make men drop oars and fishnets and swear off drinking. Down there in the water I can paint my face anything I want it to be, and I have painted my face beautiful. Why not? It's the last chance I have to make myself something I'll never get to be.

Since there isn't any moon out today (sometimes it lasts a while into the day, you know; sometimes it's there all day only you can't quite see it because of the bright light of the sun) I'll make some wishes on the sun in the water and the sun in

WORLD ONE

the sky. I guarantee I won't sound like those Egyptians. They said things like, "Holy Father of Ra, send us the fruits of your strength." I don't have anything so complicated to wish for. I just wish on the sun in the sky that I won't have to die today or even tomorrow. At least let me have my birthday. At least let me wear the gloves tonight that Mrs. Mac has knit me. I can't be sure she has, but I can't imagine her knitting those gloves for anyone else, and I know she would want me to wear them at least once. Even if it is the summer, I'll wear them tonight.

Actually, can I have four wishes? Surely you could be kind and give me four wishes. My second wish is to meet the boy of my life today. If I could only see him, I would die much more happily. A girl should go to her grave knowing the man of her life, don't you think? And not to be too demanding, I might like to get a glimpse of my first-born child. Maybe I could just close my eyes sometime today and you could draw me a picture of its face. It could be crying or smiling, I wouldn't care. I'd just like to see it once before tonight. I guess I shouldn't ask for this wish—I don't mean to profane the dead—but I might like to see my dad again, too. I only have old pictures of him that have been around for a couple of years and it's not the same thing as seeing him in the flesh. I guess you don't have requests like mine very often. But then not every day is like today and not every girl has a birthday on a day like today, so maybe you could go ahead and extend yourself and do something special on account of what's going to happen. I wouldn't tell anyone if you did these things for me. I know you wouldn't want a million people asking you for the same kinds of things. You just wouldn't have the time to arrange them. So I promise I won't go around telling everyone what you've done for me. I'm asking you for this and not the Almighty because I'm so distressed with Him. How could He allow everything to go so wrong? I don't hate Him or anything so dreadful as that. I just figure that He's so angry with everyone that He wouldn't pay any attention to my birthday wishes. You can tell me if I'm wrong, but I expect I'm right and I'm going to the proper person for wishes like this.

Are you going to keep the earth warm after today? Or

are you going to try to find some other planet to make come alive? Are you angry with all the people too? I hope you won't be. It's not everyone's fault. It's just that we people haven't been around the universe as long as you and the Almighty and we haven't learned how to keep ourselves in balance. I guess it's no use trying to make excuses. It never seems to make things better. But still, you're older and wiser and more generous than people, so I guess you and the Almighty are our only hope for the future. So maybe you could keep an eye on the people who survive, like the people I'm pouring my heart out to who will be listening to what I have to say someday. If you could just look out for them, I would appreciate it more than you know. In fact, if you would do that, I won't even ask for all my wishes to come true. I take them all back. Just try to look out for my friends who are listening to me now. They never had a chance to see the world the way I see it today. They never had all the advantages that I've had. And they have a lot of work to do. They have to rebuild the world and fix it up right this time around. You'll take care of them, won't you? I guess I won't know if you have or you haven't. But I'll trust you. I will. I have faith in you. And why shouldn't I? You made everything grow and gave everything life and made the world what it is today. You have been very good to the earth. Now it's the people on the earth who aren't going to be good to you. I can't help that. My dad tried to help that, but he was only one man in a million and one man doesn't have much say in a world where he's outnumbered. Anyway, please put in a good word for my friends to the Almighty. I know you are an acquaintance of His. He will probably listen to you more than me. It's funny. I really feel like I'm talking to you. Maybe I was an Egyptian in another life.

The white gulls are circling around and looking for fish. They won't find many at this hour though. Mornings, early mornings and evenings are the best time for fish. Ask any fisherman. He knows how nature works. He lives by nature. He respects nature and doesn't dare tred on its toes. Let's hope the white gulls have a hearty last supper. In the movies they never let people die on an empty stomach. Say you were a war prisoner and the enemy was going to execute you at dawn. They would always feed the prisoner one last meal and

WORLD ONE

then give him whatever he wanted to drink or smoke. So I hope that the gulls will have something special this evening. It's only fair, you know. I'd call it civilized. Wouldn't you?

Right where I'm sitting is a fine place to watch fires on the beach at night. When they're burning in the darkness it's like the stars are being born. Have you ever seen fires from a boat on the water at night? That's the very best. The light of the fires is reflected in the water like the sun today. And the fires make these long streams of color that extend out to the boats part way. Sometimes when I see that, I feel like I could walk on the colors—like the colors were rainbows—like the colors were a source of life and could be felt, even from a distance. Does your world have any colors? Are the colors all gone? Is there no more green or purple or red? Does the sun set, or is there any sun at all? I ask too many questions. I'm supposed to be telling you of all the beauty that I see. Well the world I see is beautiful, and it will never be the same for you after today and it wasn't my fault but I'm sorry anyway. It wasn't my dad's fault either. And it wasn't your fault. You just got in the middle of a bad time and besides you didn't know any better. If you'd known you would have done something about it, right? You wouldn't be crazy enough to live the way we've lived for all this time. It just doesn't make any sense at all. How could they have done this? It isn't fair to anyone and now there's no one around to prevent it. If you ever get mad about what's happened to you and to the world, go ahead and get mad at us. I won't be offended. You've a right to say what you want. It was us who made a mess of things, not you. But, oh, you should have seen how beautiful the sun once was in the water on this pier. It was enough to make you think it was alive and your friend.

You know, unless you're careful, it's easy to take things like the sun for granted. But not me today. Today I appreciate everything—and I hope the white gulls have a hearty last supper.

You don't know it, but you're taking a walk with me whether you want to or not. Where am I taking you on this walk? Along the rocks on the shore, of course. I only treat my friends to the best things in life and this is one of them. Ra the sun is shining down, beaming his face on me and the rocks and the sea and we are altogether happy. This is the way birthdays should always be, don't you think? I'm just bouncing from one rock to another—dipping down between the high and low ones, slipping on seaweed whenever I'm not paying the strictest of attention to each step I take. Do you hear the foam, the sizzling of the incoming foam nestling among the rocks? It sounds like fire, doesn't it?—a low hot fire when the water subsides and leaves behind its foam. Talk about a symphony. This is it. I am living in a world of symphonies. If it's not the sound of the foam, it's the calling of the gulls or the echoes of the tide rushing in and out of the caves. Here, as I told you, I feel like I'm the only one left in the world. Everyone else is gone—I am the original aborigine. I am the first-born and the last. The trumpets of the world play for me. I have been blessed by the hand of nature. I will not die, I will live on and hear the music of time until there is no time. You see how I let things go to my head when I'm out here. It will happen to you, too, if you come out here on a beautiful day and let the sun soak you up and let your ears hear everything there is to hear, and let your eyes feast, just let them feast on what is.

You know by now, I'm a nut. And no apologies necessary. Birthdays give one certain privileges. And I'm taking advantage of them. I'm taking off my clothes! First the shoes, then the pants, then my shirt, my favorite blue-striped shirt—and now I am naked under the sun like the original aborigine and my body is brown, brown like the bark on the trees. I am a blend of brown and blonde and by the hour I will get browner and more blonde. I will look pretty in my grave. I will be the tannest corpse that ever lived. People will come from miles around and look down at me in wonder, in amazement. I will be immortalized. My name will go down in the *Encyclopedia Britannica* because I looked so alive when I was dead. I'm a nut! I'm a nut! I admit it! I'm a nut! It can happen to anyone, I'm sure. I'm a nut because I like to go naked on the rocks with the fingers of the waves at my feet and the sun at my back. And most of all because I'm constantly talking into this nifty recording machine where all my friends

WORLD ONE

hide. Whoever said you had to be over twenty to be nuts? What's this world coming to when a girl just fifteen turns into a nut? You tell me. Is it the world or just me? Do the rocks make me drunk? Does the sun intoxicate me? Or is it the swell of the sea by my side that is seducing me into this state of nuthood? Does it matter? I'm happy. I'm alive. It feels good to have friends who will listen to me and stand by me. You are taking care of me—you are making my life worth something. Sonia is the girl at the end of the world—the first and the last, the last and the first. She has risen above being dead. She will have life after death. I have to flip the tape. Stand by.

Swoooooosh goes the sea. Kaw-kaw-kaw go the birds. Sizzzzzle goes the foam around the rocks. Talkity-talk goes me ... I am a chicken on my roost. I am the master of the flock. All birds obey me. I am sister to the sun—he feeds me light and clothes me with warmth. Let's go down to the caves and visit the demons.

Echo, echo go the walls of the caves. Who goes there in the darkness? Who hides there in the back of the dark? Who will you feast on for supper tonight? Not me. I have other plans. I have an invitation. I received it early this morning. It came as a telegram. An important telegram marked urgent. I have already replied. I was taught that once accepted, I was never to decline, unless I was sick. I am not sick. I am happy and in the best of health. I am very tan and very blonde. My graces are imitated and my company sought. I cannot accept your invitation in the dark. You will have to make do with others. There are many you could ask. Here, I will help you. There are men in governments who would be willing to accept. They will make good conversation before you dine. Have them all, each and every one. Serve them up on a plate and be finished with them. But do it before it gets dark outside in the world. Invite them soon. Send them telegrams at my expense. I would be happy to pay for the charge. We must take this situation seriously. We must satisfy your needs before it is too late. Tell me: Is it the law down here that you eat everyone who accepts your invitations? If so, I will accept your invitations for all those men in governments. I accept for them. Right here, right now, I accept. Eat them for supper and you will do me a great service. I will put in a good word with Ra for you—he has contacts with the Almighty. What more can you ask? You can help us all. Just invite the men in governments and have them for supper. You'll get all the credit, too. Millions of people like me will thank you. For once, dear demons, do the right thing.

I'm lying on my back now, dear friends, and I am just enjoying listening to the music of the world. Don't worry. By tonight everything will be fixed and I will be able to go back to school and grow up and marry my husband and take care of his child and all good things like that. And I'm sure I'll get to know you. You'll be coming around to my little cabin and we can talk in person. You can have coffee with me and lie on the beach with me and I'll show you the shipwreck and I won't have to show you my grave. I'll cover it up tonight and I'll tear down the cross and I'll wear my gloves that Mrs. Mac is going to give me. Yes, I'll wear my gloves if she gives them to me on my way home. I'll love those gloves. She's worked on them for such a long time. She must be very proud of them—she made them out of thin air.

Do you think we could hide underwater tonight? We could disguise ourselves as fishes and dive down deep into the bottom of the bay and go to sleep until it's all over. Do fishes sleep? Of course, they must. Though they probably don't want to. Maybe people and fishes and every living thing have to sleep so that they can have dreams of a better world to live in. Doesn't that make sense? Since we can't have it when we are awake, it makes perfect sense that we should try to get it when we're sleeping. Like I never dream about wars in my sleep. I dream of delicious things like boys and horses and

WORLD ONE

dolphins. If I could hide with you under the sea tonight, I would prefer to be an octopus. It's not the prettiest of fish, but it's certainly one of the most mobile—it gets around like mad. I could do twirls and somersaults and all sorts of acrobatics that would dazzle any discerning eye. And if any nasty fish tried to come and get me and eat me up, all I'd have to do is scrunch down in the sand and hide myself until they went away. And when the danger passed, I could go swimming. I don't know how fast an octopus swims, but with that many legs I'm sure they can outdistance many of their companions and make for safe waters even in a pinch. You might think I'd want to be a mermaid or something exotic like that, but I wouldn't. I would want to be the real thing. I don't go in for halfway measures. And besides, mermaids have always scared me. They aren't exactly human and they aren't exactly fish. It's the combination that's so creepy. I just wouldn't want to be a mermaid and that's that. But I would like to be an octopus. And I would be safe down there in the deep. The people all over the world couldn't get me. They wouldn't even know who I was if they could find me. Probably the bottom of the bay is the safest place to be tonight. I should have made that one of my wishes. Then I would be alive to know you and then we could become real friends. You wouldn't have to know me just by listening to my machine. We might even meet for my next birthday. Wouldn't that be great? We could just avoid the whole mess. All I'd have to do is hide until the danger was past and then I could change back into me and I could go on living and be there when you finally met up with me. We could go swimming as people, instead of fish! We could be just what we are. We wouldn't have to worry about anything. And the whole world would be ours. Right from the beginning we could set things right and we wouldn't have any of the problems that have finally caught up with us today. Wow! That's the answer I've been looking for! Maybe I could think up some magic spell to put myself under. Some words that have the power to change me into something I'm not. Do you think if I did that I would upset the balance of nature? I've heard that if you went back into time and misplaced a rock or killed a cat or a bird, that the whole future of the world might be changed. So I'm just wondering—if I were to change myself into an octopus, is it possible for me to change the nature of things by being there when I wasn't expected?

I guess that's not something I really need to worry about since everything is going to change so much anyway. But still it's important to think about these things so you don't make a mistake and damage the natural way of things. Anyway, what possible harm could there be in putting one more octopus into the sea? I'll think about some magic words and try to make myself a spell and see whether I can't do something to save myself so you and I can meet up and get together when the world is safe again . . .

How about this: Sisters of the bay—cousins of the universe. Accept me as one of you and hide me with you until the danger above us is past . . . Is that too much to ask? Oh Octopi, I want to go on living just like you . . .

I'm still sitting here on the rocks by the bay and nothing has happened to me yet. Maybe it takes a long time for spells to work. I don't know for sure, considering it's the first one I've ever tried. Do you have any suggestions? Also, I'm getting a little worried that I won't be able to change myself back again once I get to be what I want. You have to speak spells for them to work. Either that, or someone has to speak them for you. If when you get here I'm not here or anywhere around, then you'll know where I am. I'll be safe and sound down at the bottom of the bay. So you better try repeating just what I've said but at the end ask to have me changed back as me. If that doesn't work, then I'm in a fix and you'll have to use your imagination to come up with the right words. And if nothing ever works, then at least I'll still be alive down there in the bottom of the bay and that's better than nothing. I'd rather be a live octopus than a dead person any day of the week. You'll probably understand that after you've seen what's going to happen. For all I know, I won't even want to come back on land. It might give me terrible dreams—I might forget all about dreaming about a better world—and that

WORLD ONE

would be too bad. I couldn't stand that. On second thought, don't worry about me. It's best that I just stay down there and do the best I can. You'll still have me to listen to and that's a lot better than nothing. I'll take a deep breath and not speak for a minute. I'm probably interfering with my spell by speaking so much anyway. I'm confusing all the spiritual energy in the atmosphere. One part of me is saying that she wants to be alive after today and the other part of me is saying that she wants to be alive in a different way. I better make up my mind. Spells can't be confusing. That's the first rule. They have to be exacting or you end up somewhere else.

Well, I'm not an octopus down at the bottom of the sea and I don't think I'll ever be one. I've messed it all up on account of not thinking it all out ahead. I could try it again, but I think you only get one chance and besides I'd still rather talk to you for the rest of the day. A girl doesn't want to become an octopus on her birthday anyway. That would be very uncivilized. And anyway, I'm not a chicken. The world can do anything it wants to me. I've lived a better life than most and I still have a lot of hours left, so I'm going to make the best of them. You'll see. I'll have fun. I'll have a party and you'll be the first to be invited. You are invited. And don't worry about bringing me presents. I've got all the presents I could ever want, just being alive and out here on the rocks, basking in the sun and watching the tide and talking to you, my friends.

I wonder what time it is? Maybe ten o'clock? I don't feel in the least bit sleepy. The sun always wakes me up. You see the sun really does make you grow. I wonder how fish grow without the sun over their heads? Maybe they just need a little sun. Maybe they get all they need when they swim up close to the surface. I wish I knew more about the magic of nature. It would be helpful when I try to explain things to you. I really should have read the encyclopedia all the way through. Perhaps in another life, I will.

Do you like strawberries and raspberries? You're coming with me while I go picking. I want you to know about the natural delights of what grows on the hillsides. If you had to, you could survive on them for a long time. You could store them for the winter, too. You can use my refrigerator if you want. The idea is to keep them cold so they won't spoil. Switching off while I put on my clothes. Don't peek. I'm really a very modest girl at heart. Bye for now.

You hear the rustling? That's me climbing up this old hillside looking for the best patch of them all. The strawberry pickings are still a little lean, but by August they'll be running wild. They'll be to my right and to my left—up and down, all over, everywhere. It's as though there's nothing there one day and then the next there's an explosion of them. Bright, red, delicious, scrumptious strawberries that taste as sweet as sugar and are much better for you. You probably won't want to make jam out of them, although I have a recipe that Mrs. Mac gave me that would make you flip. I think I still have one jar left from last fall. If you're good all day long, I'll serve you some at the party. I can't wait to see your faces light up when you take the first bite. You'll be hooked. You'll never want to taste another kind of jam again, not as long as you live. You'll be spoiled like me. It's good to spoil your friends. Mrs. Mac spoiled me and I'm going to spoil you. That way everyone is happy for generation after generation. You see, people really aren't as bad as I've made them out to be. The world is full of good people. You just get the good with the bad. It's like nature having to put up with forest fires and electrical storms. The good comes with the bad. Maybe it has something to do with the balance of life. It keeps everything on its toes.

My fingers are wet with the juice of raspberries and my lips taste like the air of heaven. When I was younger I always thought it would be best to kiss a boy just after I'd eaten a lot of raspberries. I would want him to think me delicious in every sense of the word—irresistible, in fact. What better way to make an impression on him? He'd be in for the thrill of a lifetime and I'd know he was the right one for me by whether

WORLD ONE

or not he loved the taste of raspberries on my lips. That would be my test. Raspberries on my lips. If he didn't like the taste—then that would be that. I would not marry him. I'd wait for the prince who loved the taste of raspberries on my lips, and when one day I found him, I'd consent to marry him.

I don't think that way any more. There are other ways to test the boy of your dreams. It's pretty pathetic that I've wasted so much time thinking up tests when I won't even have a chance to try them out, though. Have you ever felt stupid about wasting time? You have to be careful in life not to waste the good time that you have. After all, you're not on earth forever. I'm not trying to tell you what to do with your time, I'm just telling you that it's important to use every second to the fullest. Like, I should have brought a bucket with me for these raspberries. I didn't think ahead about it and now I won't be able to take any home with me. I'd have to go home, get the bucket, come back and then go home again. Right there I've wasted maybe an hour or two. And on a day like today, I just can't afford to do that. It makes me feel stupid to just think about it. So remember buckets when you know you're going to be out by the hillside—it'll save you a lot of time, and time is the only thing you've got.

Yakity-yakity-yak! If I haven't driven you crazy by now with all my talkity-talk, I won't believe it. Maybe this isn't the most exciting recording you've ever listened to, but then I hadn't planned on doing this—it was just kind of an inspiration. Anyway, you try to describe life at a moment's notice. You won't find it such an easy thing to do. I can't paint you pictures and I don't have the time to write everything very carefully down so you'll get an exact impression of the way things are, so this is all I can do for you, considering the last minute circumstances of everything.

Do you know raspberries have little furry hairs on them? I think they're sweet. They're nature's coat and they protect the raspberry from the rains and the wind. Everything in nature has its own way of protecting itself. Isn't that amazing? Think about the bark of a tree—it's like armor. But I guess none of nature's protections will protect enough by tonight. Nature wasn't set up to protect itself against the kinds of things that man has made. That's why it's all so unnatural. That's why it's such a disgrace. That's why the world is never going to be the same again once the men in the governments let the bombs loose. None of these cute little red raspberries will stand a chance once all that poison gets into the air. You'll have to wait for a lot of summers to go by before they'll be any good again. I'm glad I won't have to wait—I couldn't stand it. It makes me sick just to think about it. But like I said, I can't waste any time. I just have to enjoy what I have now and not worry about tonight. There's too much to see and do to get wrapped up in self-pity. Not that I need to put on a smile—that would be phony and fake. I'd just like to look serene. I'd just like to feel alive and be happy for it. There's no sense in even wasting tears. Every second counts. And the more seconds I have to tell you about the world, the better off you'll be knowing what the world was like in my time.

There's a butterfly circling around the raspberry patch. It's got yellow and black wings. I can't make out the color of its eyes, but I'm pretty sure they're black. Round and black and shiny and smooth. How can it be that little creatures such as this are so perfectly made? How could anyone have the time to think them up and then put them together and make them work the way they do? Really, it's all a miracle when you get right down to thinking about it. There it goes, from one patch to another, not wasting any time. Do you think the Almighty will bother to make butterflies again? I'm hoping for your sake that He does. I've always thought butterflies were some kind of good luck. Maybe I'll be lucky today because of this black and yellow one who has come to visit me in my patch of red raspberries. You never know. The luck of butterflies is very good luck, and we could all use it today. Maybe the Almighty will send down a million more butterflies to bring us all good luck. That's one thing He could do, if He wanted to help. It would be very nice of Him.

I think I've eaten too many raspberries . . . I feel a little woozy and strange, like I'm going to be sick . . . I won't get sick, I won't get sick, I won't, I won't . . .

I got sick. I feel better. I got carried away talking to you and

WORLD ONE

eating raspberries but now I feel better. I never get sick but it's been a long night and the men on the radio made me upset and I've been trying to make a very good impression on you so you'll think that not everyone was so bad before your time. I think I need a little rest, just a minute or two to keep up my strength. I won't be gone long, I'm just not feeling so good at this moment. Suddenly I feel so much alone. I can't describe it exactly—like something just fell out of my life. I hope everything is going to be all right. I must see Mrs. Mac soon—she is so old and I have to look out for her. She's got no one to care for her . . .

But first I'll get a little sleep. I'll be myself again then. I'll switch off, so I won't waste any tape. I'll be back before you'll know I was gone.

9

I was dreaming that tomorrow was today and that today was tomorrow . . . You were with me . . . you weren't mutilated . . . you could smile . . . you liked me . . . and I liked you too . . . We had escaped, hadn't we? You were there to protect me . . . You knew what had happened but you didn't tell me because you wanted to protect me and not frighten me. Oh, that was so good of you. You see, I don't really want to know what happens. I'd rather just be with you and be happy with you and get to know each other and do everything there is to do with each other.

I was so glad to see that you were happy and alive. And I was laughing in my dream. Did you hear me laughing? One of you was doing handstands and there were others who were making funny faces, and still others were clapping, they were clapping for me. I saw myself once in the dream—I did look funny talking into this recording machine, so I could understand them laughing, but why were they clapping? Had I done something to save the world? Or were you celebrating my birthday? That must have been it. We were at the party and we were having a good time. One of you was doing a dance for me—was it a Greek dance, maybe Russian? It was a lovely dance, though I couldn't hear the music, I felt it. Were you playing the music? Sometimes in dreams you don't hear the music, even when you can see all the faces, every single expression, every color of the skin. You gave me such a nice birthday. How can I ever thank you? You must tell me all the dates of yours. I will mark them down in a book so I'll remember them. And during the year I will make each and every one of you a present. I want you to be as happy on your birthdays as you made me. It was such a happy dream, I feel so much better. I haven't wasted too much time, have I? The sun hasn't moved hardly at all. It was just a little nap—no harm done. I still have lots of time. There is still plenty that I can do. And then I have tomorrow, too. Isn't that true? I saw it. I saw tomorrow and it was there and we were together and you had remembered that it was my birthday and we were having such a good time.

Can I still keep talking to you? It seems silly to be talking to friends when you're going to see them tomorrow, but I hope it's all right. I feel lonely today and it will help me if I can still keep talking to you. I better not have anymore raspberries. I got sick, didn't I? That's why I went to sleep, wasn't it? But you were watching over me when I slept. I could feel that. You were taking care of me all that time, weren't you? I've missed having someone take care of me. You know I'm not a child and that I can take care of myself, but still, it's so nice to know that someone is looking out for me when I have to go to sleep. I'll do the same for you. And I don't need much sleep, so I'll be able to watch you for a long time. Go ahead and get some sleep if you need it now. I'll just sit here on the hill and watch over you. No one will come and get you and mutilate you. You'll be all right with me. I've seen tomorrow in my dreams and tomorrow is going to be okay ... I was so worried—really I was much more worried than I said—but now that I've seen my dream, I'm not worried anymore. You are going to be fine and we are going to have a party and you and I will be happy and the world isn't going to go anywhere.

When are you planning to come tomorrow? Have you decided when? I wish you could come today. Don't think I'm ungrateful—I'll be happy to have the party tomorrow. I was just hoping that you could make it here today. We could listen to my tape. Wouldn't that be fun? Is that why everyone was clapping for me? Did you like my tape? I've tried so hard to tell everything just right. Oh, I hope you like it. I'll make it even better by tonight. You'll get the whole picture then. There's Mrs. Mac, who I haven't introduced you to. There's Reverend Russell, who I could get to say a few words—and the doctor, Doctor Elson—I'll ask him to say something important. You'll want to know these people. They can help you if you ever get into trouble. I know I can count on them. You can too. You'll see, once you come here and listen to my tape I've made for you.

I'm up and about and walking down the dirt road from the boys' camp. The morning light is showering down—I'm practically wet with light—and the dust is lying low on the ground. We had rain a few days ago and so it's easy to walk without getting all the dust kicked up. I do hate the dust on the raspberry plants. They look so unfinished when they're that way. Sometimes I wish I could go around to every plant with a bucket of water and clean the leaves one by one. I like the leaves to be shiny. They set off the red so well and make the berries look all the more inviting.

I see a bird's nest on one of the branches of one of the pine trees. The birds know everything is going to be all right. They have more sense than those men on the radio who upset me all night. But then birds can probably dream, too. And they've probably already had their dreams about tomorrow and so that's why they aren't worried. They're just going on about their business and life is its usual self to them. Birds are lucky that they don't have to listen to the radio. They don't have to listen to anything at all, except for the noises in the fields and the woods, and the sounds coming off of the sea. They lead quite a nice life, really. They don't let

WORLD ONE

themselves get mixed up in worldly events. They are quite content to stay where they are and be what they are and do what they do. Me, too. From now on I'm going to do what I do and stay where I am and be what I am without paying any more attention to those men on the radio who are trying to get me upset on my birthday. They probably didn't mean to do that—they just don't know yet what I know and you know. How can I blame them? They live around all those other men in the governments who have nothing better to do on my birthday than to get themselves into a war. If they had just listened to what my dad and other people had to say, those men on the radio would still be playing Beethoven sonatas and helping me celebrate my fifteenth birthday.

Flippity-flop down the road I hop—and there will be a tomorrow. Hippity-hop, flippity-flop, I'm on my way back to town.

There goes a cloud covering up the sun. How could you do that to my sun, Mr. Cloud? Haven't you anything better to do then to take away that shining light? No you wouldn't, would you. I've a mind to be very unpleasant to you. I've a mind to wish you harm and put a curse on you. May you never have another drop of rain in any part of you. Though you are a lovely cloud—all puffy and round on the edges—I'd much rather see the sun today. We have so much to celebrate! Sunshine is made for celebrations—clouds are for rain and funerals. There will be no funerals today. Life will triumph over death! My sun will triumph over all and any clouds! My dream will come true and tomorrow will be like any other day—maybe even better. The men on the radio will play Beethoven again! My friends will come to my party! And I will have all the years of my life to look forward to. I will find the beautiful boy who likes the taste of raspberries on my lips! And we will be married by the sea, and he will take me to Paris for our honeymoon and we will travel around the world and we will learn more than any encyclopedia could tell. Everything is going to be okay by tomorrow, once Mr.

Cloud goes away. Clouds are for rain and for funerals. Sunlight is for days like today when nature has power over all—even men who want to ruin everything in the world.

    The sun looks so dark up there—it looks so cold and grey and dull—Ra must be angry with me. He is frowning and he is glaring and he is silent. Only once have I ever seen him look this way. It was the day the moon moved in front of him. I saw it happen here, right in this spot on the hill overlooking the Bay of Fundy. Mrs. Mac and I came up here because she knew what was going to happen. The moon was to come in front of the sun and mask out its light for a minute or two. She said it was to be an omen for the end of the world. It scared me then—I wasn't very old and I hadn't read up on eclipses and why they happen. All I knew was what Mrs. Mac told me and she told me that it was an omen that the end of the world was coming—someday not too far away. At least that's what she said the Australian aborigines believed. She said that they got down on their knees when the moon went in front of the sun and prayed—she said the natives in Africa did the same—so I got down on my knees when I saw the moon begin to go in front of the sun and cut out its edges a piece at a time—first just a slice, then more of a bite, then a bigger crunch until it ate the whole thing. And when the sun was gone, I lifted up my piece of smoky glass and looked at it. It was like it was wrapped up in white fire, crowned in white fire, its flames reaching out to the stars but not getting there. And then I looked around me and the world was in a glittering twilight. The green of the fields wasn't real anymore—it was like no light I had ever seen—a clear twilight and dawn light all rolled into one. And the sea was coal black—it glistened like oil. And then I heard the animals singing, or were they crying? The cows in the distance moaned like they were giving birth to calves, and the birds in a thousand trees sounded as if they were speaking a different language. And then suddenly they all flew up—they were trying to run away from the world—they were trying to find someplace safe to go before it was too late. But what I remember most was the silence—there was so much silence and calm, like the way the world must have been at the beginning. Every living thing was left so humbled. Though it

WORLD ONE

was beautiful the way the world quieted down and though it was beautiful the way the white fire leapt away from the sun, I knew that Mrs. Mac was right—it was all an omen of things to come. Mother nature was telling us that the world was soon never to be the same. So I said my prayers—I think Mrs. Mac did too. And then it began to be over. The moon started to slip away from the light of the sun. And bit by bit the sun was restored to its full round face. But I was never the same after that. Every day since then, I watch the sun fearing that I'll see it go away again. And whenever a cloud so much as gets in the way for even a second, I get scared and mad because I've seen what can happen to it when the moon gets in front of it. And I know what the omen means—it means the end of the world is coming and none of us want that. Not you or me or Mrs. Mac.

I haven't seen an eclipse of the sun since then. I'm glad of it, too. Maybe that's why I got so nervous this morning about the end of the world. You see, I'd seen that eclipse and I knew it was an omen, and I thought maybe the omen was going to come true—like Mrs. Mac said the aborigines believed.

The light is coming back! The cloud is passing on! It heard me! We will have no funerals today! There won't be any rain! And the moon is far away from the sun, it won't get in its way—so the sun is safe and we are safe and the world is not coming to an end. It will just go on and on like it has always done before and there will be so much more time for happiness and life. Aren't you glad? The omen was wrong!

Mrs. Mac shouldn't be so superstitious. I'll have to tell her today. It's probably because she's lived alone for so long that she believes in omens and cryptic messages that come from nowhere. But I know mother nature doesn't work that way. And why should she? She doesn't have time for meaningless messages. She has enough to do without a lot of hocus-pocus. Mother nature is above it all. She only has time to move the tides and light the sun and make the grasses turn to green. Hocus-pocus is for people who do not believe that mother nature will be here to save us all—move the moon from out in front of the sun—and keep the men in governments from ruining everything she has taken the time to make. Mother nature is looking out for us all. We can count on that. Mr. Cloud has moved away and I have had a dream about tomorrow and my friends will come to visit me and we will have a party.

I feel so in touch with the world! I've had such a lovely time and my skin feels so warm and the sun is striking the bay now—it makes the water a dazzling white, white as a field in heaven, maybe. How could anyone believe that there are things like omens when the world is lit this way? It's just not possible to think that anything could go wrong in a world as beautiful as this. So I won't believe it. I refuse to believe it. There are too many signs that tell me to think otherwise. I don't believe in omens anymore, but I do believe in signs. Like the cloud going away from the sun—that was a sign that everything was going to be fine. And it is! We just have to get through today—just get through one day and everything will be fine. You'll see. By tomorrow there won't even be a cloud in the sky. The clouds will have climbed out of this universe and only the sun will shine. And the moon won't get in the way of the sun anymore. It will have learned its lesson. It won't even need to scare people anymore, because the people will have decided to make everything better and not go to war. I'm so relieved! I just know now everything is going to be all right. And you'll be with me tomorrow. And the moon won't get in the way and Mrs. Mac won't need to be superstitious anymore. She can forget all about it. And life can go on in my village where the world is so quiet and calm and sweet.

I'm beginning to walk down the road that leads to Dead Man's Curve. I always hold my breath when I pass it, so don't expect me to be talking then. Some people hold their breaths when they pass by cemetaries. Not me. I only hold it when I go past Dead Man's Curve in honor of the person who died and the children who got hurt.

You know what's funny about this road today? I haven't seen a car on it or a truck or any other person like me walking on it for the last half mile. I don't see the old men sitting on the

WORLD ONE

porches and smoking their tobacco pipes and jawing on and on about the king crabs and the lobster poachers and the ever increasing license fees. I don't know why that is, do you? They must have gone to Digby for supplies—or maybe they're all out taking walks like me because of what the men on the radio were saying early this morning. Do you think I could have just dreamed that I had that dream? I mean, maybe I dreamed that everything was going to be all right tomorrow, but maybe that was a dream within a dream and it won't be coming true. Why have the old men gone somewhere today, anyway? I see them up there on those porches every day. It's only on the weekends that they sometimes disappear and go to Digby. There is something funny going on—I can sense that already. There should be more people on the road. I should have seen a truck pass by Dead Man's Curve. I should have seen men working on the telephone lines—one line snaps every couple of days and they're usually out here, parked by the side of the road, climbing up the ladder to fix whatever it was that went wrong. I wonder if everyone really believes what the men on the radio were saying this morning. But where would everyone go? Where would they go to hide from the poison in the air that the men said would be coming tonight? This is very strange—I feel strange all of a sudden. I wasn't expecting this. I was expecting to tell everyone that it was going to be all right, that they didn't have anything to worry about, that they were going to be okay and that there was going to be a tomorrow for all of us.

Why is everything so quiet now? Up on the hill everything was buzzing and there was so much going on—and now, now it's so quiet and strange and I don't see the old men who usually wave to me and ask me how I'm doing. "I'm doing fine," I'd say. And they'd be doing fine, and we'd all be doing fine and that was fine by all of us. But they're not doing fine now, are they? They're running away from here, aren't they? They've figured out a good place to go where it will be safe and they didn't even bother to tell me. But they couldn't have told me. I've been up on the hill looking out over the sea and they wouldn't have thought to look there on a day like today because they would have thought I would have been keeping close to my cabin where I could listen to those men on the radio. But they forgot it was my birthday. Did they even know it was my birthday? I don't suppose they would. I don't know theirs. What has happened to everyone and where are the cars? I came to tell them it would be all right and now they've disappeared. They are hiding in caves. They've had some plan all along to protect themselves on a day like today—and they didn't invite me to come along—they couldn't have cared less whether I lived or died. How could they do that to me after all the times I said hello to them and waved at them and said something nice about the weather? What kind of people are they, anyway? They don't care about me. I'm nothing to them. They only want to protect those who are kin to them. They couldn't care less that I'm going to die (unless my dream was true—and it was true. I could see you, my friends, and you were clapping for me and you were laughing and it was my birthday and we were having the best kind of party—we were happy, besides, and you were being wonderful to me and I had all the years of my life ahead of me).

You've deserted me and my friends! You've gone and hidden yourselves and not taken me with you! You left me to bake in the sun! Why does everyone want to leave me behind?

Don't worry, Sonia. Everything will be all right. Just keep walking, just keep walking down the twisting road and you will come to town and you can go and see Mrs. Mac. Mrs. Mac will be there, and if necessary, if it was only a dream, then she will take me somewhere and make it safe for me. She won't let me down. She's not afraid of the men on the radio and the men in the governments—she's not afraid of death—she's not afraid of anything at all. Just wait till you meet her, my friends. She will be a honey to you. I'll have her say a few words like I promised. She'll be glad to know that you'll be coming to my party tomorrow. We'll invite her, too. Maybe she could close down the store for a few hours—that would be so nice. She very rarely can come to my cabin and have tea with me, but maybe she'll make an exception for the day of the party . . . that would be so nice. I'd love her to come and we could all be together and I won't even think about the old men who have run away and left us here

WORLD ONE

alone, when everything was going to be all right in the first place.

I see the steeple of the white church, now. I'm not very far from home. My sun is out and happy and I'll be happy, too, when I get to see Mrs. Mac and remind her that it's my birthday. I know she won't have forgotten. She's not that kind. Now, she might pretend to have forgotten in order to be able to surprise me. But all along she won't have forgotten—she has a memory for dates. She's really neat that way. Tell her a date and ask her to remember it, and then ask her again in six months what the date was, and she'll be able to tell you without a second's pause. I wish I had her kind of mind for history class. It would be very handy indeed. I would be the star of the class, spouting out dates like they were second nature to me—like I had exactly lived in those years for me to remember them so well.

I know one thing for sure—Mrs. Mac wouldn't leave town without me. She'd make sure I left with her if she knew everything wasn't going to be okay. And she'd wait for me, too. Even if the bombs were coming down not very far away, she'd wait for me and then take me by the hand and walk me to whatever place she had found where we could be safe until it was over. But she won't have to do that. Every place will be safe. It's just that everyone doesn't know it, yet. But they will. Mrs. Mac and I will go hunting for all the people in the town who have hidden themselves wherever it is they have. And when we find them we can tell them the good news. And they'll believe me then, because Mrs. Mac will be with me, and everyone believes Mrs. Mac. Her word is like the word of the Bible, and when she says everything is going to be all right, then it is.

Me, I'm too young for people to really believe me. Most people think I don't know much and so they aren't likely to take me at my word. That's the one problem I've found in being so young. That's one reason why I wish I would grow up, and grow up fast. I want people to believe me when I have something to say. I don't want them to treat me like they treated my dad. He couldn't take that, and I guess I couldn't take that either. It's always best when people believe you. It just works out better that way. If I can only make

Mrs. Mac believe that what I dreamed was true. If only she will believe that, then we won't have to run away. We won't have to hide in some caves for a long time. I don't want to hide in caves for a long time. I like looking into caves on the shore and everything—but caves are too dark and there are sometimes evil spirits in them and I wouldn't want to spend a whole lot of time in them. I've got better things to do. I like it outside where the sun is and where the waves are and where nature is all around me and making me feel good about everything I see.

Anyway, it's not natural for people to have to hide in caves. That's for aborigines to do. Why should I want to act like an aborigine when I am who I am—nothing more or less. I'm just an ordinary girl who wants all the ordinary niceties of life. I wasn't brought up to go live in caves, either. I wouldn't live in a cave if my life depended on it. I'd rather just go on talking to you until I died, if you want to know the truth. I'd rather you remembered me the way I was instead of the way I would be living inside some kind of cave like an aborigine.

I'm on my way to see Mrs. Mac, and nobody is going to stop me. I'm on my way to see Mrs. Mac and no one is going to stop me—not the rain or the moon or the men on the radio. You will see that no one gets in my way when I go a-knocking on Mrs. Mac's door. And she will greet me and treat me to tea and we will begin to celebrate my fifteenth birthday. And you will hear a friend of mine who has been there through the thick and the thin—and she will be very glad to meet you, too.

I'm on my way to see Mrs. Mac, and nobody is going to stop me. So boo! to the men in the governments, and boo! to the men on the radio, and boo! to all those who plan to get in my way. I'll walk right through you if I have to. I'll call on Ra to push you out of the way. He will protect me and Mrs. Mac today. He will look out for everyone who is under the thumb of the bombs. Boo! to the bombs. Boo! to everything

WORLD ONE

that gets in our way. We are all going to live happily today and there will be a tomorrow—wait and see—tomorrow will come with the sun and you and I will be here, will be here, will always be here—along with Mrs. Mac.

I know I'm a lousy poet, you don't have to tell me. And I wouldn't mind even if you did. Sometimes it's the sentiment that's expressed that's even more important then how it's said. You get my point, don't you? I'm all for the living and I'm against all who are for the dying. And the friends of the living stick together like glue and can't be broken apart. Life binds us together and with us it's all for one and one for all. That's the way I see it and since you're my friends I'm sure you do too.

I'm on my way to see Mrs. Mac and we stick together like glue . . .

Knock, knock, Mrs. Mac. It's me, Sonia—why don't you answer me? I've come to see you. I'm sorry I forgot to pick up my milk . . . Mrs. Mac? Why don't you answer me? Won't you please open the door and let me inside? . . . I've got something special I'd like you to do for me . . . It would mean so much to me. I've been working on it since dawn and I want to tell you about it—you would be so proud of me. I thought it up all myself. Mrs. Mac?

I shouldn't go in—the lights are out inside—she must be sleeping—she's fallen asleep in her chair—yes, I see her through the window asleep in her chair. I really shouldn't wake her—but what if she has customers?—she could lose so much business if people don't know she's really in there. I better wake her up, don't you think? She would want that. Sometimes she just falls asleep for a nap—it's good for her health, but I know she won't want to miss any business. She would be so upset with me if she knew I let her sleep. I better go in and turn on some lights and turn the CLOSED sign around. Mrs. Mac, it won't do to sleep on a day like today. There is so much to look forward to!

I'm going in, the door's unlocked—luckily she left it

unlocked. I am going in right now—the door still squeaks in exactly the same way it's squeaked for years. I'll go easy. I'll stand on my tiptoes and walk to her quietly. I wouldn't want to startle her and give her a heart attack. She's not in the best of health. And she's too old to be frightened out of her sleep . . . Mrs. Mac? It's time to wake up. It's morning, Mrs. Mac, and the day is wasting away. I've turned the OPEN sign around. You will be expecting customers—you will not want to disappoint them. They will be coming soon, and I've come to pick up my milk. I'm here Mrs. Mac. Won't you wake up? I'm talking to you. I have something special I want you to do for me . . . Mrs. Mac! Wake up!

When I put my hand on her shoulder, she just fell over. I didn't know she would be dead. She just fell over and then I knew she was dead. You heard me, I said, "Mrs. Mac! Mrs. Mac! What's happened to you!" She was dead, though. And there were those pills by the chair—and on the floor—and the empty bottle and the half finished glass of water—and the radio was turned down low—it was so low I didn't hear it when I walked in—she had been asleep for a long time. She must have been up all night like me. Why didn't I come and see her sooner? It's my fault that she's dead. She died without saying good-bye to me. She knew it was my fault. She wanted me to come to see her. She really did. And I didn't. I would have but I was trying to have such a good time—but she wanted me to come to see her. She wouldn't have died if I had gone. And she's dead. She died there in her chair and now she looks so grey and white and sick—she looks so old and sad. But she doesn't look in pain—it doesn't look like it hurt. She just went to sleep and now she's sleeping and now you won't be able to hear her voice and hear how nice she was. I didn't do it! It was those men on the radio—they did it! I didn't do it! I wouldn't have done that to her! Not me! I loved her! I love you Mrs. Mac. I came to see you and to see how you were. And then you were asleep and I couldn't wake you and now my friends won't ever get to hear you and they will think I did this to you, but I didn't. It was those men—the same men I was listening to. I didn't think you

WORLD ONE

would pay any attention to them. I came to tell you that everything was going to be all right. You see I had this dream and in this dream there was a tomorrow and me and my friends were having this party and now I won't even be able to invite you. It's my birthday, did you know? Can I open this package on the table? It's got my name on it. TO SONIA, it says. Can I open it? You did remember that it was my birthday, didn't you? I'm opening your present, Mrs. Mac—I'm opening it now. There. I've taken off the ribbon and I'm unfolding the wrapping and there they are, Mrs. Mac. There are the gloves that I wanted so much. You knit me these gloves and they are so beautiful. And they are just the right size. I told you she was going to give me some gloves. Oh, Mrs. Mac, I love them. And you made them for me and they have made me so happy. So why are you asleep? What's gotten into you? You're not supposed to take so many pills. And the pills are for the nighttime, not the daytime. You're supposed to take one at bed. But you have your clothes on. You shouldn't be sleeping. You shouldn't be dead, Mrs. Mac. You didn't even ask me. And now look at you. You're so cold and hard and not like yourself. How could you be so alive and then dead? You did the same thing to me as my dad. How could you have done it? I would have made myself die if you had asked me, if you would have been happier without me. But you didn't even ask me. What am I going to do, Mrs. Mac?

I'm not confused, I'm not confused at all. What is there to be confused about? What on earth is the matter with me? I know what must be done. I know Mrs. Mac must have a burial, she must be laid to rest, I must think of her now. I must think of her future. She would want me to take care of these things. We've discussed them before. She knew I would be here to take care of them, and now that I am here, I will. You will listen to me while I go about my duties, won't you? You should know how to do these things yourselves. I'll tell you what I'm doing step by step, so when someone you loves dies, you will know just exactly what to do.

We will have a service. And I will be the minister and you will be the congregation and together we will mourn her death—it will be so hard for me to touch her now—she's so cold and stiff and there's no color in her face and her eyes are shut so tight. She should have a decent burial—but I will not be able to lift her. She will be too heavy for me, I will barely be able to lift her out of her chair and lay her on the floor. Then I will need a blanket. She has many blankets and I will have to choose the brightest one to match her personality. But red would be too indecent. She can't go to meet her Maker wrapped in red. It will have to be either brown or blue—blue would be nice, blue like the sea on a day like today. I wish you were here to help me. We could take her to the cemetary and I would dig a grave for her and she could lie peacefully next to mine. How she might like that. We were always best of friends when we were living together in this world. Maybe we'll be friends again in the next. Maybe we'll meet up in some distant place as energy and light. Maybe we will meet my dad there, too. I don't know. Do you know, Mrs. Mac? It would be so helpful to me if you could tell me that it's all right for you. I would never be afraid for you or for me or for anyone if I knew that it was going to be all right for them to die. I would even trade places with you if I knew it was going to be all right. But now I have to bury you. I'll try to give you the service that you would want. But I can't get you to the church and I don't have a grave for you and I'll have to do the best I can. Maybe you really wanted to be buried in your store. I can understand that. This was your store. This was your home. It is right that you should go to sleep here and be at peace here. After all, you wanted it that way, didn't you? If you had wanted it to be different, you would have gone up on that hillside above the church and gone to sleep there. But you didn't do that, now did you? You wanted to be here, and so you are here and I have found you and you are dead and my friends will be the congregation and I will be the minister and we shall bury you in a blue blanket and you will be happily buried like you wanted to be.

But why didn't you tell me you were going to do this? I

WORLD ONE

would have told you that you didn't have to. I was coming to tell you that but you were one step ahead of me and my friends. Now there's only so much we can do. I won't have a choir for you and I don't know what favorite hymns you wanted to be sung. Did you have a will—did you put your instructions in your will? Mrs. Mac, you didn't have to die. All those men were wrong. They weren't going to hurt you, they wouldn't dare hurt you. It was all a bad dream in which everyone went mad for a few hours. But it's morning now and it's all over and here you are not breathing. Why aren't you breathing anymore? Why won't you wake up and give me my present? I'm sorry I looked without asking you. But you wouldn't hand them to me . . . and I knew all along what you were knitting for me. I guessed it when you asked about the size of my hand. I'm sorry I opened my present. I did so much want you to give them to me. Will you forgive me now and come back and wake up and talk to my new friends? I promised them you would at least say hello. I've already promised them and they were looking forward to it so much. How can I tell them that you've gone to sleep and won't wake up? How can I tell them that? How, Mrs. Mac? How?

It won't be necessary. They'll understand. It wasn't your fault. You were just too tired to listen to the men on the radio. It was their fault. They shouldn't have been saying all the things they were saying. They had no right to scare you so. But they were scared, too, weren't they? They were scared and so they had to scare you. But it was the men in the governments that made them scared, wasn't it? It was them. They are the ones who are scaring everyone. That's why the men on the porches up the road have gone to hide in their caves, isn't that so? That's why everything is so quiet in town. That's why you let yourself go to sleep without saying anything to me. You didn't want to have to be the one to scare me, isn't that right Mrs. Mac? Well, I'm not scared. I won't be scared. I already know what tomorrow's going to be like and it isn't anything to be scared of. And today is my birthday and I refuse to be frightened on my birthday. I just feel sorry for everyone. I feel sorry for you, Mrs. Mac. You were such a good person. And it wasn't your fault that you were so scared. Don't worry, you can speak to me now. My friends can be trusted. I've already told them all about you. They know that it wasn't your fault that you were so scared. And they know whose fault it was. They know who's responsible. And if my tomorrow doesn't come, then they'll tell everyone they know about what happened today and about who was responsible. That's why I've been telling them everything I know. It's important for other people to know what happened to the world—if it does end tonight. Someone has to know. Don't worry. I've explained everything pretty well. They understand now what's happening. They understand that it wasn't your fault. I wish you would say something, Mrs. Mac. I wish you would say that you were going to be all right.

I have the best blanket I could find—it's blue with white specks. It's the prettiest in the store. I've marked it down on your ledger—one blue blanket: funeral expenses. And don't worry about the store. I'll lock it up tight. I don't want you to be disturbed. I want you to have a good rest. You were the nicest lady I ever knew and am likely to know. That's the way I feel about you. Did you know that? Did I ever tell you that? I'm sure I did, only I can't remember right now. But you can hear me, can't you? Even though you're not breathing you can hear me, can't you?

I've folded your hands on your chest, Mrs. Mac. You had such strong and handsome hands. You always kept them so clean. You had the cleanest hands of anyone I've ever known ... I've combed your hair as best I can, Mrs. Mac. I bunched some of it under your head so you would have something to rest on. Does that feel good? I'm trying to make it easy on you. I hope it's okay. You hair is still as soft as grass. I always envied your hair that way. I admired you more than you thought, now didn't I? I was like a daughter to you, wasn't I? And I was a good daughter, too. It's nice to be a daughter. I've missed having a mother and father so much. But I had you and you had me and we didn't need anyone else. But now you don't have me anymore. What are you going to do? Who's going to take care of you? Who's going to help you

WORLD ONE

when you're sick? Who's going to talk to you when you're lonely? I have to get some rice.

There. I'm sprinkling you with white rice. Somewhere I heard it was good to sprinkle the dead with white rice. Is that good, Mrs. Mac? I'm going to say a prayer for you. I won't tell you what it is. I want it to be between me and the Almighty. I want Him to know that I want Him to take especially good care of you. I want Him to watch out for you. You won't have me anymore, so I want someone good to see that you're going to be all right. Is that okay? Is that what you want? And I'm going to clean the store for you. Look Mrs. Mac, I sweeping the store for you so everything will be clean and just the way you like it. And when the floor is clean I'll sweep the porch and wash the windows one last time. I'll be back when I sweep the porch. I won't be gone long. And I'll always be thinking about you.

I have a sponge and a bucket of cold water and I'm washing the windows so the sunlight can get in. The sun is so warm today and I want you to feel it. You were so cold when I found you and I want you to be warm. The sun is out and it's a beautiful day. I feel so happy to be alive on my birthday. Why didn't you even wait to say happy birthday to me?

I've got to go, Mrs. Mac. The store looks beautiful and the light is shining in on you. I'm locking the door Mrs. Mac. And I'll put up the CLOSED sign just like you had it before. Are you going to miss me? Are you happier now? Are you having a good rest? Have you found my father yet? . . .

I don't care if you're cold. I'm going to kiss you goodbye . . .

I'm closing the door, Mrs. Mac. I'll try to come back a little later on and see how you're doing. But no one will disturb you today. You can sleep peacefully today. It's Wednesday today and it's my birthday today and I want you to rest all you can for your life to come. It will be a wonderful life, Mrs. Mac. People do live on, you know. You don't just live one life. There has to be more to it than that. I wish you could tell me . . . I really do . . . I love you Mrs. Mac. And my friends love you, Mrs. Mac.

No one will disturb you anymore. You just get some rest and I'll be back when I can. I'm closing the door, Mrs. Mac. When you hear it shut, I'll be gone, but I'll be thinking about you as ever.

10

I've come down to the bay while I was away. I just needed to be left alone and I feel ... I don't know how I feel, anymore. Mrs. Mac ... I can't explain it. She was here one day and then gone the next. What made her want to die that way? Was she scared of what was going to happen? She didn't want to die in the poisoned air, did she? She wanted to die by her own hand, like my dad. I could never do that. I think it takes more courage to face what's going to happen than to give in to it. But I guess she died thinking that this was the only way she could be free. She was always interested in the way my dad died. She said she could understand why he did it. She said that he knew what was coming and he didn't want to feel any more responsibility for it. He blamed himself for having failed, she said. But what I want to know is why Mrs. Mac blamed herself. Did she blame herself for what she knew was going to happen to me? Is it really going to happen to me? Am I really going to die this evening? Did she really know it was going to happen to me anyway and she didn't want to see me that way? I feel so sick. I don't know what I'm doing . . . I thought, I was sure, everything was going to be all right. I just knew it. Somehow when I had that dream of tomorrow I knew that there wasn't going to be a war and that the men on the radio were wrong. But now I don't know anymore. I wish my dad would let me know. I wish he would come and tell me everything he knew. He must know what's going to happen tonight and tomorrow. Do you know, my friends? Have I just gotten myself mixed up in a crazy dream? Have I just been wishing away the morning? You must know. Why don't you just come right out and tell me? I've already told you that I won't be scared. If I die tonight, I die tonight. I've had so much to be thankful for. But I have a right to know, now! It's different if you know that you're going to die at the end of the day than if you think you might be living for a lot longer. It is going to happen, isn't it? That's why Mrs. Mac is dead. That's why my dad is dead. They both knew it was going to happen, they just knew it at different times. And now I know it. You and I know it. Does my mom know it? Why did she have to die when I was born? She would have died soon enough even if she was still alive. At least we could have been together and known each other. Am I being punished? Have I been so bad that this is happening to me? I don't ever think I've been so lonely . . .

Swoosh, crash go the waves, the little waves on the beach bringing in the tide . . . Do you know what's going to happen tonight? I don't believe it but there are other people who do . . . But these are crazy people—these are people you and I can't trust. No one wants this thing to happen tonight, so it won't. Life just doesn't work that way—you can do anything you want—and people don't want this to happen so it won't. Isn't that right my friends? We are all together—my friends of the future, mother nature and me . . . We are all together and we don't want this to happen and so it won't. We will wish it away. All things are possible if we wish hard today. And I am wishing hard . . . you don't know how hard I'm wishing. Maybe if I wished hard enough I could bring back

WORLD ONE

Mrs. Mac—I could see my dad—I could wish for anything and it would come true. I know it would—it would have to—because I still have all the faith in the world. I believe in the world and in mother nature and in the balance of everything and in the good people who are still alive and who still want to go on living even after today.

But Mrs. Mac? Mrs. Mac, you didn't have to die so soon. You could have lived a little longer—you could have waited and died with me. Wouldn't that have been so much better? Wouldn't it really? It must have been so sad for you to have gone to sleep all alone without saying good-bye to your friends, to me. Even if you hadn't wanted to wait for me, for tonight, I would have at least been there to hold your hand. I would have stayed by you until the end. I did the best I could after it was too late. But I couldn't move you to the cemetary. I wasn't strong enough. You really wanted to be buried in your store, didn't you? That's where you lived and that's where you wanted to die. I understand that—I just wanted to be with you. It would have been better for me if I had been with you. That's selfish, I know . . .

So they're all gone . . . my dad and my mom and Mrs. Mac . . . all gone, and now their child is alone on the beach by the bay celebrating her fifteenth birthday and talking like a nut into this recording machine. Wait till my friends hear what I have to say. They won't be at my party tomorrow—but maybe in a hundred years—maybe then they'll find this machine and push the buttons and hear what I have to say. And when they hear what I have to say, they'll know who I was and who my dad was and who my mom was and who Mrs. Mac was and they will remember us for a time. They will remember us until they die—but then their children might remember us still. We will all be remembered if they can just sit down and listen to what I have to say about the way the world was in the time that I was alive.

I am going to cry now. I can't help it anymore. I'm feeling sorry for myself. You would too if you were here today. I know you would so don't laugh. Now I feel like becoming a bird and flying around the world and seeing all the things that I've always wanted to see—that would be such a nice way to end it all—having seen and done everything that there is to do. And I could tell you about everything I see. That way we'll both know what the whole wide world looked like and how it smelled on its last day when it was still fresh and alive and not damaged. I would feel so at peace then, if I could do that. Wouldn't you? Yes, that would be my idea of peace—just floating up there as close as I could come to the heavens—turning on the winds—slipping through the clouds and following the path of the sun . . . I would like to follow him—round and round the world so effortlessly. I would do that, yes, I would and I would tell you everything and that would make you so happy later on. You see, you'll never see the world that way, ever again. It just won't be the same. Everything will be changed, but you'll have this tape to remember it by—to see it by—it will be like a word picture book for you . . . You can all gather around your fires at night and listen to the next chapter, or the next verse. Won't that be nice? You can sip your coffee by the fire and listen to what I had to say on the pier where I used to catch all the perch. You can imagine how it was to ride Nimrod down the trails at dusk. If Nimrod were alive today, I would go riding, that's what I would do until I died. I would take him out along the beach at high tide and ride him into the face of the wind and we would follow the path of the sun—we might even come to the Pacific Ocean by the time evening came around. I could sit on the cliffs with him and watch the bombs fall here and there. It would be so serene looking at the sunset with him . . . He shouldn't have died so soon. Everyone I know dies so soon. It's as if no one liked me and they all wanted me to be alone. They, none of them, wanted to be with me when it came time for me to die. I don't understand that. I never did anyone any harm—and I liked people. I was always kind to them and always tried to help them. So what did I do? First my mom, and then my dad, and then Nimrod and then Mrs. Mac—and now me. I'm next. I know I'm next. It's getting to be the time and my dream of tomorrow wasn't true. There wasn't anything to it—it was just a silly girl's dream. And Mrs. Mac knew that—and you know that—because you're listening to me right now and I'm already

WORLD ONE

dead and it's probably a hundred years from now and you don't care about me either except I'm helping you see the way the world was on the day I died.

I've found a boat to row. I don't think anyone will object. I'm going to put out to sea—or at least out into the bay and there I'm going to drift and dream for a while ... Switching off while I row the boat out into the center of my world.

Lap, lap go the waves. Thud, thud go my oars on the edges of the boat. My oarlocks squeak ... What a squeak it is, like the moaning of a baby whale, like a dying gutted fish whose beating heart is caught in its throat. I think the wind off the sea is coming in to lift me up and take me around the world. I don't want to go now. It's so peaceful out here in the middle of the bay. And you and I are alone again. No one will trouble us. We don't have to think of all the grey things, the dark grey things that mix us up and put us down. We'll just drift and listen to the lap, lapping and we'll rest, there's lots of time left for us to rest. We can improve our suntans, we can dream of pictures in the light, the light of the sun on the waters. The sunny light is everywhere, haven't you noticed yet? And in each flash of light I see new things—each sparkle is a new perspective on life—each is different, like everything that exists in the world, each sparkle is a different color of light. Lappity-lap go the waves and they change the meaning of the light ... That sounds like I'm crazy. But you would have to be here to know what I'm talking about. This has to be seen. And you can't see it from the shore. You have to come out here. Place yourself out in the middle of it and let your thoughts go—that's when you can see everything so differently—see all the different lights on the water ...

I'm drifting. I'm resting. I'm dreaming again, I never can stop it. It's like a disease. It just keeps coming back and I just let it keep coming back, because it makes me happier to dream. I can see so many possibilities when I dream and let myself go. I bet you have dreams, too. Do you ever dream that one morning you're going to wake up and the world is going to be different? Maybe you dream that all the green will come back to the forests . . . the blue will come back to the sea . . . the gold will come back to the color of the sun . . . the white to the clouds . . . all colors will return if you dream hard enough. Dream, and anything can be the way you want it. You can take my word on that.

My heart keeps sinking . . . sinking down and down. One moment I'm happy, then this funny feeling comes over me and I feel my heart sinking and then I've forgotten that I was happy a moment ago . . . Isn't that strange? I can feel so high and then come down so low, the lowest I've ever been, and every time it's lower than I was before . . . Mrs. Mac is resting now, isn't she? . . . she's down very low and is going down lower because she is resting so hard, sleeping so hard . . . Then maybe she gets high again and she goes up and up and up until she is as happy as she's ever been. Don't you think that's possible? Even in death there are probably highs and lows—like waves, first they rise and then they fall and then they rise and then they fall—like me, like you, like Mrs. Mac—up and down, high and low, like leaves in the spring and fall—up and down, rise and fall. I'm low now and going down. The light on the water changes, light then dark, bright then soft, then dim, then dark, then up and light again. What a strange world we live in . . . What a cruel twist of fate . . . the dark side of mother nature . . . and the dark side of people . . . like you and me . . .

Wouldn't it be better to just let yourself go? Just to sink into the sea . . . how lovely it would all be—following it down like the path of the light on the waves—first bright, then dim, then dark—would it be very light at the bottom? Would I be happy as I drown going down, down? Happy in death, sad in life, up and down, high and low, light and dark, going down, down, down, around, around and up and down . . .

I could be happy down there, me an octopus, you up here waiting for me, the sun looking after me, waiting for the right time to bring me up and change me back to who I am . . . was once long ago . . . before this time, before tonight and tomorrow . . . I could drown. No one would mind . . . Mrs.

WORLD ONE

Mac might not even know. My dad, he's long gone. My mom, who knows? I could go right now—and I might be happiest if I went. I could go of my own free will—like dad, like Mrs. Mac. I'll leave you my little cabin. You can stay there as long as you like. If anyone asks why you're there, just play this part of the tape and they won't bother you at all. You are in my will. I give you everything I own. Would that make you happy? You'd have property of your own. You'd have a bed to sleep in, you'd have a view of the bay and you'd have memories of me . . . I was happy with that. You could be, too. We would have been happier together. We could have had that party, we could have had many more birthdays to come . . .

Should I go down? I wouldn't be lonely down there. I could just rest and sleep like Mrs. Mac and dad. I'll leave my tape up here—the boat will come into shore with the tide. You'll find it. I'll put it under the tin can—the rain won't get it . . . I could go down, you know—but I won't. I let those men on the radio get to me. The world won't get to me. Why should it? I believe in life and the world believes in death and dark and going down. I'm young and I like going up and up and up—higher still. I'm going up again and soon I will be friends with the light of the sun, like I am friends with you. It's not as crazy and as nutty as it seems—it's attitude—my teachers say I have a good attitude. My attitude is getting better. Just talking directly to you makes my attitude get better. The most important thing I can do is talk to you. You are my friends. I've become very fond of you. I hope you think the same of me. We've come a long way together today. I shouldn't spoil it now. There's so much left of the day. It's been a good day and I want to go up and up and keep on talking to you. I don't want to spoil *your* day. Your day should be a happy day, and mine too. Birthdays are for celebrating life, aren't they? I mean you don't have death days do you? Or do you? Things might be different with you . . . I could understand your having death days, after everything that will have happened . . . Yes, I can understand having death days . . . It makes sense for you to remember this day—the day the world failed to keep on living . . .

So I won't fail—if the world is going to fail, I'm not. I'll live and wait and see what happens. I'm not afraid, if you're not afraid . . . there are other things we can do, other places I can take you. It's best we go up today. We can go down tonight, but it's all up today.

Lap, lap go the waves. Up up go the waves—the light on the water is going up and I am following it—I am racing with the light—everything is happy once more. There's plenty of time to go down. There's not much time to go up. It's best to continue on my way. Anyway, there's plenty more for you and I to do. I better pick up my oars and row myself in. I don't have the time to drift out to sea. I don't have the time to take myself down. I only have time for living today. I better start living before I run out of time—that's what I mean about going up. Talking to you is going up, looking at life is going up, dreaming of tomorrow is going up and up— it's the only way to go. I know that now. Don't think I'll forget it. I wouldn't dare, not if I could live a million years.

One oar in, one oar out, I'm on my way back to shore. Pine trees high and low, low and high, all of them waiting for me. My town from here is as white as white can be, every house is painted white, that pleases me. White is my favorite color this year. Last year it was red, but red is bloody and makes me think of death too often. One oar in, one oar out, I'm getting close to shore where the beach is a lane of white, like the houses that rise up on the banking hills filled with forests of the greenest pine. In front of me as I row backwards is the gap between the arms of the land—between the arms is a gap that leads out to the sea. St. Mary's Bay leads out to sea where I will never go again—because I think that it is true, the world is coming to an end. I can't lie. It is true, the world is coming to an end. So what can I do, I can do nothing, this was meant to be, but it is so hard to believe. How can it be so true—the sky above me does not know—it goes on being blue. The sun does not know—it goes on being gold and the fishes in the deep have no idea that they are soon to be dead. Happy birthday, Sonia, happy birthday—you are all

WORLD ONE

alone. What a day it is to die ... I died on my fifteenth birthday before my dreams could have a chance to come true. It will matter to no one—everyone I know is dead or gone—those that are alive are hiding in the caves, hiding somewhere safe from me. They are cowards, it is true, but cowards are cowards because they want to live ... Who can blame them anyhow? All living things have a lust for life. They are made that way. The Almighty saw to that. So you and I are living—me here now, on my fifteenth birthday—you in the time to come. You will survive, I know. Somehow you will survive and hear what I have to say.

I am coming close to shore and the sea is very far away from me. Good-bye good sea—we will never meet again. Each of us will suffer tragedy. We, the shes, should have saved the world. They, the men, have let us down, they have led us to this day. What for, we ask? For no reason, we reply. Just because, just because, they did not understand mother nature's laws.

Wet feet on the sandy shore. It's good to be back here. I can't lift the boat to where it was—it will never reach its proper resting place. So sorry, boat. You will have to wait until my friends come up this way after I am gone.

Twenty steps and I am on the road that runs beside my town. My town is not my town—it is as still as a stagnant pool of water. It is drying up—all the life is drying up. Only I am here to say it once was a proper place to be. I was growing up right. I was growing every day, and I was going to be a woman. I was going to be all the way grown up, but now the men have gotten in my way. I could have done so much better without them. I think that's fair to say.

I'm walking through the streets ... I am Sonia and I once lived in a town called Sandy Cove, but then one day, oh, it was a long time ago, but on this day, everyone disappeared. The cowards went to hide in caves. I hope they live happily ever after on seaweed and poisoned berries—they all went away and left me here to be the princess of the town. How kind of them, I wish that I could thank them. I thank them anyway for leaving me their town. I can pick any place in which to live. I could have the grandest house or I might choose to live inside the steeple of the church. I could hear the bells at breakfast, I could lunch with them at noon, or dine with them at suppertime, if I had the mind to. I could go and live with Mrs. Mac, she would take me in—but over there, the sign on the door says, CLOSED. Has she gone to Digby? Has she gone on her summer vacation to the south? Why would she? She would not do that and not tell me. Mrs. Mac tells me everything. I am her daughter in the flesh. And I am a good daughter, really I am—she will not be ashamed of me when she gets back. My virtue will be left intact. But I would like to know a boy—he would be impressed with me. Here he would see a princess of the town who owns everything from shore to shore. Every plant is mine to care for—every window I will wash. And I will sweep the roads. I want them clean for the passing visitors. We are not a messy people. We keep our town as clean as glass. There is work to do—but I will let no one down. I must keep this town so clean. I want no trespassers from the outer world. They all have dirty hands—they all wear the color red. No hands of blood will touch this town. I want it to be free. There will be no more death inside this town. It will be clean and healthy—that is the law that I pass down. To those who will disobey, you will be punished. So do not dare. It will be unwise for you. It will be best to stay clear and do your killing elsewhere . . . I cannot prevent you from bloodying your hands. But you will not do it here. You will find plenty of blood over the hills and down to the south or to the east, etc. I see no reason to permit it here. That is the law and you will obey it or you will have to go. I will put you out to sea. You can do no harm there. If the fish don't reach up and get you, then the sun, my Ra, will . . . He will see that our town is blessed and will live in peace until I have to go away. I am his favorite daughter. He looks out for me.

Where are you, citizens of the town? Have you forgotten that it is your princess' birthday? She has not. I had expected more. I had expected to be treated to some songs—a present or two would do. Why have you abandoned this peaceful little cove? How can you be afraid of death when all of life surrounds you? Do you think I'm getting through to them?

WORLD ONE

Or have they closed their ears? Perhaps their present to me is the town—yes, they have given me this town, their whole town as a present for my birthday. How kind of you, my citizens. I will always treasure it. But you must know that a town is not a town without its citizens. I am no princess unless I have my subjects. I can't be a birthday girl without my friends ... So why have you gone and hidden yourselves from a war that is not here? I am here. Mrs. Mac is here and no one will come and touch us. They will not dare. We like to live here. And those who live are so much stronger than those who insist on death. And even if they could come and get us and take us down with them—why not enjoy your lives until the last? That is your duty to me and to your town ...

I am walking through my town, my town that is filled with handsome white wood buildings. We have handsome churches made long ago, we have houses that will withstand practically any storm, and we are protected by the bay. St. Mary's Bay protects us from the death which will try to come and get us. It will not get me. I have someone above who will protect me and our town of Sandy Cove. You did not know that, did you? You could have come and asked me. If only you had come and asked me, I would have told you so. Mrs. Mac did not ask me and now she is lying on the floor quite cold and dead. She lost her faith that we would be protected till the end.

I have not lost my faith. I have everything to live for. I am just beginning to have everything to live for ... Where are you citizens? We cannot give up now. We must fight these men who wish to make us dead. I will make a law that peace will have a home here. We will make him comfortable—happy and comfortable—and I will give him any house he wants—the high one on the hill behind the church—the one that looks like a barn up on the ridge. Take any house you want. We always have a house for peace, and we can't live without you. So come to us and make your home and bring my people with you. Can you hear me? Am I speaking loud enough? Do I need to scream? Do I need to beg you? Would you like me to dance?

I will dance for you, then you will come and make everything all right. One step here and there, round and round I go. I raise my arms above my head, four steps and five, to the right and to the left, I am dancing for your eyes. Round and round I go dancing up a storm. Have you any requests? I could do the waltz, a favorite of the gentlemen. One, two, three, four, one, two, three, four, away we go. I am waltzing through and through the streets so you will come to us and bring my people home . . .

No one's coming home. The streets are naked and sunny. I've heard no applause for my dance. You would have applauded me if you had seen me. I know you would have. I'd be the apple of your eyes—Sonia, ballerina extraordinaire.

I'm happy to be the only one left, you know . . . It isn't decent to desert the town you love. One must make a stand somewhere and I choose to do it here. I should draw a white flag up the schoolhouse flagpole. I could paint a blue circle on it. The circle would be a sign of infinity for the people who will survive, somewhere. I know it sounds strange, but I'm proud of everything the people of the world have done. We have come so far in our time and it's only been a short time, really . . . We've just barely gotten started. What we've done is quite a lot, considering we've been constantly interrupted by things like wars. We just should have been a little smarter, that's all, a little smarter would have done it for us. Maybe next time. That's why a white flag with a blue circle on it would be just the right thing to express that somehow people will manage to go on. Some will survive and then there will be others—and the world will begin again. Only I hope it's a whole lot better this time around. The blue circle is for hope and the white flag is for peace and together they say that there will be peace in infinity . . . My dad would have liked that. He was all for ideas like that. At least you'll know what the flag is all about if I actually get around to putting it up there and you come along at some time or another and see it there, up on the flagpole, flapping like a lonely orphan in the bay breezes.

How'd you like to take a journey up to the church on the

WORLD ONE

ridge of the hill? You'll like the view—the view takes in everything. And it's a proper place for a princess to see the world around her. We'll worry about the flag later on. It's a good idea, but I'd still like to think it over to make sure it's just the right thing for the occasion. Some choices you're stuck with forever, so you have to be mighty careful.

Walking up the road which leads to the church now. I hope you're not getting too tired of walking everywhere. Maybe later today I could drive you around in a car. There is a jeep parked at the gas station. I'm not old enough to drive but I don't think anyone will have an attack if they see me. They won't have time to worry about things like that, will they? Besides, the worst they would do if I got caught was to try to call Mrs. Mac—and she's fast asleep, so that's okay.

I wish you could smell the air today. It's not the least bit thick with humidity. Sometimes the humidity creeps up the coast and makes it all seem so unnatural around here. But days like that usually only come in August and we're a long way from August today. Anyway, this time of year the wild flowers are everywhere. They're not just beside the roads or along the highway—they don't stop there. They creep up in every garden, around every house and into vast fields along the slopes of the hills. There are more wild flowers out here than even stars in the sky at night—that's how many there are. And you can find any color you want. If you like pale blue, there are about a million of them. If you like gold or pink, you won't be disappointed. Sometimes Mrs. Mac and I would go out gathering wild flowers on Sundays and we would come back with our arms piled high with them. We could make a mountain with them. And I think they like to be picked by people who love them. If we go back the next Sunday it doesn't look like there are any less than the week before—they grow back practically overnight. They grow for us. They like to be put in vases and admired. And me and Mrs. Mac admire them all week long. By my bed I still have some from last week, and they aren't wilted yet and their colors aren't fading. When I give them water they just drink it up and then ask for more. It seems to me that wild flowers are quite content to be put just about anywhere as long as they have a good home and people take care of them. I do hope you'll notice them when you're here. And don't be afraid to pick them and take them home with you. Just follow my instructions about watering them and they will give you pleasure all week long. That's the way with flowers. They're here to give us pleasure.

Passing the church where nobody is right now. I would have thought Reverend Russell would have been kneeling down in front of the altar praying to the Almighty to make everything all right. But he's not here. He's probably praying in his cave along with everyone else—either that or he's telling everyone, "I told you so." Ministers have us one up that way. There are so many things that can go wrong in the world that they can always say, "I told you so." It's a good position to be in, if you ask me. That way you can hardly go wrong. And when things go right for a change, they can always say, "It was the Almighty's wish that this was so." If you want to be right most of the time, I'd advise you to take up the ministry. They have a knack for being right just about all of the time. It must be a very happy life.

I won't take you to my grave right now, even though I'm dying to show it off. We should just keep going up to the top of the ridge where we can get the best view. I'm not going to pick any wild flowers today either. I want them to live as long as they can. Switching off till the top of the ridge.

Top of the ridge of Sandy Cove overlooking St. Mary's Bay. Sonia talks to her friends about her dad. You know if these ministers are right all the time, I wonder why they didn't do something more to stop what's going to happen today. I know they thought about it. "The end of the world is coming." They had to have thought about it. It's all written in the Bible, did you know that? But if these ministers are right all the time, I really wonder why they didn't try more to help

WORLD ONE

my dad. You don't think I know the answer to that? I do. They didn't much help my dad because they believed the world could only be saved through a union of religions. They thought if the churches all over the world could get together that that would bring peace. Did you know that religions have caused many of the great wars in the world? It sounds crazy seeing as how these ministers are supposed to be so peaceful and everything, but it's true. Take the Crusades, for instance. That was strictly a religious war. And plenty of people died because of it. There was the Children's Crusade which killed young people like me, too. It was all done in the name of religion, so how they think that they could save the world with religion, I don't know. I'm not saying anything against the church. I wouldn't dare say it. But as my dad said until I got sick of hearing it, "Peace is law and law is peace." It doesn't matter what religion people are. I could go ahead and believe that the Almighty was a tree and even if everybody else in the world believed that the Almighty was a tree, it still wouldn't give people peace. People have to live by laws so that they'll know what they can do and not do. The same goes for nations. They have to know what they can do and not do. I don't mean to come down too hard on all the ministers—I've never met one who I hated for instance—but they only see the world from one point of view. That's the trouble with all the people, too. They see the world from their particular point of view and it just so happens that everyone and every nation thinks that their point of view is right. And they probably have good reason to think so too. That's why law is so important. With law there is a set of rules and there are judges to see to upholding those rules, and then everyone knows the score. If the judge says you're right then you're right. If he says you're wrong, you're wrong. But that way, everyone and every nation can get a fair hearing before a judge who isn't on the side of anyone except the side of the law. That's very clear to me and I'm no genius or anything. You could try it out if you like. The trouble you'll have is trying to convince other people that it's a good idea. That's the big trouble, like I mentioned, that my dad had—and as you can see, it didn't work. And now we're all in the same soup and everything is about to go wrong and we don't have any judges to tell these men in the governments that they're either right or wrong . . .

So I'm sitting above the church and looking down at it and wondering why the Almighty didn't step in and tell everyone that this was the right thing to do. Why didn't He do that? Why is He letting this happen when it didn't have to? And why is He going to let everyone die because we didn't have the brains to discover it ourselves? That just isn't fair. My dad tried so hard to make people see that this was such a reasonable thing to do . . . I could get mad about it again and say some things I would probably regret later on today, but I won't. Maybe this was all supposed to be, like the Bible said, but I don't think so. No Almighty would want to see His creation go up in smoke. You don't spend a couple of thousand years painting a picture and then let someone tear it up. Maybe He's doing this to us because of people like you. Maybe you're supposed to make everything over again and begin again without any wars. Maybe it's like the Great Flood when He drowns the whole world and spares just a few people like Noah and his sons and their wives and a lot of animals. Don't ask me, I'm too young to figure it all out, but maybe it's something like that. You never know . . .

I could get hysterical if I wanted to. I might sound pretty good, but I'm getting a little hysterical inside. It just doesn't make any sense. Nothing makes any sense and I'm sitting in the middle of something bigger than me that doesn't make any sense. What would you do if you were me? Would you throw a fit? Would you go out and drown yourselves? Or would you go to sleep like Mrs. Mac and not worry about anything for a while? You see, I always felt that I had all the time in the world and now it doesn't look that way at all. And now I don't know what to do or where to go. I'm getting confused again and no one is here to help me figure out what to do . . . I wish you could speak to me. I need a friend right now. It's hard to go on living when you know you're about to die. That's right, isn't it? I will die soon, if not tonight than tomorrow or the next or the next. All because people couldn't figure out what to do, when all the time the answer was right

WORLD ONE

in front of them. It's enough to make me puke—and I haven't eaten anymore raspberries.

I've decided to go ahead and take you to my grave. I'm really proud of it. I made it with my own two hands. Don't think I'd like to be a gravedigger by profession. I'm not *that* morbid. But there is something beautiful in being able to dig one's own grave. It's not particularly the world's greatest grave. There are plenty of kings and queens who are buried behind cathedral altars who will have it much better than me. I'm not complaining, though. A grave is a grave and once you're in it, that's that. You could be on the moon and it wouldn't matter to you. But right now, being alive, I'm pretty proud of it, all in all. It's got a perfect view of the bay and the sunlight shines on it from early morning till late afternoon. I plan to keep my suntan even when I'm dead.

So won't you come with me and visit my final resting place? I'd be happy to entertain you there and of course I'd be honored if you could come and visit me when you come to town. You won't have any trouble finding it. It's to the far left of the highest pine tree at the back of the cemetary. It will have the only white cross made of driftwood. I'll try to engrave it with some kind of important statement, you know, like, "She died with a full heart but a sense of grief for the people of the world." I haven't quite worked it out yet, but it will go something like that—something snappy and bright but chock full of pathos and longing.

Switching off for a minute or two while we get there. Hats off everybody!

I guess I remembered it looking better than it really is. The sides have crumbled in a little so I'll have to do a bit of cleaning up. Also it's going to be hard to make that long of an inscription. I'd forgotten how thin the sticks were. Maybe I'll have to look around for something a little wider. Thinking about that inscription I just made up, I kind of like it—it's not as sappy as I thought. It also shows that I was concerned with the lives of other people, too. Will you excuse me while I clean up around here? There are pine needles everywhere and I still haven't pulled out all of the roots that were sticking out of the sides.

That's much better now, although it occurred to me that maybe a pine needle floor for the grave wouldn't be bad at all. I won't have a casket, not even a wooden one like they have in the Westerns, so it probably would be a good idea to pad the floor with some sweet smelling pine needles—the long needle variety that smell good for a long time. You know I haven't practiced lying down in it yet. I guess I was superstitious about lying down in it before my time. I didn't want to rush things—there's no sense in asking for trouble before you have to. But I guess it's all right now. It looks long enough but I want to make sure I've got plenty of leg room. Also I guess I didn't want to soil my best white shirt. It's hell to clean white shirts of dirt stains. But I'm not going to worry about it. I figure you don't have to go to your grave in a sparkling clean shirt. Lots of people haven't, so I don't imagine I have to, either.

Feet first—lying back now—arms folded—looking up—what a gorgeous view of the sky. I really know how to pick the best views. That comes from knowing the lay of the land. I am very happy with my spot. I couldn't have asked for anything better. And I wouldn't want one of those graves behind the altar of a cathedral—it would be too dark there. Out here you have the view and you can snuggle up with mother nature. This is definitely the kind of grave I want. I don't have any question about that at all.

I think I do have enough room. It's tight but very comfortable. And I think I'll need those pine needles on the floor. It's not that the ground is too hard, but it is a little rocky, especially at the small of my back. But I've done all right considering no one helped me dig an inch of it. You know I get the funniest feeling lying down here looking up.

WORLD ONE

It's as though I was far away from the world yet at the same time right smack in the middle of it. I can't quite explain it—you'd have to be lying down here too to know what I mean. Still it's the funniest feeling knowing you're alive and seeing the sky go by and then thinking about how it will be when you're dead and looking up and not seeing anything except maybe a lot of darkness. I'm going to close my eyes and pretend I'm dead.

Who's been letting it rain on me?! I must have fallen asleep and then someone brought the rain and now I'm wet and I'm not very happy about it. Are you still working, my favorite recording machine? Let me dry you off. I don't want anything to happen to you. You are my last link with the future and I don't want you to be rusty when I'm gone . . . It's like you were taking a bath. You're all dried off now and working just fine. I'm still wet though and my white shirt is ruined. I better put down the pine needles now to keep my floor from getting muddy. It's suddenly so grey and I'm getting hungry and my mouth is all dried up like a bucket of sand and I could use a bowl of hot soup and crackers. And I'm dying for a cup of coffee. We better go on home and dry off, too. It won't do for the birthday girl to be wandering around with a wet face on the day she's supposed to be more beautiful than ever.

Anyway, I hope you like my grave. I don't imagine there will be anyone around to fill it in so maybe I could ask a favor of you. There's plenty of dirt left over from my digging, so if you could just pile it on top of me I would be very appreciative. I would ask someone else but no one seems to be around anymore, and besides, it would be a real honor if you would do it. I'm going to leave this fold-up shovel by the pine tree so you won't have to get your hands dirty lifting up the dirt. When I'm all filled in around the edges and everything, you can tamp it down and then make sure my cross is at the perfect angle, towering above my head. As I said earlier, then maybe you could say a prayer for me and continue to put in a good word for me with the Almighty. After that, you don't have to pay any attention to me at all, although I wouldn't mind if you brought some wild flowers and put them on me every week or two.

Let's go and get some soup. I think I'll have the hearty chunky beef kind that's mixed in with all the gravy. I have a pack of Saltine crackers that aren't very crisp, in fact, they're absolutely soggy and stale, but when you dunk them in the soup you can't tell. And after lunch we'll go do something neat. I'll think about it when I'm eating. Also it would be a good idea to tune in to those men on the radio. I'd just like to hear what they have to say now that I know how they've managed to upset everybody in town. I won't care what they have to say. I couldn't care less. They might get a kick out of scaring people to death, but they won't scare me. Any way I look at it, I'll be happy. If it's going to end, I've got my grave. If it's not, then I still have my cabin which will always be my home. How can I be afraid when I have everything a girl could want? And besides, it's my birthday and no one is going to ruin it for me. I'm not the kind of girl who lets herself get down . . .

11

A bullet blasts through the suffocating night. It tears a seam through the sky. Elizabeth holds high the smoking rifle. A sneaky dog backs away, caught by her alert display.
"Get back you stinking dog. Or the next shot will be for you. And I will gladly watch you spit up blood and die."
Human-dog #1 speaks up.
"Row backwards! Now! Leave these people be. We are in the middle of a story. C. J. Jones has more to tell."
I turn to Elizabeth as she lowers her rifle and once more aims it at the heart of Human-dog #1. #1 is a lucky dog today. But then, Elizabeth and I have some fine luck, too. Had she fired upon Human-dog #1 as she had threatened to do, we would presently be wading in a soup of our own blood. #1 might be dead but so would we. It was smart to fire high and warn that doglet of our firepower. It was smart to hold the peace by deterring this overanxious puppy who hoped to win some favor with his master, Human-dog #1.

Even as I ponder, I see a few more boats arrive. The word has gone out tonight. There is a show in front of Thomas Jefferson. I smile over at my wife. She grins at me from ear to ear. Her eyes seem to steam with pleasure. It seems it is a thrill to fire off a gun in the middle of the night. She has a word with #1.

"Warn your bastard men that if anyone tries that trick again, I will squeeze this trigger, just like this."

And the rifle fires in the long night, explodes in my ear like one of the atom bombs which fell four hundred and one days ago, when the world was still all right.

But Elizabeth was only kidding. Her shot barely misses Human-dog #1's left ear. She must be temporarily mad. I'm waiting for something really dreadful now to happen. But all's still. All's dead but us—Elizabeth and I and the human-dogs and their beloved families. It's only us here on the still waters which sit above a dead civilization.

"There's more of that, if you inspire me to the moment."

"I'll remember that, my dear. Someone! Pass me a bottle of water."

A doggy paddles up and greets him with a green glass bottle. He snatches it out of the doggy's hand and chugs it down. That bullet seems to have greatly unnerved him. Good for Elizabeth. She could convert the dead to her way of thinking.

I would rather call the whole thing off and have time moved back two days. At least then Elizabeth and I would have our home and our fried fish and a bed which we found very pleasant in the middle of the night.

I hear noises from within the crowd. "Get on with it," and, "Tell us more of Sonia's day, you bloody pig." Okay.

Human-dog #1 nods his head. "What happens to this little girl who finds herself alone on the day when all the world died? What happens to this pathetic person you've conjured up for our evening's entertainment?"

I look at Elizabeth. She seems hard and steady now. That wretched gun sits in her hands, its one eye fastened on the frame of #1. One day I dream a gun like that will exist no more. But

WORLD ONE

today, at this hour, there is no choice but to have it at our side and have it ever ready to bolt into action.
    But to return to Sonia. To return to her day. To return to that Wednesday four hundred and one days ago.

Okay. "Sonia, on Wednesday. . ."

As you can probably guess, I'm not feeling so damn depressed, even though it's all clouded over outside, cutting out all the dazzling sunlight that made the morning so nice. I've been sitting here eating my soup wondering what the men on the radio are saying. I've been debating whether or not I should tune in and listen to them. What do you think? Do you want to get depressed too? We don't have to believe them if we don't want to. It's up to us. We can call them fakes and frauds and laugh at them, or we can take them ever so seriously and go right out of our minds. Which will it be? I don't think I'd mind going out of my mind with you—you're the easiest people I've ever been around. And I know for a fact that you won't up and quit on me, either. You certainly pay more attention to me than anyone else I've known lately. I appreciate it, too. I really do. I'll save one of my favorite cans of soup for you. You'll have to use a can opener to get into it, but after that you won't have any trouble cooking it and you'll have the meal of your life.
    I do feel rather jolly in spite of the grey. At least I had the sun in the morning. At least I took you for a long walk. I hope you didn't get as tired as me. I was the one who did all the walking, after all. You just kind of came along for the ride. But I'd take a walk with you anytime, any time at all. I don't even miss being alone when I'm with you. You people are the greatest friends a girl could ever have. I want you to know that. It means a lot to me. I hope I haven't disappointed you. I tried my best not to.
    Shall we switch on the men on the radio? We can tune into London, if you want. Boston comes in better in the

evening, so I think London would be better, at least until tonight. By your silence I take it it's okay with you. Okay by me, too. Switching on the radio and tuning in London on my fifteenth birthday. Switching off you. I've decided I don't want you to get depressed. I don't want to break up your mood.

Sonia, back again. The news stinks. They keep on jabbing about the peace talks coming apart at the seams and everywhere in the world things are going very poorly. People are panicking right and left. It doesn't look too good for us, but then, of course, it's difficult to really tell. Why don't they just go out and stop it? Wouldn't that be the easiest thing to do? After all there isn't a person alive who really wants to die after dusk. And yet there probably aren't too many people who want to be alive after dusk, either. All in all, it's going to be a royal mess. But let's not let it get to us. Why should we? We have nothing to do with it. We are innocent bystanders who have gotten mixed up with a bunch of unsavory hoodlums—namely, these governments who have gone out of their ever living minds. I guess you have to believe me now that it really might happen. I guess I was only dreaming out there on the hill when I saw you all in my dream of tomorrow. I don't think I'll turn on the radio again. It only makes me feel guilty for being alive and not being able to do anything. Does that sound strange? If my dad were alive, he'd be trying to do something. Of course, he tried before, but you all know what happened after that. At least if he were alive and kicking today, he could have told everybody, "I told you so." There would be some satisfaction in that, I'm sure. I'll say it. He told you so you foolish men on the radio. He told you so and you didn't listen and now you're all in a real fix and can't fix it. My dad knew this was going to happen—that's why he went off and shot himself in the head. He was a man of principle, he really was. I guess Mrs. Mac was a woman of principle, too. She went to sleep her own way. I wish I had the courage to do something like that. At least I could say to my dad when I caught up with him, "I died of my own free will." He'd like that. He'd be very proud of me. So, I guess

WORLD ONE

would Mrs. Mac. If only I didn't like living so much ... if only I didn't mind dying so much ... There's so much I'd leave behind. And I wouldn't have you to talk to anymore, and you'd only have heard part of what it was like to be having a birthday on a day like today.

If I keep on talking like this, I'll get depressed again and that wouldn't do. You have to understand that there is so much to live for. And even if you get mutilated by all the bombs, you'll still have lots to live for, too. You have to keep on going. You have to try to fix up everything again. That's what I would do if I were going to be around. Maybe I will—but I'm not going to hide inside some cave for a couple of years just so I can go out and see my entire world ruined. It's just not worth it. I like it too much the way it is right now. I suppose you can tell I'm mighty keen on it. I didn't walk you around up and down the roads and shore just because I was a little fond of it. I love it and always have. I wouldn't trade places with anyone for anything. I have lots to be thankful for and I know it. You probably feel that way, too, don't you? You've got eyes and ears—you've got friends—you've got a whole lifetime to look forward to. Not even all the governments in the world can take everything away from you. Try as they might, they can't get everyone. That's why I'm counting on you to fix things up next time around. Listen to what my dad had to say. Try to do what he suggested and see how it works. Call it an experiment, or whatever you want, but do try it. I wish I could be around to see how it's going to turn out. Nothing could make me happier than to see his dream come true. You'd make him happy too. Maybe he'll even know if you succeed. He could be looking down on you and seeing you, you know. He might get to know that his dream came true. I can't promise you, but it could be. You never know about anything when it comes to the afterlife. So you might seriously consider giving it a try. I'd be ever so thankful if you would. You'd have made his and my life worth living if you could do this for us. I won't say any more about it. Nobody likes to be pressed into doing something. It's just not the way people work best. They have to want to do something before it ever really happens and happens well. So I'll shut up about it and go on about my business and not give you a pain.

I'll tell you one thing—I wasn't dreaming early this morning about hearing those men on the radio. They still sound like crying children, even more so. It's enough to make me laugh. I'm glad I didn't let you listen to them. You'd have been as ashamed of them as I am. They're all taking about how they are going to be talking to the people until the end—how brave they are! It's really nice of them to be so brave—it's just a little too late to be really brave anymore. They should have been brave a long time ago and fixed things up—that would have been brave. That would have been the smart thing to do. But now they're just crying like children about what a mess everything is and are putting on this brave act about staying with the people until the end. What a lot of crap. Who do they think they're kidding? Not you and me. We know better. We're not fools like the rest of them.

I've done it again. I've let my coffee get cool and that's one of the more exasperating things I continue to do. It may seem like a little thing on a day like today—but on a day like today I want everything to be right. I want to do and know everything. I want to live my life to the fullest and have a grand time. If there was ever a day that should be perfect, this is it. It's now or never. The last chance. The last chance for being in love with everything.

Do you know what I won't regret? I won't regret having to eat another one of these stale Saltine crackers. You see when the fog comes in almost every night, the dampness gets to them. You can't keep them dry. Even if you put them in a tin box they still get stale in a week or two. It drives me crazy because I like Saltines. I could eat them for breakfast, lunch and dinner. I could eat them for a bedtime snack. If you want to know what kind of present I'd like, I'd like a fresh box of Saltines that wouldn't get stale. That's not too much to ask for, is it?

If you could arrange that, I would die in heaven. I really would.

WORLD ONE

When I get to thinking, I like to think on my bed. There's no better place in the world to think than on one's own bed. There's just something about lying on your back and looking straight up that brings out the most creative thoughts, whether you want to think them or not. So I'm lying on my bed at just about the time when the sun is directly overhead, thinking creatively about what I should do. It's like my ceiling isn't there anymore. I don't see the planks of wood or the black electrical wires or the gaps between the beams. I don't see any of that. It's more like the roof has flown off and is out in the world spinning like a top somewhere and I can see the brooding clouds which have so much to think about, like me.

You know once when I was very young—I couldn't have been more than four or five years old (this was when my dad and I were living down south)—I tried to dig a tunnel to China. I guess I wanted to travel so much and see the whole wide world that I couldn't wait any longer until I grew up—so I wanted to get busy right away and dig a hole to China and crawl my way to the other side of the world. Nuts, wasn't it? But I believed that it was possible and so I set out to do it. I didn't get very far—only a few feet before my blisters discouraged me and I had to come in for dinner. But thinking back on it now, I don't think it was such a crazy thing to try to do. In fact, I'm wondering whether I shouldn't try to dig a hole in the earth where I can hide until everything is all right again. Don't think I'm a coward like the rest of them, either. I'm my dad's daughter, and I'm just thinking about doing the right thing. I mean, someone has to be left alive to take care of the world after it's ruined. Maybe my dad would want me to try to stay alive so I could go on telling his story to people like you. And if I stayed alive by hiding in a hole in the earth—if the Almighty allowed me to survive along with some others—then I would take that as a sign that I should go around the world like my dad. I'd go to China and Russia and America and Europe and Africa—everywhere—and I'd tell the people who survived exactly what my dad thought about how to have peace in the world. I would want to talk to everyone, too. I'd find myself the best translators in all the languages that were ever made and I would have them repeat everything I said, or my dad said, until they couldn't bear it anymore and simply buckled in and did what he said they should do—make this law for the world—this law that would save the world the next time around. Do you think my dad would want me to try to do that? He never exactly asked me to, but then he probably thought I was still too young for that kind of thing and didn't want me to get too involved and end up like him. I still have all his papers and speeches. I could use those and practice up on them so I could say them all really well. If his spirit were roaming around the earth and he happened to hear me, that would be nice too, but that wouldn't be the reason why I'd do it. I'd want to do it so everyone in the world could live in peace and not bother anymore with all these wars that have gotten worse and worse. Each time they get worse. This time will be the WORST with a capital W-O-R-S-T.

Would that make my hiding in the earth have some meaning? I wouldn't be just another coward would I? A coward who is afraid to die ... I'm not afraid because my dad wasn't afraid and Mrs. Mac wasn't afraid. I just want to make sure I live my life of my own free will and at the same time try to make it better. How could all of the people of the world let themselves get into this mess? You know how? Because they didn't respect their own free will. They didn't believe they could change things and had to change things. They didn't have the guts to believe in their own free will. Well, I do.

That's why I'm lying in bed looking up at the brooding grey clouds without taking any notice of the fact that the ceiling is off spinning around someplace in the sky. I've simply removed the ceiling from my thoughts, and this is what the people of the world should have done. They should have thought beyond what was and what had been to what could be. It wasn't as if my dad were asking them to dig a tunnel to China—that was my idea. He just believed that all governments and people had to live under one law so that there could be peace. So that's why I'm wondering whether or not it's my duty to try to survive and then go around the whole world telling everybody all this over again. It seems to me that they would have to listen then—after all, the earth would be in such a state of ruin that they could hardly say no to

WORLD ONE

trying something new. It just seems to me that the people of the world are so hardheaded that you can't tell them something new without everything falling to pieces before they'll listen. My pillow is very comfortable for this kind of thinking . . . It allows all the bad thoughts of mine to flow out of me and it keeps the good ones in. Some people like to sleep with two pillows. I never could stand that. One suits me fine and is very helpful to my thinking.

One thing troubles me though. It will take a long time to dig a hole as deep as it would have to be. And then there would be other problems—like storing food and making a door for it and keeping out the bad air. I don't know how these people expect to survive for long in their caves. Don't they know what they're in for? Don't they know that only the very, very lucky will survive—like you? But you'll survive, won't you? You'll survive and listen to my tape, and I hope you'll be happy that you've gotten to know me a little. And I hope you won't blame my dad for everything that's been done to you. And I hope you won't blame me either. A girl can't do too much until she's at least twenty-one and that's so far off I can't even dream of it except to hope that I'll be a bride and go to Paris on my honeymoon.

Right now I see the ceiling again and that's never a good sign. It usually means that my good ideas weren't such good ideas after all and that I better leave off thinking for a while. Did you know I have a red bedspread with patches of blue along the edges? Did you know my pillow case has white lace on the edges, too? It's all very nice and makes me feel cushy even when I feel blue. Sometimes at night I light a candle by my bed and read for hours until the words begin to swirl around on the pages. Then I know it's time for sleep and I blow out the candle and watch the red hot ember glow until it simply fades away. Then I fall asleep to the smell of candle smoke and forget about the world until morning when I'm all ready to go again. I'm talking about this to you because I've been wondering whether I'm ever going to sleep in this bed again. Can you imagine how strange it is to think that you're never going to sleep in your bed again? Just think about that for a while . . . A girl my age shouldn't have to think about such things—especially not on her birthday. But then I'm like everyone else. They all have this problem whether they know it or not. I don't suppose the African natives know it, or the aborigines know it or the Eskimos. I don't imagine they have radios and are spending their last day alive worrying about the rest of the world and why it's about to be ruined. Frankly, they're probably a lot better off that way. Who wants to worry about dying when there is so much living? And who wants to waste all of their time getting so upset and regretting all the things that they never had a chance to do? Not me. I want to live. I want to be happy. I want to dream away the day and celebrate my birthday, and I want to celebrate it with you—you, who are my last friends in the world. You, who don't mind me talking to you and telling you about my dad.

Have you had a nice morning, too? Have I made you happy by taking you to all my favorite places? There is so much more that we can do. We have all afternoon to do whatever we want to. I'll tell you one thing, I'm glad all this isn't happening on a day I had school. I would hate to spend the time inside the classroom with the whole wide world outside my window. And as for that hole I suggested I might go out and dig and hide in—I'm not going to do it. It's too late for that kind of thing. And as for trying to help my dad by going around the world trying to fix things up after today, I think he'd rather see me have a good birthday and talk to people like you. It was for people like you that he tried so hard. He never wanted anything to happen to you—and he never wanted me to live to see this day. He wanted me to grow up right like I'm supposed to. I wish he would come and visit me. I wish he and I could just start all over again in a new world in another time when everything wasn't so blue.

Drifting away on a grey cloud momentarily, while I sit on my porch and wish the world away. I am wishing the world away as I sit on my porch and contemplate what I will do for the rest of the day ... Dream away, dream away, dream away

WORLD ONE

day. I am so privileged to ride away on that grey cloud while wishing the world away ... I'm a lousy poet.

I don't blame myself for it. Why should I? It takes time to be a poet and I haven't had the time. It takes time to do anything, and I haven't been able to do much of that either. And the time is ticking away as the grey cloud is drifting away and I miss my dad. You know, I had a dream about him the other night. It was the first dream I'd had about him since he died. And he was laughing in this dream—his face was so happy and bright—and he was laughing, like everything was going to be all right. I can't tell you how it made me feel. I felt so free when I woke up. And I've carried that picture of him to this very moment. It was a special kind of dream that makes everything seem worthwhile. He really made me happy coming to me that way. I mean he could have been frowning or looking terribly sad, but he wasn't. He was just laughing the way he always used to even when things were bad. Maybe secretly for the past couple of days I've been hoping that he'll somehow come back to me. Wouldn't that be lovely? I keep thinking that he'll walk right down the road and show his face at my window—or there'll be a quiet knocking at the door and I'll answer and there he'll be—and he'll be laughing with joy. That's what I wish for. I wish he'd just come home to me and hold me and be happy with me. We could take walks again and talk about starting the whole world over again. That was one of his favorite subjects. If he were alive we could have done that. I would have been able to help him now. Before I was too young and I didn't understand everything he had to say, but now I do. And I want to help. I want him to come home so we can begin again. It's still not too late. The world hasn't been ruined. Maybe the men in the governments will listen to him now. Maybe they'll think favorably on his plan—and if not the governments, then maybe the people of the world will unite behind him and tell the governments what they want them to do. If my dad can come laughing into my dreams, then I don't see any reason why he can't come back to me and keep me company on my birthday. I've already been without him for half of the day—he'll be coming soon, you don't have to worry about that. He'll be coming soon and he'll be laughing before it's too late.

Wouldn't you like that? It would save you all so much grief. And I could grow up then and meet you when you come to Sandy Cove. My dad and I could find you all a place to live. There's a house for rent up on the hill—you could have that one and we could visit in the afternoons and on Sundays after church. There's no one I'd rather have for company than you and my dad. And since Mrs. Mac is gone I will need you even more. We could take care of each other and my dad could show you places that even I don't know about around here. You'll like this house up on the hill. It's got two chimneys and a large round kitchen with a view of the woods and outside it's got its own fresh water well. You will be very happy there and I'll be happy having you in town. Won't that be nice? Isn't that what you want? Isn't that what we all want? A nice town to live in in a beautiful spot of the world? If only my dad would just come back ... if only he'd just step out onto the road and laugh.

But he won't. My dreams aren't any good. I think they'll come true when I dream them, and then they don't. Don't ask me why I can have a dream that seems so real and then not have it come true. Maybe I just put all of the hopes I have in my dreams. Maybe that's what's wrong with me. Maybe if I put all of my hopes in reality they would have a better chance of coming true. I don't know how I'd do that, but if I could, I would. It's not fair to have such lovely dreams and then have them only be dreams. I'd rather that they just come true. I'd rather not even have any dreams at night and save them for the day when they wouldn't be dreams at all—but true. But my dad won't be stepping out onto the road, will he? You know that. When you're dead, you're dead. You don't come back to the people who are living. You go on—you live in a new world—you have different friends and a different family. You don't even remember who you knew from the old world. It's as different as the land and the sea. That's the way it is—I don't have to be dead to know that. Otherwise we would see all sorts of people who were dead at one time coming back and visiting with those who they loved when they were alive, and that doesn't happen, now does it? There's one time and one time only when you're alive in this world and right now it's my time. I'm not angry with my dad

WORLD ONE

for not being here. He would be here if he could. He can't. That's just another one of the laws of nature that I've been talking about. And all I have are my dreams that can't come true—can't possibly come true—and I know this and yet I still want to be able to dream them and think that they'll come true, sometime soon.

So maybe I'll just believe that my dad is coming back, like I believe in all the rest of my dreams. I can't be punished for that. And I'll be happier thinking that way. And even if my dad and I can't start the world all over again when he comes back, at least we can die together tonight. That would be a whole lot better than dying alone. I'm being morbid again. One minute I'm happy, the next minute I'm not. I think I live with two minds. I think I live in two worlds. I think I'll have two deaths—one real and one not. Either that or I'll dream that I've died when I'm not dead, or I'll be dead and dream that I'm alive. Any way you look at it, I'm getting screwed up.

I've decided to compose a song for my dad and I'm going to dedicate it to you—you who are the best friends a girl ever had. I don't have a title for it yet. Most good titles are hard to come by and song titles are the worst because all the good ones have been used up over the years—long before I got interested in thinking them up. So I can't tell you the title quite yet which is too bad because titles are also good for setting the right mood.

"We are just a family like any family in the world." Here the tempo is slow and nostalgic, almost haunting. "We lived and dreamed of things to come, never once thinking that it would end." I might change the lyrics a bit here so they more or less rhyme. "But something changed, and here we are running out of time with so much we haven't done." Did you note the deep regret I had in my voice?—that's really supposed to be the message of the song. Most songs don't try to have messages, but mine do. It's important to say something when you are expecting people to listen to you. "And so we wait for the last hour of the day when the lights will go out and the day will turn blue." Here I'm talking about a day like today, of course. "But you should always know how much I've missed you now that I'm soon to follow you."

I wouldn't call it a classic or something that would have been played on the radio in Halifax, but I like what it has to say and I hope you like it too. I made it up for you and dad. Mrs. Mac never liked my songs too much. She didn't exactly tell me she didn't, but I could tell. She would always mumble something about how pleasant they were. I hope I've improved since the last time I sang for her. Anyway, I don't think she was musically inclined. Mostly she liked to hear herself talking about the old days—that was her music and those were her dreams and they were all true. It's only me who doesn't have dreams that come true, only me . . .

Switching off now while I find a way to take you along Digby Neck. You really should hear something about the coastline. There's no more beautiful coastline in the world. That's what the guidebooks say, anyway. I wouldn't know, I haven't travelled far and wide.

I don't think anyone could ever accuse me of stealing. I'm inside an old jeep that used to belong to the gas station attendant who's long gone now, safe and warm inside some cave on some hillside somewhere. I don't think he'll mind my borrowing it for a few hours, do you? After all, Mrs. Mac taught me to drive in case of emergencies and I would consider this an emergency. And if he had really wanted to have his jeep he would have taken it with him, don't you think?

Let's see . . . turn the key—rooom—roooom! It works! Release the brake, easy now, all the way down. Now for the tricky bit—push down the clutch, it needs oiling I would say, and grind the gears into first—not too much noise, clutch all the way down, releasing clutch, gear in place and off we go— a little bumpy but straight ahead . . . rooom! roooooom! You and I are the masters of the road.

Looking down at the dials we have plenty of gas and the

WORLD ONE

oil light isn't blinking red and the whole thing started up without the choke. I forgot the choke. But when it's warm it's completely unnecessary, like a third arm or eye or ear. Off we go, away from my village of Sandy Cove, and where we will end up nobody knows. That's the fun of it . . . Grinding down into second gear to stop the whining of the engine. A little jerky, but now it's smooth, smooth as drifting on those grey brooding clouds. Wait until third gear. We will cruise like water on glass along this deserted highway that runs along Digby Neck. Do you think there's a head to Digby's Neck? Do you think there are arms and legs? I've never really thought about it. I suppose there must be. How can there be a neck without a head? Somewhere to the north or south there must be a head to Digby's Neck. I'll let you know if I come to it—it should be a gorgeous head, crowned with many curls—green curls that smell of trees. And where might be the eyes of this gorgeous head? Perhaps eyes of water, large as pools or lakes. Will they blink at me as we go by? We are going into third gear, please excuse the noise and the sudden bumps. We are in the middle of an emergency so it's okay that we've all gone for a ride . . .

There's something dreamy about flying down the highway, zooming up and down the bends of the terrain. It's the closest we'll ever come to flying today, so enjoy the feeling of accomplishment. You may never have the chance to drive again, nor I. So let's take some pleasure in watching the world go streaming by. The turns come quickly, the trees begin to blur, but my pictures of the sea are cystal clear . . . Is it watching us, too? Does it see us fly? Does it admire this ingenious form of transportation? We are in the middle of Digby's Neck. Who was Digby? I would never marry a man named Digby. Digby would be very sad to know that his land will soon be sick. But I love it, Mr. Digby. I would have put my name on it if I had been here first.

Those men in the governments want to chop off my neck—Sonia's Neck. They'll make good company for the hatchet-man. If only the hatchet-man would do his work on them, then we would be safe, then we would be free, then tonight I could go to sleep in my own bed and wake up for my party tomorrow and be with you. Hatchet-man, the people are in need of you! Go fly around the world and do your best. We are all behind you. You can be the captain of the guard and protect our citizens. If you do this for us, I will pardon you and treat you well. There will be no revenge on you for chopping off their necks. But you do not hear me, do you? You, too, are hiding in the woods or in some cave down by the sea. You are a coward like the rest of them. You treasure your neck too much to do anything for the good of everyone. Hatchet-man, I am as afraid of you as I am of the governments of men.

I am afraid, now I know I am afraid and there isn't anything I can do but talk to you. Are you still listening to me? Do you even care about the way it was when I was alive? Or are your hearts too broken to hear anymore? I understand. I sympathize. I'm just talking so I won't go mad. I don't want to be afraid. I want to enjoy this day. I want to be so happy to be alive, but I'm not. It's getting sticky for me. My mouth is drying up and the soup in my stomach is turning over and over like currents in the sea. I admit I am really scared. There's no one out here. They've all gone under and they've left me to die on Digby's Neck where I was just beginning to have such a good time.

Do you have good times where you are? Do you have fun riding automobiles? Do you have dreams about tomorrow? Are you safe and sitting by the fire thinking I'm just another nut? I wasn't always so strange. I didn't used to talk like this. I was never afraid, did you know that? But then I always knew that there would be a tomorrow and the next. I should have grown up more quickly. I should have done all the things I always wanted to do. But now what? I'm too afraid. I couldn't marry if I wanted to. I wouldn't want to have a child. I wouldn't want him to be here when I died. Who would take care of him then?

Up and down, down and up we go . . . up and up and up . . . No one's on the road but you and me. I wish we could stop and talk to someone soon or I wish they'd stop and talk to me. You must think I'm the only one who's ever lived in the world. Well, that's not true. There are more people than you can count who live in the world at this very moment. Isn't it strange that it seems like there's only me? I'm the

WORLD ONE

aborigine—the last and the first, right? I was just fooling. I am the only one who's living in the world. There was no Mrs. Mac. I imagined her for you. There was no town of Sandy Cove. I made that up too. I made everything up. I was just playing. There isn't going to be a war. There is no hatchet-man. Everything is fine and I was just fooling and we will be all right and I will go ahead and have a child. He'll be fine. We are all aborigines and that's just great by me. We live by the sea and run naked on the rocks and feast on seaweed and converse with fish. We don't build bombs and we don't have wars and lots of people don't get hurt. That's the way it is with us. We learned long ago not to do things like that. We have laws against it. We found it works best that way, and it does.

Down around we go, me and the jeep which I am using because this is an emergency. I am having an emergency on my fifteenth birthday and I am glad you are here to share it with me because I don't know what I'd do without you. And you are riding with me on Digby's Neck and searching for his head. And I am not afraid, I am not afraid of what the hatchet-man might do, because he really isn't going to come and get us and chop off Digby's Neck.

My driving is frightful. I'm glad you can't see me grinding these gears. And the owner would have a fit, I'm sure. Yet none of it really matters, does it? The countryside is floating by. The sea is on my right and is staying calm. It doesn't yet know what's going to happen to it. I'm glad of that. I wouldn't want the fishes to worry. I want them to go on living hopefully, like me. Would you like to hear some music? Maybe the men on the radio have gone home to be with their families. It won't do them any good to stay where they are. It would be better for them to go home and be with their families until tonight. They should all spend their last hours at home with the most important people that they know. The fields are streaming by to my left, gorgeous open fields and meadows which are blooming with wild flowers and high grasses. The wild flowers and high grasses don't know either. That is good. It's much better that they don't have to think about it. They will know soon enough.

I'm going to try to find some music on the radio. I'll be switching off until I do, just in case the men on the radio haven't gone home. I'll miss you while I'm gone, I really will.

Back on the air, with no music. There are men talking on the radio everywhere, from the top of the dial to the very bottom. No one's gone home and no one is playing any more music. The music is gone. It won't ever come back. Beethoven might as well have never written his sonatas and I might as well have never listened to them. Everything that ever was is now pointless. What was the use of everyone trying so hard to do great things when it all comes down to this? You don't have an answer for me, do you? Even if you could speak to me you wouldn't have an answer. There is no point. Everything has gotten to be useless and nothing is important now but living for as long as you can be happy. That's all there is. There is nothing and I am in the middle of nothing, all because the men in the governments didn't find the answer.

I am driving very badly as I said. I should have had more practice in case of emergencies. Of course I never dreamed I'd be driving with you today. I never expected any of this—not the men on the radio—not Mrs. Mac—I never in a million years would have imagined that I would become such good friends with you. I don't even know you. I don't know anyone anymore so that's okay. But you know me, don't you? You know practically everything there is to know about me and about my dad. You'll remember me, won't you? You'll remember what my dad stood for, won't you? If I can accomplish just that much, I'll die a happy girl. That's the whole point of our conversation. That's why I'm trying to do such a good job on it. It's my last chance, isn't it? It's now or never. I have to live now . . . today . . . this afternoon . . . while I still can. You can understand that, can't you? That makes sense to you, doesn't it? I'm not as nuts as I said, am I? I've got a good head on my shoulders and my dad said I was the bravest girl he ever knew. He said I had guts—and I do. I don't go and hide in caves or dig holes to hide in underground. I'm living my last hours out in the open with the only family I have—you. You are my family now. You are the ones I'm

WORLD ONE

living for now, and I'm proud of it. I'm living for the future, for the people who will survive, and I'm trying to tell them how beautiful it was to live on Digby's Neck in Sandy Cove.

I'm turning off the road now. There's a meadow I want to go and visit filled with wild flowers and high grasses, and the sun is coming out over it. The sun is showing me where I ought to be. I ought to be in this meadow with my family. You're coming along with me to the sunny spot where all the flowers grow.

In the center of it all, now . . . flowers to my right and left. The wild scents are intoxicating. I'm drunk. I never drink but I am drunk.

Dreaming of dreaming I am floating away today . . . I am looking at the boy of my dreams—this one's for me. He has brought me red and white flowers, how romantic of him. And most beautiful of all, he has brought me a ring. It has no diamonds, diamonds are such icy things. He's brought me a band of gold—gold like the early morning light of the sun. How extraordinarily happy he's made me. His ring is a perfect fit. It's so warm on my hand. The sun does not warm me like this band. How I've dreamed of this man who would find me in the meadows and ask for my hand . . . I'm glad you are with me to hear him speak. His voice is more tender than the sounds of streams . . . You wish me the best, don't you? You want us to be happy, don't you? I know you do. My dad would wish us to be too. He would like this beautiful boy. He would accept him as his son. Even now I feel him accepting this boy who has come and found me in the meadows where I always dreamed he would be when the time was finally right. And the time is right. I must die with my family. We are to be married soon. We are to be married now. I'm so happy you could be with me. We will all be silent for a while . . .

We have just returned from our honeymoon. We have so many bags to unpack and he has bought me so many clothes I hardly know what to do with them. And the doctor has just informed us that I am to have a child. It all seems so soon but it will be a gorgeous child and it will live on after me and after him and we are glad of it. You will come to know it and he will be alive when we are gone and I ask you to look out for him. If there comes a time when he does not remember us, play this tape for him. He should know me as I was and he should know about his grandfather, too. Every child should know his grandfather and what he believed in. Every child should dream about tomorrow and know about all the yesterdays that came before him. That's the way of it, I know. We will be silent for a while . . .

We've had twins—one girl like me and one boy like him. What better way to celebrate a birthday than to have twins. They will grow together and happily we will raise them and show them the beauty of the world around us. We will hide them from the hatchet-man—he will never touch them. They will be free and not fear the governments of men. They will live to change the world as you will live to change the world. And they will always remember their grandfather for what he tried to do. We will be silent for a while . . .

The children are grown and they've gone on and still it is my birthday and still my husband loves me as he loved me when he came to these meadows and brought me wild flowers and a band of gold. We are old and happy and quite grey. But we remember our lives so fondly. We have had the life of our dreams . . . and the grass is high and all the flowers are in bloom and our children have grown and gone on and today we are celebrating my birthday. He always remembers my birthday. Not once in all these years did he ever forget. How could he, though? That was the day on which he found me here waiting to live my dreams.

Did you hear that rolling thunder? Did you hear it break my dream? I am who I was before. I never had a chance to do those things. I was just hoping everything would turn out

WORLD ONE

that way—that I would marry a boy and we would have children ... You want me to have all those things, don't you? I want you to have the very best, too. I wouldn't be your friend if I didn't. That's what friends are for—to hope for the best for you. And I do hope for the best for you. I want nothing but the best for you and for your children and for all the children who will someday be born.

But I won't have that someday. I'm going to die tonight, so say the men on the radio who have taken all the music away from me. Maybe if they stopped talking the world would not end today. Maybe if the people of the world just closed their ears and paid no attention nothing would happen. Then there wouldn't be any cause for an emergency and I could take this jeep back to where it belongs and I could have a nicer birthday.

I can't help but be mad at my dad ... If he had only made the men in governments listen to him, if he had only spoken in a louder voice to the rest of the world, all this wouldn't be plaguing me. And it is plaguing me—it's been plaguing me since before dawn, since the middle of the night when I should have been sleeping in my bed and dreaming of tomorrow.

I heard my dad's voice in that rolling thunder. I heard it loud and clear. If he had only been the voice of thunder when he was living he could have made everyone hear what he had to say. He could have rolled to the far east and to the far west, south and north. He could have been everywhere at the same time and the people would have listened and they would have made their men in governments do what they wanted them to do. Why didn't the Almighty make his voice as loud as that rolling thunder? Why did He wait until now? Now when there is no time left—just a few hours more—and I haven't grown up and met the one I will love and have the children that I will love and do all the things a girl should have the opportunity to do.

I don't want to blame my dad. But he's broken my dreams. He's made me be afraid of what's going to happen. He's left me alone without any life left to live. He could have saved me if he had been the voice of rolling thunder. He still could have saved everyone if they had only had the chance to listen to me and read his notes. They won't listen to me. They would only laugh at me and call me what I am, NUTS! "She is nuts and we will put her in an institution." They will do that for my own good. You see, I wouldn't have a chance. I am just too young to try to save the world.

The world isn't going to be saved, you know that don't you? You've gotten the picture by now, even though I haven't let you listen to the men on the radio. You have enough to worry about and anyway, it's just too damn depressing and I don't want you to be depressed anymore than you probably are, considering what the world's done to you without your having any say in it.

That's why I guess I'm so depressed. I didn't have any say in it. The closest I ever got to having a say in it was through my dad, but my dad didn't have the voice of rolling thunder any more than I do. No one's had the voice of rolling thunder to tell people the right thing to do to avoid this kind of mess that we've got ourselves into today. Maybe something good will happen this afternoon. Maybe somebody on earth will be given the voice of rolling thunder and everything will turn out okay. We can at least hope for that, can't we? We can at least pray for that, can't we? I wouldn't ever want to be accused of giving in unless I absolutely, positively had to. I bet right now there are millions of people praying for and wishing for someone to have that voice of thunder. That would be only natural, wouldn't it? No one really wants to die. No one really wants to just lose everything they ever worked for and dreamed of. I'm not the only one. I'm damn sure of that. It's just that, I guess, people can't cope with things that are so much larger than them. That's the way of it, isn't it? That's why we need a big, booming voice of thunder to tell us the right thing to do—a voice that everyone hears and wants to obey. If the Almighty could just do that for us it would be about the best thing He could ever do.

I don't expect any miracles. They're not likely to happen unless all the people at once cry out with one voice—a voice we could hear all the way around the world—then something might happen, then something might change. Then we all might have a chance to live and grow up and dream about a thousand tomorrows to come.

WORLD ONE

And I wouldn't have to be so mad at my dad. Why am I blaming him? It wasn't his fault. At least he tried to help and make things better and find a way for the world to live in peace. That much he did, and that's a darn sight better than most, I'm telling you that right now, and don't you forget it.

So what am I doing sitting like a nut in the middle of this meadow dreaming about a beautiful boy I'll never ever meet? I've got better things to do than that. I guess I'm glad that rolling thunder came along. It woke me up so I wouldn't waste any more time dreaming of tomorrows that will never come. It's this minute that I should think about. It's the color of the grass and the look of all the flowers that I should think about. I should snap out of all my self-pity and get to work— get to work living as much as I can while the living is good. That's why I heard my dad's voice in the thunder. He was telling me to snap out of it and get to work and do as much as I can while I can. I'm not really mad at you, dad. I know it wasn't your fault. I just wish the world had listened to you and understood what you had to say, like I've explained all morning to my friends who will be even more upset that you didn't succeed.

It's so quiet and lovely right now. A sea wind is pushing everything gently around and the clouds are moving—they are moving very fast. Where they are going, I don't know. They're probably going to rise up into the heavens to escape what's going to happen tonight. They're probably just going to abandon us to our misery. I wouldn't blame them either, if they did. Who would want to be around when the world goes mad? Not me. Not you. Not anyone. Not even the men in the governments who can't find out how to make peace.

I better go now. I better get going and do something interesting. I guess it's still okay that I drive this jeep. We're still in the middle of an emergency, right? We still don't know whether or not everything will be all right. But I'll tell you one thing. As soon as I hear that voice of rolling thunder tell everyone what to do, or as soon as I hear all the people in the world cry out with one voice, I'll return it immediately. I won't hesitate a second. I'll drive back to Sandy Cove so fast you won't even know I was gone. That's the moment I'll be looking forward to. That's the moment that will make this birthday the happiest day of my life. And you'll hear it too. I'll make sure you hear it and I'll have it forever on tape and in some future time they'll be able to play it back again and everyone will hear the voice of rolling thunder that saved the world on Wednesday.

Do I detect the sprinkling of the rain? My rolling thunder has brought the merry rain and it has come to wash me clean, to wash away the evil spirits that make me feel on the edge of despair. How kind of them to think of me and to favor me with their presence. That is twice today that I have been touched by showers. Three times is a charm. I will have to cover you up, my friends. It will not do for you to get rusty and freeze up on me. My link to the other world must run smoothly by all means. Anything less will be quite unsatisfactory. Allow me to put you under my shirt. We can't take a chance driving on the roads while they are wet. We can't afford to have any accidents. There is no time to go to the hospital. There is no time to put a cast on my foot if I should drive into a tree and hurt myself. And every turn in the road is a possible Dead Man's Curve and you don't want me to end up like the children, do you? You don't want me to end up like the dead man who lost control, now do you? I shouldn't think so! After all, we are in this together, until the sweet or bitter end. I know you are very fond of me and I of you. You might not know it now, but you will when I am gone and there is only my voice to remember me by. In that way I'm like the world. When it's here, people are less fond of it. When it's gone they will regret it. How they will regret it. You are regretting it right now, aren't you? You are wishing right now that every one of those men in government took a bad turn on Dead Man's Curve and is lying dead in some ravine somewhere. Don't be ashamed to think like that. It's okay. I understand. If I had my way, I'd like to see them down in that ravine, too.

Raining and raining, the rain is falling, falling down on Sonia, the worldly-wise aborigine. Do the fishes in the sea

WORLD ONE

know it is raining and raining down on me, down on them, down on all of us? Would they care? Not in the least. One more drop here or there makes no difference to them at all. They expect it. They expect their world to be nourished and replenished. They have done nothing wrong to make the Almighty mad at them as we have done. We, not you. You didn't have anything to do with it, you know that. So why should the fish be punished as we are about to be? Is there no justice? At least allow the fish to live. Think of all the brothers and sisters down there. Think of all the mothers and fathers down there. Think of all the little babies and babies to be. None of them should be punished. That would be so unfair. That would be a crime. The Almighty doesn't commit crimes. He does not punish those who commit no crimes. He is above that, and He has been keeping score. He knows who is bad and who is good. He will not harm the brothers and sisters and mothers and fathers of the sea. And I am sinking down into the sea as the rain is raining down and I am underneath the water and it is so wet and it is so warm and it is so wonderful. I can't tell you how right it makes me feel. And I know that you won't get rusty. You were meant to follow me and no harm will ever come to you as long as you are with me. So don't abandon me. Stay close. Listen well. There are many things for us to experience down here.

I miss the sun. A drawback, nothing more. Did you ever think there would be tall grasses down here? They are so soft on my back. They glide with me—they make me comfortable. It is like floating on pillows. I am sinking and you are with me and the only thing we've left behind is the sun. We will not be punished down here. We have done nothing wrong. We are with our brothers and sisters and mothers and fathers and we will not be punished. We are away from everything that will harm us. Don't think I am running away. I plan to go back. I just want to visit my brothers and sisters and mothers and fathers one more time. That's not too much to ask. I know it isn't. Pretty soon everyone will want to do this—but only those people who aren't afraid are allowed to come down here and visit before the day is done. We are special people this way. And you are more special than me because you get to do this and not have to die. But you will remember that I was allowed to do this before I died, won't you? I want you to remember me as a special kind of person, a special kind of girl who was allowed to visit her friends in the sea before she went to sleep. If Mrs. Mac hadn't gone to sleep she would have come with us too. There is so much room down here for her. She would have all the room in the world ... She had many friends down here. Did you know that? She wasn't just a person—she was a spirit too. And spirits can go anywhere they want to. That's why I get to go down here. I'm a spirit, too. I get to go anywhere as long as I'm living and not hiding out in caves.

Mrs. Mac? Mrs. Mac? Do you hear me still? Are you down here with us? Has the Almighty allowed you to come in spite of your sleep? You don't have to answer me. I'll understand if that is part of the arrangement. I can understand if you're not allowed to talk to anyone, even me. I just hope the Almighty didn't punish you and not let you come and visit your friends in the sea. He wouldn't do that. He knows how special you were, how special you were to me. He knows all that so I don't have to worry. But if you can speak, I'd like to hear you. I promised my friends I'd let them hear you. I'm sorry I didn't find you before you went to sleep. That was my fault. But I had been up very late and I hadn't gotten any sleep and I wanted to show my new friends all my favorite places. I'm making excuses, I know. I should have looked in on you. I should have known the men on the radio would have upset you, but I didn't think you would pay any attention to them. And I had this dream that I wanted to tell you about—this dream about tomorrow. My friends were with me and they were laughing and we were having a party and everything was all right. I wanted you to know about that dream and I was coming to tell you when I found you fast asleep and not moving and not breathing and I did the best I could to bury you and clean up the store the way you would want it. If you are down here with us and you can speak, say something nice to me. I don't want you to be mad at me or have you think I abandoned you—I didn't. I wouldn't. That would be the last thing I'd do. I just hope you got to go down here and visit before your spirit went away, because you are

WORLD ONE

a very special person and it was your right to come down here with the rest of the innocent spirits of the sea.

    I don't think it's raining anymore upstairs. I feel much better for having been down here visiting with my brothers and sisters. I think it's time to go back upstairs where the wild flowers are in bloom and where the grass is even higher than it is down here. And I miss the sun. I'm going back up there to go on with my day. It's not every day a girl has such a birthday. It's not every day a girl has such an emergency on her special day of the year. I've told you, I want to make the best of it. I want to do everything and see everything. I want everything to be real and lovely and right.

I'm quite all right, really. I've come back from the sea and everything is fine but the sun is still gone from the sky and that makes me unhappy. But the rain has moved out to sea where the fishes expect it to be and we are alone once again. Don't tell me you're rusty. I won't believe it. I took extra precautions. I put you under my shirt so no water could spill on you. We're both okay, and doing better all the time. At least we got to be away for a while. At least we got to visit friends. At least I won't die without having said good-bye.

I don't have to say good-bye to you, do I? You're not going to abandon me. You are the ones I love, now. There's no one else but you and we have to stick together. Without you, I would be nothing. Without me, you wouldn't know what the world was like. So we must trust each other, always trust each other and never forget that we've come a long way together and must continue to do so. You are my world now. You are what I am living for. You are everything to me, my world, my future. That doesn't sound strange does it? It's only natural for a girl to want somebody to talk to and share her world with and enjoy life with. I know you don't know me. I know, too, that you probably haven't been born yet, or if you have, you're a long way away from here. Maybe you come from the Arctic? Could you be Eskimos? Could you be from Greenland? That's not too far from here. Perhaps you landed by boat like the Vikings long ago? Could you be from another world altogether? Have you come from the stars to visit our planet? Are you ashamed at what you've found? Your brothers have disgraced you, haven't they? They've ruined everything. You wouldn't do that, would you? Long ago you found the answer to peace in your time and so you came visiting to see what your brothers were up to. How I wish you had come sooner! How I wish you had come today and picked me up and taken me away. Is everyone in the world dead? Have you looked everywhere for some people who might have survived? I'm kidding myself. You haven't come from another planet—you have come from this planet, this world that has been ruined. And you are mutilated and your bones are brittle and you have been sick for many years because of the poisoned air everywhere and you are listening to me because I am one of the few people in the world who has found a way to tell you what it was like before everything happened and turned out so sadly.

Why don't you talk to me? Why don't you respond to my questions? You shouldn't be wary of me. I've never done anything to harm you and I am in need of your company right now. I want to hear another voice say something nice to me—congratulate me for not hiding in the caves and for not being a coward. You could say something nice about my dad, if not about me. You could call him a hero, sing his praises, honor his name . . . But you don't do any of this. You never speak, the cat's got your tongue and I'm running out of things to say. Here I've kept you from getting rusty—I've taken you everywhere I know and I get no thanks, not a word of thanks for all I've done. You have shameful manners, that much I know. And I was going to invite you to my party. I was going to give you the rest of my Folger's coffee after I was gone—I was even going to let you sleep in my bed and live in my cabin. But now I'm very mad at you. You are everything to me and yet you won't even say my name. You're just a machine and you don't have any heart. Well, what if I do run out of things to say. Then there won't be any conversation. Then you won't have any company. We'll just

WORLD ONE

be silent and listen to the world groan. I won't even say goodbye. I'll just let the tape run out and then you'll be sorry. Then you'll be sorry you didn't bother talking to me. It's not very much to ask for a little conversation is it? No—obviously it's a big thing for you—maybe I'm not good enough for you. Maybe I wasn't raised properly enough for you. Maybe you're mad because my dad couldn't save the world and make all of your lives so terribly cushy. Well, you have a right to be mad—I've said I wouldn't blame you—but at least you could get mad at me out loud. I'm not so vulnerable that I can't take a little verbal criticism, you know. I've been criticized before in my life and it didn't kill me. You can even say something nasty and I wouldn't mind. I don't feel guilty for what's happened to you. Why don't you blame all those men in the governments? Why don't you blame the rest of the people in the world for not making them fix everything up so there would be peace? Oh, I see. You are blaming the people through me. You're punishing me for being one of the people who didn't fix things up just right. Well, I can understand that. It's true. I am one of the people who didn't fix things up. But you have to understand. No one would have listened to me. If they didn't listen to my dad, why would they have listened to me? The world doesn't go around listening to fifteen-year-old girls whose dad had some idea about changing the world so that there would be peace. It just doesn't work that way. If you don't believe me, go ahead and ask anyone else who you might come across in your time. They'll be sure to tell you it didn't work that way. And then you'll feel bad about not speaking to me on the last day that I was alive.

I'm waiting, and I've been waiting and still you don't deign to talk to me. Well, all right. Have it your way. I could care less. I'm doing you a favor. I want you to know that. And if you don't know it now, then I hope you're smart enough to realize it later. You take everything for granted just like the people who are living now. You probably think it's my duty to talk to you and tell you about my day. Well, I've got news for you. It isn't. There are plenty of other things I could do with my day than to sit around talking like a nut into some rusting recording machine . . .

I'm sorry I got mad. I know you can't talk to me. I'm not *that* crazy. I'm just sick about the fact that I'll never get to meet you and do all the things I've been talking about with you. We would have such a good time, even if the world were in ruin. At least we could be alive together—that's better than nothing, don't you think? I don't know for sure. Maybe it would have been better for you if you had died like the rest of us. Maybe it's that bad. Is that true? Is that why you've been so angry with me? I understand. Sure, I understand. Like me, you don't have anyone to talk to. You know how it is not to have anyone to talk to. The world must be very quiet now . . . Is it dark, too?

It's very quiet now where I am . . . The wild flowers are still and the grasses aren't moving anymore and the sea way beyond the road is as still as glass and the sun has forgotten how to shine. Maybe it's gone away with the clouds to a safer place in the sky. Even the clouds don't want anything to do with us, to say nothing of the sun, who is as mad as he can be at us.

But I'll tell you one thing. I'm glad to be alive. I'm glad to at least know that I am alive and kicking and I plan to go on living right up until the last moment that I can. And don't expect me to run off and commit suicide like everybody else I know. I'm not so sure it's such a good thing to die of your own free will. Look at the world right now. It's going to die of its own free will in a way. I mean the people could have prevented all this. So by the fact that they didn't prevent it, they are all going to die of their own free will. Do you get what I mean?

One other thing. I am going to keep on talking . . . I won't stop no matter what happens. But if for some reason I have to stop, say I die or something, or I go to sleep, I hope you don't take offense with me. I'm trying to do the best thing for you and I wouldn't ever want to hurt you because I know you've been hurt so much already.

12

I'm back on the road and I'm still considering all of this an emergency, so I can't get too upset about the guy who deserted his jeep after he went with his friends to the caves. Already I wonder whether I dreamed those meadows—the world is so grey, it could have been a dream. Dreams are easier to come by when it's grey. The sunlight makes everything so crystal clear and real—the grey like the grey of the fog shrouds things in mystery—a perfect time to dream . . .

And don't think I've gotten any better at driving this machine. The seat is too high and my legs have trouble getting to the pedals and my arm isn't used to tugging at the gear. But the wheels are turning round and round and I can steer and I guess that's what matters when you come right down to it. I'll drive in silence for a while and you can have a vacation from hearing my voice.

I've come a lot further than I thought. Just up the road is the Pines Hotel and I'd almost forgotten I'd promised to meet my father there at noon. He said he'd meet me there, we've had it arranged for weeks. I got this telegram from some far away place—I couldn't tell you where it was—it could have been an island in the South Seas, but then again it could have been from one of those countries in the Far East where people worship Buddha as their God. Have you ever seen a picture of the Buddha? He must be a mile high and a half mile wide and it looks like he's made of gold, all shiny and muscular. I can see why people would want to worship him. His pictures make him look close to divine. I bet right at this very moment there are millions of people in the Far East turning to him, praying to him to make the bombs go away before it's too late. And I bet he's doing what he can to help. But he's got a big problem because of all the men in the governments. It's not easy for one Almighty to make the difference. Maybe, just maybe if all the Almighties got together and decided to do something about the people's problem, then something could be done—but it doesn't work that way. From what I understand the Buddha doesn't like my Almighty and the same goes for each of the Almighties in all the religions in the world. Sometimes they're as bad as the men in the governments when it comes to their own people. Each of the Almighties wants its people to worship them alone. And so the people think that their Almighty is the only Almighty in the world worth anything—and so it goes—people get all hot about their Almighty being the best and so on, and you know what happens? People go out and kill for their particular Almighty and we're right back where we started from. It's a damn shame that all the Almighties can't forget their differences and just be content to have the people worship anyway they want to without trying to call themselves the best—the only Almighty who is worth anything. It would make it a lot easier on the people if they could work it out that way. Then at least people wouldn't have to fight over who was the best Almighty in the world.

I'm pulling into the parking lot of the Pines Hotel where I have lots of room because there aren't any cars around here—so I take it my dad and I are going to have the whole

WORLD ONE

place to ourselves—which would be nice since we haven't seen each other in years. He'll probably be wearing his old grey suit because it's such a grey day. His shoes will be brown—the tie-up kind because my mom liked him best in those. I can tell you what color his shirt will be, but not his tie. He went in for odd colored ties and from one day to the next it was impossible to tell what kind of event he would wear around his neck. Oh, his shirt will be white and somehow it will look like it's been pressed, only it probably hasn't—it'll just look that way.

Sonia has not been received well at the door. No doorman tipped his hat to me and bowed as I came in. I'm in the lobby and I'm looking around and still I don't see anyone—yes, here he comes—that must be the concierge. I thanked him for taking my bags, a good thanks is sometimes better than even a quarter when it's a quality hotel, you know. I had better sign in so my dad will know I'm here. All he needs to do is to check the register and he'll know I'm here. I've already discussed with the manager that my dad is to be expected. He's promised he'll keep an eye out for him.

I was sitting in the meadows, wasn't I? I must look like a wreck. I've been rained on, too. I can tell because my shirt is damp and it hasn't rained since I was in the jeep. I had better take a bath and prepare myself. A daughter should always look her best for her dad, don't you think? After all, he's gone to all the trouble of raising her and seeing that she grows up right. The last thing I want to do is to disappoint him. He's probably seen lots of beautiful daughters since he's been away and I want him to think he's raised the best one of any of them, no matter how many he's seen.

I see that the porter has already taken my bags—as I said, this is a quality hotel. The conceirge has made up for the doorman who wasn't there. He bowed deeply to me as I ascended the stairs and of course, I managed a graceful curtesy. There is one thing strange about this hotel. I'm walking down the second floor hallway and I've noticed that all the doors are open to all the rooms. All the rooms are empty—and I don't see any chambermaids. I like room twenty-six. This one will do. It's got that airy feeling that I like best. Of course my porter went there instinctively, knowing how I like rooms with airy feelings. They'll put my dad across the hall so we can be in constant communication.

My airy room has windows that look out onto the sea. I've opened them to let in the noon breeze. It's a small breeze, not much more than a flutter. But it's enough to make me feel quite dreamy. I wouldn't want it to be much more than a flutter actually. If it were more than that the grey clouds might be blown away and then it would be sunny and not a good time to dream. I'd like it even more if the fog would move in. If the fog were here my dad and me would be locked in—no one could come and get us. He wouldn't have to go away to some South Sea island. We could stay right here because there are so many empty rooms and lots of parking places outside. Anyone on the road would pass this hotel right by. They wouldn't see it. They wouldn't see us. We could stay here all by ourselves and not have to worry about anything. We wouldn't mind if you were with us though. So don't get worried about not being included.

I've already unpacked my bags and the closets are filled all the way up with my finest gowns, things mostly I save for special occasions. I'm a little upset because I have only two pairs of stockings and we might be here for some time and I'll get very nervous if one rips. That'll leave me just one and I never feel the same when I have only one pair to my name. I'll wear my blue dress because it matches the color of this room. And as I think I'll probably meet my dad here, I want it to go with the decor. Can you imagine how funny I'd look in a red dress in a blue room? No—I've made up my mind and I'm going to wear my blue dress after I fix myself up and take a bath and come out looking like the best daughter in the world. I hope he brings me a whole bunch of store-bought flowers. I haven't had any of those in years and you can't expect a girl to live on wild flowers all the time. A girl likes variety, expecially when it comes to flowers.

My dad isn't coming, is he? He's not going to bring me any store-bought flowers. I knew that as soon as I stepped into my bath. The steam makes me so warm . . . and I feel so tired

WORLD ONE

now ... I shouldn't have taken this bath ... I would still believe my dad was going to come for me. It's the steam that's made me see things differently. The steam takes away my dreams, all my dreams. It's the fog that I want and need. With the fog everything is so clear and so right. Everything is as it should be. The steam makes me see everything so differently ...

But a princess has no need of her dad. If he doesn't choose to come, not to worry. There are other men who will enjoy coming to me after I am bathed. They will not mind taking my hand, after all, I am the last princess in the land. There will be no others after I am gone. I should wonder why they do not all come to me? I will soon be of age to marry. Then my dad will have to come. He will want to inspect this lucky man. And he will wish to walk me down the aisle, very much he will wish to do that.

And this man, whomever he will be, will wish to make love to me, won't he? Do not think that I am too young to think of these things. I haven't much time to live my life. I have hardly any time at all and so I think I am not too young to think of these things. I will have no other chance. I must do the best I can before I die.

I would so like to know a man before tonight. All of me would like to know him. He could lift me sweetly to the bed. He could promise me the world. I would believe him. We could make love in the fog and I could at last sleep in his arms until the night was through. The steam has made me very sleepy and I wish to go to sleep but I have no time and I must dry myself for this man is soon to come and I want to be ready for him. I want him to see his prize, the one thing he loves more than anything else in the world. I would be that for him and he could be that for me and we could lie together so happily, so still ...

I have been calling and calling and still no one answers my calls. Have they no servants? Have they no ears? I've been calling and calling and no one will answer. How can we dine without food? Here we have such a lovely view. Here we have the fog and the sea and the smell of trees. He will not come until our lunch has been prepared and I CAN GET NO ONE TO ANSWER MY CALL! There isn't anyone. They've all gone, haven't they? They've all gone to the caves like the rest of them and they refuse to answer my calls. But my man will come, he will come to claim the one he loves.

I have no perfume for my neck. It doesn't matter. He'll love me for myself. The fog has not dried my shirt and no one will come to press it and stamp the wrinkles out. That won't matter, either. I am a woman who has her youth, that's the important thing, nothing else matters, nothing matters but living, and I'm living the best way I know how. I go to the finest hotel and pick out the most airy room with a view of the sea and the fog—but I hadn't expected the steam to drive my dad away, I hadn't counted on that at all. But my man will not let me down. He was born for this day and he will not disappoint me. The phones must be broken, that's why everyone has disappeared. They can't hear me, that's why they're not coming. I had best go downstairs. We won't be disturbed down there. He will have to meet me there and we will have our lunch with the rest of the people who decided not to hide in caves.

Going downstairs, I am going downstairs and I feel light and warm and very happy. I've got someplace to go. I've got someone to meet. I've got the whole rest of the day. I've forgotten all about my emergency. What was it? Was someone sick? Did someone have an accident? Was someone in pain and crying out for help? I can't remember now what it was ... I could find it on the tape, if I wanted to. I could play it back and then I would know. I would know for sure.

I'm on my way downstairs because the phones are broken and I have to meet him here at noon. Are you happy with our hotel? This is the first time I've ever been in one. I wonder why my dad asked me to meet him here when he wasn't coming? Do you know why? Did he tell you? Did he

WORLD ONE

have some kind of plan? He was caught up in the emergency, wasn't he? That's why he's not coming. He had to go out and help people because there was an emergency . . . that must be it, that must be why he isn't coming. I understand.

I'm sitting at a table with a pink tablecloth and red store-bought roses in a vase. The napkins are folded just so, very neatly on top of my plate. They haven't lit the candles, I don't understand why. They obviously still don't know that this is a very special day for me. I wish my dad had let them know. I can't expect him to think of everything . . . He's only human, you know. And to my right is a picture window looking out onto the grass, the pretty lawn, the well-groomed hedges and beyond that the sea—always the sea around here. I can't get away from it—I don't want to, even if I could.

I wonder if I should order the wine? He will want to drink red. Is that a proper wine for noon? I like this feeling of solitude . . . it sets the right mood for things to come . . . and he will be coming, I can feel that he will be coming and he will make me happy and explain to me about my dad—how he got himself mixed up in an emergency—how everything will be all right until tonight. But that gives us plenty of time! I should keep my voice down. I don't want to disturb the rest of the guests and have them blame me for being so young. I just want to be with him and live with him and wait out the hours together . . . like a family.

I'm still waiting; it's been some time now; I'm not having a fit because I know he'll eventually come—after all, he is a man and I am a woman and we were born to meet today, weren't we? There's plenty to look at and hear here. In the next room people are dancing to some kind of music I don't recognize. It could be Brazilian, it could be a samba; it's very romantic and it makes me long for him as I've never longed for anyone before. I don't think I'd know the steps to the dance, so I hope he doesn't come until it's over. I shouldn't want to embarrass myself right away—or at any time. I'll ask him to wait for a waltz—some dance I'm familiar with. I want us to dance elegantly, it doesn't have to be sexy, just as romantic as you please, that's what I'm looking forward to, that's the way it will be . . . always.

Here he comes.

We have had wine and more wine and my mind is spinning and it is such a luxury. I've forgotten all about the past. Did we really meet only today? Haven't I been here dining for days? . . . What hour is this? What day? What year? It's the day of the year of my birthday and he came for me and you have been with me, too and we have had such a lovely party I don't ever want it to end. We have been dancing for days, spinning for years, and now he wants to take me up to my room to be with me as a husband would be with his bride. And I have consented and I am going and it will be beautiful and we will love each other in the fog of the day and I will give everything to him as he will to me. Don't you think that's all right? Don't you think I had better live for today?

The fog is still here and the candles are lit and he is by my side and it is as if we have been together all our lives. That's the way it should be, isn't it? That's when you know it's right and good and beautiful—the way the books told me it was supposed to be. He is sleeping gently now—dark hairs settled on the pillow, resting comfortably. I hear him breathing ever so quietly—like the sound of a constant sea breeze, only more special—a sea breeze especially made for me. Did you hear us talking for hours? Or was it days? He's been everywhere there is to go, even some places which are scary, places I would never go—not even with him. And he has promised to take me to Paris on our honeymoon. We will go tomorrow or the next. He is so beautiful when he sleeps. I wish I had a pencil to draw him for you—you would know why all my heart was for him—you would know why his smile is as bright as the candlelight next to us—you would know why I am in love with him forever and ever. I'll be his forever and ever

WORLD ONE

and we are going to have a life and no one will hurt us or try to come and get us. He won't let them. He has the power to turn them away and make our home safe and he wants to live with me in Sandy Cove. I even told him about the hatchet-man on Digby's Neck and still he wants to live with me in my little cabin off the road.

He is still sleeping and the fog has come into the room because I left all the windows wide open so I could smell the sea. And the candles are burning, they never want to go out—they would burn happily forever if I let them. He's been talking in his sleep . . . did you hear him? He was saying something about tomorrow. He mustn't think about tomorrow—we are here in love today—and the fog is with us making all our dreams come true and we had the pick of the rooms and our lunch was so elegant. I will never forget how it was to dance with him on the day I first met him.

I want to lay my head down next to his and dream with him. I want to be that close to him. I want to be that much a part of him. He is a gentleman and his dreams are mine—he said that to me only today. Now I'm just going to rest for a minute or two. I'll be switching off for a minute or two. I'll miss you, too. This is the happiest day of my life. I am with the one I love . . . what more could there be, really? . . . that's all.

I've been trying to wake him but he will not wake. Why don't you wake, you? Don't you want to see me anymore? Don't you want to love me anymore? Haven't you been happy with me? You said you were. You said you would always be, but now you won't talk to me and it's time for me to go. The fog has cleared and the sun has come back and I think I have to go meet my father somewhere. I want you to meet him, too. I know he'll very much approve of you, but you have to come with me to meet him. We'll find him somewhere. He's nearer than we think. Somewhere back near Sandy Cove. We'll meet him there. Why won't you wake up? Are you going to abandon me, too? Have you taken Mrs. Mac's pills and gone to sleep without telling me? Are you with her now? Did you know this was going to happen all along? You were playing with me, weren't you? All along you were frightened like the rest. You had to go to sleep to protect yourself. I love you and so I don't blame you but you didn't have to do this to me on my birthday, did you? You could have waited until tomorrow. You would have gone to sleep then and I would have never known. I'm sorry you had to do this to me . . . I really am. You don't want me to go, do you? You want me to sleep with with you—but there's no time for sleep—it's way past noon and the hotel will be filling up and they'll want our room . . . someone else will want our room and I'll have to give it to them because they'll want to go to sleep like you and Mrs. Mac and all the rest of them. Go ahead! Sleep! Forget about the world and what it's going to do to you. That's right, don't answer me—no one ever answers me—they only want me to sleep and forget about the world. I won't! I've still got plenty of time—and I have a surprise for you. I'm going to have a baby today. My first baby is going to be born on my birthday. It's a miracle, I know. Everything has happened so quickly. We only just met, but today is Wednesday and it's a good day for our child to be born. You have given me everything in the world today. I wish I could thank you, but you are so still and sleeping so soundly. You aren't breathing anymore, are you? Mrs. Mac made you do this to me, didn't she? She gave you the idea. You would have stayed if she hadn't told you to sleep and forget about the world, forget about me. Mrs. Mac wants me to go to sleep, too. That's what this is all about, isn't it? Everyone wants me to go to sleep and forget about the world. But I won't. I have a child and it will be born today and I will have to find a doctor because they say there'll be pain—much later on there'll be pain and I want to be prepared.

He still won't wake up. Do you think that means it's time for me to go? You're the only ones I can trust anymore. Everyone wants to desert me and leave me to have my baby alone. I

WORLD ONE

should go, shouldn't I? I may not have too much time left and my baby must be born before tonight. I wouldn't leave him if it weren't for the child. But his father won't wake and there is so much that I have to do to get ready. I loved this airy room. I would stay if it weren't my birthday. I would have my party right here. You could come right here—there would be lots of room for all of us . . . He still might wake after awhile . . . But I can't wait. It's too late to wait. There's still an emergency, isn't there? That's why I have the jeep, isn't it? Did you sleep too when I was resting? Did you have nice dreams? Are you happy to be with me again? Didn't we have a wonderful morning? Did you enjoy the dancing and the conversation? Were you disappointed about my dad? No one ever comes and says hello to you. And I keep on promising you that they will and they don't and that makes me feel bad. But we have to go on, don't we? We can't stand still and just forget about the world. We have to stay alive as long as we can. We have to fix the world before it's too late. We have to shout out like the voice of rolling thunder. But no one's shouting, are they? No one is making any noise . . . they're all hiding and sleeping and forgetting about the world when the world is all we have right now.

We have each other though . . . We'll always have each other. No one can take us away from each other and that's a promise. I better put on some clothes. I'll have to leave my wardrobe behind—it's not important now—he isn't going to wake and so it doesn't matter anymore. There's only you and me and the baby now. That's all of us. There aren't anymore. We once had Mrs. Mac but she's sleeping—there were others, too . . . I can't remember them though . . . perhaps you can. It's not important. We have to go on.

I left him sleeping in our room. There was nothing else I could do. It's better that we go on and live out the day as best we can. You'll be with me, so it's all right. Lots of babies have been born before this one. I'll find the doctor and he'll take care of me until everyone decides to come and visit me and care for me. You won't desert me, will you? I couldn't stand that if you did. I would kill myself if you ever did that.

But you won't, will you? I know you and you'll take care of me if no one else will. You won't let me down like the rest of the world . . . I know you. You have to like me some to listen to me for so long. I'm counting on you and you can count on me.

The doorman held open the door for me and I tipped him with my smile. I didn't have any pocket change. I hope he didn't mind. He didn't seem to mind, but you never know. Sometimes people smile when there's nothing to smile about. That could be the same with him. I'm sorry. But I have to go.

Starting it up, starting it up, I have to start the jeep up and get going. I have to drive slowly now—there's another person to think of besides myself now. I have responsibilities. I have a child I have to bring into the world before it's too late and I must find the doctor—he'll tell me what to do. He'll look after me when the time comes. It's so nice to live where people care for you.

I'm still all right, aren't I? Sometimes I feel so strange, like I wasn't living anymore, and then sometimes I feel so glad to be alive in a place where people care, and then sometimes it's as if no one ever cares and that they all want to desert me—they keep telling me I should go to sleep! I won't! I just can't. I've never heard of a woman who was asleep when a child was born. Have you?

If you have, don't tell me. I don't want to know because I don't want to go to sleep. Maybe later I will. Maybe I'll sleep after he's been born. I won't promise I will, but if the doctor says it's all right I might try to get a little rest along with everyone else.

I'm going along now and the sea is still out there to my right and the meadows are still up there on the hills and the road is still down there underneath my feet and we are still together as we were and will be and no one is going to hurt

WORLD ONE

us and no one is going to make us go to sleep and everyone will love my baby when they wake up.

Can you remember where Doctor Elson lives? Didn't I tell you where he lived a long time ago? There's something I remember about that but I can't remember what it is . . . we have to remember somehow . . . there is a way we can remember but I can't remember how . . . All the roads, they're all the same. They go up and then they go down, but I don't remember where they go anymore. I remembered once, that was a long time ago and we didn't know each other very well then, not like we know each other now, it's not like now at all.

The rain hasn't quit on us yet, has it? The rain makes so much noise, have you ever noticed that? . . . tap, tapping, down it goes, beating at my windowpane, knocking to get in. We won't let it in. We don't have the time to get wet. I just pressed my clothes and I've just cleaned you up so you won't ever get rusty again and we won't let it in, no we won't, no we can't, we won't, we won't.

He was down here somewhere, I remember him being down here somewhere and if we don't find him soon, then I'll have to call Mrs. Mac and ask her for directions. She'll know the way so we won't have anything to ever worry about again. No one can touch us and make us sick because Mrs. Mac knows the way to Doctor Elson's office and we need to go there right now. Are you feeling well? If you've been sick yourselves I'll take you to him, too, and he'll make you feel all better again and you won't feel any pain because he has some pills that make you well. So don't worry if you've been sick, you've had a hard time, he'll know, and he'll promise to take care of you because he's taken an oath to make everyone he knows feel all better again, no matter what's happened to the rest of the people of the world. That's why there are doctors, doctors like Doctor Elson. They've come to the earth to make it well again after it's been sick and suffered tragedies. Mrs. Mac always told me to go to the doctor first whenever there was something wrong with me, but there isn't anything wrong with me, is there? I'm not going there because there is something wrong with me. I'm going there because there is something right with me and I need to tell him about it so nothing will go wrong. Mrs. Mac once told me, I remember she told me, that Doctor Elson can make babies come into this world. He can do that and that's why I need to see him today so he can make my baby come into the world before it's too late for him to be born.

Are you sure we're on the right road? My baby has to be on the right road or he'll never be born and that would be such a tragedy for the rest of the world. It would be sad for me and for you, too, because we'd never get to meet him and watch him grow and become a man who could save the world. We can't let that happen to the world, can we? It wouldn't be right. It would be wrong and we can't do wrong things to the world . . . never . . . We're not allowed to do that—ask anyone you know, they'll tell you you're not supposed to do that to the rest of the world.

I was worried about my baby when I first knew he would be coming, but I'm not worried anymore because you're with me and I'm with you and together we'll be able to find the doctor and see to it that he's born into the right world. I can't think of anything worse than having my baby born into the wrong world. It wouldn't be fair to him or to me or to you or to the rest of the world because my baby is going to know how to save everyone from what's going to happen tonight. And this time around everyone is going to listen to him and he will have the voice of rolling thunder and he will speak to everyone at the same time and everyone will do away with the men in the governments who want to hurt my baby before he has a chance to save the world. If only my dad were here to see the baby born. He would be so proud to have a grandson who took after him. He would do everything to help him succeed, too. He would share his notes and speeches and everything he knows about getting some peace before it's too late. It won't be too late, though. My baby will be born in time, you'll see. I won't give up hope that he'll be born before tonight. If he can just be born before tonight everything will work out okay and we can all go on living and having such a

WORLD ONE

good time. And tomorrow we can have my party after all and we can go dancing and it won't be raining, the sun will come back and shine on us and we can even go down to the sea and run along the beaches. I should feel better then, I think I'll be rested by then. We'll have a nice little party and I promise not to do too much dancing . . .

Once there was a doctor who lived on this road but then it rained and then I couldn't find him and he couldn't take care of me and my friends and my baby, so we all died and that was too bad because my baby was about to save the world. Once there was a doctor who lived on this road but then he went away to hide in a cave and that was too bad because he died anyway without having a good day. Now there is a doctor who lives on this road who is looking for me to help me when I need him most because he knows that I'm going to have a baby who will need to have a perfect birth in order to live well in the world that wants him to be happy and alive and growing up right.

I'm driving better than I was because I can't take any chances on crashing into the sea before he's born . . . I want it to be a perfect birth with no complications at all, so I'm sitting very still and holding onto the wheel with everything I can so I won't disturb him while he's sleeping. But pretty soon he'll want to be waking and I'll have to have the doctor then because Mrs. Mac told me to go to him in case of an emergency. It's okay for me to have this jeep under me because this is an emergency—my baby has to be born right before tonight. Someone told me that he had to be born right before tonight. Do you remember who it was? Was he someone you know? I remember now . . . there was someone on the radio. I didn't know him. I didn't know where he came from, but he was telling me that my baby had to be born tonight before everything got to be an emergency. But don't worry. I'm on the right road because I can see that it's going up and down, up and down and that won't hurt my baby because I'm sitting down with you and you are taking care of me before the doctor can.

My baby will have every chance ... just like me ... he'll have a perfect birth and he won't die like my mom. No one is going to die like my mom ever again because there's a doctor down at the end of this road somewhere and he knows how to take care of everyone and protect you and me and the baby from the rest of the world, no matter what happens. That's what doctors are taught to do. That's what's in their oath that they have to take before they can help you when you're hurt and you are having an emergency.

Tap, tapping, down the road, Doctor Elson I am coming and you will be there, won't you? You'll be there to help me, won't you? You'll be so proud of me for coming right to you when I found out I was going to have a baby. Mrs. Mac sent me, Doctor Elson. Remember I was the one who had a broken finger? I didn't tell you I was having any pain but you helped me anyway and you said I could come back anytime I needed you. Well, I'm coming Doctor Elson. You are somewhere on this road that is going up and down and you won't let me die when my baby is born, will you? Some doctors let the mother die, but you won't, will you? It's not right to let the mothers die just when the baby is born. She has to be around to look after him and watch him grow up right. I have to be around so that I can tell him he has to go out and save the world before tonight. Do you understand that, Doctor Elson? I must find you and talk to you so I'll know just what to do and then if you want you can come to my party tomorrow with my friends and I'll dance with you for taking care of me and my baby who is going to do so well.

Doctor Elson must be out to lunch. He had a car, I know he had a car, and it is not here. He must be back at the hotel having lunch and I missed him there. Maybe he'll come home. You see he has to see me and tell me I'm going to be all right.

WORLD ONE

I'll just wait for him until he comes. His other patients will be expecting him. I'd better wait in line. The office is so cold—it has the feeling of the sea, it's like being down at the bottom of the sea. I am at home here. I have always been at home here, although I can't remember why. Doctor Elson are you in? You have a patient waiting. She is going to have a child and I am asking you to deliver him so he will have a perfect birth. You will not let him die, will you? You have taken an oath and therefore you will not let him die. How good of you. You could be his godfather if I can get him baptized.

I should not wait out here in the lobby. His receptionist is gone and she would want me to make myself at home until the doctor has had his lunch. He is having it now. I should have known he was at the hotel. I should have waited for him there. But the doctor is not in and I should make myself at home. I had better ask the people in line if I can go on in.

Would you mind? I hadn't realized I was going to have a child tonight. The doctor will want to see me soon, would you mind if I went on in? Thank you very much—you must know how much this means to me . . . It's not every day you have a child and I want everything to go so well.

I'm switching off while I'm undressing. I really am a modest girl. But I'll be back and then we can continue our discussion.

I'm wearing white right now. I could be an angel in this white. If I were a little taller and held a candle you would think me come from heaven. Do angels ever have children? I've never read they have. So I'm not an angel. I'm a living human being and that's just as good. Not better but just as good since it's harder to be a living person than an angel in the heavens. He is not coming, now. Doctor Elson must know I'm here. He must have gotten word that there's an angel in his office and he does not administer to angels of the heavens. He takes care of human beings—makes them live much longer. He knows that angels are never sick and they live forever. That is why he isn't coming, angels do not give birth. But I am not an angel. I am a living human being who will before tonight have her first child by the man she met in her hotel who was born to be with her. Why isn't he here? Is he still sleeping? Or has he gone back around the world to bring my father home? . . . Father, you would be happy to be here. I wish you would come and be with me tonight. If the doctor isn't coming in, then I'll be in need of you, like I was when I was young.

Should I listen to my heart? It might tell me something I should know. All the doctors do it, they listen to all their patients' hearts. I think I will. His stethoscope is cold on my chest, but I hear my heart beating. It is beating very fast, like it is glad to be alive. I have a very strong heart, I'll put that down on my chart. That way when he comes he'll know that I'm all right. "Sonia has a very good heart. It is beating like it should. It is louder than I thought."

He will like my sense of humor—"It is louder than I thought." I hope that he remembers me, I hope he got my Christmas card. I better listen to my belly—that's where the child should be. His heart is beating faintly. I am a girl who has two hearts. I never dreamed it would make me so happy. I never dreamed all this would happen so soon. My child is doing fine, you can be sure of that . . . How are *your* children, now? Did you have a doctor deliver them? Did he give all of them a perfect birth? Was it Doctor Elson who delivered them, or was it someone else? I hope your children were not born when he was having lunch.

I have nothing to worry about. Everything is fine, my baby is not due until tonight. I think he will be born at dusk. That would be a lovely time to bring a child into the world— it could be safe, hiding in the dusk. No one would want to harm him then, everyone would be about to go to sleep and it will be too early for the hatchet-man, he won't come until the night. Will you be with me when he is born? Will you celebrate with me? I would love to have you come along— together we could think up his name, her name, its name— whichever it will be. I'll be all right, won't I? I won't die like my mom died, will I? You won't let me die—but if I do die, then will you take care of my child? You will look out for him. If you have any problems, come here to Doctor Elson's— he'll be through with lunch by then and he'll know exactly

WORLD ONE

what to do. There is something thumping in my belly, can you hear it thumping away?

Thumping, thumping, my baby is thumping, bumping against me and I have two hearts, one for me and one for him. Can you hear them beating? It's a wonderful, happy sound and it's all a part of me and him and now you . . . It's such a gorgeous mystery . . . Can you explain that to me? I wish the doctor would come in. He'll know everything I want to know. He'll tell me how to have a perfect birth. He's a kind man who could make me very happy if he would just come in and take care of me before I have to go with you back home. I shouldn't stay on my feet all day. It could be dangerous.

Switching off for a second while I change again. I'll hang up my white robe for the next person in line. I didn't get it dirty so no one will mind. Do you think the doctor would let me take home his stethoscope? I might need it later on. That way I'd know when my baby was born. I'd only have one heart again—that would be the sign. But you'll tell me, won't you? I can count on you. You won't be out to lunch or hiding in a cave. You'll be here with me. You'll tell me when everything is fine. You'll tell me the second my baby is born . . . You'll tell me everything I want to know—I'm so sorry the doctor isn't in. He was such a nice man—he really would have been happy to help me, even if I were an angel from the heavens.

Back again—still in the office—I hope the people in the line don't mind. I've been inside so long. I've been thinking—there is still time to try to find my dad. He's got to be around. We have to find him—he won't want to miss his grandchild being born. Not for anything. I better leave a note for the doctor in case he comes back in. Then later on he can come to me. He should be back today. He's got all those people waiting in the line. I remember that there were so many of them. Everyone had to see him today. They all had emergencies and he was the only one who could help them, the only one. But a girl like me has learned how to take care of herself. My dad taught me to be that way. I wish everyone could learn to take care of themselves, that way there wouldn't be so many emergencies all in one day. When my baby's born, I'll teach him to take care of himself and he'll tell everyone else how to take care of themselves and then the world will be fine and we all won't have to have any more emergencies.

I feel so calm in here. I don't really want to leave. It's safe in here, isn't it? There are some places in the world where you just feel safe—like no one can come and get you and harm you. This is one of them. I wish everyone could come here. Everyone in the world. I'd like to get those men on the radio in here. They wouldn't worry then, and they wouldn't have to make everyone else feel so upset. Then there're the men in the governments. They should come here, too. Then they'd feel safe and wouldn't need to go to war. Everyone could be safe in here, if only Doctor Elson could come back from lunch and be here to take care of them.

Did you know mothers-to-be have a very special glow about them? I'm having one of those glows right now. I'm looking in the mirror and there is this glow about me that would make all the world happy if they could see me.

It's because I have two hearts and both are beating fine.

I was remembering to take some pills for the pain, wasn't I? Thank you for reminding me. It won't be an easy birth and I have to have something for the pain. Doctor Elson isn't going to mind. He would have given me them anyway if he had come back from lunch. And the people in the line won't mind because they aren't going to have a child tonight so I won't be taking any medicine from them. He's got mountains of pills for pain—they're all here in his glass cabinet and the doctor hasn't locked them up, so it's okay that I borrow some for the pain that I'm going to feel tonight when my baby is born.

My dad said that my mom was in such great pain when I was born. He said it wasn't my fault but she was in great pain

WORLD ONE

and then she died because of the complications. I don't want that to happen to me because I have to be around after my baby is born to feed him and take care of him and watch him grow up right so he can go out and save the world. My dad will be so proud of him. He'll take up where my dad had to leave off because no one would listen to what he had to say and because he didn't have a voice like rolling thunder to speak to everyone in the world at once.

You have to remind me to be careful about taking too many pills . . . Will you do that? I want the birth to be easy. I want it to be lovely, but I don't want to feel the pain tonight. Pain isn't good for people like me, no it's not. Pain isn't good for anyone. I wish Doctor Elson had enough pills for all the rest of the people in the world. They shouldn't die in pain. They should go to sleep like Mrs. Mac, like the man I love. I don't want anyone to have the pain and so I wish I could give them these pills tonight, but they won't need any pills, will they? My son is going to save the world tonight. They won't need Doctor Elson's pills. I'll have to tell the people in line that they won't need the pills I'll be taking for the pain. That should make them happy, don't you think?

One bottle, two bottles and three—"For Pain: When needed." I'm so lucky to have a Doctor Elson. I will send him another Christmas card . . . I have to give him an I.O.U. Do you think ten dollars will be enough? I better say fifteen, just in case. I don't want him to be angry with me when he comes back from lunch. I have to write it down. Switching off while I write it down. Pills for pain—fifteen dollars—I.O.U., Sonia—

Did you know that all the people in line didn't even say goodbye to me? They didn't say anything to me. It was as if I wasn't there. I don't think they liked me for going into the doctor's office when he wasn't there. But they don't understand, do they? They don't understand that there isn't time to wait in line. It's already afternoon and I have things I have to do and there isn't time to wait in line for the doctor to take care of me.

You and me and my baby are on the road and going back to where we came from and now I'm a whole new person. I have so much to live for. We have to get busy. Aren't you glad we met today? I've almost forgotten it's my birthday. So much has happened since dawn and we've gotten to know each other so much better and now we have a child to look after. I couldn't ask for a more lovely day, even though it's rained and my friends have gone to sleep. Even though everyone I know has gone to live in caves instead of living on the land. I told you I wasn't afraid. I told you everything would be all right. We just have to make sure that I don't feel any pain tonight and that my baby is born right. If we can do that then no one will have to feel the pain tonight. Everyone's just scared because my baby hasn't been born yet. But they'll see. They'll know when he's been born—because when he's born the men on the radio and the men in the governments will forget all about their bombs and their wars and they'll want to live in peace and fix everything up like my dad wanted all along. That will be so nice—and you won't have anything to worry about. You'll be just fine and we'll have our party tomorrow just like I dreamed and everyone we know will come awake and we can go dancing in the streets.

I've got my eyes on the roads and on the sides of the roads making sure I don't miss my dad. I think he said he'll be waiting for me—I can't remember where . . . He couldn't come to the hotel . . . He was going to be late . . . But he wanted to see me, he wanted to see that I was going to be all right. He said he was going to help me with the child. That makes me very happy. And I'll find him soon, I will. I'll see him at the next bend in the road, or the one after that. If not there, he'll be back in town and I'll, we'll, meet him there with the man I love. Mrs. Mac will want to see us, too. She likes to know my friends. She says it makes her feel younger when she meets my friends. I want her to live forever. Or I want to die when she does. I wouldn't be happy without her, you can understand.

So far I don't feel any pain. I hope that's a good sign. It's

WORLD ONE

too early in the day to have the baby. We've got lots of time. And I think the rain is going to stop. Yes, I think it's going to stop—and the sun will shine and all our wishes will come true—like I dreamed. And everything I see is green—gorgeous green and I love the green, every blade of grass, every branch on every tree. What would the world do without green? What would the world be if it were brown? Or grey or black? It would be a very, very sad place to be and we could not be happy there. All the colors would be gone and we would have to make them up and that would be very tiresome. All the pictures that we ever painted would have to be redone. It would be a lot of work for someone. I would feel so sorry for him. I don't think he could do it alone.

This world is my home and it will be the home for my son, if he is a son, which I hope he will be because he's got to save the world as soon as he is born. I think the wind is blowing now—coming from the sea. We should stop and let it wrap around us. But we don't have time to stop, I'm sorry but we don't. Perhaps tomorrow the wind will come and we can stop and show my baby off. Can you wait until tomorrow? We can listen to the wind tomorrow and it will sing for us and we will sing for it. The wind has always been my friend. It won't take offense that we can't stop and listen to it now.

Everything is more beautiful than I remember ... the sloping curves of the meadows and the long slanting shoulders of the road that go on down to the edge of the sea ... You are lucky to see such a lovely day. Some days when it rains it's too soggy to be beautiful, but today we have a graceful rain that makes all the colors glow—like me—we are all glowing today because it is my birthday and because I am going to have a child and because my dad is coming to be with us and because my baby is going to save the world.

We don't need the men on the radio to tell us what's going to happen. We know that the Almighty is on our side. He isn't going to punish us. He wouldn't give me this child and then punish us, would He? No, I don't think so, and you don't either. It doesn't work that way. When you're bad you get punished. But when you're good you get rewarded and we're going to get rewarded today because of everything I just said.

And you don't need to worry about me tonight because I have some pills which the doctor gave me for the pain . . . So you can rest and be comfortable and know that I'm in good hands. You never know. Maybe the doctor will finish lunch and come and visit me. He won't be like the rest and hide in caves. He took an oath to take care of you and me, so I think we'll be seeing him before the night is through and my baby is born.

Everything is fine and you are fine and he is fine and I don't have to worry about the pain that I am going to feel tonight. This is the most beautiful day of my life and I have everyone to thank for it because they have taken such good care of me when I really needed it.

13

    Did you hear that the sun is coming out again? The rain is washed away and the sun is coming out and lighting up the road and making everything around look fine and grand and very special for my birthday. If I had my way I'd like to climb up on one of those beams of light and walk right into the sun—the handsome and distinguished Ra, light of the earth, nourisher of beating hearts and other miscellaneous living things. Of course, I can't do that, as you know, but if I had my way . . .

    Would you like to take a walk with me in my neighborhood woods? I think we've got the time. I do think so. I'm very sure of it. Let's go. The sun is making it glisten in green and I always like the sound of my feet crunching on the forest floor after the rain, so let's not hesitate—I can breathe again! We don't have to worry about the pain!

Slippity, crunch, crunchity, slip—we're on our way into the woods of tranquility—our harbor away from the rest of the world where everything lives without any worries at all. Stopping by the woods, crunchity, crunch, we are free to wander here and there, we will not be chastised for taking advantage of the situation. There are no laws against taking to the woods when the raining is done and the sun is shining like it was in the morning. We are among friends—don't you forget it. They treat us like we treat them. If we're good to them, they're good to us. It's simple. It's mother nature's laws. It's the balance of everything in harmony. Trees, trees, how I adore you ever living trees, won't you come to have an interest in my friends who are here to hear what you have to say about the way things work in the world? Don't feel you have to speak right away. I want you to feel at home with us. We do not want to intrude. You remember me, don't you? I was once a child and I used to come here in the summers and the winters and I slept with you to keep you company. I felt safe with you. You never wanted to harm me and I never wanted to harm you. We got along and I respected you for what you were and you respected me for what I was and that's why we got along so well. Trees, trees, if you please, treat us to your treasures today, for we are here to celebrate my child to be. We want him to grow up tall and strong like a solid tree. We want him to have his instruction here. He can learn from you, creatures of mother nature, treasures of the woods.

I am walking among the woods where I used to sleep when I was young and didn't know anything about the world except how beautiful the trees could be and how safe they made me feel. But now I have come back and I see them differently. I see that they are wary of me and see me differently. They've been listening to the men on the radio. That must be it. They know that there are men who are plotting against them at this very moment. But they will not be able to hurt you because soon my son will be born and he will save you from them.

Didn't we have a lovely time a long, long time ago? The nights were ours, every night was ours and no one ever disturbed us and made us afraid. And you weren't afraid of

WORLD ONE

me, were you? No you weren't. I was just like you. I was alive because of the sun and the sun was alive because of the Almighty and we all got along very well together. Now it's different, isn't it? It's just not the same. It will never be the same again until my son is born and saves us all from them. You know this, don't you? Word has gotten around. Your branches have been whispering all day. You have passed the word from branch to branch that this is going to be the day when everything will turn out to be all right. Are you happy I came by to see you? Would you have missed me otherwise, or would you have forgotten to think about me at all? It doesn't matter. I'd understand if you had forgotten about our nights in the summers and the winters when I was very young. That was a long, long time ago and things have changed and you've become suspicious of people like me. But I'm different. My dad was different and my son is going to be different, too. He's going to help you. He's going to do all he can to set things right again and restore the balance between you and me and the rest of us. That's what's going to make him special. He's going to uphold the laws of nature, he's going to remind the people of the world about the laws of nature and they are going to hear him and my dad is going to be so pleased. I can't wait to tell him. I'm so glad I have a chance to tell you so you won't be so suspicious of people like me.

Do I look any different than I looked before? I've been growing older all the time, very, very quickly. A girl has to grow up quickly when everyone else is gone. At least you have your friends to take care of you and be with you. I've had to grow up so quickly today. I can't tell you how much I've grown—but I've had a big advantage—I've had some secret friends—no one on earth knows about them—it's just between me and them. But I'm going to tell you because I trust you and love you and we've known each other for such a long time.

I've been talking to friends of another world—they come from this world yet they're very different from us. They come from a time in the future—a time that early this morning I thought was going to come. But it isn't now. It's okay now. That's why we don't have to worry anymore. But early this morning I was convinced that this time was going to come when everything that was, wasn't anymore because of the men in the governments who had forgotten all about the laws of nature and what they meant to them. So all day long I've been talking to these friends from another world which would have been the world after this, if it weren't for the fact that my son was going to be born tonight to save the world from all the bombs that the men on the radio said were going to come, just like my dad said they were going to come. I'm talking to them right now, even while I'm talking to you. But they don't hear me yet because they haven't been born yet. So we're still really having a private conversation.

I do have one thing I'd like to ask of you. I'm going to have my baby today or tonight and I'd like it very much if you could help me, if you can. I don't expect you to come down to my little cabin in Sandy Cove. I know you like to stay right where you are, but if you could at least think of me later on at about the time I'm giving birth it might make all the difference. Since we're all living things it's important that we support each other in everything we do. If I can only give birth and have it be a perfect birth, then I think everything will work out like I said and that'll be my way of supporting you by making sure those men in the governments don't harm you like they want to harm me and my friends who aren't born yet. Is that too much to ask? Just think about me—and tell everyone you know, like the animals that I can't see. I know the birds will be with me. They usually fly all over Sandy Cove at dusk, so they'll be around to support me and think good thoughts for me. But I need all the help I can get, not just for me but for my friends and for my baby and for the rest of the people of the world who are sitting around waiting for everything to go bad.

You see, I don't know for sure if my dad is going to be here by tonight. I thought I was going to see him today. He sent me a telegram but then he didn't come and then this beautiful man came, but then he went to sleep and I don't see him anymore. So I can't count on anyone except for you and my friends that haven't been born yet.

If I thought I could I'd have my baby born right here in the woods right along next to you. That would be nice,

WORLD ONE

wouldn't it? That way we could be all together like the family that we are. All your babies are born here in the woods, aren't they? All the animals I've ever known have been born in the woods, too. The birds are born up in your branches and they sing to you in the mornings and the evenings, don't they? I know because I'm a good listener and I've heard them when I've been trying to get to sleep at night and when I'm trying to wake up in the morning.

Do you feel better after the rains? Does the sun make you feel warm all over? How lucky you are to be taken care of so well. The doctor gave me some pills for the pain tonight, so I've been taken care of too. And I'm taking care of my friends who haven't been born yet and that's the best I can do for right now. But wait until my son is born—then everything will be different—then all these men won't have to go to war and make everything living get so sick and die. Then everyone I know will wake up and be happy to be living again and you won't have to be worried about people like me anymore. They don't really want to hurt you. It's just that they've forgotten all about the laws of nature and the balance of everything living in the world.

Even if I can't find my dad tonight, even if he can't be around to help me give birth to my child, I'll be all right. With you thinking about me and looking out for me, we can do it together because I know you're going to be on my side because you want the world to go on living like it always has. And I'll bet you have some friends that haven't been born yet that you'd like to take care of if you can.

I really should be at home. I can't explain it really, but I really should be at home. It's been lovely here—you know it has—for you and for me, but I have to be going and I have to be going now—so I have to say good-bye. I'm taking my friends with me. I've got to look out for them and you've got to look out for yours, so think well of me this evening—give me all the luck in the world, and just maybe everything will turn out all right after all. I'll be thinking about you later on, yes I will, yes I will . . .

Back down the road I'm going, going, going back down the road towards home. What a delight it is to know that I have friends on my side. They'll be wishing me well tonight and I them and together we're going to be all right. It's such a lovely afternoon. The world's just right again. I've spent some time with my friends of the woods before it's too late and no matter what, I'm glad of it. You never know when you'll have a second chance. Never will you know when you'll have that second chance to say hello, to say good-bye to those who let you sleep in the winter and summer amongst their families . . .

They don't have to talk to me for me to know that they are speaking well of me. They don't have to talk for me to know that they are wishing me so well. I can hear their branches creaking and I can hear the scampering of the little animals that roam the forest floor, and I can hear the flying birds bounding high and low, all wishing me so well. We are lucky, you and me, we have mother nature on our side.

My dad will understand if we are late. He knows many things about mother nature's side. He loves the woods like you and me and will understand if we are late, not too late, but late. Going down the road, going, going down . . . We are on the top of the world in the middle of an emergency and they won't be able to get us now because my baby will be born. And you will be with me when he is born and you will see him change the world and make it safe for all of us who understand mother nature's laws and we will have that party in the morning and everyone we know will wake up bright and early and dance with us in all the streets of Sandy Cove, dear Sandy Cove, the gorgeous place where I have lived in happy solitude since my father went away . . . a long, long time ago.

I will not be too late for him, he has come so far to see me and to meet you. We mustn't upset him; we must make him think that everything is going to be all right. He must never know what the men on the radio have said. He will have come too far to hear all that. We must make him happy by telling him everything is fine, everything is as he always dreamed

WORLD ONE

that it should be. I'll whisper in his ear, "Mother nature's on our side—all men know her laws—they've discovered them since you've been gone."

He will want to dance with me and take me to the county fair and we will go to Front Royal to the Cherry Tree Festival and eat ourselves silly—bright red cherries for breakfast, lunch and dinner—cherries, cherries everywhere—cherries when we wake and when we sleep. You will want to come with us so you will know what delights will be in store for you when you are born and living at the top of the world ... at the top of the world—you and me and he—all of us up here—feasting on the cherries at the county fair, happy to be living in a land that is so safe from all the men in governments who want to ruin everything before mother nature wishes.

We don't want to be too late; we have a child who is hoping to be born. We shall let him have his wish, as mother nature wishes. And mother nature will look after us and oversee his birth and you and me and dad will have all our friends together in one very special place. And Mrs. Mac ... Mrs. Mac will bring me soup and Saltine crackers that will be as fresh as the day that they were made. And when the child is born we will have the soup and crackers and light a fire that will keep us warm tonight, when the fog comes in—it gets cold—and cold will not be good for baby—no, we will have a fire and soup and crackers and everyone will share and then we will all go out into the woods and thank mother nature for the miracle of my son who is hoping to be born ...

You know all this; I don't have to tell you ... children are everything ... they defy the men in the governments because they want to be born and they want to go on living. They defy all the death there is or has ever been. They only know life through birth—that's what's so special about them. They are born according to mother nature's laws. It's only later that they forget how it is that they should live ... it's only later ... like on days like today ... it's only then that they forget how it is they're supposed to live in peace. They have to go on living. All these children have to go on living. They are the ones who can change the world. And my son won't want any wars at all, he won't have time to forget about mother nature's laws and he will have the voice of rolling thunder and he will speak to everyone around the world and tell them that they must respect mother nature's laws if they are to live. And they will want to live. After all, they have children too, and their children want to live, because they remember mother nature's law. They have not lived too long to forget. That's the beauty of the child. He remembers even better than we. And he will want to remember because he wants to go on living. But now I must live for my child. Now I must be getting back home, going, going down the road, I must be getting back home so I can meet my dad, so he can get to know me all over again before my child is born. You see, I can't go to sleep. I can't go hide in a cave. I have to go on living no matter what so that I can teach my child the laws of mother nature. And I must teach him to see the woods the way they really are. He must know the language of the trees and the meaning of the moss. And he will learn to recognize the sounds—the sounds of living creatures in the woods who will want to know whether he means them any harm. And I will take him down to the sea and there I will teach him all about the tides and the currents of the bay and my good friends down deep inside. I will teach him about everything that I love and there will be plenty of time because he will save the world by speaking with the voice of rolling thunder that will wrap itself around the world from the moment he is born. And my dad will be so proud of him because of what he's done and my dad can die in peace then, because his grandson saved the world from the men who meant to go against the laws of mother nature that were meant for you and me.

And I will introduce you to my son. I will tell him all about how you and I set out this morning to try to save the world before it was too late. But we couldn't save the world, could we? We didn't have the voice that could wrap itself around the world. But he will have it and you will hear it and he will save us all. Tonight will be a good night—there could be no better—for tonight will be the evening of my birthday and the evening of the day that my dad's dreams came true because I had his grandson in the town of Sandy Cove.

WORLD ONE

Sunlight is everywhere and we are all doing fine and soon there will be no emergency. It will be forgotten in the fog. And Mrs. Mac will wake up soon and my husband will, too, and they will be with us tonight before my birthday is through. Life is so much nicer when you don't have to listen to the men on the radio. Life is so much better when you just go along on mother nature's side. We are coming home, home we come, and we will have our home forever because the sea is on our side and the woods are looking after us and all the living creatures in the world are wishing us the best today—on the day that I grew up.

I'll be switching off while I park the jeep at the gas station down from Mrs. Mac's. You don't have to worry about me while I'm gone though. My baby won't be born for several hours at least. There's plenty of time and we'll find someone to help us when the time is right. So switching off now. I hope you enjoyed our trip. Now you've been to most of the places that I know (except for Digby—we'll do that tomorrow if we can). I'm feeling better now that I'm at home. Homes are like that, you know. They make you feel better almost automatically. You don't have to do anything at all except be there. They make you feel better right away, I don't know why and it doesn't matter. Switching off in Sandy Cove while I park the jeep.

I put a note on the steering wheel for the owner of the jeep. I said that I had had an emergency and that Mrs. Mac said that I could borrow the jeep if I had an emergency and so forth and so on and I said that I hoped the owner didn't mind and that I'd make it up to him if he was mad at me. I also left an I.O.U. for five dollars for the gas that I used up while you and I were travelling down the road. Do you think the owner will be mad? I couldn't find him anywhere. I'm pretty sure he's probably hiding in some cave, so it's possible he won't know until tomorrow in which case he'll be thanking me for what my baby's going to do for him tonight. He'll probably be so glad that he doesn't have to live inside a cave after tonight that he'll end up thanking me for all I've done—for all my baby's done for him and for the rest of them. I left the I.O.U. just in case. You can't take people's thanks for granted, you know. Like my dad knows, you can't expect people to thank you for trying to save the world. They just naturally expect it of you, particularly when a baby like mine is going to be born with a talent for speaking round the world . . .

I'm really going to miss that jeep. I even mastered how to shift it into third gear. I thought I did pretty well for a girl of fifteen. I've never heard of any other girl doing so well in her first emergency. Have you?

I still hear the rumbling down beneath me like I was still travelling down the road. I guess that's to be expected, I'm not very used to travelling in automobiles. I'm used to horses and my two feet. It's a wonderful invention but in the end I think I'd rather trust my feet. With a step or two or three I can be anywhere. Even better than that all I need to do is close my eyes and I can be ten thousand miles away. My mind is my greatest form of transportation. I'd say that that goes for all people everywhere. All they have to do is close their eyes and they can be anywhere and do anything. That's why I have such faith in the people of the world, that's why I think we're all going to live to see tomorrow. Tomorrow will be so much better than today. Tomorrow all the bombs will be put away and everyone will follow mother nature's laws . . .

Won't that be nice?

. . . There's someone standing on the porch . . . I know who's standing on the porch—it's my dad—it really is my dad and he's standing on the porch and he's waiting for me like I said he would be and he's so tall and handsome, just like I remember him. Has he seen me yet? Did he see me park the jeep? Won't he be surprised when I tell him how far we drove today without any help from anyone? Just wait till you hear the sound of his voice. I can't believe this is coming true.

WORLD ONE

We are going to be altogether and we will have our party and he is going to help me have the child as I was hoping he would. He will be so impressed by how much I've grown, don't you think? Do you think he'll recognize me? I haven't changed all that much. He looks so well, doesn't he? But he's greyer than I remember him. His hair is grey not brown. How could so much happen to him in such a short time? He must have travelled a long way since I last saw him ... He will have a hundred stories to tell me—to tell us—you're part of the family now. You'll be included in everything we do. And I'll have my dad tell you exactly what he thinks about how the people should find peace. He can do all that much better than me. If I had known that he was actually going to come today I never would have told you my own interpretation ... I wouldn't have breathed a word of it. I was just trying to help the future remember him for what he was and what he did and how he tried so hard to see that all people found a way to live in peace without the bombs.

Let's run!

He was here. I know he was here. I saw him from back there—you saw him, didn't you? ... I saw him and he was standing on the porch looking very grand and grey. I wasn't sure that he saw me, but I saw him and then I decided to run and then when I got here he wasn't here anymore. He must have gone somewhere else. But where? In the cabin—he must be in the cabin having tea—or instant coffee. Opening the door—looking inside, glad to be back home, "Daddy? Have you come home to me?" Sssssssh—let him answer. Let him have time to say hello. I don't want us to frighten him. He's been away for such a long, long time. He might not know me right off the bat. We need to give him time to get used to us. "Daddy? Do you remember me? I'm your little girl and it's my fifteenth birthday."

I've looked everywhere for him and he's not here. He was here but now he's gone again and he didn't stop for tea or coffee. I could tell, the cups were all clean and none had been recently washed. Mrs. Mac must have seen him. I'll go and ask her. She knows everything there is to know in town.

Mrs. Mac isn't answering her door and the sign says, CLOSED and my dad isn't anywhere around here. I don't feel him here like I felt him when I saw him standing on the porch in the sunny afternoon. It's so strange that Mrs. Mac isn't answering her door. She's probably taking a nap because everyone else has gone to hide away from here. "I'll come back, Mrs. Mac. I don't want to disturb you now. I know how you like your sleep."

He'll be at the church. My dad liked to go to church and that's where he's gone, if I'm not mistaken. He liked the colored windows especially much and I'm sure he's up there right now admiring them. He's seen the colored windows in churches all around the world—but he always said that the color of the windows in our church up here was the nicest of any he ever found.

"Daddy, are you in here?" He's not here. He's come and gone and I am getting upset again. Why is he doing this to me? Why should he be afraid of me? I've done nothing wrong. I just want to have my child so he can save the world. I just want my dad to help him being born. That's not too much to ask . . . after all these years.

He's gone down to the shore. He's at the bay. We used to walk down by the bay and that's where he'll be—walking on the sand enjoying the sounds of the sea. He wanted me to meet him down there—just like in the old days before everything got so bad and he had to go away. He'll be down there and there I'll find him and we will go walking in the afternoon and I will tell him about my child and he will be so glad for me because I am having a chance to live like everyone else who's come before me.

WORLD ONE

I'm standing on the road, looking at the beach and at the sea. And there he is. I told you he'd be here. I was right, wasn't I? Sometimes, I'm wrong, but this time I'm right. He's walking on the sand, he's marching toward the sea and he's walking like he's happy. He must be happy now—now that he's come back home. I'll run after him and you'll come with me and we'll meet him at the edge of the sea where he wants to meet us and get to know us all over again. He's been gone so long but he's come back for my birthday and for the birth of my child, just like I always dreamed.

Don't walk into the sea, daddy. I can't follow you there. It's too deep for me—I can't go that far in ... What are you doing, daddy? Why don't you answer me and speak to me. I thought you wanted us to meet you by the edge of the sea. What's the matter with you? Why are you still unhappy? I've waited such a long time. Don't disappear. Come back and meet my friends if you don't want to talk to me. We've all got such good news for you—just listen to us before you go and disappear again. You don't have to disappear. I've worked everything out and I'm going to have a child tonight who's going to save the world just like you would do if you had the chance all over again. Don't go, daddy. I'm not mad at you for leaving me. I just always hoped that you'd come back. That's what kept me going. I knew you would return. I never gave up and felt sorry for myself—not even when I heard those men on the radio talking like you said they would. I never gave up on you, daddy—please don't disappear right now. I really need you now, like never ever before ...

I can't follow you. You've gone in too deep. I have to look out for my baby. I can't take any chances with him. If it were just me I'd follow you. I'd go with you wherever you wanted me to go. But I have to look out for my baby now. Please come back before it's all too late. You don't have to die anymore, daddy. Daddy? Daddy? Where are you daddy? I thought I saw you ... now you aren't even out there, like you were ... you were just there ... I know you were just there. Why have you gone and disappeared on the day when my baby's going to be born? Why have you gone and disappeared and left me all alone all over again when this is such an important day for me?

I can't see him anymore, no more, no more, no more . . .

I know my dad's dead. You don't have to remind me. That's not the first time I've seen him and then not seen him. Sometimes when I don't get any sleep, I think I see him, right around a corner, at the end of the street, up in the churchyard, under a late night lamppost—lots of places, even down by the shore of the sea where I saw him just now. He was there in my imagination. I really did see him in my imagination. But then I was wishing more than seeing. I was hoping more than knowing. That's the way it is when you're young. You have to count on wishes and hoping rather than reality because reality will let you down every time, every time that I've ever known. It's all very disappointing, really it is, but I guess you know that by now, having been born after today.

That's why I must go and make preparations immediately. I can't waste another second with my little girl fantasies. I have responsibilities to my child and I can't afford to waste any more time dreaming of things that can't be. And don't you do the same. It's all very fun while it lasts, and it does seem real while it's all happening, but when it's over it's very sad and makes one even more blue and distressed. I believe in all sorts of things, but I don't believe in bringing back the dead. Once you're dead you're dead and you go on somewheres else and live another life under very different circumstances. But you can't come back to earth anymore and do the things you used to do and be as happy as you were before. That's my philosophy about being dead.

I'm happy to be back alive in my little cabin in Sandy

WORLD ONE

Cove. There's so much we have to do to get ready for this evening. If you've ever had a child you'll know exactly what I mean. We should make a list of what we have to do since no one else will be around to make sure we do them. It's better to do that kind of thing when you're clear in the head and not feeling all the pain that's going to come when my baby is being born.

First the sheets on the bed must be changed. We must have clean sheets, the cleaner the better. They should sparkle like the sun was shining on them. I did the laundry last week. Mrs. Mac and I always do it together. There's something about Mrs. Mac that I can't remember. Did she say she was going away today? Did we see her this morning? I'm remembering something about seeing her this morning but I can't remember what it was or where it was or anything about it. Can you? And where did this beautiful pair of gloves come from?

First the sheets and the pillowcases. I love getting into bed when I've just changed the sheets. It makes me feel so luxurious and sweet . . . I'll use my mom's country quilt, too. She would have liked that. Her grandchild born on her favorite country quilt. She probably knew all along that this was going to happen to me. My dad always said she was very good at looking ahead and knowing what was going to happen. He said it ran in the family. He was probably right. Like I know what's going to happen tonight after my baby's been born, and you know it, too. I wonder why my dad didn't know that if it really ran in the family like he said?

I'm down on my hands and knees scrubbing the floors like I like to do once a month. I did them last week but I want to be sure that they're as clean as they can be. I don't want my baby to wake up and sit on unclean floors. You can't be too careful when it comes to babies being born. I've read all about it in books that I wasn't supposed to read. At least Mrs. Mac said I wasn't supposed to read them yet, but what if I hadn't? I would be in trouble, wouldn't I? I'd forget how clean everything was supposed to be and my baby would wake up and get sick in the world right away and then where would we all be? We'd be in trouble, that's where we'd be. My baby and you and me and the rest of them can't afford to have my baby born imperfectly and get sick right away. We wouldn't have a chance then. We only have one more chance and all our friends in the woods are counting on us to do it right.

Somewhere around here is that book I was reading about how to give birth to a child. I think I remember most of it but I want to study it one more time just in case I've forgotten anything important. Maybe it's hidden in one of my drawers ... Sometimes Mrs. Mac will come over and I hide it from her so she won't think I'm learning about life too fast for my own good. Old people are like that, you know. They think you should only know just so much before you get to be a certain age. But I bet Mrs. Mac knew everything I know when she was my age. She probably just wasn't going to have a baby so soon. But then she didn't have the men talking on the radio like they are today on her fifteenth birthday. That's the truth of it, I know.

I found the book and have put it next to my pillow so I can study it some more before this evening. Right now I'm making some food and am chopping it up into little bits so my baby can eat right away before he has to get to work saving the world. I guess I'm getting worried that I'll be rushing him into it, but I have to, don't I? Maybe when he's older he'll understand why I had to rush him into it. Just think. He doesn't even know right now what's happening in the world. That must be a nice place to be. I'd like to go there myself. I really would. And I'm not talking about hiding there. I'm talking about just resting there for a minute or two. I'm probably forgetting all sorts of things and it would be a good place to think everything over again while I still have the chance. We can't make any mistakes tonight, that's for sure. This has to be a perfect birth or there won't be any others anywhere.

I've made him some crunchy bacon that I've cut up into bits and pieces so he can chew on them right away. And I've made some more Quaker Oats which he won't have any trouble chewing at all. I'm not going to give him any sugar quite yet.

WORLD ONE

I don't want him to have bad teeth. A mother has to think about such things. It's one of the ways she can be of help. I've got a problem. I'm all out of milk—well, almost all out. I better go and see if Mrs. Mac has come back. I always get my milk from her and she'll be delighted to know that this time it's for my baby who's going to make everything all right by tonight. I hope she hasn't been listening to the men on the radio. They don't know what we know and if Mrs. Mac believes them she might get upset and depressed and her day might be completely ruined and that wouldn't be fair. After all, she's old and doesn't have much time left to enjoy everything she can.

I'm back at Mrs. Mac's and the sign on the door still says, CLOSED. I'm going to have to do a sneaky thing. I'm going to have to try to get inside to find some milk so everything will be ready by this evening. I'm just going to turn the knob on the door and if it opens then I'll waltz in and pay for it with another I.O.U. My bank's in Digby and it's too far to go right now, and besides, Mrs. Mac always knows I'm good for it. It's opening. She forgot to lock her door and I'm going in to find some milk before it's too late. Mrs. Mac, are you in here? This is Sonia and I've come to find some milk for my baby. Did you know I was going to have a baby? I was going to surprise you but I can't anymore, because I have to make preparations for everything to be all right tonight. She's not here. She's not in her chair and she's not behind the counter and the wood stove isn't at all warm. She must have gone to Digby. Maybe she's had an emergency . . . She's left a blanket on the floor and there's rice on top of it but I can't spend time cleaning up. I don't have anymore time to clean up. I've got to make preparations right now and I'm sorry Mrs. Mac, if I can I'll clean up tomorrow. You'll be back then and we'll do it together and still be in time for my party.

Maybe I'll name my child after my dad. It will be a boy, I know. But if it's a girl I'll name it after Mrs. Mac. She'll like that very much. I think I'll leave her a note that says just that. "If it's a girl, Mrs. Mac, I'm naming it after you for all you've done for me, especially when I was young." That should make her happy when she returns from Digby. She'll come right over to my cabin and she'll be as pleased as she can be with me for thinking of her—even if it's a boy which I expect it to be, she'll still be very pleased that I thought of her. And if it is a boy, then I'll promise to name my first girl after her. That way she'll always be remembered even after she's gone on to some other place where she can't come back from.

You aren't angry with me for taking a bottle of cold milk, are you? I know you don't know Mrs. Mac but I promise you she won't mind. She's got lots of bottles left and since there isn't anyone walking around the town I don't expect her to run out any time soon.

I'm closing the door now and leaving up the sign that says, CLOSED. I'd almost forgotten that on Wednesdays she goes to Digby. It's kind of her day off—the one day a week when she likes to take it easy and go into town and do whatever it is that makes her happy. But to tell you the truth, I think her trips make her more sad than happy. I think she goes into town and remembers the old days when her husband was alive and kept her company.

Do you think my baby is going to have a happy life living here with me in Sandy Cove? Or do you think he'll eventually want to go down south and live in the big cities? Questions like that make me dizzy.

I'm finally ready now for anything. I've changed my clothes, I've slipped into something very comfortable and informal for the events of the evening. I made myself a suit of loose sheets. I think I look like a Roman with a toga . . . Did you know Romans often committed suicide when they lost a battle that they were supposed to win? It was all very dignified and the proper thing to do considering their obligation to the state to which they belonged. I would have been an exceptionally pretty Roman but I wouldn't have been able to go along with the committing suicide side of things. I just don't have it in me—not even for the state to which I belonged. I'd rather go on living even if we lost a battle. At least when

WORLD ONE

you're living there's still hope. I've never heard of anyone having any hope when they're dead, have you? That may seem obvious to you but it's something I have to think about when it comes to me. You see, I have a choice. I could go to sleep and forget about everything that might happen tonight if my baby's not born, or I can stay up some more and hope that my child will born in time to change the world for the good of everyone . . . If he isn't born in time then I won't be alive to commit suicide. If I go to sleep before tonight then we won't have any chance to win the battle against the men in the governments. We won't know whether we're going to win or lose. It's much better that I stay awake and keep my hope and take my chances . . . I may look like a Roman, but you won't catch me trying to commit suicide. I've got better things to do than that, and so do you.

Do you know if the doctor will be coming? I went to see him today to see if I was all right, but I can't remember what he said about coming here this evening. I know he gave me lots of pills just in case I have some pain—yes, I think the doctor will be coming later on this afternoon. He will want to come and look over me while I'm giving birth to my child. I thought my dad would be coming, too, but he's dead and he can't make it because he committed suicide like the Romans who lost the battle with the enemy and wanted to show that they remained loyal to the state. Well, if you ask me, I'm not loyal to any state. I'm loyal to the living people who get caught up in the suicide of the state. We've all got better things to do than to commit suicide when there's so much living to be done. I guess my dad was saying that he wasn't going to be a part of the suicide of the state. Do you know that right now the world is contemplating suicide? Have you ever heard such a crazy thing? Why should we go along with them, anyway? I protest! If I don't want to commit suicide then I don't want to, and that's that. No state is going to make me do it just because they are going to. I'm loyal to the living and normal people don't want to commit suicide. It's just that they've all been living inside an unhealthy state. Like I said, I've got better things to do and so do you, so let's not talk anymore about committing suicide—just mentioning the word makes me uneasy—like I'm talking about some kind of sickness.

Do you know that when I put my hand on my stomach I can feel the baby inside of me? It's the most wonderful sensation I've ever felt and it makes me happy to know that I have the privilege of giving birth to a baby on my birthday. I think everything is ready now. There's hot water on the stove. It's just sort of simmering there for later on. It makes the cabin all steamy and warm. I don't feel a bit sleepy. I could stay up forever I feel so good. You've helped me so much to get ready just by keeping me company. I think I better study my book on giving birth for a while. I want to make sure I haven't overlooked anything and be ready for any complications that the book says can happen. I would play some music on the radio to make you feel at home while I read but I'm pretty sure that the men on the radio are still talking the way they were talking this morning and I don't want to upset you when we still have so much hope now that I'm going to have a baby who's going to save the world from committing suicide. That's fair, isn't it? Why give up before we know that we're finished? I'm not one for giving up especially when I know how nice it is to be grown up and living in the most beautiful spot in the world. Here I've got everything. You know that already. But what I've really got here is the happiness of peace. Every girl should have it. Every person in the world should have it, and everyone knows that they should have it. It's just how that's the problem ... I've told you how my dad thought they should get it. And my son will think so, too, just as soon as he is born. And it's then that the miracle will come; it's then that everyone will finally listen; it's then that the laws of mother nature will be understood by everyone who has ears to hear the voice of rolling thunder travelling round the world.

I'll be switching off while I study up. I've only got just so much tape and I want to make sure you hear my baby being born. I want to make sure you hear his voice travelling round and round the world. I want to make sure you hear the sounds of peace tonight when everything turns out to be all right. Then I'll let you listen to the men on the radio. We can listen to them together and we can all go to sleep to the

WORLD ONE

music of Beethoven's sonatas which will be coming in clear from Boston like it was last night before the men took over on the radio and made me get so upset. I don't think they wanted to ruin my birthday. I don't think they were trying to do it intentionally. Why would they want to do that? They like listening to music too. They must like living too. They must want to watch their children grow up right too. You would think if they wanted all of that, they wouldn't waste their time making other people get so upset. That makes sense, doesn't it? I think it would be better if they were spending their time trying to fix things up, after all, they have voices that can travel round the world. Why don't they use them to talk about mother nature's laws instead of telling us we'll probably all end up dead by tonight?

Switching off temporarily. Be back soon.

I haven't learned anything that I didn't know before. The book said that I really should have someone with me. I knew that, too, and I was hoping that I would have my dad if the doctor couldn't come, but the doctor will be coming if I remember correctly what he said. It's okay for me to take some pills for the pain. I looked that up right away because I didn't want to do any damage to the baby before he was born. When you're a living person like me it's your responsibility to take care of the people who aren't living yet, and that especially goes for an unborn child. But isn't it funny that it's my baby who is really going to take care of me and you and the rest of them? That's what you call an irony and that's the first irony I've thought about today. Maybe it's the second. I think it's ironic that I'm here having my birthday on the day I'm going to give birth to my first child on the day he's supposed to die, too. Only he's not going to die because he's going to save the world as soon as he comes alive which I hope won't be too late.

Everything is calm inside. The sunlight is streaming through my windows like it always does in the afternoon. Sometimes at night my little cabin makes noises that I don't recognize, but in the day it's as silent as it can be and I feel so safe here and so happy. It's hard for me to believe that the men in the governments would want to make me unhappy. I thought those men were supposed to make people happy and protect them and make sure they got lots of food and enough to drink. I always thought that governments were supposed to be good for the people and make laws for people to live by so that they could live in peace and enjoy the calm of the day. I used to think all these things until I found out that they didn't listen to my dad. Then I tried to forget about them and was doing just fine until early this morning when I heard the men talking on the radio. It's funny how everything can change in just a day. And it's just my luck that today of all days the men in the governments decided to get really mad at each other and make everybody contemplate suicide.

If you ask me, they've got a lot of damn gall and frankly, not trying to be too mean, I hope they choke on it before it's too late for everyone else who'd much rather go on living in peace.

Now I've been considering how everything's going to be when it turns out all right. I mean I've been considering how as a mother I'm going to raise my child. Mrs. Mac says it's a most trying thing to do, but I can't imagine it. After all, that's what mother's were made for, that's what they were born for, that's why they were made in the first place, don't you think? Look at it this way. If there weren't mothers in the world who found it easy and nice to raise children then we wouldn't have a world, would we? If it were just too much bother then no one would want to do it and that would be that. So it can't be too much trouble and too trying a thing to do and I'm telling you right now I'm looking forward to it and I can't wait and all that.

Now I've been sitting in this rocking chair for quite awhile thinking about the most perfect ways that I can raise my child. There're books that I could read on the subject but I think I'd rather be original about it and play it by ear. I don't want just an ordinary child—there are lots of those already.

WORLD ONE

I want him to be something very special—unusual even. I want him to grow up free and right. I want him to see the world for what it is and what it isn't. It wouldn't be fair to disappoint him by telling him right off that everything is just wonderful and as perfect as it can be. It's not like that, is it? There is no such thing as a perfect world and if you ask me that's not entirely a bad thing, considering it would be pretty boring if it were. If you didn't have problems and you didn't have to sit around and figure out the answers then there really wouldn't be much of a challenge in the living of it, now would there? So you can count on me not to paint the perfect rosy picture for my child first off. I want him to be aware of the horrible things that can happen as well as all the good and wonderful things that happen every time you step out the door and look up at the sky or down at the grass or the sea. Is that such a nutty thing to do? That's what I mean about being original. That's what I mean about giving him the whole picture about the world. But there is one thing I will tell him that is very important—to me it's the most important thing and something my dad taught me. He taught me that no matter what the good in the world always outweighs the bad by just a little bit. The bad is always struggling to outweigh the good by just that little bit, too, and that's what causes so many of the problems—big and small. That's why we have to have good laws—you know all this, I know because I've been talking to you for as long as I can remember, but I want you to know that that's the kind of thing I have to teach my child right off. I don't want to take any chances having him think that there is more bad than good in the world. Just think if that happened to every child that was born this world would never survive. Now let's talk about particulars.

I haven't had time to make him some clothes. All I have are my baby blankets that my dad saved for me. I have two of them. One's orange, the other's pink. Since it's going to be a boy I guess I'm stuck, he's stuck with the orange, although if I had my way, I'd pick out a brown or dark blue one for him. Tomorrow I'll get busy on making socks and sweaters and mittens for when it gets cold and damp outside. Mrs. Mac might help me to make up for some lost time. I don't know for sure. She might be pretty mad that I didn't tell her about the baby, but then I didn't know about him until today and she was gone by the time I went to her store. I'd forgotten that she was going to Digby today. I don't know how I forgot that. I must be losing my mind. I should never have started to listen to those men on the radio—never, never, never. I won't ever think of doing such a thing again. Not for as long as I live. And I'll teach my child that he should be careful whom he chooses to listen to because there are a lot of people out there who can make you awfully upset before you even know it. That's one lesson I've learned today and I'll never forget it.

I think babies should listen to a lot of music when they're very young ... And I mean good music, all the good music that was made a long time ago when people made music for the Almighty. I heard somewhere that if a child listens to good music from the day that he or she is born that it makes them happier. That makes a lot of sense to me because my dad used to play music for me. Even when I cried all the time, he played music for me and look how happy I've been. You won't find a happier girl anywhere on Digby's Neck and probably a lot farther away, too. I'm known for my happiness and I owe it all to listening to music when all I could do was scream in my crib and keep an eye out for my mom who never did come around because she was already dead. Most kids who don't have a mother or a father end up being mean and nasty and eventually end up running governments and ruining everything. But all that could have been avoided if the one parent left had played lots of music for the baby after he was born. I guess I have something to worry about there. If the men on the radio don't stop talking about the end of the world by the time my baby is born, then I won't be able to play any of Beethoven's sonatas and everything will start out all wrong and he'll get off on the wrong foot and it will be an uphill battle all the way after that. So let's hope the men on the radio stop talking by then. Everything is riding on it.

Of course, I'll read to him. I like reading out loud and so it will be good to have someone to be able to read to. I don't expect him to understand too much at the beginning, but slowly he will begin to comprehend the subtlest of phrases and before I know it he'll be reading to me the way Mrs. Mac

WORLD ONE

always used to read to me when she knew that I was blue and lonely. Even though it makes me dizzy to think about it, I'll take him on trips to the big cities in the south. I'd hate to lose him down there when there is so much beautiful country up here, but I can't be selfish about that kind of thing. Every child has to grow up and do what he wants and that's just one of the chances you have to take if you're going to raise a child in the world today. Would you feel the same way? Maybe if everything doesn't go right, you won't have to worry about that. There won't be any big cities for him to go to and that will take care of that. But you'll have other worries, I'm sure to make up for it, so don't think you're going to get off so easily.

    I intend to celebrate all the holidays with him, too. And I don't mean just one kind of religious holiday, either. I want him to know about all the great religions. I don't believe that there is only one religion. Of course, there are other religions and people believe in them as much as the other people believe in theirs. It's good to have different religions so I think I'll celebrate all the religious holidays with him and then later on if he wants he can pick the one or two that he thinks makes the most amount of sense to him. Now you know I'm going to teach him about mother nature and her laws—that's probably the first thing. I want him to learn that very well so he won't make the same mistake so many other people have made. He's got to help the world stay mostly good, you know, and that's where mother nature's laws come in. We'll go walking in the woods every afternoon, if we can. He should know what heaven is right away, no matter what religion or religions he decides on. Heaven is here on earth when you want it to be. That's what I say. Sure, there may be other heavens in other places of the universe, but you can't worry about them until much later on, so you might as well enjoy the one you can.

    His first birthday will be a lot better one than today's, I can guarantee you that. There won't be anything to worry about by then and there will be plenty of good music on the radio for the party. And I bet people will come far and wide to celebrate it with me. He will have a reputation by then as the one who saved the world on the evening he was born. I bet there'll be lines of hundreds of people from all over the world just waiting to get a glimpse of him. Some might even bring him presents. I can't say for sure, but some might—you never know. You might say I sound like a mother already, boasting about the accomplishments of my child. But you see the people will be so thankful for what he did for them. I mean if he wasn't going to be born today then they would all die and that would be the end of it. No more birthdays, anywhere. No more nothing. All waste and no beauty. It's too terrible to think about, really—so I don't think about it. I just think about how my child's going to be born this evening and how he's going to save the world with his voice of rolling thunder that's going to travel everywhere and tell people about how they should live by mother nature's laws so there won't be any need for anymore war.

Do you think he'll be walking by his first birthday party? I forget when children are supposed to learn to walk. But if he does learn how to walk by then, then we're going walking on the morning of his birthday and I'm going to take him on the same walk I took you on today. And I'm going to tell him all about you and me and how we got through today. He'll want to know all about it because that's part of the reason why he was born—to help you and me so we could help him go on living and grow up right. You never know, but maybe by the time he's all grown up and I've gone on he'll meet up with you in Sandy Cove—that is if he hasn't gone off to the big cities in the south and made a name for himself doing something else.

I don't care what he ends up doing as long as he's happy and as long as it's good. I'd rather he be good and happy than run all the governments in the world. But by then I guess they'll be only one big government that takes care of keeping the peace and he'll be free to do anything good that he wants. That's the kind of thing a mother wants for her child, you know—nothing else counts.

I would have been free if I hadn't been left all alone, abandoned by everybody I ever knew, left alone to have my baby here in my little cabin in Sandy Cove. I would have

WORLD ONE

done a whole lot better in the world if it wasn't for everyone else letting me down. And it's not only me—everyone who ever lived is being let down right now. If everything goes up in smoke tonight then nobody's life would have been worth anything. They might as well not even have been born. Think of all the people who died in all the wars. They would have died for absolutely nothing at all. It's all too horrible to think about, isn't it? I won't think about it. We've only got one more chance to fix things up so we're all going to have to sit tight until my baby is born. It's our only hope now and it's getting later and later and soon it will be evening and we have to pray that my baby is going to be born in time to make everything right . . .

Did you see my dad walk away from me and disappear into the sea? Did you see that? Why did he do it? Was he ashamed of me? Was he ashamed that he failed long ago? I'm remembering how he just walked away and was soon gone—swallowed up by the sea because he wanted to be . . . He didn't want to see the world die. He wasn't ready for it, like you and me and the rest of them. He couldn't bear to see it happen. He still feels guilty that he didn't succeed. But I could have made him feel better if I could have only talked to him and told him about my baby and what he was going to do when he was born. I would have told him that we had one last chance to save the world before the end. I hate him for leaving. I hate him for walking into the sea without listening to me. Do you think he could have been going to get the doctor? Do you think that that's why he left me? I could understand that. I really could. If he were going to get the doctor from where he was having lunch then I wouldn't blame him for going away and leaving me when I needed him so much. He *will* return with the doctor, if he can find him. That's why he left me and walked away and disappeared into the sea. I don't hate him. I love him and I should have known what he was doing, where he was going. He just didn't have time to stop and say hello to me. He knew that time was short—that there was so little time left—that's where he's gone and I'm thankful for that. He will make sure that the doctor will be coming to make the birth go easily and without any complications. My dad knows that his grandson is going to save the world tonight. He knows it in his heart. And he will be with us to see his old dream come true. He will return to see his dream become reality. That's why he's returned from wherever he was before. He's returned to see the world learn to live in peace. That's the only explanation that makes sense. I should never ever have doubted him. He died because he couldn't make the world understand how best to live in peace. And now he's come back to see the day when everyone comes to understand how to live by mother nature's laws. It's as simple as that. I love you daddy, I really do. I never really hated you. It's just I'm so fragile and so scared. I want so much for everything to be all right. I don't want the world to end. I want it to be happy like I am when I'm walking in the woods or playing on the shore. I want it to stay alive and be beautiful and wonderful in a million different ways. I'm with you, daddy, until the end—or until the whole wide world starts all over again—the first world that ever learned to live in peace according to mother nature's laws. How happy that will make all the people who ever lived and died. How happy that will make all the people who live on after us. This could be the greatest birthday any girl has ever had . . . If only my baby can be born before the time when the men in the governments go to war and mutilate everything that is and ever was.

Don't worry, daddy. If you can't find the doctor at the hotel where he was having lunch and you can't find him in his office—or if he's too busy with the rest of his patients, you can help me yourself. You can help my baby be born and you can listen to his voice of rolling thunder—and you will be so proud of him and me for carrying on after you and trying to do the right thing before it's too late. No one can hurt you now. It's too late for them to hurt you. Now they should know that you were right. Now everyone will love you like I love you. You didn't have to die after all. You were born so that you could teach me and so that I could teach my baby. It's all working out so well. You don't have to die anymore, daddy. You can be free to live some more and you don't have to be afraid that the world is going to die. You will be free and we will be free and the rest of the people in

WORLD ONE

the world will finally be free from the men in the governments who don't know how to live in peace.

But try to come back before it gets too dark. The sky is beginning to be red in the west which means that the day is beginning to come to an end. It's all blue to the east and it's getting colder, yes it is getting colder, I can tell because my house is damp and I have to start a fire in the stove. I should make some coffee, too. I'll make enough for you. I know how you like your coffee, without sugar—very strong. I won't pour it yet—not until I see you coming through the door with the doctor. I don't know what he likes to drink. Perhaps he likes tea. I've got plenty of tea and even some honey. He could have tea while you and I have coffee, while we all discuss how to make the birth so easy for me. But if you can't make it, daddy—if you can't find the doctor or you get stuck on the road somewhere because of the dark, I'll try to understand. I won't hold it against you, because now I understand that you've come back to try to help me with the birth. I promise I won't hate you ever again. I understand why you were so scared for the world and why you decided to commit suicide. I really understand that now. It's so terrible to feel so helpless when you know the world is coming to an end because nobody wants to pay attention to what the laws of mother nature have to say.

If he doesn't come—then it's just you and me. We'll have to do it together if my dad and doctor don't come. I'm not saying that they won't—not by any means, but we have to be prepared for all eventualities—we can't take any chances not being prepared. And remember. We have the woods and creatures of the forests on our side. They want us to succeed. They desperately want us to succeed. They won't have a home anymore if we don't. They won't have a place in the world if my baby isn't born just perfectly. You will always be with me. You are my true friends and I won't ever forget you for how you've been with me today and made me feel so good to be alive on my fifteenth birthday. No one can ever say that you tried to or had to abandon me. It's just not in your nature to do such a thing. You don't even go to sleep on me like the rest of them. And you don't go and hide in caves to be safe when there's so much to do to try to make things all right.

I love you my friends. I love you as much as I love Mrs. Mac and my dad. I love you as much as I love me. I love you as much as the creatures in the woods and the winds above the woods and the woods themselves. Even if I had to die tonight, I would never forget you and I would love you always. Do you know why? I love you because you listen. You hear what's being said, and you know as I know how important the laws of mother nature are for making the world have peace. That shows how smart you are. You're smarter than anyone else right now. They'll all be smart soon—soon as my baby is born. But right now you're smarter than all of them and I'm very proud of you. Before this morning you didn't even know me. You didn't know about my dad and what he tried to do. But now you know everything there is to know, and I love you because you took the time to listen. And you know how important it is for the world to go on living. Without the world none of us have anything—everything is meaningless—and worse—everything will be dead. And you won't be born—and my baby will die and that won't do anyone any good. The world will be just a bunch of dead and lonely memories, looking around desperately for life.

I swear to you one thing. We will be together until the end—or until the beginning of a whole new way of life when the world gets a chance to start all over again without any wars.

Sonia swears she will never abandon her friends—not even at the end, not even then.

14

Far out along the watery horizon, small explosions are visible, like fireworks from ages ago. Following the sprays of white light, syncopated blasts are heard, like half-thunder, cut off in mid-sound. I think: Human-dogs are at it some more, battling each other for rooftops, islands of firm footing, waging war because it is the code of the day. All human-dogs are watching the blasts, the shattering balloons of round white light. Water carries noises wonderfully, so we are treated to exceptional clarity. I think I hear a groan, a guttural groan of something dying a hard, hard death. It's too far to see who or what it is. But, I know. I know that it's a human-dog like one of the ones in front of Elizabeth and me. I know that it is a dying human-dog, coming to the end of its living state of misery.

"One of yours?" I ask Human-dog #1.

Human-dog #1 doesn't answer quite yet. He is looking across the way at the place where the sound was heard. I bet he is thinking of life after death. Is there life after death, he is *thinking? I wish I could answer him if that's what he really is thinking. It would be easy to face death if we knew that life simply went on in a heavenly way.*

Back to the soup. Back to the smelly place where I sit. Back to the torchlight and drawn, uncomplicated faces that have been listening to violence and death. We're all scared, all weak, all vulnerable, all on the verge of death at any moment. It is possible that we could die at any moment.

I sigh.

The explosions have stopped. The lake is silent and somewhat cold. The tiniest of breezes is passing our way. I fantasize that it picks up Elizabeth and I and carries us on—to any place other than this.

Human-dog #1: "Death is never happy."

Elizabeth: "Death is never easy."

And me: "But death is acceptable when it's a great deal more natural, when it fits into the . . . balance."

The human-dogs beyond us seem so still. They are at this moment statues in their boats. Their eyes are set on us, on this foursome—Human-dog #1 and his wife, Elizabeth and I. It is presently uncomfortable to be the center of so much attention.

#1's eyes study the surface of the bobbing water. He is caught between this world and Sonia's—I can tell. Then comes another distant explosion. Little bombs are exploding far behind the assembly of human-dogs in boats. They all turn and look. I already see. New, fresh white flashes burn the lower rim of the sky, then vanish, followed by the impact of the jolting noise.

"Death is never happy," I say.

"Death is more acceptable when it's natural," Human-dog #1 interjects as he faces the new direction from which the sound has come.

"And some deaths are easier to take than others," Elizabeth chimes in. "Easier and less tragic."

Less tragic, I think. That's part of what we want. Less tragic deaths, more constructive lives. But I am dreaming while I'm sitting in the dark of this night that has been thrust upon me.

"Please continue, Mr. Jones," says #1's scrawny wife. She should be entertaining at candlelit dinners, rather than sitting out here in the stink of the world.

But I am pleased that she is so polite. I will continue now

WORLD ONE

that the sounds have faded down to the whispers of breezes. I will continue to press my tragedy home.

All right then, I will: "Sonia is waking, on Wednesday. . . ."

I was resting and when I opened my eyes it was later than I thought and I know now that I have been sleeping. I wasted away the rest of the afternoon and now it is getting on towards evening and I have awoken in pain. I can't describe the pain exactly. It's like my stomach is all twisted up inside, like I'm going to be sick at any minute, like I could die if I wanted to. I don't want to. It's just my baby wanting to be born. They say in the books it's all normal to feel the pain this way so you won't have to be worried about me. I'll be all right and together we'll get through anything that happens. It's all been planned that way. You and me, you and me and my baby. He'll be coming any time now. I don't know exactly when. No one knows exactly when. Maybe the doctor would know but he's still not come. Not him or my dad or even the animals outside. Wait—I hear them outside. Birds must be flying high overhead. They're cheering me on, I know what they say, I've lived with them for a long time. They're saying nice things to me and wishing me well. Mother nature supports her friends.

It's okay that nobody's come. I really didn't expect them to come. I don't know why. Maybe it seems so much more natural for you to be with me on the evening my baby is going to be born. After all, you've been with me since the beginning. It's only right that you be here at the end. I don't know why. It just seems best that way. If the doctor does come, I won't mind, but if he doesn't we'll all get along okay. The blue is beautiful out my windows. I wish you could see as well as hear. That way you could enjoy more of the atmosphere. It's later than I thought. It's almost six, no seven. It's much later than I thought and now I'm scared that there isn't much time. There's so much to do . . . So much to be said and not enough time to live the way we did this morning when the whole world was ours, when every blade of grass could keep us company and be a part of our lives. Now all that is over. We've had our special day. Now we only have time to save the world and make sure my child is born just perfectly.

I am in a little bit of agony. Every once in awhile I have a terrific pain in my side. The book says that that's the first sign that the baby will be coming soon. I'm very excited. I'm very excited, I want you to know that. Before today I never thought there would be time for me to have a baby, before today I never knew I could have such good friends. Before today I was just a little girl who wanted to live for herself—not for anybody else. I never really thought about anybody else at all. I only thought about the people I knew. But I've changed. Now I want everyone to go on living and I want to help save everyone I can. I can't do it myself. That's why my baby is going to be born. The Almighty is looking out after us. Mother nature is on our side. We are going to win and all the men in the governments will hear what my baby has to say and the people will follow them and everyone will be okay. And if the men in the governments don't hear my baby's voice of rolling thunder then the people will hear it and they will make the men in the governments abide by mother nature's laws. And tonight we will all go to sleep and we will wake up in the morning and start all over again in a brand-new world—a world where peace is everywhere, where peace is . . . I'm feeling the same pain now—but this time it's deeper. I feel less sick in my stomach, but I'm finding it harder to breathe . . . It's so much harder to breathe than it was before I went to sleep . . . I better take something for the pain. I remember . . . I am remembering that the doctor gave me something for the pain. I had a bottle of pills, didn't I? He gave me a bottle of pills that he said would be good for the pain and I think I better take one now. I better take one while I can. I have to keep alert and keep strong and I can't give in to the pain because my child has to be born so very perfectly . . . as perfect a birth as there has ever been . . .

I found the pills on the kitchen table. I put them there, I remember, when I last came in. The pills are very pretty. They're bright yellow—not a color that suits me particularly

WORLD ONE

but in the bottle they look pretty and they should make me feel better and better as the evening wears on. I should take it with a glass of water. I've heard you shouldn't drink down pills with coffee. I want to be careful—you know how careful I want to be. We can't take any chances on something going wrong. I'll just take one for now. If I really start to hurt, I might take another. I have over thirty of them. I won't need all of them, I'm sure. No pain can be *that* bad ... Isn't that right? It can't be that painful to give birth to a child. The book said that there would be pain, but I don't think they meant thirty pills worth of pain. Do you? No, you don't. You don't think I should take the pills at all. I wouldn't take one, but I'm not feeling too well—maybe I'm frightened more than I think. The men on the radio said that the end would come in the evening or by tonight. And I've wasted some time by sleeping when I should have been giving birth to my child. I'm sorry for that. I won't do it again. It's just that I've been up all night and have only slept a little from time to time today and because I wasn't feeling too well, I fell asleep in my chair. I promise, I won't do it again, never again—never, never ever until my baby's been born.

There now. I've taken a pill and I hope you're not going to be mad at me. We don't have time for you to be mad at me. I think I'll just sit still for a minute or two until I'm feeling better. It won't take long. I haven't eaten much today so it should take even less time. That's very good—the shorter the time the better. You and I and everyone is running out of time, so we can't dwell over anything. I wish the doctor were here. I wish my dad were here. I'm glad you're here, very glad you're here, but I would be feeling a little better if I knew for certain that the doctor and my dad were coming. I've never been though this before and I'm so afraid I won't do everything just right. I hate the taste of cold coffee. I should have had a drink of water. I forgot that I had some ice water in the refrigerator next to the bottle of milk.

Do you think Mrs. Mac would be back by now? Sometimes she dines in Digby and isn't back until eight. She dreams about her dead husband over dinner, you know. It's not so strange—it's good for her—only if you didn't know her you might think she was nuts, but she isn't. She just likes to remember how it was in the old days when she was young and very happy. That's not bad, is it? There's nothing wrong with that, is there? I like to dream too and you probably like it as well and I know everyone does it about one thing or another. It's the way with people. They like to live and they like to dream and they like to dream and live and be happy. Not everything in this world is all so serious that you can't be happy for a while . . . We were happy today, weren't we? We didn't let the men on the radio bother us and make us sad. We didn't go in hiding like the rest of them either. We're braver than that. No one's braver than us. We want to live right up until the last minute. I'm feeling better now. It's so good to be feeling better. I was getting worried I was going to have complications and that there wouldn't be anyone around to help me when I needed it. But the pill is making me feel so much better. You can hear it in my voice, can't you? You know I feel better now and that I'm going to be all right. I won't need thirty of these pills. One will do. I'll leave them for you just in case you ever have a pain that is making you feel sick in the stomach. Take one with water, not cold coffee, and then sit still for a while so you'll feel better.

You have no idea how beautiful the evening sky is out my window. If I could paint it for you, it would be a masterpiece. The last clouds of the day would be edged in gold and purple and red. And the sea would be textured like blue velvet. Did you know that the Almighty makes masterpieces every day? They're nothing to Him. Of course He's had years and years of practice, making them just right and as beautiful as they can be. But still to do it every day is really something. It really makes you understand that you're just a small, wonderful thing next to all the big, beautiful things that are everywhere the eye can see. But at least it's nice to know that we're all part of it—pieces of the masterpiece. Yes, that's what we are.

What I am is the birthday girl—had you forgotten, too? It's been hard to keep track of everything that's been happening today, hasn't it? One thing happens and then another and

WORLD ONE

then yet another and everything that happens kind of covers over the last thing that happened and before you know it, you've forgotten what's come before the last thing that happened. You know I'm beginning to feel ever so much better when I begin to talk like this. It's like waves of pleasure are falling over me—not one wave at a time, but thousands of them, thousands of waves that make me feel better and it's all because of the pill I took for the pain. I don't think I'll ever mind pain again. It's a pleasure to have pain. All I have to do is to take a pill and then I have pleasure and no more pain and everything around me is like the blue outside my windows. Everything around fits into everything else so perfectly. Of course, it makes me forget things too. Like I'd almost forgotten that today's been my birthday. I remember that I knew about that earlier today but so much has happened to us since then that it's getting harder and harder to remember all the nice things that can come to you in just a simple ordinary day.

Weren't we going to have a party? Wasn't that the plan? Somewhere I remember having a dream about today—or maybe it was about tomorrow—yes, it *was* about tomorrow and we were all dancing in the streets of Sandy Cove because we were celebrating my new birthday in a very special way. Happiest of birthdays, Sonia. Happiest of days, Sonia. Just plain happy to be alive.

I better not eat anything, the food might not go too well with the pain. I am starving and I am hungry and I wish I could sit down to eat a dinner of lobster and melted butter and cranberry sauce. That's my idea of something next to divine. And there would be candles on the table, but this time I would have many more of them. I would put them in every window, on every part of the floor. I would have them on the stove and in the sink and lined in rows along the white railing of the porch. And people would come from miles around to take a look at the little cabin of a hundred lights. And each flame would be a symbol of thanksgiving and hope. No house anywhere at anytime would have so much hope. That's what would make it so extra special, so particularly nice—festive and gay—more brilliant than all the pale stars in the night. Candles, candles everywhere. What would you say to that if you came along and saw that? Would you know that the candles were put there by me? Would you come down and celebrate? Would you bring all of your friends with you? Candles give off a very special light . . . I would like to have a cake . . . chocolate or strawberry or lemon would do. Sprinkled with peppermint and loads of tiny ever-burning candles which I could never blow out. You can get them in Digby at the toy store. A cake would be so nice and each time I blew out the candles I could make another wish. I could make wishes all night long. I would have plenty of time to make wishes for everyone. A cake would be ever so nice. It would be hard to cut the cake. I might never cut it. I might just leave it the way it was—perfectly round and delicious looking. I might sneak some of the frosting when nobody was looking. Frosting I like better even than the cake. I really don't think I could resist sneaking some of the frosting, but I wouldn't cut the cake. No, I wouldn't. I'd let the candles burn and burn, like the candles in the house, until all my wishes came true. Then I wouldn't mind eating the cake with you. We would have something to celebrate then. We would have everything to celebrate then. That's when it's okay to eat the cake, not before—never before. I'm getting ahead of myself because I feel so good. Was I really in pain before I took the pill? If I was I'm having a very hard time remembering it. Why do you think a beautiful baby would want to give you pain? Doesn't it want to be born? Doesn't it want to get out and start to live like everyone else? Or do they know something about what's supposed to happen today? If they do, then I don't blame them one single bit. I wouldn't want to be born either if I knew what I know. We won't celebrate until my child is born. That's that and don't try to change my mind. I wouldn't feel at all good about it until I knew that he was safe and that he had saved the world. There's nothing to celebrate until then—nothing at all except for the fact that I don't have anymore pain from my baby who really is trying to be born because he knows that he's going to have to save us the minute he's alive and out in the world like the rest of us. He wouldn't want to celebrate until then, either. He isn't made like that. First things first for him. Happiness comes later. Duty to the world comes first. He's a baby of priorities.

WORLD ONE

But then, when that's all over with, when everything is settled and good, when the people of the world have taken charge over their lives like they should, then we'll all get together. You and me and him. And then we'll celebrate like we've never done before. That's when we'll have the party and the dancing in the streets. That's when everyone will come from miles around and look at my little cabin with the hundred flames of light symbolizing our never-ending hope for the people of the world. Now isn't that the proper time to celebrate—when everything is right and peaceful and calm? I'm getting very excited just thinking about it. Why didn't I think about all of this a long time ago? What took me so long to think things out and put them in the proper perspective? When I think about it, it's obvious that I've wasted so much time. I could have helped the world so long ago if I had been thinking correctly. If it weren't for you, I might never have started to think the right way. You have given me everything. You have given me the proper perspective to think about the meaning of life and about what's important and about what to do to help the world get out of its troubles. And the beauty of all of this is that it's still not too late to do something about it. How lucky can we be! If it weren't for you I wouldn't be having my baby today. I would have had a very dreary birthday because Mrs. Mac would have been in Digby and I would have been all alone, without any new friends at all. It's true I could have gotten along pretty well on the walks by myself. You know what they mean to me. But I wouldn't have had the same kind of human company that makes me warm and glad to be alive. Sonia is very, very lucky and she is very, very thankful for having so much luck on a day like today—Wednesday, my fifteenth birthday.

So we'll wait until he's born to celebrate. It won't be too much longer, I'm sure. I can't tell you exactly when but you know it's got to be before it gets too dark because that's when all the trouble is supposed to begin. So I'm going to rock in my chair and dream about tomorrow and try to imagine what my baby is going to look like. There's nothing wrong with that is there? I expect that all mothers-to-be think like that. I bet they spend all sorts of hours picturing their babies one way or another. It's natural to be curious about the way he's going to look and what color his eyes will be—the color of his hair. You name it and mothers-to-be imagine it. It's kind of a privilege that goes along with her position as the one bringing the baby into the world—for better or for best. I wonder if any other mothers are having babies today? If so, do you think that they believe their babies are going to save the world the moment they are born? They might think so but then they aren't likely to have the key that will make things work in the world ever so peacefully. And you have to have the key. Without the key another baby born is just another baby born in a world that has gone crazy. The baby won't do the world any good and the world won't do the baby any good. That's the way it's been working for a very long time and that's why it's time for it to stop and that's why my baby is going to be born and that's why the Almighty is going to give him the voice of rolling thunder so that he can speak to everyone at one time and make them understand that the world is going to die tonight unless the governments of men learn to live by mother nature's laws. It's simple, isn't it? I'm just so lucky that my special child is going to be able to make everything turn out all right. If I didn't know that, I think I would die. I wouldn't have anything to live for and that's got to be the worst—the worst of all possible ways to live and I'm telling you right now I don't have any intention of living that way—not on your life. It just doesn't make any sense, not any sense at all.

I never thought of this until just now. It never even occurred to me. I think I've gotten everything backwards. I bet, I mean I really bet, that my dad thinks that I'm already dead. I bet somehow he found out what was going to happen today and he figured that I'd want to go to sleep like the rest of them and not trouble myself by being around at the end. That kind of thinking makes a great deal of sense to me. And if he really thinks I'm going to go to sleep and be dead like him, then he's probably waiting for me at this very second up at my grave in the cemetary. That would be the natural place

WORLD ONE

to look for me, wouldn't it? Don't you think it would be a good idea to go up there and have a look? I don't know where he gets his information—that's not for me to question. But if he does know about what was supposed to happen today, then I'm pretty sure that he also knows about the grave I dug for myself when I didn't know I was going to have a baby that was going to save the world.

I shouldn't keep him waiting, should I? He's come a long way to see me even when I'm supposed to be sleeping and so I think I have a duty to go and see him and let him know that I really am all right and that I haven't gone to sleep like the rest of them and that I'm going to have this baby very, very soon, hopefully in time to straighten things out and allow everyone to go on living just the way they've all been living since the time of the Egyptians—back when they worshipped the sun instead of the Almighty.

Do you think Ra might have told my dad where I might be? I hope he didn't upset him. I wouldn't want my dad to think I was dead and sleeping when I was alive and living and going to have a child. It's impossible for me to know one way or another. I'm just going on my feelings and feelings can sometimes be wrong. Do you think it's possible that my dad knows that I'm going to die? Do you think he has that kind of information? Can he look ahead and see what's going to happen—to you—to me—to everyone who is living? I wouldn't want to be able to look ahead like that. I wouldn't want to know everything that's going to happen. How could you live that way? Maybe if you're already dead it's okay, but not when you're living. Who wants to know who's going to die and who's going to live? That's too much responsibility. And besides, how could you go to sleep at night knowing all that? And just think. Everyone would be after you asking you to tell them what was going to happen to them and when. You wouldn't have any peace. There would always be someone knocking at your door at whatever time of the day or night, asking to know when they were going to stop living. That would drive me crazy. I hope that never happens to me. If my dad knows, well, that's just fine. But I don't want to know. I just don't think it's natural for a person to know that kind of thing. You've heard what I have to say on that, so I won't say anymore. I just have to decide whether I should take a chance and leave my cabin and go up to my grave and see if my dad isn't there looking for me. If I go, I better go now. The sun is setting and the sky is dark and black and blue and I'm pretty sure my baby will be coming very soon after the sun goes completely down and out of sight. I was thinking, wasn't I, that my dad was going to come here with the doctor? Wasn't I thinking like that a long time ago? Maybe I was thinking that before the pills stopped the pain. It's often hard to remember what you were thinking some time ago. It's easier to remember what you were doing, harder to remember what you were thinking. That's why I've made a special point of talking to you on this nifty recording machine because whenever I have a mind to I can play back all of my thoughts and know then exactly what I was thinking and when. Not everyone can do that. Not everyone goes around talking into a recording machine. That's something special I do and I do it for you.

Switching off for a second while I think what I should do about my dad.

I may be making all of this up—it's not as if I've gotten any secret information that he's at my grave, but since I thought of the idea maybe it could be real. I don't think I can take a chance on it not being real. I think I better go to the grave and see for myself. I'm not in pain, like I told you before. In fact, I feel more like myself than ever before. Mothers probably tend to feel that way before they give birth. I've never read about it, but my instincts tell me that what I'm feeling is just how it's supposed to be, nothing more or less—just right.

Should I take anything for my dad just in case he is there? Can you think of anything he might like that he's missed since he's been gone? I still have his pipe and some old tobacco that's very dry. He might like that. Where he's been they probably don't like people to smoke, especially if he's been somewhere pure and heavenly and innocent. I'll put it in my pocket and take it up to him and if he's there, he can decide if he wants to have a smoke for old time's sake. I've never

WORLD ONE

taken up smoking so I guess I can't imagine how nice it is to have a smoke after not having a smoke for a long time. It's probably something like going swimming in the sea after not having been swimming for two summers in a row. I think I'll make him happy with his pipe.

Happiness is rocking, rocking, one way and then another and then back the same way I came. Happiness is knowing that I'll soon be swimming again. Happiness is hoping that tomorrow will be coming and we'll be rocking, rocking, one way and then another. Happiness is knowing that my baby's going to be born, not tomorrow but today, tonight, this evening, soon. Happiness is knowing you and I are going to be all right. Rocking, rocking by the sea where only you and I can be—wide-awake and without pain. Rock, rock until the day is done.

Switching on and off, off and on, one way and then another, am I confusing you? Switching on and off, here and there, open and shut, dead and born, live and die, on and off, rocking on, rocking off—switching, switching, which will it be? On or off? On or off? Tomorrow or today. Switching, switching, switching one way or the other . . . this is fun.

Are you listening to me you men on the radio—you men who have hidden all the Beethoven from me and from my friends? You didn't need to do that, after all. I was going to tell you, then you wouldn't listen, then I didn't remember to tell you that you didn't need to do that. You see, I have Ra and the Almighty on my side. It's all right to tell you that because my baby is going to be born and he will find the Beethoven that you've hidden since last night. He has very sharp eyes, you know. He has a very strong voice, too. So don't worry about those men inside the governments. They're going to be listening to him soon along with the rest of the people who want to go on living. They want their Beethoven back. They want their tomorrow, too. They want their peace by the sea and they are going to get it whether you're on our side or not. I would like to talk to you some more but you see I have to go and see if my dad is waiting for me because I have his pipe and he will want to have a smoke after all this time. You probably know my dad but I won't go into that. You weren't very nice to him a long, long time ago and you made him get very upset so he had to commit suicide which wasn't right because he was really just trying to help the world and make it right and not have a day like today. It wasn't all your fault. Those men in the governments helped you. And the rest of the people didn't bother to listen very carefully. And he was weak—what with him having one voice out of millions, but don't worry. We're going to fix all that this evening, very soon we'll be fixing that and then won't you bring my Beethoven back?

I better leave a note for the doctor just in case he comes and I'm not here. I wouldn't want him to think that I'm avoiding him. I wouldn't want him to think that I don't care about a perfect birth. I'll leave a note for him and tell him I'll be right back. I'll tell him to fix himself a cup of hot chocolate or coffee. I don't know what he likes to drink. He's never been a guest in my house before. I should leave out an apple for him too. I got a bushel of them when I was in Digby last week. I went to Digby last week, did you know? I was there for a whole day with Mrs. Mac and we bought apples and grapefruits and some Chinese teas. Are you familiar with Chinese teas? I haven't learned yet how to pronounce some of the more complicated names. I go by the color of the tins which they're stored in. The red one is my favorite one. It's got orange pekoe in it and I like the flavor of orange, especially as something tasty to drink in the late afternoons. Honey goes well with it too. I wouldn't think of drinking it with milk. As you know, milk and orange don't mix, never have, never will.

Is there anything you'd like me to put in my note to the doctor? Any special greetings from the future? I know he'd care about you if he knew you. Doctors by birth want to take

WORLD ONE

care of everyone they know. It's bred into them, comes all very naturally to them. That's why we can count on them to care for us when we're sick and in the dumps. If my dad wasn't what he was, he would have been a very good doctor. If my musical career doesn't work out for one reason or another, I might consider it myself. Only I think I'd like to be an animal doctor and fix horses with broken legs and birds with broken wings and squirrels with cut noses. I don't think I have the nerve to take care of people. What if something went wrong? What if one of my patients died on me because I forgot to give him the right kind of shot at the right time? I would feel so horrible and guilty. I might even kill myself and then I wouldn't get to know you when you are born and come to Sandy Cove. No, I think if my musical career doesn't work out the way I want, I'll go into making sick animals feel a whole lot better. I think I have a knack when it comes to helping mother nature's creatures. At least I hope I do. Back to the doctor.

"Dear Doctor Elson: You are probably wondering where I am. I don't blame you. I was here but then I had this thought: I had this thought that maybe my dad was waiting for me up at the grave I dug in the church's cemetary because he thought that I was going to die today. Don't ask me where he got his information. That's his secret, not ours. Anyway, I have gone up to my grave (the one with the white cross that I put together myself) and I hope to find him there. If not, then I'll be back very soon. If he is there, I might be a bit longer because I haven't spoken to him in several years and we'll want to catch up on what's been happening to each other since then. I've left you some apples and some Chinese orange pekoe tea. I've found that the tea tastes much better without milk, but maybe you think differently. That's okay with me. You go right ahead and fix it the way you want. If I can get my dad to come back with me to help us with the baby being born, you'll have a perfect helper. He loves me and will do everything he can to make sure the birth comes easily. You might think about what he can do. He doesn't have much experience in these matters, and it's possible that he's even afraid of children being born because my mom died giving birth to me. I tell you this just in case he's a bit nervous when you see him. That was all a long time ago and he might have forgotten about it by now, especially considering where he's been since he died. One more thing. I thought we might have a party after my baby is born. I'm hoping there will be plenty to celebrate. I won't go into that now. You'll see for yourself if you don't have another emergency right after he's been born.

"Did you get my note about the pills? I remembered that I was going to have some pain before the baby was born, so I took some pills for the pain that you had in the glass cabinet of your office. I've already taken one and it's been making me feel good and calm. I feel ever so much better now although every so often I feel a sharp kick in my stomach, like something wants to get out very soon. It's nice to know that you can take care of me even when I'm far away from you. You must be very happy to be a doctor, knowing how you're helping people like me all the time. Do you remember me? I am Sonia and once you fixed up my finger when it got broken and then I sent you a Christmas card. It had a star on it that was shining brightly over a dark and lonely field. I thought it was all very symbolic and I hope you appreciated the subtlety. I'm running out of room on this piece of paper so I'll say good-bye for now while I go up to the cemetary and try to find my dad who probably has some strange notion about me being dead. That sounds crazy, doesn't it? Especially since today is my fifteenth birthday and the day my first baby is going to be born in a world that is going to be starting all over again very soon. Sonia."

Did you think that my note had a nice ring to it? I hope it makes a good impression on him and that he won't be mad at me for taking my pills. Sometimes doctors are touchy about their patients taking medicine. But I know how much to take and when. I'm very good at reading instructions. Some people aren't, you know.

I've decided to take another pill before I go. I wasn't kidding when I told the doctor about that kicking pain I sometimes feel in my stomach. I felt it even when I was writing the note. That's why I thought to write it. If I take another pill now,

WORLD ONE

then I'll be okay for when I see my dad. He wouldn't want me to feel any pain. He's just like you and the doctor. It's a good feeling to know that everyone is on your side . . . after all, we all have to stick together in life. That's the only way it works. That's the only way we can all be happy and do the good things we want to do. Like taking care of birds with broken wings.

I've been sitting here in my chair waiting for the pill to make the kicking inside of me go away. But it's not going away. I feel it more and more. Something is going to happen to me very soon. I know that now. I think I'll have just enough time to go see my dad up there on the hillside. I'm cutting it very close, I know, but this is important. I don't want him to be upset and think that I am dead. That wouldn't be fair of me, not after all he's tried to do for me—for all of us. Sometimes I think my chair is rocking even when I'm pretty sure it's not. The pills make everything very dreamy and cool. I wonder what would happen if I took a hundred of them? What kind of dreams would I have then? Would I be asleep and dream that I was awake? Would I be awake and dream that I was asleep? It's hard to know, isn't it? I don't have time to experiment right now, but I'll ask the doctor when he comes what would be the most likely thing to happen to me.

I'm going to be standing in a second. My chair is definitely rocking, but I'm definitely going to be standing and then walking and then going out the door to bring my dad back home. Yes, I am walking now and I am not rocking. That's all behind me. The floor is bending here and there because it is getting dark outside and the light isn't right the way it used to be. We're having trouble with our walking, aren't we? I never thought you'd have any trouble walking with me and keeping up with me. It's different from this morning, isn't it now? So much can happen with the darkness coming. You never know from one day to the next.

Did you remember that I was thoughtful enough to leave the doctor a note? I remember that. So it's time to go even though you're having some trouble walking on the floor. Hold on to me if you feel like you're going to fall. I have good eyes and can usually see in the dark—no matter how dark it is. Mrs. Mac says I have eyes like a cat, and cats can see better than people in the dark.

I'm having—right now I'm having more pain than I can ever remember having and I think this is what the book meant by being in labor. That's a good sign that the baby is going to be born tonight. It should be pretty soon now. Don't hold your breath, but it'll be sooner than any of us think. We still have time to see my dad and bring him back home if he has time and wants to still take care of me. So hold on to me. It's time to walk and don't be afraid. Remember, I can see like a cat in the dark.

Everywhere the wind is up as I am walking along the streets of my dear town of Sandy Cove. If the town were not so small, I could walk in it forever. Happy to be here, happy to stay, will you keep me through the night, my dear town of Sandy Cove?

I am a citizen of Sandy Cove and pledge to defend it against all foes, while I can. I want to see it grow and I want all its people to come back. Mrs. Mac? Have you heard the news? I, Sonia of Sandy Cove, am going to have a baby tonight which is born to save the world. I bet you never thought it would be me, I bet you never did, Mrs. Mac. Big surprises often come in small packages and often when you least expect them, isn't that so, Mrs. Mac? You don't hear me, I know. You've gone to Digby to avoid hearing the men on the radio. I would rather have you here, but then at dawn I didn't know my baby was going to be born. You would have stayed with me, wouldn't you have? Yes, you would have. Either that or you would have taken me to Digby and put me in a hospital bed with all the comforts of home. Would you have brought me store-bought flowers and found me a doctor who would have taken care of me? Would you have been there when my child was born? Would you have told the people of Sandy Cove to stay home and wait for the miracle to come? Would you have liked my new and understanding

WORLD ONE

friends? They wanted to hear you speak. I promised them you would speak to them. They were so disappointed that you had gone to town. But they understand. Every Wednesday you go to town and dine. How nice it would have been if we had all had a chance to go together. Don't you agree? Mrs. Mac! I really love you, too. I'm hoping you'll come back home before my baby's born. I'm hoping all the people of Sandy Cove will come back as soon as he's been born. Everything will be all right then. I have it on authority. Everything will be calm just as soon as he's been born. There won't be a reason to hide in caves and go so far underground that you can't even see the stars at night. No one will have to be afraid and they can go to sleep knowing that tomorrow will come and that it will be a better day—the day that Beethoven came back and flooded all the airwaves and drowned out the men, the talking men on the talking radio. Sandy Cove, tomorrow you will be happy again and our lives will go on and on like nothing ever happened. Anything is possible. Any dream can come true. Just have faith in the good things men can do.

Hello churches and your steeples. Hello houses and your windows. Hello streets and street lights. Aren't you so happy to be where you are? But don't you miss the people who used to love to be around you? Don't you miss them very much? Let's all wish for them to come back to town tonight. Let's all wish very hard for that. If we do, if we close our eyes and drum our feet and clench our fists and bite down very tight, they might come back to visit us very, very soon.

Why, hello, Mrs. Watson. Good evening, Mr. Henderson. How nice to see you back. We've been missing you and it was our wish that you come back and be with us like it was before you got the news. Hello, Mrs. Lambert. Good evening, Mr. Hudson. Did you know? Did you know that I am to be a mother tonight and that today is my fifteenth birthday on top of that? Fifteen years ago today I had a mother and then she had me and then she died and I lived and now I am going to be a mother and when my baby is born we both are going to live and then my baby's dad is going to wake and won't even have to commit suicide. Isn't that wonderful news? We should have a parade. Isn't there a high school band in Digby that could come? Why aren't you talking to me? Can you only hear the men on the radio? Are those the only voices you are trained to hear? I have a voice for you to listen to. You won't hear it right now. But wait, wait just a little longer and you will hear it and it will make everything all right again and there will be no more men on the radio disturbing you and making you run and hide and fear and hate and forget about what it is to live the way we always did before we listened to the radios.

    You will come to my party, won't you, Mrs. Watson, Mr. Henderson, Mrs. Lambert, Mr. Hudson? I have some friends that I want you to meet. They haven't been born but they are with me and they will live for us long after we are gone to some other place far away that we don't know about yet. I want you to meet them so you'll know that our town of Sandy Cove will live on and be in good hands and won't be ruined by them.

    No one has accepted my invitation. What is it with you? Have you forgotten how to speak? Would you rather have me telephone? Or would you rather have me speak to you on the radio? That's all you ever listen to. You've forgotten how to hear anything else. Shame on you. I was just trying to be friendly and invite you to my party where we could all have a good time and forget about the troubles of the day. Oh, well. I can't stand here all night. Come if you want to. You'll still be welcome. You know where I live. I have a little cabin on the bay and there'll be lighted candles in the windows and along the porch. You'll always be welcome because you're a part of our town of Sandy Cove.

    Sometimes I think there's only you and me, my friends. You're the only ones who ever really listen to me. The rest— the rest they've forgotten how to listen like I just told them. It all comes down to you and me and my baby and tonight. You want to listen because you don't want to make the same mistakes that all the rest of them have made. They'll be lucky this time—but there can always be a next time, another time when people forget how to have the peace that they're always

WORLD ONE

saying they so desperately want. It all comes down to the fact that you're so much smarter than them. Since you haven't been born, you don't take anything for granted. You want to be born so you want to understand how to keep on living when you are born. It's as simple as that. It's so easy to explain. How I love you for it. How I wish the best for you. I'm doing everything I can to help you and you're doing everything you can to help me and that will go on and on until we die a natural death which is all any of us could ever want. Me, I'd like to die in bed on an evening before a storm. I'd be happy to hear a clap of thunder, maybe two, before I went away. Also, I'd like to be able to say good-bye to you. I wouldn't want to leave without saying good-bye to you and then to my dear friends in the woods. Would you remember me then the next day? Would you come to visit me where they put me down to rest? Yes, you would. I can feel that you would. And you will remember how I liked to live and go for drives along the road to Digby.

She went to Digby when she could, though she wasn't very good at driving in case of emergencies . . . Oh, well, she had other qualities that went beyond all that. Lucky for her she did. She wasn't very good at driving in case of emergencies. She had a child, you know. She was very good at that. She had a very special child, you know. Not one of those everyday childs. This child she had had a voice that wrapped itself around the world and changed it the moment he was born. Lucky for her and for us, she did. Otherwise, she wouldn't have been much help in the case of the emergency. Just remember her name, if you will. Sonia, was her name. Sonia lived in Sandy Cove. Sonia thought that it was the most beautiful spot in all the world, though she hadn't travelled very far—she had travelled far enough to know that what she had was good.

You've been listening to me, haven't you? I knew you would. I knew I could count on you. What better friends could there be than you? No better and that's the truth of it.

We've said our hellos, we can't do much more than that. It's time to go. My dad's waiting for me up on the hill. Night you are a pleasant sight. I'm sorry you'll be all dark and black so soon. But never mind. That's mother nature's way of letting us sleep so that we can wake and be bright and happy by tomorrow.

You know in the darkness I just had a thought. What am I going to do about baptizing my child? Aren't mothers supposed to baptize their children almost as soon as they've been born? I heard the minister, our sterling Reverend Russell talk about that. He said that babies should be baptized practically right after they've been born to keep the bad spirits away from them for the rest of their lives. And I wouldn't want my baby to have any bad spirits swooping round him the second he's been born. Is that the same kind of thing that you've heard? What do you think I should do about it? I won't hardly have any time to do all the things I'm supposed to do when my baby's born. I have to give him a name; I have to be there when he speaks out to the world; I have to baptize him before the bad spirits come and get him. This is all much more complicated than I thought. But you will help me, won't you? You won't let me down, will you? I should say not. We stick together you and me. We have to depend on each other. No one else will do. I better try to find the minister up at the church. He's an expert in baptizing little babies that have just been born. Reverend Russell, I choose you to bless my baby's birth.

Knocking on the old church door in the evening light of dusk. Knock, knock, knocking on the old church door, waiting for the man to answer. The door is locked and the lights are out and Reverend Russell appears not to be at home. Someone must have died today and he is at their funeral. But how about blessing the living instead of the dead? How about coming home when you're needed most? Why does everyone go away just when I really need them? Shame on you and you and you. Ministers of faith are supposed to be at home

WORLD ONE

where they can help the living. I'm sorry one of our people is dead. But there will be just so many more if my baby is not born tonight and all the bad spirits are not kept away so that he can speak to all the people of the world at once. Reverend Russell, my mother would want her grandchild to be baptized, she really would. It's really been of help to me. I've lived so long without the bad spirits on top of me. They don't bother me and I don't bother them. It works very well that way. And I want that for my baby. He has his rights, now that he is soon to be born and take a step out into the world where all the bad spirits are—where they are now at play. And I know my dad will insist on it. He was the one who had me baptized. I think it made him very happy, I can't remember very well at all, but I'm pretty sure it made him happy and that's after all what counts.

Reverend Russell, are you there? We don't have too many minutes left. This is not a good time for you to go away. You have a job to do, like me. So much depends upon this perfect birth. Don't you want me to succeed? Don't you want the people of the world to live? Or do you think that all the people of the world will get what they deserve? I've heard you speak of it before. You scared me half to death. But my baby has the answer. He was born to give the answer to the people of the world and now there's no stopping him from doing it, unless the bad spirits get him first. But we won't let them, will we? We'll stop them in their tracks. And then they'll go away because they don't like the word called peace. What's that you say? You won't be back until tomorrow? Oh, dear, oh dear. That could be a tragedy. Tomorrow will be too late. Ask anyone you know. Tomorrow will be too late. You should have stayed home. You should be here right now. How am I going to explain this to my child? I'm pretty sure that tomorrow will be too late. Why aren't you answering my knocking on the old church door? Don't you like people anymore? Do you want them all to die? It could happen anytime and why? Why because people like you and me and them and those haven't learned to live by mother nature's laws. The Almighty wants it to be that way, at least I'm pretty sure He does. He made the world that way. I wish you would be home. What am I going to tell my dad when he finds out that you've gone away and won't be here to baptize the one who will mean so much to us after he's been born?

Do you think he knows something we don't know? Has he heard that everything is going to be all right? Has he been listening to the men on the radio? Have they changed their minds? Will the world go on living for another day? Has another baby changed the world? I haven't heard a voice like rolling thunder since I came back to Sandy Cove. I'm pretty sure I would have heard it, I have very good ears, you know. I can hear a snapping in the woods even when it's buried in the dark. I would have heard it, yes I would. He doesn't know anything more than we. I just wanted to be sure. Tomorrow will not come, unless we have a baby born tonight. This is the way it's supposed to be. It's the only thing which makes any sense. I've been trying to make some sense all day. This has not been an easy day. No one is ever home. They've all left me here on my own—except for you whom I am very grateful for.

I hope the Almighty will not mind if I baptize my baby boy. He will want the bad spirits kept away and so do I and so do you and so that's what we have to do. I hope I can remember how it's done. Regular stream water will do. And I can make up some prayers that will be as good as any Reverend Russell would use. In times like these, you have to make do.

Knock, knock, knocking on the old church door, Reverend Russell, sorry we bothered you. I hope you chased away the bad spirits from the dead man, too. It's hard to do everything you're supposed to do, I know. Just to make sure I did everything right, I'll come back to you tomorrow and tell you how the baptism went and what I said to drive the bad spirits as far away as I could. It would have been better with you, but we are running out of time, so good-bye and wish us luck.

The birds in the forest are quiet this evening. They don't know what to do. They are listening to the sounds of the world. They worry like ordinary people do. And the wind is

WORLD ONE

very still. Someone must have locked it up in a bottle so all the people of the world could hear my baby cry. It's nice to know I'm being helped, mother nature's on my side, our side, everyone's side. She wants tomorrow as much as we. That's good news, my friends. Pretty soon we'll be going home and sleeping in our beds.

It might be a little late for our party. I'll be so sorry to see my birthday go. It's been such a special day, the best I've ever had. But we will always remember how it was. And no matter what, we'll have proof that we lived today. That's what I really want. I want you to know that I lived today even when the rest of the world was going mad and hiding in caves and avoiding me and going to sleep before the proper time. It doesn't matter about the party. You can have a party any day. We'll forget the party. It's not important now. What's important is that I give birth to a perfect child. What's important is that my child speak with a voice of rolling thunder to the people of the world and tell them about how they should learn to live by mother nature's laws before it is too late. We're agreed on that I know. I just want to get things straight. I don't want to take any chances and make any kind of mistake. I know what I want and what needs to be done, and that's good—that's better than some who would rather see it all come to an end before my baby has a chance to live like all the babies before.

It's getting harder to do things myself. I wish the future were now and that you were here with me and helping me so that you could be born and live in peace ever so grateful that the people of the world heard what my baby boy had to say on my fifteenth birthday.

We know we've come a long way today and yet we haven't come far enough to go home. We know we've come a long way today but not far enough to make it count. Good-bye dear setting sun, once more you have turned your back on us and we are here holding onto the empty dark. Remember my wishes, won't you? Remember what I said to you when I was on the shore this morning and you were shining ever so bright and magically. Remember all of that and I will be happy and sleep ever so peacefully.

How are you my warm hillside? Are you happy to see me again? I haven't been gone too long, have I? I've been in the middle of an emergency and I haven't had time to come back until now. Are you keeping my dad hidden from me? Father, are you hiding in my grave? That was meant for me, not you. You already have a grave. I remember going there and bringing you flowers and sitting beside you even when it was cold and damp outside—I didn't mind. I was happy to be near you, just to be close to you. It's funny how just a little happiness can make all the difference to a girl who is trying to grow up on her own. Thank you for everything, I told you. And I meant it. You were very brave and very true to what you believed and that's always been important for me to remember. I don't know why. It just has been. It always will.

You didn't come, did you? I was right the first time. You couldn't come. It just wasn't possible. They wouldn't let you out from wherever you were. I can understand. Some things just aren't possible in this world. There are some things you just can't change no matter how much you wish and dream for them to be the way you want. You knew that, didn't you? That's why you committed suicide, wasn't it? You knew you couldn't change the world and that killed you, yes, that's why you died and didn't live with me anymore. I'm not mad at you, dad. I'm not mad at anyone anymore. It's just the way it is, nothing more and nothing much less. Though I must say how I regret it.

You would like the view from here. It's what you could call majestic. That's why I picked out this spot to be buried. I wanted a view that was majestic. I don't think I'll be seeing much of a view if I die. But if I don't I'll always remember

WORLD ONE

with pride how I picked out the most majestic view so that even when I was dead I could be reminded of it. That's silly, isn't it? Really very silly. After all, I'm all grown up and I should know better than to think like that. But I don't care. There's nothing wrong with being silly when things have gotten to be so bad. I came up here—I came up here to see you, but that was silly, too, because you were never here, just like you were never down on the beach, never on the porch of the little cabin, never, never even near me. They wouldn't let you out, that's all. I'm sorry you couldn't get out. I guess I wouldn't mind dying if I could be with you.

Baby is coming, I can feel him coming and I am very frightened now because baby is coming and I don't know what to do. When it was light, I knew. I had it all planned out and I was ready and then there was some pain. I remember the pain. There was lots of pain and I took a pill and then I felt better and I was talking to my friends. Here are my friends, I'm holding them in my hands and they are listening to me talking to you and I'm glad that they hear me because I want them to remember who you were and what you stood for and why it was you had to die. You didn't want to live to see an evening like this.

There's plenty of pain in me, dad, but I have some pills and they will make me feel better when I take some more. If I walk the pain returns, I don't know why, it just does. But that's good because I still know that I'm alive and that's good because I know I'm going to have a baby boy who will change the world and make everything all right. Then won't they let you go, let you come to me here and see my majestic view? My baby is coming and the sun is down and the lights are out and nobody's here to take care of me. That's the way it is in the world. That's the way I've found it to be. Is that the way you felt it was? No one was taking care of you, either. And you didn't have any friends that you could talk to because everyone turned against you because of what you believed in. I've been lucky, dad. I've found these friends that haven't been born and I can talk to them anytime I want to and they will listen because they want to learn from you and from me all about mother nature's laws—about what it is to live with her. You would have liked them, dad. I love them very much.

I'm remembering right now that all the clean sheets are back at the cabin and I don't know now whether I have the time to get back before my baby is born. What should I do? My clean sheets are back at the cabin and that is where the doctor is—waiting for me, reading my note and fixing himself a cup of tea and honey. I hope he likes the Chinese Pekoe tea and I hope he doesn't put any milk in it because that spoils it and ruins it and we wouldn't want it to be ruined, would we? I can't go back now, maybe later I'll go back, but now there is pain and more pain and I don't think I'll be able to lift my little feet and find my way back in the empty dark. I should be silent while I get through this pain but I don't want to leave any of you for a second. Not you, dad, not you, my friends. Not all the creatures in the woods—I don't, I can't lose touch with mother nature. Besides, I know I have to have her on my side—not only now, but before and after and all the time that I am living. We all have to have mother nature on our side. It's the only way we can get through it and live and be happy and warm when it is so cold and damp outside and when so many people want to hurt you and spoil everything with their wars that make everyone else feel so bad.

I am going to lie down in my grave. I am not going to die. I'm just going to lie down there and rest and try to make the pain go away. Will it go away when my baby is born? Is that how it works? Is that how it happens? I think it must. Lying down I am and cool and comfortable it all feels and that is good and just the way I wanted it. There is plenty of time for pain but I think I better take another pill—two pills, I'll have for supper while I lie down and wait for the pain to die and to go to some other place where it won't hurt me anymore. Didn't the doctor say it was okay to take the pills for the pain?

WORLD ONE

You were there, you should know. I was there but I am having trouble remembering when it was and why it happened—things like that. You were there and you saw me and you said it was okay and so I'm going to take some more pills to make the birth come easily and quietly and naturally, like the book said.

Do you know that when I get up I'll probably be holding my baby boy? Did you know that? I am very fond of you and am trying to do the best I can so that you can live even after I am gone. It's lonely now and the woods are silent and the trees above my head aren't moving like they were today when it was raining and when the clouds were settling in. But that was a long time ago and I don't remember too much of what I had to say, but you will remember it all someday when you listen to what's on my nifty little recording machine.

15

Now I know he's coming. There isn't any doubt that he's coming anymore and there isn't any doubt that I'm going to be by myself when he's born and there isn't anything I can do about it. No, there isn't anything to be done but give birth and I have to give birth to him in time because there's so little time and everything depends on it being a perfect birth and I have to count on my friends in the woods to pull me through—and you—of course, I can count on you . . . Happy birthday, Sonia, happy birthday . . . happiest of happy birthdays, Sonia, we're all counting on you and your beautiful baby boy to make everything turn out all right.

I've been taken over by the pills. I'm sure I have. That's what I wanted, wasn't it? I wanted it that way so that I could have a mild and easy birth and wouldn't feel the pain so badly. But the pain's still here; it won't go away magically the way

WORLD ONE

it's supposed to. I'm stuck with it. Maybe I should take more pills before it's too late. Who knows what pills I should take? I was hoping I might have a little help. There goes the wind up in the branches of the high trees. Good for the wind. It's come to me. It's surrounding me. It's with us now and we have no worries. Soon the creatures in the forest will be here to look over me and guide me through the thick of it—through the beauty of the birth that was meant to save the world and make it all one—yes it would be so nice to have a world one starting all over again.

I really have to scream and I should be switching off while I have to scream, what should I do? Can you listen to me scream or would you rather not hear it at all and just wait in silence for it all to be over with? Switching off, yes, no, maybe—off.

Go ahead and be born. We can't wait any longer! It's the evening—it's getting to be night! You're all we have—you are our last hope and we've been hoping to see you all day and to hear your voice travel round and round the world. Don't let us down! Come quickly! Show yourself! I was born to deliver you and so I will and nothing is going to stop me, nothing, not even the end of the world.

I'm pushing for you—with every ounce of my strength I'm pushing for you to be born—right here—right now—right here in my grave that I made before I knew that you were going to be born. I'm pushing, dear boy, but you won't come. What's the matter with you? What's the matter with me? What's the matter, what's the matter? Should I drive my fists into the earth to make you come? What is it? Why don't you be born before it's too late? They said—the men on the radio said that in the evening the bombs would come and then after that the poison would be everywhere and we would all die and that would be the end of it until my friends were born in some distant time. But the men on the radio didn't know about you and I didn't tell them when I found out and so they still think that the bombs are going to come. That's why you have to be born now—so there'll still be time to fix things up so we all don't have to die before our time. Be born, be born, be born . . .

Sonia is pounding her fists on the floor of her grave where once upon a time ago she lay down pine needles so her white shirt wouldn't get too dirty when it rained. Why aren't you coming yet when I've made everything ready for you? We can't wait for the doctor. I don't have the strength to get back to the cabin. You won't be born on clean sheets, dear boy. I had them ready for you but that was all so far back when I thought the doctor was going to be there. But I can't call him to come and see us here because I don't have a telephone and I'm in terrible pain and I've waited so long already and Mrs. Mac isn't back from Digby. Switching off because of the pain.

I could be sick and I wouldn't know it. I could die and I wouldn't feel it. I could be alive and I could be dead and I wouldn't know the difference. What's happened to us? The darkness is making me sad and sick and I wouldn't mind if I had to die—but please baby be born. Everyone is waiting for you and everyone is counting on you and I don't mind if I have to die—like my mom—she died for me and my dad died for us and I'm willing to die, too, so that you can be born and save the world from the end. Do you hear me? I'm ready and willing to die tonight for you! Steady now, Sonia. Steady now, my friends. I don't know what's going to happen and I might not be here anymore very soon and I'll miss you when I'm gone and I don't think I'll be able to come and visit you. The pain is easing off. But you can listen to me any time you want and that should make you feel better. Pain is coming back and the pills don't seem to want to work the way they did when it was still light and the sun was still up and high in the sky and you and I were talking the way we normally do. Some time ago it was—we did do that, didn't we? I remember we had a day that was my birthday. I remember that much and I won't forget it no matter how bad the pain.

WORLD ONE

Will you be born? Let me die—it's okay—I've lived enough. I've had a good life and I am happy to die for the rest of the world and for my baby boy. You will take care of my child if I die, won't you? That's all I ask of you—it's not too much when we've been such close friends and have learned about each other even though we don't know each other. I'm just wanting my baby to be born so that you can have a life of your own and grow up right and fix up the world so that it wants to live by mother nature's laws—like my dad said—like my dad wanted it to be—like we all want it to be—like it must be if we are to be happy and do good.

Pain is away, away and Sonia is breathing evenly and the wind is still up high in the trees and the moon is certain to be coming up at any time and I would like to stay alive so that I could see it one more time before I have to die and give up my life so that my child can do what is right. Just one good look at the moon is all I ask—that—and for you to take care of my child. You promise me? Yes, you do. I know you do. You are one of us—one of us who wants to help the world so you don't grow up mutilated and feeling bad about what we did to the world before you were born.

I've been listening to the silence of the world from my grave and I've been listening, waiting to hear the heart of my baby, the crying of my baby, and I'm still listening, still waiting, still hoping that everything is going to be all right very soon—right now—right away—no more waiting, no more listening, no more pain—just happy and happy, nothing more—that's enough.

If I raise up my head I can see the bay even while it's dark and I can hear the wash of the water and somewhere I hear the gulls and they are with me and they are telling the world that the baby is soon to be born and I am happy that it's worked out that way because I want everyone to know that there will be the voice of rolling thunder travelling around the world so that they will come out of their houses and put their ears up to the sky and listen carefully. I never knew that the gulls would do that for me but I should have known. They've been friends of mine for years and they want to help, too, and now they are helping and they are telling people to go out and listen to the voice of my child who is coming to save the world before the end of time. There isn't much time. The time is going with the end of the light that I was seeing in the sky some time ago. I wish I had a radio. I would like to listen to the radio and hear that everything is going to be all right as soon as I am well and have forgotten all about the pain that I'm feeling right now.

Just be born, just be born, my baby boy. It will mean so much to all of us who don't want to die today—who all want to live to see tomorrow come up with the sun.

Something funny is happening to me and I didn't know it for a while, but now I do. I know what it is and I can tell you about it because it's all over and it is better, you see, the pain has gone away and I am myself again—like I was before the pain started and crippled me. Yes, I like resting here in my home and I won't mind sleeping though I'm not tired yet—just relieved that the pain has subsided and gone on to some other place where it can't touch me and cripple me like it did before I had a chance to take some pills to make my life easier to bear on a day like today.

Yes, I like the resting part of this. I read that it is good to rest after the baby comes so that's what I'm doing and I'm not going to apologize for it at all. Breathe evenly, Sonia, and take in the breadth of the sky which is your home, too. I have many homes, you know. One down by the bay, one up here on the edge of the woods, one up there in the sky. That one's just waiting for me and I can have it when I want. It's mine for the asking. I don't want it just yet—not now . . . later, later when it's right—when everything is right—that's when I'll go there and claim my majestic view of the world above and below. . .

Do you hear anyone crying? I thought I did, now I'm not so sure. Are you sure? Or are you just hoping like me that I

WORLD ONE

hear a crying sound. There's supposed to be a crying sound. After the pain—that's when it's supposed to come. But I'm not sure I hear it and I'm counting on you to tell me if it's there. Is it? Is it? Is it? Was it? Was it? Was it?

Was it baby who was crying loud and clear? Was it the new voice of my baby boy? Is he here at last to save us from the world? Beautiful boy, don't cry if you are here. There's no time to cry anymore . . . no one has any time anymore . . . I'm sorry to tell you, but you have to grow up very quickly now and tell the world what it needs to know. Baby boy? Was it you who was crying after the pain went away and I was lying here in the dark? And what's happened to the voices of the party—where are the ones who came to celebrate? You can come out now. The birth is over and the baby's been crying, hasn't he?

What are you waiting for? I can't lie here all night! Pretty soon I'll be running out of tape and then where will I be? I won't have anyone then. It will just be me without Mrs. Mac and without my dad and without my friends. There will only be me and mother nature in the woods and my baby boy. Where is that boy? Where has he gone to? What is he up to—mischief already? It's time to speak my beautiful boy. It's time to say out loud to all the people of the world what you were born to say the moment you were born. Ready now—ready with the voice of rolling thunder? I'm leaving it all to you. Where is everyone who wanted to be here when you were brought into the world?

I don't hear my father's voice—he isn't telling me everything is going to be all right. When are you going to tell me, dad? What are you waiting for? It's now or never. This time or none. What's it going to be, dad? Where's my baby boy?

Sitting up and looking around and still no sound of the one I love. Come back you little rascal, you have work to do. Your mother wants to get a good look at you. Beautiful boy, I'm not here to hurt you. I'm not here to give you any pain. And if you have pain I have some pills that will make you feel better like they did for me. After you've done what you've been born to do, we can all go to sleep—rest up for tomorrow—rest up so we can rise early to see the sun. Baby, baby, why don't you come to me? I went through so much to have you in my arms. Don't desert me. I'm here to take care of you like I'm supposed to do. It's only natural for us to be together now. Now is the time for mother and child to be together . . . So silent you are . . . so quiet . . . so silent . . . so quiet . . . You're not here.

There is no baby boy. You knew that, didn't you? He knew he wasn't here, but you didn't have the courage to tell me he had gone. But he *is* here. There! Next to the white cross! Lying under the white cross in the dark is my baby boy. Why isn't he moving? Why isn't he crying? Why isn't he living anymore? He's dead. Baby was born dead. Baby was living, then he was dying, now he's dead and gone beyond to where my father is. Why wasn't it me? I should die and he should live . . . Let me look at you—let me hold you and make you warm. You shouldn't be out here in the dark. At home I have clean sheets. That would be the place to go. When I have the strength, we'll be home soon.

You see, he would have been a gorgeous baby boy. He had his father's eyes. And smile. Why is he smiling that way at me? Why are his eyes glued to me? Why wasn't he crying the moment he was born? If the doctor had been here he would have cried. The doctor did it. The doctor made him die. The doctor didn't care for him the way he was supposed to and now he's dead and looking that way at me and making me feel like I should die and be with him when all I wanted was for him to live. And he would have saved the world, you know. Someone told me he would have a voice which could wrap itself around the world . . . I remember . . . I remember that that was supposed to be what he was going to do the moment he was born . . . Why didn't my dream come true? He wasn't going to fail—not like my dad. And now what are we going to do? Is it still too late to have another child? Has everyone gone to sleep? Has everyone abandoned me? He wasn't supposed to fail but now he's failed and what am I

WORLD ONE

supposed to do when the hour is dark and the men on the radio haven't brought Beethoven back?

It wasn't my fault. I didn't know he was going to be born dead. No one told me that this was going to happen. The doctor said everything would be all right if I just took the pills. And mother nature was supposed to help me have a perfect birth. But it's a perfect death, isn't it? My baby didn't want to live in the world that was going to die. He just didn't want to live in it and I don't blame him. I don't want to live in it either. I have better things to do. I have a place in the sky to go to. There'll be more baby boys up there. It would be better to live up there than down here where babies are born dead because it's too late for them to save the world. That's the way it is, isn't it? That's why he died, wasn't it? And now the world is going to die like the men on the radio said it would and there's nothing Sonia and her baby can do for it except to die with it and go to the home in the sky where we can start all over again like we were trying to do before . . .

You don't hate me, do you? You know how much I tried to help you. And I've still helped you a little, haven't I? You'll still know what the world was like today—Wednesday—my birthday—the day I was going to have a child that was going to save the world. That's something, isn't it? Even if they mutilate you you'll still be able to listen to me and what I have to say. You won't be as lonely as you would have been. And I promise I'll put all my tapes in one place so you can have them when you want. Please don't hate me. Please don't push me out of your lives. I wanted you to be so happy and now everything's gone wrong and it's not possible to do everything you want. Sometimes things don't turn out just the way you want. I didn't know that before. I always thought that anything was possible. But I've failed like my dad failed like my baby failed because of us. It was our fault. We should have had the voices to speak around the world. We should have been able to do it before it was too late. But that's over now. Now it *is* too late and nothing's to be done anymore and I can understand why everyone's gone to hide in caves and gone to sleep before their time ...

That's what happened to Mrs. Mac ... She never went ... I have to go ... I can't stay here anymore ... There's something I have to do before I can't do it anymore ... What is it? What is it? Tell me, tell me, I have to do it ... I have to do it now or wait forever. There's no forever, only now, and I have to do it now because forever isn't anymore.

First let's get out of this grave. We can't do what I have to do here. There's just no way I can do it here, so let's get out and up and on with it. Ssssssh. Isn't the world wonderful when it's so silent that you can hear just about anything there is to hear? Ssssssh. Let's listen while we still can. We must remember this. We must.

Say good-bye to the sun, my friends. It's gone for another day and there's nothing I can do to bring it back. Such a gorgeous sun today. It will bring us our wishes soon. It wants to come back tomorrow, too. It likes being with us and watching over us and giving us the life that we need.

The pine needles worked. My shirt is still clean and my trousers aren't wet and I was very comfortable down there. It's a perfect place to rest. It's the perfect place to go to sleep on a summer's day. It was very thoughtful of me to dig my own grave. I won't have to put anyone else to any trouble when my time comes to go away and go on and up to some other place far away. They will say that Sonia was a very thoughtful girl. That pleases me. Thought is all that we have. You know what I mean. Intelligent thinking is all that we have. Sane reason is the best that we have to offer, guided by mother nature's laws and all that. Down went the sun over

WORLD ONE

the sea, up went Sonia to do what she had to do. What a lovely evening. What a beautiful day. Ssssssh.

What was it we were going to do? Sssssssh—let me hear myself think. I was thinking that we had to do something and it was all very important, you know. Something about my baby boy and Mrs. Mac and later on this evening. Something about there being so little time. Will you give me a hint? I'm remembering less and less as the evening goes on ... I was doing so well earlier today.

Someone took my baby boy. Yes, thank you for reminding me. I had almost forgotten what happened when I was down in the grave looking up at the world in the evening. Someone took my baby boy before he was even baptized. How could they do that to him? What are their plans for him? Why didn't they even give me a chance to baptize him before he had to go to sleep with me? Don't you remember that we had so many plans? I told you about the plans, didn't I? I don't remember that I did, but I think I did, I'm sure I did. I just can't remember right now.

What about the party we had planned? I know I told you about the party we had planned. That was supposed to be this evening—or at the latest tomorrow. My baby boy and I didn't have the party before they took him away. If I were they, where would I take him to? I have to think creatively. If I were them I would want to protect him and I would want to take him to some place safe ... First of all, they would take him someplace safe until they knew that he was going to be all right. After that, who knows? Do you think they might have started the party without me? Why wouldn't they have invited us? That isn't very fair of them, considering we've all been together since the beginning of the day. And why wouldn't they let me do the things with him that I'd planned?

No, there isn't much sense in all of this. There isn't much intelligent thinking going on around here. Someone is not doing it very well and I hate to see my baby boy get mixed up in all of this. He was supposed to help fix things up, not get mixed up in it and wind up like the rest of us. If I ever have another child, I'm not going to take my eyes off him. I'm going to hold him to me until I know that he's all right and nobody is going to take him away until I know he's safe.

I really have to find him so we can do the things we had planned to do. I can't make mistakes right from the beginning. I can't be like the rest of the mothers in the world. I have a duty like the doctor to take care of my child—even though the doctor didn't come and take care of me when I really needed it. I can't be like the rest of them and let my child down. I have to keep him safe, safe to save the world, safe to live until tomorrow—safe until he reaches his fifteenth birthday. At least until then, at least until he has had a chance to live for as long as me. That's my duty to my child and no one can take that duty away from me. No one. Not even the men in the governments and the men on the radio and the men who took my baby boy away.

Intelligent thinking is what we need now and you can help me if you want. So let's go looking. Let's go finding. Let's show the rest of them that they can't do this to us because we know what is right and how it should be and what we want. They don't know that we've been listening to mother nature all day long. They don't know that about us and that's why we're ahead of them and always have been. Good for us. Very good for us.

I can see the sea down there. It's part of my majestic view. It's the reason why I'm up here. I don't feel the physical pain anymore. I once felt the pain but not any longer. I've erased it. Done away with it. But something else is creeping inside of me—it's a different kind of pain. The doctor would call it

WORLD ONE

emotional pain and I have it bad. You would have it too if they took your child away before you could even speak to him and make him laugh. You would have it too if you didn't know for sure whether he was going to have a fifteenth birthday. It's easy for us to face what's going to happen. But a baby boy. He hasn't lived very long and he doesn't know what beauty there is in it and so he won't understand about dying on the day that he was born. He doesn't have our kind of intelligence. He just expects everything to be okay until he's old enough to understand the way some things have to work out.

I'm going to take another and another yellow pill. It's not the physical pain I mind so much. It's the deep down inside pain that is making trouble for me. And I can't do anything about that. I wasn't made to stand that kind of pain. I was made to do something with my good feelings—not do something because of my bad feelings. Are you still listening to me? Are you still hearing what I have to say on a day like today? I'm pretty sure you won't have to be listening to me for too much longer. I told you what the men on the radio said. They said that this evening was going to be the evening when everything there ever was goes bad. And I'm feeling it. I wasn't before but I am now and I'm sick because of it. Sick way down inside and that's the emotional pain I was talking about and that's why I think I better take another and another yellow pill. I have to think intelligently—without pain—physical or emotional. Thinking hard about what I have to do and where I have to go . . .

And it helps me to know that you are with me, whether you're still listening to me or not. One pill, two pills, down they go and round and round inside me they will go to help me think intelligently. Did you know everyone is missing now? Not you—but all the rest of them. There was dad and the doctor and Mrs. Mac . . . she's been missing for a long time and I thought I could explain it a while ago, but not now—she's missing, too—the minister, too—the people in the town who were all here yesterday and the day before, but now they're all gone, too, and the caves must be full of them. I'm the only one in town. You and me are the only citizens of this town of Sandy Cove and we should be proud of that. Yes, we should. There aren't any people like us around and that makes us special. All we need to do is find my baby boy and then no one will be missing for us. We'll all be together again, like before and then we'll have so much to look forward to that no one will be able to hurt us and make us die and go to sleep before we've had a chance to live a long, long time.

Ready everyone? Sonia says it's time to go and find out what they did to my baby boy after we went to so much trouble to see that he was born just ever so perfectly and intelligently.

Away goes the pain and you and me—my dear friends inside . . . inside of me.

So we're up and out. Out of that old grave where dead people lie and moan and worry about the world that's put them there. What a joke we played on the world. They thought that we were down and out and soon to be dead. Not us! Not you and me! We've had it. We're tired of people disappearing in the day and night. We're tired of feeling any pain. We won't put up with it anymore, you hear! Stop this fighting you men in the governments who have better things to do. Take care of us or we'll all do you in, right now! Either you follow mother nature's laws or she'll slap you down and crush you under her weight and then where will you be? You won't have any governments at all. And you won't have any people to give you your power. You see, we'll all be dead and gone and won't be of any use to you at all. Ha! That would serve you right, I'd say. It would almost be worth dying to do that to you. You silly little boys. You silly bearded boys! Mother nature should have spanked you right from the start. That would have been a much better way to cope with your arrogance and stupidity. Ha! She'll have the last laugh when you've ruined everything there is to ruin. She'll bury us all

WORLD ONE

and start all over again, all by herself—and this time she'll know better than to put her trust in men. I only wish the men on the radio would be there to tell you what they see. I would like you to be informed. I would like you to know what you've missed. I would like you to know what you've done. I would like you to choke on it, my fellow men.

You must think I'm very rude to say these things to people who I don't even know by name. It's very true. I'm rude. But I've explained all this to you. You understand. You're with me. We're sticking together like moss and rock. Let's walk!

Walking is trouble for me and you. My legs feel like plastic sticks. And the ground is a sponge and one step makes me go up, the other makes me go down. This is a new experience for us. The ups and the downs all the way to town. I'm glad no one can see us. I would be angry if they laughed at us. Walking is trouble for you and me. Trouble is walking down to town.

I feel like the black sky. Deep inside my sky is black. Will I get light inside when tomorrow comes? Or will I be black forever inside? I could walk on the sky if I wanted to. I could walk on the sea if I dared. I could walk upsidedown and under and over, around and through. If I only knew where it was that I was walking to . . .

It's true. I feel like me. But then when I turn around I feel like you. What do you suppose that means? I know the future and you know the past. That's our nifty arrangement. That's the one that's gotten us all through the day. If I had a hat, I'd take it off to us. Instead, I'll say thanks a lot! Still going through the trouble of walking to town in the dark. But I can see because I'm blacker inside than out. I'm going to give that doctor a good talking to. I'm going to chew off his ear for not being here. I'm going to report him to the rest of the doctors in the world because he didn't live up to his oath of taking care of you and me when we really needed it. He won't like me after that, I'm sure. Oh, well. I'll send him another Christmas card next year.

You never did get to meet that Mrs. Mac. I'll scold her, too. Sleeping late. Never getting up in time to start the day and make it right. Mrs. Mac needs discipline. To bed without her dinner! Upstairs to her cold and damp room! And only lumpy porridge in the morning. She's got to learn that tardiness is not tolerated. She's got to learn her responsibilities in life. We will teach her—you and I—and she will come to understand the meaning of it all.

I've got to learn to take more medicine. How much better I feel than I did before. There's something in those pills that I like. They make me have some trouble walking to town, you know. Oh, well. At least I'm feeling light. At least I'm feeling strong. At least I know what I'm about. I am and am some more. I have life and live some more. Second by second I live some more and I will not rest until I live to death. Ha! We understand the magic of intelligence. We understand the purpose of our lives—to live today for all tomorrow by our blessed mother nature's laws.

Up and down, down and out—right and wrong—slow and fast—up, up, up to my pillow in the air. I will get there before I'm gone. Don't worry, I'll take you there. As long as I can talk to you I'll take you anywhere I want. We are the history and future of all. We are the original aborigines . . . the first and the last . . . last, but first. First but last. Happy to be here—sorry to leave. Up and down and around on the path back to town. Slow down, take some more medicine for the fall.

Goodness to the last. Goodness at the first. Goodness is the message that goes all the way through. Down go the pills—inside of the dark and the black and the belly of me. Has

WORLD ONE

anybody had the time to see my child? I am looking for him to take him away before he has to die and be gone in the black. Which way you say? To the right or to the left? Up or down? I'm counting on you to tell me which way. Is this a plot to keep my baby boy away from me?

I really am feeling better before it's too late. Or it's too late and I'm feeling much better, thank you. Nice of you to look in after me. It would have been better before, but oh, well, can't change that. Can't change anything. All things are not possible. Babies can't be born on birthdays. Worlds can't be saved on Wednesdays. Lives can't be spared at night. Futures can't come and histories can't go. Trouble is is that I'm having trouble walking to town.

Sonia sees the church in sight. What a lovely sight. No less than my majestic view. Once I had a view and then it got all dark and black and then it vanished like the rest of them. Yesterday we had everything. Now there's only you and me and a baby boy who is lost in the middle of an emergency. I should drive the jeep. This is an emergency. Mrs. Mac said that it would be all right in case of a general emergency. You know that. But it won't help us now. Now it is too late to drive the jeep. I don't know why. It just seems that way ... up and down and around and through. The church is my majestic view and we will get there pretty soon if I can keep on walking on to town.

I better save some pills for later on. You never know when it's time to use them. Time could be right ahead. I'll try to save you some of my pills. They're very good for pain. Or when you're feeling black inside they make it so you can't see it—very good of them, you know. Otherwise it would be black above and black within and then we couldn't see or know anything except to remember the way it was before the darkness came and blinded us and locked us in. I've got a feeling I won't be talking too much longer . . . You've got the picture, though. You've been with me all the way—ever since the very beginning—that was some time ago, wasn't it? Once we had a morning and now it's gone and then we had a day, but that's gone too, and then we had an afternoon and that went too. What is it now we have, my friends? Blackness coming on and on without any help from the sun. I don't know if my wishes are going to come true. I can't promise because I don't know—but I'll be hoping along with you.

I'm down the hill and ready to face the evening. Voice of rolling thunder, where are you? Baby boy, won't you cry even a little for me?

Beautiful baby boy, where have you gone? Don't you even want to get to know your mother who brought you into this world? Don't let those men take you away. They will take you nowhere—or else someplace that's not good for you. Don't let them. We have better things to do. Now stand up and let me know where you are. I want to hear you crying. I want to know that you're alive and feeling fine. That's my duty to you to make sure you're doing fine. You didn't even get a chance to wish me happy birthday. And I never got a chance to wish you the same. We can't let them do this to us. It just won't do and we have to stop them now, or else it will be too late. Then there won't be anything we can do. This is our last chance. Evening is here. The world is going to die. Just speak to me once. That's all I want. Then I can go and die in peace and you and I can go see my dad. He'll want to know you. He wanted so much to be with you. I'm afraid he just couldn't make it today. We will have other times and other joys. But now while I'm still living and liking to look on at the world, I would like so much to be with you, dear boy—my last and only hope for a better world to be.

WORLD ONE

Is that you? Over in the stream—is that you? What are you doing down there—taking a bath so soon? Let me look at you. How did you find your way down to the stream? Who brought you here? Why didn't you tell me you were coming here? I should spank you for scaring me to death. It is you, isn't it?

Come here, little boy. Mommy's here and happy now. She's found her newborn boy sitting in a stream. We won't tell the Reverend that you've taken up in his shallow stream behind the garden gate. I won't even mention it. That way I won't have to tell a lie. He'll never know that you came here on the evening you were born. And by the time you're grown, you won't even remember what you did—just after you were born into such a gorgeous world.

Yes now, let me lift you up. You've gotten yourself so wet! You're so lucky I found you before you caught cold. Colds are not good for infants—no matter how beautiful they are. There you are. You're home and safe and soon will be warm. No one's going to take you away. You're going to be nice and safe with me forever and ever. Are you happy to be with me? I bet you didn't recognize me at first. You'll have to spend some time getting used to me. But I promise you—I'm the only mom you have and I won't ever, ever leave you.

Now—let me wash your face—you've gotten it so dirty. And so soon! I'll have to teach you some manners. My baby boy doesn't go off and get his face dirty the second he is born. That's not the way we do things. It doesn't suit your position in life. You're going to have lots to do if you're going to make things all right. And remember, we're all counting on you. We've been counting on you all day. There—face is clean—clean as moonshine. I wouldn't mind showing you off to anyone now but before we do there's something that has to be done. It's important. I've wanted to do this for a long time but the Reverend wasn't in. So it looks like it's just you and me. We're going to have a baptism right here in the stream. I can't think of a more perfect place. And mother nature's going to be watching over us to make sure we do everything just right.

First things first. Get everything in order and then everything else is going to be all right. That's what we believe. And that's what my friends are counting on too. I bet you didn't know you'd be having such distinguished company so suddenly. Mother nature's all around. My good friends are listening to us now. You are one lucky boy. I wish I'd been so lucky. I never even had a mother, you know. She couldn't come to my baptism. Something went wrong when I was born and then she died and left me all alone with just me dad. And then he died later on and now it's just you and me and mother nature and my friends that I've been talking to.

Now, take some water in my hand—very cool it is for this time of the day. I thought the rain was supposed to make it warm. It's cold, my boy. I hope you won't mind. There's a drop and now two, three and four. That should do. Now, now, you're not going to cry. No, you're not crying and that is good. I didn't think you were going to cry. You are so brave and strong. You're the one for me, all right. There now. Quiet now. Let me say a prayer or two in the shadow of the church. I don't want the Reverend telling me that it wasn't done right.

Bless this child of mine who came into the world today on my fifteenth birthday. Give him the strength to save the world and grow up in a peaceful one. And give him the knowledge to show the world that they should live by mother nature's laws. If you could do this a lot of people would be happy and would be grateful that they didn't have to die today—on such a pretty day—on a day that will never come again if my baby boy doesn't speak out and save the world from the dead.

WORLD ONE

I think I've prayed enough. I don't know how much is enough and what is too little but I think I prayed enough. Do you think I said the right things? I'm talking to you my friends inside my nifty little recording machine. Sometimes when I'm talking I'm not talking to you, but this time I am. I said enough, didn't I? Right—good—it's done.

Wiping off the water, I am and a good thing since it's cold when really it should be warm. We did have rain today, didn't we? I was sure we had some rain. That's why I put those pine needles on my grave. Now we mustn't stay too long. Remember it's evening and you have work to do. I can't wait to hear your voice of rolling thunder. You've been told, haven't you? You know what you have to do, don't you? . . . Of course, you do. You're just a little quiet now—thinking things over—planning out what you're going to do. That's right. You've only got one chance. You better do it just ever so perfectly. We don't have any time to make mistakes. You were born for this and there are so many people counting on you. They don't know it, but they are.

After you've fixed everything up just right do you think you could help me find my dad? I've been looking—just ask my friends—they know—but I haven't had any luck and I thought perhaps you could help me when you've time. Then maybe you could find the doctor. He was supposed to be here. I left a note for him back at the cabin. He might be there. He'll want to take a look at you and see that you're all right. He's a nice man and I like him very much. He gave me lots of pills to help me with the pain that I was having. It's even hard to remember that. I don't feel the pain. I only feel the happiness. Then when you've seen the doctor maybe we could find the minister who's gone on to a funeral. I'd like him to record that you were born today. I'd like to tell him what I said when you were baptized so there won't be any question that I did it right. And then there's Mrs. Mac. Maybe she'll be back from town. She rarely ever comes back after dark. We will all get to see her again. You and me and my best friends in the whole wide world. She won't be mad at me for taking some milk today, if I show her who it was for. She'll be so surprised! You'll make her so happy. You had better mind your manners with her. She's never liked a dirty face so I'll have to scrub you through and through before we go and see her. Are you hungry now?

He said he was hungry and so I better be taking him home where I've prepared some food. Are you happy for me? Isn't my baby boy as beautiful as we all dreamed? I'm going to take him home before anybody else comes and gets him and takes him away from me. After he's had some supper you will hear his voice of rolling thunder and then we can all sleep better tonight, knowing that the world is going to be safe and won't do any of us any harm, anymore.

I guess I only hope that I did the baptism just right . . .

16

You'll be so happy when I get you home. How does it feel to be born? Is it everything you expected? Is it more? I wish you were all grown up and could talk to me. I haven't talked to anyone all day except for my friends who won't be able to talk back until later on. It's funny how one can miss conversation when one doesn't have it. It's like the rest of the things in life—once you don't have them, you miss them. Well, I'm going to raise you so you don't take anything for granted, that's the way I'm going to raise you. No one should take what they have for granted. It could end at any time. And think how we'd miss it all then. It would be pretty sad, don't you think? Yes, it would. I don't need anyone to tell me that. I've been around and then some. I know what I know and am what I am and I don't take any of it for granted—especially you, my boy, especially you.

Out of the cemetary and down the road and through the streets of Sandy Cove. Feet forward, one by one, me and my baby on the way home. And no one's going to take that away—not even you, my men on the radio. You can't hurt us while we're here. No you won't, no you can't. You won't even dare because my baby is going to fix everything up just right.

Open the door, look in and around to see if they're here. No one's here. It's all right. A very safe place it is to go. Do you like it the way I made it up for you? Is it the home where you wanted to be? Yes, my boy, I understand, you'd like some homemade food. But let's light some candles to celebrate. Let's make everything cozy and warm. We want all the world to see that you were born. We will show them by the light. A hundred candles lit at night—a hundred candles surrounding Sonia's house. Come one, come all. Witness the birth of the one who's going to save us all.

I'm going to have that birthday party. I can't take a chance on missing it tomorrow. Today is today. Nothing else counts. Here today, gone tomorrow. We can't take the chance. So you sit there. Sit there on the bed where I have made it up with clean white sheets and pillows and soft blankets. Sit tight, my boy, while I light the candles to show the world that we were born to help the world.

One by one, strike match, light candle, one by one the flames come on and burn. What a glorious sight. What a splendid show. Quite the right way to go and celebrate. Don't you feel all nice and warm? Isn't the world beautiful this way? I wish the world would light all its candles and glow and glow all through the night. Little flames to the east and little flames to the west. Little flames, little flames everywhere we look. They would make everyone so happy. They would make everything turn out all right. Little boy, I'm glad you're here to see the flames. I'm glad you're here to celebrate our

WORLD ONE

birthdays. I must light the ones on the porch. I want Mrs. Mac to see that we are in.

Now we have biscuits and tea and coffee and milk. I'm afraid I haven't any cake—no frosting, too. But I have some supper for you. I made it myself. Would you care for a bite to eat?

Sitting there on the bed, you make me happy. I was so afraid you wouldn't be born in time. But you're here, safe and sound and they didn't get you and take you away. Mother nature has been so good to us. She looks after her kind—those that want to live under her laws, those that care for her as she cares for us. I hope she can see the candles now. I'm sure she's looking down on us, I'm sure she likes what she sees. But don't you dare ever light candles in the woods. When it comes to fires, she frightens easily. Candles are meant to be burned at home—on special occasions like this—for birthdays and babies and to celebrate life. That's what candles are for and always will be. I'm going outside. Don't go away.

It's all done. And there's not too much wind to blow them out. Just enough to make them flicker in the night. Anyone who passes will know that you've been born. We're showing them the right sign—candles at night. Would you like to listen to the radio? I'm sure they've started to play the music by now. They must know that you've been born and that everything is going to be all right. Sometimes at night they play Beethoven on the radio and it puts me in the most wonderful mood. We can stay up for hours—all night if you like. I won't mind not sleeping for another day. A day like this comes once in your life. You have to enjoy it while you can. What would you like?

Would you like me to sing to you instead? I'm told I have a very good voice. I've been known to sing to the woods on rainy afternoons. I've been known to sing when the sun comes up. And I've been known to sing even when it's dark and grey and snow's on the ground. I sing for all seasons. Can you hear it? There's music somewhere ... Over there, over here, everywhere I listen I hear the music. It's not coming from the radio. Are you singing to me? Have you learned how to sing already? Are you practicing to sing to the world out there? I'll just sit here and listen. And anytime you want to sing, go right ahead. I won't make a sound. I won't disturb you. I know you have lots to do and so little time. After all, it's night and this is when it's supposed to all happen.

I'll be quiet while I fix you some milk ... Mrs. Mac wanted you to have some fresh milk. I just remembered ... the doctor didn't come and find my note. I wrote him a note and he didn't even come to read what I said. That's the way it is sometimes, my child. We're all by ourselves even when we don't want to be—it was so lonely when you weren't here. But now there's music coming from everywhere made by you and I am not lonely anymore and I don't need the doctor or anyone else. I just need you and I hope you need me—that's all we have in life, we're all by ourselves, by ourselves, by ourselves without any help.

Candles and music and you and me and all of mother nature out there. But I said I'd be quiet while you practiced your singing. I can't hear the music when I'm talking. Can you hear it in there? Have you heard my baby sing? Didn't I tell you he was going to make everything all right. He's not even an hour old and already he's singing to save the world. After he's had his supper his voice is going to travel round the world and then everyone is going to be listening to what he has to say and to what my dad had to say and what I have to say—all through my beautiful baby boy who has a voice like the voice of rolling thunder that will be heard around the world before it is too late.

Happiness is living with my child in Sandy Cove on Digby's Neck. And I haven't seen the hatchet-man and I don't think he's coming anymore. I think he knows what's in store for

WORLD ONE

him and he wouldn't dare to raise his head while my baby is here and ready to sing for the world. Hatchet-man? How does it feel to be dead?

Hatchet-man is dead, la, la, la. Hatchet-man is no more, la, la, la. He won't find us anymore. Good, good, good, he is dead. There is so much to celebrate. Come one, come all and join the party here and now. The world is safe because my baby's born. Hope, hope, hope has come our way and we are not afraid. Come out of the woods, come out of the caves, come out of your deep sleep. Tomorrow is another day and we must stand up for our rights. The people of the world will rule, the governments of man will be tamed and made to live under mother nature's laws. Just wait until you hear my baby's voice travel round and round the world! All the creatures far and wide will shout out and celebrate his song of harmony. Sing well, my child, sing well.

Now dance with me. Hold on to me. Place your hand on your mother's shoulder. It is time to do the dance of life. Tum-ti-dum-ti-tum, away we go through candlelight and starlight and lamplight. You are in time to make the peace, you are in time to dance with me, you are in time to save the world. Ready go! Ready now. This world was made for you and me and all the rest of them out there and all the ones to come. No one has the right to take that away from us, not one of them, especially not the hatchet-man—he the least of all. But now he can't hurt us anymore. Just sing your song and sing it well and all the creatures will come pouring out of the woods as happy as they can be.

Around and around we dance tonight in the cabin where I have lived, where I have been, not having lived until today. And I owe it all to my friends who are listening to me. I won't forget my friends who have been near me all this time, hoping for their time to dance the dance of life. Sonia hopes for them, Sonia hopes for everyone, Sonia hopes that she gets her wish before she goes to sleep tonight—before she wakes up to see tomorrow shining in the light. Round and round we go, my child celebrating in the candlelight that can be seen on every shore across the waters in the dark. And very soon we will have our Beethoven back.

Sonia is so dizzy—round and round makes her very dizzy, but do not fear, it is better than the pain, the pain has gone away and only the dizziness remains. Are you dizzy, my boy? I will slow the dance. It is slowing down and the day has turned to evening, darkening into night. But we have conquered all. We have had our day. We have had our birthday. No one can take that away—not now or ever. We've had it now, and that is that. It's time for you to change the world. But round and round we go. Just one more dance. Just one more chance at life before the world begins again, before we are all born again into a land where dreams come true and where nothing is impossible and where most everything is right and lives according to mother nature's laws.

I am dizzy and getting dizzier and I can't stop myself from going round and round. Hold on, my baby boy. Hold on tight just one more time. Round and round. I think I'm falling down—slowly falling, slowly coming down—I'm going to black out . . .

What's the smoke? Who's been lighting fires in here? What time is it? Where is my baby boy? Sonia wants to know where her baby boy is gone? Who's been lighting fires in my house?

Over there a candle burns . . . Who knocked it over? There again another candle burns—on the floor, in my house, lighting curtains, going up in smoke. Burning cabin in the

WORLD ONE

night. Candlelight has turned to fire. When did all this happen, why did it happen, where is my baby boy?

He is somewhere on the floor. I remember falling, falling slowly down. He is somewhere underneath the smoke. Why is my cabin smoking now? I'm holding on to you, my friends—but we must find my baby child. Can you see him now? Is he underneath the bed? Is he underneath the fire? Is he underneath the smoke that is making me cry? The curtains are smoking more and more. I'm not dizzy anymore.

Crawling, crawling on the floor . . . looking east and west for my baby boy. Hatchet-man, have you taken him? I didn't see you come right in! That's not fair. You were dead. My baby was alive. You weren't supposed to be here now. We had taken care of you. It's very hard to breathe. I wish the candles were out, where is my boy, he hasn't had his first supper of his life. I had fixed it for him. I even had some milk, but then I was dancing with him and then I got so dizzy I had to go down onto the floor and then I looked up and then there was smoke and then there was fire and now I can't find him anywhere at all.

Holding on to you. I don't want to leave you, can you still hear me? I am not doing fine. Everything is not all right. I need all your help. I must save my child. It's so hot and I can't breathe. Hold on to me, never let me go. My baby boy is somewhere near, if he were near I would hear him crying and then I could find him and then I could save him. I'm beginning to choke and it is getting hotter and I can't stand much more. I must find the door.

My hand is on the door, I feel the bottom of the door, up along the edge, up along the crack, my hand is on the window sill. Still no baby boy—just sounds of fire, the smell of heat. Turn the knob, Sonia. Turn it now before it's all too late.

Your baby boy is dying in the fire—all because of you—all because you lit the candles too soon. You should have waited until he had his chance to save the world. He hadn't time to live. Only time to change the world. It's your fault. It's your fault. You waited too long and now he's gone. Opening the door.

What have I done to my baby boy? He's in there, in the smoke and fire and my house is burning down and the candles aren't my friends anymore. Did you hear that? They've killed my baby boy!

I have to lie down and breathe and be quiet and gain my strength and feel the cold of the air which is warm compared with the heat that was inside—the fire that was everywhere—the fire that is burning, burning my baby as I speak. And we were having such a good time and we were so happy for a while in there—and no one could hurt us—no one except for ourselves—and we hurt ourselves and I am to blame because I was playing in the fire, playing with my baby in the fire and then the candles fell and then the candles burned and then my child was lost and died when I couldn't find him down there on the floor . . .

Sonia—tell your friends that you have killed the world—your world and your baby's world—their world and their children's world—it was all your fault that your child didn't have the chance to save the world from death by fire . . .

Now I'm here, out here. I never wanted to be out here. I always wanted to be in there with my child, but now I'm out here and everything is burning down when it had been so nice and safe and sound. Did you hear that? Everything I ever had is burning down and the water shows the color of

WORLD ONE

the flames and the flames are very bright against the darkness that is everywhere. All dark. All gone. All dead, now, even my little cabin beside the bay.

The candles killed my baby. They killed my baby! Look at them. All of them. I see everyone of them inside those flames and they all know what they did to my boy! They killed him! They let him die. They didn't watch over him like they were supposed to and now he's dead and now he'll never come back and you won't get to know him, nor will I. None of us will ever get to know him the way we should. And it's all because of them! They did it! I did it. I killed my beautiful baby boy. I didn't mean to. We were supposed to have a party. We were supposed to be happy. We were all supposed to be having such a good time—because there wasn't much time left for us anymore . . .

They did it. I did it. They've burned him up inside and the candles aren't my friends anymore—they hurt me like the rest of the people who aren't here anymore.

So what are you going to do about it? There isn't time to have another child! Who's going to save the world? Who's going to put an end to all the misery that's going to happen tonight? I've let you down, my friends. I didn't know this was going to happen to us. I felt sure that my baby would still be alive and try to save you and me and the rest of us. But he's burning inside and he's dead inside and there isn't a thing I can do about it but watch the flames go higher and higher— all the way up into the sky—the black sky, the same black that I feel inside . . . I was so hoping and now I'm not hoping anymore. All of it's gone. All of it's ended. All of it's dead, eaten up by the flames from the candles that were supposed to help us celebrate my fifteenth birthday and the birthday of my child.

You can say I did it. I won't hate you if you say I did it. But it wasn't only me . . . my dad did it, too. The doctor did it, too. The minister did it, too—and Mrs. Mac—they all did it, too. You see, they should have been here to help me and my baby boy. I wasn't asking too much was I? Older people are supposed to take care of you. A girl like me can't do very much. I can't control the world around me. And mother nature can only do so much. She can only be our guide, like my father said. They all should have helped me and looked out after me and taken care of me and my child instead of going away to some other place where I couldn't find them and ask them what to do.

What am I going to do now? My baby could have done something. He was born to save us but now he's not able to. He can't help us—can't help you—can't even help the people of Sandy Cove—can't ask them to come back and live like they used to. This is very bad and I feel so sick and feel so much pain and it's all on the inside—all black on the inside—all dead on the inside. There is nothing there and it's all supposed to happen right now. The men on the radio said it was all supposed to happen right about now and there just isn't time anymore. And I don't have a home to go into. I loved my little home. It was very special to me and I was going to give it to you if I had to die today. Now I still think I'm going to have to die but now I won't have anything to give to you except for what I've had to say today on my nifty little recording machine. Is that enough? Will that mean something to you anyway? I have the tapes in my pocket. I won't let them get wet in the rain, if it rains before I have to die. And I'll hold my recording machine under me while I'm dying. It won't get rusty that way. You'll be able to play it when you come to Sandy Cove and find me in my grave. This has turned out to be the worst day of my life and I wish I never had had a birthday and I wish I had never had my baby boy. It would have been better to leave life to the past—remember it the way it was some time ago. I don't want to think about it anymore. They should have been here to help me, I wish they had been here to help me. I wish I had just slept all day—like Mrs. Mac. She's been sleeping, she knew what was going to happen. That's why she went to sleep. She wasn't in Digby. I just made that up. I knew all along that

WORLD ONE

she was sleeping and that she was dead and wasn't coming back anymore. I just made all that up so you wouldn't be too afraid for me. But now you have to be afraid for me because I'm going to die. If not tonight, then tomorrow or the day after that. That's why everyone I ever knew in Sandy Cove is hiding in the caves. They knew what was going to happen today. They listened to the men on the radio and they believed them like I believe them now. No baby can save the world—it's way too late for that. I'm sorry. I tried. I failed like my father did. I'm ashamed and I'll never forgive myself for what I've done to you and to my baby boy and to the people of the world who were counting on me and on him. Now it's going to be up to you—you good people of the future. You're the ones who are going to have to keep on living even if you're mutilated and not like us at all. I tried everything I knew to save you—you heard me—it's on the tape. You know what I tried to do. I failed, that's all, and now there isn't anything any of us can do but wait until the end.

Did you know that I've grown to love you as much as myself? I bet you didn't know that. I do. I love you as much as myself—maybe more—you're really just me—the later on me—and you're the later on everyone else, too. Everyone no matter who they are counted on you to be born and to live and to carry on and to do the best you could for the memory of everyone else who came before you ... That's the way it works and that's the way it's supposed to be—people living on, trying to get along. Well, we didn't get along and we've let you down and you can hate us if you want, no one will blame you, I'm just so sorry that it ended this way.

And my house is falling down and there won't be anything left of it in awhile and I can't stand here and look at it and think of my baby inside. I feel sick and I feel I'm in pain and I wish I had died before I was born. I wish I had never lived. I wish I hadn't known the world the way it is because now when I die I'll have memories of other days when the sea was calm and the sun was so shiny and bright that it made me feel glad to be part of it. You at least got to hear something about it. You at least got to go for a walk with me and see the things that I really liked. I'm sorry you didn't get to meet all the wonderful, nice people in town. They were smarter than me. They went hiding because they knew my baby wasn't going to save the world. They knew he was going to die when he had just started to live and they didn't want to be around when they saw how much this has hurt me—I—I—I—don't want to die but the candles made my house burn down and no one is here anymore and there isn't anything to live for now that I know that the men on the radio were right. There isn't time to fix it up and make it right. Mother nature must be very sad too—why doesn't anyone listen to her? Why didn't they listen to my dad? Why did they kill my beautiful baby boy before he had a chance to live?

There's only you and only me and that isn't very much anymore ... And I'm running out of tape and once that's gone there won't even be you—just me, just Sonia in Sandy Cove without anything, anyone, anywhere to go ... but to sleep.

But I can't go to sleep in my house anymore. I would go to sleep there if I could, I really would, but it's burning down around my baby boy and it's not safe in there and I don't want to die in the flames, I don't want to die at all, I just want to go to sleep for a long, long time until the world is better and until the men on the radio say it's safe to wake up and live again. At least then I'd be sleeping along with Mrs. Mac and it would be all very peaceful and calm if I were sleeping along with Mrs. Mac. Don't burn little cabin, don't burn all the way down. I had it fixed up so nicely and I loved it so much and it would have been the perfect home for my baby. He would have grown up right in it and everyone would have come from far and wide to see where he had lived when

WORLD ONE

he had the voice of rolling thunder that saved the world from the end.

There's only one place left to go. I should have stayed there in the first place. I should never have come home. My baby would be alive right now if I hadn't come home and hadn't lit the candles and hadn't danced before it was time. I should have waited until my child had saved the world. Then we should have had our party together. Then all the other guests could have come and been with us and then nothing would have happened. Everyone would have been safe and I would have a home and a child and a life to look forward to—but now it's different, now I think it's best that I go to sleep and dream and be with Mrs. Mac until it's safe to live again. I should go back up to the cemetary and get some sleep—lie down and close my eyes and let the sleep come and take me away to some other place where no harm can come to me. If I do that then everything will be all right. It would be so nice to have everything all right. Don't you think? You could rest, too. It's time for you to rest. You've been with me all day and you must be getting tired now—yes, you must be getting tired and maybe you would like to get some sleep along with me and Mrs. Mac. Now is the perfect time to go to sleep. Everything is calm and quiet, everything is still and it's not scary anymore. I'm not afraid of anything, it's just time to sleep, that's all . . .

And I have just the thing to help me sleep. Remember? I have some pills that are good for the pain which I was feeling before my child was born and then after my child was born and now, now . . . I thought I had gotten rid of it but it's still here and it's a pain that goes way down deep inside and it sticks with me no matter what I say or what I think. The pain is everywhere I look and in everything I see and it seems as though I just have to learn to live with all this pain. There's nothing I can do about it—only the pills will take it away, make it leave me alone—allow me to go to sleep and dream and forget about everything that's happened today and is going to happen tonight. Pretty soon now, the men on the radio said it would happen pretty soon and it's true. They were right and I was wrong.

Take the pills, Sonia. Take the pills now, Sonia. There isn't time not to take the pills. Mrs. Mac took the pills and then she went to sleep and now she is so much better off than I. I want to go where she is. I want to be with her. I want to thank her for my gloves that she gave me for my birthday. I want her to know how much I appreciate them—how much they mean to me, how much they will always mean to me because she meant so much to me. I'm going to count the pills—five and six, nine and ten, fourteen and eighteen—twenty, twenty-two. Twenty-two pills and everything's right. Twenty-two pills and time to sleep. They look so pretty in my hands—yellow, yellow, yellow pills in the fire light. I wish I had some water to help me drink them down. I wish I had a cup of Folger's coffee. I wish, I wish that you were here beside me, then all of us could go to sleep and take our dreams into a better world where everything was right.

Down they go—six and seven and eight. Take a breath, down they go—nine and ten and eleven and twelve. Take a breath, swallow hard, don't worry about the heat and flames. They can't do you any harm. They just go on and on without any thought about tomorrow. But I can fix it up for us. I know the way to go to sleep. And I've seen it done before. I saw Mrs. Mac asleep when it was morning. She knew that it was time to go. Mrs. Mac was always smarter than me—she was practically my mother you know. And you are my brothers and my sisters. We are brothers and sisters in this world which is about to go to sleep. So burn yourself down my little cabin in Sandy Cove. I have other places to go. And where I'm going, you can't come—even if you didn't have any flames inside of you.

Thirteen and fourteen, happy birthday, Sonia, fifteen and sixteen and seventeen and eighteen and nineteen and twenty. Two more to go. Two more to make me dream some happy

WORLD ONE

dreams. Then all I'll have to do is to go and find my grave—my grave underneath the trees, protected from the rain with pine needles on the floor to keep my shirt clean and warm my back while mother nature watches over me and helps me dream. So take them all, Sonia, take them while you can. You never know what's going to happen to you and everyone needs rest. Twenty-one, twenty-two. You've done it and that is good. They can't take that away from you. No one can keep you from sleeping now and you're protected from the pain—that great pain that makes you black inside—all the way inside.

So before the pills take me away and put me to sleep we can watch my happy cabin burn right on down to the ground—right on top of my little boy who never had a chance to save the world. You don't mind watching with me? It's the last time we'll ever get to see it—the last time anyone will ever get to see it. It was all I ever had. It was all my dad left me before he went on like I'm going to go on, like we'll all going to go on because today is my fifteenth birthday and nothing has turned out right. I'm sorry, I'm sorry that I was ever born. I'm sorry, I'm sorry that I didn't work everything out. I'm sorry, I'm sorry I killed my child. Mother nature will you ever forgive me? And will you ever forgive me—will anyone ever forgive me for what I've done to the world that was my home?

Falling down, it's falling down. I told you it was going to fall down and bury everything I ever had in ash. But you're safe with me. I told you that and I mean that. You won't get rusty and our story will be safe and I want you to get some sleep along with me so you'll have a better day tomorrow. It's time I said good-bye to my home. It was my home, I know. And I lived in it for a time before I started listening to the men on the radio. But when they took my Beethoven away it wasn't my home anymore—and then they took my child away and now I don't ever remember living there. And if I ever did—it was a long, long time ago and everything was different then, not like it is now. I don't mind. I have a place to go. I dug a hole in the ground so I could hide in it when things went black outside.

And things are black outside and inside and everywhere I turn it's not the way it used to be. I remember liking it much better before. You liked it better too. We all liked it better before, but that was yesterday and today is today and there's nothing we can do anymore but find another home.

So I'm sorry you had to die, my little cabin by the bay. I'm sorry you had to die, my beautiful little boy. It'll take more than you or me to save the world. It'll take everybody alive to save the world but then we should have thought about that a long, long time ago. Oh, well. I can't be gloomy for the rest of the day. I have to go on and find another home—a home away from home. Wouldn't it be nice to have just one home? I hate this moving every other minute or two. It really wears me down. It makes me sleepy. I need to find a bed in which to sleep, just a bed will do. Then I'll worry about another home. Then I'll worry about another child. Then I'll worry about finding everyone I've ever known. I'll do all that later—after I get up and the morning is here again and the sun is making me warm and I'm feeling like myself again.

So good-bye. Now Sonia must walk—go back up the road, through the streets of the town where she lived and was so happy for a while . . . Can you think of a tune to sing, Sonia? Is there one special tune you would like to sing to your friends who will soon be sleeping too? Something happy would do. Leave them happy, Sonia, and they will remember you even when you're sleeping in your bed. Quiet now, thinking now, waiting for that special tune to come into my head. It is coming from somewhere deep inside where it is still a little light. I knew I had a little light left inside. I knew

WORLD ONE

it wouldn't be all gone. I knew I would find it, too—that last little special light inside that would give me a tune to sing to my friends before I had to go to bed. It's Beethoven's Moonlight Sonata, you know. That's the special tune I have for you. It's all feelings to me—both happy and sad, fearless and calm, but always beautiful—like people, like the world, like this evening, like the morning. It doesn't matter if the men on the radio won't play him anymore. I still remember the way it sounds—I couldn't forget that. I know the music by heart and I love his music because it feels for all things—all living things that once had a place in the world before it got to be too late.

And now I have all the time in the world to sing it out loud. There's nothing else I'd rather do than to sing this tune to you—you can always have it that way, and any time you're feeling blue and want to know how it was to live in this other world—just play my tune and you will know the beauty of what we had when we were all alive and living so well. Sonia has all the time in the world—that is good. She has no place to go, but to sleep—that is good, too. She's been up for many hours—she didn't get any sleep last night—she wanted to get to know you before she didn't have any time anymore. Well, she knows you a little now—that's better than not. That's something to remember at least. Sonia can sleep remembering you and thinking of you and knowing that she went to sleep in the company of friends who wanted to know how it was to live in a world where there was light and sun and music and sea. Sonia doesn't have to worry anymore. No, there is nothing to worry about because everything is the way it is and Sonia knows now that that is the way it was supposed to be. Mother nature wanted it this way. She wanted the people of the world to learn their lessons and this is the way she has chosen to do it, so you can see, I haven't a thing to worry about. That is good, that is right. Better to sleep in peace knowing that everything is the way it is supposed to be.

Strolling through the streets, up through the winding streets of the town—will I ever see it again? I hope you do. I'll be up at my grave and I give you permission to wake me. Will you bring me a cup of coffee? I like having a cup of coffee as soon as I'm awake. I can see the world better that way. I like Folger's Instant Coffee the best, if you can manage it. Just shake my arm and I'll be up—but I won't wake until you shake me. I'll just go on dreaming and dreaming until you come and wake me with a cup of instant coffee.

Now if by chance you can't wake me up—if I've been sleeping too long and I just won't wake up—remember that I'll still be alive in this nifty little recording machine. So if you can't wake me, just turn it on and I'll be there and that way we'll be together until the day you die. Mostly I've forgotten what I've said to you today—but it's all there—everything I said. You might like parts of it better than others. That's okay. I won't be offended if you want to skip over some of it. If I wasn't so tired, I'd go back over it and erase the parts that were boring to you, but then I wouldn't be sure which they would be because I don't know you well enough yet. So it's better if I just leave it alone and let you be the judge of what's good.

Did I tell you I know of a bed where I can sleep? I was just there a while ago. I made it myself and it has a blanket of pine needles which will keep me warm in the night. And there are trees over head that will protect me if it rains. And best of all, it's out in the woods where I like to sleep because I can sleep next to the creatures in the woods and mother nature can watch over me to see that no harm ever comes to me while I'm dreaming about happiness and the good things in life. I'm taking you there right now. It's up by the church. It's on a high hill with a majestic view of the bay. It's getting too dark to see the view, but in the morning, in the morning the sun will make it shine.

Don't you think we've had a splendid birthday together? I don't think there is anyone else in the world I'd rather have shared it with. You've been so understanding and gone with

WORLD ONE

me everywhere I wanted to go. And you never complained and you never got tired and you always wanted to please me and help me even when I was having emergencies. That says a lot about you. Not many people would do that you know. A lot of people would have only stayed with me for the dawn or for the morning or for the afternoon or for the evening— but you, you my friends, have stayed with me all through the day and have made it a very special day.

I don't think there will be anybody up by my bed. I used to think I'd see my other friends from time to time today. But they never came and now I don't think they'll ever come and that's too bad and everything but I've come to accept it and don't blame them anymore. They've had other things to do and just couldn't get here to celebrate. That happens sometimes . . . sometimes that just happens and it's not good to blame anyone for it.

You would think that I'd like to look back and see my cabin— what's left of my cabin. I don't want to. There's no reason to be sad anymore. Sometimes things just happen even when you don't want them to. I've learned about that. You can't expect everything in this life to turn out the way you want it to. Not everything is possible no matter how much you might think that it is. And I know now that one person can't change the world and keep it from dying. It takes lots of people to change the world in the right way. I just mention these things to show off how much I've learned since I first met you. I guess my dad knew this—that's probably why he committed suicide and died the way he did. But I don't feel as bad as him. At least I got to know you. And I wouldn't ever think of committing suicide. Even if I was in the greatest of pain I would never want to shoot myself. If anything, I think I'd just like to go to sleep—like Mrs. Mac. That way no one could call me a coward and say that I was taking after my dad. And no one could accuse me of hiding in caves. I would never ever want to be accused of that. That's about the worst, if you ask me.

No, I think I'd just go to sleep in my bed and hope that tomorrow would be better than today—hope that there would be a miracle or something that would make everything all right. I never thought about this before, but maybe, maybe it's just possible that there is another baby somewhere around the world that has been born today, and that this baby is going to be the one with the voice of rolling thunder that is going to save the world. Anything is possible, you know. You just have to keep your faith about these things and hope for the best and sleep through the bad parts that you don't want to see. That's what I'm going to do. I'm just going to curl up with you and get some sleep and dream about the new sun coming up over the bay in the morning.

This is the hour when all the things in the night come out. This is the hour that the men on the radio were waiting for. This is the hour when you and I retreat. We'll leave behind the troubles of the day. We had some troubles, but a lot of it was good, very special for a birthday, very special for this time in my life. Twilight has turned to night. Aren't they a little late? I thought surely it would be over by now. I had expected it. I don't like to be kept waiting in suspense. Ever since I was a little girl I never liked suspense. I like things to happen when they're supposed to happen—not before, not after. What's taking them all so long? I don't believe they're fixing things up for us. I would have heard that voice of rolling thunder. I'm sure I would have heard it coming in over the bay from the sea—from the land to the west. We would have heard, I'm sure. Did you hear it when I wasn't listening? You would have told me if you had, isn't that right? We've become friends and friends tell each other what they want to know. I've been listening but I haven't heard and so I know that they are late and that they are keeping everyone in suspense which isn't very kind of them. We'd all rather get it over with. I don't know whether I can wait up for it. You see, I am really rather tired now. I thought that I could stay up for days and days, but my birthday has taken a lot out of

WORLD ONE

me—what with all the walking and my bad driving and my baby being born. If it had been an easier day I'm sure I could have stayed up for the event. But it's late and I'm sleepy and I might have to miss all the excitement after all. I'm not made of stone, after all. I'm a person, just like you. Except I'm a person who lived before all the excitement and that makes me a little different than you. I have a perfect nose and eyes and cheeks. No one can ever say that I was mutilated in any way. I must have had a perfect birth. When they dig me up out of my grave, they'll know that I wasn't one of the mutilated ones that came after the excitement of tonight.

What's that I hear? You heard it, didn't you? Rumbling, low, low rumbling from somewhere out over the middle of the sea. I'm sure I heard the rumbling—listen carefully—faint sounds, long low howls, like thunder underground, like thunder coming down from heaven, like the voice, the very voice of rolling thunder that we were talking about awhile ago. And there! Over there—flashes on the sea—milky white, faint and light, like moving pictures of a storm—but it's not close—it's happening somewhere else, not close to you and me. That's good. It's better that way. That way we can really see it instead of being in the middle of it all. Like, like white shadows in a dark room—and low rumblings like a train on the railroad tracks ... We had better hurry up—there's no telling what's going to happen next. We're safe now. We're okay right now, but later on everything might change and we might find each other in the middle of it before we have a chance to get some sleep.

Sonia is marching up the road on the way to bed and nothing is going to take her from her bed. She has a right to sleep, you know. So do you. We all have a right to get some sleep in peace without being disturbed by the low rumblings and the white flashes and white shadows on the painted night. Sonia is climbing up the hill—once more she climbs, but this time she will not return to town until she's had her sleep and dreams about tomorrow. I'm sorry I don't have the time to introduce you to all the people in the town—we tried today, but we were too late—we should have come around yesterday—it would have been better then. I would have been so glad to introduce you. I really did know the people in this town of Sandy Cove. I wasn't making them all up. I still don't know why they all decided to desert me—maybe they came by for me when I was with you on the other side of the bay—that's probably it. They came for me and I wasn't there. They must have known that I was with you and they decided not to disturb us, knowing that it was my birthday.

Up she goes, like a fish in the stream, like a jeep on the road, like a rising moon, like a spirit in space—all these things are me as I climb up the hill to my bed to the sounds of low rumblings and to the light of white shadows far away and to the east. What a pretty picture the grave markers make. They have the white shadows on them—they are glowing to the sounds. I wish I had my camera, but I had to leave it in the cabin along with my baby boy and I can't go back for it. Anyway I'd have to go all the way to Digby to buy some film and it's too late for that and I couldn't drive the jeep because I'm only supposed to use that in case of an emergency—and picture taking isn't any emergency—it would be nice, but it's not an emergency. Sorry. You'll have to use your imaginations to picture just right the way the white shadows make their marks on the crosses that watch over all the beds in the night.

Looking so nice, white crosses in the night, looking so nice, it's good to be home. Hearing so nice, I'm hearing so nice, the sounds of rolling thunder, rumbling thunder. Aren't I? There was another child, wasn't there? Mine was not the only child that was meant to save the world. The Almighty took care to make two. Mine and some other. He must be very disappointed in me. But He must have known that one wouldn't make it. And it was mine and it was because of me. It's okay though. I'm hearing the voice of rolling thunder. It will come closer too. So listen hard and try to make out what it has to say. There will be a message in it—my dad's message

WORLD ONE

and mother nature's message. Everyone is trying to help us hear the message. Do you think it will be in English, or do you suppose it will be in every language said at the same time? I can't make out the words—but when it comes closer we'll all hear the words together along with the rest of the people of the world. One voice that travels round the world at once. That's kind of a miracle, you know. It's not every day that that can happen, but this is a special day like I said before and wonderful things can happen on special days.

Right now the markers on the graves are swimming in front of me. If I didn't know better I'd say they were fish come up from the bay to say good-bye to me. Swimming they are right in front of me—just like they do when they're under the sea. I can't explain that. I can't explain what I see. I thought I said good-bye to them. Now I guess they're saying good-bye to me. But they don't understand. I'm only going to sleep for a while. I'll be back by morning, I'm sure. They've gone to a lot of trouble just to say goodnight. Goodnight to you, my favorite fishes of the sea. Thank you for coming to see me to my bed. You make pretty patterns in this light. You are one of those masterpieces I was talking about. You should see them, swimming to my left and right. You should see them swimming upsidedown. And when the light from the shadows catches their eyes the whole front of the dark lights up and it's as if the hillside were lit with flames from the shadows. And the eyes of the flames are the eyes of the fishes that have come to see me to bed. I can't describe it any better than that. I wish I could, but I can't and since I don't have a camera to take pictures with, that will have to do. Some night you might come up here and see if you can see them. They might come up for you, knowing that you're friends of mine. I've found fishes to be such loyal friends—they treat you right if you don't bother them and try to catch them and fry them for supper. I haven't had any dinner, have you? It's not good to go to bed hungry. It's bad for your dreams. But I won't catch any fish to fry them and I'll just have to take my chances on having bad dreams, because I'm just too tired for any of this.

I can be tired but that won't ruin my favorite time of the day. This is the time of the day when I like to think, I think best when the sun has just set and the moon hasn't risen and I'm all alone minding the dark and watching out for my friends. It's a good feeling to be alone at this time of the day. I wish I could describe all my thinking. I think you'd be rather impressed. But these kinds of thoughts can't often be described. If I had a camera I would take a picture of them. But right now I think I'll just be alone with my thoughts—if that doesn't offend you. It's the last chance I'll have to think for a while and it's best to take the time to think right now before the voice of rolling thunder gets too close and interrupts my favorite time of the day.

Sonia switches off in white shadows and distant rumbles. Sonia gives thanks for the fishes she can see. Sonia gives thanks for the end of the day . . .

Sonia coming back out of her thinking after being there for such a long time. Sonia is here to stay now, she's thought of all the things that she can. Sonia has reached the crest of the hill with the majestic view and she still hears the low rumblings and still sees from time to time the white shadows on the distant horizon. Sonia is running out of tape and she hasn't anymore. She did have some, but that's all back in the cabin and she can't go there anymore because it's been burned down to the ground and she only has some clean white sheets that she pulled from her bed to sleep on. Much better to sleep on clean sheets than on the dirty ground . . .

My bed looks small to me. I remember it being so much bigger than this. It's funny how things can change in such a short time. But it will have to do. There isn't time to dig another bed. The sleepiness has gotten to me and it is demanding that I go to sleep and that is good because I am running out of tape and I won't be able to buy any until next Wednesday when Mrs. Mac goes to town. If I could stay

WORLD ONE

awake until then then I wouldn't miss anything. I could stay up to see the dawn, hear all the creatures in the woods wake up and worship the early morning sun. And I would get to see the majestic view again—sun and sea, beach and sand—listen to the lapping of the waves down below as they creep closer and closer to the shore. No, I'd rather not go to sleep. I do have so much to look forward to. I have so many more thoughts I'd like to think. And I'm getting better at thinking those thoughts. It's been a great help to have you near me so that I could practice thinking those thoughts and all the while to have some company. I really don't know what I'd have done without you. I couldn't very well just talk to myself all day long—think what other people would think. They would really think that I was nuts! Well, it's true, I do have a little nuts in me. I'm a little crazy, too. But we're all like that sometimes—that's just part of being alive—it's all pretty harmless when you come right down to it. Without being a little nuts then you wouldn't know when you were sane. Isn't that right? You'll be a little crazy, too. After tonight the whole world is going to be nuts—the only sane thing will be what's left of mother nature—she's the only sane one among us. That's because she was here at the beginning and she's had a longer time to sort out her thoughts. But if you want my advice, you better learn to live with her and under her laws. She knows best. She's wiser than the rest of us and you must show her respect.

I really am getting sleepy now. My birthday doesn't seem to end . . . It just goes on and on as long as I'm awake. I wonder what I'll be doing next year for my sixteenth birthday? I hope I'll have a chance to see the rest of the world—fly like a bird from one end to the other—get to know everyone there is to know. That's what's so nice about the future. You never know what's going to happen or where you might end up. It could be anywhere. I could be doing anything, seeing anything, thinking any thoughts I wanted to. All I need is time and I can go anywhere and do anything and be anyone I want to be. I just have to hope that everything is going to be all right. It will, won't it? They won't take the world away from me, will they? It wouldn't be fair if they did. You see, I haven't lived as long as some others. I haven't had the chances that other people have had. And don't think I'm complaining. At least I've lived until my fifteenth birthday. That's better than some, you know. There are some children out there that are only four and five years old. Not very old. They haven't even begun to think their best thoughts. They haven't even seen what I've seen. And they never got to know people like Mrs. Mac and Doctor Elson and Reverend Russell—never even got to know their dads. I would feel sorry for them if they didn't even have a chance to get to know their dads.

You know, up here, on the hill, by my bed, I feel calm. I can't quite explain the feeling. It's one of those mysterious feelings that only older people can describe. Since I'm not old—not really old—I won't try. But it's something like contentment—a kind of peace that goes over you just before you fall off to sleep. Just while you're on the edges of your dreams that are coming down to swoop you away from the whole of the living—into the world of the dreaming. That doesn't explain it quite right but I'm sure you get my meaning. If I had one wish right now I think I'd make a wish for tomorrow. I'd like to see the sun rising up out of the sea, the clouds breaking away making room for it to climb up higher and higher. Then I'd like to see the tide come in and go out—all in a few seconds. What I'm saying is that I'd like to see a whole day pass by from up here, from the most beautifully majestic view of them all. It wouldn't have to take very long. Everything could go very fast. To see a whole day pass by in a minute—all the colors and the changes of the winds—and the movements of the creatures in the woods—the noises in the forests—the sunlight shifting over the water. Just have it all happen almost at once. Wouldn't that be kind of nice? See it all come and go in an instant. Here one second and then gone the next. But think of it. Those few seconds would be such a rich experience. You could see life so clearly. It wouldn't be all drawn out like it is when you're living it. It would be all there for you to enjoy like a good cup of instant coffee. I don't think anyone would want to hurt the world if

WORLD ONE

they could see it like that. It would make them too happy to see everything so alive and changing, changing so quickly before their eyes. And of course, they could really see the power of mother nature and what she does for the world every day of the week. And then people might take a special notice of her and learn to live according to her laws. It would be natural then for all the people of the world to want to live by her laws—because she's learned how to live forever and you know she would never want to destroy herself. She can't destroy herself. She's found a balance that makes everything come out all right. And she takes care of her kind and watches over them and sees to it that everything has a chance to go on living.

I guess that's why I always liked sleeping in the woods. I felt safe with mother nature watching over me. And there I didn't have to listen to the men on the radio. They couldn't find me there. And the men in the governments were even farther away. They didn't exist for me at all. I could be happy there in the woods, knowing that she was watching over me and would see to it that I didn't come to any harm. Well, that's the way I want it tonight. I'll go to sleep in the woods, knowing that I'll be safe from harm because she is everywhere and taking care of me, knowing she'll be there in the morning when I wake up, knowing she'll be there all day, morning, noon and night. I don't know how much longer I can stay awake . . . I'm remembering now that I have so little time . . . I had so much time but now there's so little and I'm sleepy and I haven't finished talking to you.

Well, let me say some things I think I've forgotten to say. I want to thank everyone for being so kind to me. I really have had such a wonderful life. And I was taken care of for a time—ever since I was born I have been taken care of and I'm thankful for that, really I am. And all through my life I always had some company so I was never too lonely. And then I met you and now I'll never be lonely again. I'll always remember you and what we've meant to each other. Friends like you don't come along every day and so you can be sure how much I appreciate you and you were so nice about the death of my beautiful baby boy and about my cabin burning down. I'm sorry I can't give you my cabin anymore. Maybe one of my neighbors will let you sleep with them. And if you want you can play this recording for them, too. Maybe you could remember to thank them for me for everything they've done for me. Would that be asking too much? I don't want to put you to any trouble. It's just that I don't think I have time to write them anymore notes. Sometimes you just run out of time—sometimes there just isn't anymore. I don't know why—but I've found that to be true.

Quiet now—listening to the trees, now—thinking about sleeping, thinking about you. How nice it will be to sleep in some peace—if only I could remember what it is I'd like to do tomorrow . . .

I better lie down. Wrap myself up in my clean white sheets and lie down. Wasn't there a time today when we were by the bay? Wasn't there a time today when we were listening to the sounds of the waves lapping against the hull of the ship that had been wrecked on the shore? I remember something about that. You and I were listening to those sounds and those were the sounds I was hoping to sleep by . . . Somewhere on this tape I have those sounds—it would be so nice to hear them before I sleep. If I can't hear them tonight would you someday find them for me and listen to them and think of me? If you listen closely you might hear my voice in those sounds. I don't know what I'll be saying but I think it will be something like I love you and miss you, my friends. That's what I would want to say to you even if I can't. It's so warm down here in my bed and when I look up I feel safe because I know that mother nature is watching over me—she is taking care of me because I respect what she has to say—and I know, too, that

WORLD ONE

she is taking care of my dad because he loved her even more than me.

Are you comfortable underneath my arms? Don't worry, I won't let any harm come to you. My clean white sheets will protect you from the rain and the rust—you'll be okay without me.

Did you hear that? That was the voice of rolling thunder again. It's louder now—it's coming closer now and the sky sometimes lights up like someone was taking a picture of it. That's good—everyone around the world is hearing the voice of thunder—and they will soon know what they have to know to go on living and sleeping and having days like today. That's good. I'm very glad of it. I was worried that it wouldn't come in time—but it is coming and everything is going to be all right. You won't have to worry about being mutilated now. And pretty soon you'll be able to listen to Beethoven on the radio. I can usually get it coming in from Boston during the day. And at night they have music coming in from London. They won't have those men on the radio anymore. They will all have gone home and gone to bed. They will be much happier that way and I'm glad for them. They should all be home with their families listening to Beethoven on the radio and sipping a cup of Chinese Pekoe tea. The English like their tea at the strangest times. I like coffee any time.

You know, if I could see myself right now I bet I would see myself smiling. I often smile a lot before I go to sleep. I think it's because I'm remembering what I did during the day. And I think if I smile before I go to sleep I have more beautiful dreams and it's at times like that that I think anything is possible and it makes me look forward to tomorrow when I can get up and try it again. So I bet if I had a mirror right now, I would see myself smiling out here on the hill above the church on the edge of the woods. But I don't need a mirror. I know I'm smiling. I know I'm happy. I know how glad I am just to be alive talking to you.

You don't even have a picture of me! Maybe if the fire in the cabin didn't burn everything down you could go and try to find a picture of me so you would know what I looked like while you were listening to me. I forgot that you wouldn't be able to see me. I guess I was hoping that I could meet you sometime when everything was all right again and that you could see me in person. But that won't happen will it? I'll be asleep when you come to Sandy Cove. All I can say is that I hope I'll look the same when I'm asleep as when I'm awake. My dad used to say that I smiled when I was sleeping. I hope I'm smiling for you. I wouldn't dream of having you find me frowning at you. I'll do my very best to be smiling at the instant when I fall off to sleep. I want you to have a good impression of me. I want to look my best here under the trees.

Did you hear that again? More thunder—closer now—the voice is travelling round the world—just like I said it would. You see, there really is someone taking care of us. And the sky is turning white again—brighter now—whiter than it was before. It is a very powerful voice. It wants to be seen as well as heard. That's good. Everyone should see and hear it. It's our only hope. We have to have everyone in the world hear the voice of rolling thunder before it's too late. And it's not too late. Anything is possible. Everything is going to be all right in the end. I'm glad I was here to see it and hear it. You can hear it, too, can't you? It's low and powerful and great like the Almighty was speaking to us and like mother nature was speaking to us—like everything living was speaking to us at the very same time. We've been so lucky today. It all could have worked out so badly—it all could have worked out so wrong. But they didn't let us down. They wouldn't let us all die. They wanted us to live and go on and be at peace in the world. They respect us people, too, you know. We are all part of the masterpiece and the miracle and it wouldn't be

WORLD ONE

the same without us. That's the beauty of the plan. It's right that we're all here together. It's right that we all live side by side. I wonder why it took so long to understand that? I wonder why it took so long for the voice of rolling thunder to come and rescue us? I wonder why they didn't listen to my dad a long, long time ago? I can't pretend to know why. I haven't lived long enough to know all the answers to everything there is to know. Maybe there're some things that I'm just not supposed to know. But I know that we're all going to be safe. I know that everyone is listening now. And I know that this time they won't forget what mother nature has to say.

It's so nice down here and I feel so at home, but I do need some sleep. We've been up for such a long time—I can't remember when I last had some sleep. Thinking back and trying to remember I think this is the best birthday I've ever had. I didn't think it was going to be, but somehow it just worked out that way. We went to so many places and saw so many things—and all of them were beautiful. I didn't get many presents but I don't mind. I had the best present of them all. I was able to show you a part of my life. I was able to tell you about my dad. I was able to share with you the finest things in my life, and you never once got too tired to listen. I'm very proud of you.

Sonia is sleepy now . . . she might be sleeping any moment. She's in that peaceful place just on the edge of dreams where everything is calm and quiet the way it's supposed to be. And Sonia is smiling, content with life, happy that she had the best birthday of her life.

Sonia has had such a long day and Sonia has been through so much but now she knows that there's no emergency and that it's safe to get some sleep. Today was Wednesday, wasn't it? And tomorrow will be Thursday, won't it? And then Friday will come and then after that Saturday and then Sunday. And you know what? Pretty soon it will be Wednesday again and I'll have only my dreams to remember you by, but they will be so nice and will keep me smiling all day long.

Goodnight, my friends. I hope to see you in the morning when everything's all right.

17

Torches are quietly burning. The littered water beneath us is smooth and lifeless. I am sweating. And beside me, Elizabeth looks pale, due to her vigilant duty. Before me, Human-dog #1 and his wife and children are overcome. Dog-wife reins in her grief, pulling her dirty smock more tightly about her. #1 is a mad dog weeping. Slippery tears rain down and join hands with the sea. And the children, two girls and a boy, huddle close to dog-wife, their faces distorted by emotion.

Beyond, the human-dogs sigh in a muddled silence. All women and children and human-dog men reflect twisted, bitter feelings. This is quite a different lot from the one before. Can these be the same people who came to kill us, kill Elizabeth and me? Can the human-dog men really want to take our monument and my beloved Thomas Jefferson? A few feet away from me sit my fellow citizens. They are living through the same catastrophe as we. They knew the world before the atom bombs went off. They knew this country before, before four hundred and one days ago. This afterlife has made a mess of them. This afterlife has made them into human-dogs, doggies of relentless violence, doggies of indecency. But here they are in the night and all of them feel tragedy, all of them know the misery of a world and country undone by the ultimate violence, political warfare mated with atomic weaponry.

Elizabeth shifts in her seat. She arches her back. She gently stamps her feet. I put my hand on her neck. She turns her head this way and that. But always her eyes are on Human-dog #1, along with the barrel of her gun. I look up at the hideous black sky. I am not thinking. I am simply feeling. Here in the world am I. Elizabeth and I. Elizabeth and I and Human-dog #1. Elizabeth and I and Human-dog #1 and his wife and children. Elizabeth and I and Human-dog #1 and his wife and children and all of the other human-dogs and their wives and their children and on and on around the world.

I stop my thinking and return to my feelings. The hideous sky created by war and the ultimate violence. But war in any form is the ultimate violence no matter what the weaponry. I return to my feelings and think of nothing. I am resting on this black river in the night, surrounded by human-dogs with their wives and their children, attempting to defend my home with words and ideas rather than by force of arms, or am I?

And while I rest more human-dogs come to join us. Elizabeth and I are surrounded by torches, wives and children, boats, human-dogs and debris. We are the center of everything here, here in the dead capital city. Eyes look to mine. I look to them. These are people, not dogs. These are people distrupted by war, warped by circumstance, made dirty by the soot of an old civilization.

"What do you think of my people? Our children and wives, nearly a hundred of them, here to hear you, C. J. Jones. Here to listen to your story of tragedy and hope."

"I fear them less up close."

"What can we do with these people? They need places to live; they need land, but everywhere there is water. The freestanding rooftops are crowded. There is not enough space. We need more land, a new land, not simply one more monument."

WORLD ONE

Human-dog #1 lifts his lips to a smile. I like this man now. He is looking out for the needs of his people, albeit violently. He is less a dog than a product of the old civilization. Americus, I am thinking, these are your new people.

Elizabeth points out: "So you will not want our home, our handsome monument you swore to take only last evening. That is good. I would have to kill you otherwise."

I am glad to hear Elizabeth say this. I shouldn't be, I know. But with her rifle aimed at Human-dog #1's heart, I know I am safe, at least temporarily. But that's just it, I'm temporarily safe. I'm safe for a moment, not much longer than that. And that's the way of it—with violence or with the threat of it one's safe for only those moments when no one has any desire to practice it. But once that desire's given leash, it's over, it's ended, safety predicated on violence or the threat of it is a dream.

"Why don't you join with us, with Elizabeth and me, and build a new country—a place I call Americus?"

"What's in it for us?"

"Safety from people like me. Safety from people like you. Safety from immediate violence, violent death. Together and with others we will restore this country, build it up and then wage peace across the world, wage peace across all seas, everywhere."

"Don't trust him," Elizabeth snarls. She's been at it too long, I think. She's had her eye on him for too many hours, ready to end his life.

"You might be right," I say. "You might be very right."

Beyond our immediate circle, we hear singing. In the light of the high flames we hear voices making music, children and women and young men singing in the night, singing songs from another age, another world, another place altogether.

The voices carry up to the sky. They seem to break the dark and open the night to a strong light. I look down and then up and the light is as before. It is black stained by the glow of smouldering fires.

Voices lessen and then die out. A wind spreads its face across the way. We are in the center of the night and already I am looking forward to dawn, the small, dim dawn which imperceptibly ushers in the new dark day.

Behind Human-dog #1 and his wife and children, a sickening cry. Three dogs now are at it, sticking each other with knives and opening bright red wounds. #1 reels round. He howls; he howls, capturing everyone's attention. Even the attention of the perpetrators of violence, even as they gape in disbelief at their afflicted bodies.

"No more! No more! There will be no more bodies for this lake! There will be no more killing; violence among us has ended—Goodnight to it. No more! None of it. C. J. Jones, did you hear that?"

Dead, I would have heard it. Alive, how could I possibly not? The wounded dogs are lying on their sides, in the arms of their friends and companions. A boy heaves while spitting up blood. His teeth rattle and his eyes seem to float in his head. Now he sighs; now he expires. An unseen woman weeps, a child cries out in sudden horror. Human-dog #1 bows his mangy head and curses the choppy waters. His wife places her thick hand on his knee while she cradles her bewildered children. Elizabeth seems on the way to tears. I am throughly disgusted. Disgusted with the killing and the wounding and the ruin. Hateful of the waste and the constant misery. Even before Americus can truly begin, it seems destined to begin at the feet of the dead.

"I hear you."

The boat carrying the boy's lifeless body moves out across the waters. Our congregation stares at it under the long, deep light of the night. Oars lift and fall and slice the trashy surface of the water. We watch it disappear, Human-dog #1, his wife and children, and the rest of what is left of our old civilization. With all of the dead who have come before, strangely this is the one that seems to affect us most. I put my hand on Elizabeth's back. I gently stroke between her shoulder blades. Relief moves her face. She arches her back and for a moment releases her eyes to the sky.

Nothing happens. She is not struck down by stone or cut by a concealed knife. She takes in the sights above her head and then, and only then, returns to her duty, her vigilant watch with my rifle.

Human-dog #1's eyes have never left her. They followed her

WORLD ONE

gaze upwards and then downwards. They met hers once more from across way. Then they met mine. Human-dog #1 and C. J. Jones.

"We've had it," say I. "We've had it with war and warfare. Strife is for animals, angry dogs, human-dogs which you are not."

But as soon as I say this, a human-dog leaps out at us. It seems to fly toward Elizabeth with a dull blade exposed, eyes white with raging anticipation, teeth protruding unnaturally. And its flight takes forever. It ascends in a high arc, gaining momentum and velocity. Its right arm lifts back still farther. The blade will split Elizabeth's back. I am helpless to defend her. It is too late. She's protected me and I have failed her.

But Human-dog #1 has not. A small polished gun magically appears in his hand and explodes in a burst of violent energy. The shot breaks open the human-dog's hideous face. Where the face once was, mangled flesh stands instantly revealed. Where open eyes once were, pools of human blood swirl.

The bloodied body crashes with a monsterous noise before us—between Human-dog #1 and Elizabeth and I. Its sheer weight takes it down. It sinks unceremoniously into the polluted deep.

Now panic sets in. Children are screaming and mothers cower in terror. And the other human-dogs aim their derringers at our hearts, along with Human-dog #1. A smile of delight crosses his wild face. His pistol smokes. He announces, "I have just saved your life."

He tosses his derringer aside and addresses his men. "Put those things down. They serve no purpose this evening. They don't serve our interests, anymore. Am I right C. J. Jones? Am I getting the picture clearly?"

Elizabeth is pale and sweaty. But her rifle's aim is true, though her eyes focus on Human-dog #1's abandoned tool. I see nothing but the feverish light of smoky torches and the shadowy faces of too many people, too many children and women, and I see the black eyes of too many cleverly concealed derringers, pointed in our direction.

Now the guns slowly, hestitantly vanish in the night. There are low and high voiced cheers. Torches are rising and then fall-

ing, moving this way, moving that way . . . I am dreaming, no I'm not.

I remember Human-dog #1's questions. I instinctively respond.

"You are seeing things quite clearly. Thank you for saving Elizabeth's life."

"One good deed certainly deserves another, old man. If the hour is not too late, if you have sufficiently recovered from your fright, tell us one more tale—tell us the ultimate tale of a new world without war, of the world as it was before, but new. C. J. Jones, give us a picture of where Americus might lead us on into the centuries."

I look at the faces before me. All of the faces in the scattered light of the smouldering torches. I think of the old world, the dead civilization. I think of the world tomorrow and of how we will get there. I think of Mr. Thomas Jefferson and his oath against tyranny. But then I see a light in my mind, a curious light sparkling like sunshine. And I see the face of a girl in this light, not Sonia, but perhaps her twin. It could be her miracle twin—a sister born into a new age. And her presence inspires me, lifts me above the swamp and the night. Takes me to a new world, the world of W*O*D*E*N.

All right then. "Tanya is writing her first report in a world called W*O*D*E*N. . ."

Entry #1: Dawn. I'm rid of the ice. Bless my eyes, I'm rid of it. Blue grey water is all I see. No sign of sunshine. No matter. The ice is gone. I left it in the south. I was raised on ice and rocks and wind. I was raised at the bottom of the world. I haven't lived long enough to see the top. I hear there's ice up there, but between me and it, I know there's an earth full of green. Green hills and fields. Green mountains,

WORLD ONE

too. There's more green on earth than white ice. I'm going to drink down all the green and all the sunshine until I make myself sick. But I don't expect to get sick any time soon. Maybe in a thousand years, but no time soon.

Entry #2: Mid-morning. Daddy's on the bridge. I went to see him and ask him to breakfast. He'd already eaten his scrambled eggs. He'd already had two cups of coffee. I had to eat in the mess all alone. Sailors get up long before girls. I have to practice getting up before it's light. I'm a little behind. My clock is still set on bottom-of-the-world time. I'm an Antarcticus baby. I'm a baby who was born into a whole new time. That used to be something really rather special. Now it's just commonplace. They call people like me W*O*D*E*N babies. W*O*D*E*N's capital is where I came from and where I never hope to be again.

Entry #3: Afternoon. It's two weeks before Christmas and I wish I had some evergreen. I'd wrap it round the porthole and spread it as thick as moss along my cabin bunk. Down where I come from Christmas is in the middle of the summer. I've never had a Christmas in the middle of the winter. I've never even had a Christmas tree. Trees don't grow in ice. Nothing grows in ice, except maybe underwater fish. I grew up on the ice, not in it. I wish I had been born much, much higher up. As it was I got stuck in Antarcticus. I got stuck in the capital of the world. You would have thought that someone could have found a better place for it. You would have thought they would have put it in the middle of some green. As it was the only place that they could settle on was an island choked by ice.

My daddy didn't mind. He got to leave it every month. I used to call him Mr. Medicine Man. You know why? It's this ship of his. It's a cargo ship. And under me is a small mountain of medical supplies. I will be healthy just as long as I stay where I am. We've got enough supplies for half the people of the world. It seems that way to me. It took one week to fill the belly of this ship. They make lots of medicine where I used to live. I say "lived" because I'm never going back there. I'm going to be travelling with my daddy until the day I die. He'll never get me back to school. I've had enough. Now I want experience. Now I want to go with him and help the people of the world. Maybe I'll even become a woman doctor. I might even run for President. I'll be the second woman President of the World. But first, as I said, I need a few years of experience.

Entry #4: The beginning of the evening. Daddy's in a less than happy mood. He said this to me at dinner. "Tanya, fourteen-year-old girls don't leave home forever. You will *not* spend the rest of your life travelling on the sea. You have to continue with your education. And that, my dear, is that!" I like that! It didn't do any good to remind him that he went off to sea when he was as young as me. In fact, it only made him mad. I think I should have waited to talk to him at some other time. Maybe I'll bring it up again in another month. In the meantime, I'll make myself indispensable to him. I'll learn to steer the ship. I'll save him in a storm. I'll think up some ways to really impress him. I have no intention of ever going back to school. I'll send postcards to my mother when I have a chance. She won't miss me as much as she thinks. I'll send her snappy notes. She'll get used to having a seafaring daughter. She got used to daddy being gone. Why not me?

The gloomy sun is setting on the water. I guess it's dawn at the very top of the world. I guess the Eskimos are getting up. I guess it's the middle of the day in the green in between parts of the world. Right now I bet my mother's fixing dinner. She's cooking in our wooden house. She's looking out on rocks and ice. She's staring at the never setting sun. It's really hard to get some sleep when the sun is out and going round and round the bottom of the sky. In the winters it's nighttime all the time. Summers it's always light. You can understand why I want to sail and sail and sail. I like variation. I like things to change. I like to know about all kinds of possibilities. I'm curious for the sake of curiosity. I'm a sea goat like my daddy. That's just the kind of person I've turned out to be. My mother's the one who likes everything the same. That's

WORLD ONE

why she and daddy always get along. The two together work out perfectly. I think the sun's down. It's time to turn on the cabin lights. I should talk to daddy on the bridge. I should say I'm sorry. I didn't mean to get him angry. He seems a little sad these days. He's been talking very darkly. His early life wasn't very happy. Still, I wish I had been born before the time I was.

A brand-new day. Up before the light. I'm catching on. I had scrambled eggs and coffee with my dad. It was a smart idea to talk to him last night. It never hurts to apologize. We talked until midnight. Then I must have fallen asleep. I woke up and found myself in bed. Daddy must have carried me there. When I sleep, not even a hurricane can wake me up.

Last night I dreamed that daddy died. It was horrible from start to finish. If it wasn't for the coffee, I'd be feeling sad. It must have been something daddy said that made me dream that dream. Daddy's had a troublesome life. He remembers all the wars. He still hears cannons booming in his head. I don't understand why it was all so bad. Way back when, he had so much to do. He had wars to fight and victories to enjoy. He got to travel the world about a dozen times. He belonged to the United States Navy. They took him everywhere. And all he had to do was to fight for them. That doesn't seem so bad to me. Think of all that he experienced. He had some kind of action almost every day. I can't see any reason why he should be so bitter about what happened. At least the world was filled with dramatic action. These peaceful times aren't nearly so lively. There just isn't much to do. Peace can be a problem. Peace leaves holes in life. I bet you think I'm queer. But, you try living on the ice. There's nothing in it for a girl who wants to follow in the footsteps of her daddy. Nothing in it at all.

Daddy fought in two world wars. He was a captain in the navy. He commanded battleships. He defeated many enemies. He helped bring nations to their knees. He was even wounded in his leg. You'd have to say that, all in all, his life was terribly romantic. I try to cheer him up when he moans about the past. He feels he wasted all those years. I tell him, "But, look what you experienced!" I tell him, "Look, you won all those wars." If you ask me, he wasted nothing. He had everything. My mother keeps his ribbons hung high above the fireplace. He says he'd rather hang up a picture of the sea. I think the ribbons look just right. I wish I had a photo of them. I wish he'd wear them on the bridge. I wish he'd write a book entitled *War Stories: Things that I have seen and known*. Instead, all he writes are jerky poems about the days to come. My daddy isn't me. If I were him, I'd write about the past. I'd write about the action. I'd tell it like it was, including every single gory detail. I'm not proud to be a W*O*D*E*N baby. The world was much, much better way back when, I'm sure. These days the world is just so . . . quiet. And quiet is for night.

Entry #6, isn't it? Have I told you where we're headed for? We're headed for the coast of Africa. We should be there by the first of the year. I hope to bring it in while standing off the Ivory Coast. They need medicine up there. My daddy says they're having an epidemic. They have some virus that is making everyone desperately sick. We have tons of vaccinations which should help all those people in the future. We're looking out for all the future children. My dad says that this is the kind of thing that makes his life worth living. Of course, I like to think that I add some color to it, too. I'm his only oldest daughter. He doesn't have a son. That's why it's important for me to follow in his footsteps. That's why I've gone into summer training. He won't live forever. He's got to have a substitute. And I'm the one it's going to be. I'll be a captain by the time I'm twenty-one. I'll command the fleets of W*O*D*E*N before I'm thirty-one. After that, I'll start thinking about being President.

I stood on the deck of the ship this morning. The morning sun was still shrouded in the clouds. Pretty soon I'll see it full and bright. Pretty soon I'll have that suntan. All the sailors have one. Each and every face looks like it's had just the right amount of experience. I suppose when my face begins to look like theirs, I'll know that I'm ready for anything.

WORLD ONE

Daddy gave me a radio! He said that it would help expand my knowledge of the world. So far I've only heard a lot of Spanish. In a couple of days we'll be rounding the South American peninsula. It's part of the 9th Society. It's called Columbius. There are nine Societies in the W*O*D*E*N world. That doesn't include Antarcticus which is where I've been for all this time. They used to have nations. Now they have states within Societies. I guess it's not much different from the way it was. It's just that now there's a President who sits on top.

I hear the bell which means it's time for lunch. Billy the cook told me we'll be having shepherd's pie. I'm getting to like the food we eat. And with each meal I feel more and more like my dad.

Entry #7: Sitting back with a glass of milk. Lunch was very significant. Daddy made a speech. It made all the sailors quiet down. When he taps his glass with the side of his spoon, everyone shuts up including me. He said this: "There have been reports of fighting between Liberia and the Ivory Coast. From my information the skirmish is still contained. Evidently, it's a simple border clash. The two sides have been enjoined against any further action. But it may take weeks to straighten everything out. A fleet of naval ships has been dispatched. We should see them pass by morning. So far, we've been directed to continue on our course. If the situation worsens, we may have to abort our journey until the dispute is settled. Are there any questions?"

I wasn't happy to hear this news. How could I be? The people of the Ivory Coast need vaccinations. And we have a mountain of them. But still, I was excited. We are heading toward a war. I've never been to war. I've never seen the signs of smoke. Personally, I hope the battle lasts until the day we get there. I wouldn't mind at all hearing a cannon boom. I wouldn't mind at all watching a battleship go down. I'm ready to face the action. Don't think I'd ever dare mention this to my dad. He'd scalp me if he ever heard me say this. When he spoke his face was pale. He looks so worn and tired. I should fix him tea and tuck him into bed. I should read him a story or a piece of poetry. I could stomach some for him. I'll read him a verse from the *Canterbury Tales*. Knights in shining armor. Flags and maidens fair. He'll cheer up and snooze then. A person can never get too much action. It's far, far better than tranquility. Tranquility is for birds and animals. I can't wait to see some battle smoke. I'll have my fingers crossed that I'll get to see one day of it. After that, I hope it all dies down. Those people really need our medicine. And we've been told to bring it to them. I'm sure our President has her eye on us. She wants us to get through. Maybe the navy will escort us. I'll be up to see them in the morning. I'll be on deck to wave them on. They should have left Antarcticus by now. I bet the men are glad to leave the ice. I bet they're glad to have something really important to do. Africa is in the 5th Society. And those two states shouldn't be doing what they're doing. But this happens from time to time. I believe their leaders will have to go before the Court. I wouldn't want to be in their shoes. They could go to prison. Fighting isn't permitted anymore. Not since W*O*D*E*N came to be. It came to be to put an end to war. So far it's all been working really rather well.

I couldn't get to sleep last night. I tossed and turned until I had a fit. It gets lonely in my cabin. I imagine it's because of all the strange noise. For instance, I hear pumps and pressure valves. I hear distant clanging bells. Sometimes it seems as though the floor is rumbling. I have about a thousand engines down below me. It's like we have a myriad of horses pulling us, pulling us to the north. If I open my porthole, the sea sounds like gentle crashing thunder. It's downright scary in the night. I feel better now that it is dawn. The thunder seems to fade away. It's still there, it just seems quieter.

Daddy took his tea and let me tuck him into bed. He told me not to tell the other sailors how I treated him. He said they'd all ask to have their daughters come aboard. As it is, I'm very lucky to be here. In the olden days, girls brought bad luck to men at sea. That's a superstition. It has nothing

WORLD ONE

to do with me. I think girls are good for ships. They tend to soften its metal qualities. Daddy fell asleep while I sung him a childhood lullaby. When he began to snore, I lowered his cabin lights and then kissed him on the cheek. I said, "Goodnight, daddy. I hope you dream about the moon." Then I came back here. I had to travel down a hundred steps. All the corridors are lit in a murky red. Sailors always sleep with the lights on. Red is the darkest light that they can do it in.

I was going to make an entry even late last night. But, I was in a very somber mood. Daddy shook me up by what he said. He said he hadn't even told my mother. Daddy said that he'll retire when we get back home. He said his time had come. Fifty years on the sea was all he had to give. He said it brought back just too many memories.

I think my daddy was wounded in more than just his leg. I think his heart was cut in half. I think he lives on half a heart. The other half was chewed up long ago. He's seen too much battle smoke. He can't seem to repair all the damage that's been done. He's haunted, always haunted by his dark and eerie memories of the way it was in the time before I even came into the world. I'll try to make him better. I'll try to get him happy. But I don't know if there is any hope of it. I can't give him back what his experience took away. Still, I'll try to pep him up. I can be funny when I want to. My mother says that I can make a wall laugh. She's always flattering me that way. I see myself much more seriously. I guess I throw the laughter in to hide that side of me.

Entry #9: I've just come down off the deck. I've seen the W*O*D*E*N Navy on the high seas. It's a splendid sight. I remember most a skyline full of flags. Each ship bears one hundred and fifty flags for each of the states around the world. And towering above them is the W*O*D*E*N flag. A huge blue circle on a plane of white. I stood at attention and saluted as all the ships steamed by. They're on a mission of importance. You could see they knew where they were going. I was breathless for a moment. I've never seen those ships at sea. I've only seen them in the harbor or returning from the north, creeping slowly back through ice. They can cut through any thickness of ice. They can travel in the winter months. Daddy says that it's a miracle of engineering. To see them thrashing through the open waters on their way to stop the troubles is about as beautiful a thing as I have ever seen.

I feel invigorated. We're now following in their wake. Soon they'll be far ahead of us. All those ships will be pinpoints on the lower edge of the sky. Daddy let me look at them through his high powered binoculars. I could see the massive cannons on both the bow and stern of each and every ship. I saw the turning radar framed against the sky. Three of the ships had jets. Daddy says that in times of combat they can land twenty jets a minute. I hope to see a jet take off one day. I hope to be around to see it land. I have to say that I feel safe with all those ships ahead of us. There isn't a state in the world that can do us any harm. About when I was born, all those states handed over their navies and arms to the W*O*D*E*N government. Now it's *the* most powerful government in the world. That's the way it's supposed to be. It's here to protect each girl like me wherever she might be living.

Entry #10: Daddy and I just had a long-distance radio conversation with my mother. He and I went down to the radio room and rung her up on a kind of telephone. It was mighty nice to talk to her. She sounded like she missed us. I guess I miss her, too. After all, she is my mother and she's locked down there on the ice.

I told her about the fleet of ships. I told her that I was taking care of dad for her. I even told her not to worry. She said she'd heard about the border clash and was hoping we'd turn around and come back home. I told her we'd all be fine. I even told her I was excited. How many girls my age ever get this kind of experience? That made her pause for a second and then she asked to speak to my dad.

Then daddy suggested I go for a walk. I took him up on it. The radio room is very cramped and I think the operator was thankful for a bit more air. Anyway, daddy had said that he wanted to talk to mom alone. I think he'd decided to tell her that he'd be coming home for good. I didn't want to stick

WORLD ONE

around and hear him tell her that. It makes me sick to think about it. This may be my last chance to sail around the world until I'm old enough to do it on my own. I'll have to work on daddy and get him better from heart to head. I think he should be sailing until the day he dies. What's he going to do at home? He can't sit and watch the fire forever. It will break his heart to be standing on the docks while all the ships depart. He was born to live on the sea. Have I told you he was born in the middle of the sea? When his mother was alive and going to have him, she decided she wanted him to be born out there on the sea. "She didn't want me born with my two feet on any nation. That's the kind of woman she was. It took some time for me to understand her. When I finally understood, it was too late." Oftentimes, my daddy says that he wished that she had seen this world I'm living in. I can understand this to a point. It's much safter now than it was way back when. But then she'd already seen some wars and been raised for action. She'd had the best years of her life filled up with experience. People forget that when they look at me. How lucky I am, they say. How lucky you can be.

    I better see if daddy's back up on the bridge. I'd like to ask him how he thought my mother was. Actually, I'd like to find out what she said about his plans to come back home for good. I think she knows he belongs on the seas. She's said as much to me.

Bringing you up-to-date: Yesterday daddy told my mother that this trip out was going to be his last. I was really stunned when he told me the news. I guess I expected it, but it was a big blow all the same. I boycotted dinner because of it. I've been in my cabin ever since then and haven't had a bite to eat since yesterday lunch. Daddy came to my cabin last night, but I wouldn't let him in. I've been sulking and feeling sorry for myself. Isn't that ridiculous? Here I am on the high seas and having the opportunity of a lifetime and I'm acting like a kid. I should be ashamed of myself. I guess I'm that and more. It's not daddy's fault that he's gotten old. It's not his fault that his heart's dried up. I'll be recovering from my despondency. I just have to learn to face the facts. He's had a painful life and that is that. Me, my only problem has been living on the ice. I've got a whole lifetime ahead of me. I have endless possibilities before me. Maybe daddy wants to spend his last years living with my mom. Maybe they'll decide to move back to the middle of the world. I'll go with them naturally. Until I'm grown I'll be able to have a happy time in some land where all the trees are green. Anything would be better than living in Antarcticus. Come to think of it, this could be very, very good news.

The sky's still slate grey out my porthole window. The sun still hides its face. Any time now we'll be passing by the Falkland Islands. They're a group of islands off the Argentine coast. They used to belong to the British. Britian is in the 2nd Society, along with the United States. In the olden days, they had a war down here. It was a short, short war as far as wars can go. The British brought their battleships and fastest jets. The Argentineans weren't much of a match for them. They lost the war and that was that until W*O*D*E*N came to be. When the people of the world got tired of always fighting wars and having to prepare for them, they formed this one gigantic government. It was a miracle of politics, I've heard my daddy say. And when this happened, the Argentineans went to court to lay a claim to these islands that they said were theirs. I think they call it suing. They sued the British state. They went before the Grand Tribunal. Each side hired a lawyer and presented their case to the sixty judges. And in the end, Argentina of Columbius won the battle without spilling any more blood. That's what daddy calls the civilized approach. From my perspective, it all seems rather boring. I've seen film footage of the war. I've seen the pictures of those jets swooping down from out of the clear blue sky. I've seen the men landing on the beaches and firing mortars left and right. I've seen them raise the flag and call out victory. If you ask me, that's ever so much more colorful than a court of law. Who wants to hear sixty, stodgy judges spout off their individual opinions? I'd much rather have won the case on the open battlefield. I'm all for noble sacrifice

WORLD ONE

and marching infantries. I bet you think I'm bad. I bet you think I'm spoiled. Who knows? Probably I am.

Entry #12: Billy the cook just came in and brought me a tray of toast and coffee and scrambled eggs. He also brought in orange juice. I could of kissed him I was so appreciative. He thought I had been sick. He said he hadn't seen me last night at supper and noticed the grim look on my daddy's face. I told him that I was as healthy as a bean. Then I told him all about the troubles. He said, "Don't worry, child. You'll understand the way of it before you go back home."

What he meant by that is a little beyond my imagination. Billy the cook's the mystic type when he's not out there making chow. I think maybe he can read fortunes on the waves, or see the past on cloudy days. But whatever he can see, he's rather comforting.

I have an invitation! Billy says that if I want some fun and if I can keep a secret, I can come to the kitchen after ten tonight. He says there'll be a social poker game. Won't that be nice! I can play five card stud and I like it when something's wild. I don't have too much money to throw around but I expect the sailors will let me bet with nickels instead of paper bills.

Billy the cook is my friend. He understands about daughters and their fathers. He says he has a child who's just about as old as me. He says that daddy's very lucky to be able to take me along. He says he wishes he had that kind of luck. He'd trade his pans in for it any day. I should count my blessings, Billy says. And I do. I'm thankful for my mom and dad and for Billy, too.

Entry #13, I think: It must be midnight and it could be later. I'm a little drunk. By little, I mean a lot. I had three-quarters of a bottle of beer. I'm sworn to secrecy. I wasn't to let anyone know. But I can tell you.

I'm rich, too. Everyone called it beginner's luck. Billy the cook said that it was a fateful hour when he invited me to play some hands of poker. I'll have to hide my earnings underneath my mattress. I can't afford to have to explain how I got so rich. This is supposed to be my summer vacation. I'm not supposed to make my fortune.

I'm a little woozy from all the cigarettes and lack of air. I'm glad I'm back where I belong. I'm not used to such extravagance. Sailors do it every other night of the week, sometimes more. Me, I'm wet behind the ears, also green in every sense. My bunk wavers when I take a look at it. I think I better curl up and go to sleep. My daddy expects me at breakfast in the morning. He left me a note on my cabin door. It said, "Tanya, enough is enough. Your mother wants me home. Let's talk about it at breakfast." I can't hide from him forever. There are just so many places on this ship to hide. Maybe if I hid among the piles of medicine it would take him one long week to find me. But what's the use? I have to face reality. I just have a fit when I think about going back to the ice. Still, who knows what might happen tomorrow? We could run aground and have to live it out on some interesting island. All I can do is to pray that fate will intervene. If it's right for me to stay away then fate will see to it I do.

I had a lovely night. I'm ready to face my daddy in the morning. I have to say that now I know this life's for me. I could earn a fortune out here on the seas. I could buy a ship like this in no time flat. Of course, by then, no sailor would ever want to sail with me. Goodnight to you. Remember, you're sworn to secrecy.

I woke up with a hangover. It was enough to make me swear off drinking. I don't know how those sailors do it. They must have heads of iron. The doctor gave me Bromo Seltzer and I feel better. I don't remember much of what I did last night. I remember only that I won a lot of money. I have to go and meet my dad. I'll let you know what happens. I hope he's in a better mood than me. I could make a lion jump if he dared come near me.

Daddy said, "Let's bury the hatchet. Let's call a truce and not look back." He held his napkin up like a white flag. I said I was sorry for acting so atrociously. He smiled and asked me

WORLD ONE

how my night was. I told him it was very interesting to get to know the sailors on the ship. He said I had a future on the sea if I could get along with them. That made me happy because he seemed to be encouraging me in the right direction. After that we gobbled down our breakfast and then took a stroll on the deck. It's a fine, fine morning. The clouds are beginning to wear away. And for the first time I even slightly missed our home. It's strange to look around and see nothing but endless seas. There's no place to walk except up and down, up and down the deck. It's rather limiting. On the ice you can walk for miles and never finish walking. On the ice the world looks so much different. It amazes me to think of how they built those buildings. They built a mile round city off a place called McMurdo Sound. It's on the edge of a chunk of ice called the Ross Ice Shelf that's adjacent to the Ross Sea. In the winter that sea freezes up and only ships like this and naval vessels can get through. It's a pretty sight to see a storm crossing it. Grey on white makes for a lovely picture. That's enough of homesick reminiscing. I'm really glad not to be walking on icy streets. I'm really glad not to be feeling warm when it's just twenty degrees outside. I like it when I'm with my dad and a blast of sea slaps us in the face. I'd rather be wet than cold. I'd rather brace myself for danger than sit by the fire and knit another pair of winter mittens. I'd rather walk down forty flights of stairs to the local library than have to cross town on a snow mobile to get there. At least on ship you can avoid the outside when you want to. Down in Antarcticus, I have to sled on ice to even get my teeth cleaned. Once I had to brave a blizzard just to buy some Chap Stick. On this ship, everything's at my fingertips. It's just too bad they didn't think to build the capital of W*O*D*E*N that way. I'd have been happy if they had.

Entry #15: I've been resting up during the afternoon. I can't say I really had a choice not to. I have to take it easy and restore myself to health. I've been spending my time listening to the radio. I've also been lying straight out on my bunk. My neck feels like someone pinched it with tweezers while I slept last night. My stomach has gotten back to normal, thanks to the doctor and his Bromo Seltzer.

I've managed to tune in New York City loud and clear. Sometimes the signal falters, but then I fine tune the dial and it all comes back again. Right now they're playing a cool sort of midnight jazz. It's kind of bluesy and it's kind of dynamite. New York City is a place I'd like to go. Daddy's been there countless times. He's steered ships in and out of it. I might live there for a while as soon as I'm free to go. But who knows where I'll go when I'm ready for real action? I'm a citizen of the world. I have a passport that will let me go anywhere. It has nine stamps on it for each of the nine Societies. I'm awfully interested in going to Atlantia. That's the region where the United States is. And daddy says that Moscow is pretty in the springtime. I'd like to stop by there. I have a stamp that says that I can go there. That's in the 3rd Society. That Society has my favorite name. It's called Eurasius. Isn't that a pretty name? It sounds so ancient and mysterious.

Getting back to New York City. Daddy says that in the olden days it housed the United Nations. That was the infant form of the W*O*D*E*N government. But like babies, it could barely walk. It was made to help with the troubles of the world. It was supposed to feed the poor and settle wars and generally take care of everything. It had some good points but mostly it went bad. Daddy said it never had the muscle to do the things it should. All the governments of the world sent spokesmen there to debate any one of a thousand points. But in the end, that's all they did. When they got through debating that was just about the end of it. They were never men of action. Too many of the nations could veto action and then everything would come to a shrieking halt. It never stopped a war, maybe it held it up, but it never stopped it. That was the trouble with it. It didn't have muscle—not like the W*O*D*E*N government. No nation goes to war while it sits on top. And the world gets fed now much more easily. Nations don't have to spend all their money to keep the W*O*D*E*N world in place. It's much less costly to live in a world of peace. It's much less entertaining, too. But what can I do? I was born after all the excitement was done. I can't

WORLD ONE

turn back the clocks of history. I have to make the best of a harmonic situation. Sometimes I feel like those singers on the radio. I feel blue.

Entry #16: I just had a horrible sight. I can't get the picture of it out of my mind. It's stuck there like a sore on my mouth. I just saw daddy crying on the bridge. He was crying there all alone. I saw the side of his face lit in red and I could see him trembling. I stood by the window of the door not knowing how to move. I couldn't go backwards and I couldn't go forwards. Daddy was weeping like a child of six. What is the matter with him? I thought he'd be happy to be going home for good. I thought he'd be happy to have me here. Now I don't know anything. Do you think it's because of all his memories? Do you think he's frightened because of the battle on the Ivory Coast? I couldn't make myself go in to see him. I thought it over and decided he wouldn't want me there. But now I'm not so sure. I've never seen my daddy cry. He's seen me cry plenty. But daddies aren't supposed to cry. He's grieving because of me, isn't he? I've been very bad and that's why he's upset. I swear I'll never be bad again. I'll do exactly as he wants. I'll go back to school gladly and I won't make a fuss. I'll get straight As and study books until I'm thirty-one. I never wanted him to get so blue. I don't know what I'm going to do!

That was daddy knocking at my door. He came down here to tuck me into bed. By the look of him, I wouldn't have known that he'd been crying. His cheeks were bright and his eyes were clear. I asked him if he was all right. Then he told me the truth. It's those old memories of the way it was. It's those old wars that he had to fight in. He says now that there is peace, now that there is hope, all the guilt of what he's had to do is tearing him apart. That's the reason why, he says, he's going home for good. He wants to forget all those old missions on the seas. And even now the seas just bring those memories back. Night and day, sleep or wake, they zero in on him. He can't stand the pain. He says he's like a fish that's been harpooned. He can't shake off the spear. Then daddy told me stories until he thought I was asleep. But when he left I got up to tell you all that's been happening to him. And the worst part of it is that there's nothing I can do. All I can do is to safely see him home. I promise you that I'll do that. I promise you he'll shake the spear and land where he belongs.

18

When I woke up this morning I had a piece of sunlight in my eyes. I can't say it was a big one, just a slice or two. I put on my jeans and knitted sweater and dashed up to the deck. But before I got there, it had slipped back behind the clouds, once again holding back its very colorful light. That's the way it is, isn't it? Just a glimpse and then no more. But I have hope that it will be coming out again. Won't that be news?

I do have some other kind of news. Early this morning there was a fire in the kitchen. Billy the cook burned his hands and face. The doctor says he's going to live, but Billy's in great misery. I went to see him, you see. I bought him a *Sports Illustrated* magazine. He wears a bandage on his head but it has slits in it. His eyes can read between the holes and I know he was very grateful. If I had my way, I'd do his cooking for him. I could use some practice serving up some soup. I threw a coin over the side of the ship after I went to see him. I made a wish on it. I wished for him to get better right away. I hope I don't jeopardize the wish by telling you about it. What's really bad is that Billy's going to miss some poker nights. On the other hand, that might be good. He might save some money. All the sailors were grumpy this morning because breakfast was served several hours late. They were sorry to hear about Billy but their stomachs were much less sympathetic. Sailors always like to be fed on time, no matter what the tragedy. That's the kind of thing I'm storing in the back of my memory. It's all part of what makes a ship work. It's as necessary as the steering wheel.

Entry #18, of course. I've been sweating out my summer reading. For English class I have to read that old book, *Moby Dick*. And for Civics class I've been studying the W*O*D*E*N constitution. Mostly, it's a bore, but there are parts of it that I find to be inspiring. Take this section: "We, the people of mankind, do hereby join together for the common advancement of mankind. Justice and peace stand or fall together. Universal peace is the prerequisite if universal justice is to be achieved. War and lawlessness stem from the anarchy of sovereign states. The age of nations must end for the sake of all humanity."

It goes something like that. I wrote it out from memory so don't expect it to be perfect. I'm not a tape recording machine and I don't have a photographic, computer memory. But I think you can get the point of what it has to say.

I've been brushing up on history, too. It seems like all I ever read about is war. A war here, a war there, there are dozens and dozens of them in all shapes and varieties. Once I bothered to scratch a mark in the margin of all the pages that mentioned wars just in the last seventy-five years. When I got through I set out to count them up. Can you guess how many there were? Twenty? Fifty? One hundred? Two hundred? Try again. There were more like three or four hundred wars with millions upon millions of people getting killed. I almost lost my breath when I got through finishing counting. And you wonder why my daddy feels so upset? It's a wonder his heart hasn't turned to stone. It's a wonder he

WORLD ONE

can still breathe anymore. It's a wonder that I'm even here to tell of it. I could have been any number of those people who had to die. It's just a miracle that I escaped all the tragedy. It's a miracle of W*O*D*E*N, if you want to know the truth. Without W*O*D*E*N here to protect me and all the rest of us, I'd be sure of one thing in my life—I'm sure that I'd be dead. And I don't need my daddy to have to tell me that. All I need to do is to look back in those books and count the marks along the margins. It's as simple as that. When they write the history books on W*O*D*E*N, I'll bet I can count the wars on one hand. And the one we're heading for may be one of them. What a glorious thing it will be for me to be able to say, "I saw one of the W*O*D*E*N wars."

Entry #19: This has been a fateful night. Billy the cook died. I'm so full of grief I don't know what to say. Around about eight o'clock his heart suffered a massive heart attack. The doctor couldn't revive him. They said he pounded on his chest until it was no use. Billy the cook died at exactly 8:06 p.m. It was because of the burns that he died. The burns made him have a heart attack. He would have gotten better if only his heart hadn't been so shocked at what had happened to his face and hands. The doctor said he died just before he was about to go to sleep. What is his daughter going to do? Daddy said he had to radio his wife and tell her the dreadful news. She asked us to bury him at sea. In the morning we're going to do that. He'll have a flag draped around his casket. He asked to have a W*O*D*E*N flag wrapped around his person. That's what his wife told dad. I've never known a person to die before. It's all so permanent. He was doing fine and then he died. Billy the cook was a friend of mine.

I just came down from up on the deck. A new moon is shining on the seas. Even the heavy clouds have parted in honor of him. I stood on the deck and watched the waters part and then fold back over. I was imagining how Billy would feel down at the bottom of the sea. I was imagining how his daughter was feeling right now. Poor girl. She should have been able to come with him for his last days on the sea.

At least Billy had the life he wanted, I think. He seemed happy to be taking care of all of us. Sure, he grumbled about his pots and pans but I know he liked to serve up soup. He took pride in his scrambled eggs. He boasted about his nectar coffee and his flag steak. And he was one for enjoying his after hours and including others in the fun. Billy the cook will be remembered for all that he has done. I should write his daughter and tell her how kind he was to me. Billy the cook was a seaman of the highest order. I'll suggest my daddy send his wife a medal. I'll leave it up to him to pick out the best one. This is a day I wish I hadn't seen. This is a day I'll always have to live with. It'll always be floating somewhere in back of my memory. I'll remember Billy the cook each time I drink a cup of coffee or dive into a plate of scrambled eggs. In a way, I guess you could say that he's become a part of me. He's touched my life and made me rich in the very best kind of way.

Rest easy, Billy. There are many people who will go on remembering you. You were a credit to the world and all the people in it.

I just came back from a beautiful ceremony. We buried Billy the cook this morning. The chaplain read some prayers, my daddy said some words, and then all the sailors joined in to sing a hymn for him before they let the casket slide down into the hungry waters. I stood by daddy all the time. I made every effort not to cry. I peeled my fingernail off in an attempt not to do it. It was a sad, sad event for the members of this ship. I could see that the doctor felt especially bad. I think he feels he should have been able to save him. I'm sure he did the best he could.

The sailors saluted Billy as he went down. I saluted, too, even though I'm not a sailor by profession. Daddy gave every sign of being moved by the experience. Billy had served with him for a long, long time. Daddy says that Billy came to his

WORLD ONE

ship nearly eight years ago. Daddy said that there was never a better cook on all the seas. He died too young, he said. He was only forty-two. He had many years left in which to cook and he could have been hired by any ship he wanted. But Billy liked this cargo ship. He liked the captain and his crew. He liked the purpose of the missions he was sent on. At least Billy died in his right place. That's more than some can boast, I'm sure.

I think I'm going to go into a period of mourning. I think I'll wear my pleated navy blue skirt for about a week. I'll dye my white scarves black and wear them even when I go to sleep. I want people to understand how I felt about my friend. I'll get down to writing his daughter, too. I'll ask daddy for her address. I think he came from the deep South in America. I think he joined my daddy's ship to help support his family. Daddy says he only got to see them three or four times a year. It's a wonder to me that he had such an even temperment. I would have thought he would have gone crazy being away from them. I know he wrote them letters each and every week. Maybe he told his daughter about me. I think his daughter would like to hear from me. I'm going to ask daddy for her address. I'll tell her how sorry I am for all the tragedy. Daddy's already written a heartfelt letter to his wife. That's his duty and this is mine. I think his daughter's name is Alice. She's probably in tears at this very moment.

Entry #21: Back and snug inside my cabin. Daddy and I have been chasing whales all afternoon. We've been chasing the bottle-nosed variety. They are sleek and fast but very short. They escorted us for about ten miles. Such gorgeous creatures you have probably never seen! I'd like to take one home with me. I'd like to carve out a harbor for it in the ice. Daddy says they look like porpoises. They live in these waters all year round. I can't remember ever having so much fun. Daddy and I were laughing in the wind and spray. We laughed until we cried, or until tears rolled down our cheeks. It seemed like they knew what they were doing. They were following us until they just got tired. Then they moved on to the west. Maybe they were going home to have their dinner.

I got a good look at them through daddy's high powered binoculars. Each one had a fin right in the center of its back. And their backs were glossy. They shone nicely in the spots of sunshine. How I'd like to ride one. How I'd like to sit up on one's shoulder and let it take me where it wanted to. I'd like to dive down deep with it. I'd like to be carried across the sea by it. All in all, daddy and I are in a fabulous mood. I'm hungry, too. All that running up and down the deck to watch the circus come to town was enough to make me famished. If Billy were alive he'd let me sneak a piece of toast before the supper bell. If Billy were alive I could tell him what I saw. I saw lane of whales, Billy. I saw mommy and daddy and baby whales. They looked as happy as me and were probably showing off. They must know how elegant they are. They must be proud to live on the seas and raise their families.

That's an interesting thought. If I ever do want to have a family and I still want to live on the sea, I could marry a sailor who could come with me. That way we'd be all together, right where we belong. It's a thought that I could take seriously.

There goes the dinner bell. And after dinner daddy's taking me to see the movie. I don't know the title of it. It's probably a romance. Daddy says the sailors like romantic movies. I guess I had better get used to them if I want to enjoy my time on board.

For your information, I've already taken care of my letter to Billy's daughter. Daddy radioed the contents of it back to base and someone will type it out and then put it on a plane for her. Daddy said it sounded just right. A real "daughter to daughter" letter. See you after the movie, if I'm still awake.

Entry #22: Never have I seen a movie that was ever quite like this. Talk about romance. It was gushing with it. It also had a lot of war and slippery action. It's called *Casablanca* and stars a man named Humphrey Bogart. He wears a white dinner jacket and goes around morosely tidying up affairs in his North African saloon. He says he went there for the

WORLD ONE

waters but when he got there he discovered that there weren't any. He wasn't very bright when it came to navigation.

What later happens in the plot is that he turns out to be a hero. He helps a freedom fighter escape the clutches of the Nazi people. He does this and more. He sacrifices his one true love so she can go on and aid this noble freedom fighter in his cause. For some reason, this sappy woman has trouble making up her mind about which man she wants to spend her life with. From my point of view, I wouldn't have given it a second thought. I would have gone any day with the freedom fighter. Who wants to be tied up for the rest of their lives in a dusty Moroccan saloon?

I liked the movie anyway. It made my blood rush. It was all about victory and sacrifice. It brought back to me the glory of the olden days. My daddy was in that war, although he was stationed miles away in the Pacific Ocean. Daddy said that the movie "painted an accurate picture of the atmosphere of the times." He said the movie held up well over time, too. There was a black piano player named Sam who was Humphrey Bogart's all-time friend. He looked like Billy sometimes and every time he came on the screen, I got choked up and wished that he was with me. I suppose I shouldn't have gone to see the movie tonight. I should be in my period of mourning. But daddy said he wanted me to see this film. He said it would paint a certain kind of picture of wartime for me. It did do that. I see the excitement of it. But afterwards he sat with me in the movie theater and told me otherwise. He said that that war was one of the worst wars in history. And then he said that he thought it never should have happened. A madman was on the loose. He went on like that for maybe twenty minutes. But his point was this. He said that if W*O*D*E*N had come about at the turn of the twentieth century that that war and the other very bad one couldn't have happened either. He said it would have been impossible. I guess he wanted me to think (like everybody else) just how lucky I really am. I don't care to see it that way. A movie like that seems perfectly right to me. It's just another sign to me that tells me that I should have been born way back when. My daddy should have been born when I was born and I should have been born when he was born and that's the best that I can make of it.

If a freedom fighter came to me and asked me to go with him and fight the Nazi men, I would do it in a second. And I'd leave my father safe and sound in Casablanca or wherever he thought he would be safe. You know, my dad has a lot in common with that Humphrey Bogart. He's so morose when he talks about his past. They both need some enlightening. They both should have been born in the time when this world was suffering peace.

Goodnight and farewell, Billy. I wish you had been alive to see this wonderful movie.

Daddy was grave and grim at breakfast. He tapped his spoon again and made another speech. It doesn't sound good for the people of the Ivory Coast. They have problems at every turn. "The border war's expanding and the epidemic is reaching frightening proportions. We have been instructed to continue on our course. The Navy is still three days out. Meanwhile, W*O*D*E*N ground troops have been sent in from Atlantia. That is all the news I have to offer. Are there any questions?"

Then one sailor raised his hand and asked if we would reach the coastline by New Year's Eve. Daddy said we would. That was the first good news of the day. I'll be on the shores of the Ivory Coast to celebrate a whole new year. Can you think of anything more romantic?

The President is the Protector of the Peace. She's doing all the ordering and is in charge of trying to contain the conflict. Underneath her is the Chamber of Guardians. There are six of them elected by the Grand Tribunal. They are in charge of holding up the peace. They have a lot to do. I wouldn't be in their shoes for anything right now. What a way to spend the week before Christmas. I'm sure all of the people would much rather be out buying some Christmas gifts and hanging up the holly.

I wish I had some colored bulbs. If I can't have a Christmas

WORLD ONE

tree then I'd at least like to have some Christmas bulbs. I'd like the ones that flash on and off, on and off. It's a dream to go to sleep by them. That way I see flashing colors all night long.

By the way, I'm a little nervous about what my daddy had to say. Not only is the epidemic worsening but the conflict, too. I really might see those cannons booming after all. I hope I don't catch the virus. If I did, I wouldn't have to worry. I'm sitting on the biggest medical ship in the Atlantic Ocean.

I should think about Christmas, not the war up there. I have to plan out a present for my dad. He's a hard one to dream up anything for. Last year I wasn't with him during Christmas. Mom and me sent him a cable which read, "You come home for New Year's now. We miss you and wish you a smooth and clear Christmas morning." He was in the China Sea last year. I think he was sailing somewhere near the mouth of the Yangtze River. He sent me an ancient Chinese relic. China is part of the 7th Society—Asia Major. China is practically the oldest civilization in the world today. They invented paper there and fireworks. Gunpowder, too. You won't find them having Christmas lights in China. They have different kinds of religion. I'd like to go there and find out what they are. I'm interested in just about anything that exists above the ice. And I'll be free to see it all one day pretty soon.

Entry #24: Hallelujah! The sun is finally out and glittering on the surface of endless waters. But I haven't had much time to celebrate. Daddy got a distress call over the ship's emergency radio. Somewhere out there is a vessel in distress. Even as I'm sitting here we're steaming toward it very quickly. Daddy says we'll be there in about a half an hour. It's probably a whaling ship or some South Georgia Island tourist boat drifted way off course. Could it be some pirates run aground? Could we be heading into an awful trap? We'll know shortly what our fate is. S O S is all we heard. I'll be up on deck to see what's happening.

When daddy told me about the call, he seemed to be exhilarated. Yes, exhilarated is exactly the right word for his present disposition. He's got the same brightness in his eye as that stunning sun up in the sky. Daddy's looking forward to being a certain kind of hero. There's a certain part of him that likes to rescue people. I don't blame him. If I were captain I would like that, too. Even from my point of view, it's better to rescue people than defeat them.

Daddy just hurried in and said, "Tanya, twenty minutes." That's my cue to wrap this up. I've never seen him quite so bouncy. He looks almost as young as me. You see what I mean about it being good for him to be here on the sea? If he goes back to the ice, he'll become a rock. A nice rock, but nonetheless a rock. Out here he's got opportunities. Out here he can mend those brutal wounds. He can help people right and left and not have to worry about the ancient past. History is history and I think he should forget it. Me, I have a perfect right to dwell on what's been going on. I may be nervous about what looms ahead, but still I'm looking forward to it. Daddy's got nothing to look forward to except to continue to bandage up his past and try to breathe a little easier in this brand-new world of ours.

Got to go and monitor the rescue. I'll be back to report the captain's brand of victory.

Entry #25 and how! All the drama has finally settled down. It was a drama of magnificent proportions. Daddy snatched a wayward prince right out of the sea. If it hadn't been for daddy, the prince of Rio de Janeiro would likely be dead. As it is he's suffering from dehydration and fatigue. He was a sorry sight to look upon. He had a beard about a mile long and his eyes were like the eyes of owls and he was as thin as the broken mast of his wandering sailboat. His name is Santiago and one month ago he set out from Brazil to sail his way down into the hazardous south. He was on his way to Antarcticus when the storms began to blow him east instead of down. Then his mast snapped and his food and drink supplies began to dwindle and as of three days ago all he had

WORLD ONE

left was his emergency radio that he's been tapping out messages on when he's had the strength. Poor Prince!

Daddy says he's eighteen. He looks more like a noble twenty-five to me. I should say I tingle when I think of him. I can see him being lifted up on ship in the rescue basket. Even though he looked something like a chicken sitting on its nest, he still maintained his dignity. And do you know why our Prince was out there? Do you know why he had set sail for Antarcticus? I'll tell you why. He was on his way to plead his case before the Tribune of the People. It's the Tribune's job to defend the civil rights and natural rights of all individuals everywhere against any violation or neglect of the Government. The Tribune is there to uphold the letter and spirit of our Constitution, and Santiago was on his way to see him. Santiago claims his rights have been violated by his state government. Santiago is all for saving whales and certain kinds of fish that exist off the coastal waters of his native home. He wants the Tribune of the People to go before the Grand Tribunal and, if necessary, before even the Supreme Court to make his government stop pestering and slaughtering those fish that are so dear to him. I could tell that daddy was impressed with him. Although he spoke very little English, his meaning still came through: "I go to save my heritage. I go and speak of life before blood!"

Santiago's sipping soup and eating wheat bread. I'm sure he's on about his eleventh mug of fruit juice. Now he's going to have to come with us and will be delayed in his action in Antarcticus. But it's better that he lives and is a little late than dies in his rotting sailboat. And I'll have a handsome companion for the rest of the journey. I might set out to teach him a phrase or two of English and he might do the same for me with Spanish. Already I'm paying more attention to how I look. I don't know what's come over me. I'm a sucker for freedom fighters. They seem to stir up the high emotions in me.

"Long live all whales and fishes in the sea!!!"

Santiago's still blissfully sleeping in Billy the cook's old bed. He's been sleeping for almost twelve hours. I expect he'll sleep another twelve. Wouldn't you under the circumstances? I would if I were him.

Only five more days till Christmas!

I still have my mind on Santiago's face. Down in Antarcticus, there aren't young men like him. There are blonde boys who come from the state of Germany whose mothers and fathers work in the government in one capacity or another. There are boys from the state of Niger and Egypt and Zaire. They're unusually tall and stride about like ostriches. I've never kept them in my mind for long. I don't know why. It just never happened. And the blonde boys always look so pale. They seem to be translucent against the piles of ice. But Santiago is a different story. His face would go well against any background—sea or ice—land or sky. Can you believe I'm bothering with these kinds of thoughts? Before Santiago came aboard I had my mind set only on the rolling sea. Now the sea is beginning to pale in comparison to him. I'll get over it soon. These feelings could be dangerous to me. My mother said it wasn't good for a girl to fall in love too soon. I can sense that she was right. I'm feeling like a ship without a compass. If I'm not too careful I could stray off course. I could end up west instead of east. I could end up going down instead of up. I could tangle myself instead of cutting loose. You see the problem, don't you? I'll avoid Santiago at every hall. I'll ignore his handsome face. I'll study navigation charts rather than attempt to digest Spanish. I wish I could tell my mom just how I feel about this man. She might have a good suggestion for how I might dampen my emotions.

I feel pretty silly having spent the larger part of last night manicuring my fingernails and then painting them a star burst red.

Entry #27: A sunny afternoon in the middle of the ocean. All's calm on board our ship. Santiago hasn't stirred yet. Daddy seems happy about his sea-lift rescue. Me, I'm neither here nor there. I suggested to daddy that we radio mother. Daddy said we'd do it after supper. I don't know if I can wait

WORLD ONE

that long. Any time now, my freedom fighter will be waking. I'd rather sort me out before I see him again. Will mother even understand my perilous predicament? And will I have the privacy to talk to her alone? I don't want the radioman to listen in on me. And I mustn't let daddy hear. I'm in a fix. Woe is Tanya on this sunny afternoon.

The doctor has come and gone. He came in to see how I was doing. I think daddy sent him here. I've noticed daddy always works behind the scenes. Doctor Lin is the doctor's name. His speciality is sea medicine. He knows how to treat every kind of illness that one can catch while travelling. Daddy sent him to me to talk about the medical profession. Daddy's meddling, I can tell.

Doctor Lin asked me to think over what he had to say. And I have been thinking it over. If I went to school for years and years and years I could become like him. I could treat the sick and make them well. There's glory in it, Doctor Lin tells me. Maybe yes and maybe no. That kind of life sounds a bit sterile to me. Of course, Doctor Lin gets to ride the seas. He gets to go everywhere a ship like this will take him. That's a plus. There are minuses, too. A lot of it's routine. Doctor Lin has spent many bored hours on ships like this. And he's suffered failures. Take Billy the cook, for instance. I was discreet and didn't mention him to him. I thought about it. Basically, I'm angry at him. What's the good of doctoring if people still die in front of you? It was Doctor Lin who mentioned failures, not me. He said it just wasn't possible to save everyone. Still, he said, medicines are getting better all the time—and people are living longer. "Dr. Tanya has a very nice ring." I should say it does. So does Captain Tanya or President Tanya or even just plain Tanya. I'm going to talk to dad about how I might go about becoming president one day. I'd like to get it clear what all my alternatives are. There's no sense in jumping into one profession when another might be better. I think what I really want to do right now is abandon myself to the profession of love. I think Mrs. Santiago sounds the best of all.

Entry #28: Santiago sat at the dinner table with me and dad and Doctor Lin. He must have eaten three or four steaks and as much as a bucket of mashed potatoes. I kept track out of the corner of my eye. Santiago has a fierce appetite and an even more fierce personality. You should have heard a few of the things he said. He's practically a revolutionary. I thought my dad would throw him overboard. But nothing happened of the kind. I guess daddy's heard those lines before. It was all new and sharp to me. I'll try to tell it like he said it: "What good is government if it still feeds on the fish? What good, tell me, is people in peace when they make wars on helpless beauties? You tell me what good and I listen. What good is a world that feeds its hungry on the backs of our ancient ancestors? Are we not a civilized population? Are we not a credit to our universe?

"Captain, I am one grateful one to be here eating at your open table. But tell me why we have to kill that which has rights just like us?"

Santiago doesn't needle daddy. Santiago has a way of painting questions that are food for thought. Daddy said, "Better fish than people. Better to feed people and stamp out war then let all fish dominate all oceans."

But Santiago stood his ground. I was proud of him. He said, "Captain, have you no heart for smaller ones than us? Were they not made by the same one which made us? We must protect what is given us. They give us no harm. Man should eat wheat and fruit of branches. You understand. We are all . . . right in our places."

Daddy toasted Santiago. I lifted my glass to him, too. Daddy thinks Santiago's got a fine personality. He told me so after supper. And when we went to ring up mom, I didn't feel the need to tell her my problem. I'm happy to live with it for as long as I can.

Daddy told her about the rescue. He must have gone on about it for half of ten minutes. It charges him up to consider the good that he did. He saved a man's life who would have otherwise died on the seas. Then I talked to mother. I told her that dad was bright and handsome. I told her that we'd been getting along fine. I told her that Santiago might need a place to have dinner when we all came back home.

WORLD ONE

Now it's midnight again and the engines are groaning. My cabin smells damp and I'm sensing my own eerie feelings. Daddy is happier, that much I've seen. But it's a foggy kind of happiness. What do you think that means?

I've spent the morning plotting out my daddy's Christmas gift. After a few false starts, I've finally decided on something. I've drawn a page-size medal for him. It should be made of bronze or silver or even gold but since I don't have those particular materials with me, I've had to work it out on paper. Oh, well.

The shape of the medal is oval. And halfway up the oval I've drawn the choppy line of the sea. Now, sitting on the sea is a picture of a ship like this. Obviously, it's a medical cargo ship. I had to restrain myself from drawing a battleship. Then in the space that I left for the sky, I wrote an inscription. The inscription is the meaning of it all. The inscription reads: "Merry Christmas to an honorable and courageous captain. With love from his sea goat daughter." I signed my name below it.

I have plans for where he can hang it on his wall. There's a beautiful space between his bunk and his walnut desk. I'll suggest he put it there. I've always thought he should have a medal with him. This should serve the purpose well.

No sign of Santiago this morning. He didn't show his face at breakfast. Probably he's still sleeping in. Probably he's dreaming his revolutionary thoughts. I hope he saves his whales and fishes. He has a point, you know. I think the Tribune of the People will listen to him. Anyone who can speak like him should be listened to. I'll help him if I can. Being a captain's daughter, I have certain connections. You never know. We might make a powerful alliance. And according to the Constitution, Santiago may have an ironclad case. You see, all the people of the world have a claim on the earth and air and water. Even energy. W*O*D*E*N's here to protect those rights. It's all laid out on the first page of the Constitution.

Someone's knocking at my door . . .

Entry #30: I've just come back from seeing daddy. Doctor Lin took me there. Daddy doesn't feel well and the doctor says he has a fever. It must be something he ate for breakfast. Now do you see the importance of a cook like Billy? He mixed the food just right. Daddy never got sick when Billy was aboard. He was too much of an expert to let anything happen to his customers.

Daddy's snug in bed. Doctor Lin wants to give him a day of rest. I want him to have it, too. There's no sense in allowing the fever to play on him. It's always best to rub it out at the beginning.

I thought about calling mom but then I thought better of it. I'm supposed to be the one taking care of daddy. There's no sense in upsetting her down there on the ice. There's no sense in having her pace around like a bird in a cage. I'm in charge and I'll monitor the situation.

I must say daddy looked a little frail. He spends too many hours up there on the bridge. It will do him good to rest up and go to bed early. Tomorrow the sun will shine and his head will be cooled down and he'll be like his old self again. Daddy told me not to worry. He said, "Tanya, it happens every year or two. Don't fret and don't be glum. My old body is as young as ever." So I'm not fretting and I'm not glum. Concerned is more like the way I am. You never know about the hearts of grownups. Sometimes they just give out. Anything can set them off. Anything can do them in. It's enough to make a daughter have sleepless nights. I hope the first lieutenant knows the way to go. I wouldn't want to end up in another place from the one we're going. You see how jumpy I get when daddy isn't well.

One more thing. Doctor Lin spotted Santiago on deck. That's all he said. He said he saw him. I have a feeling that that doctor knows what's going on inside my heart. He not only specializes in body medicine. He specializes in heart medicine, too. I might go up and stroll around and pretend I've run into him. I'd like to know more about his plans. I'd like to hear something about his family, too. I imagine he's

WORLD ONE

an orphan. He just has that look. Any man who would set sail for Antarcticus in a boat the size of a raft can't have too many people depending on him. If he is an orphan, maybe he'd like to add a member to his family. I know just the person for the job. And I bet this person would even volunteer.

Entry #31???? Does he love me or does he not? Will he love me or will he not? Am I for him? Is he for me? There are just so many unanswered questions. And I have no way of knowing what's to become of me. Woe is Tanya on this melancholy evening. She spent the afternoon looking into his lovely eyes. And it is true. He is an orphan and he lives by his wits and his family is the fish of the sea.

We sighted whales, he and I. I wish I could have steered our ship to them. I yearned to take Santiago to them. Maybe some day we'll build a house on the sea and with each morning we'll wake and watch the whales circle our home. That should make Santiago happy. He needs to be with his friends. He needs to have a family. My life seems so far away. And between here and then I'll have to waste so much time.

Better see daddy before he sleeps. I almost forgot about him. I'm turning into a lovesick, seafaring daughter.

Daddy was sleeping when I went in. Doctor Lin wasn't around. I sat by daddy and listened to him breathe. I felt his forehead and it was still hot. Then daddy began to talk. He wasn't talking to me. He was talking to a person inside of him. It scared me and jarred me. It was like he was talking to shadows of ghosts.

"Let me sleep," he said. "I wish it was over and I wish I was gone and I wish and I wish . . . Get out! Get out!" That was all he said. Words like that. I was listening to daddy's troubled side. He's afraid down deep. He's in pain down deep. The old world keeps coming back to him. More when he sleeps than when he wakes. I wish I could sweep out his ghosts. I wish I could scrub his mind clean. I wish my daddy had been born when I was born. Santiago, I'm sure, has beautiful dreams. He must dream of whales. He must dream of sunshine in the deep. Daddy dreams of skeletons. Daddy fights skeletons while he sleeps. How can two worlds be so different? And why did daddy have to be born into his?

I'll be up early to look in on daddy. And I'm going to talk to Doctor Lin about how to stop those dreams. He must have some medicine to put a stop to them. Maybe some vanishing memory cream.

Daddy's head is cool while mine is getting hot. I just came back from having breakfast with him. We had it in his stateroom. The steward brought us a silver pot of coffee and white toast and marmalade. Daddy was still a bit too weak to wolf down scrambled eggs. I told daddy he'd been talking in his sleep. He grinned and said, "I hope I wasn't scolding you." I told him he was murmuring something about the past.

Then daddy got a phone call. It came in on the black telephone next to his cushy chair. That call didn't make the atmosphere for convalescing any better. Daddy greyed all over and then lit up a cigarette. The war on the Ivory Coast isn't settling down. And the W*O*D*E*N ground forces are now caught up in the middle of it and there are plenty of people who are going to be in a lot of trouble when everything is said and done. But don't worry. We're still directed to continue on our course. It'll still be over a week before we get there. And the Navy should be there any time. The Navy will take care of all the action. It'll water it down. Daddy assures me that this will be. Once those cannons start to boom, each side will buckle under and make a beeline for the courts.

Then I asked dad what I'd have to do to become the President. I could see a haze come up before his eyes. I think he'd rather have me considering other things. Well, I'll consider them all. I'd like to be in charge of the Chamber of the Guardians. I'd like to order them about. "Go east and fix it. Go west and squash it. Protect this and that—help here and there. And don't come back until it's done." You can see the appeal in that. It's a life of mild action. Not as good as it

WORLD ONE

was before, but nothing to be ashamed of. And always interesting.

It goes like this: First I'd have to be elected to the Federal Convention. That's no easy thing to do. The delegates get elected by the people of the world. One delegate for each million or so of the population. Within the Federal Convention there are nine Electoral Colleges (for each of the nine Societies) and these colleges nominate twenty-seven candidates for president. Then the Federal Convention secretly selects three and then elects one of three by a two-thirds majority. It's a long way to go, I can see that. I'd have to do many years of campaigning and even then my success wouldn't be assured. But that's the way it's done. Hopeless sounding, isn't it? Maybe there's something easier I could attempt to do. I'd be so old by the time I sat on top and by then it might be too late for me to have a family. I can see why daddy is pushing me back to school. I can see why he didn't run for President. He'd have been 99 by the time he got there. And think of all the time he would have lost out here on the sea.

Good grief. Wasn't there any easier way? Doesn't talent count for anything? Anyway, daddy's well.

Entry #33: While daddy's been recuperating, I've been exploring the cargo bays. Really they're vast rooms about the size of football fields. And they're laiden with treasures—boxes and cartons and crates. It's the perfect place to run into a disease. Anything could attack me there and I'd come out of it as healthy as a country lamb. I guess treasures like that mean more to some people than crowns of jewels and gold. In the long run there isn't much more valuable cargo than what we've got on board. If we were to sink or be kidnapped, it would hurt many more people than us.

It was a good feeling to be down in the hole. Though the light was dim and the air was thin, I felt as if I was in an oasis.

Entry #34: So there!—I went head to head with Santiago this evening. He's a brute and not at all a gentleman. If I were him, I wouldn't count on having dinner with us when we get home. I wouldn't want him in my house. I take back everything I ever said about that man. Freedom fighter or not, I have no use for him. It would have been better if daddy had never even rescued him. That's how mad I am at him. SANTIAGO IS A CREEP!

Here's why. Early tonight I went out for a stroll up on deck. I was minding my own business, just taking in the smell of the heavenly breeze and listening to the roll of the sea. Then I bumped into Santiago. He was out smoking a hand rolled cigarette. I guess daddy gave him some privileges at the canteen. He got the tobacco from somewhere. Santiago says to me, "How is your father's health?" I said he'd be fine by morning. Then just for the sake of conversation I asked him if he was excited by the new news of the war on the Ivory Coast. I said doesn't it sound exciting? That's when he turned on me. And that was all I said, too. "Doesn't it sound exciting?" Well, instead of saying yes, he said, "TANea, you are a stupid little girl. Men die and you like the news of it? Men in pain and they make you excited?" Santiago said some other things which I won't reiterate. But what sticks in me is his phrase, "TANea, you are a stupid little girl." Why he can't even pronounce my name. What makes him think he can say those things to me? My daddy was the one who rescued him. We fished him up out of the sea. And here he is now calling me names. And I was just trying to be polite. I didn't even have to speak to him. I could have been talking to Doctor Lin instead. I could have stayed with daddy and played a game of chess. I could have been doing any one of a million things, but instead I went out of my way to talk to him to make him feel at home. And this is what I get. A slap on the tongue. He's got a temper, that one. And he's got a head the size of a balloon. I suppose he thinks that there's nothing exciting in this world but saving whales and fish and sailing until he almost sinks. I suppose he thinks that a little bit of war is the end of everything. I suppose he thinks this world is heaven where nothing ever goes wrong and no people ever get hurt. Well, I have something to tell him! No place is perfect and no place is heaven but heaven itself. And what happens, happens and nothing and nobody can ever change that.

WORLD ONE

When Santiago called me a stupid little girl, he practically cracked my heart. There I was trying to get to know him and then he did that to me. I came right down here after that. And I haven't moved since. I hope he's fallen over and drowned in the deep.

19

I woke up in a blue funk. I haven't had my breakfast and I haven't had my shower and I haven't even gotten out of my pajamas. I might never leave this cabin again. I had bad dreams all night long. I dreamed that Santiago tied me up and then wrapped me in straw. He made me into a scarecrow. And of course, I didn't scare one bird. In fact, they all flocked to me. I was out in a golden field. That part was nice. I was in a warm golden field and all the birds flocked to me and sat at my feet and made their music until the sun went down. And Santiago just went away, leaving me there. He didn't even take the time to look back. Now what's a dream like that supposed to mean?

I've also been listening to New York City on the shortwave radio. It's just dawn back there. People are rising and stretching. People are drinking their morning coffee and munching on breakfast rolls. I wish I was up there to join them. I wish I was anywhere but here. How can I go out of

WORLD ONE

my cabin and face that monster again? He's ruined my journey and he's spoiled my vacation and probably my Christmas, too. I'm going to paint a table knife black and then give it to him. That's what he's done, he's knifed me. And I'll be bleeding until I know I'll never see him again. This is the worst day of my life. Maybe I should be the one to drown. Maybe I should be the one to end my own misery. I haven't had any training in matters of unrequited love. And I can't call my mom without my dad and I don't want dad to know anything about what Santiago said. Help! I'm a prisoner on the high seas. And a pirate's throttling me.

Entry #36: I've been hiding out in the Engine Room. Daddy asked me to go down there with him to help him investigate a malfunctioning pump. Such a whirlpool of noise I've never heard. It sounded as if I was in the middle of a combat zone. And the sailors down there were as greasy as bicycle chains. It was good to be down there because I knew I was safe. I tried to stay as long as I could. I stayed and asked questions until I knew I was a nuisance. Daddy had left long before me. The malfunctioning pump was only a minor problem. In fact, one of the greasers fixed it by tapping his wrench against it. Daddy saluted him for his "brilliant craftsmanship" and then shuffled back upstairs. I said I'd stay behind to continue to monitor the situation.

Well, here's the big news. When I dared come back up (hoping the coast was clear), I found a note pinned to my door. It read: "Tanya: Forgive me for my trespasses against you. Affectionately, Santiago." At least he can *spell* my name right. And the tone was appropriately contrite. How about that? Santiago is asking me for forgiveness. I've taped the note above my bunk. I've read it a thousand times. I guess he's thought better of what he said. I guess now he's excited by what's ahead. It's a fact—freedom fighters always like to mix with battles. They can't resist the lure of action. Santiago's no different from the rest of them. I bet he's itching to see the first smoke.

I forgive him, of course. I won't run to him and show just how glad I was to receive his note, but I won't avoid him either. We've drawn a truce. The white flag is up and the battle's concluded and I feel better because of it. Santiago isn't such a monster after all. I can love him again if I feel like it. And my invitation to dinner still stands. I'm going to take my shower.

Fresh and clean and smelling like daisies. I've splashed on daisy smelling perfume. And I've put on my blue and white dress. Before the night is done he'll be asking me to marry him. I can't, of course. Not yet, anyway. I'll only do that when I've decided on what my life will be. I should be spending my time thinking up a gift to give Santiago. He deserves a gift from me. Do you have any ideas on what to give an orphan for Christmas?
  Give him love, naturally.

Entry #37: (black night, bad news) Daddy's had a relapse. He felt faint at supper. Doctor Lin escorted him back to his cabin. I followed after that. Daddy was up and about before his time. He should have laid in bed one day longer. Now I'm worried he'll miss Christmas. He's been coughing, too. "And no more cigarettes!" That was the order of Doctor Lin. When Doctor Lin wants to he can come down hard on his sickly patients. And all of this is happening when I thought everything was going to go so well.
  Santiago and I didn't have a chance to speak. He was at the table and I sensed he was being friendly to me, but there wasn't time to strike up an understanding conversation. Daddy dropped his fork and then slumped back. He was breathing very slowly and his forehead was perspiring. Now daddy's back in bed, right where he belongs. It just goes to show that he has to be awfully careful of his health. And no more cigarettes! Those are the doctor's orders. I told him that again when I tucked him into bed. He said, "No more smoking, Tanya. No more smoking . . ." And then he drifted off. Poor daddy must have some kind of flu. He looks so old when he's fast asleep. I'm really worried and think daddy should be home. Maybe his retirement is just the thing for him. Maybe

WORLD ONE

he should fly back when we get to Africa. Mom will know what to do with him once he steps back on the ice.
Tomorrow is Christmas Eve.

That was Santiago. He came to tell me Doctor Lin wants to see me. I have to go. I have to look in on my daddy. I may sit up with him all through the night. I'll bring a candle for his room. I'll be there in case he has more nightmares.

Early Christmas Eve morning and daddy's been hollering in his sleep. He's had an attack of his darkest memories. They're like demons that eat his heart. He's afraid he's going to hell. He sees faces of the dead when the fever's on him. I put cold washcloths on his forehead but the ugly things then only hide away. They come back right away, just as soon as I lift them off. Once when daddy was calm and sleeping soundly, I thought I saw them in the room. They were dancing just above the flame of my lighted candle. I was scared and I almost woke up Doctor Lin so he could chase them out. But then they disappeared. They vanished through the porthole. I dozed off then. I've just now come awake.

I'll need some sleeping time. Not right now but soon. I'm remembering what the doctor said to me. He said, "Tanya, your father's not well. He is weaker than I thought. Tomorrow I want us to call your mother. It is my opinion that your father should be flown home once we reach port. Will you be prepared to go with him?" Of course, I would, I said. I told him that I had already thought of it. Daddy needs rest. Daddy needs relaxation. Daddy needs to get in shape for his years of retirement. That's obvious to anyone who looks.

I hate the past for what it's done to dad. It should have been much more kindly on him. If he hadn't gone to battles and had to fight in wars, daddy would be sleeping better, fever or not. I could take those demons. At least I think I could. But daddy's not as young as me. I have more resilience. I have a stronger constitution. Daddy's been gnawed at in the dark. His lungs are filled with smoke. And not just the smoke of cigarettes. You can blame it on the battle smoke any time you want.

Entry #39: Christmas Eve afternoon, off the coast of Africa. Merry Christmas Eve. That's what mother said to me. I could only cry at her. But she kept saying, "Merry Christmas Eve, Tanya. No need to worry, your father will be fine." But I'm not sure. Doctor Lin didn't sound so positive. He brought her up-to-date. I heard everything he said. He mentioned fever #1 and #2. The two together are enough to really scare me. One is fine, but two, two is one too much.

Daddy's sleeping. When I'll be able to give him his Christmas present, I don't know. When I was young, we gave each other gifts on Christmas Eve. This year, though, we might have to wait until tomorrow morning. How can mother sound so relaxed? How can Doctor Lin speak so easily of daddy going home? Don't they know how much he'll miss his ship? Don't they know how much he'll miss the lanes of whales? Don't they know how he won't want to go home? And who's going to tell him that his time is up? Cut short. Cheated of his final hours on the sea.

Someone's put on Christmas music over the loudspeakers. It's comforting to hear that merry music. The thought of Christmas is very strange out here on the sea. Somehow, right now, it all seems out of place. I'm disoriented. My sleeping patterns have been disrupted. I've only slept for five hours since I came back to my cabin. And where is Santiago? What's he been up to? And why hasn't he come to see me? I'm lonely and I'm upset. I haven't eaten right and slept right. I'm in distress, too. And I wish mother had been more upset. But then, she wasn't there to hear daddy moan and cry in his sleep. She didn't see the demons in his room. I'm the one who saw them. I'm the one who heard him. I'm the one who stayed up all night long and watched my father's pain. I'm the only one who knows what's been happening to him.

I need to calm myself. I need to brush my fears away. I need to think of Christmas and listen only to the music. I need to try to be happy that the world is different now. I

WORLD ONE

have to try to believe that we're better off with less action and more tranquility. I've just had a thought: There must be millions of people in this world who have to live with demons. And these same people always have to fight them. If I were one of them, would I like to have to fight them on a day like Christmas Eve? Would I like to have them circling me and haunting me and gnawing at my heart? That's a question that I can't answer. What is the matter with me?

Merry Christmas Eve on the W*O*D*E*N seas. I'm in between what was and is and it's an awkward place to be for me.

Entry #40: Santiago is ... Santiago is ... Santiago is ... HEAVEN. Do you know what he did? While I was sleeping in this morning he was up to something. Do you know what it was? Santiago was making arrangements for the captain's Christmas party. He was in the kitchen making punch. He was in his room making Christmas ornaments. He was hopping right and left extending invitations. He was in the spirit of being Santa Claus. And I've just come back from a glorious party—the most merry that I've ever been to. And we owe it all to Santiago, the shipwrecked freedom fighter who is also good at giving parties.

Doctor Lin said it would be all right. And I could tell that daddy didn't mind. Daddy loves to have his crew surround him and that's exactly what they did, right there in his not so enormous stateroom. There was happy music on the loudspeakers. There was laughter mixed with sailor talk. And daddy was beaming right there in the center of it all. There he was. He and his devoted crew. And there I was a part of it, too.

But this was more than just a get-well party. More than just a Christmas bash. It was like a farewell party. The word has gotten out. And I think I know by who. The radioman was the only one who heard what Doctor Lin had to tell my mom. It was the radioman who spread the news that daddy must go home. I think right now everyone but daddy knows what's going on. Doctor Lin promised me he'd tell him in the morning. Some Christmas gift that will be! But I'll be there to soften the blow and I still have my boat-made present to give to him. That should brighten up his Christmas morning. That should ease his agony. He'll always have my medal to remind him of our journey to the Ivory Coast.

Daddy stayed in bed throughout the party. He didn't seem ashamed. He never tires of feeling like the captain. The crew gave him something, too. They gave him a life preserver with a phrase on it. "TO OUR CAPTAIN FROM HIS CREW." Then Santiago made a speech. It was a perfect speech. He said, "If not for this man, I would be one helpless, dried-out fish. Without this man, the people we go to meet would have many sickly years. And without this man, we might end up where I began."

Everyone applauded then. And daddy was bursting with a smile. I've never seen him look so happy. I hardly even recognized him. I thought: Is that my daddy? Is he the one that was so grim? Not anymore he's not. He just needed some encouragement.

After the party, I went up to breathe some air. And Santiago came to breathe some, too. He said, "TANea, your father will die a happy man." It was a crazy thing to say, I know. But I took it right this time. I know Santiago thinks the world of daddy. And I hope it's true, too. I do hope daddy dies a happy man—about a hundred years from now.

My world is full of dazzling and dramatic news! Item One was a news flash from Antarcticus. Daddy received it while I was in his room. No more war in Liberia and the Ivory Coast. How's that for Christmas music? A light went on in daddy's eyes when he heard the words. By the look of him I thought maybe my mom was going to have a baby. But it isn't so. But it does mean that the women of the Ivory Coast will be free to have thousands of them now that the war is stopped—only the epidemic needs to be contained from here on out. We'll see to that and we'll see to the health of all the future children born today and tomorrow and after that and after that.

Item Two was less than happy news. The doctor came in

WORLD ONE

and told my dad that he had no choice but to go on home. Daddy bristled when he heard what the doctor had to say. I must admit, I bristled, too. It was odd to hear a doctor order my daddy about. Doctors don't have the rank of captains and the ordering should be done the other way around. But daddy wasn't too surprised. In fact, he didn't make a fuss. He just stared at the wall where the crew hung the life preserver and then finally said, "I'd always thought I'd die out here on the seas."

Then Doctor Lin let us be. He tiptoed out while daddy thought, and closed the door very quietly behind him. Right then and there I gave daddy his Christmas present. I wasn't going to wait a second longer. In my mind there wasn't any sense in allowing him to catch the blues, not even for a second. Daddy nearly cried when he saw what I had written. I guess he liked what I had to say. He hugged me then. He squeezed me tight. I felt like a mushy teddy bear.

Daddy then ordered me to go to chapel. I would have stayed with him but he gave me no choice. I had to go and listen to the chaplain. He was in full swing and jolly with the news of Christmas Day. Then he closed the service with a blessing. He said, "God bless the people of the world. God keep the world in peace. God bless all Societies and the W*O*D*E*N government. God bless our captain and keep him well. Merry Christmas everyone."

I prayed along with all his words. I even prayed for peace. Why not? It seems to make my daddy so happy. And it doesn't exactly tear anyone else up, either.

Entry #42: Well, my Christmas Day is now complete. You know beautiful who slipped an invitation underneath my door. The invitation slyly pointed out that the issuer had a present for me. I scrubbed my face and twirled a ribbon in my hair and then set out to Billy the cook's old cabin. On the way I spent some time thinking about Billy being gone. I wish I could have another taste of beer and I wouldn't mind some more poker winnings and most of all I'd like to have Billy back for good company.

Santiago greeted me at the door. He was standing there

looking like a Latin Santa Claus. He was slimmer than my childhood one but was by far much handsomer. And he had a glimmer in his eye and was holding something small behind his back. I said, "I received your invitation . . ." Then I lost what I had planned to say. It was him at the door that made me choke. I wasn't prepared for such a sudden confrontation. But Santiago smoothed it over nicely. He said, "TANea, I have a gift from me to you. We are Christmas friends. We have only good thoughts between us."

Then Santiago put his present in my hand. It was small and wrapped up very roughly. I think he used a shoestring for the bow. It was white and fluffy. I untied the bow and then folded back the colored paper. And what was inside surprised me. I guess I had hoped for more. Why? Don't ask me why. I had visions of bracelets and rings and necklaces. But what I got was something very useful. I got a pack of poker cards from him. It was a new box, too. It hadn't even been opened. My daddy gave Santiago very generous canteen privileges. We played blackjack for a while.

I, of course, gave my friend a kiss. I had planned to do it all along. "Give him love," I kept thinking to myself. Orphans are always the loneliest at Christmas. Santiago didn't kiss me back. I thought he did at first, but then I knew he didn't. I didn't feel any warmness on my cheek. I could have used that feeling. I wanted to have that feeling, but it wasn't my luck to have it. But then I beat him at cards, five or six times. I let him win once, for the sake of sportsmanship. Anyway, all in all, it was a lovely afternoon. I thanked Santiago for his beautiful present. Now I wonder if my gift of love was obvious enough. I'm not sure he understood it. I don't know for sure. Love is like a deck of cards. You have to break it in.

Entry #43: The sea is rushing past, like storms in sleep. The porthole window is open wide and the air is spicy like smelling salts. I'm in the mood for some miracle to happen. I'm in the mood to fly. I can't explain my mood. It's neither here nor there. It's just unknowable. Christmas brings out the mystery in me. It takes me to another world—part me and part the people around me and the new people I'll one day meet.

WORLD ONE

I ask myself, why was I born? I ask myself, why am I here? I ask myself, why am I me and not a star, for instance? I am flooding with thoughts such as these. The sea opens up my gates. I'm free to consider all matters in the air and sky and land and sea. Have you ever had those moments when all the world is yours to contemplate?

I'm changing, I can tell. Which way is an unknown quantity. Free feeling as I am right now, I can imagine changing to a fish or a patch of sea. Why am I here on earth and why was I born when I was?

My radio's turned down low. I'm tuned in to strange and exotic African tongues. They could be speaking of vegetables for all I know. But what does it matter? It's Christmas night and all is well, even though daddy's still sick.

Last night I dreamed that I was President. What an unlikely dream. I should tell daddy about this dream. Then he might become more encouraging on the subject. I can't tell you more because the landscape was so murky. I was walking maybe on the ice—it could have been in a grand hall, it was partly white at least—and I was thinking presidential thoughts. I was worrying about energy supplies and taxes and immigration. I was also fretting about worldwide transportation and shipping lanes. One thing I wasn't worried about though was my reelection. In the W*O*D*E*N government I can be president only once, for six years give or take a month. That's long enough for anyone, even long enough for me.

As you can understand, I woke up exhausted. I sat in bed and mulled over the implications of what had been going through my head. Is what I dreamed a sign of what my future's going to be? Should I be heading off in that direction? It's hard to say with dreams. Sometimes they play tricks. Like once I dreamed I passed an arithmetic exam when it turned out that I hadn't. Sometimes dreams are merely wishes come into your sleep. But sometimes wishes can turn into real, living dreams.

When I was growing up, I always wanted to journey with

my daddy. It was more than a wish, I dreamed of it many times. And now look at me. I'm on the seas. I'm floating high above the waters. I'm heading for the Ivory Coast where they speak strange and exotic tongues. I'll be consulting with daddy soon. I'll repeat to him what I've said to you. I might even mention it to my friend, Santiago. He doesn't even know all the ambitions I have. And he might be of help to me. He might help me sort them out. I don't know. I'm just glad I had that dream.

Entry #45: Just when things were slowing down, we've started up some action. When I was in his room, daddy got the call from the radioman. Miles and miles up ahead is a ship that's in distress. It's on our path, maybe some 1000 miles off the coast of Africa. Daddy gave the command to intercept and rescue them. But what daddy thinks is so strange is that they won't answer questions about their problems. All they do is signal S O S, S O S, S O S . . . I told daddy that they were pirates for sure. I told daddy that he ought to be very careful about approaching an unknown quantity. But daddy says this kind of call has happened before and that there's nothing to worry about except getting there on time—before it sinks, or before whatever damage worsens.

So it's double full steam ahead to rescue pirates and their stolen treasures. Daddy says we'll meet up with the pirates in another day. He says ship and I say pirates. I wish daddy would avoid this kind of rescue. Wasn't rescuing Santiago quite enough for one journey across the sea? Not for daddy it isn't. Daddy would rescue people all day long if he had the opportunity. For every person he gets to rescue, he feels that much better. But what if these pirates take us hostage? What if they steal all of our medical supplies? They could sell them for a fortune in the black markets. And they could kill us, too. We don't have cannons on board. We are virtually defenseless. This ship wasn't made to do battle with anyone. For the first time in my life, I fear an early death.

If I were older, I'd relieve daddy of his command. I'd say it was the fever that was luring him into this trap. But I can't do one thing or another. I have to go with what the captain

WORLD ONE

says. I'll have nightmares tonight. Of that you can be sure. I'm not ready to see battle smoke when it's our ship that will be going up in jagged flames. Right now I'd rather just float our way to port and then take my daddy home. I never wanted to spend the rest of my life in captivity. All I wanted to do was to make the right choice.

S O S ... We're heading toward disaster.

Entry #46: Santiago thinks I've lost "my nonsense." I didn't have the heart to tell him I may or may not have lost my sense. But nonetheless, I told him I was scared. Pirates are an ugly lot. They live in another world. They hijack ships and murder crews and then sail off safely and hide in coves. Santiago made fun of me. He said, "But TANea, you will have excitement. You may yet come heart to heart with war. Isn't that what you wanted? Weren't you hopeful of it before?"

I said, "Cut it out. We are in danger of losing our lives. Don't you think I want to live? Don't you think I want everyone to live?" Then Santiago said, "But you had hope of seeing war. You were hungry for experience. You may get your wish and then not want it after all." I am trembling here and there. I just know we're in for it. I just know we're facing trouble. If anyone should be signaling S O S, it's us, not that ship we're going to meet. How am I going to sleep when tomorrow I may die? And Santiago may die, too. And even daddy. Should I call my mom and have her talk to dad? Maybe she can persuade him of what I know will happen. Right now I wish I was back safely on the ice. At least down there I had W*O*D*E*N to protect me from pirates on the sea. Santiago, I don't understand why you think everything is right. I don't understand why daddy can be so calm. You would think that with his fever better, he would be thinking right. But no, all he wants to do is rescue people in distress and then fall into their trap.

If Billy were here, he would understand the dangers to the north. He would know that we should steer a little to the east. He would know the ways of pirates and the best course to avoid them. Billy, won't you come back and help daddy with his reason? I pray that Billy hears me now. I pray that

Billy somehow intervenes. I pray that Billy puts his shield or net or whatever all the way over us. If he were here, he wouldn't want us to end up dead. And he would want our medical supplies to go untouched and land intact in port. This is a dreadful evening and this has been a fearful day. And by tomorrow it will only be getting worse.

Good-bye for now. I'll be trembling in my sleep and dreaming of the way it was when I was so happy back in Antarcticus.

I hardly said a word at breakfast. I could hardly eat my eggs. I drank my juice and then loaded up on coffee. But the coffee only made my heart want to explode. Santiago was nice to me, but I know what he thinks of my speculations. Daddy patted me on the head and said, "If you're afraid, lock the door to your cabin." I said daddy I think you ought to signal S O S. He just shook his head.

Daddy looks okay but I know the fever's got him. It's in his blood and in his brain—it's taken over him. We're a ship without a captain and the pirates like that fine. They're waiting for us now with daggers in their hands. And the leader of the pirates has a crooked foot. And his pirate crew eat rats when their stolen food runs out. One of the first things that they'll do is raid the kitchen and seize the eggs. I've missed my last chance to eat a normal breakfast.

I've just come back from crying at Doctor Lin. I thought if no one else would understand certainly he would. But he didn't. And he says the fever has not infected daddy. He says daddy's brain is fine. He says the captain is the captain and that is always that. I'm alone with all my trembling. There's no one else to turn to. If I could drug the radioman and put him fast asleep, I would signal S O S. I'd call in the W*O*D*E*N Navy. They could be turning back already. They could meet us and check that ship for pirates. You don't think I know what the future holds? You think I'm the one who's got the fever? You think I'm the one who should be in bed? Well, maybe so. But I have premonitions. I see what lies

WORLD ONE

up ahead. After all, I am the captain's daughter. And I naturally fear for the lives of everyone.

Doctor Lin just sent me a glass of warm milk. And with the milk he gave me a pill. He said it would calm me down. I drank the milk but didn't take the pill. I want to be alert for my execution.

Entry #48: Because the seas are high, we've been slowing down. It's rocky where I am and my stomach's ill at ease. I can't tell if I'll just be sick or if I'll die. I'm twisted up with anxieties. I'm praying that we'll be blown off course and run aground on some gorgeous island. There I could relax and nurse a luscious tan. There daddy could stamp out his fever once and for all. And there he could regain his perspective and see the folly of his ways. We won't meet up with the pirates until very late tonight. I might go to sleep before we meet our doom. I might not stay up to see the bloody action. I'll lock my cabin door and barricade it, too. There's no sense in giving up to them without putting up a fight.

I had a conference with Santiago. I know he thought I was a fool, but he'll know better soon. I told Santiago that if the pirates should attack the ship, if we should be brought directly under their control, that he's to make his way someway to the radio room. He's the only one I know who can signal S O S. I told him that everyone would be counting on him after it was too late. He said, "TANea, you have a brave imagination. Someday you will be a good captain on the sea."

He was making fun of me, don't you think I know that? It's true, of course. I'll make a captain someday—just as long as I don't have to fight off pirates. I wouldn't have the nerve for that. If I knew that pirates would be coming, I'd turn right around and take my sailors home. I'd avoid them without a second thought. I have no need for pirates in my life. And I have no wish for them to ever get the better of me. I like it best when everything is calm and floating along peacefully. Pirates belong to another world that I never wish to know. They belong to a world that shouldn't exist at all.

I'm torn up about what I should do. Should I go and stand with daddy on the bridge? Should I stay by his side until the hour of my death? It might be nice to die together. It might be nice to have some company then. Or should I go and stay with Santiago? Wouldn't it be more heroic to die in the arms of my beloved freedom fighter? I can't believe I have to talk like this. When I came on board I never dreamed I'd ever be . . . afraid.

I've washed my hands and face. I feel more sturdy now. I think I'll go for a walk up on deck. It will be nice to breathe in the salty air. It will be nice to feel alive before the pirates cut me up and feed me to the fish.

This may be my last communication.

Entry #49: It's too late for me. I've been with daddy on the bridge and we've been talking hour by hour but we're still not near the rescue point. The seas are rough because we're approaching wintertime and leaving the summertime of the south behind. There's one good piece of news. It's good news for me—not such good news for the possible pirates. The ship has responded to our questions. They've signaled that their engines are down and a fire's just broken out. It's hot on board that ship! Daddy's now sure that we won't meet up with pirates. Me, I won't be sure until I see their stripes. Daddy's in a blissful mood. Me, I'm cranky and looking forward to sleep. I could sleep a hundred hours and then a dozen more. But daddy won't need sleep until the rescue's over.

Daddy was talking about the future tonight. It was good to hear him think ahead. I suppose these rescues are a form of medicine for him. With each rescue, I believe, he erases another deadly memory. But more importantly he enjoys the thought of what my life will be. When he entertains those thoughts, his past life doesn't seem to matter. He's all for forward thinking now—he's all for young people like me and Santiago. He says the world is ours to have and to hold. Sometimes daddies get sentimental, you know?

WORLD ONE

I asked daddy what his best memory was. He thought and thought about that one for a while. Then he coughed it up. He said, "Tanya, when you were very young, I remember standing in the harbor of McMurdo Sound. You and your mother were there and all the people of the W*O*D*E*N government. And standing with us all was the world's first woman president. And altogether we watched the Navy set sail. Do you remember that?" I remember something of it. I was eight and very cold. Beyond that it is just a cloudy memory, something I could have even dreamed. But I'll take my daddy's word for it. He should know his life's best memory.

Santiago was hiding out tonight. I expected to see him but he never showed his face. Maybe he's been thinking over my theory of this afternoon. Maybe he's planning his route to the radio room if the worst should ever happen. Well, I hope he's planned it well. If I wake up and find myself a captive of the pirates, I'll be expecting him to rescue me by calling in the Navy.

My lip is stiff and my eyes are narrowed and I am the one who told them so. I told them it would happen and, of course, it happened. Late last night when I was curled up safe and sound underneath my blankets, the pirates made their move. They seized the ship and killed a man—they just threw him overboard. He's now down there with the fish. He's past the stage of drowning. He's with Billy the cook and a hundred thousand long gone sailors. Daddy's locked in his stateroom. There's a pirate guard outside his door. And all of the phones have been disconnected. He won't be radioing W*O*D*E*N for any help.

What the pirates want is this. They want food and all of our medical supplies. Isn't that what I said? I said that that's exactly what they'd want and get if we didn't change our course. But daddy had to have his way. He had to throw the dice and the dice came up snake eyes and here we are in captivity, just exactly like I said.

The captain of the pirates is named Abu. He wears a

turban rather than a cap. He wears a flowing robe rather than a suit. He has a pistol hanging from his belt. And he has serpent eyes and a shiny, dark tanned face. He's in charge of the unloading operations. And he's in charge of my fate and the fate of all the sailors on this ship. You may wonder how I know about everything that's been going on. Here's how I know.

I woke up to the noisy sounds of men running down the corridors right outside my door. At first I thought I was having unfriendly nightmares. But when I sat up in bed and listened hard I knew the sounds for what they were. They were sounds of men in panic. I put on my clothes and went out to investigate. And when I saw a pirate wearing robes, I pretended to be sick. I held my stomach like I had a burning ulcer. I moaned and spun my eyes. Then I fell down at his feet. And I began to cry. I said, "I'm so sick and I want my daddy!" Then to my surprise the ten foot pirate smiled down at me so nicely. He picked me up and carried me in the direction that I pointed. His hands were like locks on both my neck and ankles. But he took me to the captain's door and I went in to see my dad, crying out in pain, until he closed the door.

Daddy was pale and had a bruise just below his eye. I winked at him and whispered that I was fine. Then I said, "What's the damage, daddy?" That put a smile back on his face. He hugged me and gave out a little laugh. Daddy was fooled all right. The pirates did it very cunningly. They had made their ship look like it was going up in smoke. And when daddy's ship had come up alongside, the chief pirate and his men had swarmed on board, pulling guns out from beneath their robes. Daddy said he was sick when he saw those guns. But then, of course, it was too late for anything constructive to be done. And now we're at the mercy of the pirates and with each passing hour we're losing more and more medicine that should be going to the Ivory Coast. And along with the more and more medicine, we're being robbed of all our food. This is a tragedy. This is death. This is more than I can take. Daddy, too. Now I have to think up a way to rid daddy of the pirates. At least I am free to roam around because I am a "little petite." That's what Abu has come to call me. Abu

WORLD ONE

came to daddy's cabin when I was there and he said words like this: "Your majesty Captain, I am Abu and your ship is trespassing out here on my waters. I am the King of Law in this wilderness. And you have infringed upon my sacred territory. Therefore, you must pay a token to pass by well. Your ship will live if we are paid most highly. Do not struggle, do not plead. Be good and gentle and you shall have no harm. We shall be gone before two days are done."

Abu is a speaking pirate and a very good one. But daddy was not impressed. He said back to him, "You will grow old in imprisonment. You will never reach the shore." When daddy said that I thought his life would end. I thought Abu would fire a shot at him. But Abu smiled and then left us sitting there. Daddy said that I should stay with him. I said all right, but first let me bring some things from my cabin. I'm back here now considering what to do. I should make my way to Santiago and get him to the radio room. There's no time to waste. We must be very smart. We must play pirate when we're at war with pirates. We must save what we have for the people who really need it. We have a duty that's higher than our lives and no pirate King of Law will hurt those desperate people who have need of our provisions.

Entry #51: Reporting back and in command. Operation Rescue is proceeding rather well. Phase One is underway. I turned Santiago into an ugly pirate. I wrapped him up in sheets. I made his turban out of cloth. He's on his way right this minute up to the radio room. I have my fingers crossed that he will go undiscovered. If he's caught, it might be the end of us. But we agreed, we have to take the chance. We have to fight the pirates to keep the people well.

What Santiago's going to do is to signal S O S. I'm pretty sure the pirates have long since tied up the radioman. They went to find him just as soon as they climbed on board. They've probably gagged him, too. Let's just hope they haven't cut his throat. He's got a wife and family to support. And he's got a right to live just like all the rest of us.

What I'm counting on is this. If Santiago can get through, if he can signal the Navy right away, then all we have to do is stall. We have to keep the pirates here, not let them sail away. If we can do that, maybe the W*O*D*E*N Navy can come in time to rescue us and save our medicines. It's my job to think up a plan to keep the pirates here. If I can hold them here for half a day, maybe less or maybe more, then who knows? We might be safe.

It's murder, waiting here. Each time I hear a footstep outside Santiago's door, I think it will be him. Each time I hear a footstep, I think it might be them. Daddy's probably been wondering where I am. I'd like to let him know, but I can't leave yet. I'm bound to wait for Santiago. I have to know if Phase One is going to work. After that, I'll need Phase Two.

Just before Santiago left, he said, "If I am to die, I am proud to die on your father's ship. He saved me and now I go to save him. If I die, go and bury me in the sea. TANea, stay safe and be a captain when you can." Then he left. He slipped right out the door. I know he made it down the first corridor because I watched him till he disappeared. I hope my plan is right. I hope my daddy will approve of . . .

The S O S is on its way. Phase One has been accomplished and Santiago is back with me. I said it right, they've tied up the radioman, but Santiago said he winked while he signaled our distress.

Entry #52: Daddy's furious with me. I've never seen him quite so livid. He's sitting in his chair right now, casting nasty looks at me. But what in the world does he expect? We have to save our ship and we have to fulfill our mission and if he's going to get us caught then I have to find the way to be released. Daddy said, "You, my child, will get us killed. What will the pirates do when they see the Navy coming? Do you really think they'll raise their hands in surrender? Do you really think they'll turn in their pistols to go to prison? Think, Tanya, think. You have put all our lives in jeopardy!"

Ha! I've done no such thing. If daddy had given me a chance, I would have explained Phase Two. But he didn't

WORLD ONE

want to hear it. He said I wasn't to move. He said, "Let's hope the W*O*D*E*N Navy is headed north instead of south." Could it be that my daddy's turned into a coward? Could it be that he's afraid to fight for justice in this world? What's this world about now but justice anyhow? He's the one who seemed so pleased with it just a day ago.

Since I'm stuck here for a while, I'll detail my thinking on Phase Two. It's a powerful plan based on my experience with a poker night. I'll need a little bit of Doctor Lin's help for this. But I think Doctor Lin will help me as long as daddy doesn't know. If there's anyone on board this ship who wants to see those vaccinations reach their destination, it's Doctor Lin. He'll take a chance, I know.

Phase Two is this. Sometime tomorrow when daddy is distracted, I'll go out for a stroll. And on my stroll I'll bump into Abu, King of Law. And to Abu I'll make a friendly suggestion. "Your Majesty," I'll say, "your men are in need of sustenance. And I have just the ticket for them. Why don't you come with me? . . ." Meanwhile, Doctor Lin will be very busy. He'll be down in the kitchen lacing the bottles of beer with sleeping potion. Now I think you'll understand the meaning of Phase Two. All the pirates will be drunk and sleeping when our Navy comes. They'll be dreaming of riches and wonderlands while the Navy steps on board. And just so the Navy understands the situation, I'll run up a black flag to show them who's on board.

I think the plan will work. Pirates must love beer as much as any sailors. And Doctor Lin has plenty of those sleeping pills. I wish I could tell daddy of my plan. I wish he'd understand. He should have more faith in this ship's future captain.

20

Up early with the stormy winds. Winter's begun to whip us right and left. Still the pirates continue to unload, despite the winds coming from the west. I slept in daddy's bed last night. Daddy was noble enough to sleep on the floor. He's been sneezing since before sunrise—a trace of flu stays with him.

The pirates gave us bread and water for breakfast. How generous of them! I'm really rather snappish. I've been deprived of my morning coffee. We are prisoners and I don't like the taste of it. We haven't even had a trial. Abu, King of Law, is a shameful man and not so honorable. He seems to like to break the laws. Well, I'll tell you this. If he came before my court, I'd put *him* on bread and water until the age of sixty-one. After that I'd graduate him to bread and milk until the age of seventy-one. After that I might have mercy on him and set him free. I can be severe for only just so long.

I have to rendezvous with Doctor Lin. I'll mention to

WORLD ONE

daddy that I have some stomach pains. He'll let me go if I say that. He'll want me to get immediate medical attention. "Go and see Doctor Lin." He'll say exactly that. I can count on daddy to say certain things every time.

Daddy was laughing in his sleep last night. I've never heard anyone ever laugh in their sleep at night before. He was having a jolly time dreaming of whatever he was dreaming. I asked him over bread and water just what he was dreaming of. He said he didn't know. I imagine he was dreaming of being home and happy. I imagine he was dreaming of his future life back down on the ice. Me, I dreamed that daddy died in a battle with the pirates. I was holding his wounded arm and patting him on the head and before he died he smiled at me and said, "Be a captain when you can."

In a few more minutes I'll be coming down with stomach pains. Then shortly after that I'll be on my way to visit Doctor Lin. I figure by tonight the pirates will want to sail away. But before they do, I should think they'd want to drink some ice-cold bottles of beer.

Entry #54: We've spiked three hundred bottles of beer. We unscrewed each cap and sprinkled sleeping potion in each one. I've got blisters on my fingers and the muscles in my right arm ache, but the deed is done. Everything is ready for the pirate's sleeping party. And I've just come up with another idea. I have a notion that pirates love movies. If this is true, I have just the movie for them. One that they can identify with, more or less. I plan to have a rerun of the movie, *Casablanca*. Probably they will identify with the unfriendly Nazi men. On the other hand, I don't really care who they choose to like. What's important is that they drink themselves to sleep in the theater tonight.

On my way back from my mission with the doctor, I went up top to engage in conversation with Abu. He's not a pretty man and he isn't so polite. But what in the world should I expect from a savage pirate who's stealing right and left. I said, "Your Majesty, what are you going to do with all that medicine? Do you have so many sick people on your ship? If you do, I am truly sorry. We would have helped you if you had asked." Abu studied me. Gradually, he split a smile. He said, "Maybe I will kidnap you! Maybe you will come with me and serve me supper, lunch and dinner. We have a place for you." I was worried for a moment. It hit me then that he might do just what he said. I pretended it wouldn't bother me. I pretended that it was a very interesting proposition.

"Your Majesty," I said. "Why don't you try me out? Daddy isn't very happy with me wanting to spend my life travelling far and wide. Me, I like to travel. I could travel till I die. Why don't you let me show you what I can do." Abu sensed something that I know he didn't like. But he couldn't put his finger on it. He thought awhile as he studied me. "What, little petite, is in your mind?" He was testing me. He was probing me. I steadied myself and said, "I know where the liquor is. If you won't hurt my daddy and his men, I'll give it all to you. You and your men should have something to celebrate with—after you've finished with your chores."

Abu, King of Law, liked me better then. But I liked him less. For the chief of pirates, he isn't very smart. I was surprised that he didn't know exactly what I'd planned. He told me to stand by. I am standing by. I am here with daddy standing by, just waiting for my call. My only fear is that the Navy won't be here on time. Tomorrow morning is many hours away. And, of course, I can't be sure that the Navy will even come by then. But I have to take this desperate chance. I have to do it for the people of the Ivory Coast. I have to do it for my daddy's name. If I were a captain I sure wouldn't want to retire on such a note. I'd rather die than go out with a pirate taking all my medicine, wouldn't you?

Entry #55: I don't know what's going to happen but everything's in progress. The movie's running on and on and the pirates are swallowing down all the beer. When last I left, the pirates were getting groggy and fights were breaking out. One of the meanest pirates threw a bottle at Humphrey Bogart. That was okay with me, just as long as he respected the image of the freedom fighter.

Santiago played host with me. He passed out bottles of beer. The only trouble is is that Abu doesn't drink. He is the

WORLD ONE

purest pirate that there ever was. I just hope that everyone else drinks down their fill and falls down into sleep. We can handle Abu on his own. At least daddy says we can. We'll have to handle him and the pirate stationed outside our door. Other than that, everything else will be easy.

Daddy liked my trick. He just told me how fine he thought it was. He said, "Tanya, you are even smarter than your captain. I am very proud of you." Well, I was flabbergasted that he praised me. I thought sure he'd yell at me and then lock me in my room. But daddy knows a good plan when he sees one. Now we'll just wait it out and hope to tie the pirates up while they're dreaming and sleeping and off their guard.

After I told daddy of all that I had done, he went into fits of laughter. He must have laughed a full five minutes. I'd never seen my daddy laugh so long. If I hadn't known otherwise, I might have thought that he was drunk. After all that has happened, I was glad to see him rolling over. I was glad to see him on the verge of happy tears. Even if my plan doesn't work, it was worth the try to get that laughter out of daddy. He's practically a whole new man. If his health weren't so fragile, if he were down a year or two in age, I'd be the first to say that he should go on sailing.

I suppose what daddy likes about what I did is this. I made a stab at rescuing us. I made a stab at rescuing us and saving all our medicine. That's what this world's about now anyway. It's all about rescuing people and helping them out with medicine and keeping them safe from war and pirates. I think I like the world I'm in. Well, I like it better than I did. It's all this experience that makes me see it better than I did.

Daddy says it's time to move. He has a plan to do in the pirate stationed just outside our door. My stomach pains are about to happen. And daddy's positioning himself behind the door armed with a life preserver. When I cry out and the pirate comes in, daddy will drop the life preserver over his head and shoulders. My next job is to relieve him of his pistol. After that, we'll tie him up and go in search of Abu.

Wish us lots of luck.

It was a long and triumphant night. I haven't slept and I don't think I will at least until the W*O*D*E*N Navy comes. They should be here early this afternoon. And when they come, we'll be cheering for them. They've already sent us a cable of congratulations. And they've promised to take the pirates off our hands. Right now all the pirates are locked up tight down inside the movie theater. Even Abu is locked up with them. He's the poorest pirate (and only pirate) I've ever known. If anyone should be retiring, it's him. He let a girl like me get the better of him. Here's what happened.

After daddy and I tied that unsuspecting pirate up, we gathered up some of the heartiest crew. Then we all headed off to where the pirates were stumbling around. You've never seen so many drunken, stumbling pirates. They were falling over chairs and bumping heads and mumbling in their sleep. I went in and distracted Abu for a second. That was all the time we needed. Daddy hit Abu on the head with the butt of the pistol and he fell over instantly. Santiago grabbed his gun while the other members of the crew stole the guns off of the rest of them. After that, we locked the door, just as the movie was ending. It was very poetic the way the freedom fighter was flying off at that very moment. I would have to say that we have a lot of hot and angry pirates down inside that room. And daddy said he's not about to give them any breakfast. He's waiting for the Navy to come by before he opens that door. I don't blame him. They're probably acting like a pack of bees and we want the Navy to be here before we let them out.

Daddy is beaming very proudly. I told *him* that I was proud of him. You can bet he liked that compliment. I suppose all daddies like to show off in front of their daughters. We called my mother, too. She was horrified. But daddy calmed her down. He told her exactly what I had done. I'm sure my mother never thought that I could do that. I never even thought I could until I did it. This journey has had many suprises for me. Like daddy, I feel like a whole new person, too. But to tell you the truth, I wouldn't want to have to do it again, not any time too soon. It was harder than it looked and I was lucky because Abu is a sucker for little petites like me.

WORLD ONE

Entry #57, zzzzzzzzzzzzzz! I'm crazy with agitation. How I could have done this, I don't know. I missed the boat, so to speak. I was fast asleep when all the action happened. I was counting sheep when I should have been counting Navy men. I'm very upset as you can tell. I didn't have the chance to say good-bye to Abu. He was spirited away in the middle of this afternoon and now he's gone to go before the courts, along with his not-so-deadly crew. But daddy told me something that he said. Abu, King of Law, had a personal message for me. Abu said, "Tell her . . . I am sorry she did not come with me. Tell her . . . she should be a captain, Captain. Tell her . . . in all my years, I have never been so undone." After that was said, Abu was carted off. Daddy said he thought Abu was a very tired pirate. Daddy said, "He'd been too long at sea. A rest will do him good. And people like us, too." Me, too.

All the medicines are back on board! And we have all our lovely food back, too. I'm on my way to dinner. I'm about as hungry as I've ever been. I'm looking forward to steak and biscuits and hot potatoes. I'm looking forward to sitting next to daddy. And Santiago will be there as will Doctor Lin. I think tonight we should all celebrate. We should drink plènty of bottles of beer. I won't need mine to be spiked. I'll be able to sleep tonight. I won't have any trouble with that at all. I'm still under a dreamy haze. I'm still savoring the daring deeds of last night. It's a night that I'll remember until the day I die.

Just wait till all the girls back home hear about what I got to do. I'll be famous by the time I get home. I might even win a medal from the Navy or maybe even the President. I might be offered a ship when I graduate from high school. All things are possible now that I'm a hero. Who would have thought my summer vacation would have turned out this way? Lucky for daddy that I came on board. Lucky for the people of the Ivory Coast that pirates love beer. And lucky for me I had a friend like Billy the cook. If it hadn't been for him, I never would have come up with the idea. Billy was watching over me all right. He was seeing me through. Billy, wherever you are, thanks for all your help. You are a credit to your nation, even outside of life.

I'm off to have my supper before I get some more sleep. Tanya signing off, back on her way to the Ivory Coast.

Entry #58: Tonight was my night. I was honored at a party. I was toasted several times. Everyone from my daddy on down stood up and said how much I helped. But the best thing of all is this. Tomorrow I am to be a Captain for a Day. I'm to wear my daddy's cap and order us north at our capacity. I'm to watch out for pirates and any abandoned ships. I'm to do the things that all captains get to do. What'd you think of that?

Santiago was a sweetheart. He said out loud to everyone that he wished he had a sister like me. At first it made me sad because you know how I feel about him. But then on second thought, I was really rather glad. It's nice to know that he thinks I could belong with him. And it's important to know that he has some affection for me. Maybe in a few more years he'll think about me differently. After all, he still has those court battles to win to help save the fishes and the whales. And me, I still have my education to complete. If I'm to be a full-fledged captain one day, I'll need to have more information. Until that day, I can wait. I'm just happy he said those words about me. It's nice to know that I can belong just about anywhere. I guess that's nice for anyone.

Daddy said a few kind words about our Navy, too. He said that without the Navy the seas might be full of pirates and that ships like ours would live more dangerously. There's no doubt about that from where I sit. It's good to have a Navy helping to keep the world safe and full of peace. In some ways though, I think I'd rather follow in the footsteps of my dad. I could join the Navy and fight pirates and settle border disputes, but I still think in the end I'd rather go about carrying loads of medicine. If I can't carry medicine then I'll settle for food. I'd be happy to sail plenty of food to anywhere in the world. I'd be happy to do that on behalf of the W*O*D*E*N government, wouldn't you? I know you would. It would be an honor to do that and a good way to spend a life. It's even better than occasionally getting to see battle smoke. Who wants to see smoke when there are millions

WORLD ONE

of smiles to see? Who wants to have action when all the action I need is to steer a ship in the right direction? It's possible I'll change my mind, of course. I reserve the right to do just that. But from where I am I think I know what's best for me. I even think I know the reason why I was born. I was born to take my daddy's place.

I'll be a captain in the morning and try it out. Goodnight, goodnight and wish me well.

Tanya reporting on her morning. The waves have been thrashing and the ship has been heaving, but we're still pushing full steam ahead.

At breakfast I gave the crew a pep talk. I tapped my spoon against my glass and then everyone quieted down. I cleared my throat and said this. "Members of the crew, I hope you all slept well. I know I did. It is a pleasure to sleep without pirates aboard. Now hear this. Let's work extra hard today to make this ship look shining. Let's polish the rails and clean the decks and press the flags just perfectly. We want this ship to look fine when we sail into port. And as this is New Year's Eve, we want to bring in the new year well. By tomorrow night we should be off of the Ivory Coast. We are one day behind because of the irregularity. But at least when we get to port, the skies should be clear and free from the dark clouds of war. Now let's get to work and show the world just how pretty we can look. I want you to be as proud of us as I am of you."

I got a cheer when I said that. If there's one thing sailors like it's to have occasional compliments. Not too many to make them vain, but enough to keep them cheerful and happy. I'm up on the bridge right now. And my words seem to be working, although no sailors can scrub the decks in this kind of weather. Oh, well. Perhaps daddy will ask them to finish the job tomorrow.

It's glorious to be in charge of a fine ship like this. It's like nothing I've ever known. Sometimes when I was down on the ice, I'd try to imagine what my daddy was feeling like—standing where I am, looking where I'm looking, doing what I'm doing. I never imagined it right, that's for sure. There's no way to imagine a time like this. It's part great and part small. Out beyond is all the world and before me are all the dials that allow me to get there. Who could ask for more? Who would want it to be different? I can hardly wait to get back down to Antarcticus and tell it all.

Entry #60: This afternoon I ordered daddy and Santiago to help me watch for whales. They followed my orders exactly. The sea was calm and the blue was back in the sky and my ship was running smoothly. It was a serene and gentle afternoon. Santiago was the first to spot a family of whales to the east. How grand they looked lining the low horizon. Truly, whales are my favorite mammals now. I wish I could bring one home.

    Daddy's spirits are high and happy. Is this the daddy that I once knew? Has he completely forgotten about all his old memories? I should say that he has. Either that or he's just so glad to have a daughter like me in this brand-new world. I should ask him about that for the record. I'd like to know how he could change so much in such a short while. I've never seen a person change so much in my life!

    I ordered the newly pressed flag up the flagpole. A bright circle of blue floats over all. The W*O*D*E*N flag is the prettiest flag in the whole wide world. I'd like to have one on my wall in my bedroom. I'll ask daddy if he has one to spare. Maybe he'd even like to hang it over the fireplace for a while. He can put away all his medals, not including the one that I gave him for Christmas. I'll take this matter up with him first thing this evening. I wonder why daddy isn't upset that he has to retire?

    After an hour or two of watching whales, all three of us went to the bridge to have coffee. Santiago served while I checked in with the engineers. Everything was going along fine. So to keep up the morale of the crew, I got on the loudspeaker system and said a few words to all on ship. I said, "It's a beautiful day to be on the seas. It's a beautiful day to sail under our flag. I hope you are all very proud of

WORLD ONE

your mission in life. I know as your captain I am. Let's just keep it that way, all right?"

I didn't hear if the crew cheered or not. I suppose they did, but I couldn't hear. But daddy heard and Santiago heard and I heard what I said. I don't think I would have said something like that when I started out. I was more interested in other things that I've said. I think that daddy and Santiago have been very good influences on me. And you know what, I don't think Santiago will ever call me a "stupid little girl" again. And furthermore, I think I finally understand why he did.

Captain Tanya will report back this evening. Until then it's a beautiful world out here and I'll never forget the honor I've been given.

Entry #61: Your captain had a heart to heart talk with her dad tonight. We could have gone on forever, but I got sleepy out there on the deck. Now that I'm back inside, I feel more than wide-awake. I feel keyed up and bursting with new found energy. I don't want to fall asleep and wake up tomorrow morning and not be captain. It suits me to be just who I am right now.

Daddy thanked me once again for all my help tonight. He sounded as if I had saved his life. In fact he said that I had saved him from "drowning." I suppose I made him happier when he was being so sad. I'd hardly call that saving him from drowning. Daddy put it this way. He said, "I'm a new man. We both have a future beyond any future that there's ever been. The past is past, Tanya. It doesn't do to anguish over it. We have so much to live for, me and you. There is a better peace now . . . There is."

I think what daddy meant is that this W*O*D*E*N world has turned out all right. It's working better than ever before. That's good. It just so happens that I was lucky enough to be born when I was. I'd have hated to have dark memories like my dad. It could have ruined my life, made me sad when I should be glad. I realize this now. I just wish both dad and me could have been born in the time when I was. Mother, too. She's had to cope with daddy's dark memories a lot longer than I. She's seen more of the bad times than good. She deserved a better life than she's had. But I can't change the past. I can only open my arms to the future. Right now both daddy and I have our arms spread wide open, ready and waiting for whatever good things will happen.

Daddy explained something to me tonight that I've never understood before. I asked him how it was that W*O*D*E*N was born. He said that it went like this: "There was a time when the people of the world knew war more than peace. It was a horrible time of division and desperation. But at last, when the people were faced with a choice, a choice between final war and lasting peace, the vast majority of them voted to bring in the one all-powerful W*O*D*E*N government. We voted for the best peace at a time when we were faced with the worst war. That's how it happened, Tanya. We made the great choice, we accomplished what had never been done before."

Well, so they did. Good for them. Who am I to suggest otherwise? But, if you ask me, everything still could be better. I mean, what about that skirmish on the Ivory Coast? What about those pirates holding us captive on the seas? What about stamping out epidemics and feeding more people food? What about this problem and that? Surely, Santiago and I can do better than that? We can't stop now, can we? We have to do better and better, don't we? These times may be better than those, but who's to say that the next times can't be better than these? I don't know. I expect I should be satisfied and let it go at that. But there's something inside of me that wants everything to be perfect. Maybe when I get to be my daddy's age the world will be more perfect than now. I can at least hope for this, can't I? Maybe by then Santiago will have managed to save both the fishes and the whales. Maybe by then we will have tied up the rest of the pirates. Maybe by then there will be no more disease and plenty of good food for everyone. We can't stop now. We have to go on and make this world better yet. I'll do what I can to help out. I think I've begun by knowing which is the right direction. Now all we need to do is to go full steam ahead.

WORLD ONE

Daddy died in his sleep last night. Doctor Lin came in and told me. Doctor Lin knocked three times, very quietly. Somehow I knew that it was going to be bad news. Somehow I knew that it was fate knocking at my door. I didn't want to open it. I nearly pretended that I was asleep. But when Doctor Lin whispered, "Tanya . . . Tanya," I was drawn to open the door.

Daddy's been dead for five hours. Daddy died of one of those heart attacks. Doctor Lin finally told me the truth. Daddy has had a weak heart for the past three years. That's the reason why both he and mother and even daddy thought it would be best for him to retire. I wish they had told me. I wish I'd been more informed. No wonder daddy wasn't so upset about having to retire. Probably he suspected that he might die. Probably he even had a premonition of what lay ahead for him. This isn't like Billy the cook dying so unexpectedly. Daddy knew that the end was near. Mother, too. And they didn't even bother to tell me.

I'm here with you because I can't move. I haven't left the room since the moment I was told that daddy had died. I'm waiting for the spirit of daddy to come visit me. I'm waiting to feel his presence in my room. I know he'll be here. He's probably not far away. Maybe he went down to visit my mother. Maybe his spirit is with her right now. I have to call her soon. Doctor Lin asked me if I would want to give her a call. I said, "Yes, but not right this second." That was five hours ago and I still haven't moved. I'm waiting for daddy to come. I'm waiting for him to tell me good-bye. He won't leave forever without saying good-bye. I know my daddy and he won't do that. He'll be here and I'll feel him once more. Daddy died without saying good-bye.

Twenty minutes have passed and still he's not come. Santiago has come and gone. I couldn't speak to him. The ship seems quiet though the sea's rushing past. I've opened my window to make sure that daddy can still get in. I have to call my mom. I don't want to call my mom. I want Doctor Lin to call my mom and tell her the . . . tell her that daddy has died.

Twenty more minutes have passed. I'm afraid to leave my room. I don't want to miss him. I want to feel him here. Doctor Lin has come and gone. He called my mother for me. He told her the news and he told her that I couldn't come to the phone. Daddy, why did you die so suddenly? Why did you die when we had our arms spread wide open? Why can't you come and visit with me?

Twenty more minutes have passed.

Entry #63: I've been down all alone in the cargo bays. I've been sitting among the mountains of medicine. I've been having some words with daddy down there. I've just come up to tell you of them.

I can't remember if I spoke first or if daddy did. It was cold and damp down there, but when daddy came by it warmed up considerably. I went down there because I knew no one would look for me there—it's my special place to be all alone.

I suppose it was I who spoke first. I said, "Look where I am daddy! I'm sitting in the heart of your ship. I'm sitting under the trees of your oasis. I'm by the fresh waters and it's cool and soothing . . . How are you?"

Daddy whispers now that he's gone. If anyone else had been down there with me, they wouldn't have heard him, they couldn't have listened to him. He said, "Tanya, thank you for saving my life . . . thank you for making me better. Tanya, this world is yours to have and to hold."

Daddy was being sentimental again. And his voice was filled with good feeling. You may think that I've flipped my lid, but I really did hear him down in the cargo bays, I really, really did.

Then it got warm, well, it warmed up a bit. Maybe it was just that the sun came out up on top. In any event, I was warmer than I had been. And I basked in the warmth that was daddy moving around me.

Now I'm back where I started from. I don't like where I am anymore. When daddy was alive and running the ship, I

WORLD ONE

liked it here. I liked the view out the porthole window. But not anymore. I'd rather be up on deck. I'd rather watch a thousand whales go by. I'd rather put my face in the sun and glory in the light of this beautiful day. I say beautiful because daddy did come by to say good-bye to me. I told you he would and he did. Daddy wouldn't leave me hanging high. He had to soothe me by the fresh waters. He had to make me feel that everything was still all right and that it was the time for him to die.

I'll be up on deck if you need me. I'll be watching for whales, if you care. I'll be thinking of how daddy looked on the night before he died.

Entry #64: My radio's chattering on in front of me. Daddy was the one who gave it to me. I guess he gave it to me so that I could tune in all the world. Thank you for my present, daddy, I'll always keep it with me.

We're due in port tonight. The horizon of the Ivory Coast is coming up. It's New Year's Night. Daddy died on the first day of a whole new year. He made it all this way without his heart giving out.

I talked to my mother tonight. She told me that she and Doctor Lin had made arrangements to fly both me and daddy home. We'll be flying home tomorrow evening. We'll be flying home by jet. I've never been on a jet before. I've never been up in the air.

I told mother two things. First I told her that Santiago had to come with me. I told her that he had important business back home. I asked her if he could stay with us for a while. She said, yes, immediately. I haven't had a chance to tell him the news. I hope he'll want to come.

After I got a yes, I got a no. I told mother that I thought daddy should be buried at sea. I said, "Mother, don't you think he'd want it that way? Don't you think that's where he belongs?" No, she didn't. She said that daddy asked to be buried back on the ice of Antarcticus. She said that he wanted to be buried down there.

I wanted to fight her. I couldn't believe what she said. After all daddy's years on the seas, I was sure that he would wish to go down to the deep. Why Antarcticus? I asked. Why there instead of out here? She said this. "Your father was so proud of what W*O*D*E*N stood for. He said he belonged to this world."

I didn't fight mother too long. How could I? I'm all for what daddy would want. I was just surprised, that's all. After dozens of years on the seas it seemed natural to me that daddy would want to sink into his sea. But then, I'm remembering how he looked last night when he talked of my world and of how it came to be.

I'll be taking daddy home with me. I'll be taking daddy right back where he belongs. Like me, daddy is part of a whole new world and that is just how it should be. And this journey with me made him forget how it was to have lived in the past. And my journey with him opened my eyes to a world full of future that is right for us all and was right for him.

Daddy, I'll take you back home. Mother and I will bury you on the ice. And I'll come and see you whenever I can. And I won't leave home until I'm ready to take your place. And when I'm ready, daddy, I'll make the best captain the world has ever known.

The morning came in fine and cool and clear. There's no trace of battle smoke anywhere up in the air. The ship is busy being unloaded right now. I spent a part of the morning with Santiago watching the boxes lifted and lowered. Santiago was very gentle with me. He expressed his sorrow. He's gone into mourning just like me. He said, "TANea, my girl, the captain is smiling high above us. He will follow us all the way home. Your daddy will be with you always in your life. I will remember him, too. Sea captains stay close to sea captains, in life and in death. That is the way with them. You will be all right, TANea. You will travel with him far and wide."

Santiago knows just what to say. And when he says it it turns out just right. Santiago will go a long way in this world. Already I feel sorry for the members of the courts who'll

WORLD ONE

have to worry over him. Maybe even one distant day away, Santiago will become our President. I'd vote for him. And I'd follow his commands. If he ordered me to the North Pole, I'd sail off right away. If he ordered me to some tropical island, I'd be there two days ahead of when I was due. Santiago's the one who should be President. Me, I'm the one who should be free to glide on the seas with mountains of medicines and tons of food.

Santiago graciously accepted my invitation to come back to Antarcticus with me. I told him my mother had invited him, too. He was honored, I know. He's anxious to get on with his fate. Every day that he's not in court, he loses another family of fish. I expect he'll be in court by late tomorrow afternoon. And the day after that, I know he'll be with me when we bury daddy under the ice of his new home.

I have to see Doctor Lin and talk about details. I have to pack my bags, too. I want to remember to take daddy's present from his crew. I've already decided that it will definitely hang above our fireplace. And my medal to daddy will be tacked on his grave. That way he'll have me near wherever I go.

Entry #66: This will be my last communication. This will be my last entry before leaving for home. I'm all set to step back on land and return to where I began. Doctor Lin has said his good-byes. I told him that I didn't think I'd ever get to be like him. He said that that was all right. That there'd be plenty of people like him to do what had to be done. That's good. I was relieved. I didn't want him to think that I was abandoning him or all of the people who are in need of medicine. I'll let those other people take Doctor Lin's place in life. My fate lies in taking daddy's place. My fate lies in sailing the seas and enjoying its beauty and peace. Also it's my fate to stay out of the way of pirates. I never want to run into them again. If I ever get an S O S over the radio, I'll check it out ten times before I take any action. I never want to be in the position of jeopardizing our stores again. I won't make that mistake. I've learned what can happen when there are pirates about. I've learned what can happen when there's an Abu, King of Law, out there. I'd like not to experience that ever again. That was enough excitement for a whole lifetime. It was more than enough action for a person like me.

Here I am in my cabin. My porthole window is open and a breeze is blowing my way. Outside the sky is clear and white clouds float up high. It's pleasant and peaceful for as far as the eye can see. And that's exactly the way it's supposed to be. That's what my daddy was living to see. And that's what I'll be living to see for the rest of my life. That's what I am, all right. I'm a W*O*D*E*N baby born in the flesh. And I'm proud to be one. It's not every girl who's had a chance like this. It's not every girl who's had a daddy like mine. I think there's one last thing I'd like to do before I step back on land. I'd like to go up on deck and stand before our flag. I'd like it if Santiago could escort me. I can picture us now. We'll be there with our hands on our hearts. And we'll be looking up at a white and blue flag flapping its heart out in the African breeze.

21

The grubby sky stands before me. A pallid dawn will break within hours. And still Elizabeth and I are alive. We are alive because I spin tales, weave them around these human-dogs who surround us and stink of mud and wretched waste carried up from the sewerage beneath us.

Human-dog #1 is grinning. My, what a lovely smile. He reminds me of a crocodile. But he has no teeth. Rotted, no doubt. Lost in warfare, perhaps. But Human-dog #1 purrs. Bliss is his, I see. And his bliss makes for our sanctuary.

"Bless you, C. J. Jones. Bless that little tongue of yours."

He turns to his doggy friends.

"Applause for this man! Give him a great roar!"

And his command becomes a wave of glad chatter. Children and women and plenty of dogmen allow themselves a good roar. And I must say, I love it. I am getting through. I may have gotten through to these violent beings who choose war over words, war over a nice peace . . . war, war, war.

Human-dog #1 looks beyond for a moment. He takes in the magnificent sight of Thomas Jefferson. I know what he is seeing. I've seen it a hundred times before myself. He's seeing a spirit, like a gliding bird, and this spirit is singing a melody which lifts up one's heart and delivers it to a place of strength and magnanimity. I'm there with him, though he doesn't know it. Elizabeth and I are perched with him in this place. For a second, we're all there. Human-dog #1, Thomas Jefferson, Elizabeth and I. Now the second is past. It's over, but Human-dog #1 has changed. His eyes sail back to me. Elizabeth has his belly in her sights. Everything is different now, but everything is as it was before—human-dogs galore, flames shimmering in the dirty night. We are on the verge of battle, but somehow, for some odd reason, I have no fear of it. It just seems like it couldn't possibly happen now—not after what's just been told, not after we've all experienced life and death through my tales of the imagination.

The applause dies down. I am on stage. I have lights. I have an audience. I even have a backdrop. Lucky, me. I have Thomas Jefferson and his marble hall.

"Give us an encore, Jones. Tell us what became of Tanya and her world of W*O*D*E*N. Elizabeth, your husband grips my imagination."

"I like his stories, too. But he is dreaming in the dark, so long as you meet us less than halfway. But I am not here to lecture you. I am only here to protect what's ours—our home and lives," Elizabeth calmly insists.

What a pair these two have turned out to be. Good God am I impressed. Elizabeth can match the best of them—the worst of them—any of them. I married well. I give myself lots of credit.

"Let's finish this night and then everyone will be free to draw their own conclusions. Either we fight and kill or we all go home in peace. But let's get it done."

"Fine," says Human-dog #1's wife.

"Fine," I say.

"C. J. Jones will speak again! Listen, my friends! Encore! Encore! Encore!"

And then all of the human-dogs begin to chant. And the

WORLD ONE

noise grows fierce and my ears shudder deep down inside. "Encore! Encore!"

Okay, you dogs. Okay you poor people who have nothing but nothing. I will give you an encore . . .

I reach down one last time. And I don't even need Mr. Jefferson to light up my mind. I need only the thought of a world peace in place which is tempered by age and experience.

To wit: "Tanya Shepherd is dreaming of a time when she was a name in the world of W*O*D*E*N . . ."

If there was ever a night to remember, it had to be that night, that time, in a place which is a long time away in my life. I will tell you of that night because my life and the lives of my children were changed from that time forward. Old women may knit and young ones may embrace, but being in between, being on either side of old and young age, I remember with increasing joy what took place when my children were young and my husband was behind the walls of his ship.

Since that time I have stayed on the ice and watched my children leave for the north, only one year, another the next. Then two years later the last went away and left me behind. That is how it should be, we all know. But what is left for me? Who do I have to sing to? Who will stir my heart with joy and proud promises? Not my children, not anymore. My husband is here, but his pipe is a better companion to him than the sound of my voice. His quiet mind follows the patterns of light, lifting smoke. He settles himself by the smouldering fire. He closes his eyes when the wood crackles hard. He leaves me to drift one way, then another. Up and down stream, over fast and slow currents, racing toward death or back to a moment of sunlight when I was a name in the world.

My story begins one stark summer night on the ice of Antarcticus. I remember this woman who was me, sitting with children and singing. It was a song my father used to sing. He used it to soothe me before he sailed off to sea. "Father," I would say in a half happy sleep. "Will you be back tomorrow?" He would be back after not too many tomorrows. And one day, he promised, I would join him and we would conquer the seas together.

But on this stark summer night, when the sun was high and unwilling to set, the rebels came in swarms. They came like hot men melting ice. And we, the villagers, were the flags of their cause. We went with them away from the harbors of Antarcticus. And the lights of the capital of W*O*D*E*N were lost to the smouldering sun above.

My children did not scream. A fist at the door and a breaking of glass and an English voice demanding submission. Those are the sounds I remember. I wonder, can my children still hear them? I do on odd nights. For eighteen years I have heard them. But when I hear them I do not hear my children whimpering. How brave two boys and a girl can be. And how proud their mother is of them. Even now.

We were made to wrap food in blankets and pillows. We were made to put on our boots and not rattle our tongues. I did as I was commanded. I saw the hate in their eyes, those keen rebel eyes and I was not about to hammer at them. Perhaps I bowed my head and prayed. Perhaps I wished for my husband to come, to return from his ship unexpectedly. He did not come, he was sleeping right then as we had been sleeping and I knew he would not be walking toward us. We were alone on the ice that night. And we were to be pawns in the service of a desperate and nomadic people.

"Children, get your things quickly. Snap, snap. These men would like us to go with them. Gregory, you do not have time to wash your face. No brushing of hair at this time of night. We'll leave that for the morning." It is easy to hurry children at night. When awakened, they commit to command. I remember seeing no pistols pointed at me. The eyes of these men were daggers enough. I needed no proof of sincerity. I needed only to hurry my children and tie up their boots.

WORLD ONE

The lights burned in our clear windows. Once I turned back. With one silent girl in my arms, I turned. I had to see our dear house again. I had to have a picture of it standing calm. And I would hold on to this picture as I held the legs of my child. She looked back, too. Was she wondering if we were off to see daddy? Had she thought that daddy had finally asked us to come? The lights burned in our windows and I would have died to have had the privilege of taking my children back and laying them softly in sleep on their pillows.

That would not be my privilege, however. I would have no privileges for some time. All the villagers knew this, too. We were leaving the shores of Antarcticus and the lights of our village and W*O*D*E*N and its sounds could have been one thousand miles to the west instead of ten. It need not have existed at all at that time. Its defenses were helpless against our intrusive enemies. And so we marched. Women and children and summertime fishermen. We dragged our feet over ice and blankets of rock. The walking birds kept out of our way. They hid and pretended to sleep. They would risk not a squeal for our lives. They had fish on their minds for the morning.

Down we went, women and children and summertime fishermen. We were walking to death, we knew. A summertime death with the sun holding high and the breath of rebels clouding our tracks. "Tanya," I said to myself. "Do nothing to frighten these men. Do not look in their eyes, do not nod the wrong way. Go quietly. Go happily. They won't hurt us tonight when we are sleepy." Perhaps they would. I knew nothing of what lay ahead. We were leaving our soil and there was a dark ship, a ship with no lights to which we were headed. These rebels meant to take us for an early morning voyage. How delightful and kind and certainly how generous. I hadn't been on a ship since the death of my father. I hadn't left my village since then. How long ago? Twenty good years? This was to be our summer vacation. This was to be the beginning of my night to remember. And I walked on and prayed for the sight of my husband and the ships of the Navy.

But they were high in other waters. They were not there and not due back until tomorrow. So alone we went, stepping over soft summer ice and the sun bore down and down and down. There was to be no quick relief.

W*O*D*E*N, I thought. Why have these strangers come? What is the meaning of this? Who are these men to deprive us of sleep? Who are these men who live in dark ships? But I would not ask questions. I would go where my captains led me. Father had always said, "The captain is king while on ship."

Down to small boats we were led. Now children were crying, but not mine. Old women were dragging their husbands ahead. Young boys were pulling their blankets around them. It was icy as the sun stared down from the sky. It was hopeless to try to run.

Villagers in boats, that's what we were. Gregory caught sight of a flying bird. I did not notice it in time. We were moving toward the ship with no lights and Peter was putting his hand in the water and Julia was holding her foot in my lap. It's hard, even now, for me to say why. Perhaps her boot had irritated it. My fingers were sweaty despite the cold and the clean air seemed to be making me sick. But it was the fear that gripped me the most. Had I ever had such a fear before? "Father," I thought. "The S O S is on its way. The Navy will be here by morning." Father was irate when I told him that. The pirates would hang us high. Oh, well. I was so young and wanted to be a hero.

Two hundred yards to the ship with no eyes. Gregory was staring up at the sun. He would not damage his eyes. The sun was a smear on the low edge of the sky and the sky was a mantle of homespun wool, fluffed up just right for the occasion. I remember the sky and the way it held still. I wanted to tug at its fabric and lift us away. I wanted Gregory to shout, "They're here! Mother, W*O*D*E*N's come!" But Gregory was watching the sway of the sea and Julia was sucking her thumb and Peter was playing a game with the village idiot. I was helpless then as I am helpless now. I couldn't pull us up and hide behind the almighty sun. We closed in and closed in and my summer vacation was beginning all over again. But now it would begin with my children and me and not with my father and I.

WORLD ONE

The old and the young were made to climb. The ropes were creaky and wet. The steel of the hull was warm against my hand. Julia clung to my neck and sometimes shielded my eyes with her hands. "I have to see, Julia. Take off your hands." Julia grabbed my neck as we climbed higher. There, up above, was Gregory. His leg was lifting over the edge. Peter had reached the last rung of the ladder. Now he would be safe from the deep waters below. My footing was weak. But I would not fall. Julia said, "Mother, we're almost there." Julia was an encouraging navigator.

On deck, we were happy. Why were we happy? We had stayed alive thus far. The rebels, I knew then, needed our presence for some lovely purpose. We were guests at a banquet on board ship. We were important visitors come to be entertained. Gregory said, "When will daddy come?" And Peter said with shocking maturity, "Not for a while, Gregory. Mother will let us know." How Peter knew of our fortunes, I could not guess. Perhaps he had read of rebels and pirates and cargo ships. We stood on the deck of an unlighted ship and waited for the rest of the villagers to climb up from the boats. Then one old man, I didn't see his face, fell back, fell far, fell down into the black waters and sank with a groan and then disappeared forever. A woman screamed. His wife, no doubt. The ropes were wet and his hands were weak and perhaps he wanted to die more naturally. I turned the children's faces away and looked up at an ancient British flag lying limp at the top of the mast. We were to be guests of rebel Atlantians. And we were to be instruments of political warfare, that was obvious.

Herded together now, we all stood under the eye of the never setting sun. The women breathed hard and there was much coughing among the men. My children leaned up against me. The other children huddled close to their mothers and fathers. Even children are not brave in the night. Mine, least of all.

Then Marcus stepped forward. His name was Marcus or Tarcus or Sarcus. A wind blew his name out to sea. He spoke politely. He did not wish to interrupt our lives anymore than he had to. Marcus was brave in front of his men. His glittery voice still annoys me as I recall it for you. Peter whispered to me, "Will he kill us?"

Marcus wore a sheep's vest and was the proud possessor of iron red curls. These curls were reflected in a form on his face. And his eyes were like razors, like slits across wounds. I was trembling a bit. I slapped my leg to keep it still. Then Gregory put his hand on it. He held it in place as the words continued. Thank God they speak English, I heard myself thinking.

"Good evening, friends of Antarcticus. We have displaced you abruptly, I know. But we are not enemies. We are friends for a cause. You will be temporarily unhappy as we have been unhappy for one generation of our unfortunate children. To wit, let me speak.

"You will stay with us until W*O*D*E*N makes a decision. To the west, now look. See you the shining lights of the capital city? See you the pale lights against the pale, cloudy night? W*O*D*E*N is our target today. And tomorrow, if necessary. I hope not. We do not wish to ruin your sleep or expose your children to cold or deprive you of food and nourishment. What we wish for is this: We wish to reclaim our homeland. We wish to leave the Salleny Islands behind—they do not make a proper home for our children. We would rather live in ships than sleep on unloved soil. We have made the decision to force W*O*D*E*N's hand. And you will join us to pursue this end, or we will die together and sleep well in another land."

Marcus was not a young man. But old, he was not that either. Marcus was a warrior, lost somewhere at sea. He was a model from a world long before the world of my children and I. Marcus was a spirit crossed by the laws of the land. And we would now pay for his many years of loneliness and neglect. Marcus, Marcus are you still living? Or did you die one night of old age, still a thousand steps from the state of your making? I do not know the answer. But, Marcus, somehow you've managed to survive in me. I hear what you say and what you said to the villagers of Antarcticus. Let Marcus continue for me.

"You people are guilty of crimes against us. Did you not know that? Do you plead that you were miserably informed?

WORLD ONE

I will inform you for your benefit. No good people should die unaccused. You must understand the reasons for your unhealthy position.

"First, listen sharply. Children, too. Perhaps, children most of all. When your government was born, when it rose to its position of fine trust, we cheered its construction. W*O*D*E*N would be good for us all. Is that not what we said? We blessed along with you the wisdom of men for founding a new heart to the world. But that was before our land was seized by the Great Court of indiscretion. That was before the Argentines walked back across our shores and set up new homes in our houses. Even now they steal the wool from our sheep, the oil from our wells. Even now they spend our profits. Even now they bury their dead among our fathers and mothers, our people.

"We have you to reverse this great indiscretion. We claim the Falklands and its far islands. We claim by royal right our homeland. And we will trade lives to retrieve it. We will trade your lives, my friends, to sleep in our houses again. Goodnight."

Villagers are not practiced in dissension. No fists were thrown and no throats were slit from our side. We had no pistols nor knives nor munitions. We had voices but they were unwilling to speak. And besides, Marcus had said it all. Marcus had held his court and delivered his verdict. We were to be held for ransom. Our children were like lots of land. One child per acre. One woman might bring two. One young man in good health might bring three or four more.

We were ushered downward then. Marcus and his men had been thoughtful. They provided for us a hole in which to live. The empty bays of the ship were open to us. We climbed down and settled in. We gathered close to ward off the chill. We gathered together in hopeless submission. "When will daddy be coming?" Gregory asked.

The wife of the old man who had escaped so early by death lingered for a time by the rail. She had no wish to follow her love and she had no wish to follow our fate. She gazed down at the sea. She whispered a last thought to the water. "Husband, you were a fine lover and friend."

We, the villagers of Antarcticus, were not alone on this ship out at sea east of W*O*D*E*N. We were families among families. All kin to the rebels were with them. Little rebel children and homely rebel wives, grandfathers and grandmothers, were sleeping in cabins, on floors, wherever there was room enough to lay down feet and rest heads. I was not certain of this when I first came on board. It was in the morning that I found out. While napping in the hold, I once looked up and saw the surprised faces of young and old strangers. The white sky was moving above them. I heard the rumbling drive of the engines. Below my back the engines were running. Our ship, for the moment, was crossing the wide Ross Sea. In summer, the ice dissolves and the mouth of the waters open, yawn slowly and allow visitors to come and to go. We were going somewhere. Was it north to the Amundsen and Bellingshausen Seas? The noise of travelling made me forget the curious faces peering down from on high. It felt better to travel than to sit still in calm, deep waters.

I remember a dream of that morning. I wanted to dream so I dreamed. Father and I were watching a lane, many families of whales spirit their way north along the coast of Africa. Father was roaring with glee. All manner of whales had been his constant companions. For how many years? Over how many seas? Whales are a universal mammal. And father was a universal man. I was a W*O*D*E*N baby and my children were a second generation of the same, but father and the great men and women of his age were universal like the whales, for they had founded the new world of W*O*D*E*N.

In my light dream, in the dream that held my attention that morning, I followed once more the path of the family of whales. I took the drive of the engines to be the roar of father's delight and excitement. Father was with me again on

WORLD ONE

that morning. Perhaps, I thought when I opened my eyes to the day, father had returned for a time to instruct me. But instruct me in what? How to sit in submission before rebels? How to calm my little children's nightmarish fears? I had no ready answer for father's sudden return. I only knew that he was to be with me, that he was with me, on this ship that was taking us somewhere for reasons of which I was painfully aware.

Gregory woke up first. "Will we be having breakfast this morning, mother?" Our fellow friends woke one by one after that. Peter immediately started waving to the curious faces of the children high above our heads. Julia woke up crying. My lap had been an uncomfortable bed. And Julia was thirsty for milk.

"Mother, when will we be leaving for home?" "Has father arrived in the night?" "Will we be allowed to play or do we still have to be quiet?" Questions like these, I could answer easily. No, we will not be leaving for home. Father has not yet arrived. You will have to be quiet for a while longer. I'm sure there'll be time for playing soon. But the answers to my questions were harder to find, least of all to accept. We were important nonpersons for the moment. Were we more valuable alive or dead? And how would we die if the time came? Had W*O*D*E*N been informed of the rebels' demand? And why were we hurrying away from the capital city?

How I wished then that my husband was there. He would have stood tall, I knew. He would have challenged Marcus and his men. He would have thoughts of escape and bold confrontation. But not me. My thoughts were as weak as a pool of standing water. I had not been a hero since that time on my father's ship. A fourteen-year-old hero, I had been. I was the one to dream up the plan. I was the one who put the pirates asleep. I had been the one to call in the Navy. And they had come. They had come for me and for father and for the sake of W*O*D*E*N. And because of my actions, because of my fearless disposition, the good people of the Ivory Coast received their shipments of vaccinations, their mountains of medicines. And for my accomplishments, I had been made Captain for a Day—the day before daddy died from his violent heart attack.

Like father, those days were gone. I had not even told my own children of this bright little story. Now down in the hold, I was remembering it. Where was my journal now? In a trunk, no doubt. In the basement, probably. Under sweaters or blankets or old baby clothes. How I wished then that I had something to write on. Day #1: We have been kidnapped by rebels from the Salleny Islands. Marcus is a small threat to civilization. He will repossess his good peoples' homeland or my children and I will die. But when?

With no paper and pen, I strained to remember each detail. Marcus would be remembered for the slits of his wounded eyes. And Gregory would be remembered for his direct and pertinent questions. We ate bread that morning in the bays of the ship. And we drank cool water from the lip of a thermos. I would save the cold can of soup for dinner. But how would I open it?

The morning was a moving white sky. The children above had gone to their cabins or perhaps back to bed. And Peter was asking where he might go to the bathroom. It was the delicate manner in which he asked the question that made me roar like father with laughter. And it was my laughter that set off the spark. All villagers quickly turned their attention to me. I was suddenly beheld as some kind of folk celebrity. If this woman can laugh, if she can hold up a smile in this damp and frigid hole, then why is she not protecting us? Why is she not beating the floor and demanding release? Why is she not speaking on our behalf? I read their looks and wanted no part of their entreaties. Who was I but a mother of three? Who was I but a woman without her husband? Who was I but a grown-up captain's daughter who had once, long ago, tricked pirates and radioed S O S to the Navy? I demurred and lay back down with my children. I tried to rub out the faces and hands outstretched to me. I was too old for heroics. I was too afraid to defy fate. If fate held us, then fate would win. If fate released us, then the rebels would have won their cause. I was no match for them. I was barely a good mother to my children. But as I closed my eyes and hid from the stares of my companions in life, I heard the slow breathing of father. Was he sleeping somewhere or just watching? Was he above me or below me? Was

WORLD ONE

he asking or answering? Go back to your place, father, I thought. Leave me to lie uncomfortably. But his breath became voices and the voices of many called my name, "Tanya ... Tanya Shepherd, you must speak to Marcus. You must speak for us. Your husband is a man in the Navy. Marcus will listen to you. Marcus must know that W*O*D*E*N will never give in. Marcus must know that we are no good to him dead. Plead with him, Tanya. Plead with him to spare us."

I was compelled to respond to these mischief-makers. I could not shake off the grip of their demands. Tanya, mother of three, rose from her place and put Julia in between Peter and Gregory. I had no idea what I would say. I thought of father at breakfast on his ship with his crew. In the mornings he would tap his juice glass with the side of his spoon and then cleverly ease into his orders for the day. I had no spoon or glass on which to tap. I had no crew to carry out my orders. I had only women and children and summertime fishermen waiting for some cooked up gospel of truth. I remember at that moment hearing the faint cries of birds, of gulls, of airy creatures at some distance away. The slow breathing of father was no longer audible. The demanding voices had ceased to exist. I stood in a damp void of silence. I stood waiting for the Muse to speak through me.

"We are held by a people who have suffered pain. While a justice was served an injustice remains. It is not for me to right the wrong. I, like you, have no power in this situation. I am not the voice of the President. I am not a member of the Federal Convention, neither am I a part of the legislative body. All that you have before you is a mother of three. And all that I have to offer you is hope. Let W*O*D*E*N negotiate for us. Let W*O*D*E*N work out a fair settlement. These rebels will not murder us unless W*O*D*E*N acts arrogantly."

My words sputtered then. I have no accounting for this. Sometimes they come and then sometimes they stop—a wall of silence goes up. It was not my place to speak more, think more, do anything. I was one woman in the hold of a ship heading north. I was one woman under a white moving sky. I was one woman being carried far away from her home and her husband. Who was I to hold out a banner of courage? I sat back down and comforted my children who now stared at the villagers suspiciously.

The eternal day passed uneventfully. I was not summoned to speak by the friends that I knew. I was again one among them. I sang to Julia who was curled in my arms. Peter was pacing out the length and width of the bay. Gregory was napping and losing sleep to the troubles in his dreams. The villagers sat like dumb dogs awaiting their extermination. This was not a good day for cheer. Afternoon: Day #1. Where is Marcus now? And where is the great W*O*D*E*N Navy? A fine thing it is when it protects the coasts of the world. A worthless thing it is when rebels snatch up weak people like us. When will Marcus return? And what news will he bring? I can hear the laughter of children up on deck. I can hear the sighs of old women down here. What is it that I should be doing?

My thoughts turned to the comforts on shore. How I missed the walkways of ice and the sight of the bobbing heads of the fishermen as they set their boats in the water. How I missed the noon toll of the bell in the church, the still heart of the village square where school children performed skits for their parents in the evenings. Wasn't Peter supposed to play a dragon tomorrow night? Where will we be by then?

My husband and I had planned a rendezvous in W*O*D*E*N the night after that. We were to be free for a night. The children would be safely amused with friends. My husband and I would be busy in bed under sheets. We would have earlier dined on a fine boulevard and wistfully discussed moving one day to Atlantia. But my husband was then behind the walls of his ship and my children and I were locked together under a white moving sky, and now I had disappointed my friends.

Marcus disrupted my meditation. Marcus would continue to display this habit. I wrenched my neck to get a good look at him. He was unrecognizeable from this distance. But his voice rung true and I knew it was him. "Father," I thought. "Will he kill us?"

WORLD ONE

Marcus was no evil man but his voice and his words betrayed his lack of innocence. He was a man who dreamed of justice. Justice is and was a funny word. Justice for him was injustice for us. Justice for us was injustice for him. What court of W*O*D*E*N could solve that? I was not solving, I was listening.

"You shall have the good news when it comes to us. And when it's bad, you shall have it, too. Our demands have been announced to the world. And the world has been made to listen. How well they listen now. What a crime it was that they did not listen before. Such is power. Power hears power, nothing else. How are your lives down there?"

Not well enough, I thought.

"As you can see, our people gave up room for you. You are now sharing their beds. We are a generous people. It will be helpful if you understand us. But we do not expect you to love us. You have been treated unfairly, I know. We are two peoples who cry out for justice. I am willing to listen to complaints. We have food to share and will provide you with hot water for tea and coffee. And we will keep you alive for as long as we can. W*O*D*E*N will move quickly and decide our fates. And I will negotiate for all of our lives. Pray hard, my friends, that I have the mind of our President. She was chosen by us for her nimble alertness. Let us all hope she has compassion while under attack. She will want to review our case and bring it once again to the attention of the Supreme Court of indiscretion."

Thinking back on the words of this man, I begin to appreciate his kind of clarity. He painted a portrait of a world without shadings. How wonderful that must have been for him. And what a nuisance it was for us. Yet, I wondered. Did not Marcus vote to bring in the W*O*D*E*N government? Did he not cast his ballot for justice and peace in the world? Did he not know when he did it that justice rears its head in many forms? And if his vote was for peace, how could he turn his face away from this great theme now? Marcus, I knew then, was a man of conflicting complexities. More simply put, Marcus was a man who wished to be rid of the Salleny Islands that lay off shore south of Antarcticus. Perhaps the climate is a bit better in the Falklands.

Evening, Day #1: Children and I are eating cold soup and the imposition of fear has faded. How quiet it seems in the hold of this ship. The grating noise of the engines has been transformed into a comforting melody, the rhythms of which I now know by heart. Peter is playing once again with his friend, the one who can't speak but knows how to smile. Village idiot, I wish I had your courage. I wish my smile would pay off the ransom.

Marcus came back in the evening. He broadcast no good news. But, then of course, he hadn't expected to. W*O*D*E*N was informed and W*O*D*E*N had responded. There would be no talk of justice until we were freed. There wasn't much of a surprise in that. And Marcus's response was just as easily read. By a federal decree their homeland would be returned or in fifteen days we would all be dead.

With that news my children and I went to bed.

Marcus must have entered Gregory's dreams that night. While my husband's warm and naked figure came into mine, Gregory was besieged by fits of fear and tugged at my arm while I dreamed of breathless pleasure. "He dropped me in the sea, mother. He dropped me by my ankles which were tied with rope." Gregory's mild hysteria woke up Julia and then the sleeping lion, Peter. I was forced to try to lull them back to sleep, cast a spell of calm and ease directly over them.

"Once when I was young and my daddy was still alive, he took me with him out to sea, he took me out beyond the waters of Antarcticus. My daddy was the captain of his ship. He went north and east and west, wherever he was sent to bring relief to all Societies of the world. We set sail for the Ivory Coast on the western shores of Africa. I was on my way to see the world and my mother was kind enough to let me go.

"My father had lived in the world before W*O*D*E*N came to be. He had fought as a sailor in the United States Navy. He had seen great victories and defeats. He had been raised in a world when combat was an instrument for peace.

WORLD ONE

I had heard stories of these times from the time I was your age. I had imagined how exciting it must have been for him to have been so heroic. I even longed to live like him—to see twisting clouds of battle smoke and hear gunfire scrape the seams of a deadly quiet night. But your grandfather, my father, was a sick and haunted man. He had nightmares and saw the hateful memories of ghosts. He was a sad man, really, a sad and sick man, really. One night on ship when his temperature was rising, I heard him cry out, 'Get out, get out!' He slapped the air around him and then punched it with his fist. Grandfather had nightmares, too, Gregory. In part, he had a wretched life. Even after W*O*D*E*N was born, his memories haunted him and drove him. This all took place many, many years ago before I even knew your father, before I knew the horrors of the old and savage world.

"Your grandfather fought for the sake of his great country. He fought for peace and for prosperity. But the world was out of balance then, countries crouched in conflict with each other and the people suffered greatly. Now countries live no more. The nine Societies were born and the W*O*D*E*N government sits in trust above them. Each dead country is now a state, a member state of one of the world's Societies. And men like grandfather do not get sick from battle and the heroics of our age can be found in the words of the W*O*D*E*N Constitution. What has happened to us now is an aberration of the pledge made by the people of this earth to fight for causes peacefully. Marcus has betrayed a world that he consented to. It is a better world now, children. It is a world where justice can be found if men obey its laws. Marcus has made a reckless mistake, not only for him but for his people. Marcus will one day pay for his mistake. He will have years of nightmares, too. Children, it is time for us to sleep. The world will look better in the morning. Marcus will not haunt us for long. W*O*D*E*N will protect us. It is strong and Marcus is a brittle man. Sleep now and dream of flying birds and water sounds. I will stay awake and watch over you."

My children were fast asleep by then. I continued speaking to soothe myself, not my children. It made me sad to think of father. His young life was a pit of ugly memories. But how glad he was to have seen the day when the peoples of the world called upon their governments to consolidate. How I wish I had been alive to have been a witness to that time. Nine world Societies and one great government rose to power one fine August night. And all arms were surrendered by the stroke of twelve as the newly elected President made a broadcast to the world. His words were translated into a hundred languages. In English he said this: "History has been changed. The rage of war is dead. Life and all time is before us. Disease and hunger will be banished now. The certain knowledge of lasting peace cannot be erased. We have stepped together into a new frontier of destiny. I as your President for the next six years will uphold all laws of our constitution. I pledge my mind and heart to you and to this time of open peace."

Our first President died the year that I was born. But his name is one of the truly great names in history. I thought of him that night when Gregory woke with nightmares. I thought of those words which I had read. And despite my certain fears, I was profoundly happy. I understood how little power these rebels had at their command. Even if we were to die, it would not matter much. No rebels of a certain cause could destroy our government. No states within Societies could break the hands of law. I with my husband and children lived within the fields of an all-embracing peace. We had the best of what could be. And we had known it for all our lives. The ones who I had pity for were the peoples who came before. I had pity for those who had lost their lives throughout the ravages of history. I could not conceive of dying for a worthless cause, or a cause made worthless by unbalanced justice. But I would die for this W*O*D*E*N world. I would stand and die for it. True peace and prosperity is worth a small sacrifice of life—even my life and my children's.

The night wore on as I lay watching the strangely lighted sky. Perhaps I drifted off from time to time, perhaps I only thought I did. But shortly before the brighter light of morning came, I heard the cautious whisper of my father's voice. I heard him say, "You must take the charge for peace and act accordingly." Absurd, you say? Whispered words in the southern night? Maybe yes and maybe no. I could have dreamt

WORLD ONE

those words. I could have created them and spun them in the air. But truly, I did not wish to hear them. I wished to sit and wait and calm my only children. I wished that others would come and settle this and then take us neatly home. I wished my husband would appear on board and break Marcus's back in half.

Morning was bright as we travelled north and fast. The shouts of happy children sailed ceaselessly down to me. Peter shouted back. "I could play with you. What is it that you're doing?" Gregory was in a less than goodwilled mood. He said, "What makes you think you have the right to keep us here? Why don't you tell your mothers and fathers to come and get us out!" Julia, being young and shy and unaware, simply combed my hair.

Later, when Gregory had checked his anger, Julia had asked, "Why was Gregory shouting at the sky?"

Day 2 was blissfully dull. Marcus did not show his face to us. We, the villagers, passed around our food. We shared bread and fruit and water. By afternoon, we had all begun to sing. What better way to pass the time while we waited for more news. And Peter performed his dragon dance for our friends and neighbors. Peter had told me many times that he one day wished to join the circus. After his performance, I was convinced that he should. He flipped his imaginary tail for all to see. He told us stories of how hard his life had been. Set upon by knights he'd been. Driven from his land of opportunity. He was a tired and friendly dragon now. All he wanted was to find a way to extinguish the fire that he breathed every time he opened his mouth.

The climax of Peter's play was how he managed to do this. He met a she-dragon in the woods and fell in love and then moved to show his love. He proposed to her but had to speak while looking up. In between his breath of fire he said, "If you will marry me and rid me of my fire, I will take you back to my ancient land of opportunity. The knights will love me too, if I do not breathe on them with fire. Kiss me and say you love me and my fire will go out."

And that is what the she-dragon did. She kissed him and then married him. And as soon as this was done, the dragon's breath was cool. Then Peter bowed to all of us. He sat down and blushed. Every one of us applauded him for his rich performance. Julia patted Peter on the head and then Gregory got up next. Gregory said, "Guess who I am?" He marched around us and scowled at us until the village idiot pointed up. Everyone knew who Gregory was but he had to say it nonetheless. "I am Marcus, king of you. I will never take you home. I want more friends and so I have kidnapped you. I am not a bad man; I am just unfriendly. No crying now. I don't like crying friends."

Then Gregory stabbed himself and died. After a moment or two of death, he got up again. He shook his fist at the sky and said for all of us, "Just you wait until the Navy comes. Just you wait until they tie you up!"

Marcus came that night. He had news for us. Marcus was in a jolly frame of mind. He strutted back and forth above us. He paused for emphasis. He was obviously enjoying his temporary state of power.

"We have company on the seas. The W*O*D*E*N Navy follows us. From where I stand I see three ships—to the right and left and center. They mean to hold our hands and escort us safely to wherever I am going. I won't tell you where. I will save that surprise for later. Let me tell you now what W*O*D*E*N says. I promised to inform you.

"It seems I have no choice. I must release you so that I and my men can be sentenced. The Tribune of the People has guaranteed a lenient punishment for our crimes, if we let you go. Perhaps even suspended sentences. Perhaps no more than a slap on the wrist and a threatening reprimand. I would like to make this choice for you. I know you would like it, too. But I can't. I will only trade you for our land. You will have your lives if we will have our land. That seems fair to me. I will right two wrongs. We will never go back to the Salleny Islands. When at first we were made a gift of them, we had no choice but to accept them. The Supreme Court of indiscretion ruled against our claim to the Falklands

WORLD ONE

and so we had to go. We had to have a home. But there the land is rocky and cruel.

"Nomads live in deserts, not on mountain tops. Fishermen live at sea, not in the middle of some city. We must live where we were meant to live. If not, it does not matter if we die."

Marcus paused to hear the echo of his noise. If better days had come to him, he might have run for President. He might have made it, too. But bad days were all he knew and now we shared his unhappy life.

"You think I am a bitter man. I am. I am passing my bitterness on to you. But now you listen to us, don't you? You listen to us well. So why not our government? Are they not people like you and me? Are they not one with us? I simply want to change a law. I simply want to call attention to a claim. Is that so bad? Is that so wrong? I do not think so. Sleep well tonight and I will tell you of our response tomorrow."

Marcus disappeared and went to wherever he found rest. But we, the villagers, could not rest. We saw the situation. I remember thinking, Why don't Marcus and his people come and live with us? Why don't we build new homes for him and for the families and their children? Why not indeed? Why not share the gifts of W*O*D*E*N with our fellow adversaries? I wondered what father would have to say to this. I forced his voice to speak to me. I heard him whisper sweetly.

"You must take the charge for peace and act accordingly." But how, father? How would I do this from my hole? And why would Marcus listen to me when all of W*O*D*E*N heard him speak. I knew no way to capture this rebel man's attention. I was a mother of three and not much more. I feared for my own safety just like all the rest. I had children to protect and a husband who even then was probably following me. Yes, my husband was behind me. He was in his ship and he knew that I was here. He would advise me to be quiet, to let W*O*D*E*N steer us clear. But W*O*D*E*N was not bending to Marcus's demands. It would never bend to force of arms. It would not defy its own constitution—it could not do this for us. Either Marcus would put aside his claim or a time would surely come when steel clashed with steel.

Marcus came back in the middle of the night. He had received another threat from the voices of our government. If one of us should die by whatever circumstances, then Marcus and his men would be tried for murder. If one of us should die, then the families of these men, as refugees, might be scattered across the world, made citizens of other Societies. Marcus shook his head at us. He found these threats amusing. Here he was ready to die at any time and yet they threatened him with prison sentences. "No worse life I think it will be to live in prison than to live on unloved soil. What makes this government think so stupidly? Tell me now. Any of you. Can any one of you understand why our President would want to think this way?"

No one answered him. I wanted to, but didn't. He left us then and I felt foolish and embarrassed. Why hadn't I spoken up? Why had I not faced down my fellow citizen? I should have shouted up, "What makes you think we have so much to fear from death?"

If I had, I knew, Gregory and Peter would have backed me up.

22

Night light came and went and morning light broke anew. How many miles had we travelled? And where was our destination? Where was Marcus taking us and why? When would those three ships act? When would W*O*D*E*N force the rebels' hand? I remember walking back to childhood memories then. I pulled on those events for strength. Could I ever be a courageous hero again? Or had time softened the fibers of my character? What would Abu, great King of Law, think of me and my fearful face? What had happened to this aging pirate? I never knew.

Tell the little petite that she should be a captain . . . Those were Abu's last words for me. As the W*O*D*E*N Navy took charge of him, he whispered them to father. And father proudly told them to me. Imagine that! A king of pirates thought enough of me to suggest that I should one day be a captain. I never was, of course. I got distracted after father's death. I lost my sense of overriding purpose. I could have been so happy on the seas. I could have commanded a fleet of cargo ships. I could have followed in my father's place and seen all lands and peoples of this world. But I was to marry and give life to children. Did father think that I had abandoned him? Should I have entered into politics as he wanted me to? "Fight for justice, Tanya. Help move the world for good." Father, I have disappointed you, I announced to him that morning. On Day 3 I was thinking, I have wasted one calling in my life . . . Father should have lived and led me to a life of meaning . . . Am I now paying for this misdirection? Will I now pay for it with my life?

"Children, sit down and be quiet!" I was angry with my place. I would die having lived a wasted life. Any woman of age could have her children. Any woman of age could have her husband and her home. But father had other dreams for me. "Tanya, this world is yours to have and to hold. Take it and do good with it. The new world's life is just beginning."

Abu, pirate, great King of Law, I tricked you well that night. You had seized my father's ship and were stealing our treasures of medicine. I would not stand for that. You had no business trading on other people's lives. Thus, I offered you and your men some beer. You were thirsty, high seas pirates. You were greedy for all we had on ship. But I put you to sleep that night now, didn't I? We locked you in the theater while you fell asleep to *Casablanca*. It was Doctor Lin and I who laced your drinks with some magic sleeping potion. We had you sleeping while the Navy came aboard. We had you sleeping while you should have been sailing free. I was a captain when I was fourteen. I had promise and courage then. I feared no pirate and his men.

On Day 3 I was thinking, I am the village idiot. I speak no better than he. And I have disappointed my villagers and friends. I hear my children shout. How lovely and naive they are. They have no fear of death. But I sit and shake. So do old women and men and summertime fishermen. And Marcus walks above us. We are his silent pawns. Yet he is the one who disregards our laws. He and his people had their day before the courts. But now his discontent is sharp. He suffers and is cruel. He uses violence easily and rejects the spirit of our nation. I do not pity him, nor the longings of his people.

WORLD ONE

Without our laws, father's savage world would return and the bloody spirits with it. Violence and justice do not mix. Violence is injustice. And we, the villagers, are the proof of it.

A shy time it was for me. Yet I was growing bolder. Father's voice was with me and the captain's daughter heard it. I could no longer face the knowledge of my lack of courage. I could not face it with my father near me. I had to act. I had to make a stand for us. I had to risk my life for my father's faith.

W*O*D*E*N is yours to have and to hold. Words like that flew at me. I am the mother of three and not much more. I fear for my own safety. Then Marcus showed his face.

"I hope you do not tire of me. Are you in need of food? Say the word and you will have fresh treats. We must keep you well. We must play this game with rules. All's well then?"

Bastard, I was thinking. Don't dangle meat before us. Perhaps we will all starve in protest of your actions . . . Then where will you be? What power will you have? Our deaths will be your end to power. And we will raise no sword.

"I sadly say that we have been repelled by W*O*D*E*N's generous offer. It is not enough for us to go quietly to prison. We are forging north. At this very moment we are moving toward our homeland. How fresh the air will be and how beautiful the sea. You will be our guests when we step back onto land. Have any of you ever seen the Falklands? Have you ever seen the old green hills lit by dawn's grey light?

"You will understand our needs when we take you there. You will understand the love we have for this place of ours. It is time the Argentines return to the mainland. I will gladly loan them this rotten cargo ship. And we will let them live so long as W*O*D*E*N relents to our demands. We are not spiteful people. We are loving people lost in a world which holds great power over us.

"When the land is ours again, I will release you. And you will have our love for what you have done for us. Citizens of W*O*D*E*N, I respect you. W*O*D*E*N will give in or one of you will hang."

It was time for me to speak. It was time to put an end to pity for ourselves and speak like patriots. I put Julia in

Gregory's lap. I grabbed Peter by the arm and sat him down. He had been standing to get a better view of Marcus who loomed so high above us. I rose up tall and wrapped my cloak around me. I brushed back my hair and shook it loose. Tanya Shepherd was now fourteen. Tanya Shepherd was now the captain's daughter. Tanya Shepherd would put this pirate to sleep.

"You may call me Tanya Shepherd. I speak for us, the recently oppressed. I have no pity for your cause."

Even against the strange white moving sky, I saw his interest spark. He leaned a little farther forward and searched for the body of my voice. Now he saw me, this tiny mother of three. And he seemed pleased to have a partner with which to engage in conversation. But first, he stamped me with his mark. He wished to have the edge before opening up the floor. Marcus shamelessly announced that I would be the first to hang should W*O*D*E*N cause him any problems. And I for some strange reason said, "It will be my honor."

He came Abu, pirate, great King of Law. He came Marcus, master rebel of the Falklands. And there was little Tanya plotting bold and courageous strategies. There was Tanya Shepherd waking up from years of sleep. But where was my father's voice? I expected him to come and shape my thoughts. Did I feel a warm and gentle wind running through the ways? Or did my heart create a sudden storm in the chilly cargo bay? Marcus and Abu came down to me and little Tanya and Tanya Shepherd found each other waiting in the exact same open space. How fine it felt to be so young. How fine it felt to stand in strength before my children and my friends.

While Marcus made his way to me a crowd of little and not so little rebels gathered round the iron mouth of the cargo bay. We were the lions in the pit and Marcus was to come and tame us, tame me, tame this tiny mother of three. Gregory said, "Mother, I will bite his leg." No you won't, I said. Peter said, "I will jump on him and ride him like a

WORLD ONE

pony." You will not, I said. And bewildered Julia advised me to sit down. "In just a while, I will. Now be silent, children."

Marcus now came from a dark and empty corner of the steely room. He had come to see me and look directly in my face. I had won an easy sort of victory. He had come to me. I no longer had to strain my neck to see him. And I no longer had to shout. All the villagers were as quiet as my children. Marcus questioned me. "I beg your pardon, but what will be your honor?"

"To die peacefully," I said.

Marcus would have laughed if I had not held his gaze with mine. I held his eyes and I would not let them go. I had fear of what would happen if I did. Little petite, little petite, she should be a captain.

"You are a righteous one. You believe in foolish sacrifice. But what about your children? Will you leave them motherless?" Marcus spoke as if to his entire congregation. He was a circus master. He had a whip to tame the lions. And he had a woman to harrass. Little petite, little petite, how will you ever put this man to sleep?

"And will you leave your people leaderless? Will you allow them to be scattered across the globe? You and your people commit crimes against the foundations of our nation. You break laws like sticks. You would have had a better time in the old, inhumane world. But you were born too late. Your flight of fancy is patterned after the formless rules of an ancient era." Marcus had no use for my compelling lessons of history. More to the point, he had found new use for the formless rules of ancient history.

"And what would you do, dear, if you were I? How would you go about restoring ancient property? By right of possession, we owned that land. It should have been a simple claim. But unfair justice is more complex than that. Even older rights of possession were taken into account. And so we lost our claim by the highhanded judgement of sixty injudicious fellow citizens. What would you have us do? Beg on bended knee before the court? Pray for divine intervention? Weep before the world and hope for the pity of the people? You must understand, Tanya Shepherd, the courts have turned their faces to other fair and unfair claims. They listen to us no more. We are forgotten people. The courts would rather address more exciting subjects. Land disputes in Africa. Squabbles in the Society of Asia Major. We are little people with little problems. We had lost our voice until we took you up. W*O*D*E*N hears us speak for the first time in thirty years."

I could have loved a man like this, I thought. And I despised myself for thinking it. But there was a beautiful passion in his heart, a passion made bold by desperation. Yet I could not forgive his actions. He was more deadly than Abu, aging pirate and nomad on the seas. Abu stole for riches but Marcus threatened life for land and struck at the heart of our constitution. Abu was no better man but his dreams were less destructive. Little petite, little petite, speak as a captain should.

"But there was recourse left to you," I muttered passively.

Marcus crooned softly, "Change the world in twenty days by nonviolent resistance . . . Change the world in twenty days by sitting in the sand . . ." Marcus spit at my feet and then lit up a laugh. I had no idea I possessed the powers of a comedian. I had no idea I could ever make a rebel laugh. But I did with the suggestion of implementing one of the major principles of W*O*D*E*N.

"You must take the charge for peace and act accordingly." Father had come again to bother me. Gregory stood up and held my hand while Peter began to slowly clap, why, I'll never know. But as he clapped so my other friends joined with him. And in that suspended moment of time, a whole chorus joined him. And the clapping was like fire under me and I played Peter's dragon.

"Where will it end, Marcus? We have been through this before. Any student knows the sick tragedy of our people's past. Where will it end, Marcus? Where will the flames go out? If you win your land by violent means then what's to stop the world from returning to dangerous days? I see no end, Marcus. You have no right to breach your contract with the world. You have no right to stab at its integrity."

The chorus of sound was violent now. And the helpless villagers put one name to song. "Marcus, Marcus, Marcus . . . ," the sound thundering like cannons of the past.

WORLD ONE

Marcus demanded silence. "Be quiet or your lady hangs. We are in the middle of a conversation. Please be more polite."

I held a feeble hand up. Peter put his hands underneath his bottom while Julia overcame the sudden silence with her spontaneous weeping. Gregory gripped my other hand and squeezed it as if holding onto life. And I, the little petite, the pitiful mother of three, suffered humiliation gladly and said no more to Marcus.

But neither did Marcus rejoin the conversation. I suppose that he had other things to do. Marcus was a busy man. He had the world's attention. He had a President and a Federal Convention and even all the members of the courts interested in him. And how he liked to shine! How he liked to play the part of the circus master taming all the lions. But remembering now, I must say I liked my part as well as he liked his. Motherhood is one thing, but standing somewhat firm in the face of death was as rewarding, if not more, as giving birth to children.

Marcus left us happy and relieved. I, for one, curled up and let my mind breathe. But one by one the villagers came to me and thanked me. I nodded graciously and then fell into a sleep. I brought my children with me. All of us were swimming in my sleep. And above us were the whales. I looked up and counted them. All the whales in all the world had come to swim above us. A ridiculous dream, now really. But it did not seem so at the time. I took this dream to be a message. I was young then and had a peculiar imagination. I saw the fleet of the W*O*D*E*N Navy in those many whales. Our Navy shadowed us to protect us. Yet we were running out of breath. "Swim up, swim up," I tried to cry. But the water muffled what I had to say. I was not communicating with my children. I was communicating with no one but the soundless sea.

Day 4 was a refreshing change. Marcus marched us up on deck. We were made to stand on the stern of that old ship. And to the south, one long mile behind us, were the

W*O*D*E*N ships. The sight of them was of little comfort. A reach away, a world away, they followed at a safe, respectful distance. Marcus suggested that we wave. There was no need to encourage us.

Then Marcus took us for a walk. Round and round the upper deck we went. It was good to stretch and breathe the air, the temperate summer air off the coast of Antarcticus. I asked Marcus where we were. He said, "My love, the Bellingshausen Sea is right before us. Soon we will be passing Peter Island. It is a beautiful place to lie in wait for birds. If our lives were free, I would take you there. Summertime on Peter Island is like returning to the beginning of the world."

I was touched by Marcus's romantic attitude. I let his words seduce me. I found strange comfort in them. This man was a beautiful and ugly savage. I fought off my sympathetic feeling. I divided him in half. I closed one eye and stared at his warped heart.

"Then why not put us down there? Why not free us and let us take our flight? Let the children go, at least. Have you no children of your own?" Marcus would not answer me. He understood my game. All he said was, "Children should have their homeland." With that said, we were instructed to descend. I went below thinking of my husband.

Had he seen us crowded on the deck? Surely Marcus brought us up to be seen by men like him. We were property that W*O*D*E*N demanded to inspect. We were like bits of fertile land. Now what would W*O*D*E*N do? What course of action was it likely to pursue? I did not dwell on this for long. Our government could not capitulate. To do so would set a nasty precedent. I could sense the heated, watchful eye of our impatient Navy. I could sense the coming of certain grief.

Hazy day turned to misty twilight. Great lumps of cheese and bread were brought for us. The cheese was fresh but the bread was hard and stale. I broke a tooth while eating. Even now when I look in the mirror, I probe for that empty place. Marcus is a permanent memory with me. I never wished to have it fixed. It is a badge of honor for me.

No whales crossed my dreams that night. I did no swimming either. Instead, I tried to remember my husband's noble

WORLD ONE

face. I tried to remember everything about him—the way he wore his naval suit, the way he brushed his hair. I saw him walking on the ice, leading our children to their favorite place to play. I saw him drinking coffee and setting wood to burn in the fireplace. I saw him studying navigational charts on the kitchen table. I saw him in every way but making love to me in bed. I knew then that my lover was dead.

Julia was singing happily. She asked me if I saw daddy wave. I told her that I hadn't. She informed me that she had. Peter and Gregory were huddling in a corner. No doubt they were plotting our escape. Silently, I wished them well. I prayed for their success. But with each prayer and thought, I unconsciously excluded myself.

So now you think me wretched. I suppose I was and am. But Marcus was a man whom I could understand. Though his vision of justice was not mine, he brought my father to me. And with my father near me, I recalled my better self.

Who was this better self? A woman who fought for peace. I had lifted no hand to maintain it. I had done too little for far too long. I was made little by my inactivity. I had not contributed my mind to my nation in any way. I had not risked my safety for anything but for bringing up the children. It was a modest curse, I knew. But a curse that I had finally recognized, thanks to Marcus and his reckless thought.

The engines turned beneath me and the light was dim and sterile. My children slept and sometimes muttered partial words and incoherent phrases. But I was resting on a wave. I was moving with the current. I was naked in a pool of lovely warm water. And my heart was beating rapidly. I could taste the fruit of a purposeful, noble death. Good God, I thought. Let me be remembered for something other than my children.

Julia woke once claiming that beetles were eating at her hair. I brushed her hair like she had done for me. "Julia," I whispered. "You are a special girl . . ." I wanted to say more. I wanted to tell her who I was. But I did not know. I had been a child like her. I had been a W*O*D*E*N baby just like her. But now, what was I? And who was I? And where would I be going? What had happened to my childhood dreams and my promises to father? And why had mother died so few years after father's death? If she had lived perhaps I would have found my way. I might have taken father's place and commanded cargo ships. I might have become some instrument for peace and justice. I might have contributed a breath of something to this awesome world. But instead I married quickly, became a mother on that first night. And years of strength had passed me by, had evaporated into ice.

But now the time had come. My small fire was eating at the ice. "Julia," I whispered. "There are no beetles in your hair. But I will watch for them."

Julia floated down to sleep cradled in my arms. I rocked her sweetly and envied her. Oh, to be a child again with a field of choices.

On Day 5, we, the villagers of Antarcticus, waited for something that did not happen. We expected W*O*D*E*N to strike, to bear its teeth at Marcus and his men. Every noise above the engines turning was a suspect sound. On that morning, Gregory was a little spooked. With each unaccounted noise he heard, he stood up and strained his ears. "Mother, they're finally coming for us. Mother, that was a gunshot, wasn't it? Mother, what's taking daddy so long?"

But Peter was the rational one. He would say to Gregory, "They won't come and rescue us because Marcus will hurt our mother. They won't come and rescue us because daddy wants us all to live." For all my worries, I hoped that Peter was right. What could the W*O*D*E*N Navy do? What good was their strength when Marcus held us close? I expected no heroics from our Navy. And I expected no fine ending to our story, either. I suppose I expected death for all of us. When would it come? was the question.

The children of our captors ringed the upper edges of the cargo bay and delighted in tossing down ripe oranges to us. We gladly caught them, peeled and ate them. It was a

WORLD ONE

wonderous sight to see a hundred falling balls of fruit. It gave the children up above something fun to do. And Peter and Gregory enjoyed this game. They ran one way then another to catch as many as they could. Then they passed them out, presenting them as gifts.

With sweet, bitter juices now inside of us, we passed the day pensively. It was natural for all of us to be thinking of our deaths. The fruits made the thoughts pass more easily. Or maybe it had more to do with the sight of those children providing us with tasty nourishment. We only hoped that they would do the same tomorrow. And tomorrow. When the fruits failed to fall, we would all be forced to say good-bye. How does a mother say good-bye? I couldn't allow myself to think of it. I studied the active outlines of the captors' children. Would they die in this conflict, too? Probably they would. Children are usually among the first to die in their parent's battles.

In the vague and slanted light of afternoon, Julia surprised me. Out of nowhere, her question came at me. "How did our world begin?" Gregory and Peter heard her speak and stopped their playful ruckus. Even the village idiot was curious as to how our world began. I had four sets of ears tuned to my answer. I heard my father near me, too. I said to Julia, "An even better question is why our world began."

Children can be the best of listeners when they have the minds to. I felt fortunate to have such an attentive audience. I hurried into the details of a world that I had never known. "Once there was a world of nations and not Societies. There were great and little nations which sometimes went to war and sometimes basked in peace. But there came a time when the weapons of war, the great guns of these nations, proved much too powerful for any of them. They had the strength to destroy the world and end all life forever. But this was only half of it. A majority of the people in our world then were cold and hungry and needed more than they had to live. They needed medicine and shelter, boots and shoes to tie onto their feet. They needed basic necessities—simple things that you and I now take for granted. They needed water when the droughts came and food when there was famine. But in this world that was, it was not possible for the rulers of these big and little nations to provide for their people. Too many resources were spent on weapons of death and destruction. Why? Why didn't these rulers take care of all their people's needs? Because many of these nations feared each other, feared their intentions and indeed, their actions. Little wars, civil wars were raging in dozens of places round the world. And, of course, the last great war was an aching probability. Weapons with godlike powers slept underground, just waiting to be stirred awake. The world then was a terrifying place. No one knew when the end might come. But the people began to be afraid. They began to look for a certain way to live in peace. And the people of the world now took the lead. After all, their rulers had not succeeded. War could no longer be called a luxury, an easy way to settle griefs. Nuclear war threatened everyone. And so a beautiful debate began. The citizens of nations called to each other and in time sorted out a plan. That plan would deny the nations of earth the freedom to resort to violent actions to settle problems of any kind. That plan made the people of this earth citizens of a different kind. One parent government was formed. And the world Societies were like their children. They were free to live as they chose, but under certain rules. These rules made it a crime to be violent—that was the most important rule. And it has given us peace. Why did this world begin? It began so that you and I could live without the constant fear of death. It began so that the world could be a safer place to live. And W*O*D*E*N has done well, despite the likes of Marcus who is but one man discontented by the ruling of our courts."

The children were wide-awake when I had finished speaking. The village idiot with his happy grin clapped three times then nodded seriously. As if to say, no, no, he pointed up and shook his head. It was obvious to me that Marcus stood condemned before this child who spoke with eyes and fingers and without a tongue in his head. I said, "Yes, that's right. Marcus is a naughty child. And his parents will come and punish him."

I was the one who fell asleep. My night of solitary thought had caught up with me. I leaned a little to the right, then swayed the other way. Then I happily gave in to my inclina-

WORLD ONE

tions. I leaned lower, then rested on my hands. How warm a pillow hands can be when the wood is hard below them. Like Julia had the night before, I floated down to sleep. And I was cradled in the comfort of knowing how wise our village idiot actually was. Clapping hands and nodding head and pointing up . . . Peter said goodnight to me and Julia kissed my cheek.

Now father beamed his face at me. Hello, father. Hello youth. I've come back to you. Instead of swimming underwater, I was running on a bright and glorious morning. I was running down the deck, not as a child, but as me. On the sea again with the soaking wind. On my father's ship again, following a majestic line of whales. We all return to happier dreams when the day outside is dim. And I was returning to mine. The joy of little Tanya had found its way to me. Now Tanya Shepherd lifted her face and joined it with the sun. Father had his face up to it, too. Wet wind and stroking sunlight and pleasure fresh and new. The whales were going somewhere, had a destination firmly in mind. But I did not care where I was going in that dream. I was on the endless seas and happy to be there.

I was not so happy to have the morning greet me. My fragile peace was snapped in two by the boom of cannons. Little children screamed around me and up above me. The W*O*D*E*N Navy was sending early warnings. By the sound of them the bombs were dropping on either side of us. I could almost hear the commander issuing instructions to his men. "Twenty degrees to the right. Now that again to the left. And one for luck fifty yards ahead." Gregory was shouting, "Daddy's coming, mother. Get up! Get up! Daddy's almost here!" Peter was more frightened. He huddled in a corner and buried his head between his knees. Julia clung to my waist and wet my cloak with tears. "Tell them to stop it, mother. The noise is hurting my ears."

I took the children up and met Peter in his corner. We all crouched down and embraced each other. Our ship was rocking like a basket in a storm. We were like a nest of birds on a windy mountain top. Then an eerie silence rained down. Our ship began to steady. The W*O*D*E*N Navy had made its point and now they waited for Marcus to react.

Marcus was a time in coming. No doubt he was consulting the commander of the fleet. No doubt he was issuing orders of his own. The stink of death came to me. I could smell it where we sat. Where were the children with the oranges? Where were the bright, falling balls of fruit? When the noise of the running engines overwhelmed the silence, Marcus showed his violent face.

"How dare they bluff us to our knees! How dare they risk your lives. Have I not been good to you? Have I not provided you with everything? Now hear me, children and citizens alike. You will come up here with me. We have a drama to perform. And none of you will need a costume. You are all actors in my play. Now climb the ladders and prepare for Act 1."

We did as Marcus said. Children first, then the rest of us. The sky was a holy white. The summer sun was held hostage behind the curtain of the clouds. Beyond the stern, three warlike ships followed in pursuit. But this time it was not within our thoughts to wave. If anything, we wished to see them disappear. One terror was enough for us. Two terrors made us sick. Now three of us would die.

"I warned them, did I not? I warned them not to interfere. Now three of you will pay for it. I'm sorry, but this has to be. We will not fold and be like sheep. We will not hand you over. No is as simple a word as yes. I've said my no to them. I have not heard their yes. Which of you would like to die? It is a pretty day for it. The weather's just right."

Old women and summertime fishermen wept. And Marcus picked out three. His eyes avoided me. He would save my neck for later. Marcus had discriminating taste when it came to death. Two old men and one pathetic grandmother were chosen for this fitful demonstration. Their hands were tied up quickly. And eyeless hoods were set down over their heads. The ropes were hung and the nooses tightened. The boxes on which they stood were kicked away and their bodies performed an ugly dance. I noticed Marcus did not look.

WORLD ONE

Marcus was looking toward the naval ships. How dare they force him in this way. How dare they make a spectacle when this was his play.

Our fellow friends and villagers expired while Marcus took his look. I held my children close and held their faces to me. I looked up to the sky and cried. How could men be so cruel for the sake of land? It was a stupid question. And I was a stupid woman. Bastard, I thought. And bastard I said.

Marcus turned to me. Were his eyes wet with grief or glee? I did not know and never did. His voice was even and direct. "A bastard, I am. But I warned your government of this. I warned them many times. I am sorry. Now my men will take you down. And there will be oranges for all. Let us hope this play is done."

The children did not speak for hours. And I was ashamed to look at them. I was ashamed for all of us—the children, my friends . . . Why had W*O*D*E*N acted? Did they think that Marcus was a boy? Did they think he collected people for fun? And now what would happen? Violence gives birth to violence. Ask any child of reason. Ask the village idiot and he will somehow tell you.

Evening on Day 6 was a graceless evening. A sick fear had grown among us. We saw no children up above us. We saw only the outlines of Marcus and his men. Where were their wives and mistresses? Why were these women not plotting to hand them over to the Navy and release us before anymore harm was done? And what was my husband doing? He had seen the dangling figures. He had seen the effects of his Navy's actions. Why was he not demanding clean negotiations? Why was he not crying out for a peaceful resolution?

The dimmer light of night revealed itself to us. And with that night came the formless face of Marcus. Marcus had been drinking. His words were slurred and his balance was uneven. Marcus had no stomach for anything but dreams.

"You people blame me, hate me . . . I know what you are thinking. So what! So come and kill me. So come and hang me and watch me die. I have already failed. I have lost my claim for justice. I have become a violent, insane person. I deserve to die.

"Tanya Shepherd, you are listening to me? I have killed today for the sake of property. Now the world will know that I am a crazy man. But will they know what W*O*D*E*N did? Will they know of W*O*D*E*N's use of force? If I die, please tell them. Tell them how it was. Tell them we were sleeping when it happened. I made threats, yes. But I didn't want to kill you. I was forced to do it. I am the leader! I must protect my people, provide them with food and land and houses. I must see that they have clothes, hats and scarves for winter. I must see that they have a little money in their pockets and can raise their families. My ends are good and right. But now, I am a murderous drunkard. Now I am condemned to kill, to continue down the road. I care nothing for my life. I will go to prison and die in peace there. But my people must have a new life—they must not be isolated on a rocky, little island. They need a broader stretch of land. They are lawful people. And, indeed, our children are just as fine as yours. Help them, won't you? Stand up for them and see that they are treated right. Forgive me, Tanya Shepherd."

Marcus went away but left his thoughts with me. And once again that night I didn't sleep. I stayed awake and cried. I stayed awake to see those dangling feet. Two old men and one pathetic grandmother died in the name of one man's dubious justice. I stayed awake to remember the pain of it. And how richly that pain was felt.

Pain became rage by morning. I would sit and stew no longer. Marcus had had his fun. So, too, had our Navy. Like a game that had been played out for too long, I was weary of its challenge. I had better things to do than to witness worthless death. I was moved to action. I was moved to verbal confrontation. "Marcus, murderous drunkard of the Falklands! Wake from your guilty slumber. Tanya Shepherd requests the pleasure of your company. Let me join you and we will speak. We are nothing to you dead. We are priceless so very much alive. Wake, Marcus! Treat your captives with respect!"

WORLD ONE

Marcus was a time in coming. His stupor dragged him down. Whiskey was like a plague to him. It made him slow and weak. It sapped his mind of vitality, drowned his pain only temporarily. I wondered what distorted dreams he had had that night. Had he dreamed of fields of flowers or had he dreamed of flowers crushed by ice? Had he dreamed of children running free or had he dreamed of naked children choking on dying fish? Had he dreamed of making love or of cutting holes in bodies? What does a bastard dream when his reality is sick and devoid of meaning?

Marcus ordered me up. My children asked me not to go. "Mother, he will hit you . . . Mother, he will torture you." I kissed my children and then went the way I had to go. And as I climbed, I heard my father say, "The whales are singing today." He said that often when I was with him on his ship. And each time he said it, I wondered what it meant. But I never asked him, I would have felt a fool. "The whales are singing today." Yes, I thought. The whales are singing today . . .

When I reached the deck, I was a welcome guest. In fact, I was invited to have coffee with biscuits dipped in honey. Marcus led me to his cabin. It was fine to walk; I would have liked to run. The day was cool and right for running. I remembered how when I fell in love I used to run alone along the plains of ice. I was fired by my passion. Was I running from or to my love? Or was I running with it? Marcus smelled of sleep. His red curls were like snakes of blood. I said nothing to Marcus on the way. I listened instead to the sounds of families waking behind closed doors. The deposed people of the Falklands, the fatigued people of the Salleny Islands, the outcasts of the world . . . I dared to pity them. They had not heard the singing of the whales, not today nor yesterday, perhaps not ever. What did it mean to think one heard them sing? Father was as cryptic as my husband. And now I was the cryptic one. "The whales are singing today." Father and I were happy.

"My wife and children were drowned at sea. I had no strength to save them. Now it appears that it would have been best if

I had followed them. How lovely death can seem. How peaceful it must be . . . More coffee?"

I accepted one more biscuit. "So now you punish us. Kill us because of them. Deprive us of our happiness, haunt us while we sleep. Did you sleep well last night, or did you sleep at all? I thought of you last night. You have become an evil man. Conflict does not suit you. Your murders will now destroy you. Set us free, Marcus. Save your people while you can. W*O*D*E*N will not be moved. It will use force to conquer you. It has the right. We granted it the power . . . Do you know that my husband is on a ship behind us? He is a naval officer, kind and gentle with the children. He is a friend and I love him. But in these days ahead, I could come to hate him. I could hate him as I hate you. Why? Because of his course of violence. He and the government have the right. You have provided them with cause and justice sits with them. But violence is a hated face. It leads us all to death. I would break all violence if I could—W*O*D*E*N's or yours. I can hardly tell the difference."

Marcus poured me coffee and then put his pistol on the table. The fate of Abu would be his. Pirate, rebel, government were all the same with pistols out. And the sameness was so unappealing. It made us all so weak, feeble and confused. Marcus stared at me and said, "It is a last resort. Now end it for me. Pick it up and shoot and you will steer this ship. Pick it up and shoot and I will trust you to care for all the families. Do it or the violence will continue. Do it, Tanya. This is your chance for peace."

For all that I had said, Marcus had not heard me. And I made my scorn known to him. I spit up a laugh and slid the gun aside. I would not dabble on this murky stage of senseless action. I would rather die on it then become a part of it. "Marcus, I am happy as I am. Look at me. I am only a mother of three. I have a husband with a noble face. I live in a world where people have enough to eat. I have it all. And you had it, too. I'm sorry you have lost it. But I will not trade peace for violent grief, not even for the luxury of freedom."

My uncertain rebel was a thousand miles away. Was he watching his children drown or was he walking through a field of flowers? Were the flowers crushed by ice or were they

WORLD ONE

lapping up the sun? Marcus waved vaguely, a sign for me to go. I walked away and left this lonely man, left him sitting by a table with a pistol on it. I had failed him, I knew. And I had failed my people, too.

The villagers of Antarcticus and my children stood when I returned. I was led to them by Marcus's leaderless men. What had I said, what had Marcus done? Those were the questions that were put to me. And I refused to answer. "Marcus will continue on his course. We will not go free. He is a man who is drowning. I can do nothing for him and even less for us." My, how I disappointed them. They had expected me to save them. But who was I but one? One little woman who had heard the whales singing in the morning. I crept in a hole. I passed the day that way. I sought refuge in the fact that I had not taken Marcus's life. I could have ended it and perhaps our troubles, too. But I was a W*O*D*E*N woman and would not stoop to one woman's dubious justice.

Day 8 was a mixture of hope and inspiration. I had spent the day before dreaming up alternatives for all of us to take. And why not? Marcus's plan would never succeed and W*O*D*E*N's mandate would only serve to bring about more pain. I had a right to think. I had a right to dream. I had a right to enter into the negotiations. In fact, I had a duty to. You would have felt this duty, too, had you been with us on the Bellingshausen Sea.

As every schoolgirl knows, Antarcticus is the seventh continent of the world. Though much of the ice was uninhabitable, there were parts of it that were beautiful and fit for human life. As I lay thinking in the morning, turning over the same thoughts of yesterday, I decided that my plan might work. Further north and east was the Antarcticus Peninsula. Its furthest reach lay a thousand miles to the south of the Falkland Islands. Why not deed this stretch of land as a homeland for these people? Why not negotiate this settlement for peace? Marcus might enjoy the thought of this—a new land for his people.

It was possible, I knew. After all, we lived on the shores of ice. And the capital was built on it. Build your villages and raise your children. It had worked for us. Why not for these deposed people of the Falklands?

Marcus was well that morning. He looked young and bold and was happy to hear me out. He and I walked the deck, from bow to stern, and listened to each other. I felt no contempt for him. Our encounter of yesterday had vanished with the day. Today was the only day that mattered.

We could have been in love. We could have been brother and sister. Certainly we were not enemies. Not on that day of thought. The winds at sea were warm on us, though the sun was shaded white. A distant happiness had come to us. What wind had brought it here? We spoke as if tomorrow were today, with all differences laid to rest. I remember Marcus laughing when I mentioned singing whales. He had never heard them sing until that very day.

"My people might accept this neck of land. It might right a wrong. Think of it, Tanya, your villagers would have new distant neighbors. People of Antarcticus . . . it has a ring to it. But would W*O*D*E*N really accept this?"

Probably not, I thought. Not right away, at least. But in time they might, when the violence was done and the waters had cooled and Marcus was in prison.

We watched the W*O*D*E*N ships for hours. We watched families of flying birds swoop high and low and then disappear from sight. And in the middle of it all, I felt comfortable. I was working for a cause. I was grasping for the heart of peace. I was lifting up my eyes to a calm and dreamy sky. "Why was Gregory shouting at the sky?" At that moment the voices of anger had stopped. We were in a quiet time, safe from death and violence. We were listening to the world and to each other's thoughts. We were listening to the singing of a parade of invisible whales. Then a sudden sadness overtook the magic of the music. I thought of Marcus condemned to prison for his crimes against our government. He would die in isolation, far from his home and people. He would die alone for his mistakes. And Marcus knew his fate. He knew

WORLD ONE

the time was coming and he accepted this. But he would go to it and know that it was right.

"Tanya, I will go to my people and suggest this plan of action. We will vote on it and decide our fate together. I wish to end this hopeless undertaking. I wish to settle it without violence. Will you stay with me a moment longer?"

I stayed with Marcus while the sun descended to the glowing rim of the sky. Once while we stood and followed the thrashing of the waves with our eyes, he touched my hand, then held it tight as if he'd just married me. At that moment I thought perhaps he had. We knew peace together. And joy. We saw the world as one, we loved it separately. I longed to have my children with me. I wanted them to see this man . . . I wanted them to see this citizen of W*O*D*E*N.

Marcus offered my children and me a cabin in which to sleep. I refused his gesture of kindness and he escorted me back. When I looked down at the villagers of Antarcticus, I wondered how far I would go to serve their needs. If they believed that justice had been unfair to them, what measures would I take? Would I risk a life of prison to see that they were fed? Would I commit violence for the sake of our homeland? I could not answer this. I had never had the responsibility to care for anyone other than my husband and my children. But who can say? My questions were disturbing. More so, because I had no ready answers.

That night, while we waited word from Marcus, we began to celebrate. The music came from voices as we, the villagers, danced. The children went round and round, clapping gleefully. I tired quickly and watched the people's faces. Here, in this cargo bay, all the villagers were one—made one at first by terror and now by joy.

But Marcus did not come that night. I made excuses for him. Perhaps he was waiting until morning to speak to the W*O*D*E*N government. I dared not think beyond that. I had too much hope to blur it with suspicion. I only wanted to hear him say, "You are free to go."

Gregory was excited and very proud of me. "Mother, won't you get a medal? Won't they put you in the paper? Can

I be there when they take your picture?" Peter was a bit more circumspect. Peter worried over me. "What if Marcus decides to keep you, mother? He likes you more than us. I won't go unless you go. I want you to be with me."

I told Peter that Marcus would be going to a place where I could not go. I told him not to worry. Yet somewhere deep inside of me, I knew that if the time had been different, I might have followed him, set out across the sea with him and never returned home. Marcus and I would have made some lovely children. And we would have loved them dearly.

Julia was rolling back and forth on the cold, hard floor of the bay. She found amusement in her movements. Up and down, right and left, over and over. She was a perfect, bubbly child. Over and over, up and down and right and left, she rolled. Her smile was as sure as the feelings in my heart. I was in love with another man—a murderous pirate, rebel on the seas. I loved him for his change of heart, for his passion for his people, for the way he touched my hand while we listened to the singing of the whales while watching flying birds swoop up and down.

23

The ghost of father came like death into my dreams that night. He walked across a field of ice toward me. I remember I was crouching down as if to protect myself from a raging storm. A barrage of snow hurtled at me. I looked up just long enough to see the ghost of my father coming. And when he stood before me, the snow began to lessen and the wind began to slow and soon it was all gone, only father's ghost remained to stand above me.

Father reached out to touch my face. I let him touch me. His icy fingers made me warm. "Hello, father. How is it where you are?"

I think I said that in my dream. What else could I say? Even in my dreams I was prepared to be polite to all types of walking ghosts. But when I spoke to father he was no more. He left as quickly as he came. He did not tell me that he was well. He did not tell me from what place he had come. I had no doubt that he had journeyed far. I should have kept my quiet and listened to his thoughts. He had come to tell me something. His words now went unspoken. I dreamed on and on and walked through fields of sunshine. It was of great relief to me to have conjured up this place. I would have stayed there if I could. I would have settled there and made a home with Marcus and my children. I would have wished away my former life to have taken up a new one. How I wished that dream had been transformed into reality. But this was not to be. I woke to Marcus shouting obscenities at me.

"You break my heart by calling me a bastard. And so I am when I am made to murder. But I tell you this. W*O*D*E*N is the supreme bastard of them all. It has a hide of ice as thick as the land on which it sits. Tanya Shepherd, they have turned your noble proposition down. They refuse to bargain anymore. 'First, justice must be served.' First, I must be tried and sent to prison. But what guarantees do I have that my people will be treated fairly? None, they say. 'The W*O*D*E*N government does not negotiate with criminals.' That is not good enough for us. We must have a more sound future than that. We must know what will happen before we give you up. Tanya, what would you suggest I do?"

Let me dream more, I thought. Let me go back to the fields of sunshine. Let me erase the day and week. Let me pretend this never happened. Let me return to the way I was, before I ever knew you.

To this unhappy music, all the villagers were lifted from their sleep. The celebration of the night before was not recalled. We looked at each other and feared once more. Like a host of fish washed ashore, we longed for the soothing waters of the peaceful deep.

"Say nothing, children. Be good and sit up straight." I walked below where Marcus stood. I had no ideas and no words to fill the void. I was like my father's muted ghost.

Marcus showered me with words. Now once again, he was the wronged and aggrieved party. He had offered peace in the name of justice. He had acted righteously for the sake of everyone. Indeed, he was prepared to sacrifice himself for his people's future. But no more. He would seize the Falklands, claim them for his own. And he dared the President

WORLD ONE

of W*O*D*E*N to intervene. He dared the world at large to resist his righteous strike. Had he thought of it, he would have dared God, the Almighty. But Marcus was content to take on secular orders.

"What else did W*O*D*E*N say?" I asked.

Marcus leered at me. He was a wounded wolf. He was a sick romantic. He was a child of yesteryear. He let his hate be known.

"Our people accepted your thoughtful inspiration, Tanya. We praised your name, we did. A beautiful stretch of land is far better than a rock infested island. And a peaceful resolution is far better than tragic revolution. But W*O*D*E*N spit at us. It shook its fist at us. I am a marked man. I presume I have few days to live. But I will live to see our homeland and I will live to die on it. There is no finer place to die than where one was born."

"What else did W*O*D*E*N say?" I asked.

"Nothing!" Marcus screamed. The word rocked the rolling cargo bay. It shattered our hopes into tiny fragments of pain. Once again we faced the wrench of death. Once again we sat under the eye of terror.

"I am sorry, Marcus. I am sorry for all of us."

"Damn them, Tanya. Let them come for me. And when they do, we all go to death together. That's the way of it, sometimes."

Twenty minutes after Marcus left, the children dropped down oranges for us. I must admit, I found hope in this. Marcus thought of us as allies. We were the ones who listened to his tempers. We had become witnesses to his crumbling cause. We were citizens of W*O*D*E*N sitting in judgement on the conflict.

Now the villagers of Antarcticus turned to me. Now I was to blame for their sense of grief. Now it was for me to defend myself. Now where was that proper little mother of three? I wished to sleep.

The afternoon was empty of all passion, hope and news. We all sat and stared like the speechless village idiot. We listened to the rumblings of the engines and studied the trembling of our fingers. Julia complained that she hadn't had enough to eat. Gregory fought with Peter over the rules of a paper, scissor and rock game. I felt seasick and buried my head in my hands. I wondered what my husband was doing behind the walls of his ship. I wondered why my fate had come to this—why us, why me, why now, why ever? W*O*D*E*N had been created to put a stop to violence, yet violence looked at us like light. It touched our every move. It followed us like the eternal summer sun. Oh, for the darkness of an endless winter's peace.

I thought of young Tanya on the seas. I thought of her tucking father into bed. I thought of father reading her a story. I thought of young Tanya playing poker with the men. And then I thought of father dying in his sleep. I never fulfilled his dreams for me. Because I married young, I never entered into politics, I never strove to shape the world, I never fought injustice, I never, I never . . .

But then I thought, never is not now. Now is ever. Now I had my chance. In the morning I would try again, in the morning I would lead the charge. In the morning I would speak to the W*O*D*E*N government on behalf of us, for Marcus and his people, but most of all for Marcus. I would lead the charge for peace and act accordingly. I released the words of my muted father's ghost.

By morning it seemed too late to speak. By morning the Navy cannons boomed and shells shrieked overhead. Another forceful warning was the unmistakeable message sent to Marcus and his men. The Bellingshausen Sea seethed in turmoil round about us. Were dead fish flying through the sky? I think that probably they were. I was sick to my stomach. I clapped my hands over Julia's ears. Her screams overwhelmed the noise of the ugly racket. Gregory and Peter held each other tightly, forgetting their sharp quarrels of yesterday. It was all I could do to shout up to the sky, "Stop it! Stop it! Stop it!"

Some commander must have heard me. The shelling

WORLD ONE

ceased and the waters calmed and Julia lay limp in my arms. What madness had overcome my husband and his kind? Would they be pleased to sentence more of us to death? Our ship continued on its course. It would stop for nothing. W*O*D*E*N would have to destroy us before our engines slowed and stilled. This attempt to intimidate the rebels was a fool's folly and no one knew this more than Marcus. Before the stench of smoke had cleared, he showed his ruthless face to us. He ordered three old women up. And I was asked to witness this hideous execution. They dangled high from ropes. Their bodies swayed according to the breeze. And I wished to be the fourth. "Take my neck and break it, Marcus. Show the world who you really are. If you will not break it, then I will. Or I will take a step into the sea. I will die peacefully in protest of all violence—yours and theirs. And my death will be the one that is remembered. Watch and I will show you."

Marcus dispatched his men to seize me. I was taken by the wrists and led down the ways to his steely cabin. But as I went I saw no halls or doorways. I saw no floors or fixtures. I saw only the dangling bodies of the women who died without protest.

In his death-stained room, my hand was fitted with a phone. Marcus gently placed it to my ear. I heard the oceans storm in it. I heard hollow booms. Then the sounds subsided and I registered a voice. And the voice said, "Marcus, that was your last warning."

"You are speaking to Tanya Shepherd. I am a citizen of W*O*D*E*N. I speak for my fellow villagers when I say hold your distance and stop your bloody tactics. If you persist, he will kill us all. Why do you continue to make the same mistake?"

The channel faded then. Marcus had switched us off. I had said exactly what he had wanted me to say. I said it without rehearsal. Marcus thanked me for my intuitive brilliance. "Tanya, you negotiate better than I. Why don't you have a cup of coffee and we will plan our strategy and enjoy the quiet of the seas."

I slapped Marcus across the face. I would have beat him like a madwoman but for the weakness of my body. Marcus caught my hand and easily pushed me back into my chair. I slumped down low and felt too much pain to cry. I neither looked at Marcus nor at my stinging hand. I looked beyond and saw my father's sorry face. He had come into the room. He observed my tattered state. He moved close to me and touched my hand. It was then that I was lit by the beauty of his fire. It was then that I turned my eyes to Marcus and challenged his authority.

"Let me speak to the ship again. I will plead for you. I want no more killings. We have had enough. My conscience will bear no more, ever." Did I really speak or was I dreaming that I did? Did I really see my father? Did he really touch my hand? I was sleeping with my husband, wasn't I? I was waking Gregory from a nightmare. I was in my house on the silent shores of Antarcticus. I was safe and warm there. It was time to wake and fix my children's breakfast. It was time to take a shower. Didn't Peter have an appointment to see the doctor this morning? And who would sit with Julia for the afternoon? I had things to do. I had to see my husband off. Wasn't he leaving for the week? Hadn't we made love the night before because he would be away again? It was time to take a shower. It was time to begin the day.

"Tanya, you are here with me. Your children are very safe. I will let you speak to anyone. Just don't go mad on me. Have coffee. I'll see to it you have biscuits dipped in honey. I am here with you, Tanya. What is done is done—do not worry over it." Marcus led me back to the thought of death. I was lying in my coffin. I was not scratching to get out. I was lying still and a pillow held my head in place. "I need you, Tanya. You can help us end this conflict. You can help us all live."

And so I rose up from the dead. I saw the steely room and red, bloody curls. I was Tanya Shepherd, mother of three, again. I was ready for biscuits dipped in honey. I was thirsty for a cup of coffee. I had come back to a world of noxious violence. But where was love? I did not love this man in front of me. I did not love the man who shared my bed. I only loved my children who were captives on this ship.

"Give me the phone."

Marcus dutifully obeyed. If I was frightened, he was more. But was I frightened? Had fear come and gone forever?

WORLD ONE

Good riddance, if it had. I had nothing to fear but the failure to find peace. I took the phone and heard the oceans storm. Marcus looked at me as though I was his spirit of salvation. I was nothing of the kind. I was simply a woman who feared no man, no government while speaking words of peace.

"There is nothing to negotiate, Marcus. Release your prisoners and surrender now. Your time is running out."

I heard a man then, didn't I? He phrased his words succinctly. But this man threatened me with violence, threatened me through Marcus. There I sat with terror on either side of me, yet I felt none of it. Now I was the aggrieved party. Now I held the higher ground. And I swore to myself that I would be the one to end the violence when the time was right. "I am Tanya Shepherd and it is your duty to listen to me. My time will never run out as long as I call for a peaceful resolution to this hopeless play."

I did not hear what the voice of this man said next. I was compelled to stare at the breathless smile upon my father's understanding face. He had come from far away to be with me in this trial. He had walked the earth to stand by me and fortify my mind. He was still teaching me. He was still looking after me. He was still loving my world despite this situation.

I was prepared to speak to him, to ask him what to do. But his happy eyes said not to. His happy eyes told me to continue as a child of W*O*D*E*N should. And I did.

"You, commander, have broken a fundamental law of W*O*D*E*N. Is this your doing or do you have the consent of our President? Your tactics are better suited to a previous age. Violence in our day must never be used unless all other channels of negotiation have been ended by all parties concerned." I said that and more. This commander to whom I spoke was anxious to end his voyage. Perhaps his wife demanded he come home. Perhaps one of his children had whooping cough. Perhaps he simply did not like the sound of Marcus's arrogant voice. It was not my place to interrogate his motives. It was only my place to raise a hand for peace and to put myself between the sparring factions. I did this and more. I accused the W*O*D*E*N Navy of violating universal law. I held the Navy in contempt, held them accountable for any further violence. Imagine Tanya Shepherd being as bold as this. Now when I think of it, my heart beats faster and my cheeks begin to burn. Who would have thought a captain's daughter would have lived to have known a day like this? Who would have thought Tanya Shepherd would have lived beyond it to recall it?

I steadied my nerve and awaited the commander's response. What would he say to the one he had come to save? From that time on all the world would know what I had accused the W*O*D*E*N Navy of and indirectly the W*O*D*E*N government, too. I was brash at thirty-two, I admit. But I had seen terror meet terror and I was not about to sanction it. I heralded our principles of peace and defied both Marcus and the Navy to honor them. The ghost of my father had disappeared. I knew then that all was well. I knew I followed his spirit and spoke the words that were satisfactory to him. Farewell, father, I thought. I will see you again when good words lose ground to unlawful actions.

"We have committed no violence, Mrs. Shepherd. We are here to assist you and free you. There are fifty of you we have responsibilities for. Please do not second guess our course of action." Stated like a man of wisdom. Bravo! "Your husband is here to speak to you . . ."

At that, Marcus nearly snatched the phone. But I avoided the trite assault by saying that I had no wish to chat with him. I was a wretched wife, was I not? I shut the door on the voice of my husband. But he was of no less threat to me and my friends then was Marcus. I had made my point for the moment and I had been heard. The W*O*D*E*N Navy was in violation of the laws of nonviolence. It was a plain and irrefutable fact. Of course, Marcus had done worse than that. But for Marcus's part, he was still willing to settle his claim in a more acceptable way.

Marcus thanked me as the line went dead. I had no idea why. I only sought to uphold our laws, my father's world's laws, so that we all might live and see another tomorrow.

I was released and went back to where I belonged. And

WORLD ONE

after me came rich stores of food. Marcus had decided to treat us right that day. Somehow he seemed certain that I would pave the way for his people's better life of freedom. Maybe I could—small miracles had happened before and would happen again and again when principles of peace were at stake. But for the rest of the day I was more interested in eating fruits and chomping on carrots and fresh celery. I was more interested in thinking my way through the events that surely lay ahead. What would happen when Marcus led his people ashore? Then what would the W*O*D*E*N Navy be commanded to do? In between bites of red apples and spoonfuls of hot onion soup, I shuddered at the thought of the coming collision. I knew that near day would not be bright. I knew too well what Marcus's actions would mean.

The quiet cloak of fog settled in on the eleventh day of our captivity. To Marcus, this day seemed to mark some kind of anniversary. I was in no mood to celebrate with champagne, or even coffee. On that morning, Marcus announced that we were but a full day out from the Falkland Islands. And best of all, he said, the fog was a sign that divine justice had chosen his cause to be right. I had no spare courage with which to argue with him. Marcus was most kind when his hostages tended to agree with him. So we agreed. The fog was a sign that justice had rendered a verdict. And now Marcus could safely make his way to shore and direct the denouement of his lavish production.

Marcus had surprises for me by afternoon. He had received a promise from the W*O*D*E*N fleet that they would initiate no more actions. "Your President walks backwards today, my friends. She sees the world better that way. You may not have to die on the fifteen day if she continues to walk in the direction she's going." What was clear to me was that the Federal Convention had intervened. Not even our dear President had the right to bend the laws of the nation. And the balance of power was such that it was wise for her to retreat.

Take a step backwards, lose a little face—better that than impeachment and disgrace.

Although Marcus gladly received the credit for this move, it was I who put the fire to her feet. I was the one who invoked the cry for nonviolent behavior. And my words had been carried round the world. The eyes of law were on everyone—President and Marcus alike. The power of good law was a glory to see, even from a hole in the heart of a ship moving nearer and nearer to the frontiers of war.

I settled in for the night. The fog was a source of cruel tension. Its presence made the bones of old women ache and it found fertile ground in the lungs of our children. Through the white moving night, the fog did not lift. It lingered and burrowed down deep. I staved off the insidious cold by dreaming of mugs of hot chocolate. The illusions provided for a pleasant relief. But my children had more sophisticated methods than I. They played games of "Tag" along the vacant sides of the cargo bay. One was It, then another. The other was It, then another. The village idiot was the only one who resisted the warm temptation to play. He lay curled in his coat to the right of me. He sucked his thumb until the rescue of sleep released him. I wondered what dreams he was having while I watched his transition from slumber to sleep.

When the hour seemed late, I clapped my hands as a signal to my children to stop their game. As good children will, they obeyed. I believe that Peter was the last to be It. But in all truth, that wasn't the case. When they came to me, they wore wickedly mischievous expressions. What little plan had they cooked up? What game was I soon to be included in? I should have guessed it immediately.

You see, when they touched me, I was It.

The time had come to land by morning. We were but a thousand yards off of the south coast of the Falklands and it was there that the engines slowed to a halt. The shield of fog

WORLD ONE

remained to aid Marcus's move. Small boats were lowered into the choppy waters and we, the villagers of Antarcticus, were once more ordered up to participate in the final act of this tragedy.

Peter was delighted at the prospect of setting foot back on land. Gregory searched the fogbound distance for low flying birds. Julia swatted the fog as she paced up on deck. "Mother, is it okay that I try to brush it away?" Marcus overheard Julia's question. It seemed to amuse him greatly. "My dear child," he said, "please wait until we are safely on land." Julia refrained from her chore without question. She held her busy hands behind her back. She had no desire to anger a giant. "I was just trying to help us all see, mother."

Then one by one we made our way down to the boats. First the old women and men. Then the children and summertime fishermen. I followed last and had words with Marcus. "You know what this means, my dear man?" Marcus grinned like a wolf before breakfast. "It means, Tanya Shepherd, that we are on the way to reclaim our homeland. Now go with my men and our people will follow. The fog will be lifting by midday. W*O*D*E*N must not know of our passage until then."

"Goodbye, Marcus," I said. "You have committed the ultimate folly. This act is an act of war." Marcus paid no attention to me. He had preparations to make. He had families to please and more boats to lower. Would he set fire to his ship? It would be a beautiful statement of arrogance. I expected he'd do it. But he didn't.

The waters were warmer than those off our shores of Antarcticus. Through the banks of fog I saw the rising green land of the Falklands. It was an enchanting land and as old as any on earth. So this was what my friends had been hanged for. A surge of fog covered it over. Only the dipping of the oars could be heard as we moved briskly.

It was true, I knew. Marcus might die on his homeland. We might die on his homeland. And so might his people. An act of war is an act of war. The W*O*D*E*N government would have all legal rights now to take action. What possible good could this do for Marcus? The Navy would set down an ultimatum. They would force Marcus's hand. And surely we would die on the fifteenth day of our journey. And to what end, I asked? To no end, I replied. To no end.

The scent of land was keen and the fog thinned as we stepped on wet sand. Marcus's men held pistols to us. We marched to a point where sand met green. And it was there that we waited through the hours of the day while Marcus and his people returned to their homeland. And when all had come ashore, the fog did lift. Beyond the ship in which we had lived, there stood in the green grey waters the three ships of W*O*D*E*N. The world now knew that Marcus was at war.

At that moment of the afternoon, there was new found cheer among Marcus and his people. There was dancing on the beach and the ring of laughter was everywhere. We, the villagers of Antarcticus, were made to sit on our hands and contemplate the certainty of our pathetic fate. A fire was made and its light rose up and painted the landscape with red. To the south was our ship and the Navy. The scene on the beach must have made for good watching. All in all, it was a virtuoso performance. Children come back to reclaim their playground, children showing off their daring. To my mind, theirs was the truly pathetic fate. Ours was just a sad one.

By early evening Marcus had been in contact with the fleet. He had been thoughtful enough to bring along with him a radio for the relay of messages. At least Marcus could think that far ahead. At least he still had a few wits about him. At least he still cared to attempt to negotiate. But I saw no way out for either party. I saw no way out for anyone. Was there nothing left I could do? Perhaps Marcus could be persuaded to let the children go free. They could make for the towns in the north. Let the older ones face death together. How would W*O*D*E*N attack? Would they shell the beach and then land? Would my husband be among the first to land? Would he land to find my burnt body? Perhaps, I thought, I should write him a note. I regretted then not having spoken to him. I had too many regrets as I sat on the sand and admired the glow of the twilight.

WORLD ONE

In the night Marcus was so kind as to come and inform us of what had been said in the day. "The Navy is poised to attack. They now think nothing of you. They have larger issues with which to contend. You see, my friends, we are at war with the Falklands and thus with W*O*D*E*N. Of course, we all know that we will not win. How could we? We do not have the privilege of having the strength of the world behind us. We only have pistols with which to commit suicide. That's what we are doing, are we not? But, you see, we have won. We will die on our homeland and lie in graves on our soil. It is better this way, don't you think? When W*O*D*E*N attacks there will be enough pistols to go around. And bullets have been saved for each of you, including the children, I'm sorry to say."

My children began to cry. I could do nothing to comfort them. I could do nothing but sit in the sand and picture the aftermath of the slaughter. Why the children too? I heard myself screaming. Why any of us, at all? Marcus disappeared as fast as he came. He was not anxious to face us with such grim news. He never once looked at me. He spoke as if to the fog, as if to the green grasses above us. I could not tell if he was serious.

Luckily the children were able to cry themselves to sleep. For them now the world was harmless and sweet, but I kept remembering yesterday evening when Peter and Gregory tagged me It. What was it to be It? What was it to act accordingly? How could I prevent W*O*D*E*N from attacking and how could I force Marcus to change his mind—to surrender and find a better justice for his people? And where was the ghost of my father? The children were asleep and he could come and visit me and speak. But as the light dimmed down and the world around me was blessed with silence, I was a woman left alone on a beach without peace.

24

Hours before dawn on the thirteenth day of our trial, I was shook from sleep by a radiant apparition. To this day there is no way for me to be sure if I dreamt this ghost or actually saw it. But either in my dreams or in a blissful reality, I saw the golden frame of my father and heard his round words of wisdom.

We went for a walk on the beach. The tide was high and the dew had set in and I had no cares. I had been transported out of myself and had been granted a stay of relief. How fine it was to live a whole day before dawn. Father guided me by the light of his form. I simply followed, looked and listened.

And as we travelled I seemed to be reliving the night before his death. He seemed to be the way he was on that night—a man of hope and vitality. His sentences were the same as before, his gestures identical. Everything was the same except for the landscape. We were on the beach and not on his ship. And I was thirty-two and not fourteen.

WORLD ONE

So when he spoke, I knew what he was about to say. How wonderfully strange that time was . . . what a rich encounter it turned out to be. The ghost of my father was continuing my education.

"Always remember this, Tanya. Always remember that your peace is founded on law and nonviolent resistance for change. That is the key to the world of W*O*D*E*N and to all men's destiny for tomorrow and tomorrows to come. This is my generation's gift to you and to your children and theirs. Without this gift, surely you might not have been born. Surely your mother and I would have died long before in some great war at some sad time. Our generation took the great step forward. We made the hard choice for peace. We opened our minds and took the chance. Through your life you must continue to do the same. You must do it for your children and their children. And their children must do it for theirs. With justice comes peace and with peace comes plenty. It is the best man can do as children of God. It is the best man can do for his children."

We walked on. I was neither happy nor sad. I had no regrets for the death of my father. It was enough to be with him for a time, to hear his mild voice once again. I was not moved to utter a word. I only wished to listen and remember. Sometimes it is so sweet to remember. My memories in life were not fraught with pain. I had lived the life of a golden child. Now I walked with the golden ghost of my father down a beach before dawn.

And then father slowly stepped away. With one step he was gone. He had stepped toward the sea. I followed. He was gone. I looked out across the low endless waters. I searched the sky for his light. I turned back and sought his form striding up over the hills. He was gone. And I knew I would never see the joy in his face again.

But then his joy would never leave me. His joy would follow me all my days. I would see it in the faces of my children. I would see it in my eyes when I was old and plain.

I remember that night on the Falklands and cherish that stream of feeling. I remember those words to this day. I remember the surge of power behind them. And so when the hours before dawn were done, I found myself back with my children. I found myself in the sands of Marcus's camp. The fire still blazed and the wood still snapped and my children slept soundly as did I.

We fried fish for breakfast in the morning. It was a glorious day and the sun was out and the blue of the heavens was ours. The fish needed salt, but no matter. The fish was fresh and the meat was hot and it was good to be alive.

Marcus and his people waited like soldiers for death. We villagers waited for a miracle of some kind, any kind. The three ships of W*O*D*E*N sat dead in the waters. What was the President's thinking? . . . What was mine? It was a day of nondecisions. It was a day of rest before the battle. It was a day of peace before war. What was the President's thinking? . . . What was mine?

Dusk followed day without confrontation. Perhaps Marcus himself was waiting for some miracle to happen. He walked the beach in front of us with his head bowed low. He stood in the wash of the tide and glared at the Navy. From time to time he'd bend down and wash his face with sea water. I wanted to reach out to him. I wanted to shake his head in my hands. I wanted to lead him away from this place and his people, too. But I did not know how. I did not know where to take them. I had been helpless that day and still helpless at dusk and a blind fury began to rage in me. Father had come and father had gone and still I was not moved to action. Was the time still not right? Would I know what to do when it was? I would, I would, I said over and over. I would, I would . . . I must.

Night followed dusk without confrontation. The stars shone and the sea swayed. The three ships of W*O*D*E*N sat dead in the waters. What was the President's thinking? . . . What was mine?

When Marcus had retired I walked to where he had stood by the sea. I looked for where he had looked. I saw the world for a while from his place. I cried out for help as did he. I longed to end this tiresome tragedy. Had he? Who knew what Marcus was thinking? Who knew how far he would go? I could not measure his mind, nor the mind of W*O*D*E*N's

WORLD ONE

President. But I could measure mine. I could measure the minds of the villagers of Antarcticus. It was time we put an end to this—whether for death or for peace, I didn't know. But it had to be. The fifteenth day was coming. And the fifteenth day would be the day of decision. The fifteenth day would be the end of the journey. The high tide crashed at my feet. The waters were warm and inviting. The waters had a peace all their own.

I bent down as Marcus had done and bathed my face in brine. Oh, what a fine feeling. Marcus had had that same feeling, had known the same taste of salt on his lips. What was this man, this pirate, this rebel thinking? Why had he stood here and looked and listened?

I closed my mind to all thought. I watched the roll of the tide coming in, coming in. I wanted to swim far out to safety and leave the terror behind. But I could not swim. I had no talent for it. I never learned to swim off the shores of Antarcticus. Twenty steps out and I would sink and be lost to the tides forever.

My children summoned me to Marcus in the morning. I had slept an hour after the sun had come up. Gregory pulled at my hand and whispered urgently. "Marcus is unhappy this morning, mother. He very much wants to see you. Did you hear what I said, mother?" Peter boldly stated that he would go with me and Julia warned me not to go at all. "He's not a nice man, mother. He's not like father. I think you should go on sleeping."

My first sight of the world that morning was the brilliant line of the sea. Then Gregory's dear face came into view. But I quickly returned my gaze to the sea. The sea was It, not me. The warm and almighty sea . . . I got to my feet understanding for the first time exactly what I was thinking. The sea would provide us with our means to justice. And I would put both W*O*D*E*N and the rebels to the sticky test. I would challenge both man and nation to reaffirm the spirit of nonviolent resistance for change. The time was coming and my mind was set. I walked across smooth sand and found Marcus waiting for me on the top of a rock in the center of an island of green. "Good morning, Tanya," he said. "It seems we have been given an ultimatum. It seems that death threatens you from both ends. There will be no heroes in this last act of my play. It is a pity for us all, don't you think?"

I could have cared less what Marcus said to me on that morning. A pleasant breeze was up and the flying birds were calling and the green rising hills sloped gracefully down to the sea. I turned to the sea and put one ear in the direction of Marcus. I knew what I was thinking and I knew how to lead the charge for peace and I knew now how to act accordingly. Father and I had determined the answer together. Father and I feared no man or nation when living by the law of the world.

"I think little of you, Marcus. And as for W*O*D*E*N, it continues to make mistakes. What is the ultimatum? How many hours are left?"

I could feel the weak strength of Marcus. I could sense his uncertain resolve. But strangely enough, I detected his love. He loved this mother of three. He loved me.

"Twenty-four hours, Tanya. Twenty-four hours are left to us. How shall we spend them? Will you walk with me? Twenty-four hours can be all the time in the world. I would prefer to die with those memories. What memories do you wish to take with you? Would you rather stay with your children?"

His remarks, of course, were preposterous. His romantic vision of death was foolish and pathetic. Though he denied it, he believed himself heroic. He believed himself to be a ward of noble history. The child in this man was dreaming. Perhaps this child of yesterday would be better off dead. I didn't know. But I had no desire to belittle my friends and children by following in his wake. I would make my own choice for death, if necessary. I would make my claim on history in my own way. I would not suffer a meaningless death, nor, I hoped, would the villagers of Antarcticus.

"When the time is right, Marcus, I will submit to you my own ultimatum. I will submit it to you as well as to W*O*D*E*N. You will do me the favor of transmitting my

WORLD ONE

statement, will you not? I can trust you to do that, can't I? I will not die for nothing. You may, if you wish. You have the freedom of choice as do your people. Choose what you like. I prefer to be remembered as a guardian of life."

Marcus was uneasy up on his rock. Now it was I who was directing the play. Now Marcus was but a mere actor in it. I looked to the sea and the sea was It. I was but a mere actor in It. And what a sure feeling it was to be. At that moment I felt the power of greatness in me. It was a power that took me out to the heavens and then down to the sea. It took me for a walk around the world. Yes, I went all those places in that moment. I was ready for death if it had to be. I was ready to take my place in history.

Marcus sat on his rock that day. I withdrew to where I belonged. And I belonged with the children of W*O*D*E*N, simple old women and men and children and summertime fishermen. I gloried in peace with these few who possessed the heart of our nation. We spoke of the sea and the morning to come. We spoke of life after death—could it be? And the children understood what we proposed. There was no fearful crying and pain. There was only the knowledge of what was right, right for us and for the heart of W*O*D*E*N. And the reward for our thought was a measure of hope. All things were possible in the name of peace. We, the villagers of Antarcticus, had only to act accordingly. Or so we believed as the light of the sun showered down from the sky.

We refused all food to eat that last day before the end of our journey. We took nothing to drink. We sat on the beach and clapped our hands. We moved neither forward or backwards. We sat where we were like rocks, like statues, like pillars of strength and nobility. And our thoughts turned to the next morning when we would deliver our ultimatum to Marcus and W*O*D*E*N. It was a joy to feel free. It was a joy to hold high the hope of W*O*D*E*N. There was no child who questioned our purpose. Gregory and Peter and Julia heard the singing of the whales. We all heard them sing. Though no whales were in sight, their music was there. The village idiot heard it, too. But to Marcus and his people the whales did not sing. They sang not to warriors, only citizens. The day finally faded away.

With twelve hours before morning our hearts still had not changed. The stars seemed to shower us with light. The bonfire on the beach seemed to dim with their ever increasing intensity. But this occurrence was only visible to us, to those who lifted themselves above the fire of the world and resided elsewhere. I do not overstate what took place. I do not overstate the magnificence of how we all felt. It would be impossible to do this and I have not. The stars seemed to shower us with light and our hearts beat with pride for the spirit of our nation.

And as the moon rose and fell, I knew no longings. If I had to die then our actions would make it the best possible death, if death can be looked on that way. And the same applied to my children. If they had to die then their consent made it worth something and allowed their young lives to have meaning beyond all expectations.

This was the way I was thinking that night on the beach below the rising green hills of the Falklands. The great sea was It and we were beckoned to It. We, the villagers of Antarcticus, had requested it.

Morning was upon us and we had but an hour left. Marcus and his people stood along the line of green and we sat where we had been and watched a gold sun make its ascent. It was a perfect morning to die. It was a perfect morning to be alive. It was a perfect morning because the time was right for nonviolent action against those who would have it be otherwise.

Time ticked away to the roll of the sea. I counted the waves as minutes on a clock. Come minutes, come waves. Come peace or death. Come people of W*O*D*E*N to victory.

The three ships of W*O*D*E*N sat poised to attack from their soft spot in the waters. Marcus and his people stood ready to commit the ultimate act. And we were prepared to

WORLD ONE

please only ourselves by stepping forward again and again and again.

Time ticked away to the roll of the sea. I counted the waves as minutes on a clock. Come minutes, come waves. Come peace or death. Come people of W*O*D*E*N to victory.

We waited in the splendor of silence for the time to be up. It was then that we would put all parties to the sticky test. It was then that we would test the foundations of W*O*D*E*N. All things are possible in the name of justice. All unbalanced passions could be cooled by nonviolent dissent. Or so I prayed as the time drew nigh.

And now it was time. The sun was as high as it had been yesterday. I saw the glitter of pistols behind us. I saw the shine of cannons before us. I smelled for the first time in my life the currents of warfare—like overheated wires laid down on paper. So this was the scent that my father had known and forgotten. So this was the scent of ancient history. "It is time to stand," I said.

Marcus, I knew, would not come near us. He had no heart left for other people's executions. He had only heart enough for his own. But now I would attempt one final time to help him. I would attempt one final time to amend his warped thinking. I called out to him as I had promised I would. "Marcus, this is our ultimatum. Listen well and report it to the forces of W*O*D*E*N."

He had been waiting for me over there by the green. He and his people were no more than fifty yards away. But it was a world away—they stood on the other side of a sea. Their grouping looked small under the shower of sunshine. The three ships of W*O*D*E*N looked slight against the clear blue blaze of the day. But from where I stood, we appeared to have the strength of a thousand armies. I wondered then if all the world was listening. Surely my next words would be monitored. I cut my thoughts and delivered my words to Marcus—to W*O*D*E*N—to my friends and children—to my dear husband out at sea.

"Today we have been captives for fifteen days. By the threats of two sides we await execution. By an unlucky chance we have found ourselves in the center of war. But we, the villagers of Antarcticus, are true citizens of W*O*D*E*N.

Even at death we will not divorce ourselves from the great spirit of our nation. I, for one, was born to preserve my father's heritage. I will not desert the noble cause of his generation. I will not. Nor will my friends who once lived in peace on the ice.

"Before both W*O*D*E*N and Marcus, we stand in protest. Before Marcus for his fifteen days of violence in the name of dubious justice. Before W*O*D*E*N for its declaration of war against Marcus and its unwillingness to bend and negotiate. To my mind, to our minds, both parties have violated the fundamental law of our nation, the great nation of W*O*D*E*N. And that law is the law of nonviolence. And because of this we now stand in protest and do issue our ultimatum as you have issued yours.

"Now hear this, Marcus. Now hear this, W*O*D*E*N. Unless you pledge yourselves to a peaceful resolution to this conflict, we will take a walk to the sea and we will follow the tide where it takes us. It is better for us to choose our own deaths, than to find death in violence and stupidity. And perhaps most important to us is the fact that we resist your actions nonviolently. Both sides now have one minute to consider their positions. When this time is up, then the time is right for us to begin—to walk in protest and find peace in death."

We, the villagers of Antarcticus, joined hands. There were Julia and Peter and Gregory and the dear village idiot. There were the old men and women and the summertime fishermen. And there in the center was me, the mother of three, whose husband looked on from the ship and whose lover stood behind speaking, I hoped, to the fleet. Was he? I did not strain to listen. My mind was on the roll of the sea. I looked to either side and smiled one last time at my children. They did not notice me. They studied the sea. Each had the courage of Marcus times ten. Each had the courage of a thousand armies. Truly, these were the children of W*O*D*E*N. These were my father's great grandchildren. And their time had come to an end.

"Let us walk."

On that morning fifty villagers of Antarcticus took their steps for peace. On that morning fifty villagers of Antarcticus spoke with one voice for nonviolent resistance for change.

WORLD ONE

And the sand was hot on our feet. And the gold sun above us was like the doorway to heaven, yes, like the entrance to a garden so fine and full of life. Together we walked without question toward It. And the It was the sea and ourselves together. It was a declaration for nonviolent action. And never was there an action so powerful and great.

"Let us walk."

And the warmth of the sea touched us. The sea encircled our feet. But no child or old man gasped. The sea was like the water of a bath and we would cleanse ourselves that day and be remembered for our actions of peace.

The waves moved aside as we walked. The water was deep then deeper. The sun seemed higher then higher. Julia went under, then Peter. The village idiot sucked for air. Gregory squeezed my hand tight but his face was not frightened. Better to die this way . . . Better to die for this . . .

Then like the trumpets of the world sounding, the horns of the ships did blast. Then like the cries of all people everywhere, the rebels of the Falklands did shout. But it was Marcus's voice that I heard. And I heard his love for me in that cry, or was it for the love of a world he had lost and found? I never knew which. And I never knew why he surrendered or why W*O*D*E*N agreed to a settlement. But I knew why the horns of the ships had sounded. W*O*D*E*N had to surrender its claim for action when people like us protested nonviolently. Come people of W*O*D*E*N to victory.

In the next moment Julia and Peter were in my arms and Gregory lifted the village idiot up. And down the long line we looked at each other and knew what we had done. And far beyond the noise of the horns and the cries of the rebels we listened to music on the edge of the sea. We heard the whales sing, the singing of the whales, and their music in that time circled the world and all people for a time stopped and listened.

I never saw Marcus again. When the boats of W*O*D*E*N came ashore, he and his people were taken to one of the ships. We were delivered to another. We were delivered to the ship where my husband had stood and watched us walk toward the sea. He would not speak to me when we arrived. He clutched the children and wept over them. In his eyes I had committed a crime. I risked too much for a statement. I risked all for the maintenance of peace. But to me, I had risked nothing. With the foundations of our nation destroyed, what was life but anarchy? And what was anarchy but death?—death to all who supported its ways. I had risked nothing. And I had achieved everything. I had achieved the one thing in life worth having. My husband was simply too close to see this. He saw only the children sinking down. He saw only his legacy near death.

The years passed and Marcus was tried and sentenced. He was sentenced to spend the rest of his life in prison—the worst possible punishment under the laws of W*O*D*E*N. It was I who took care to look after his people. It was I who saw to it that their cause was brought to the courts. And they now live on the Antarcticus Peninsula in peace and prosperity.

I live with my husband in our house and wait for tomorrow. Gregory is a member of the Federal Convention and represents in part the Society of Atlantia. We see him only every six months and he now has a wife and two children of his own to care for. Peter has followed in the footsteps of his grandfather, my father, and commands a fleet of cargo ships. He travels from sea to sea and from shore to shore and I haven't seen him for the last three years. And Julia, precious Julia, has recently become a doctor. She is living with her husband in the heart of the Society of Africa. Every month she telephones and tells us how many lives she's saved and how many were too far beyond help. She was a beautiful child and I often close my eyes and think of her combing my hair.

Since that time on the beach, father has not come to me. I knew when he stepped away that I would never see him again. I knew when he disappeared that he was gone forever. But I remember feeling him close to me as my family and I stood on the deck of my husband's ship. We had travelled far since that day on the Falklands and the slow moving white sky had returned and the evening sun would not sink below a point in the sky and the lights of the capital of W*O*D*E*N were near. Julia, I think, was complaining that she hadn't

WORLD ONE

been able to see the moon in the sky that previous night. Peter was happily clapping his hands while sitting atop his father's shoulders. And Gregory was running up and down the deck with his fast friend, the village idiot. But only part of me was there. Really, I was in three places at once. I longed to be asleep in my own bed and dreaming of whatever might come. And I longed to stay where I was—on the deck of a ship out at sea. I wanted to savor my victory forever. And why not? It was the one time in my life when I knew I had lived as my father had wished me to live. I did not want to lose that time. I did not want it to fade or ever be forgotten. And the third place that I was was with Marcus. A part of me sat with him in his cell. A part of me comforted him. For all that he had done, I still cared for him. I cared that he had cared for the lives of his people. It was his means that destroyed him. And perhaps, it was his love for me that saved me. He never intended to kill us. He never intended to commit mass suicide. All that poor man wanted was a home for his people and a place in the world for himself. Perhaps all that poor man wanted was a wife like me and children like Julia and Peter and Gregory. Now he has nothing but four walls and a window that overlooks ice. I wonder, if he's still alive, how often he thinks of me. I wonder if he regrets what he did to the old women and men who died for his dubious justice.

As my husband's ship came to shore, the banks of Antarcticus were lined with people who had followed the course of our captivity. Were there hundreds or thousands? They looked like millions. It was as if all citizens of W*O*D*E*N had come out to greet us. I had never seen so many people in my life. And since that time I never have again. And their cheers still break into my dreams. The sight of those people waving flags still empties my heart of all pain when I think of them there on the shore. They came to see us, the villagers of Antarcticus. They came to honor our will to live by the law of the world—to die, if need be, for the laws of W*O*D*E*N. And we did all of that. We the people of this great world.

It was then that I felt my father closest to me. Did I hear him whisper? I thought so. If it wasn't he who whispered then surely it was something he said to me as a child that had come back. "This world is yours to have and to hold. With justice comes peace and with peace comes plenty. It is the best man can do as children of God. It is the best man can do for his children." That's what father whispered to me. That's what my father once said.

As our ship made its way toward land and as the people cheered and shook the white moving sky, I felt the long lasting pride of my father and I knew the great achievement of his generation. And it was then that I knew I had become a part of it. I had joined hands with my father as I had joined hands with my children and my fellow friends and villagers. "Father," I said. "I've come home."

And at home I've stayed. I watched my children grow up and go on. I've seen my husband settle in and read hundreds of books by the fire. And I've seen my face age and the light in my eyes grow dimmer. But this is no great curse in life. It is no curse when you have lived through a time when you had the chance to help secure the foundations for peace. And this I did. And now you will remember it and I can die well satisfied knowing that as a child of W*O*D*E*N, I once gave my heart to it. I can die well satisfied knowing that my children will be safe and that theirs will live on as long as the World One Democratic Nation exists.

And I remember the cries of the people on the shores of Antarcticus as they welcomed us home, "World One . . . World One . . . World One."

25

The anemic light of dawn grazes the faces of the people in front of me, beside me, behind me. Once more the sewer of water in which we all sit is still. Some children are sleeping in the arms of their mothers. Others are wide-eyed from the long night of entertainment. I am ready to take Elizabeth home, make up our bed and step into dreams. I am prepared to die, if I have to. I am numb with fatigue. But I am happy to be alive, even here. Even here on this river, this lake cluttered with garbage and filth from another time.

I turn my eyes to the sky, all ashy and pale. There above me a wedge appears between great rolling clouds. And for a moment I think I see the glitter of a star, one star shining like light beyond the haze of it all.

I look over at Elizabeth. She can barely hold open her eyes. But true to me, her rifle points where it has before—at Human-dog #1. It is time to take it. I gently lift it from Elizabeth's hands. She does not resist. And with the sweep of my arm I toss *it gracefully into the dawn's sea. There it goes. It goes down and drowns. A violent death for an instrument of violence. Human-dog #1 smiles broadly. And then he stretches out his hand to me. I take it. Our hands are joined for the first time. For the first time we recognize each other as something other than enemies. Perhaps I am a fool, or foolhardy. Perhaps I am making a mistake. I will know soon. I may die soon. But I must take this risk. I must wage peace with all that I have. And I must try to do it without violence and without inflicting pain. It may be too hard, I know. It is probably impossible, too. But what am I? What are we? Are we animals or are we humans? Are we people of the wilderness or are we the founders of civilization? I choose to be a founder. I dream of founding the first civilization which has as its base freedom from violence and warfare. This is Americus and this is World One—this is our future and will be our legacy because the human-dogs and I have come to an understanding, I can tell. I can see it in Human-dog #1's eyes. At least with him there is an understanding. We have made a silent statement together. We have committed ourselves to a new frontier, an unknown destination. Who knows if we'll get there? It may take our lifetime to travel halfway there. It may take another one hundred years. Of course, it may never happen. We may live out our lives in this sewer and so may all of the other survivors around the globe.*

They are there now. They sit in places like this with the wreckage of all things rotting about them. I pity them, I do. I would change it if I could. But perhaps even now, people and human-dogs are meeting and making progress towards peace. No doubt they are thinking as I am thinking about the other poor wretches sitting in polluted soups the world over. I can imagine them dreaming of their Americuses. I can imagine them dreaming of a worldwide peaceful settlement, not unlike the one which I have outlined. However ugly this may sound though, I can picture an opposite scenario. I can see a return to all-out warfare, to never ending national conflicts, to perpetually dying infantries locked in perennial combat. I've seen enough. I'd rather think ahead to what Americus will do now that its first battle has been won. Elizabeth and I have won the first battle, yes, that's right. Human-dog #1 is our new ally. And behind him, we have a hundred others. This is the begin-

WORLD ONE

ning, the beginning of World One, the beginning of the beginning, the beginning of the beginning of the end of war between men and men of nations. War is our common enemy. War is what we survivors must overcome. And if we do this, all will not be a waste. The dead bodies below us will have served at least some kind of purpose. Perhaps I am dreaming before sleep. I am presently dreaming of sleep and peace. Elizabeth has just kissed my cheek.

"It's time to rest, old man. It's time Elizabeth takes you home. You have waged peace all evening. And you have won. We are defeated and triumphant simultaneously. We will accompany you to Americus and beyond. You have my word on that."

This is Human-dog #1. If I had not just heard it, I would swear I was dreaming. But Human-dog #1 said it. I am awake. I am listening. He said it. And I believe I can trust him.

"Goodnight," he says. "Welcome to Americus."

The people around us cheer. It is a warm and heartfelt cheer in support of something deeply felt, tacitly understood. And it seems that within these people lies the heart of civilization, of at least a new beginning, a measure of hope tempered by the knowledge of possible tragedy. This is progress, I think. This is a long step forward, I hope. But why did it have to happen like this? Why this way, why all of the damage? Why didn't we succeed before this? Certainly this is the question I will always ask. Why not before this?—and will we succeed even now? Violence is a part of us. It is memory. It is history. It is present with us every day. But it can also be undone, both rooted out and de-institutionalized. I say this confidently because before my eyes the human-dogs have been tamed with words and ideas, rather than with war. It seems simple enough. It seems impossible, too. That's my tomorrow's problem, not today's. Today, Elizabeth and I will sleep. It is a warm dawn and I think we will sleep at the base of Mr. Jefferson's high statue. We will wrap ourselves in a bright light cloth and dream on into the early evening.

Human-dog #1 is departing and his people follow. The war is over and a new peace reigns. The tyranny of war has been overcome by our hostility toward it, our hostility, Elizabeth's *and mine and Thomas Jefferson's. The torches are dim in the muddy dawn light. Elizabeth and I watch the wide procession row out. Oars rise and fall. Our fortunes are rising now, I think.*

And then out in the middle of the black lake, #1 turns around and has another look at us. I can see that he's curious about whether we've stayed to see them off. He raises his hand, his right hand high. "World One," he cries. "World One."

Elizabeth and I return the gesture and repeat the cry. We are all partners now in civilization.

I would like to acknowledge my debt to Emery Reves and his work, *The Anatomy of Peace,* as well as to the Committee to Frame a World Constitution and its *Preliminary Draft of a World Constitution,* without which the writing of this novel would have been impossible.